U0051619

# NEW TOEIC

附MP3音檔連結

## 必考單字快速記憶

美式音律快記法
押韻輕鬆記字串

一舉突破750分!

Carolyn G. Choong 著

笛藤出版

# introdiction 前言

您知道美國小朋友是怎樣記單字的嗎？他們除了利用字卡，在上面寫下單字、例句、用法跟同義字之外，也經常利用押韻來記單字哦！他們背單字時，會把單字唸出來，一邊開口唸一邊練習拼字，同時了解單字的意思與用法。對美國人來說，押韻的單字因為帶有韻律，就如哼歌一般容易深植人心，而一再重複的尾音，就是加深記憶的主要原因。

書中利用「押韻分類法」，將押韻的單字「串」在一起，這些字尾發音相同、拼法一樣的單字串就像個大家庭，家中每個成員的外貌都有雷同之處，聲音也很類似，一起唱誦記憶，學習效率事半功倍！本書由《TOEIC字串王》一書改版，從光碟改為MP3音檔連結，隨處聆聽複習更便利、印象更深刻。

在準備TOEIC考試的過程中，背誦單字被視為加強實力的不二法門，只要利用單字串押韻的特性，就可以輕鬆記住，加速提升單字實力。

## 全書依5大母音A・E・I・O・U分為5大單元，主要特色如下：

- 以發音為分類依歸，只要開口唸出押韻單字串，或聽MP3中專業錄音員的示範，就能感受單字間流動的節奏與韻律。
- 利用單字字尾重複的發音，自然而然幫助記憶。
- 以單字串的尾韻作為標題，並用紅色字標記押韻部分，一目瞭然。
- 單字＋詞組＋句子的組合，學習一氣呵成。
- 在TOEIC頻出單字前面加註＊號，提醒讀者特別注意。
- 精心錄製的MP3，收錄全書英文單字與例句。可利用各種零碎時間，或入睡前的片刻，把MP3當成背景音樂來聽，固定的節奏與重複的韻律加深對單字的印象，達到有效記憶。

**♪ MP3音檔請掃右方QR code或至下方連結下載：**

https://bit.ly/TOEICaeiou

★ 請注意英文字母大小寫區別 ★

MP3英語發聲｜Rachel Yang・Robert Fehr・Brian Funshine

## 使用小叮嚀

**1** 有時單字群組會跟不同拼法?發音相同的群組銜接，這是因為本書以發音為出發點，所以將發音相同的群組放在一起，讓讀者可一併學習。
例：(eak)[ik]群組後接著是(ique)[ik]群組，雖然拼法不同，但發音一樣屬於同韻字，可以一起學習記憶。

**2** 本書附有單字尾韻索引，統整全書單字的尾韻，讀者可以好好利用。
例：如果想找(eam)[im]結尾的單字，可以參考單字尾韻索引，就能找到114頁以(eam)結尾的單字群。

**3** 本書也附有單字索引，方便讀者找出單字所在的頁數，並將單字的尾韻用紅色標記，可以很清楚看出單字押的尾韻，及所屬群組。例：在單字索引看到**architect**，就知道它是歸類在(ect)群組下，押(ect)的尾韻。如果想知道跟**architect**同一群組的單字，只要翻到**architect**所在的95頁，就能學到群組內所有單字。

**4** 詞性對照表

| | | | | | |
|---|---|---|---|---|---|
| 名 | 名詞 | 動 | 動詞 | 形 | 形容詞 |
| 副 | 副詞 | 介 | 介系詞 | 連 | 連接詞 |
| 代 | 代名詞 | 感 | 感嘆詞 | 助 | 助動詞 |

## MP3的內容

以 01，第6頁的(ab)群組為例

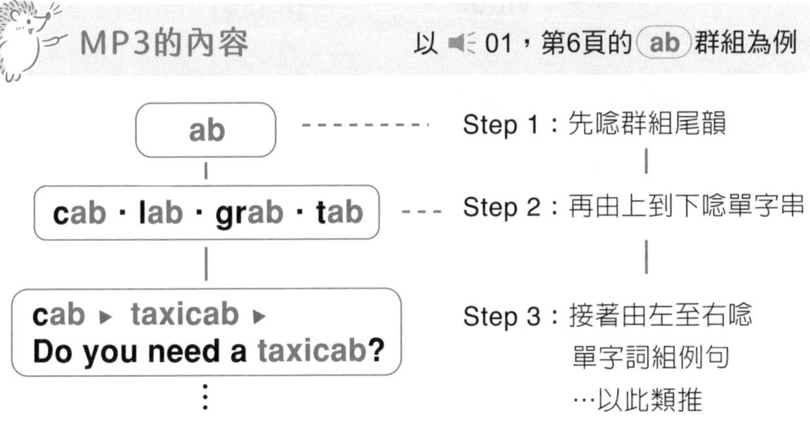

# contents 目錄

# 1. 押 A 韻的單字

## ab [æb]

 01

| | | |
|---|---|---|
| **cab** [kæb] 名 計程車 | taxicab 計程車 | Do you need a taxicab? 你需要叫計程車嗎？ |
| * **lab** [læb] 名 實驗室 | medical lab 醫學實驗室 | They study diseases at that medical lab. 他們在醫學實驗室研究疾病。 |
| * **grab** [græb] 動 抓取 | grab hold of 抓住 | You need to grab hold of something so you don't fall down. 為了避免跌倒，你得找東西抓著。 |
| **tab** [tæb] 名 拉環、標籤 | silver tab 銀拉環 | The silver tab on the can will help you open it. 易開罐上的銀拉環方便你把罐子打開。 |

## ace [es]

| | | |
|---|---|---|
| * **ace** [es] 形 一流的 名 么點 | ace of spades 黑桃A | In many card games, the ace of spades is the highest card. 在很多撲克牌遊戲中，黑桃A都是最大的。 |
| * **face** [fes] 名 臉 動 面向 | face reality 面對現實 | You need to face reality in order to be true to yourself. 對自己誠實的方法就是面對現實。 |
| **deface** [dɪ'fes] 動 損壞 | deface property 破壞物品 | Some teenagers deface property by writing graffiti on the walls. 有些青少年在牆上塗鴉來搞破壞。 |

| | | |
|---|---|---|
| * **place** [ples] 名 地方 動 放置 | take place 發生、舉行 | The meeting will take place here. 會議會在這裡舉行。 |
| * **replace** [rɪ`ples] 動 取代 | replace what's broken 更換壞的部分 | You better replace what's broken. 你最好把壞的部分換掉。 |
| **pace** [pes] 名 一步、步伐 | quick pace 步伐很快 | She walked at a quick pace. 她走路的步伐很快。 |
| * **space** [spes] 名 空間、太空 | space shuttle 太空梭 | The space shuttle took off for the moon. 太空梭向月球的方向行進。 |
| * **race** [res] 名 賽跑、種族 | race horse 賽馬<br>black race 黑人 | Which race horse do you bet on? 你賭哪一匹馬贏？<br>The Black race is made up of many different ethnicities. 黑人是由很多種族組成的。 |
| **embrace** [ɪm`bres] 名 動 擁抱 | warm embrace 溫暖的擁抱 | He longed for the warm embrace of his lover's arms. 他渴望戀人給他一個溫暖的擁抱。 |
| * **grace** [gres] 名 優雅、恩典 | Amazing Grace 奇異恩典 | "Amazing Grace" is an American spiritual song. 《奇異恩典》是美國的宗教歌曲。 |
| **disgrace** [dɪs`gres] 名 丟臉、恥辱 | what a disgrace 奇恥大辱 | "What a disgrace!" 「真是奇恥大辱！」 |

| | | |
|---|---|---|
| **trace** [tres] 名痕跡 動 追蹤 | ▶ without a trace 沒有任何蹤跡 | ▶ He disappeared without a trace. 他就這樣無聲無息地消失。 |

## ase [es]

| | | |
|---|---|---|
| * **base** [bes] 名基礎、基地 | ▶ home base 本壘 | ▶ In baseball, home base is the center of action. 棒球比賽中，本壘是比賽的重心。 |
| * **case** [kes] 名事例、案件 | ▶ divorce case 離婚訴訟 | ▶ She is filing a divorce case. 她正在訴請離婚。 |
| **chase** [tʃes] 動追逐 | ▶ chase the robber 追捕搶匪 | ▶ The police chased the robber down the street. 警察在馬路上追捕搶匪。 |
| **erase** [ɪˋres] 動擦掉 | ▶ erase the blackboard 擦黑板 | ▶ At the end of the day, students must erase the blackboard. 上完課後，學生要擦黑板。 |

## acial [ˋeʃəl]

| | | |
|---|---|---|
| * **facial** [ˋfeʃəl] 形面部的、表面的 | ▶ facial expression 臉部表情 | ▶ Although she tried to hide her feelings, her facial expression gave her away. 雖然她試圖隱藏她的感受，但她的表情早已表露無遺。 |

| | | |
|---|---|---|
| * **racial** [ˋreʃəl] 形 人種的、種族的 | racial prejudice 種族歧視 | There is so much racial prejudice in the world. 世界上存在著很多種族歧視。 |

## acity [ˋæsətɪ]

| | | |
|---|---|---|
| * **capacity** [kəˋpæsətɪ] 名 容量 | maximum capacity 最大容量 | We've reached maximum capacity in this room. 這個房間已經爆滿。 |
| * **veracity** [vəˋræsətɪ] 名 誠實 | truth and veracity 真理與真誠 | Truth and veracity are virtues that every culture honors. 真理與真誠是每個文化都讚揚的美德。 |

## ack [æk]

| | | |
|---|---|---|
| * **back** [bæk] 名 背部 副 向後 | back and forth 來來回回 | He went back and forth on his decision. 他猶豫不決，無法做決定。 |
| * **lack** [læk] 動 名 缺少 | lack of 缺少 | There is a serious lack of food in starving countries. 在飢餓貧窮的國家，食物短缺的問題很嚴重。 |
| **black** [blæk] 形 黑色的 名 黑色 | black book 秘密名冊 | Many men keep a black book full of women's telephone numbers. 很多男人都有一本記錄女生電話的秘密名冊。 |

| | | |
| --- | --- | --- |
| **slack**<br>[slæk]<br>動 鬆弛 | slack off<br>鬆懈 | Don't slack off in school.<br>求學千萬不可以鬆懈下來。 |
| * **pack**<br>[pæk]<br>名 包 動 打包 | backpack<br>背包 | My backpack is too heavy.<br>我的背包很重。 |
| * **unpack**<br>[ʌn`pæk]<br>動 卸下、打開 | unpack the suitcase<br>打開行李 | You have to unpack the suitcase when you come home.<br>回到家時你得打開行李整理。 |
| **rack**<br>[ræk]<br>名 架子 | laundry rack<br>衣架 | Clothes hang to dry on the laundry racks.<br>衣服掛在衣架上晾乾。 |
| * **crack**<br>[kræk]<br>動 使破裂、弄開 | crack a safe<br>撬開保險箱 | Robbers know how to crack a safe.<br>搶匪懂得如何撬開保險箱。 |
| * **track**<br>[træk]<br>名 行蹤、軌道 | keep track of<br>記錄 | It's hard to keep track of everything.<br>把每件事情都記下來是很困難的。 |
| * **tack**<br>[tæk]<br>名 大頭釘、圖釘 | box of tacks<br>圖釘盒 | The box of tacks fell on the floor.<br>圖釘盒掉到地上了。 |
| * **attack**<br>[ə`tæk]<br>動 名 攻擊 | heart attack<br>心臟病 | He died of a heart attack.<br>他死於心臟病發作。 |

## ackle [ˋækl̩]

| | | |
|---|---|---|
| **shackle** [ˋʃækl̩] 名 腳鐐、手銬 ▶ | pair of shackles 一副手銬 ▶ | The prisoner was bound in a pair of shackles. 囚犯被銬上手銬。 |
| **crackle** [ˋkrækl̩] 動 發出爆裂聲 ▶ | crackling noises 劈啪聲 ▶ | Deep-frying usually makes crackling noises. 油炸通常會發出劈啪聲。 |
| * **tackle** [ˋtækl̩] 動 處理 ▶ | tackle a problem 處理問題 ▶ | You need to learn how to tackle a problem to survive in this world. 為了生存，你必須學會如何解決問題。 |

## actical [ˋæktɪkl̩]

| | | |
|---|---|---|
| * **practical** [ˋpræktɪkl̩] 形 實際的 ▶ | practical joke 惡作劇 ▶ | Don't play a practical joke on people. 不要對別人惡作劇。 |
| * **impractical** [ɪmˋpræktɪkl̩] 形 不切實際的 ▶ | impractical plan 不切實際的計畫 ▶ | That is an impractical plan and it won't work. 那是不切實際的計畫，是不可能成功的。 |

## action [ˋækʃən]

| | | |
|---|---|---|
| * **action** [ˋækʃən] 名 行動、動作 ▶ | take action 採取行動 ▶ | You must learn to take action when necessary. 在必要的時候，你必須學會採取行動。 |

| | | |
|---|---|---|
| * **reaction** [rɪ`ækʃən] 名 反應 | ▶ chemical reaction 化學反應 | ▶ There is a chemical reaction in almost everything you see. 幾乎每件你所看到的東西都歷經化學反應的過程。 |
| * **subtraction** [səb`trækʃən] 名 減 | ▶ addition and subtraction 加減法 | ▶ We learn addition and subtraction in grade school. 我們在小學時學加減法。 |
| * **distraction** [dɪ`strækʃən] 名 分心 | ▶ mental distraction 分心 | ▶ I don't like mental distractions when I'm working. 我工作時不喜歡有東西讓我分心。 |
| * **transaction** [træn`zækʃən] 名 辦理、交易 | ▶ money transaction 金錢交易 | ▶ I made a money transaction at the ATM. 我用ATM做金錢交易。 |

## active [`æktɪv]

| | | |
|---|---|---|
| * **active** [`æktɪv] 形 活躍的 | ▶ active sports 動態運動 | ▶ What kind of active sports do you like to play? 你喜歡從事什麼樣的動態運動？ |
| * **attractive** [ə`træktɪv] 形 有吸引力的 | ▶ attractive woman 有吸引力的女人 | ▶ That attractive woman has many suitors. 那個迷人的女子有很多追求者。 |

## ad [æd]

| | | |
|---|---|---|
| * **ad**<br>[æd]<br>名 廣告 | ▶ TV ad<br>電視廣告 | ▶ Did you see that new TV ad for Coke?<br>你看過新的可口可樂電視廣告了嗎？ |
| **bad**<br>[bæd]<br>形 壞的 | ▶ bad sign<br>不好的預兆 | ▶ It's a bad sign to see a coff-in in your dream.<br>夢見棺材是不好的預兆。 |
| **fad**<br>[fæd]<br>名 一時的流行 | ▶ fad diet<br>流行減肥法 | ▶ Drinking lemonade is just a fad diet.<br>喝檸檬水減肥只是一時的流行。 |
| * **mad**<br>[mæd]<br>形 發瘋的、瘋狂的 | ▶ mad scientist<br>瘋狂科學家 | ▶ There is a myth that mad sci-entists create monsters.<br>傳說瘋狂科學家創造了怪物。 |
| **pad**<br>[pæd]<br>名 墊、便條簿 | ▶ pad of paper<br>便條紙 | ▶ Hand me that pad of paper please.<br>請把便條紙遞給我。 |
| **grad**<br>[græd]<br>名 研究生 | ▶ grad student<br>研究生 | ▶ He is a grad student, not a college student.<br>他是研究生，不是大學生。 |

## ade [ed]

| | | |
|---|---|---|
| * **decade**<br>[ˋdɛked]<br>名 十年 | ▶ three decades<br>30年 | ▶ In three decades, there may not be any use for Styrofoam.<br>三十年後，可能就沒有人在使用保麗龍了。 |

| 單字 | 片語 | 例句 |
| --- | --- | --- |
| **fade** [fed] 動 枯萎、褪去 | fade away 消逝 | I hope that my love for you won't fade away. 希望我對你的愛永遠不會消逝。 |
| **shade** [ʃed] 名 陰暗處 | in the shade 在陰涼處 | It's nice to sit in the shade in summer. 夏天的時候，能坐在陰涼處是件很幸福的事。 |
| **blockade** [blɑ`ked] 動 封鎖 名 道路阻塞 | road blockade 道路封鎖 | You can't go that way; there is a road blockade there now. 那裡不能走，因為道路被封起來了。 |
| **blade** [bled] 名 刀片 | razorblade 刮鬍刀片 | He cut himself shaving with a razorblade. 他用刮鬍刀片刮鬍子時刮傷了自己。 |
| * **made** [med] 形 製造的 | made in Taiwan 台灣製造 | In the seventies, there were many things that were made in Taiwan. 在70年代，很多東西都是台灣製造的。 |
| **unmade** [ʌn`med] 形 尚未做好的 | unmade plans 未做好的計畫 | Without efforts, there are unmade plans. 沒有努力，計畫永遠都沒辦法做好。 |
| **parade** [pə`red] 名 動 遊行 | Macy's parade 梅西大遊行 | In New York City, the Macy's parade is one of the biggest parades of the year. 在紐約，梅西百貨遊行是每年最盛大的遊行之一。 |
| **grade** [gred] 名 等級、成績 | good grades 好成績 | I want good grades so that I can get into a good college. 為了進入好大學，我要爭取好成績。 |

| | | |
|---|---|---|
| * **trade** [tred] 名 貿易、交易 | trade market 貿易市場 | The trade market for publishing changes almost weekly. 出版業的貿易市場行情幾乎每個星期都在改變。 |
| * **persuade** [pɚˋswed] 動 說服 | easily persuaded 容易被說服 | That girl is very easily persuaded. 那個女生很容易被說服。 |
| **invade** [ɪnˋved] 動 侵略 | illegally invade 非法侵略 | Some war criminals illegally invade national borders. 有些戰犯非法入侵國界。 |

## aid [ed]

| | | |
|---|---|---|
| * **aid** [ed] 名 動 幫助 | financial aid 補助貸款 | Many American students receive financial aid for college. 很多美國大學生都有助學貸款的補助。 |
| * **paid** [ped] 形 有薪津的 | paid leave 有薪假 | The employees of the company are entitled to an annual paid leave of 10 days. 這家公司的員工一年有十天有薪假。 |
| **unpaid** [ʌnˋped] 形 無薪資的 | unpaid leave 無薪假 | She took an unpaid leave for 9 months. 她請了九個月的無薪假。 |

## aide [ed]

| | | |
|---|---|---|
| **aide**<br>[ed]<br>名 助手 | nurse's aide<br>助理護士 | The nurse's aide helps the nurse with daily duties. 助理護士幫護士處理每日的例行公事。 |

## ater [`etɚ]

03

| | | |
|---|---|---|
| **cater**<br>[`ketɚ]<br>動 提供飲食 | cater food<br>承辦食物 | That company caters food.<br>那家公司負責承辦食物的業務。 |
| * **later**<br>[`letɚ]<br>形 較晚的 副 後來 | see you later<br>再見 | "See you later" means the same as "Bye." "See you later" 和 "Bye" 是同樣的意思。 |

## ator [`etɚ]

| | | |
|---|---|---|
| * **creator**<br>[krɪ`etɚ]<br>名 創造者 | creator of the Earth<br>造物者 | Many people think that the creator of the Earth is God.<br>很多人認為上帝是萬物的創造者。 |
| * **elevator**<br>[`ɛləvetɚ]<br>名 電梯 | take the elevator<br>搭電梯 | He took the elevator to the 5th floor.<br>他搭電梯到五樓。 |
| * **escalator**<br>[`ɛskə͵letɚ]<br>名 電扶梯 | escalator belt<br>電扶梯輸送帶 | The escalator belt got stuck so it stopped working. 電扶梯輸送帶卡到了所以沒辦法運轉。 |

| 單字 | 搭配 | 例句 |
| --- | --- | --- |
| * **legislator** [ˋlɛdʒɪsˏletɚ] 名 立法委員 | political legislator 政黨立委 | That political legislator is corrupt. 那個政黨立委貪污。 |
| * **translator** [trænsˋletɚ] 名 翻譯者 | Chinese translator 中文譯者 | It is hard to be a Chinese translator. 當中文譯者很難。 |
| * **calculator** [ˋkælkjəˏletɚ] 名 計算機 | electronic calculator 電子計算機 | I can't survive without an electronic calculator. 沒有電子計算機我活不下去。 |
| **regulator** [ˋrɛgjəˏletɚ] 名 管理者、調節器 | gas regulator 瓦斯調節器 | That gas regulator makes the water warm in the shower. 瓦斯調節器能加熱洗澡水。 |
| **coordinator** [koˋɔrdn̩ˏetɚ] 名 協調者 | volunteer coordinator 義工調度者 | Every non-profit organization needs a volunteer coordinator. 每個非營利團體都需要義工調度者。 |
| * **operator** [ˋɑpəˏretɚ] 名 操作者 | machine operator 機械作業員 | Machine operators risk their lives using dangerous equipment. 機械作業員冒著生命危險操作危險設備。 |
| **narrator** [næˋretɚ] 名 敘述者 | narrator of the book 書中的敘述者 | The narrator of the book is a young boy of age 13. 這本書是以一個13歲的小男孩為敘述主角。 |
| **spectator** [spɛkˋtetɚ] 名 旁觀者、目擊者 | spectator at a football game 橄欖球賽的觀眾 | There are many spectators at a football game in America. 在美國橄欖球賽現場有很多觀眾。 |

## aff [æf]

| | | |
|---|---|---|
| * **staff** [stæf] 名 職員 | ▶ members of the staff 員工 | ▶ All the members of the staff will be given a raise starting next year. 明年開始全體員工都會加薪。 |

## alf [æf]

| | | |
|---|---|---|
| * **half** [hæf] 名 一半 形 一半的 | ▶ half full 半滿 | ▶ People who look on the bright side say a glass is half full. 樂觀的人會說杯子是半滿。 |
| * **behalf** [bɪˋhæf] 名 代表、利益 | ▶ on behalf of 代表 | ▶ I'd like to write on behalf of my sister. 我謹代表我姊姊寫這封信。 |

## aph [æf]

| | | |
|---|---|---|
| * **graph** [græf] 名 圖表 | ▶ graph paper 座標紙 | ▶ The only time I ever needed graph paper was in math class. 我唯一一次要用到座標紙是在數學課的時候。 |

## aft [æft]

| | | |
|---|---|---|
| **craft** [kræft] 名 工藝 | ▶ arts and crafts 手工藝 | ▶ I'm not good at arts and crafts. 我對手工藝沒轍。 |

| | | |
|---|---|---|
| * **draft**<br>[dræft]<br>名 草稿 | rough draft<br>大略的初稿 | You need to make a rough draft of it first.<br>你必須先做一個大略的初稿才行。 |

## after [ˋæftɚ]

| | | |
|---|---|---|
| * **after**<br>[ˋæftɚ]<br>介 在…之後 | after class<br>放學後 | I'm going to the movies after class.<br>放學後我要去看電影。 |

## ag [æg]

| | | |
|---|---|---|
| **lag**<br>[læg]<br>動 名 落後 | lag behind<br>落後 | Don't lag behind the group.<br>不要落後團隊進度。 |
| **flag**<br>[flæg]<br>名 旗子 | national flag<br>國旗 | Which national flag do you like best?<br>你最喜歡哪一國國旗？ |
| **brag**<br>[bræg]<br>動 吹牛 | brag about<br>吹噓 | He likes to brag about his pretty girlfriend.<br>他喜歡吹噓他女朋友有多漂亮。 |
| **drag**<br>[dræg]<br>動 拖 | drag along<br>拖去 | I don't want to be dragged along to the party.<br>我不想要被拖去參加派對。 |

| | | |
|---|---|---|
| **sag**<br>[sæg]<br>動 下跌 | ▶ stock prices sag<br>股價下跌 | ▶ It's normal when stock prices sag.<br>股價下跌是很正常的事。 |
| * **tag**<br>[tæg]<br>名 標籤 | ▶ clothing tag<br>衣服標籤 | ▶ I looked at the clothing tag for the price.<br>我看了一下衣服標籤上的標價。 |

## age [edʒ]

| | | |
|---|---|---|
| * **age**<br>[edʒ]<br>名 年齡 動 變老 | ▶ old age<br>老年 | ▶ I want to travel a lot in my old age.<br>我老的時候要常去旅行。 |
| * **engage**<br>[ɪnˋgedʒ]<br>動 使從事、使忙於 | ▶ engage in<br>忙於 | ▶ What have you been engaged in lately?<br>你最近在忙什麼啊？ |
| * **page**<br>[pedʒ]<br>名 頁數 | ▶ page 12<br>第12頁 | ▶ Turn to page 12.<br>翻到第12頁。 |
| **rage**<br>[redʒ]<br>名 狂怒 | ▶ full of rage<br>大發雷霆 | ▶ What he did to me made me full of rage.<br>他對我做的事讓我大發脾氣。 |
| * **wage**<br>[wedʒ]<br>名 薪水 | ▶ minimum wage<br>最低薪資 | ▶ Hopefully everyone can earn at least minimum wage.<br>希望每個人都至少達到最低薪資。 |

## age [ɪdʒ]

| | | |
|---|---|---|
| **garbage** [`garbɪdʒ] 名 垃圾 | take out the garbage 把垃圾拿出去丟 | Can you take out the garbage? 你能把垃圾拿出去丟嗎？ |
| * **encourage** [ɪn`kɝɪdʒ] 動 鼓勵 | encourage her dependence 鼓勵她的依賴習慣 | Don't encourage her dependence on you. 別鼓勵她養成依賴你的習慣。 |
| * **percentage** [pɚ`sɛntɪdʒ] 名 百分比 | percentage of profit 利潤百分比 | What is the percentage of profit attached to the mugs? 這些馬克杯的利潤是多少？ |

## age [ɑʒ]

| | | |
|---|---|---|
| **camouflage** [`kæmə͵flɑʒ] 名 動 偽裝 | in camouflage 偽裝 | You can't see them because they are in camouflage. 你看不到他們，因為他們已經偽裝起來了。 |
| * **garage** [gə`rɑʒ] 名 車庫 | parking garage 停車場 | I circled for blocks before I found a parking garage. 我繞了好幾個街區才找到停車場。 |
| **entourage** [͵ɑntu`rɑʒ] 名 隨行人員 | entourage of fans 歌迷隨行 | That band always has a huge entourage of fans following them. 那個樂團總是被一大群歌迷追隨。 |
| * **massage** [mə`sɑʒ] 名 動 按摩 | back massage 背部按摩 | I need a back massage. 我需要背部按摩。 |

## aim [em]

04

| | | |
|---|---|---|
| **aim** [em] 動 名 瞄準 | ▶ good aim 好好瞄準 | ▶ Did you have a good aim at the target? 你有好好瞄準目標嗎？ |
| * **claim** [klem] 動 名 要求 | ▶ claim to fame 以…出名 | ▶ Stunning looks are most models' claim to fame. 大部分模特兒都是以佼好的外貌闖出名氣。 |
| * **acclaim** [ə`klem] 動 稱讚 | ▶ critically acclaimed 廣受好評 | ▶ That movie was critically acclaimed by the usually harsh critics. 那部電影廣受一般嚴苛的影評青睞。 |
| **reclaim** [rɪ`klem] 動 使悔改、收回 | ▶ reclaim land 收回土地 | ▶ Native Americans wanted to reclaim land which was stolen from them. 印地安人想收復被奪取的失土。 |
| **exclaim** [ɪks`klem] 動 呼喊 | ▶ exclaim loudly 大叫 | ▶ You don't have to exclaim loudly. 你也不需要叫得這麼大聲。 |

## ame [em]

| | | |
|---|---|---|
| **fame** [fem] 名 聲譽 | ▶ come to fame 成名 | ▶ He came to fame when he was eleven years old. 他11歲時就成名了。 |
| * **shame** [ʃem] 名 羞恥 動 使羞愧 | ▶ full of shame 顏面盡失 | ▶ She was full of shame after she lost the game. 她輸了比賽後顏面盡失。 |

| | | |
| --- | --- | --- |
| * **blame** [blem] 動 名 責備 | blame yourself 責怪自己 | Don't blame yourself for everything. 不要每件事情都歸咎到自己身上。 |
| **flame** [flem] 名 火焰 | eternal flame 永恆之火 | Is an eternal flame possible? 真的可能會有永恆之火嗎？ |
| * **name** [nem] 名 名字 動 指定 | name your price 定價格 | You are not allowed to name your price for groceries. 你無法訂定商品的價格。 |
| * **surname** [ˋsɝ͵nem] 名 姓 | what's your surname 你姓什麼 | "what's your surname?" the policeman asked. 警察問：「你姓什麼？」 |
| * **frame** [frem] 名 框架 | picture frame 相框 | He hung the picture frame on the wall. 他把相框掛在牆上。 |
| * **same** [sem] 形 同樣的 | not the same 不同 | It is not the same. 這不同。 |

## ain [en]

| | | |
| --- | --- | --- |
| * **gain** [gen] 動 名 獲得 | gain weight 增重 | It's so easy to gain weight. 體重增加是一件很容易的事。 |

| | | |
| --- | --- | --- |
| * **chain**<br>[tʃen]<br>名 鏈條、連鎖 | chain reaction<br>連鎖效應 | There is a chain reaction to almost everything. 幾乎每件事情都是連鎖效應下的產物。 |
| * **complain**<br>[kəm`plen]<br>動 抱怨 | complain all the time<br>老是抱怨 | Spoiled children complain all the time. 被寵壞的小孩總是抱怨東抱怨西的。 |
| * **explain**<br>[ɪk`splen]<br>動 解釋、說明 | explain clearly<br>清楚解說 | Good teachers know how to explain clearly.<br>好的老師知道該怎麼清楚解說。 |
| * **main**<br>[men]<br>形 主要的 | main idea<br>主要的意思 | Did you get the main idea of the reading passage?<br>你了解這一段最主要的意思嗎？ |
| **domain**<br>[do`men]<br>名 領土 | domain of Japan<br>日本領土 | Taiwan used to be under the domain of Japan.<br>台灣曾經是日本的一部分。 |
| * **remain**<br>[rɪ`men]<br>動 剩下、保持 | remain friends<br>維持友誼關係 | They have remained friends for over fifty years.<br>他們之間的友誼超過了50年。 |
| **pain**<br>[pen]<br>名 疼痛 | sharp pain<br>劇痛 | I have a sharp pain in my stomach.<br>我的胃劇烈疼痛。 |
| **Spain**<br>[spen]<br>名 西班牙 | culture of Spain<br>西班牙文化 | The culture of Spain is very interesting.<br>西班牙文化很有意思。 |

| | | |
|---|---|---|
| * **brain** [bren] 名 腦袋 | brain damage ▶ 腦部受傷 | ▶ You can get brain damage from using drugs. 吸毒會使腦部受創。 |
| **drain** [dren] 動 排出 | drain water ▶ 排水 | ▶ Please drain the water from the cup. 請把杯子的水倒掉。 |
| **refrain** [rɪ`fren] 動 抑制 | refrain from smoking ▶ 禁菸 | ▶ You must refrain from smoking in this room. 在這房間裡你不能吸菸。 |
| **sprain** [spren] 動 名 扭傷 | sprain my ankle ▶ 扭傷腳踝 | ▶ I sprained my ankle playing tennis the other day. 前幾天打網球時我扭到腳踝。 |
| **train** [tren] 名 火車 | train station ▶ 火車站 | ▶ Do you know where the nearest train station is? 你知道最近的火車站在哪嗎？ |
| **strain** [stren] 動 拉緊 | strain my back ▶ 背部拉傷 | ▶ I strained my back lifting a heavy box. 抬重箱子時我拉傷了背部。 |
| * **obtain** [əb`ten] 動 獲得 | obtain knowledge ▶ 獲得知識 | ▶ You have to obtain knowledge from school and experiences. 你必須從學校和經驗中獲取知識。 |
| * **maintain** [men`ten] 動 維持 | maintain peace ▶ 維護治安 | ▶ Police try to maintain peace in the streets. 警察試圖維護街道上的治安。 |

| | | |
|---|---|---|
| * **contain** [kən`ten] 動 包含 | contain vitamins 含有維他命 | The food contains a lot of vitamins. 這種食品富含維他命。 |
| **sustain** [sə`sten] 動 支撐、維持 | sustain life 維持生命 | You need to eat to sustain life. 我們都需要進食來維持生命。 |
| **vain** [ven] 形 徒然的 | in vain 白費力氣 | All your efforts will not be in vain. 你所做的努力都不會白費。 |

## agne [en]

| | | |
|---|---|---|
| **champagne** [ʃæm`pen] 名 香檳酒 | champagne bottle 香檳酒瓶 | Do you know how to open a champagne bottle? 你知道如何開香檳嗎？ |

## aign [en]

| | | |
|---|---|---|
| **campaign** [kæm`pen] 名 戰役、活動 | political campaign 政黨造勢活動 | Political campaigns are very competitive before elections. 政黨造勢活動在選舉前競爭激烈。 |

## air [ɛr]

| | | |
|---|---|---|
| * **air** [ɛr] 名 空氣 | ▶ clean air 乾淨的空氣 | ▶ I like to get out of the city and breathe clean air. 我喜歡遠離市區，呼吸乾淨的空氣。 |
| * **fair** [fɛr] 形 公正的 | ▶ fair play 公平的比賽 | ▶ No one cheated during the game; there was fair play all around. 比賽中沒有人作弊，這是一場公平的對決。 |
| * **unfair** [ʌnˋfɛr] 形 不公平的 | ▶ unfair assessment 不公平的評價 | ▶ The teacher made an unfair assessment of the situation. 老師對這個情況作出不公平的評價。 |
| * **affair** [əˋfɛr] 名 事件 | ▶ have an affair 外遇 | ▶ Her husband doesn't know that she has an affair. 她丈夫不知道她外遇的事情。 |
| * **repair** [rɪˋpɛr] 動 名 修理 | ▶ repair the damage 修理損壞部分 | ▶ Do you know how to repair the damage? 你知道如何修理損壞的部分嗎？ |
| **despair** [dɪˋspɛr] 名 動 絕望 | ▶ feelings of despair 絕望的情緒 | ▶ After she got fired, she's been wallowing in her feelings of despair. 在被革職後，她深陷在絕望的情緒之中。 |

## are [ɛr]

| | | |
|---|---|---|
| **care** [kɛr] 名 動 關懷 | ▶ intensive care 特別照顧 | ▶ He has to stay in the intensive care unit of the hospital. 他必須要待在醫院的加護病房。 |

| | | |
|---|---|---|
| * **fare**<br>[fɛr]<br>名 票價 | car fare<br>車資 | I need car fare to get home.<br>我需要買車票的錢才能回家。 |
| * **share**<br>[ʃɛr]<br>動 分享 名 一份 | share a room<br>共用一間房間 | I share a room with someone so my rent is cheaper.<br>我和別人共用一間房間，所以房租比較便宜。 |
| * **declare**<br>[dɪˋklɛr]<br>動 宣佈 | declare war<br>宣戰 | There will always be a country that will declare war on another country.<br>國對國宣戰總是會發生。 |
| * **prepare**<br>[prɪˋpɛr]<br>動 準備 | prepare dinner<br>準備晚餐 | It takes a long time to prepare dinner.<br>做晚餐很費時。 |
| * **compare**<br>[kəmˋpɛr]<br>動 比較 | compare and contrast<br>比較異同 | It's hard to compare and contrast everything you see.<br>去比較你所看到的一切其中的差異是很困難的。 |
| * **spare**<br>[spɛr]<br>動 騰出 形 多餘的 | spare time<br>空閒時間 | Do you use your spare time wisely?<br>你有善用你空閒的時間嗎？ |
| * **rare**<br>[rɛr]<br>形 稀有的 | rare find<br>罕見的發現 | That bracelet from the Tang Dynasty is a rare find.<br>唐朝的手鐲很少見。 |
| * **ware**<br>[wɛr]<br>名 …製品、…物品 | housewares<br>廚具 | Do you know where the housewares section of the department store is?<br>你知道百貨公司的廚具部在哪裡嗎？ |

| | | |
|---|---|---|
| * **aware** [ə`wɛr] 形 察覺的 ▶ | politically aware 熱衷政治 ▶ | Even though she's young, she's very politically aware. 雖然她很年輕，但很熱衷政治。 |
| * **beware** [bɪ`wɛr] 動 當心 ▶ | beware of 注意 ▶ | Beware of falling rocks. 注意落石。 |

## ake [ek]

05

| | | |
|---|---|---|
| * **fake** [fek] 形 假的 ▶ | fake diamond 假鑽 ▶ | That is a fake diamond. 這是假鑽。 |
| * **sake** [sek] 名 緣故 ▶ | for the sake of 看在…份上 ▶ | I won't do that just for the sake of saving a few pennies. 我才不會為了省那些小錢而這樣做。 |
| * **mistake** [mɪ`stek] 名 錯誤 動 弄錯 ▶ | make mistakes 犯錯 ▶ | Everybody makes mistakes. 每個人都會犯錯。 |
| * **wake** [wek] 動 醒來 ▶ | wake up 醒來 ▶ | You better wake up soon, or you'll be late for work. 你最好趕快起床，不然你上班就要遲到了。 |
| **awake** [ə`wek] 形 醒著的 動 喚醒 ▶ | wide awake 十分清醒 ▶ | It's hard to stay wide awake during a boring class. 在無聊的課堂上要保持清醒是很困難的。 |

## ache [ek]

| | | |
|---|---|---|
| **ache** [ek] 名 動 (持續性)疼痛 | ▶ stomachache 胃痛 | ▶ I have a stomachache because I ate too much. 因為我吃太多所以胃痛。 |
| **headache** [ˋhɛdˏek] 名 頭痛 | ▶ headache 頭痛 | ▶ I have a bad headache; do you have any aspirin? 我的頭超痛，你有阿斯匹靈嗎？ |

## eak [ek]

| | | |
|---|---|---|
| * **break** [brek] 動 打破 | ▶ break up 解散、分手 | ▶ Break up the fight. 不要再打架了。 |
| **outbreak** [ˋautˏbrek] 名 爆發 | ▶ outbreak of war 戰爭爆發 | ▶ It looks like there will be an outbreak of war soon. 看樣子戰爭就要爆發了。 |
| **steak** [stek] 名 牛排 | ▶ juicy steak 鮮嫩多汁的牛排 | ▶ Even though he's a vegetarian, he still likes a juicy steak once in a while. 雖然他是素食主義者，但偶爾還是會想吃鮮嫩多汁的牛排。 |

## ale [el]

| | | |
|---|---|---|
| * **scale** [skel] 名 刻度、秤 | ▶ weighing scale 體重計 | ▶ I weighed myself on the weighing scale. 我站在體重計上量體重。 |

| | | |
|---|---|---|
| **inhale**<br>[ɪn`hel]<br>動 吸入 | ▶ inhale smoke<br>吸二手菸 | ▶ I'd like to sit in the non-smoking section because I don't like to inhale smoke. 我想坐非吸菸區，因為我不喜歡吸二手菸。 |
| **exhale**<br>[ɛks`hel]<br>動 呼出 | ▶ exhale air<br>吐氣 | ▶ Don't forget to exhale air when you exercise.<br>運動時不要忘了吐氣。 |
| * **male**<br>[mel]<br>形 男性的 名 男性 | ▶ male dog<br>公狗 | ▶ That male dog is known for attacking the female ones.<br>那隻公狗以攻擊母狗出名。 |
| * **female**<br>[`fimel]<br>形 女性的 名 女性 | ▶ female friend<br>女性朋友 | ▶ Don't you have any female friends?<br>你都沒有女性朋友嗎？ |
| * **sale**<br>[sel]<br>名 出售、拍賣 | ▶ on sale<br>特價 | ▶ Is that shirt on sale?<br>那件襯衫有特價嗎？ |
| **stale**<br>[stel]<br>形 腐壞的 | ▶ stale crackers<br>餿掉的餅乾 | ▶ You should throw those stale crackers out.<br>你應該把那些餿掉的餅乾丟掉。 |

## ail [el]

| | | |
|---|---|---|
| **bail**<br>[bel]<br>名 動 保釋 | ▶ out on bail<br>交保釋放 | ▶ He was only in jail for 10 days before he got out on bail.<br>他在看守所待了十天就被保釋了。 |

| | | |
|---|---|---|
| * **fail**<br>[fel]<br>名動 失敗 | ▶ without fail<br>不失敗 | ▶ I will succeed without fail.<br>我會一口氣就成功的。 |
| * **mail**<br>[mel]<br>名 郵遞、信件 | ▶ mail order<br>郵購 | ▶ You can only get that book by mail order.<br>你只能用郵購的方式買到那本書。 |
| **tail**<br>[tel]<br>名 尾巴 | ▶ wag its tail<br>搖尾巴 | ▶ My dog wags its tail when it's happy.<br>我的狗快樂的時候會搖尾巴。 |
| * **detail**<br>[`ditel]<br>名 細節 | ▶ in detail<br>詳細地 | ▶ Can you explain that to me in detail? 你可以從頭到尾仔細跟我解釋清楚嗎？ |
| * **retail**<br>[`ritel]<br>名 零售 | ▶ retail price<br>零售價、定價 | ▶ The retail price is $26.00 while the sale price is $20.00.<br>這東西定價26美金，但只賣20美金。 |
| **prevail**<br>[prɪ`vel]<br>動 勝過 | ▶ truth will prevail<br>真理勝過一切 | ▶ "The truth will prevail" is a common proverb. 「真理勝過一切」是很常聽到的諺語。 |

## ality [`ɑlətɪ]

| | | |
|---|---|---|
| * **quality**<br>[`kwɑlətɪ]<br>名 品質 | ▶ bad quality<br>品質不良 | ▶ That store sells a lot of clothes that are cheap, but of bad quality. 這家店的衣服雖然便宜，但品質很不好。 |

| | | |
|---|---|---|
| * **equality** [i`kwɑlətɪ] 名 平等 | racial equality 種族平等 | Will there ever be racial equality in the world? 種族平等的夢想在這世上會有實現的一天嗎？ |
| **inequality** [ɪnɪ`kwɑlətɪ] 名 不平等 | inequality between the sexes 男女不平等 | The inequality between the sexes makes many women frustrated. 男女不平等的待遇讓很多女性很有挫折感。 |

## all [ɔl]

| | | |
|---|---|---|
| * **all** [ɔl] 形 所有的 代 全部 | all at once 突然 | I felt like so many things in my life were happening all at once. 我覺得生命中許多事情好像突然接踵而至。 |
| * **hall** [hɔl] 名 大廳 | dining hall 餐廳 | That school's dining hall serves terrible food. 學校餐廳的菜真是有夠難吃。 |
| **mall** [mɔl] 名 購物中心 | shopping mall 購物中心 | Do you want to go to the shopping mall after work? 你下班後想去購物中心嗎？ |
| * **small** [smɔl] 形 小的 | small size 小尺寸 | Make sure you buy the small size shirt. 記得要買S號襯衫。 |
| * **tall** [tɔl] 形 高大的 | tall building 高的建築物 | It's easy to recognize a tall building. 高大的建築物比較容易被認出來。 |

| * install<br>[ɪn`stɔl]<br>動 安裝 | ▶ | install a program<br>安裝程式 | ▶ | Could you install a program on omy computer?<br>你可以幫我在電腦上安裝程式嗎？ |
|---|---|---|---|---|
| wall<br>[wɔl]<br>名 牆壁 | ▶ | wall paper<br>壁紙 | ▶ | I want to put red wall paper in my living room.<br>我要在客廳的牆壁上貼上紅色壁紙。 |

## ally [`ælɪ]

| rally<br>[`rælɪ]<br>名 集合、集會 | ▶ | student rally<br>學生集會 | ▶ | There is a student rally today against the use of fur.<br>今天有個主張反皮草的學生集會。 |
|---|---|---|---|---|
| tally<br>[`tælɪ]<br>名 動 計算 | ▶ | tally the score<br>計算分數 | ▶ | The teacher will tally the score once the game is over.<br>遊戲一旦結束老師就會計算總分。 |

## allow [ə`laʊ]

| * allow<br>[ə`laʊ]<br>動 允許 | ▶ | allow for<br>允許 | ▶ | Will you allow for mistakes?<br>你會允許錯誤發生嗎？ |
|---|---|---|---|---|

## alter [`ɔltɚ]

| | | |
|---|---|---|
| **alter**<br>[ˋɔltɚ]<br>動 改變 | alter the size<br>改尺寸 | Since she gave me her clothes and she's bigger than me, I need to alter the size of them.<br>她給我她的衣服，但她比較大隻，所以我得改衣服的尺寸。 |

## ault [ɔlt]

| | | |
|---|---|---|
| * **fault**<br>[fɔlt]<br>名 缺點 | not at fault<br>沒有錯 | Don't look at me. I'm not at fault.<br>別看我，不是我的錯。 |
| * **default**<br>[dɪˋfɔlt]<br>名 預設值 動 拖欠 | default settings<br>預設值 | The computer comes with default settings if you don't change them. 如果你不做任何變更，你的電腦就會照著預設值跑。 |
| **vault**<br>[vɔlt]<br>名 地窖、金庫 | money vault<br>保險庫 | They broke in the company's money vault.<br>他們闖入公司的保險庫。 |

## am [æm]

| | | |
|---|---|---|
| **jam**<br>[dʒæm]<br>動 名 堵塞 | traffic jam<br>塞車 | It's so frustrating to be stuck in a traffic jam.<br>卡在車陣當中真是令人洩氣。 |
| * **gram**<br>[græm]<br>名 克 | one gram<br>一克 | It will only take one gram of medicine a day.<br>一天只要一公克的藥就行了。 |

| | | |
|---|---|---|
| * **diagram** [ˋdaɪə͵græm] 名 圖表 | draw a diagram 畫圖表 | Children learn to draw diagrams in school. 小朋友在學校學畫圖表。 |
| **telegram** [ˋtɛlə͵græm] 名 電報 | receive a telegram 收到一封電報 | Did you receive a telegram from them? 你有收到他們發的一封電報嗎？ |
| **milligram** [ˋmɪlɪ͵græm] 名 毫克 | milligram of salt 一毫克的鹽巴 | There is a milligram of salt in my water. 我的水裡有一毫克的鹽。 |
| * **program** [ˋprogræm] 名 節目單、程式 | TV program 電視節目 | I love that TV program. 我喜歡那個電視節目。 |
| * **exam** [ɪgˋzæm] 名 考試 | final exam 期末考 | You'd better study hard for the final exam. 你期末考最好認真準備。 |

## an [æn]

| | | |
|---|---|---|
| * **ban** [bæn] 動 名 禁止 | ban on alcohol 禁酒 | There was a ban on alcohol in America in the 1920s. 1920年代美國是禁酒的。 |
| * **scan** [skæn] 動 名 審視、掃描 | scan a picture 掃描照片 | You can now scan a picture into the computer. 你現在可以把照片掃描到電腦裡了。 |

| | | |
|---|---|---|
| **fan** [fæn] 名 扇子 | ceiling fan 吊扇 | The ceiling fan helps cool the room down. 吊扇能降低房間的溫度。 |
| * **than** [ðæn] 連 比較 | more than 比…多 | I like this more than that. 我喜歡這個勝於那個。 |
| **Pakistan** [ˏpækɪˋstæn] 名 巴基斯坦 | government of Pakistan 巴基斯坦政府 | The government of Pakistan is divided over the India issue. 巴基斯坦政府在印度議題上分歧。 |
| **Afghanistan** [æfˋgænəˏstæn] 名 阿富汗 | country of Afghanistan 阿富汗 | The country of Afghanistan has had a turbulent history. 阿富汗這個國家一直以來都處於動盪不安的狀態。 |
| **van** [væn] 名 小貨車 | red van 紅色小貨車 | I saw a red van drive by. 我看見一輛紅色小貨車開過去。 |

## ance [æns]

06

| | | |
|---|---|---|
| **dance** [dæns] 動 名 跳舞 | dance club 舞廳 | Let's go to a dance club tonight. 我們今晚去舞廳跳舞吧。 |
| * **chance** [tʃæns] 名 機會 | good chance 好機會、很大的機會 | There's a good chance that he will be fired for his dishonesty. 他因為不誠實，很有可能會被開除。 |

| | | |
|---|---|---|
| * **enhance** [ɪnˋhæns] 動 增加 | ▶ enhance the color 加深顏色 | ▶ You can enhance the color by changing the settings. 你可以改變設定來加深顏色。 |
| * **finance** [faɪˋnæns] 名 金融 | ▶ finance company 財務公司 | ▶ He's worked at that finance company for 30 years. 他在財務公司已經工作了30年。 |
| **France** [fræns] 名 法國 | ▶ country of France 法國 | ▶ The country of France is now using the Euro as their currency. 法國現在進行的貨幣是歐元。 |
| * **entrance** [ˋɛntrəns] 名 入口 | ▶ front entrance 前門 | ▶ Where's the front entrance of the building? 這棟大樓的前門在哪裡？ |
| * **circumstance** [ˋsɝkəm͵stæns] 名 情況 | ▶ unfortunate circumstance 不幸的境遇 | ▶ Maybe she can help us out in this unfortunate circumstance. 或許她能幫我們擺脫這不幸的境遇。 |

## and [ænd]

| | | |
|---|---|---|
| **Thailand** [ˋtaɪlænd] 名 泰國 | ▶ made in Thailand 泰國製造 | ▶ That purse was made in Thailand. 那個錢包是泰國製造的。 |
| * **demand** [dɪˋmænd] 名 動 要求、需求 | ▶ in demand 有需求的 | ▶ That color is in demand this year. 今年這個顏色很流行。 |

| | | |
|---|---|---|
| * **command** [kə`mænd] 動 名 命令 | ▸ chain of command 一連串的命令 | ▸ You have to follow the chain of command when you're in the army. 在軍中必須要服從一連串的命令。 |
| * **expand** [ɪk`spænd] 動 展開 | ▸ enlarge and expand 擴展 | ▸ That business will enlarge and expand in the future. 那個產業的前景看俏。 |
| * **brand** [brænd] 名 品牌 | ▸ brand name 名牌 | ▸ She only wears clothes that have a brand name. 她只穿名牌的衣服。 |
| **grand** [grænd] 形 雄偉的 | ▸ grand scale 大規模 | ▸ He robs banks on a grand scale. 他搶了銀行鉅額的錢。 |
| * **understand** [ˏʌndə`stænd] 動 理解 | ▸ do you understand 你了解嗎 | ▸ Do you understand? 你了解嗎？ |

## ange [endʒ]

| | | |
|---|---|---|
| * **change** [tʃendʒ] 動 名 改變 | ▸ change of plans 計畫改變 | ▸ There has been a sudden change of plans. 計畫突然改變。 |
| * **exchange** [ɪks`tʃendʒ] 動 名 交換 | ▸ exchange rate 匯率 | ▸ Do you know what the exchange rate for U.S. currency is? 你知道美金匯率是多少嗎？ |

| | | |
|---|---|---|
| * **range** [rendʒ] 名 範圍 | out of range 超出範圍 | The radio is out of range here. 收音機在這裡收不到訊號。 |
| * **arrange** [əˋrendʒ] 動 安排 | arrange the furniture 打點家具 | We have to arrange the furniture for the party. 你要打點辦派對用的家具。 |
| **strange** [strendʒ] 形 奇怪的、陌生的 | strange place 奇怪的地方 | Get me out of this strange place! 讓我離開這個奇怪的地方！ |

## ank [æŋk]

| | | |
|---|---|---|
| * **bank** [bæŋk] 名 銀行 | bank account 銀行帳戶 | I need to open a bank account. 我需要開個銀行帳戶。 |
| * **blank** [blæŋk] 形 空白的 | blank paper 空白紙 | Can you give me a piece of blank paper? 可以給我一張空白紙嗎？ |
| * **rank** [ræŋk] 名 等級 | high rank 高階 | He has a high rank in the police force. 他在警界有很高的位階。 |
| * **frank** [fræŋk] 形 坦白的 | be frank 坦白說 | I want to improve, so please be frank in your criticism. 我想進步，所以請盡量批評指教。 |

## anner [`ænɚ]

| | | |
|---|---|---|
| **banner** [`bænɚ] 名 旗幟、大標題 | ▶ hang a banner 掛旗幟 | ▶ We should hang a banner to welcome him home from the hospital. 我們應該掛個旗幟歡迎他出院回家。 |
| * **scanner** [`skænɚ] 名 掃描器 | ▶ computer scanner 電腦掃描器 | ▶ With our new computer scanner, we can send pictures by email. 有了這台新的電腦掃描器，我們可以用email傳照片了。 |
| **manner** [`mænɚ] 名 方式、態度 | ▶ pleasant manner 隨和的態度 | ▶ Everyone likes her because of her pleasant manner. 她的個性隨和，每個人都很喜歡她。 |

## ant [ænt]

| | | |
|---|---|---|
| **implant** [ɪm`plænt] 動 植入 名 植入物 | ▶ breast implant 隆乳 | ▶ That woman probably has breast implants. 那個女人很可能有去隆乳。 |
| **transplant** [træns`plænt] 動 名 移植 | ▶ liver transplant 肝臟移植 | ▶ He drank too much alcohol and now needs a liver transplant. 他喝酒過量所以需要肝臟移植。 |
| * **grant** [grænt] 動 准予、答應 | ▶ grant wishes 答應願望 | ▶ Mothers grant wishes to their children all the time. 母親總是試著去達成小孩的願望。 |

## ap [æp]

| | | |
|---|---|---|
| **handicap**<br>[ˋhændɪˏkæp]<br>名 動 障礙 | handicap parking<br>殘障停車位 | Handicap parking is usually reserved closest to the entrance. 殘障停車位通常會規劃在靠近入口的地方。 |
| **gap**<br>[gæp]<br>名 缺口、代溝 | generation gap<br>代溝 | There is a generation gap between most parents and children.<br>親子之間多半有代溝的問題。 |
| **overlap**<br>[ˋovɚˋlæp]<br>動 重疊 | overlap each other<br>互相重疊 | Some subjects overlap each other.<br>有些議題互相重疊。 |
| * **map**<br>[mæp]<br>名 地圖 | map of the world<br>世界地圖 | There is a map of the world hanging in my living room.<br>我的客廳掛了一張世界地圖。 |
| **nap**<br>[næp]<br>名 打盹 | take a nap<br>睡一下 | When you are tired, take a nap.<br>你若覺得累可以先睡一下。 |
| **kidnap**<br>[ˋkɪdnæp]<br>動 綁架 | kidnap his son<br>綁架他兒子 | Will they kidnap his son for money?<br>他們會為了錢而綁架他的孩子嗎？ |
| **strap**<br>[stræp]<br>動 捆綁 | strap on<br>綁住 | Strap on your backpack. We're going hiking!<br>綁好你的背包，我們要去遠足了！ |
| **wrap**<br>[ræp]<br>動 包裝 | wrap up<br>包起來 | Can you wrap up the leftovers for me?<br>你可以幫我把剩菜打包起來嗎？ |

| | | |
|---|---|---|
| **unwrap** [ʌnˋræp] 動 打開 | ▶ unwrap a present 打開禮物 | ▶ It's time to unwrap your present! 拆禮物的時間到囉！ |
| **tap** [tæp] 動 輕拍 | ▶ tap lightly 輕拍 | ▶ Tap lightly on the door. Don't bang on it! 你可以輕輕敲門，不要用撞的。 |

## ape [ep]

| | | |
|---|---|---|
| **landscape** [ˋlændˏskep] 名 景色 | ▶ landscape painting 風景畫 | ▶ Some painters prefer landscape paintings to portraits. 有些畫家喜歡風景畫勝於人像畫。 |
| **escape** [əˋskep] 名 動 逃脫 | ▶ no escape 無法逃脫 | ▶ There is supposedly no escape from prison. 監獄理當無法逃脫。 |
| * **shape** [ʃep] 名 形狀、狀態 | ▶ get in shape 保持好體態 | ▶ I have to get in shape. 我得保持好體態。 |
| **tape** [tep] 名 卡帶、膠帶 | ▶ video tape 錄影帶 | ▶ I have a video tape of their wedding. 我有他們婚禮的錄影帶。 |

## ar [ɑr]

| | | |
|---|---|---|
| **bazaar** [bə`zɑr] 名 市集 | shopping bazaar 市集 | Did you go to the shopping bazaar? 你有去市集嗎？ |
| **bar** [bɑr] 名 酒吧、條 | bar of soap 一條肥皂 | Don't forget to buy a bar of soap at the supermarket. 到了超市別忘了買條肥皂回來。 |
| * **car** [kɑr] 名 車 | car wash 洗車 | There's no use in getting a car wash today because it's raining. 今天下雨，洗車是沒用的。 |
| **scar** [skɑr] 名 疤痕 | have any scars 有任何疤痕 | Do you have any scars? 你有任何疤痕嗎？ |
| **seminar** [`sɛmə͵nɑr] 名 討論會 | health seminar 健康座談會 | There is a health seminar on smoking tonight at 6:00. 今晚六點有個吸菸的健康座談會。 |
| **registrar** [`rɛdʒɪ͵strɑr] 名 註冊主任 | registrar's office 註冊組辦公室 | You have to take care of transcripts, course changes, and other business at the registrar's office. 辦理成績單申請、改課之類的事情要到註冊組辦公室。 |

## arre [ɑr]

| | | |
|---|---|---|
| **bizarre** [bɪ`zɑr] 形 奇異的 | bizarre phenomenon 怪異現象 | That snow storm in the middle of August was surely a bizarre phenomenon. 八月天下雪純屬怪異現象。 |

## ara [ˋærə]



| | | |
|---|---|---|
| **mascara** [mæsˋkærə] 名 睫毛膏 | black mascara 黑色睫毛膏 | Black mascara is the most popular color for mascara. 黑色睫毛膏是最常見的顏色。 |
| **Sahara** [səˋhærə] 名 撒哈拉沙漠 | Sahara desert 撒哈拉沙漠 | Many people have died in the Sahara desert. 很多人死在撒哈拉沙漠。 |

## ard [ɑrd]

| | | |
|---|---|---|
| **bombard** [bɑmˋbɑrd] 動 轟炸 | bombard with 疲勞轟炸 | I'm so busy, please don't bombard me with other work. 我很忙，請不要再拿其他工作來煩我。 |
| * **card** [kɑrd] 名 紙牌、卡片 | get-well card 早日康復卡 | I need to make a get-well card for my friend in the hospital. 我得做卡片給住院的朋友，祝他早日康復。 |
| **postcard** [ˋpostˏkɑrd] 名 明信片 | send a postcard 寄明信片 | When you are traveling, don't forget to send a postcard from wherever you are. 旅行的時候，別忘了寄張明信片給我。 |
| * **regard** [rɪˋgɑrd] 名 動 考慮、留意 | with regard to 留意 | Please play with regard to the valuables around you. 請留意身邊的貴重物品。 |
| * **hard** [hɑrd] 形 困難的、硬的 | hard to please 很難取悅 | She is so hard to please. 她很難搞定。 |

| | | |
|---|---|---|
| **guard**<br>[gɑrd]<br>名 守衛 | security guard<br>警衛 | The security guard did not let me in the building.<br>警衛不讓我進去大樓。 |
| **lifeguard**<br>[ˋlaɪf͵gɑrd]<br>名 救生員 | lifeguard on duty<br>執勤的救生員 | Is there a lifeguard on duty at nighttime?<br>晚上有救生員執勤嗎？ |
| **yard**<br>[jɑrd]<br>名 碼、院子 | yard sale<br>庭院二手拍賣 | There is a yard sale you can not miss this Saturday.<br>這個星期六有個二手拍賣，你一定不能錯過。 |
| **graveyard**<br>[ˋgrev͵jɑrd]<br>名 墓地 | graveyard shift<br>大夜班 | He works the graveyard shift so he sleeps during the day.<br>他上大夜班，白天睡覺。 |
| **backyard**<br>[ˋbækjɑrd]<br>名 後院 | in the backyard<br>在後院 | I want to have a barbecue in the backyard for my birthday.<br>我生日想要在後院辦烤肉會。 |

## arent [ˋɛrənt]

| | | |
|---|---|---|
| * **parent**<br>[ˋpɛrənt]<br>名 雙親 | my parents<br>我的父母 | My parents are both doctors.<br>我爸媽都是醫生。 |
| **grandparent**<br>[ˋgrænd͵pɛrənt]<br>名 祖父母 | grandparents' house<br>爺爺奶奶家 | I like to go to my grandparents' house for vacation.<br>我喜歡去爺爺奶奶家度假。 |

| | | |
|---|---|---|
| **transparent** [træns`pɛrənt] 形 透明的 | ▸ transparent cover 透明套 | ▸ I put a transparent cover on my report. 我在我的報告書上加上透明套。 |

## arge [ɑrdʒ]

| | | |
|---|---|---|
| * **charge** [tʃɑrdʒ] 動 收費 名 費用 | ▸ free of charge 免費 | ▸ This meal is free of charge. 這份餐點是免費的。 |
| **recharge** [ri`tʃɑrdʒ] 動 再充電 | ▸ recharge batteries 充好電池 | ▸ I need to recharge my batteries tonight. 今天晚上我得充好電池。 |
| **overcharge** [`ovɚ`tʃɑrdʒ] 動 收價過高 | ▸ overcharge you 超收費用 | ▸ Tourist areas will often overcharge you. 觀光景點通常收費都比較貴。 |
| **discharge** [dɪs`tʃɑrdʒ] 動 釋放 | ▸ discharge from the hospital 出院 | ▸ The doctor will discharge the patient from the hospital when he gets well. 病人康復後醫生會讓他出院。 |
| **large** [lɑrdʒ] 形 大的 | ▸ large quantity 大量 | ▸ I bought a large quantity of nuts today. 我今天買了一大堆堅果。 |
| **enlarge** [ɪn`lɑrdʒ] 動 擴大 | ▸ enlarge the picture 放大照片 | ▸ She will enlarge the picture of her boyfriend. 她會把她男友的照片放大。 |

## arious [ˋɛrɪəs]

| | | |
|---|---|---|
| **precarious**<br>[prɪˋkɛrɪəs]<br>形 不穩的、危險的 | ▶ precarious situation<br>狀況不穩定 | ▶ We are in a precarious situation right now.<br>我們現在的情況不是很穩定。 |
| **various**<br>[ˋvɛrɪəs]<br>形 各式各樣的 | ▶ various possibilities<br>各種可能性 | ▶ There are always various possibilities for every situation.<br>每一種情況都有許多可能性。 |

## arity [ˋærətɪ]

| | | |
|---|---|---|
| **charity**<br>[ˋtʃærətɪ]<br>名 慈善 | ▶ donate to charity<br>捐助慈善機構 | ▶ Many people donate their old clothes to charity.<br>很多人會捐舊衣給慈善機構。 |
| **clarity**<br>[ˋklærətɪ]<br>名 清楚 | ▶ speak with clarity<br>講話清楚 | ▶ When you are giving a speech, you must speak with clarity.<br>演講時，口條和思路一定要清楚。 |
| **solidarity**<br>[ˏsɑləˋdærətɪ]<br>名 團結 | ▶ solidarity among our group<br>團隊團結 | ▶ We must create solidarity among our group.<br>我們這一隊一定要團結。 |

## arm [ɑrm]

| | | |
|---|---|---|
| * **arm**<br>[ɑrm]<br>名 手臂 | ▶ break his arm<br>撞斷手臂 | ▶ He broke his arm playing baseball.<br>他在打棒球時撞斷手臂。 |

| | | |
|---|---|---|
| * **farm** [fɑrm] 名 農場 ▶ | farm animals 農場動物 ▶ | Farm animals are hard to work with. 農場動物很難管理。 |
| * **harm** [hɑrm] 名 動 損傷 ▶ | without harm 毫髮無傷 ▶ | She escaped without harm. 她毫髮無傷順利逃脫了。 |
| **charm** [tʃɑrm] 名 魅力 ▶ | full of charm 充滿魅力 ▶ | You must be full of charm to win her over. 你一定要很有魅力才能贏得她的芳心。 |
| **alarm** [ə`lɑrm] 名 警報 ▶ | alarm clock 鬧鐘 ▶ | Remember to set your alarm clock before you go to bed. 上床睡覺之前記得要設定鬧鐘。 |

## arat [`ærət]

| | | |
|---|---|---|
| **carat** [`kærət] 名 克拉、開 ▶ | 24 carat gold 24開(K)純金 ▶ | This necklace is made of 24 carat gold. 這條項鍊是24K純金做的。 |

## art [ɑrt]

| | | |
|---|---|---|
| * **art** [ɑrt] 名 藝術 ▶ | art museum 美術館 ▶ | Let's go to the art museum today. 我們今天去美術館吧。 |

| | | |
|---|---|---|
| * **chart** [tʃɑrt] 名 圖表 | ▶ flow chart 流程圖 | ▶ Look at the flow chart and follow the lecture. 邊看流程圖邊聽演講。 |
| * **mart** [mɑrt] 名 市場 | ▶ mini mart 迷你市場 | ▶ There are so many mini marts in Taiwan. 台灣有很多小型市場。 |
| * **smart** [smɑrt] 形 聰明的 | ▶ smart dog 聰明的狗 | ▶ He has a smart dog which can do many tricks. 他有隻很會表演的聰明狗狗。 |
| **outsmart** [ˋaʊtˋsmɑrt] 動 智取 | ▶ outsmart your opponent 智取你的對手 | ▶ You need to outsmart your opponent in the game. 你必須在這場比賽中智取你的對手。 |
| * **part** [pɑrt] 名 部分 | ▶ play a part in 參與 | ▶ I want to play a part in making a difference. 我想要參與改造計畫。 |
| * **apart** [əˋpɑrt] 副 分開地 | ▶ break us apart 拆散我們 | ▶ Nothing will break us apart. 沒有任何事情能拆散我們。 |
| **depart** [dɪˋpɑrt] 動 出發、離開 | ▶ depart from 從…出發 | ▶ We'll depart from New York at 3. 我們3點會從紐約出發。 |

## ary [ˋɛrɪ]

| | | |
|---|---|---|
| **legendary**<br>[ˋlɛdʒənd͵ɛrɪ]<br>形 傳說的、傳奇的 | legendary talent<br>傳奇天才 | Mozart is a legendary talent.<br>莫札特是傳奇性的天才人物。 |
| **secondary**<br>[ˋsɛkən͵dɛrɪ]<br>形 第二的、中等的 | secondary school<br>中學 | Secondary school is hard for most adolescents. 大部分的青少年在中學期間都會比較叛逆。 |
| **vocabulary**<br>[vəˋkæbjə͵lɛrɪ]<br>名 字彙 | vocabulary list<br>單字表 | You should keep a vocabulary list of words you don't know.<br>你應該把不知道的單字列成一張表。 |
| * **ordinary**<br>[ˋɔrdn̩͵ɛrɪ]<br>形 普通的 | ordinary life<br>平凡生活 | He led an ordinary life.<br>他過著簡單平凡的生活。 |
| * **extraordinary**<br>[ɪkˋstrɔrdn̩͵ɛrɪ]<br>形 特別的、非凡的 | extraordinary student<br>不凡的學生 | She was an extraordinary student in high school.<br>她在高中時是個不凡的學生。 |
| **disciplinary**<br>[ˋdɪsəplɪn͵ɛrɪ]<br>形 懲罰的 | disciplinary action<br>懲處 | Teachers will take disciplinary action on students when they cheat.<br>若學生作弊的話，老師會實行懲處。 |
| **preliminary**<br>[prɪˋlɪmə͵nɛrɪ]<br>形 初步的 | preliminary round<br>第一輪 | He made the preliminary round of tryouts.<br>他通過了第一輪的選拔。 |
| * **revolutionary**<br>[͵rɛvəˋluʃən͵ɛrɪ]<br>形 革新的 | revolutionary idea<br>創新的想法 | What a revolutionary idea!<br>真是創新的想法！ |

| | | |
|---|---|---|
| * **temporary** [ˋtɛmpə͵rɛrɪ] 形 臨時的 | temporary job 臨時工作 | I want to get a temporary job to make some more money. 我要找份臨時工作賺外快。 |
| * **voluntary** [ˋvɑlən͵tɛrɪ] 形 自願的、志願的 | voluntary service 志願服務 | Will you participate in voluntary service? 你有意願當志工嗎？ |

## ash [æʃ]

08

| | | |
|---|---|---|
| **ash** [æʃ] 名 灰燼 | ashtray 菸灰缸 | Please use the ashtray and not my floor! 請使用菸灰缸，不要弄到地上！ |
| * **cash** [kæʃ] 名 現金 | pay by cash 付現 | Will you pay by cash, or by credit card? 你要付現或是用信用卡付款？ |
| **crash** [kræʃ] 動 名 碰撞 | car crash 車禍 | They got into a car crash yesterday. 他們昨天發生車禍。 |

## asion [ˋeʒən]

| | | |
|---|---|---|
| * **occasion** [əˋkeʒən] 名 場合 | special occasion 特別場合 | You should wear something nice for this special occasion. 在這個特別場合你要穿好看一點。 |

| | | |
|---|---|---|
| * **persuasion** [pə`sweʒən] 名說服 | ▶ a lot of persuasion 花很大力氣說服 | ▶ It took a lot of persuasion to convince them that it was right. 我們花了很大的力氣去說服他們那是對的。 |

## ask [æsk]

| | | |
|---|---|---|
| * **ask** [æsk] 動詢問、要求 | ▶ ask about 詢問 | ▶ Will you ask about it for me? 你會幫我問嗎？ |
| * **task** [tæsk] 名任務 | ▶ multiple tasks 好幾項工作 | ▶ Can you handle multiple tasks at once? 你能馬上處理好幾項工作嗎？ |

## asm [`æzəm]

| | | |
|---|---|---|
| **sarcasm** [`sɑrkæzəm] 名諷刺、挖苦 | ▶ full of sarcasm 充滿諷刺 | ▶ You can sometimes offend someone when you are full of sarcasm. 一味諷刺有時會得罪別人。 |
| * **enthusiasm** [ɪn`θjuzɪˏæzəm] 名熱心、熱情 | ▶ little enthusiasm 沒啥熱忱 | ▶ You have little enthusiasm for learning English. 你對學習英文興趣缺缺。 |

## ass [æs]

| | | |
|---|---|---|
| * **class** [klæs] 名 階級、課 | science class 自然課 | When is your science class? 你什麼時候有自然課？ |
| **glass** [glæs] 名 玻璃、玻璃杯 | glass of water 一杯水 | Bring me a glass of water, please. 請拿一杯水給我。 |
| **hourglass** [ˋaʊr͵glæs] 名 沙漏 | shaped like an hourglass 狀似沙漏 | Some men prefer women whose figures are shaped like an hourglass. 有些男人喜歡身材玲瓏有緻的女人。 |
| **mass** [mæs] 名 團、大眾 | mass of people 一大群人 | There is a mass of people waiting outside for autographs. 一大群人在外面等著要簽名。 |
| * **pass** [pæs] 動 通過 | pass through 通過 | Let the movie star pass through. 讓電影明星通過。 |
| **surpass** [sɚˋpæs] 動 超過、勝過 | surpass expectations 超乎預期 | You will surpass your parents' expectations if you go to Harvard. 如果你上哈佛將會超乎父母的期望。 |
| **harass** [həˋræs] 動 煩擾 | sexually harass 性騷擾 | No one is allowed to sexually harass others. 每個人都不得性騷擾別人。 |

## ast [æst]

| | | |
|---|---|---|
| * **broadcast** [ˋbrɔdˏkæst] 動名 廣播 | ▶ broadcast a program 播出節目 | ▶ He can broadcast a program from his basement. 他可以從他的地下室播送節目。 |
| **forecast** [ˋforˏkæst] 動名 預測 | ▶ weather forecast 天氣預報 | ▶ The weather forecast said it would rain tonight. 天氣預報表示今晚會下雨。 |
| * **contrast** [ˋkɑnˏtræst] [kənˋtræst] 名動 對比 | ▶ in contrast to 跟…對比 | ▶ In contrast to the past, we can now communicate with each other over the internet. 跟過去相比，現在我們可以透過網路交流。 |

## aster [ˋæstɚ]

| | | |
|---|---|---|
| **newscaster** [ˋnjuzˏkæstɚ] 名 新聞播報員 | ▶ TV newscaster 電視新聞播報員 | ▶ That TV newscaster annoys me. 那個電視新聞播報員讓我很不爽。 |
| **master** [ˋmæstɚ] 名 主人 | ▶ master of the house 房子的主人 | ▶ The master of the house is often the father. 一家之主通常是父親。 |
| **disaster** [dɪˋzæstɚ] 名 災難 | ▶ terrible disaster 可怕的災難 | ▶ What happened on 9-11-01 was a terrible disaster. 911事件是場可怕的災難。 |

## atch [ætʃ]

| | | |
|---|---|---|
| **catch** [kætʃ] 動 接住、抓住 | ▶ catch fish 抓魚 | ▶ I like to catch fish. 我喜歡抓魚。 |
| * **match** [mætʃ] 動 比得上、使成對 | ▶ match each other 速配 | ▶ They match each other perfectly. 他們倆是完美的速配組合。 |
| **patch** [pætʃ] 動 修補 | ▶ patch up 修補 | ▶ Can you patch up my torn jeans for me? 你能幫我把牛仔褲的破洞補起來嗎？ |
| * **dispatch** [dɪˋspætʃ] 動 名 派遣 | ▶ dispatch a car 派車 | ▶ The taxi service dispatches a car for you after you call. 你打通電話計程車行就派車給你。 |

## ach [ætʃ]

| | | |
|---|---|---|
| **detach** [dɪˋtætʃ] 動 分開、拆卸 | ▶ detach it from 拆下來 | ▶ You can detach it from the chain. 你可以把它從鏈子上拆下來。 |
| * **attach** [əˋtætʃ] 動 貼上、附加 | ▶ attach a note 附上便條 | ▶ Should I attach a note to his desk? 我該把便條貼在他的桌上嗎？ |

## ate [et]

 09

| | | |
|---|---|---|
| **debate**<br>[dɪˋbet]<br>動 名 辯論 | ▸ controversial debate<br>爭議性的辯論 | ▸ The two candidates got into a controversial debate.<br>兩位候選人陷入爭議性的辯論之中。 |
| **dedicate**<br>[ˋdɛdəˏket]<br>動 奉獻 | ▸ dedicate a song<br>點歌 | ▸ You can dedicate a song to someone on the radio.<br>你可以在廣播節目裡點歌送人。 |
| * **complicate**<br>[ˋkɑmpləˏket]<br>動 使複雜化 | ▸ complicate an issue<br>把問題複雜化 | ▸ Don't complicate the issue.<br>不要讓問題變得更複雜。 |
| * **communicate**<br>[kəˋmjunəˏket]<br>動 傳達、溝通 | ▸ communicate with<br>跟…溝通 | ▸ She said that she could communicate with aliens.<br>她說她能跟外星人溝通。 |
| **locate**<br>[loˋket]<br>動 把…設置在、找出 | ▸ locate the missing pieces<br>找出遺失物的下落 | ▸ Do you know how to locate the missing pieces?<br>你知道要怎麼找出遺失物的下落嗎？ |
| **allocate**<br>[ˋæləˏket]<br>動 分派、分配 | ▸ allocate funds<br>分配資金 | ▸ How will they allocate the funds?<br>他們會怎麼分配資金？ |
| **dislocate**<br>[ˋdɪsləˏket]<br>動 使脫臼 | ▸ dislocate your shoulder<br>使你的肩膀脫臼 | ▸ You will dislocate your shoulder if you do that.<br>你那麼做的話，你的肩膀會脫臼的。 |
| * **advocate**<br>[ˋædvəˏket]<br>動 提倡、主張 | ▸ advocate protecting<br>主張保護 | ▸ He advocates protecting abused children.<br>他主張保護受虐兒。 |

| | | |
|---|---|---|
| * **educate** [ˋɛdʒəˏket] 動 教育、培養 | educate children 教育小孩 | What is the best way to educate children? 教育小孩最好的方法是什麼？ |
| * **date** [det] 名 日期、約會 | go on a date 去約會 | Do you wanna go on a date? 你想要去約會嗎？ |
| * **create** [krɪˋet] 動 創造 | create a plan 想出計畫 | We need to create a plan before we move on. 我們出發前要想好計畫。 |
| * **accommodate** [əˋkɑməˏdet] 動 能容納、供應 | accommodate needs 滿足需求 | People in customer service try to accommodate your needs. 客服人員會盡量滿足你的需求。 |
| **update** [ʌpˋdet] 動 更新 | update old files 更新舊檔案 | It's time to update old files. 是更新舊檔案的時候了。 |
| * **associate** [əˋsoʃɪˏet] 動 聯想、交往 | associate with 和…交往 | Do you associate with him? 你跟他有往來嗎？ |
| **initiate** [ɪˋnɪʃɪˏet] 動 開始、創始 | initiate the process 開始進行程序 | We should initiate the process as soon as possible. 我們應該盡快開始進行程序。 |
| **deviate** [ˋdivɪˏet] 動 脫離、偏離 | deviate from 偏離 | If you go that way, you will deviate from the main roads. 如果你往那邊走，會偏離主要道路。 |

| | | |
| --- | --- | --- |
| **alleviate** [ə`livɪ͵et] 動減輕 | ▶ alleviate the pain 減輕疼痛 | ▶ Take some medicine to alleviate the pain. 吃點藥可以減輕疼痛。 |
| **abbreviate** [ə`brivɪ͵et] 動縮寫、使簡短 | ▶ abbreviate the book 節略這本書 | ▶ I wish I could abbreviate the book. 我希望我能縮短這本書的篇幅。 |
| * **relate** [rɪ`let] 動有關、認同 | ▶ relate to 認同 | ▶ I can relate to your sentiment. 我能認同你的意見。 |
| * **validate** [`vælə͵det] 動使生效、認證 | ▶ validate parking ticket 認證停車券 | ▶ Validate your parking ticket here. 在這裡認證你的停車券。 |
| * **translate** [træns`let] 動翻譯 | ▶ translate a book 翻譯一本書 | ▶ How long does it take to translate a book? 翻譯一本書要花多久時間？ |
| * **calculate** [`kælkjə͵let] 動計算、估計 | ▶ calculate the price 計算價錢 | ▶ I will calculate the price with the discount. 我會算好打折後的價錢。 |
| **circulate** [`sɝkjə͵let] 動循環 | ▶ circulate the air 讓空氣流通 | ▶ Using a fan will help circulate the air. 電風扇會讓空氣流通。 |
| **stimulate** [`stɪmjə͵let] 動刺激、促進 | ▶ stimulate conversation 促進談話 | ▶ Please try to stimulate conversation between those two shy students. 請設法讓那兩位害羞的學生的交談熱絡起來。 |

| Word | Phrase | Example |
| --- | --- | --- |
| **formulate**<br>[ˋfɔrmjə͵let]<br>動 公式化、闡述 | formulate a question<br>闡述問題 | Can you formulate a question about the reading?<br>你能闡述關於這篇閱讀的問題嗎？ |
| * **accumulate**<br>[əˋkjumjə͵let]<br>動 累積 | accumulate data<br>累積資料 | She will accumulate data on monkeys over the summer.<br>她夏天時要收集累積猴子的資料。 |
| * **manipulate**<br>[məˋnɪpjə͵let]<br>動 操作 | manipulate the situation<br>操縱局面 | He knows how to manipulate the situation to his advantage.<br>他知道怎麼樣操縱局面取得優勢。 |
| * **congratulate**<br>[kənˋgrætʃə͵let]<br>動 祝賀 | congratulate the winner<br>恭賀贏家 | Let's congratulate the winner!<br>讓我們來恭喜贏家吧！ |
| * **mate**<br>[met]<br>名 同伴、配偶 | mate for life<br>終生伴侶 | My wife has been my mate for life.<br>我的妻子一直是我的終生伴侶。 |
| * **estimate**<br>[ˋɛstə͵met]<br>動 估計 | estimate the expenses<br>估計費用 | The mechanic can estimate the expenses for the car crash.<br>汽車技師能預估車禍修車的費用。 |
| **coordinate**<br>[koˋɔrdn̩et]<br>動 協調、調節 | coordinate a dinner party<br>籌備晚宴 | We should coordinate a dinner party.<br>我們該籌備一下晚宴。 |
| **eliminate**<br>[ɪˋlɪmə͵net]<br>動 排除、消除 | eliminate an odor<br>消除異味 | Use room spray to eliminate an odor.<br>用房間芳香劑去除異味。 |

| | | |
| --- | --- | --- |
| **contaminate**<br>[kən`tæmə͵net]<br>動 污染 | ▶ contaminate the room<br>污染房間 | ▶ The chemical fire in the kitchen has really contaminated the room.<br>廚房裡的化學火災污染了房間。 |
| **discriminate**<br>[dɪ`skrɪmə͵net]<br>動 區別、歧視 | ▶ discriminate against<br>歧視 | ▶ You shouldn't discriminate against others.<br>你不該歧視他人。 |
| **nominate**<br>[`nɑmə͵net]<br>動 提名、任命 | ▶ nominate a candidate<br>提名候選人 | ▶ It's time to nominate a candidate for class president.<br>是提名班長人選的時候了。 |
| **terminate**<br>[`tɝmə͵net]<br>動 使停止、終止 | ▶ terminate the program<br>終止計劃 | ▶ They will terminate the program because of the lack of funding. 他們因為缺乏資金所以要終止這個計劃。 |
| **donate**<br>[`donet]<br>動 捐獻 | ▶ donate to charity<br>捐給慈善機構 | ▶ Let's donate our old clothes to charity.<br>我們把舊衣服捐給慈善機構吧。 |
| * **anticipate**<br>[æn`tɪsə͵pet]<br>動 預期、期望 | ▶ anticipate a bright future<br>期望光明的未來 | ▶ She anticipates a bright future.<br>她期望有個光明的未來。 |
| **participate**<br>[pɑr`tɪsə͵pet]<br>動 參加、分享 | ▶ participate in<br>參與 | ▶ He likes to participate in lots of activities.<br>他喜歡參加很多活動。 |
| * **rate**<br>[ret]<br>名 價格、率 | ▶ fixed rate<br>固定價格 | ▶ By taxi, there is a fixed rate from Taipei city to the airport. 從台北市到機場搭計程車的價格是固定的。 |

| | | |
|---|---|---|
| **separate** [ˋsɛpəˏret] 動分隔 | separate from 和…分離 | Do you separate the whites from the colors when doing the laundry? 你洗衣服時有把白色衣物跟有色的分開來嗎？ |
| * **celebrate** [ˋsɛləˏbret] 動慶祝 | celebrate the occasion 慶祝 | Let's celebrate the occasion by going out tonight. 我們今晚出去慶祝吧。 |
| **deliberate** [dɪˋlɪbəˏret] 動思考 | deliberate a problem 思考問題 | When you are stuck, just deliberate the problem. 當你遇到瓶頸時，好好思考問題所在。 |
| **accelerate** [ækˋsɛləˏret] 動增加、加速 | accelerate the process 加速過程 | We can accelerate the process by being more efficient. 我們更有效率的話過程就會加快。 |
| **tolerate** [ˋtɑləˏret] 動容忍 | tolerate mistakes 容忍錯誤 | That teacher does not tolerate mistakes. 那位老師不能容忍錯誤。 |
| * **generate** [ˋdʒɛnəˏret] 動產生、造成 | generate confusion 造成困惑 | This problem will generate confusion. 這個問題會造成困惑。 |
| * **operate** [ˋɑpəˏret] 動操作、動手術 | operate a copy machine 操作影印機 | Do you know how to operate a copy machine? 你知道怎麼使用影印機嗎？ |
| **cooperate** [koˋɑpəˏret] 動合作 | cooperate with 和…合作 | Please cooperate with each other. 請互相合作。 |

| | | |
| --- | --- | --- |
| **reiterate**<br>[ri`ɪtə͵ret]<br>動 重申、反覆說 | reiterate the sentence<br>重複句子 | What? Please reiterate the sentence.<br>什麼？請再重複那個句子。 |
| * **integrate**<br>[`ɪntə͵gret]<br>動 整合、使合併 | integrate them together<br>合併它們 | The new plan will be to integrate them together.<br>新計畫是將它們合併。 |
| **elaborate**<br>[ɪ`læbə͵ret]<br>動 闡述 | elaborate on<br>闡述 | Can you elaborate on the subject?<br>你可以對這個主題多加闡述嗎？ |
| * **decorate**<br>[`dɛkə͵ret]<br>動 裝飾 | decorate with<br>用…裝飾 | What will you decorate the living room with?<br>你會用什麼東西佈置客廳？ |
| * **demonstrate**<br>[`dɛmən͵stret]<br>動 示範 | demonstrate by<br>用…示範 | Can you demonstrate it by using your hands?<br>你可以用你的手示範嗎？ |
| **hesitate**<br>[`hɛzə͵tet]<br>動 猶豫 | hesitate on<br>猶豫 | Are you going to hesitate on your decision?<br>你猶豫不決嗎？ |
| * **state**<br>[stet]<br>名 狀況、狀態 | state of<br>狀態 | This is a state of political unrest.<br>政治情勢動盪不安。 |
| * **estate**<br>[ɪs`tet]<br>名 資產 | real estate<br>不動產 | The real estate here is really expensive.<br>這裡的不動產很貴。 |

| | | |
| --- | --- | --- |
| **elevate** [ˋɛlə͵vet] 動舉起、抬起 | elevate your mood 振奮你的情緒 | What can elevate your mood? 什麼能讓你心情變好？ |
| **activate** [ˋæktə͵vet] 動使活動起來 | activate the students 帶動學生 | Does that teacher activate the students? 那位老師有帶動學生嗎？ |
| **motivate** [ˋmotə͵vet] 動給…動機、激發 | motivated by 被…激發 | What are you motivated by? 你被什麼激發？ |

## ait [et]

| | | |
| --- | --- | --- |
| **trait** [tret] 名特徵、特點 | physical trait 身體特徵 | Can you describe his physical traits? 你可以描述一下他的身體特徵嗎？ |
| **strait** [stret] 名海峽 | Taiwan strait 台灣海峽 | Where is the Taiwan strait? 台灣海峽在哪裡？ |
| * **wait** [wet] 動等待 | wait in line 排隊等待 | No one likes to wait in line. 沒人喜歡排隊等候。 |
| **await** [əˋwet] 動等候 | await the day 等著那天 | I await the day I make a lot of money. 我等著賺大錢那天的來臨。 |

## aight [et]

10

| | | |
|---|---|---|
| * **straight** [stret] 形 筆直的 | ▶ straight line 筆直的線 | ▶ Can you draw a straight line without a ruler? 你可以不用尺畫出一條筆直的線嗎？ |

## ation [ˋeʃən]

| | | |
|---|---|---|
| * **vacation** [veˋkeʃən] 名 假期 | ▶ go on vacation 度假 | ▶ I want to go on vacation. 我想去度假。 |
| **dedication** [ˏdɛdəˋkeʃən] 名 奉獻、獻詞 | ▶ make a dedication 獻詞 | ▶ She will make a dedication to her mother at the party. 她會在派對上獻給她媽媽一段話。 |
| * **qualification** [ˏkwɑləfəˋkeʃən] 名 資格 | ▶ have the qualification 有資格 | ▶ Do you have the qualifications for this job? 你符合這份工作的資格嗎？ |
| **justification** [ˏdʒʌstəfəˋkeʃən] 名 辯解、理由 | ▶ no justification 沒有理由 | ▶ There is no justification for your mistakes. 你的過失沒有理由好解釋。 |
| **complication** [ˏkɑmpləˋkeʃən] 名 複雜、併發症 | ▶ medical complication 醫學併發症 | ▶ There was a medical complication during the surgery. 手術過程出現併發症。 |
| * **application** [ˏæpləˋkeʃən] 名 應用、申請 | ▶ application for 申請 | ▶ He made an application for the position. 他申請了這個職位。 |

| 單字 | 片語 | 例句 |
| --- | --- | --- |
| * **communication** [kə͵mjunə`keʃən] 名 傳達、交流 | communication with 和…交流 | Have you ever had communication with aliens? 你跟外星人交流過嗎？ |
| **fabrication** [͵fæbrɪ`keʃən] 名 製造、虛構物 | fabrication of 虛構 | That was a fabrication of the story. 那是個虛構的故事。 |
| * **location** [lo`keʃən] 名 位置 | central location 中心地帶 | I love this house because of its central location. 我愛這棟房子，因為它地處中心地帶。 |
| * **recommendation** [͵rɛkəmɛn`deʃən] 名 推薦 | recommendation letter 推薦信 | My favorite teacher wrote my recommendation letter. 我喜歡的老師幫我寫推薦信。 |
| * **foundation** [faʊn`deʃən] 名 創辦、基礎 | good foundation 好基礎 | She has a good foundation in math. 她數學基礎很好。 |
| * **creation** [krɪ`eʃən] 名 創造、創立 | creation of 創立 | He helped with the creation of the club after the war. 戰後他幫忙創立這間俱樂部。 |
| * **recreation** [͵rɛkrɪ`eʃən] 名 消遣、娛樂 | recreation hall 娛樂廳 | This recreation hall needs new toys and games. 娛樂中心需要新的玩具跟遊戲。 |
| **segregation** [͵sɛgrɪ`geʃən] 名 隔離、分開 | segregation of 隔離 | There is always going to be some sort of segregation of races. 種族隔離一直都存在。 |

| | | |
|---|---|---|
| **obligation** [ˌɑbləˋgeʃən] 名義務、責任 | obligation to 義務 | It says that there is no obligation to buy. 上面寫著沒有義務購買。 |
| * **investigation** [ɪnˋvɛstəˋgeʃən] 名調查 | private investigation 私下調查 | They are conducting a private investigation. 他們正在進行私下調查。 |
| **interrogation** [ɪnˌtɛrəˋgeʃən] 名訊問、審問 | interrogation of 訊問 | The police participated in the interrogation of the criminal. 警方參與訊問罪犯的過程。 |
| **appreciation** [əˌpriʃɪˋeʃən] 名欣賞、鑑賞 | appreciation of 鑑賞力 | Do you have an appreciation of flowers? 你對花有鑑賞能力嗎？ |
| **abbreviation** [əˌbrivɪˋeʃən] 名縮寫 | abbreviation for 縮寫 | What's the abbreviation for the United States of America? "The United States of America" 的縮寫是什麼？ |
| **revelation** [rɛvl̩ˋeʃən] 名揭示、暴露 | sudden revelation 突然明白 | She has a sudden revelation that she is old. 她突然體認到她老了。 |
| * **cancellation** [ˌkænsl̩ˋeʃən] 名取消 | no cancellation 不能取消 | No cancellations are allowed. 不能取消。 |
| **violation** [ˌvaɪəˋleʃən] 名違反、違背 | violation of a law 違法 | That is in violation of a law. 那是違法的。 |

| | | |
| --- | --- | --- |
| **legislation**<br>[ˏlɛdʒɪsˋleʃən]<br>名法規、立法 | new legislation<br>新法令 | Things will be different with the new legislation.<br>新的法令立定後情況就不一樣了。 |
| **speculation**<br>[ˏspɛkjəˋleʃən]<br>名沈思、推測 | make a speculation<br>推測 | It's hard to make a speculation about that house's price.<br>很難推測那棟房子的價錢。 |
| **calculation**<br>[ˏkælkjəˋleʃən]<br>名計算 | calculation of<br>計算 | I think the waiter's calculation of the price of the meal is wrong.<br>我覺得服務生算錯這份餐的價錢了。 |
| * **regulation**<br>[ˏrɛgjəˋleʃən]<br>名規則、規定 | regulation for<br>規定 | What are the regulations for opening a bar in this city?<br>在這座城市開酒吧有什麼規定？ |
| **manipulation**<br>[məˏnɪpjʊˋleʃən]<br>名操作、控制 | manipulation of<br>控制 | He always tries to get away with the manipulation of your feelings.<br>他總是試圖要成功控制你的情感。 |
| * **population**<br>[ˏpɑpjəˋleʃən]<br>名人口 | population of<br>人口 | The population of this town is really small.<br>這個城鎮的人口實在很少。 |
| * **confirmation**<br>[ˏkɑnfɚˋmeʃən]<br>名確認 | confirmation of<br>確認 | Do you have a confirmation of your flight reservations?<br>你有確認你的班機嗎？ |
| * **information**<br>[ˏɪnfɚˋmeʃən]<br>名消息、資訊 | important information<br>重要消息 | There is some important information here!<br>這裡有重要消息要宣佈！ |

| | | |
|---|---|---|
| * **nation** [ˋneʃən] 名國家、民族 | the nation of Islam 伊斯蘭教民族 | The nation of Islam consists of several countries. 伊斯蘭教民族包含好幾個國家。 |
| * **explanation** [ˏɛksplәˋneʃən] 名說明、解釋 | reasonable explanation 合理的解釋 | There had better be a reasonable explanation for what you did. 你最好對你做的事有個合理解釋。 |
| * **resignation** [ˏrɛzɪgˋneʃən] 名辭職、辭呈 | hand in your resignation 遞辭呈 | When are you going to hand in your resignation? 你何時要遞辭呈？ |
| * **combination** [ˏkambәˋneʃən] 名結合 | combination of 結合 | This sauce is a combination of ketchup and mustard. 這個醬汁是由蕃茄醬跟芥末醬混合而成。 |
| **coordination** [koˋɔrdn̩ˏeʃən] 名協調 | coordination with 和…協調 | We work in coordination with them. 我們跟他們協調合作。 |
| **domination** [ˏdamәˋneʃən] 名支配、統治 | domination of 統治 | During Japan's domination of Taiwan, people learned Japanese in schools. 日本統治台灣時期，人們在學校學習日文。 |
| **destination** [ˏdɛstәˋneʃən] 名目的地、目標 | final destination 最終目標 | What is your final destination? 你的最終目標是什麼？ |
| * **occupation** [ˏakjәˋpeʃən] 名職業 | current occupation 目前的職業 | What is your current occupation? 你目前的職業是什麼？ |

| 單字 | 片語 | 例句 |
| --- | --- | --- |
| * **declaration** [ˏdɛkləˋreʃən] 名宣佈、宣告 | declaration of war 宣戰 | I heard that the president made a declaration of war. 我聽說總統宣戰。 |
| **separation** [ˏsɛpəˋreʃən] 名分開、分離 | separation of 分開 | When was the separation of the two states? 這兩個州是何時分裂的？ |
| **consideration** [kənsɪdəˋreʃən] 名考慮 | careful consideration 仔細考慮 | Put a lot of careful consideration into your report. 你要多用點心思在報告裡。 |
| * **generation** [ˏdʒɛnəˋreʃən] 名世代 | my generation 我的世代 | Are there common ideals for my generation? 我們這個世代有共同的理想嗎？ |
| * **cooperation** [koˏɑpəˋreʃən] 名合作 | cooperation of 合作 | We need the cooperation of the police and the government for this event. 警方跟政府必須合作處理這起事件。 |
| **admiration** [ˏædməˋreʃən] 名欽佩、讚美 | admiration of 對…的讚美 | I'm concerned about his admiration of powerful politicians. 我關心他對有力政治人物的讚美。 |
| **inspiration** [ˏɪnspəˋreʃən] 名靈感、好辦法 | sudden inspiration 突然靈光一閃 | I've got the sudden inspiration to go for a swim. 我突然靈光一閃想去游泳。 |
| **exploration** [ˏɛkspləˋreʃən] 名探索 | exploration of 探索 | When do you think was the first exploration of this area? 你認為這個地區首次被探勘是何時？ |

| | | |
| --- | --- | --- |
| * **corporation** [ˌkɔrpəˋreʃən] 名 公司 | big corporation 大公司 | That big corporation took over many smaller stores. 那個大公司接管了許多較小的商店。 |
| **concentration** [ˌkɑnsɛnˋtreʃən] 名 集中、專心 | concentration of 集中 | There is a high concentration of Asians in this area. 這個地區亞洲人高度集中。 |
| **registration** [ˌrɛdʒɪˋstreʃən] 名 登記、註冊 | registration card 註冊卡 | Where is your registration card? 你的註冊卡在哪裡？ |
| **illustration** [ɪˌlʌsˋtreʃən] 名 圖解、插圖 | small illustration 小插圖 | I like the small illustrations in that book. 我喜歡那本書裡的小插圖。 |
| **duration** [djʊˋreʃən] 名 持續、期間 | duration of 期間 | You are not allowed to leave during the duration of the movie. 電影放映期間你不可離場。 |
| * **conversation** [ˌkɑnvəˋseʃən] 名 會話 | boring conversation 無聊的會話 | What a boring conversation! 真是無聊的會話！ |
| **expectation** [ˌɛkspɛkˋteʃən] 名 期待、預期 | high expectations 高度期望 | Most parents have high expectations for their children. 大多數家長對孩子有著高度期許。 |
| **limitation** [ˌlɪməˋteʃən] 名 限制 | limitation of 限制 | There is a limitation of space in this room. 這個房間有空間限制。 |

| | | |
| --- | --- | --- |
| * **presentation** [ˏprizɛn`teʃən] 名 呈現、演出 | oral presentation 口頭報告 | I hate making oral presentations! 我討厭做口頭報告！ |
| **quotation** [kwo`teʃən] 名 引用、引文 | quotation from 引文出自… | Where is that quotation from? 那句引文出自哪裡？ |
| **transportation** [ˏtrænspɚ`teʃən] 名 運輸 | public transportation 大眾交通工具 | Do you know how to take public transportation? 你知道怎麼搭乘大眾交通工具嗎？ |
| * **reputation** [ˏrɛpjə`teʃən] 名 名譽、名聲 | bad reputation 壞名聲 | She has a bad reputation for being late. 她常遲到所以名聲不佳。 |
| **elevation** [ˏɛlə`veʃən] 名 高度、海拔 | high elevation 高海拔 | This city's high elevation makes it difficult to breathe during strenuous exercise. 在這座海拔高的城市做激烈運動會呼吸困難。 |
| * **motivation** [ˏmotə`veʃən] 名 動力、動機 | lose motivation 失去動力 | Try not to lose motivation. 盡量不要失去動力。 |
| **innovation** [ˏɪnə`veʃən] 名 革新、引進 | innovation of 引進 | When was the innovation of the ballpoint pen? 原子筆是何時引進的？ |
| **observation** [ˏɑbzɝ`veʃən] 名 觀察 | keen observation 敏銳的觀察 | He made a keen observation about the movie. 他對這部電影有著敏銳的觀察。 |

| | | |
| --- | --- | --- |
| * **reservation** [ˌrɛzɚˋveʃən] 名 保留、預約 | make a reservation 預約 | Did you make a reservation for tonight's dinner? 今天晚餐你有預約嗎？ |
| **realization** [ˌrɪələˋzeʃən] 名 領悟 | sudden realization 突然領悟 | She had the sudden realization that she loved him. 她突然了解到自己愛上了他。 |
| **civilization** [ˌsɪvl̩əˋzeʃən] 名 文明 | ancient civilization 古文明 | Sometimes I wish I lived in some ancient civilization. 有時候我希望自己活在古文明時代。 |

## ause [ɔz]

11

| | | |
| --- | --- | --- |
| **cause** [kɔz] 名 原因 動 導致 | cause and effect 因果關係 | Do you think that there is a cause and effect for everything? 你認為每件事都有因果關係嗎？ |
| * **because** [bɪˋkɔz] 連 因為 | because of 因為 | He left because of the bad weather. 因為天氣不好他離開了。 |
| **clause** [klɔz] 名 條款、子句 | independent clause 獨立子句 | An independent clause can be a complete sentence. 獨立子句可以是完整的句子。 |
| **pause** [pɔz] 動 名 暫停、中斷 | pause for a second 暫停一下 | Can you just pause for a second? 你可不可以暫停一下？ |

## ave [ev]

| | | |
|---|---|---|
| * **save** [sev] 動 儲蓄、救 | save lives ▶ 拯救生命 | ▶ Firefighters save lives for a living. 消防隊員以拯救生命為職業。 |
| **wave** [wev] 動 揮動 名 波浪 | wave your hand ▶ 揮手 | ▶ Wave your hand in the air if you vote yes. 如果你贊成就在空中揮手。 |
| **microwave** [ˋmaɪkro͵wev] 名 微波 | microwave oven ▶ 微波爐 | ▶ You could heat this up in a microwave oven. 你可以用微波爐把這個加熱。 |

## aw [ɔ]

| | | |
|---|---|---|
| * **law** [lɔ] 名 法律 | against the law ▶ 違法 | ▶ It is against the law to smoke inside an airplane. 在飛機上抽菸是違法的。 |
| **outlaw** [ˋaut͵lɔ] 名 罪犯 | wanted outlaw ▶ 通緝犯 | ▶ He is a wanted outlaw in 5 states. 他是五個州的通緝犯。 |
| **draw** [drɔ] 動 畫、拉 | draw a line ▶ 畫線 | ▶ Can you draw a line from here to there? 你可以從這裡到那裡畫一條線嗎？ |
| **withdraw** [wɪðˋdrɔ] 動 移開、退出 | withdraw from school ▶ 退學 | ▶ I want to withdraw from school. 我想退學。 |

## awed [ɔd]

| | | |
|---|---|---|
| * **flawed** [flɔd] 形 有缺點的 | flawed diamond 有瑕疵的鑽石 | Do you know how to tell a flawed diamond from a good one? 你知道怎麼分辨有瑕疵的鑽石跟完好的鑽石嗎？ |

## ax [æks]

| | | |
|---|---|---|
| * **fax** [fæks] 名 傳真機 | fax machine 傳真機 | The fax machine in our office is broken. 我們辦公室的傳真機壞了。 |
| **relax** [rɪˋlæks] 動 放鬆、休息 | relax at home 在家休息 | Today is a good day to relax at home. 今天適合在家休息。 |
| **climax** [ˋklaɪmæks] 名 頂點、高潮 | climax of the movie 電影的高潮 | I was disappointed with the climax of the movie. 我對電影的高潮感到失望。 |
| * **tax** [tæks] 名 稅金 | tax returns 納稅申報單 | Have you filled out your tax returns yet? 你填好納稅申報單了嗎？ |

## ay [e]

| | | |
|---|---|---|
| * **holiday** [ˋhɑlə͵de] 名 節日、假日 | holiday celebration 節日慶祝會 | Our company will have a holiday celebration at the boss's house. 我們公司要在老闆家裡舉辦節日慶祝會。 |

| | | |
|---|---|---|
| **today**<br>[tə`de]<br>名 今天 | today's specials<br>今日特餐 | Today's specials are the Chicken Noodle Soup and the Striped Bass.<br>今日特餐是麵條雞湯跟斑紋鱸魚。 |
| **yesterday**<br>[`jɛstəde]<br>名 昨天 | yesterday morning<br>昨天早上 | Yesterday morning, we took the new car to the beach.<br>昨天早上我們開新車去海邊。 |
| * **delay**<br>[dɪ`le]<br>動 名 耽擱、延遲 | delayed flight<br>班機延誤 | I am waiting for my husband's delayed flight.<br>我在等我先生延誤的班機。 |
| **play**<br>[ple]<br>動 玩、演奏 名 戲劇 | school play<br>校內話劇比賽 | There is a school play for each class every year.<br>每年每班都會參加校內話劇比賽。 |
| **display**<br>[dɪ`sple]<br>動 名 陳列、展示 | display case<br>展示箱 | The robbers broke the display case.<br>強盜砸壞了展示箱。 |
| **may**<br>[me]<br>助 可能、可以 | may I<br>我可以…嗎 | May I call you again?<br>我可以再打給你嗎？ |
| * **pay**<br>[pe]<br>動 付款 名 薪水 | pay day<br>發薪日 | Friday is pay day.<br>星期五是發薪日。 |
| * **way**<br>[we]<br>名 道路、方法 | which way<br>哪條路 | Which way to Texas?<br>往德州要走哪條路？ |

| | | |
|---|---|---|
| **away** [ə`we] 副離開、不在 | ▶ go away 離開 | ▶ I want you to go away. 我要你走開。 |
| **subway** [`sʌb͵we] 名地下鐵 | ▶ subway station 地鐵站 | ▶ Where is the closest subway station? 最近的地鐵站在哪裡？ |
| **halfway** [`hæf`we] 形中途的 | ▶ halfway point 中途點 | ▶ What is the halfway point from here to New York City? 從這裡到紐約市的中途點是哪裡？ |
| **highway** [`haɪ͵we] 名公路 | ▶ highway patrol 公路巡警 | ▶ The highway patrol pulled me over for speeding. 公路巡警因為我超速把我攔下來。 |
| **railway** [`rel͵we] 名鐵路 | ▶ railway station 火車站 | ▶ How do you get to the railway station? 你怎麼到火車站？ |
| **hallway** [`hɔl͵we] 名玄關、走廊 | ▶ down the hallway 沿著走廊 | ▶ The bathroom is down the hallway, through the last door on your right. 沿著走廊，穿過右手邊最後一扇門就是廁所。 |

## ayer [`eɚ]

| | | |
|---|---|---|
| **layer** [`leɚ] 名層、階層 | ▶ outer layer 外層 | ▶ She didn't eat the outer layer of the cake. 她沒吃蛋糕外層部分。 |

| | | |
|---|---|---|
| **player**<br>[ˋpleɚ]<br>名 球員、演員 | ▸ basketball player<br>籃球員 | ▸ Who is your favorite basketball player?<br>你最喜歡的籃球員是誰？ |
| * **taxpayer**<br>[ˋtæksˏpeɚ]<br>名 納稅人 | ▸ honest taxpayer<br>誠實納稅人 | ▸ He's an honest taxpayer.<br>他是誠實的納稅人。 |

## ayor [ˋeɚ]

| | | |
|---|---|---|
| **mayor**<br>[ˋmeɚ]<br>名 市長 | ▸ mayor of New York City<br>紐約市長 | ▸ The mayor of New York City had a tough job keeping the residents calm during 9-11.<br>911期間，讓市民保持鎮靜是紐約市長艱難的職責。 |

# 2. 押 E 韻的單字

## each [itʃ]

12

| | | |
|---|---|---|
| * **each** [itʃ] 形 每 代 每個 | each other ▸ 互相 | We love each other. ▸ 我們彼此相愛。 |
| **beach** [bitʃ] 名 海灘 | go to the beach ▸ 去海邊 | She goes to the beach with her friends every hot weekend. ▸ 每個炎熱的週末她都會和朋友去海邊。 |
| **peach** [pitʃ] 名 桃子 | a peach ▸ 一顆桃子 | Would you like to eat a peach? ▸ 你想要吃桃子嗎？ |
| * **reach** [ritʃ] 動 抵達 名 可及範圍 | out of reach ▸ 搆不著 | My mobile is out of reach. ▸ 我的手機收不到訊號。 |
| * **teach** [titʃ] 動 講授 | teach English ▸ 教英文 | Most foreigners who live in Taiwan teach English. ▸ 大部分住台灣的外國人在教英文。 |

## eech [itʃ]

| | | |
|---|---|---|
| * **speech** [spitʃ] 名 說話、演講 | give a speech ▸ 發表演說 | The president will give a speech to the whole school tomorrow. ▸ 校長明天將對全校發表演說。 |
| **screech** [skritʃ] 名 尖銳刺耳之聲 | a screech of brakes ▸ 煞車聲 | I heard a screech of brakes outside my house. ▸ 我聽到屋外的煞車聲。 |

## eacher [ˋitʃɚ]

| | | |
|---|---|---|
| **preacher** [ˋpritʃɚ] 名 牧師 | a good preacher ▶ 一位好牧師 | He is a good preacher. ▶ 他是一位好牧師。 |
| * **teacher** [ˋtitʃɚ] 名 老師 | English teacher ▶ 英文老師 | I want a new English teacher. ▶ 我想要一位新的英文老師。 |

## eature [ˋitʃɚ]

| | | |
|---|---|---|
| * **feature** [ˋfitʃɚ] 名 特色、專題 | an interesting feature of ▶ 有趣的特色<br>a special feature 特別專題 | The strange steering wheel is an interesting feature of that model of car. 奇特的方向盤是該款車型迷人的特色。<br>There is a special feature on TV tonight about rats. 今晚有個老鼠特輯的電視節目。 |
| **creature** [ˋkritʃɚ] 名 生物、人 | a creature of habit ▶ 受習慣支配的人<br>a lovely creature 可愛的動物 | He never changes; he's a creature of habit. 他不曾改變，他是改不掉習慣的人。<br>What a lovely creature! It's adorable! 多可愛的動物啊！真可愛！ |

## eady [ˋɛdɪ]

| | | |
|---|---|---|
| * **ready** [ˋrɛdɪ] 形 準備好的 | get ready to ▶ 準備好要… | Let's get ready to play ball! ▶ 我們快準備去打球吧！ |

| | | |
|---|---|---|
| * **already** [ɔlˋrɛdɪ] 副 已經 | ▶ he had already gone 他已經走了 | ▶ He had already gone when we arrived. 我們到達時他已經走了。 |
| * **steady** [ˋstɛdɪ] 形 穩固的 | ▶ a steady faith 堅定的信仰 | ▶ She has always trusted in me and kept a steady faith in my abilities. 她一直信任我，也相信我的能力。 |
| **unsteady** [ʌnˋstɛdɪ] 形 不平穩的 | ▶ an unsteady mind 心神不寧 | ▶ Please forgive my behavior because I have an unsteady mind now. 請原諒我的行為，因為我現在心神不寧。 |

## eague [ig]

| | | |
|---|---|---|
| **league** [lig] 名 聯盟、社團 | ▶ baseball league 棒球聯盟 | ▶ Which baseball league do they watch? 他們看的是哪個棒球聯賽？ |
| * **colleague** [ˋkɑlig] 名 同事 | ▶ a colleague of mine 我的一位同事 | ▶ An old colleague of mine called me last night. 我的一位老同事昨晚打電話給我。 |

## eaker [ˋikɚ]

| | | |
|---|---|---|
| **loudspeaker** [ˋlaudˋspikɚ] 名 擴音器 | ▶ electrical loudspeaker 電子擴音器 | ▶ The electrical loudspeaker blasted through the hallways. 電子擴音器的聲音響徹走廊。 |

| **speaker** [ˋspikɚ] 名 演講者、說某種語言的人 | a poor speaker 蹩腳的演講者 French speaker 講法語的人 | He is a poor speaker when he has a large audience. 面對廣大聽眾時，他是個蹩腳的演講者。 There are many French speakers in Canada. 加拿大有很多講法語的人。 |
|---|---|---|

## ealous [ˋɛləs]

| | | |
|---|---|---|
| * **jealous** [ˋdʒɛləs] 形 嫉妒的 | jealous of 嫉妒 | She is jealous of her friend's beauty. 她很嫉妒她朋友的美。 |
| **zealous** [ˋzɛləs] 形 熱心的、熱情的 | overzealous 過度熱心的 | He gets overzealous sometimes when he talks about sports. 他講到運動有時會興奮過度。 |

## ease [is]

| | | |
|---|---|---|
| **cease** [sis] 動 終止 | cease firing 停止開槍 | You must cease firing your guns! 你一定要停止開槍！ |
| * **lease** [lis] 動 租借 名 租賃 | lease a car 租車 for lease 出租 | Can I lease a car with my credit? 我可以刷信用卡租車嗎？ That house is for lease. 那間房子待出租。 |

| | | |
|---|---|---|
| * **release** [rɪˋlis] 動 名 釋放、發行 | release from prison 從監獄中釋放 the latest release 最新發行 | He is finally released from prison. 他終於出獄了。 The latest release from the press just came out. 報社才剛發出最新的新聞稿。 |
| * **decrease** [dɪˋkris] [ˋdikris] 動 名 減少 | decrease in numbers 數目減少 | The amount of people on strike has decreased in numbers. 罷工的人數已經減少了。 |
| * **increase** [ɪnˋkris] [ˋɪnkris] 動 名 增加 | on the increase 增加中 | Shopping malls in Taipei are on the increase. 台北的購物中心不斷增加中。 |
| **grease** [gris] 名 油脂 動 賄賂 | shiny with grease 油得發亮 | His hair was shiny with grease. 他的頭髮油油亮亮。 |

## eason [ˋizn̩]

| | | |
|---|---|---|
| * **reason** [ˋrizn̩] 名 理由 動 勸說 | reason with 規勸 | He won't listen to me, but see if you can reason with him. 他不會聽我的，不過看看你是否可以勸他。 |
| **season** [ˋsizn̩] 名 季節 動 調味 | the four seasons 四季 | I like living in a place that has the four seasons. 我喜歡住在四季分明的地方。 |

## east [ist]

| | | |
|---|---|---|
| * **east**<br>[ist]<br>名 東方 形 東方的 | go east<br>往東方 | You should go east if you want to see that.<br>如果你想看那個，應該往東方走。 |
| **feast**<br>[fist]<br>名 盛宴 | prepare the feast<br>準備盛宴 | We prepared the feast for the wedding.<br>我們為婚禮準備了筵席。 |
| * **least**<br>[list]<br>名 最少 形 最少的 | at least<br>至少 | There are at least ten people in love with me!<br>至少有十個人愛上我！ |
| **yeast**<br>[jist]<br>名 酵母 | live yeast<br>活酵母 | Some people use live yeast for making bread.<br>有些人會用活酵母來做麵包。 |

## easure [ˋɛʒɚ]

| | | |
|---|---|---|
| **pleasure**<br>[ˋplɛʒɚ]<br>名 愉快 | It's a pleasure to<br>很高興… | It's a pleasure to meet you.<br>很高興認識你。 |
| * **measure**<br>[ˋmɛʒɚ]<br>動 測量 名 措施 | take measures<br>採取措施 | We'll take measures to stop global warming.<br>我們會採取措施阻止全球暖化。 |
| **treasure**<br>[ˋtrɛʒɚ]<br>名 財富 動 珍愛 | art treasures<br>藝術珍寶 | We went to see the art treasures of China in the museum.<br>我們到博物館看中國的藝術珍寶。 |

## easy [ˋizɪ]

 13

| | | |
|---|---|---|
| **easy** [ˋizɪ] 形 容易的 ▸ | come easy 變容易 ▸ | Don't worry, it will come easy to you when the time comes. 別擔心，到時事情就會變得容易。 |
| **uneasy** [ʌnˋizɪ] 形 擔心的 ▸ | uneasy about 為…擔心 ▸ | I'm really uneasy about the test. 我真的很擔心那個測驗。 |

## eath [ɛθ]

| | | |
|---|---|---|
| **death** [dɛθ] 名 死亡 ▸ | put her to death 處死她 ▸ | He put her to her death with a gun. 他開槍殺了她。 |
| **breath** [brɛθ] 名 呼吸 ▸ | hold your breath 屏住呼吸 ▸ | How long can you hold your breath for? 你可以閉氣多久？ |

## eath [iθ]

| | | |
|---|---|---|
| **beneath** [bɪˋniθ] 介 在…之下 ▸ | beneath the table 在桌下 ▸ | The child hid beneath the table. 這個小孩躲在桌下。 |
| **wreath** [riθ] 名 花圈 ▸ | Christmas wreath 聖誕花環 ▸ | Most people put Christmas wreaths on their front door during the holiday season. 聖誕節期間大多數的人會在門前掛聖誕花環。 |

## eeth [iθ]

| | | |
|---|---|---|
| **teeth** [tiθ] 名 牙齒 | ▶ brush teeth 刷牙 | ▶ I don't think he brushes his teeth much because his breath stinks. 我想他不常刷牙，因為他有口臭。 |

## eather [ˋɛðɚ]

| | | |
|---|---|---|
| **feather** [ˋfɛðɚ] 名 羽毛 | ▶ feather bed 羽毛床 | ▶ I want a feather bed for Christmas. 我想要一張羽毛床當聖誕節禮物。 |
| **leather** [ˋlɛðɚ] 名 皮革 | ▶ leather gloves 皮手套 | ▶ Leather gloves are not only stylish, but also warm. 皮手套不僅時髦而且暖和。 |
| **weather** [ˋwɛðɚ] 名 天氣 | ▶ weather forecast 天氣預報 | ▶ What's the weather forecast for tomorrow? 天氣預報說明天天氣怎樣？ |

## ether [ˋɛðɚ]

| | | |
|---|---|---|
| **together** [təˋgɛðɚ] 副 一起 | ▶ work together 合作 | ▶ We need to work together. 我們得攜手合作。 |
| **altogether** [ˏɔltəˋgɛðɚ] 副 完全、全部 | ▶ come altogether 全部（一起）來 | ▶ Will you come altogether, or separately? 你們會一起來還是各自來？ |

## eave [iv]

| | | |
|---|---|---|
| * **leave** [liv] 動 離開 名 休假 | leave for 前往 | When will you leave for New York? 你何時要前往紐約？ |
| **weave** [wiv] 動 編織 | weave a story 編故事 | She is good at weaving a story. 她很會編故事。 |

## eeve [iv]

| | | |
|---|---|---|
| **sleeve** [sliv] 名 袖子 | roll up sleeves 捲起袖子 | Roll up your sleeves and get ready to do some work! 捲起你的袖子準備工作吧！ |

## eive [iv]

| | | |
|---|---|---|
| **deceive** [dɪ`siv] 動 欺騙 | deceive yourself 欺騙自己 | Don't deceive yourself about the facts. 要勇於面對事實，別欺騙自己。 |
| * **receive** [rɪ`siv] 動 收到、受到 | receive a letter 收到一封信<br>receive criticism 遭受批評 | Have you received a letter from your mother yet? 你收到你媽媽的來信了沒？<br>Her unconventional style caused her to receive criticism from many people. 她異於常人的風格讓她遭到許多人的批評。 |

| | | |
|---|---|---|
| **conceive**<br>[kən`siv]<br>動 構想出、懷孕 | conceive a plan<br>構思一個計劃<br>conceive a child<br>懷小孩 | Let's conceive a plan to win this match.<br>讓我們想個計劃贏得這場比賽。<br>To conceive a child is apparently an interesting experience.<br>懷孕顯然是個有趣的經驗。 |

## eve [iv]

| | | |
|---|---|---|
| **eve**<br>[iv]<br>名 前夕 | Christmas eve<br>聖誕節前夕 | On Christmas eve, most families get together for a huge traditional dinner.<br>聖誕節前夕，大部分家庭會聚在一起享用豐盛的傳統晚餐。 |

## ieve [iv]

| | | |
|---|---|---|
| * **achieve**<br>[ə`tʃiv]<br>動 實現、達到 | achieve a goal<br>達到目標 | Sometimes it's hard to achieve a goal.<br>有時要達到目標很難。 |
| * **believe**<br>[bɪ`liv]<br>動 相信 | believe in a faith<br>相信信仰 | For some people, if you can believe in a faith, you will feel more at peace. 對某些人而言，堅定信仰就會感到更平靜。 |
| **relieve**<br>[rɪ`liv]<br>動 減輕、使放心 | relieve the pain<br>減輕疼痛<br>feel relieved<br>感到放心 | She took some medicine to relieve the pain.<br>她吃藥以減輕疼痛。<br>I feel so relieved that I passed the exam.<br>考試及格讓我鬆了一口氣。 |

| | | |
|---|---|---|
| **grieve**<br>[griv]<br>動 使悲傷 | grieve the loss of loved ones<br>為失去所愛的人悲傷 | It is so painful to grieve the loss of loved ones.<br>失去所愛的人是如此悲痛。 |
| **retrieve**<br>[rɪˋtriv]<br>動 重新得到 | retrieve my backpack<br>取回背包 | I need to retrieve my backpack from the locker before I go home. 回家前，我必須去置物櫃拿我的背包。 |

## ever [ˋivɚ]

| | | |
|---|---|---|
| **fever**<br>[ˋfivɚ]<br>名 動 發燒 | have a fever<br>發燒 | You should rest when you have a fever.<br>發燒時你應該要休息。 |

## eiver [ˋivɚ]

| | | |
|---|---|---|
| **receiver**<br>[rɪˋsivɚ]<br>名 接待人、聽筒 | pick up the receiver<br>拿起話筒 | Pick up the receiver! The phone's been ringing for so long.<br>快接電話！電話已經響很久了。 |

## eck [ɛk]

| | | |
|---|---|---|
| **check**<br>[tʃɛk]<br>動 名 檢查 | check out<br>檢查、看 | Did you check out the new girl in our class?<br>你看過我們班上新來的女生嗎？ |

| | | |
|---|---|---|
| * **paycheck** [ˋpe͵tʃɛk] 名 薪資 | ▶ a large paycheck 大筆薪資 | ▶ I'm waiting for a large paycheck. 我正在等一大筆薪資進來。 |
| **neck** [nɛk] 名 脖子 | ▶ long neck 長脖子 | ▶ Giraffes have long necks. 長頸鹿有長長的脖子。 |

## ecord [ˋɛkɚd]

| | | |
|---|---|---|
| **record** [ˋrɛkɚd] 名 紀錄、唱片 | ▶ break an all-time record 打破紀錄<br>jazz records 爵士唱片 | ▶ She broke an all-time record in the swimming race. 她打破游泳比賽紀錄。<br>I found a bunch of jazz records in the basement of my grandparents' house. 我在祖父母家的地下室發現一堆爵士唱片。 |

## ect [ɛkt]

14

| | | |
|---|---|---|
| **defect** [ˋdifɛkt] 名 缺陷 | ▶ a birth defect 天生缺陷 | ▶ Her one closed eye is the result of a birth defect. 她的一隻眼睜不開是因為先天缺陷。 |
| * **affect** [əˋfɛkt] 動 影響 | ▶ affect people 影響人們 | ▶ He has really affected people in a good way. 他為人們帶來了正面的影響。 |
| * **effect** [ɪˋfɛkt] 名 影響、效果 | ▶ have an effect on 對…有影響 | ▶ I think this lotion has an effect on my skin's texture. 我認為這種化妝水會影響我的膚質。 |

| | | |
|---|---|---|
| * **infect** [ɪnˋfɛkt] 動 傳染、感染 | ▶ infect the crowds 感染群眾 | ▶ That band really knows how to infect the crowds. 那個樂團很會帶動群眾。 |
| * **object** [əbˋdʒɛkt] 動 反對 | ▶ object to 反對 | ▶ I hope you don't object to what I'm saying. 我希望你不反對我說的話。 |
| * **subject** [səbˋdʒɛkt] 動 使服從 | ▶ subject to 使服從 | ▶ She subjects his will to her own. 她要他服從她的意願。 |
| **eject** [ɪˋdʒɛkt] 動 噴射 | ▶ eject smoke 排放廢氣 | ▶ Many factories eject smoke into the air. 許多工廠排放廢氣到空氣中。 |
| * **reject** [rɪˋdʒɛkt] 動 拒絕 | ▶ reject all our ideas 拒絕我們所有的點子 | ▶ My boss rejected all our ideas. 我的老板否決我們所有的點子。 |
| **inject** [ɪnˋdʒɛkt] 動 注射 | ▶ inject him with a drug 為他打針 | ▶ The nurses have to inject him with a drug to calm him down. 護士必須為他打針好讓他平靜下來。 |
| **project** [prəˋdʒɛkt] [ˋprɑdʒɛkt] 動 計劃 名 企劃 | ▶ project a tax decrease 規劃減稅 | ▶ The economists have projected a tax decrease for next year. 經濟學家已計劃明年減稅。 |
| **elect** [ɪˋlɛkt] 動 選舉 | ▶ elect a president 選總統 | ▶ Democratic countries have the people vote to elect a president. 民主國家由人民投票選總統。 |

| | | |
|---|---|---|
| **neglect** [nɪg`lɛkt] 動 忽視 | neglect his duty 怠忽職守 | Don't let him neglect his duty of washing the dishes. 別讓他忘了洗碗。 |
| * **intellect** [`ɪntḷ͵ɛkt] 名 智力 | a man of superior intellect 智力出眾的人 | He is a man of superior intellect. 他是一個非常聰穎的人。 |
| * **collect** [kə`lɛkt] 動 收集 | collect stamps 集郵 | She collects stamps as a hobby. 她有集郵的嗜好。 |
| **recollect** [͵rɛkə`lɛkt] 動 回憶 | recollect memories 回憶往事 | I find it hard to recollect any memories from my early childhood. 我發現喚起童年記憶是件難事。 |
| * **connect** [kə`nɛkt] 動 連接 | connect with 與…聯繫 | We think it is easy to connect with each other. 我們認為互相聯繫是很容易的事。 |
| **disconnect** [͵dɪskə`nɛkt] 動 分開 | disconnect from 分開 | She feels disconnected from the rest of the class. 她覺得跟班上其他人有隔閡。 |
| * **respect** [rɪ`spɛkt] 名 動 尊敬 | show him a lot of respect 對他表示崇高的敬意 | Everybody shows him a lot of respect. 每個人都對他表示崇高的敬意。 |
| **disrespect** [͵dɪsrɪ`spɛkt] 名 動 不敬 | no disrespect intended 並無不敬之意 | There was no disrespect intended when he left early. 他提早離開，其實並無不敬之意。 |

| | | |
|---|---|---|
| **inspect**<br>[ɪnˋspɛkt]<br>動 檢查 | inspect the roof for leaks<br>檢查屋頂的漏洞 | My mother hired someone to inspect the roof for leaks.<br>我媽媽雇人檢查屋頂的漏洞。 |
| * **prospect**<br>[ˋprɑspɛkt]<br>名 預期、可能性 | prospect of his return<br>他回來的可能性 | Are there any prospects for his return?<br>他有可能回來嗎？ |
| * **expect**<br>[ɪkˋspɛkt]<br>動 期待 | more than we had expected<br>超乎我們期待 | A lot more people showed up for our play than we had expected.<br>來看表演的人比我們預期的多很多。 |
| **suspect**<br>[səˋspɛkt] [ˋsʌspɛkt]<br>動 懷疑 名 嫌疑犯 | suspect your motives<br>懷疑你的動機<br>suspects of the robbery<br>搶劫的嫌疑犯 | She suspects your motives for being so nice to her all of a sudden.<br>她懷疑你突然對她那麼好的動機。<br>The suspects of the robbery were rounded up at the police station.<br>搶劫的嫌疑犯都被圍捕到了警察局。 |
| **direct**<br>[dəˋrɛkt]<br>形 直接的 | in direct contact with<br>與…直接聯繫 | Are you in direct contact with him, or do you go through someone else?<br>您是直接聯絡他，還是透過其他人？ |
| **indirect**<br>[ˏɪndəˋrɛkt]<br>形 間接的 | an indirect route<br>間接路線 | That's an indirect route to the store; it'll take forever.<br>那條路不直接通到那家商店，會花太多時間。 |
| **correct**<br>[kəˋrɛkt]<br>形 正確的 動 改正 | correct answers<br>正確的答案<br>correct mistakes<br>修正錯誤 | How many correct answers did you have on the test?<br>你在測驗中答對幾題？<br>Can you correct my mistakes?<br>你可以修正我的錯誤嗎？ |

| | | |
|---|---|---|
| **incorrect**<br>[ˏɪnkə`rɛkt]<br>形 不正確的 | an incorrect report<br>不正確的報告 | They sent an incorrect report to the agency.<br>他們寄給代理商一份錯誤的報表。 |
| **sect**<br>[sɛkt]<br>名 派別 | belong to different sects<br>屬於不同的派別 | Although they are all Christian, they do belong to different sects. 雖然他們都是基督徒，但屬於不同的教派。 |
| **insect**<br>[`ɪnsɛkt]<br>名 昆蟲 | an insect bite<br>昆蟲咬傷 | I got an insect bite.<br>我被昆蟲咬了。 |
| **intersect**<br>[ˏɪntɚ`sɛkt]<br>動 貫穿、交叉 | intersect to form a right angle<br>交叉成直角 | Two lines must intersect perpendicularly to form a right angle.<br>兩條線必須垂直相交才能形成直角。 |
| **dissect**<br>[daɪ`sɛkt]<br>動 解剖 | dissect a frog<br>解剖青蛙 | I refused to dissect a frog in my seventh grade science class. 上七年級的自然課時，我拒絕解剖青蛙。 |
| **detect**<br>[dɪ`tɛkt]<br>動 察覺 | detect anger in her voice<br>察覺她語帶氣憤 | Is she mad? Can you detect anger in her voice?<br>她生氣了嗎？你有發現她說話語帶氣憤嗎？ |
| **architect**<br>[`ɑrkəˏtɛkt]<br>名 建築師 | a well-known architect<br>知名建築師 | A well-known architect designed this building.<br>一位知名建築師設計了這棟建築物。 |
| **protect**<br>[prə`tɛkt]<br>動 保護 | protect from<br>保護…免受（傷害） | My parents try hard to protect me from the cruel world outside. 我的父母努力保護我避免受到外面殘酷世界的傷害。 |

# ective [ˋɛktɪv]

| | | |
| --- | --- | --- |
| * **effective** [ɪˋfɛktɪv] 形 有效的 | effective in 對…有效的 | He is effective in persuading others. 他很能有效地說服別人。 |
| **ineffective** [ɪnəˋfɛktɪv] 形 無效果的 | ineffective in 對…無效的 | She is ineffective in telling others "no." 她無法對別人說「不」。 |
| * **objective** [əbˋdʒɛktɪv] 形 客觀的 名 目的 | the objective reality 客觀事實 | Can you tell the objective reality from the subjective one? 你能分辨客觀事實跟主觀事實嗎？ |
| * **subjective** [səbˋdʒɛktɪv] 形 主觀的 | a subjective judgment 主觀判斷 | A subjective judgment can sometimes be biased. 主觀判斷有時可能是帶有偏見的。 |
| **elective** [ɪˋlɛktɪv] 形 選修的 | elective courses 選修課 | What elective courses are you taking this semester? 你這學期要選什麼選修課程？ |
| **selective** [səˋlɛktɪv] 形 有選擇性的 | be selective 具有選擇性的 | You must be selective in choosing a new sofa. 你必須有所取捨地挑選一組新沙發。 |
| **collective** [kəˋlɛktɪv] 形 集體的 | the collective effort 集體努力 | We will need the collective effort of the whole team to win. 我們必須集全隊之力贏得勝利。 |
| * **perspective** [pəˋspɛktɪv] 形 透視的 名 觀點 | a different perspective 不同的觀點 | Let's ask her for a different perspective. 讓我們請教她不同的觀點。 |

| | | |
|---|---|---|
| **detective** [dɪˋtɛktɪv] 名 偵探 形 偵探的 | ▶ detective stories 偵探小說 | ▶ I liked to read detective stories when I was young. 年輕時我喜歡看偵探小說。 |

## ector [ˋɛktɚ]

| | | |
|---|---|---|
| **projector** [prəˋdʒɛktɚ] 名 投影機 | ▶ an overhead projector 高射投影機 | ▶ The overhead projector is broken so we can't view slides today. 投影機壞了，所以我們今天無法看投影片。 |
| * **collector** [kəˋlɛktɚ] 名 收藏家 | ▶ a collector of antiques 古董收藏家 | ▶ It's costly to be a collector of antiques. 成為古董收藏家要很有錢。 |
| **inspector** [ɪnˋspɛktɚ] 名 視察員 | ▶ a ticket inspector 剪票員 | ▶ The ticket inspector threw out anyone who didn't have a ticket. 剪票員不讓沒有票的人進場。 |
| * **director** [dəˋrɛktɚ] 名 主管、導演 | ▶ a film director 電影導演 | ▶ He wants to be a film director one day. 他希望有一天能成為電影導演。 |
| **detector** [dɪˋtɛktɚ] 名 探測器 | ▶ a lie detector 測謊器 | ▶ They hooked up a lie detector to see if he was lying. 他們用測謊器測試他是否說謊。 |
| **protector** [prəˋtɛktɚ] 名 保護者 | ▶ protectors of wildlife animals 野生動物保育者 | ▶ There aren't many protectors of wildlife animals today. 現在的野生動物保育者不多了。 |

## ed [ɛd]



| | | |
|---|---|---|
| **bed** [bɛd] 名 床 | go to bed ▶ 上床睡覺 | It's time to go to bed. ▶ 睡覺的時間到了。 |
| **sled** [slɛd] 名 雪橇 | pull sleds ▶ 拉雪橇 | In Alaska, dogs pull sleds. ▶ 在阿拉斯加，狗會拉雪橇。 |
| **coed** [ˋkoˋɛd] 形 男女同校的 | coed school ▶ 男女合校 | I went to coed schools all my life. ▶ 我一直都上男女合校的學校。 |
| **biped** [ˋbaɪˏpɛd] 形 兩足的 | biped mammal ▶ 兩足哺乳動物 | Humans are the only biped mammals that can talk. ▶ 人類是唯一會講話的兩足哺乳動物。 |
| **red** [rɛd] 形 紅色的 名 紅色 | a red carpet ▶ 紅毯 | I dream of walking down a red carpet wearing a beautiful fancy dress. ▶ 我夢想穿著漂亮別緻的禮服走過紅毯。 |

## ead [ɛd]

| | | |
|---|---|---|
| **dead** [dɛd] 形 死的 | a dead end ▶ 困境、死角 | You have to turn around. This road leads to a dead end. ▶ 你必須迴轉，這條路是死巷。 |
| * **ahead** [əˋhɛd] 副 在前 | go ahead ▶ 先走 | Go ahead and leave. ▶ 先走吧。 |

| | | |
|---|---|---|
| **forehead** [ˋfɔr͵hɛd] 名 前額 | ▸ high forehead 高額頭 | ▸ He has a really high forehead. 他的額頭很高。 |
| **letterhead** [ˋlɛtɚ͵hɛd] 名 信頭 | ▸ use the letterhead 使用信頭 | ▸ Use the letterhead when you send something from the company. 當你從公司寄信時，要使用信頭。 |
| **overhead** [ˋovɚˋhɛd] 副 在頭頂上 | ▸ fly overhead 在頭頂上飛 | ▸ I saw a flock of geese fly overhead just now. 我剛才看到一群鵝飛過我頭頂。 |
| **lead** [lɛd] 名 鉛 | ▸ lead pipes 鉛管 | ▸ The lead pipes in this house are beginning to wear out. 這房子的鉛管開始破裂了。 |
| **bread** [brɛd] 名 麵包 | ▸ bread and butter 麵包和奶油、謀生之道 | ▸ Can you pass the bread and butter please? 請把麵包和奶油遞給我好嗎？ |
| **dread** [drɛd] 動 懼怕 | ▸ dread snakes 怕蛇 | ▸ Many brave men dread snakes. 很多勇敢的人都怕蛇。 |
| **thread** [θrɛd] 名 線 | ▸ a piece of thread 一段線 | ▸ I can't get this piece of thread through the needle. 我沒辦法把這段線穿過針孔。 |
| * **spread** [sprɛd] 動 使伸展 | ▸ spread his arms 伸展他的手臂 | ▸ He spread his arms out for the tailor to measure his size. 他伸直手臂讓裁縫師量他的尺寸。 |

| | | |
|---|---|---|
| * **instead** [ɪn`stɛd] 副 作為替代、反而 | instead of 代替 | Instead of going home, why don't you come out to dinner with me? 與其回家，何不出來跟我吃晚餐？ |

## ettle [`ɛtl̩]

| | | |
|---|---|---|
| **kettle** [`kɛtl̩] 名 水壺 | put the kettle on the stove 把茶壺放在爐上 | Can you put the kettle on the stove to boil some water for tea? 你可以把茶壺放在爐上煮點水來泡茶嗎？ |
| * **settle** [`sɛtl̩] 動 解決（問題等） | settle the matter 解決問題 | Let's settle the matter quietly. 讓我們安靜地解決問題。 |

## etal [`ɛtl̩]

| | | |
|---|---|---|
| **metal** [`mɛtl̩] 名 金屬 | a metal detector 金屬探測器 | Take out the stuff in your pockets before you go through a metal detector. 你通過金屬探測器之前要取出口袋裡的雜物。 |
| **petal** [`pɛtl̩] 名 花瓣 | flower petals 花瓣 | The flower petals have already started to shrivel up and die. 花瓣已經開始枯萎凋謝了。 |

## edge [ɛdʒ]

| | | |
|---|---|---|
| **edge**<br>[ɛdʒ]<br>名 邊緣 | on the edge of<br>在…邊緣 | He's on the edge of the cliff.<br>他在懸崖邊。 |
| **pledge**<br>[plɛdʒ]<br>名 動 保證 | give him my pledge<br>我向他保證 | I give him my pledge to tell the truth.<br>我向他保證會說出真相。 |

## ee [i]

| | | |
|---|---|---|
| **bee**<br>[bi]<br>名 蜜蜂 | busy as a bee<br>忙得像蜜蜂 | You've been as busy as a bee lately; I haven't gotten a chance to speak to you.<br>你最近很忙，我都沒機會和你說話。 |
| * **fee**<br>[fi]<br>名 費用 | the doctor's fee<br>看診費 | The doctor's fee is cheaper than the medicine.<br>看診費比藥便宜。 |
| **refugee**<br>[ˏrɛfjuˋdʒi]<br>名 難民 | a refugee camp<br>難民營 | He volunteered at the refugee camp during his free time.<br>他有空時就到難民營當義工。 |
| **flee**<br>[fli]<br>動 逃走 | flee the burning house<br>逃出火燒屋 | She didn't have time to flee the burning house.<br>她沒有時間逃出火燒屋。 |
| **nominee**<br>[ˏnɑməˋni]<br>名 被提名人 | Oscar nominee<br>奧斯卡被提名人 | Who are the Oscar nominees for best actor this year?<br>今年奧斯卡最佳男演員被提名人有誰？ |

| 單字 | 片語 | 例句 |
|---|---|---|
| **knee**<br>[ni]<br>名 膝蓋 | on his knees<br>他跪著 | He got down on his knees to propose to her.<br>他跪下來向她求婚。 |
| * **free**<br>[fri]<br>形 自由的、免費的 | a free country<br>自由的國家<br>free of charge<br>免費 | Is this a free country?<br>這是一個自由的國家嗎？<br>He gave me a haircut, free of charge. 他免費幫我理髮。 |
| **carefree**<br>[ˋkɛr͵fri]<br>形 無憂無慮的 | feel carefree<br>感覺無憂無慮 | It's good to feel carefree.<br>無憂無慮是很棒的。 |
| * **agree**<br>[əˋgri]<br>動 同意 | agree with<br>同意 | Do you agree with me?<br>你認同我嗎？ |
| * **disagree**<br>[͵dɪsəˋgri]<br>動 不同意 | disagree with<br>不同意 | I disagree with you.<br>我不同意你的說法。 |
| * **degree**<br>[dɪˋgri]<br>名 程度、學位 | to some degree<br>在某種程度上<br>a bachelor's degree<br>學士學位 | He seems mean, but to some degree he's just insecure.<br>他似乎很不友善，但某種程度上來說只是沒有安全感而已。<br>Do you have a bachelor's degree? 你有學士學位嗎？ |
| **tree**<br>[tri]<br>名 樹 | a cherry tree<br>櫻桃樹 | George Washington chopped down a cherry tree.<br>喬治華盛頓砍倒櫻桃樹。 |
| * **oversee**<br>[ˋovəˋsi]<br>動 監督 | oversee the workers<br>監督員工 | The manager's job is to oversee the workers.<br>經理的工作是監督員工。 |

| | | |
|---|---|---|
| **sightsee** [ˋsaɪtˏsi] 動 觀光 | go sightseeing 觀光 | Where should we go sightseeing? 我們該去哪裡觀光？ |
| **absentee** [ˏæbsn̩ˋti] 名 缺席者 | an absentee ballot 缺席選票 | Since I go to school in Connecticut, I will have to vote by absentee ballot this year. 我在康乃迪克讀書，所以今年我勢必得用缺席選票選舉。 |
| * **guarantee** [ˏgærənˋti] 名 動 保證 | my guarantee 我的保證 | I give you my guarantee that I will win. 我跟你保證我會贏。 |
| * **employee** [ˏɛmplɔɪˋi] 名 雇員 | a government employee 政府官員 | Government employees receive many extra benefits. 政府官員收受很多好處。 |
| **chimpanzee** [ˏtʃɪmpænˋzi] 名 黑猩猩 | cute chimpanzee 可愛的黑猩猩 | I want a cute chimpanzee for a pet. 我想要有隻可愛的黑猩猩當寵物。 |

## ea [i]

| | | |
|---|---|---|
| **plea** [pli] 名 懇求 | plea for 懇求 | He will make a plea for the victim's safety. 他將請求讓受害者保持安全。 |
| **pea** [pi] 名 豌豆 | like two peas in a pod 十分相似 | We're like two peas in a pod. 我們倆像同個模子印出來的。 ※用豆莢內的豌豆比喻兩者非常相似。 |

| | | |
|---|---|---|
| **sea**<br>[si]<br>名 海洋 | under the sea<br>海底下 | There are many creatures under the sea.<br>海底有很多生物。 |
| **tea**<br>[ti]<br>名 茶 | a cup of tea<br>一杯茶 | Could you pour me a cup of tea please?<br>可以請你倒杯茶給我嗎？ |

## ey [i]

| | | |
|---|---|---|
| * **key**<br>[ki]<br>名 鑰匙、關鍵 | car keys<br>車鑰匙 | I lost my car keys.<br>我的車鑰匙不見了。 |
| * **money**<br>[`mʌnɪ]<br>名 錢 | cost a lot of money<br>花很多錢 | That dress costs a lot of money.<br>這套衣服很貴。 |

## eed [id]

| | | |
|---|---|---|
| * **proceed**<br>[prə`sid]<br>動 繼續進行 | proceed with his story<br>繼續講他的故事 | He proceeded with his story even though the lights went out.<br>即使熄燈了他還是繼續講他的故事。 |
| * **succeed**<br>[sək`sid]<br>動 成功 | succeed in<br>成功 | I want to succeed in business.<br>我想要事業有成。 |

| | | |
|---|---|---|
| **exceed** [ɪkˋsid] 動 超過 | ▶ exceed my expectation 超乎我的預期 | ▶ The amount of donations we received exceeded my expectations. 我們收到的捐款金額超乎預期。 |
| **indeed** [ɪnˋdid] 副 確實 | ▶ yes, indeed 是的，沒錯 | ▶ Yes, indeed, that is a good idea. 是的，沒錯，那是個好點子。 |
| **feed** [fid] 動 餵養 | ▶ feed the birds 餵鳥 | ▶ Do not feed the birds in the park. 請勿在公園餵鳥。 |
| **bleed** [blid] 動 流血 | ▶ bleed a lot 流很多血 | ▶ I fell and my knee is bleeding a lot. 我跌倒了，膝蓋流了很多血。 |
| * **need** [nid] 動 名 需要 | ▶ no need to 不需要 | ▶ There is no need to panic. 不必驚慌。 |
| * **speed** [spid] 名 速度 | ▶ at a high speed 高速 | ▶ Slow down! You're driving at a high speed! 慢一點！你開得太快了！ |
| **breed** [brid] 動 繁殖 | ▶ breed fish 養殖魚 | ▶ A lot of places in Taiwan breed fish to sell as food. 台灣很多地方養殖食用魚供販賣。 |
| **greed** [grid] 名 貪婪 | ▶ full of greed 充滿貪婪 | ▶ You shouldn't be so full of greed. 你不應該這麼貪婪。 |

| | | |
| --- | --- | --- |
| **seed**<br>[sid]<br>名 種子 | a bag of seeds<br>一包種子 | I bought a bag of seeds for the bird feeder in my back-yard.<br>我買了一包種子放在後院的餵鳥器。 |
| **weed**<br>[wid]<br>名 雜草 | pull out the weeds<br>拔雜草 | I hire a gardener to pull out the weeds in my yard.<br>我雇用園丁幫我在院子裡拔雜草。 |
| **seaweed**<br>[ˋsi͵wid]<br>名 海藻 | green seaweed<br>綠海藻 | Some people don't like to eat green seaweed.<br>有些人不喜歡吃綠海藻。 |

## ead [id]

| | | |
| --- | --- | --- |
| **bead**<br>[bid]<br>名 有孔小珠 | string of beads<br>一串珠子 | This string of beads is going to be used to make a necklace.<br>這一串珠子將被做成項鍊。 |
| * **lead**<br>[lid]<br>動 領導 | lead the fight<br>主導論戰 | She will lead the fight against sexism in the debate today.<br>她將在今天的辯論中，主導反對性別歧視的論戰。 |
| **plead**<br>[plid]<br>動 辯護 | plead innocent<br>辯稱無罪 | The accused man pleads innocent.<br>被告辯稱無罪。 |
| **mislead**<br>[mɪsˋlid]<br>動 誤導、欺騙 | mislead voters<br>誤導選民 | Honest candidates try not to mislead voters.<br>誠實的候選人會盡量不去誤導選民。 |

| | | |
|---|---|---|
| **read**<br>[rid]<br>動 閱讀 | ▶ read the newspaper<br>閱讀報紙 | ▶ Do you read the newspaper every day?<br>你每天都看報嗎？ |

## ede [id]

| | | |
|---|---|---|
| **recede**<br>[rɪˋsid]<br>動 後退 | ▶ recede from<br>後退 | ▶ I watched them recede from the line.<br>我看著他們退到線後。 |
| **precede**<br>[priˋsid]<br>動 處在…之前、優於 | ▶ precedes the Ming Dynasty<br>明朝以前 | ▶ That vase precedes the Ming Dynasty.<br>那是明朝以前的花瓶。 |
| **concede**<br>[kənˋsid]<br>動 承認、讓給 | ▶ concede defeat<br>承認失敗 | ▶ The blue team finally conceded defeat.<br>藍隊最後認輸了。 |

## eter [ˋitɚ]

16

| | | |
|---|---|---|
| **meter**<br>[ˋmitɚ]<br>名 儀錶 | ▶ the gas meter<br>油錶 | ▶ It looks like the gas meter is running on empty.<br>從油錶看來好像沒油了。 |
| **centimeter**<br>[ˋsɛntəˏmitɚ]<br>名 公分 | ▶ one centimeter<br>一公分 | ▶ My nails are only one centimeter long.<br>我的指甲只有一公分長。 |

| | | |
|---|---|---|
| **kilometer**<br>[ˋkɪlə͵mitɚ]<br>名 公里 | ▶ two kilometers<br>兩公里 | ▶ The road from the post office to my house is about two kilometers long.<br>從郵局到我家大約兩公里。 |

## eaty [ˋitɪ]

| | | |
|---|---|---|
| **meaty**<br>[ˋmitɪ]<br>形 肉的、豐富的 | ▶ meaty dish<br>有肉的菜餚 | ▶ I'm craving a really meaty dish.<br>我好想吃肉喔。 |
| **treaty**<br>[ˋtritɪ]<br>名 條約 | ▶ sign a treaty with<br>與…簽條約 | ▶ Japan signed a treaty with China.<br>日本與中國簽定條約。 |

## eek [ik]

| | | |
|---|---|---|
| **cheek**<br>[tʃik]<br>名 臉頰 | ▶ rosy cheeks<br>紅潤的臉頰 | ▶ She gets rosy cheeks after she exercises.<br>她運動後臉頰變得很紅。 |
| **peek**<br>[pik]<br>動 名 窺視 | ▶ take a peek at<br>偷看 | ▶ Did you take a peek at the answers?<br>你有偷看答案嗎？ |
| **creek**<br>[krik]<br>名 小河 | ▶ by the creek<br>沿著小河 | ▶ We used to play by the creek when I was little.<br>小時候我們常常沿著小河玩耍。 |

| | | |
|---|---|---|
| **Greek** [grik] 形 希臘的 | ▶ the Greek islands 希臘島嶼 | ▶ I hear the Greek islands are amazingly beautiful. 我聽說希臘島嶼的美讓人驚豔。 |
| **seek** [sik] 動 尋找 | ▶ seek answers 尋找答案 | ▶ Some people look to a god to seek answers. 有些人期待神明能給予解答。 |
| **week** [wik] 名 星期 | ▶ once a week 一星期一次 | ▶ He showers only once a week! 他一星期只洗一次澡！ |

## eak [ik]

| | | |
|---|---|---|
| * **leak** [lik] 名 裂縫 | ▶ a leak in the roof 屋頂的裂縫 | ▶ There is a leak in the roof. 屋頂有個裂縫。 |
| **sneak** [snik] 動 溜走 | ▶ sneak past the guard 越過警衛溜走 | ▶ The prisoners tried to sneak past the guard, but didn't make it. 犯人試著越過警衛溜走，但沒成功。 |
| * **peak** [pik] 名 尖端 | ▶ the mountain peak 山峰 | ▶ Have you ever made it to the top of a mountain peak? 你曾成功登頂嗎？ |
| * **speak** [spik] 動 說話 | ▶ speak to 與…說話 | ▶ I want to speak to the manager. 我要跟經理說話。 |

| | | |
|---|---|---|
| **freak** [frik] 形 怪異的 名 怪人 | a freak accident ▶ 奇怪的事故 | ▶ I don't know how it happened; it must've been a freak accident. 我不知道是怎麼發生的，這真是個奇怪的意外。 |
| **streak** [strik] 名 條紋 | lucky streak ▶ 幸運連線 | ▶ She's had a lucky streak on the slot machines today. 她今天玩吃角子老虎贏得一個幸運連線。 |
| **weak** [wik] 形 弱的 | a weak man ▶ 懦弱的男人 | ▶ He's a weak man. 他是一個懦弱的男人。 |

## ique [ik]

| | | |
|---|---|---|
| * **technique** [tɛk`nik] 名 技術 | new techniques ▶ 新技術 | ▶ He's been doing this for twenty years, but he doesn't know new techniques. 他做這個已經20年了，卻不知道任何新技術。 |
| * **unique** [ju`nik] 形 獨特的 | unique to the region ▶ 這一區特有的 | ▶ This style of noodles is unique to the region. 這種麵的風味是這一區特有的。 |
| **critique** [krɪ`tik] 名 評論 | critique of the novel ▶ 小說評論 | ▶ I read the critique of the novel, but I didn't agree with what it said. 我讀了小說的評論，但我並不認同這樣的說法。 |
| * **antique** [æn`tik] 名 古董 形 古董的 | antique chair ▶ 古董椅 | ▶ Please handle that antique chair carefully. 請小心拿古董椅。 |

| | | |
|---|---|---|
| **boutique** [bu`tik] 名 精品店 | fashion boutique 流行精品店 | Her dream is to open a fashion boutique of her own. 她夢想開一家自己的流行精品店。 |

## eel [il]

| | | |
|---|---|---|
| **eel** [il] 名 鰻魚 | slimy eels 黏滑的鰻魚 | Some people like to eat slimy eels. 有些人喜歡吃黏滑的鰻魚。 |
| * **feel** [fil] 動 感覺 | feel ashamed 感到羞愧 | She feels ashamed because she lost the contest. 她感到很丟臉，因為她比賽輸了。 |
| **kneel** [nil] 名 跪 | kneel down 跪下 | Kneel down and pay your respects to your ancestors. 跪下對你的祖先表示敬意。 |
| **heel** [hil] 名 腳後跟、高跟鞋 | high heels 高跟鞋 | It is a skill to walk in high heels. 穿高跟鞋走路要有技巧。 |
| **wheel** [hwil] 名 輪子、方向盤 | four wheels 四輪<br>take the wheel 開車 | All cars have four wheels. 所有的汽車都有四個輪子。<br>Could you take the wheel while I put on some lipstick? 我擦口紅時，你可以幫我開車嗎？ |
| **peel** [pil] 動 削皮 | peel potatoes 削馬鈴薯 | Do you peel potatoes with a knife, or a peeler? 你削馬鈴薯是用刀子還是削皮器？ |

| | | |
|---|---|---|
| **reel**<br>[ril]<br>動 捲 名 捲軸 | ▶ reel in his fishing line<br>捲起他的釣線 | ▶ When he reeled in his fishing line, nothing was on the line.<br>當他捲起釣線時，根本沒有東西上鉤。 |
| **steel**<br>[stil]<br>名 鋼鐵 | ▶ made of steel<br>鋼鐵做的 | ▶ This kitchen counter is made of steel.<br>這個廚房流理台是用鋼鐵做的。 |

## eal [il]

| | | |
|---|---|---|
| **conceal**<br>[kən`sil]<br>動 隱藏 | ▶ conceal his real motives<br>隱瞞他真實的動機 | ▶ The criminal tried to conceal his real motives.<br>犯人試圖隱瞞他真實的動機。 |
| **deal**<br>[dil]<br>名 交易<br>動 處理、發牌 | ▶ business deal<br>商業交易<br>his turn to deal<br>輪到他發牌 | ▶ We had a business deal with that company.<br>我們跟那家公司有生意往來。<br>Give the cards to him; it's his turn to deal.<br>把牌給他，輪到他發牌了。 |
| * **heal**<br>[hil]<br>動 治癒 | ▶ heal the sick<br>治好病人 | ▶ He wants to be a doctor and heal the sick.<br>他想成為醫生治好生病的人。 |
| **meal**<br>[mil]<br>名 一餐 | ▶ delicious meals<br>美味的餐點 | ▶ That restaurant offers delicious meals.<br>那家餐廳供應美味的餐點。 |
| * **appeal**<br>[ə`pil]<br>動 呼籲、有吸引力 | ▶ appeal to<br>對…有吸引力 | ▶ Which crowd does this appeal to?<br>這可以吸引哪個族群？ |

| | | |
|---|---|---|
| **unreal**<br>[ʌn`ril]<br>形 假的 | ▶ look unreal<br>看起來像假的 | ▶ That must be fake. Its looks unreal.<br>那個一定是仿冒的，它看起來很假。 |
| **seal**<br>[sil]<br>名 印章 動 封 | ▶ affix his seal<br>簽章<br>seal the envelope<br>封住信封 | ▶ He affixed his seal on the document. 他在文件上簽章。<br>Don't forget to seal the envelope. 別忘了要封好信封。 |
| **steal**<br>[stil]<br>動 偷 | ▶ steal my wallet<br>偷我的皮夾 | ▶ Those kids tried to steal my wallet!<br>那些小孩想偷我的皮夾！ |
| **reveal**<br>[rɪ`vil]<br>動 名 展現、洩露 | ▶ reveal his secrets<br>洩露他的秘密 | ▶ He can't keep a secret, because he always reveals his secrets.<br>他不能守密，因為他總是洩露自己的秘密。 |
| **zeal**<br>[zil]<br>名 熱忱 | ▶ her zeal for work<br>她對工作的熱忱 | ▶ Her zeal for work is the foundation for her success.<br>她對工作的熱忱是她成功的基礎。 |

## eem [im]

| | | |
|---|---|---|
| **redeem**<br>[rɪ`dim]<br>動 贖回、兌換 | ▶ redeem the points<br>兌換點數 | ▶ You can redeem the points you win at the counter.<br>你可以在櫃台兌換你贏的點數。 |
| **seem**<br>[sim]<br>動 似乎 | ▶ seem strong<br>似乎很強壯 | ▶ That little girl seems strong.<br>那個小女孩似乎很強壯。 |

| | | |
|---|---|---|
| **esteem**<br>[ɪsˋtim]<br>名動 尊重 | self-esteem<br>自尊 | You shouldn't have such low self-esteem; you underestimate yourself.<br>你不應該自貶，你低估了你自己。 |

## eam [im]

| | | |
|---|---|---|
| **beam**<br>[bim]<br>名光束 | a laser beam<br>雷射光 | I saw a laser beam come out of that building!<br>我看到一束雷射光從那棟建築物發射出來！ |
| **gleam**<br>[glim]<br>名動 閃光 | a gleam of sunshine<br>閃耀的陽光 | As long as there is a gleam of sunshine, there's still hope.<br>只要有陽光，就有希望。 |
| **scream**<br>[skrim]<br>動名 尖叫 | scream out<br>尖叫 | I heard someone scream out for help!<br>我聽到有人尖叫求救！ |
| **dream**<br>[drim]<br>名夢 動 做夢 | a good dream<br>一場好夢 | I wish I could have a good dream every night.<br>我希望每晚都有個好夢。 |
| **stream**<br>[strim]<br>名溪流 動 流動 | in the stream<br>在溪流中 | Look! There is something gold floating in the stream!<br>看！溪中有一個金色漂流物！ |
| * **team**<br>[tim]<br>名隊 | a football team<br>足球隊 | I want to join a football team.<br>我想參加橄欖球隊。 |

| | | |
|---|---|---|
| **steam**<br>[stim]<br>動 蒸 名 蒸氣 | ▶ steamed fish<br>蒸魚 | ▶ Do you like to eat steamed fish?<br>你喜歡吃蒸魚嗎？ |

## eme [im]

| | | |
|---|---|---|
| * **scheme**<br>[skim]<br>名 方案、計劃 | ▶ a scheme for raising money<br>籌資計劃 | ▶ Do you have a scheme for raising money for the party?<br>你有沒有為派對募款的計劃？ |
| * **theme**<br>[θim]<br>名 主題 | ▶ the theme of the story<br>故事主題 | ▶ What is the theme of the story?<br>這個故事的主題是什麼？ |
| **supreme**<br>[su`prim]<br>形 最高的 | ▶ the supreme court<br>最高法院 | ▶ That case went all the way to the supreme court.<br>那個案子已達最高法院。 |
| **extreme**<br>[ɪk`strim]<br>形 極端的 名 極端 | ▶ go to the extreme<br>達到極致 | ▶ He goes to the extreme in everything he does.<br>他對每件事都要求做到最好。 |

## een [in]

17

| | | |
|---|---|---|
| **keen**<br>[kin]<br>形 熱衷的 | ▶ keen on art<br>熱衷藝術 | ▶ You need a sense of aesthetics to be keen on art.<br>你要有美感才會熱衷藝術。 |

| | | |
|---|---|---|
| **screen**<br>[skrin]<br>名 螢幕 | TV screen<br>電視螢幕 | Don't sit so close to the TV screen.<br>不要坐得那麼靠近電視。 |
| **green**<br>[grin]<br>形 綠的 名 綠色 | green hills<br>綠色山丘 | The green hills of the countryside make me feel at peace.<br>鄉下的綠色山丘讓我感到寧靜。 |
| **evergreen**<br>[ˋɛvɚˏgrin]<br>形 常綠的 | evergreen trees<br>常綠樹 | Evergreen trees are always green.<br>常綠樹一直保持綠色。 |
| **unseen**<br>[ʌnˋsin]<br>形 未被察覺的、看不見的 | unseen reality<br>未被察覺的事實 | There is an unseen reality that the television is unwilling to show. 電視台不願揭露某個沒被察覺的事實。 |
| **teen**<br>[tin]<br>形 十幾歲的 名 青少年 | in her teens<br>她十幾歲時 | She died of cancer when she was only in her teens.<br>她才十幾歲就死於癌症。 |
| * **between**<br>[bɪˋtwin]<br>介 副 在…之間 | between two buildings<br>在兩棟樓之間 | There is an alley between two buildings.<br>在兩棟大樓之間有條小巷。 |

## ean [in]

| | | |
|---|---|---|
| **bean**<br>[bin]<br>名 豆 | green beans<br>綠豆 | Green beans are very good to eat.<br>綠豆是非常好吃的。 |

| | | |
|---|---|---|
| **lean**<br>[lin]<br>動 傾斜、倚靠 | ▶ lean against the wall<br>靠在牆上 | ▶ You can lean against the wall if you're tired.<br>你如果累了可以靠在牆上。 |
| **clean**<br>[klin]<br>形 乾淨的 | ▶ a clean room<br>乾淨的房間 | ▶ Can't you ever keep a clean room?<br>你就沒辦法保持房間的乾淨嗎？ |
| **mean**<br>[min]<br>形 卑鄙的<br>動 意指、意圖 | ▶ mean lady<br>差勁的小姐<br>mean to say<br>想要說 | ▶ Did you see what she did to me? What a mean lady!<br>你有看到她怎麼對我的嗎？真是個差勁的小姐！<br>What I mean to say is, I love you. 我想說的是，我愛你。 |

## ene [in]

| | | |
|---|---|---|
| * **scene**<br>[sin]<br>名 景象、場景 | ▶ the scene of the play<br>戲的場景 | ▶ The scene of the play is set in Italy.<br>這齣戲的場景在義大利。 |
| **obscene**<br>[əb`sin]<br>形 猥褻的 | ▶ obscene magazines<br>色情雜誌 | ▶ Do you look at obscene magazines?<br>你有看色情雜誌嗎？ |
| * **gene**<br>[dʒin]<br>名 基因 | ▶ gene mutation<br>基因突變 | ▶ That animal looks strange because it went through gene mutations. 因為基因突變，所以那個動物看起來很怪。 |
| **serene**<br>[sə`rin]<br>形 寧靜的 | ▶ calm and serene<br>寧靜的 | ▶ Do you prefer a calm and serene night, or an exciting, lively night? 你比較喜歡寧靜的夜晚，還是激情熱鬧的夜晚？ |

| | | |
|---|---|---|
| * **convene** [kən`vin] 動 召集 | ▶ convene a meeting 召開會議 | ▶ The managers will convene a meeting tonight. 經理們今晚將召開會議。 |
| * **intervene** [ˏɪntɚ`vin] 動 介入 | ▶ intervene between 介入…之間 | ▶ Don't intervene between the two opposing sides. 不要介入對立的兩方之間。 |

## ine [in]

| | | |
|---|---|---|
| * **vaccine** [`væksin] 名 疫苗 | ▶ rabies vaccine 狂犬病疫苗 | ▶ Did your dog get a rabies vaccine before you brought him in? 你在養狗以前有幫牠打狂犬病疫苗嗎？ |
| **sardine** [sɑr`din] 名 沙丁魚 | ▶ like sardines 像擠沙丁魚 | ▶ During rush hour, people in the MRT are packed in like sardines. 在尖峰時刻搭捷運像在擠沙丁魚。 |
| * **machine** [mə`ʃin] 名 機器 | ▶ a washing machine 洗衣機 | ▶ Do you have a washing machine at home? 你家裡有洗衣機嗎？ |
| **Vaseline** [`væsḷˏin] 名 凡士林 | ▶ a jar of Vaseline 一罐凡士林 | ▶ A jar of Vaseline is good for dried lips. 凡士林對嘴唇乾裂很有效。 |
| * **gasoline** [`gæsəˏlin] 名 汽油 | ▶ out of gasoline 用盡汽油 | ▶ You better find a gas station before you run out of gasoline. 你最好在沒油以前找到加油站。 |

| | | |
|---|---|---|
| **marine** [mə`rin] 形 海的 ▶ | marine animals 海洋動物 ▶ | What kind of marine animals do you like to eat? 你喜歡吃哪種海生動物？ |
| **submarine** [`sʌbmə͵rin] 名 潛艇 ▶ | a nuclear-powered submarine 原子能潛艇 ▶ | Have you ever seen a nuclear-powered submarine? 你曾看過原子能潛艇嗎？ |
| **cuisine** [kwɪ`zin] 名 烹飪、菜 ▶ | French cuisine 法國菜 ▶ | French cuisine is usually expensive. 法國料理通常很貴。 |
| **limousine** [`lɪmə͵zin] 名 豪華轎車 ▶ | a bulletproof limousine 防彈車 ▶ | His dream is to own a bullet-proof limousine. 他的夢想是擁有一輛防彈車。 |
| **nicotine** [`nɪkə͵tin] 名 尼古丁 ▶ | addiction to nicotine 尼古丁成癮 ▶ | Some people can't quit smok-ing because of their addic-tion to nicotine. 有些人戒不了菸，因為他們對尼古丁上了癮。 |
| * **routine** [ru`tin] 名 例行公事 ▶ | the daily routine 每天的例行公事 ▶ | Most people have some sort of daily routine. 大部分的人都有些每天習慣要做的事。 |
| **magazine** [͵mægə`zin] 名 雜誌 ▶ | a monthly magazine 月刊 ▶ | Do you have a subscription to any monthly magazines? 你有訂閱月刊嗎？ |

## eep [ip]

| | | |
|---|---|---|
| **beep**<br>[bip]<br>名 嗶聲 | sound of the beep<br>嗶嗶聲 | Please leave your message at the sound of the beep.<br>請在嗶一聲後留言。 |
| **deep**<br>[dip]<br>形 深的 | the deep forest<br>濃密的森林 | Some people are terrified of the deep forest.<br>有些人害怕濃密的森林。 |
| **sheep**<br>[ʃip]<br>名 綿羊 | a flock of sheep<br>一群綿羊 | Herding a flock of sheep must be hard to do.<br>牧一群羊必定很辛苦。 |
| **jeep**<br>[dʒip]<br>名 吉普車 | by jeep<br>開吉普車 | Traveling by jeep is fun.<br>開吉普車旅行很好玩。 |
| * **keep**<br>[kip]<br>動 保持 | keep quiet<br>保持安靜 | Make sure to keep quiet during the movie.<br>在電影播放期間一定要保持安靜。 |
| * **sleep**<br>[slip]<br>動 睡覺 | sleep in late<br>睡得晚 | I love to sleep in late.<br>我喜歡睡得晚。 |
| **asleep**<br>[əˋslip]<br>形 睡著的 | fall asleep<br>睡著 | It took me a long time to fall asleep last night.<br>昨晚我躺很久才睡著。 |
| **peep**<br>[pip]<br>名 動 偷看 | peep through the keyhole<br>從鑰匙孔偷窺 | I saw him try to peep through the keyhole of her room.<br>我看到他試圖從她房間鑰匙孔偷窺。 |

| | | |
|---|---|---|
| **steep** [stip] 形 陡峭的 ▶ | the steep hill 陡峭的山丘 ▶ | We were so tired after we climbed over the steep hill. 我們爬過陡峭的山丘後都覺得很累。 |
| **weep** [wip] 動 哭泣 ▶ | weep over their sad fate 為她們悲慘的命運哭泣 ▶ | In fairy tales, many princesses weep over their sad fate. 童話故事裡，很多公主都為自己悲慘的命運而哭泣。 |
| **sweep** [swip] 動 清掃 ▶ | sweep the floor 掃地 ▶ | The floor is so dirty; please sweep the floor. 地板很髒，請掃一下。 |

## eap [ip]

| | | |
|---|---|---|
| **heap** [hip] 名 動 堆積 ▶ | a heap of 一堆 ▶ | There is a huge heap of clothes that we need to do for laundry. 有一大堆衣服要洗。 |
| * **cheap** [tʃip] 形 便宜的 ▶ | cheap clothes 便宜的衣服 ▶ | Where can I buy cheap clothes around here? 這附近哪裡可以買到便宜的衣服？ |
| **leap** [lip] 動 跳躍 ▶ | leap out of the water 跳出水面 ▶ | Frogs leap out of the water. 青蛙跳出水面。 |

## eepy [`ipɪ]

| | | |
|---|---|---|
| **sleepy** [ˋslipɪ] 形 想睡的 | feel sleepy 覺得想睡 | I feel sleepy because I didn't get much sleep last night. 我覺得想睡，因為我昨晚沒睡好。 |
| **creepy** [ˋkripɪ] 形 令人毛骨悚然的 | a creepy movie 恐怖電影 | What a creepy movie! 好恐怖的電影！ |

## eer [ɪr]

| | | |
|---|---|---|
| **beer** [bɪr] 名 啤酒 | glass of beer 一杯啤酒 | Can you give me a glass of beer? 可以給我一杯啤酒嗎？ |
| **deer** [dɪr] 名 鹿 | hunt deer 獵鹿 | Some people hunt deer as a hobby. 有些人把獵鹿當作嗜好。 |
| **cheer** [tʃɪr] 名 動 歡呼、喝采 | cheer up 使…高興 | They tried to cheer me up. 他們設法讓我高興。 |
| * **engineer** [ˏɛndʒəˋnɪr] 名 工程師 | an electrical engineer 電機工程師 | He's been studying to become an electrical engineer. 他一直努力讀書，想成為一名電機工程師。 |
| **pioneer** [ˏpaɪəˋnɪr] 名 拓荒者、先驅者 | a pioneer in the field of 領域的先驅 | She is a pioneer in the field of sociology. 她是社會學領域的先驅。 |

| | | |
|---|---|---|
| **peer**<br>[pɪr]<br>動 凝視 名 同輩 | ▶ peer at<br>盯著看<br>peer pressure<br>同儕壓力 | ▶ They peer at her through judgmental eyes.<br>他們帶著批判的眼光盯著她看。<br>Most teenagers suffer a lot of peer pressure.<br>多數青少年遭受很大的同儕壓力。 |
| * **volunteer**<br>[͵vɑlən`tɪr]<br>名 義工 動 自願 | ▶ volunteer for community service<br>自願參加社區服務 | ▶ It is good to volunteer for community service.<br>自願參加社區服務是件好事。 |

## ear [ɪr]

| | | |
|---|---|---|
| **ear**<br>[ɪr]<br>名 耳朵、音感 | ▶ have a good ear<br>很有鑑賞力 | ▶ She has a good ear for classical music.<br>她對古典樂很有鑑賞力。 |
| **dear**<br>[dɪr]<br>形 親愛的 | ▶ dear friends<br>親愛的朋友 | ▶ My dear friends are scattered all over the world.<br>我親愛的朋友遍及全世界。 |
| **fear**<br>[fɪr]<br>名 動 害怕 | ▶ fear of water<br>怕水 | ▶ My brother has had a fear of water ever since he was 12 years old.<br>我弟從12歲那年開始就怕水了。 |
| * **hear**<br>[hɪr]<br>動 聽見、聽說 | ▶ hear someone knocking<br>聽到有人敲門 | ▶ I hear someone knocking on the door.<br>我聽到有人在敲門。 |
| **overhear**<br>[͵ovɚ`hɪr]<br>動 無意中聽到 | ▶ overhear what he said<br>無意中聽到他說的話 | ▶ I wish I didn't overhear what he said. 我真希望我沒有無意間聽到他說的話。 |

| | | |
|---|---|---|
| **clear**<br>[klɪr]<br>形 清澈的 動 清除 | in the clear water<br>在清澈的水中 | He played with the fish in the clear water.<br>他在清澈的水中跟魚玩耍。 |
| **unclear**<br>[ʌnˋklɪr]<br>形 不清楚的 | unclear conditions<br>不清楚的狀況 | You'd better be careful because there are unclear conditions on the road today.<br>你最好小心點，今天路況不明。 |
| **near**<br>[nɪr]<br>介 在…附近 | near the door<br>門附近 | I keep the umbrellas near the door.<br>我把雨傘放在門口。 |
| * **appear**<br>[əˋpɪr]<br>動 出現 | appear out of nowhere<br>突然出現 | He appeared out of nowhere.<br>他突然出現。 |
| * **disappear**<br>[ˏdɪsəˋpɪr]<br>動 消失不見 | disappear with<br>跟著…消失 | I think she disappeared with that guy at the coffee shop.<br>我想她跟那個人在咖啡館裡一起消失了。 |
| * **rear**<br>[rɪr]<br>名 後面 | in the rear<br>在後面 | The dumpster is in the rear.<br>大型垃圾車在後面。 |
| **tear**<br>[tɪr]<br>名 眼淚 | the tears falling down her face<br>她臉上滴落的淚水 | It was hard not to notice the tears falling down her face.<br>很難不去注意她臉上滴落的淚水。 |
| **year**<br>[jɪr]<br>名 年 | this year<br>今年 | This year, things are going to change.<br>今年，事情會有所改變。 |

| | | |
| --- | --- | --- |
| * **sincere** [sɪn`sɪr] 形 真誠的 | sincere apology 誠心的道歉 | I appreciated his sincere apology. 我欣賞他誠心的道歉。 |
| **insincere** [ˏɪnsɪn`sɪr] 形 無誠意的 | an insincere smile 無誠意的笑 | It's natural to crack an insincere smile every once in a while. 偶爾出現假笑的情況是很正常的。 |
| * **interfere** [ˏɪntɚ`fɪr] 動 妨礙、干涉 | interfere with 干涉 | We are not allowed to interfere with other projects. 我們不得干涉其他計劃。 |
| **here** [hɪr] 名 副 這裡 | come here 來這裡 | They will come here for the meeting. 他們會來這裡開會。 |
| * **adhere** [əd`hɪr] 動 黏附、遵守 | adhere to 遵守 | We must adhere to the company's policy. 我們必須遵守公司的政策。 |
| * **atmosphere** [`ætməsˏfɪr] 名 氣氛 | a cordial atmosphere 融洽的氣氛 | He knows how to create a cordial atmosphere. 他很懂得營造融洽的氣氛。 |
| **severe** [sə`vɪr] 形 嚴重的 | under severe strain 在沈重壓力下 | She's been under severe strain lately. 她最近承受不少壓力。 |
| * **persevere** [ˏpɝsə`vɪr] 動 堅持不懈 | persevere through hard times 堅持不懈度過困難期 | He is a strong person who can persevere through hard times. 他很堅強，能堅持不懈度過困難期。 |

## eet [it]

| | | |
|---|---|---|
| **feet** [fit] 名 腳 | ▶ back on my two feet 恢復健康 | ▶ It feels good to get back on my two feet again. 重新恢復健康的感覺很棒。 |
| **sheet** [ʃit] 名 床單 | ▶ change the sheets 換床單 | ▶ It's about time to change the sheets. 該換床單了。 |
| * **meet** [mit] 動 遇見 | ▶ meet again 再次見面 | ▶ When will we meet again? 我們何時會再見面？ |
| **discreet** [dɪˋskrit] 形 謹慎的 | ▶ a discreet reply 謹慎回覆 | ▶ He gave a discreet reply even though he was actually angry. 雖然他很生氣，但還是謹慎回覆。 |
| * **greet** [grit] 動 問候、迎接 | ▶ greet the guests 迎接來賓 | ▶ He has a maid to greet the guests. 他有個女傭負責迎接來賓。 |
| **street** [strit] 名 街道 | ▶ on the street 在街上 | ▶ They play hockey on the street. 他們在街上打曲棍球。 |
| **sweet** [swit] 形 甜的 | ▶ taste sweet 味道很甜 | ▶ This candy tastes sweet. 這顆糖果很甜。 |

## eat [it]

| | | |
|---|---|---|
| **eat**<br>[it]<br>動 吃 | eat breakfast<br>吃早餐 | What did you eat for breakfast this morning?<br>你今天早餐吃什麼？ |
| **beat**<br>[bit]<br>動 擊打 | beat a drum<br>打鼓 | It's satisfying to beat a drum really hard.<br>用力打鼓是很快樂的事。 |
| **feat**<br>[fit]<br>名 功績、事蹟 | marvelous feat<br>驚人的事蹟 | That was a marvelous feat.<br>那是件驚人的事蹟。 |
| * **defeat**<br>[dɪ`fit]<br>動 名 擊敗 | defeat the other team<br>打敗另一隊 | I can't believe they defeated the other team.<br>我無法相信他們打敗了另一隊。 |
| **heat**<br>[hit]<br>動 加熱 | heat the room<br>使房間暖和 | We need to buy a space heater to heat the room.<br>我們需要買個暖氣機使房間暖和。 |
| * **cheat**<br>[tʃit]<br>動 欺騙 | cheat on a test<br>考試作弊 | If you cheat on a test, you will be severely punished.<br>如果你考試作弊，會受到嚴厲懲罰。 |
| **wheat**<br>[hwit]<br>名 小麥 | a field of wheat<br>小麥田 | You will find the train station next to a field of wheat.<br>你會在小麥田旁找到火車站。 |
| **meat**<br>[mit]<br>名 肉 | slice of meat<br>一片肉片 | Please add another slice of meat to the sandwich.<br>請在三明治中多加一片肉。 |

| | | |
|---|---|---|
| **neat** [nit] 形 整齊的 | neat writing 工整的筆跡 | The boss likes her to write memos because she has neat writing. 老板喜歡讓她寫備忘錄，因為她的筆跡很工整。 |
| * **repeat** [rɪˋpit] 動 重複 | repeat the word 重複說 | Please repeat the word again. 請再重複一次。 |
| * **treat** [trit] 動 對待、看待 | treat as a joke 把…當成玩笑 | You shouldn't treat this as a joke! 你不應該把這當作玩笑！ |
| **retreat** [rɪˋtrit] 動 撤退 | retreat from the fire 從火場中撤退 | I saw the firefighters retreat from the fire. 我看到消防人員從火場撤退。 |
| **mistreat** [mɪsˋtrit] 動 虐待 | mistreat his wife 虐待他的太太 | They got a divorce because the man often mistreated his wife. 他們離婚了，因為這男人時常虐待他老婆。 |
| **seat** [sit] 名 座位 | take a seat 坐下 | Please take a seat. 請坐下。 |

## eit [it]

| | | |
|---|---|---|
| **deceit** [dɪˋsit] 名 欺騙、詐欺 | a man of deceit 奸詐的人 | He is a man of deceit, who you shouldn't trust. 他是個奸詐的人，你不應該相信他。 |

| | | |
|---|---|---|
| **conceit**<br>[kən`sit]<br>名 自大、自負 | ▶ intolerable conceit<br>難以忍受的自大 | ▶ I can't stand his intolerable conceit.<br>我無法忍受他的自大。 |

## ete [it]

| | | |
|---|---|---|
| * **delete**<br>[dɪ`lit]<br>動 刪除 | ▶ delete his name<br>刪除他的名字 | ▶ Please delete his name from the list.<br>請從名單上刪除他的名字。 |
| **athlete**<br>[`æθlit]<br>名 運動員 | ▶ good athlete<br>好運動員 | ▶ I want to know a man who is a good athlete.<br>我想認識一位好運動員。 |
| * **complete**<br>[kəm`plit]<br>形 完整的 | ▶ a complete sentence<br>完整的句子 | ▶ He can't even make a complete sentence.<br>他甚至不能造一個完整的句子。 |
| **incomplete**<br>[͵ɪnkəm`plit]<br>形 不完整的 | ▶ the incomplete novel<br>不完整的小說 | ▶ The publishing company wanted to see his incomplete novel.<br>出版社想要看他未完成的小說。 |
| * **compete**<br>[kəm`pit]<br>動 競爭 | ▶ compete with<br>與…競爭 | ▶ How can you compete with her?<br>你怎麼跟她競爭呢？ |
| * **concrete**<br>[`kankrit]<br>形 具體的 | ▶ concrete objects<br>具體的物體 | ▶ It's easier to imagine concrete objects, than it is to imagine abstract ideas.<br>具體的實物比抽象觀念較容易想像。 |

## eathe [ið]

| | | |
|---|---|---|
| **breathe** [brið] 動 呼吸 | breathe fresh air ▶ 呼吸新鮮空氣 | ▶ It's nice to be outside of the city and breathe fresh air. 在城外呼吸新鮮空氣感覺很好。 |

## eeze [iz]

| | | |
|---|---|---|
| **breeze** [briz] 名 微風 | in the breeze ▶ 在微風中 | ▶ How wonderful it is to be in the breeze. 置身微風中真是太棒了。 |
| **sneeze** [sniz] 動 打噴嚏 名 噴嚏 | a loud sneeze ▶ 大聲打噴嚏 | ▶ His loud sneeze startled everyone in the office. 他的噴嚏很大聲，嚇到辦公室裡的每個人。 |

## eese [iz]

| | | |
|---|---|---|
| **cheese** [tʃiz] 名 乳酪 | French cheeses ▶ 法國乳酪 | ▶ There are at least 350 different kinds of French cheeses. 至少有350種不同的法國乳酪。 |

## ease [iz]

| | | |
|---|---|---|
| **ease** [iz] 動 減輕 名 容易 | with ease ▶ 輕鬆 | ▶ She handles the truck with ease. 她很輕鬆地操縱卡車。 |

| | | |
|---|---|---|
| **please** [pliz] 動 取悅 | please everyone 取悅每個人 | He's always trying to please everyone. 他一直努力取悅每個人。 |
| * **disease** [dɪ`ziz] 名 疾病 | mental disease 精神疾病 | Mental disease can be difficult to cope with. 精神疾病有時很難處理。 |
| **tease** [tiz] 動 名 逗弄 | tease the cat 逗弄貓 | The naughty boy likes to tease the cat. 這個頑皮的男孩喜歡逗弄貓。 |

## eezer [`izɚ]

19

| | | |
|---|---|---|
| **freezer** [`frizɚ] 名 冷凍庫 | freezer compartment 冷凍庫隔間 | There are some barbecue chicken wings in the freezer compartment. 冷凍庫裡有些烤肉用的雞翅。 |

## ef [ɛf]

| | | |
|---|---|---|
| **chef** [ʃɛf] 名 主廚 | pastry chef 點心師傅 | That pastry chef is supposed to be the best in town. 那位點心師傅被認為是鎮上最好的。 |
| **ref** [rɛf] 名 裁判員 | the basketball ref 籃球裁判員 | Everyone thinks that the basketball ref is unfair. 每個人都認為籃球裁判不公平。 |

## eaf [ɛf]

| | | |
|---|---|---|
| **deaf**<br>[dɛf]<br>形 聾的 | ▶ deaf in one ear<br>一隻耳朵聾了 | ▶ She was born deaf in one ear.<br>她生下來一隻耳朵就聾了。 |

## eg [ɛg]

| | | |
|---|---|---|
| **beg**<br>[bɛg]<br>動 乞討 | ▶ beg for a living<br>乞討為生 | ▶ I feel sorry for people who have to beg for a living.<br>我對必須乞討為生的人感到難過。 |
| **leg**<br>[lɛg]<br>名 腿 | ▶ the pain in my leg<br>腿部疼痛 | ▶ The pain in my leg is getting worse and worse.<br>我的腿愈來愈痛。 |

## egg [ɛg]

| | | |
|---|---|---|
| **egg**<br>[ɛg]<br>名 蛋 | ▶ egg rolls<br>蛋捲 | ▶ You can find egg rolls in most Chinese restaurants in the U.S.A. 你可以在美國大多數中國餐館找到蛋捲。 |

## egal [ˋigl̩]

| | | |
|---|---|---|
| **legal**<br>[ˋligl̩]<br>形 合法的 | ▶ take legal action<br>提出訴訟 | ▶ You must take legal action, or else you will regret it.<br>你必須提出訴訟，不然你會後悔。 |

| | | |
|---|---|---|
| **illegal**<br>[ɪˋligḷ]<br>形 不合法的 | an illegal immigrant<br>非法移民 | She is afraid the police might find out she is an illegal immigrant.<br>她害怕警察會發現她是非法移民。 |

## egion [ˋidʒən]

| | | |
|---|---|---|
| **region**<br>[ˋridʒən]<br>名 地區 | in a cold region<br>在寒冷地區 | Do you prefer to live in a cold region, or a hot region?<br>你比較喜歡住在寒帶還是熱帶？ |

## elf [ɛlf]

| | | |
|---|---|---|
| **shelf**<br>[ʃɛlf]<br>名 架子 | on the shelf<br>在架子上 | Place the object on the shelf.<br>把這個東西放在架上。 |
| **bookshelf**<br>[ˋbʊk͵ʃɛlf]<br>名 書架 | on the bookshelf<br>在書架上 | There are at least 300 books on the bookshelf.<br>書架上至少有300本書。 |
| **self**<br>[sɛlf]<br>名 自身 | self-confidence<br>自信 | Self-confidence is a virtue and a curse.<br>有自信是好事也是壞事。 |
| **himself**<br>[hɪmˋsɛlf]<br>代 他自己 | introduce himself<br>介紹他自己 | He introduces himself as a doctor, although he's not one yet. 雖然他還不是醫生，但他介紹自己是醫生。 |

| | | |
|---|---|---|
| **itself**<br>[ɪtˋsɛlf]<br>代 它自己 | the work itself<br>工作本身 | Being a doctor has its rewards, but the work itself must be hard. 成為醫生有它的好處，但工作本身必定很辛苦。 |
| **myself**<br>[maɪˋsɛlf]<br>代 我自己 | teach myself<br>自修 | I taught myself Japanese.<br>我自修日文。 |

## ell [ɛl]

| | | |
|---|---|---|
| **bell**<br>[bɛl]<br>名 鐘 | school bell<br>校鐘 | The school bell rings when class is over.<br>下課時校鐘響起。 |
| **cell**<br>[sɛl]<br>名 單人牢房、細胞 | in his prison cell<br>在他的牢房裡<br>blood cell<br>血球 | He's been living in his prison cell for over fifty years.<br>他住在監獄牢房裡超過50年了。<br>Are his blood cells healthy?<br>他的血球健康嗎？ |
| **hell**<br>[hɛl]<br>名 地獄 | go to hell<br>下地獄 | Some people are very afraid they may go to hell.<br>有些人非常害怕自己會下地獄。 |
| **shell**<br>[ʃɛl]<br>名 殼 | seashells<br>貝殼 | I like collecting sea shells at the seashore.<br>我喜歡在海邊收集貝殼。 |
| **smell**<br>[smɛl]<br>動 嗅 | smell something burning<br>聞到燒焦味 | Go check the stove, I smell something burning.<br>快去看爐子，我聞到燒焦味。 |

| | | |
|---|---|---|
| **spell**<br>[spɛl]<br>動 拼寫 | spell your name<br>拼寫你的名字 | How do you spell your name?<br>你的名字怎麼拼？ |
| **sell**<br>[sɛl]<br>動 銷售 | sell stamps<br>賣郵票 | Where do they sell stamps around here?<br>他們在這附近哪裡賣郵票？ |
| **tell**<br>[tɛl]<br>動 告訴 | tell a story<br>講故事 | He really knows how to tell a story well.<br>他知道要怎麼把故事說好。 |
| **retell**<br>[riˋtɛl]<br>動 重述 | retell the story<br>重講故事 | I had to retell the story because she wasn't listening.<br>我必須重講故事，因為她沒在聽。 |
| **well**<br>[wɛl]<br>副 很好 | eat well<br>吃得好 | People in Taiwan eat well.<br>台灣人吃得好。 |
| **dwell**<br>[dwɛl]<br>動 居住 | dwell in London<br>住在倫敦 | That lad dwells in London.<br>那位少年住在倫敦。 |
| **farewell**<br>[ˋfɛrˋwɛl]<br>名 告別 | wave farewell to<br>對…揮手告別 | It was sad when he waved farewell to me.<br>當他揮手跟我告別時是很感傷的。 |
| **swell**<br>[swɛl]<br>動 腫脹 | swell up<br>腫脹 | This bruise will probably swell up by tomorrow.<br>這個擦傷明天可能會腫起來。 |

| | | |
|---|---|---|
| **yell**<br>[jɛl]<br>動 叫喊 | ▶ yell at<br>叫喊 | ▶ I hate it when my parents yell at me.<br>我討厭我的父母對我大吼大叫。 |

## el [ɛl]

| | | |
|---|---|---|
| **excel**<br>[ɪk\`sɛl]<br>動 勝過、突出 | ▶ excel in English<br>擅長英文 | ▶ You will excel in English when you're finished with this book.<br>你讀完這本書後，英文就會很厲害。 |
| **gel**<br>[dʒɛl]<br>名 凝膠 | ▶ hair gel<br>髮膠 | ▶ I need to buy new hair gel.<br>我需要買新髮膠。 |
| **parallel**<br>[\`pærə͵lɛl]<br>形 平行的 | ▶ parallel lines<br>平行線 | ▶ Please draw two parallel lines right here.<br>請在此畫兩條平行線。 |
| **personnel**<br>[͵pɜsn̩\`ɛl]<br>名 人員 | ▶ the personnel of the company<br>公司員工 | ▶ The personnel of the company are upset about the pay cuts.<br>薪水被減，公司的員工都很沮喪。 |
| **compel**<br>[kəm\`pɛl]<br>動 強迫 | ▶ feel compelled to<br>被迫、不得不 | ▶ Even when I'm on vacation, for some reason I feel compelled to do some work.<br>即使是在休假時，我還是不得不做點工作。 |
| **expel**<br>[ɪk\`spɛl]<br>動 驅逐、開除 | ▶ expel from school<br>被學校開除 | ▶ He was expelled from school for cheating.<br>他因為作弊而被學校開除。 |

| | | |
|---|---|---|
| **carousel**<br>[ˏkærʊˋzɛl]<br>名 旋轉木馬 | ▶ go on the carousel<br>坐旋轉木馬 | ▶ Mommy, can I please go on the carousel?<br>媽咪，我可以去坐旋轉木馬嗎？ |
| **hotel**<br>[hoˋtɛl]<br>名 旅館 | ▶ resort hotel<br>度假飯店 | ▶ That resort hotel is really fancy.<br>那間度假飯店很貴。 |
| **motel**<br>[moˋtɛl]<br>名 汽車旅館 | ▶ business motel<br>商業汽車旅館 | ▶ The business motel on the corner of our street is always busy. 街角的商業汽車旅館生意一直很好。 |

## ellow [ˋɛlo]

20

| | | |
|---|---|---|
| **fellow**<br>[ˋfɛlo]<br>名 同伴 | ▶ his fellow traveler<br>他的旅伴 | ▶ His fellow traveler took all his money and belongings.<br>他的旅伴拿走他身上所有財物。 |
| **mellow**<br>[ˋmɛlo]<br>形 微醺而愉快的 | ▶ in a mellow mood<br>愉快的心情 | ▶ I don't feel like going out tonight; I'm in a mellow mood.<br>我今晚不想出去，因為我心情很好。 |
| **yellow**<br>[ˋjɛlo]<br>形 黃色的 名 黃色 | ▶ that yellow taxi<br>黃色計程車 | ▶ Hail that yellow taxi!<br>叫計程車！ |

## elly [ˋɛlɪ]

| | | |
|---|---|---|
| **belly**<br>[ˋbɛlɪ]<br>名 肚子 | on my belly<br>在我肚子上 | When he jumped in the swimming pool, he landed on my belly.<br>他跳入游泳池時降落在我的肚子上。 |
| **jelly**<br>[ˋdʒɛlɪ]<br>名 果凍 | eat some jelly<br>吃些果凍 | You can eat some jelly if you are on a diet.<br>如果你在減肥，你可以吃點果凍。 |
| **smelly**<br>[ˋsmɛlɪ]<br>形 臭的 | smelly socks<br>臭襪子 | Please wash those smelly socks!<br>請將那些臭襪子洗乾淨！ |

## elp [ɛlp]

| | | |
|---|---|---|
| **help**<br>[hɛlp]<br>動 名 幫助 | help with<br>幫助 | Can you please help me with this problem?<br>可以請你幫我解決這個問題嗎？ |

## elt [ɛlt]

| | | |
|---|---|---|
| **belt**<br>[bɛlt]<br>名 腰帶 | leather belt<br>皮帶 | I lost my leather belt.<br>我的皮帶不見了。 |
| **heartfelt**<br>[ˋhɑrtˏfɛlt]<br>形 衷心的 | heartfelt apology<br>誠心的道歉 | I forgave him after he gave me his heartfelt apology.<br>在他誠心向我道歉後，我原諒他了。 |

## em [ɛm]

| | | |
|---|---|---|
| **them** [ðɛm] 代 他們 | ▶ love them 愛他們 | ▶ I miss my family; I love them very much. 我想念我的家人，我非常愛他們。 |
| **stem** [stɛm] 名 莖 | ▶ flower stem 花莖 | ▶ Please cut the flower stem here. 請在這兒切斷花莖。 |

## emn [ɛm]

| | | |
|---|---|---|
| **condemn** [kən`dɛm] 動 責難、責備 | ▶ condemn his behavior 責備他的行為 | ▶ You shouldn't condemn his behavior. 你不應該責備他的行為。 |

## ember [`ɛmbɚ]

| | | |
|---|---|---|
| **December** [dɪ`sɛmbɚ] 名 十二月 | ▶ in December 在十二月 | ▶ There is a long vacation for students in December. 十二月時學生有很長的假期。 |
| **member** [`mɛmbɚ] 名 成員 | ▶ the members of the family 家庭成員 | ▶ Could you contact the members of the family to inform them about this? 你可以通知家庭成員這件事嗎？ |
| **remember** [rɪ`mɛmbɚ] 動 記得 | ▶ remember the phone number 記得電話號碼 | ▶ I can never remember the phone number. 我從來都記不得電話號碼。 |

| | | |
|---|---|---|
| **September**<br>[sɛp`tɛmbɚ]<br>名 九月 | in September<br>在九月 | Students have to go back to school in September.<br>學生九月時必須回學校上課。 |
| **November**<br>[no`vɛmbɚ]<br>名 十一月 | in November<br>在十一月 | Thanksgiving is in November.<br>感恩節在十一月。 |

## emble [`ɛmbl̩]

| | | |
|---|---|---|
| **tremble**<br>[`trɛmbl̩]<br>動 發抖 | tremble with fear<br>因害怕而發抖 | He trembled with fear when he was lost in the woods.<br>當他迷失在森林中，他害怕得發抖。 |
| **resemble**<br>[rɪ`zɛmbl̩]<br>動 類似 | resemble her mother<br>像她的母親 | She really resembles her mother.<br>她真的很像她媽媽。 |
| **assemble**<br>[ə`sɛmbl̩]<br>動 集合 | assemble at the airport<br>在機場集合 | We have to assemble at the airport early.<br>我們必須早點在機場集合。 |

## empt [ɛmpt]

| | | |
|---|---|---|
| **tempt**<br>[tɛmpt]<br>動 引誘 | tempt me to<br>引誘我 | He wants to tempt me to go on a vacation.<br>他想誘惑我去度假。 |

| | | |
|---|---|---|
| **contempt**<br>[kən`tɛmpt]<br>名 蔑視 | ▶ contempt of court<br>藐視法庭 | ▶ The judge held the witness in contempt of court because the witness was cursing.<br>因為證人罵髒話，所以法官認為他藐視法庭。 |
| **attempt**<br>[ə`tɛmpt]<br>動 名 企圖 | ▶ attempt to<br>企圖 | ▶ I will attempt to try my best.<br>我會盡力而為。 |
| **exempt**<br>[ɪg`zɛmpt]<br>動 免除 | ▶ exempt from<br>免於 | ▶ Government employees are exempted from paying certain taxes.<br>政府官員不必付某些稅。 |

## en [ɛn]

| | | |
|---|---|---|
| **then**<br>[ðɛn]<br>副 那時、然後 | ▶ and then<br>接著 | ▶ I'd like to go out and then I should go home.<br>我想出去，接著回家。 |
| **when**<br>[hwɛn]<br>連 當…時 副 何時 | ▶ when is a good time to<br>何時適合… | ▶ When is a good time to come over?<br>什麼時候過來比較好？ |
| **men**<br>[mɛn]<br>名 人、男人 | ▶ two men<br>兩個男人 | ▶ I saw two men rob the store.<br>我看到兩個男人搶商店。 |
| **pen**<br>[pɛn]<br>名 鋼筆、筆 | ▶ write with a pen<br>用鋼筆寫字 | ▶ Please write with a pen and not a pencil on these forms.<br>填寫這些表格請用鋼筆別用鉛筆。 |

| | | |
|---|---|---|
| **ten**<br>[tɛn]<br>形 十個的 名 十 | ▶ ten dollars<br>十元 | ▶ I found ten dollars on the street today.<br>我今天在街上發現十元。 |
| **yen**<br>[jɛn]<br>名 日圓 | ▶ one hundred yen<br>一百日圓 | ▶ That meal only cost one hundred yen.<br>那一餐只要一百日圓。 |

## ench [ɛntʃ]

| | | |
|---|---|---|
| **bench**<br>[bɛntʃ]<br>名 長凳、長椅 | ▶ on the bench<br>在長椅上 | ▶ They ate their sandwiches together on the bench.<br>他們一起坐在長椅上吃三明治。 |
| **French**<br>[frɛntʃ]<br>名 法國人、法語 | ▶ speak French<br>說法語 | ▶ Do you know how to speak French?<br>你知道怎麼說法語嗎？ |
| **wrench**<br>[rɛntʃ]<br>動 扭擰 名 扳手 | ▶ use a wrench<br>用扳手 | ▶ You must use a wrench to unscrew this one.<br>你必須用扳手鬆開這個。 |

## encil [`ɛnsl̩]

| | | |
|---|---|---|
| **pencil**<br>[`pɛnsl̩]<br>名 鉛筆 | ▶ pencil case<br>鉛筆盒 | ▶ I bought a new pencil case at the bookstore today.<br>我今天在書店買了一個新鉛筆盒。 |

## ensil [ˋɛnsl̩]

| | | |
|---|---|---|
| **utensil** [juˋtɛnsl̩] 名 用具 | cooking utensils 烹煮器具 | You need a variety of cooking utensils in a standard kitchen. 標準廚房裡要有各式的烹煮器具。 |

## end [ɛnd]

| | | |
|---|---|---|
| **end** [ɛnd] 名 末端 動 終了 | at the end of 在…末端 | I lose my concentration at the end of the day. 在一天結束之際我根本無法專心。 |
| **bend** [bɛnd] 動 折彎 | bend the iron bar 將鐵棍折彎 | He's so strong he can bend an iron bar. 他強壯到可折彎鐵棍。 |
| **unbend** [ʌnˋbɛnd] 動 弄直 | unbend your arm 把你的手臂伸直 | Does it hurt when you unbend your arm? 你伸直手臂時會痛嗎？ |
| **ascend** [əˋsɛnd] 動 登高、上升 | ascend to the sky 升向天空 | The balloon will ascend to the sky if you let go of it outside. 如果你在外面放開氣球，它會飄到天空中。 |
| **descend** [dɪˋsɛnd] 動 下降 | descend on foot 走下來 | She descended on foot gracefully. 她優雅地走下來。 |
| **transcend** [trænˋsɛnd] 動 超越 | transcend human understanding 超出人類理解 | There are probably many things in this world that transcend human understanding. 世界上可能有很多事情是人類無法理解的。 |

| | | |
|---|---|---|
| **offend** [ə`fɛnd] 動 冒犯 | ▶ offend many people 冒犯很多人 | ▶ His attitude offends many people. 他的態度冒犯很多人。 |
| **defend** [dɪ`fɛnd] 動 防禦 | ▶ defend our city 保衛我們的城市 | ▶ If we were at war, who would defend our city? 如果發生了戰爭，誰會保護我們的城市？ |
| **comprehend** [ˏkɑmprɪ`hɛnd] 動 了解 | ▶ comprehend the text 理解文意 | ▶ Could you comprehend the text? 你能理解這段文字的意思嗎？ |
| * **lend** [lɛnd] 動 借出 | ▶ lend you the bike 把腳踏車借給你 | ▶ I can lend you the bike for the weekend. 週末我可以借你腳踏車。 |
| **blend** [blɛnd] 動 混和 | ▶ blended juice 混合果汁 | ▶ I really want some blended juice now. 我現在好想要喝點混合果汁。 |
| * **recommend** [ˏrɛkə`mɛnd] 動 推薦 | ▶ recommend me a book 推薦我一本書 | ▶ She recommended me a book that she thought I would like. 她覺得我可能喜歡這本書，所以推薦給我。 |
| * **depend** [dɪ`pɛnd] 動 依賴、取決於 | ▶ depend on 依賴 | ▶ He depends on his girlfriend too much. 他太依賴他的女友。 |
| * **spend** [spɛnd] 動 花費 | ▶ spend $50 on 花50元在… | ▶ The teacher spent fifty dollars on a new textbook. 老師花50元買了一本新教科書。 |

| | | |
|---|---|---|
| **suspend** [sə`spɛnd] 動 懸掛 | suspended from the ceiling 掛在天花板上 | All chandeliers are suspended from the ceiling. 所有的吊燈都被掛在天花板上。 |
| **trend** [trɛnd] 名 趨勢 | a new trend 新趨勢 | Celebrities are often the ones who start a new trend. 名人常引領新風潮。 |
| **send** [sɛnd] 動 發送、寄 | send the letter 寄信 | When will you send the letter to your mom? 你何時要寄信給你媽媽？ |
| **tend** [tɛnd] 動 趨向、傾向 | tend to 有…的傾向 | He tends to think too much. 他容易想太多。 |
| * **intend** [ɪn`tɛnd] 動 打算 | intend to 打算 | Do you intend to go back to school? 你打算回學校嗎？ |
| * **attend** [ə`tɛnd] 動 出席 | attend the meeting 出席會議 | Will you be able to attend the meeting this afternoon? 你今天下午可以參加會議嗎？ |
| * **extend** [ɪk`stɛnd] 動 延伸、伸出 | extend your arm 伸出你的手臂 | Please extend your arm so the doctor can give you a shot. 請把手臂伸出來，這樣醫生才能幫你打針。 |

## ender [`ɛndɚ]

| | | |
|---|---|---|
| **gender**<br>[`dʒɛndɚ]<br>名 性別 | gender difference<br>性別差異 | Many people argue about the importance of gender difference.<br>很多人爭論性別差異的重要性。 |
| **slender**<br>[`slɛndɚ]<br>形 苗條的 | a slender figure<br>苗條身材 | All models in this day and age have a slender figure.<br>現今的模特兒都有苗條的身材。 |
| **surrender**<br>[sə`rɛndɚ]<br>動 名 投降 | surrender to<br>投降 | They will never surrender to you!<br>他們絕不會向你投降！ |
| **sender**<br>[`sɛndɚ]<br>名 寄件人 | block the sender<br>封鎖寄件人 | Since we receive a lot of unwanted e-mail, you can now block the sender.<br>我們收到很多垃圾郵件，你現在可以封鎖寄件人了。 |
| **tender**<br>[`tɛndɚ]<br>形 柔軟的、嫩的 | tender blossoms<br>嬌嫩的花 | Your love is like tender blossoms on a cherry tree.<br>你的愛就像櫻花樹上嬌嫩的花。 |
| **bartender**<br>[`bɑr͵tɛndɚ]<br>名 酒保 | busy bartender<br>忙碌的酒保 | That poor, busy bartender has been working too many hours. 那可憐的忙碌酒保已經超時工作了。 |

## endor [`ɛndɚ]

| | | |
|---|---|---|
| **splendor**<br>[`splɛndɚ]<br>名 光輝、壯麗 | the splendor of the scenery<br>壯麗的景色 | It's nice to take in the splendor of the scenery.<br>很高興能看到這壯麗的景色。 |

| | | |
|---|---|---|
| **vendor**<br>[ˋvɛndɚ]<br>名 小販 | ▶ busy vendor<br>忙碌的小販 | ▶ This night market has so many busy vendors.<br>這個夜市有很多忙碌的小販。 |

## ength [ɛŋθ]

| | | |
|---|---|---|
| **length**<br>[lɛŋθ]<br>名 長度、期間 | ▶ the length of the movie<br>電影片長 | ▶ What is the length of the movie?<br>這部電影片長多少？ |
| **strength**<br>[strɛŋθ]<br>名 力量、效力 | ▶ lose its strength<br>失效 | ▶ The glue will lose its strength after a while.<br>膠水放一陣子後就會失效。 |

## enny [ˋɛnɪ]

| | | |
|---|---|---|
| **penny**<br>[ˋpɛnɪ]<br>名 便士、一分硬幣 | ▶ ten pennies<br>十便士、十分錢 | ▶ Ten pennies are worth the same as a dime.<br>十分錢等於一角。 |

## ense [ɛns]

| | | |
|---|---|---|
| **incense**<br>[ˋɪnsɛns]<br>名 香 | ▶ incense holder<br>香器 | ▶ I need to buy an incense holder for my room.<br>我得替我房間買個香器。 |

| | | |
|---|---|---|
| **dense**<br>[dɛns]<br>形 密集的 | the dense forest<br>濃密森林 | I'm afraid of the dense forest.<br>我害怕濃密的森林。 |
| **condense**<br>[kən`dɛns]<br>動 濃縮 | condensed milk<br>濃縮牛奶 | Condensed milk can be stored for a long time.<br>濃縮牛奶可以存放很久。 |
| **immense**<br>[ɪ`mɛns]<br>形 巨大的 | immense gratitude<br>無比感激 | The winner showed immense gratitude for the prize.<br>勝利者對於得獎表現出無比的感激。 |
| **dispense**<br>[dɪ`spɛns]<br>動 分配、發放 | dispense food to the homeless<br>發放食物給無家可歸者 | Some churches dispense food to the homeless.<br>有些教堂提供食物給無家可歸者。 |
| **suspense**<br>[sə`spɛns]<br>名 掛慮、懸疑 | in suspense<br>掛慮著 | Please tell me what happened. I'm sick of being in suspense.<br>請你告訴我怎麼了，我很討厭一直掛慮著。 |
| **expense**<br>[ɪk`spɛns]<br>名 費用 | afford the expense<br>付得起費用 | Can you afford the expenses of car maintenance?<br>你付得起車子的維修費嗎？ |
| **sense**<br>[sɛns]<br>名 意識 | sense of responsibility<br>責任感 | You should develop a sense of responsibility before you have a child. 在你有小孩之前應該先培養責任感。 |
| **nonsense**<br>[`nɑnsɛns]<br>名 胡説 | talk nonsense<br>胡説 | He always talks nonsense.<br>他老是胡說八道。 |

| | | |
|---|---|---|
| **tense**<br>[tɛns]<br>形 拉緊的、緊張的 | tense shoulders<br>肩膀很緊 | When I gave her a massage, I noticed she had tense shoulders. 我幫她按摩時，注意到她的肩膀很緊。 |
| **pretense**<br>[prɪ`tɛns]<br>名 假裝 | make pretense<br>假裝 | You shouldn't make any pretense of liking him.<br>你不應該假裝喜歡他。 |
| **intense**<br>[ɪn`tɛns]<br>形 劇烈的 | intense pain<br>劇痛 | I feel intense pain in my knee from falling earlier.<br>之前跌倒讓我的膝蓋劇烈疼痛。 |

## ence [ɛns]

| | | |
|---|---|---|
| **fence**<br>[fɛns]<br>名 柵欄 | build a fence<br>建柵欄 | My father built a fence around the house over the summer.<br>我爸爸夏天時在房子周圍建了柵欄。 |
| **consequence**<br>[`kɑnsə͵kwɛns]<br>名 結果 | accept the consequence<br>接受結果 | You need to learn to accept the consequences of your actions.<br>你必須學習接受自己行為的後果。 |

## ensity [`ɛnsətɪ]

22

| | | |
|---|---|---|
| **density**<br>[`dɛnsətɪ]<br>名 密集度 | population density<br>人口密度 | The population density of most states is centralized in the cities.<br>大多數州的人口都集中在城市。 |

| | | |
|---|---|---|
| **immensity** [ɪ`mɛnsətɪ] 名 無限、巨大 | ▶ the immensity of space 宇宙的浩瀚 | ▶ Have you ever wondered about the immensity of space? 你曾經對浩瀚宇宙感到疑惑嗎？ |
| **intensity** [ɪn`tɛnsətɪ] 名 強烈、強度 | ▶ the intensity of the light 光的強度 | ▶ The intensity of the light can hurt your eyes. 光的強度可能會傷害眼睛。 |

## ensive [`ɛnsɪv]

| | | |
|---|---|---|
| **defensive** [dɪ`fɛnsɪv] 形 防禦的 | ▶ defensive front 防禦的前線 | ▶ The army's defensive front should be up and ready by tomorrow. 軍隊的防禦前線明天之前應該要做好準備。 |
| **offensive** [ə`fɛnsɪv] 形 冒犯的 | ▶ offensive remarks 冒犯人的評論 | ▶ He made some offensive remarks to his supervisor. 他對主管作了不當的評論。 |
| * **comprehensive** [ˏkɑmprɪ`hɛnsɪv] 形 廣泛的 | ▶ comprehensive text 內容廣泛的課本 | ▶ This comprehensive text covers everything you need to know about blood cells. 這本內容廣泛的課本涵蓋所有關於血球的知識。 |
| **pensive** [`pɛnsɪv] 形 沈思的、悲傷的 | ▶ in a pensive mood 悲傷的心情 | ▶ She's been in a pensive mood ever since her mother passed away. 自從她母親去世後，她的心情一直很難過。 |
| * **expensive** [ɪk`spɛnsɪv] 形 昂貴的 | ▶ an expensive toy 昂貴的玩具 | ▶ He wants an expensive toy for Christmas. 他想要很貴的玩具當聖誕禮物。 |

| | | |
|---|---|---|
| **inexpensive** [ˌɪnɪkˋspɛnsɪv] 形 不貴的 | ▶ inexpensive shoes 便宜的鞋子 | ▶ I found these inexpensive shoes. 我找到這些便宜的鞋子。 |
| **intensive** [ɪnˋtɛnsɪv] 形 密集的、精深的 | ▶ intensive reading 精讀 | ▶ I have to do a lot of intensive reading for school. 我必須為上課做大量深入閱讀。 |
| **extensive** [ɪkˋstɛnsɪv] 形 廣泛的 | ▶ extensive discussions 廣泛的討論 | ▶ This seminar will hold extensive discussions on Monet. 這個研討會將廣泛討論莫內。 |

## ent [ɛnt]

| | | |
|---|---|---|
| **cent** [sɛnt] 形 分、一分錢 | ▶ one cent 一分 | ▶ I wouldn't give him one cent. 我一分錢也不會給他。 |
| * **percent** [pɚˋsɛnt] 名 百分之一 | ▶ thirty percent of 百分之三十 | ▶ His contract states that he is entitled to thirty percent of the money. 他的合約中聲明他有權得到百分之三十的錢。 |
| **scent** [sɛnt] 名 氣味 | ▶ the scent of the flowers 花香 | ▶ I love the scent of flowers. 我愛花香。 |
| **descent** [dɪˋsɛnt] 名 下降、下坡 | ▶ steep descent 陡峭的坡道 | ▶ Be careful of the steep descent of the mountain. 當心陡峭的山坡路。 |

| | | |
|---|---|---|
| **dent**<br>[dɛnt]<br>名 凹痕 | dent in my car<br>我車子的凹痕 | Where did the dent in my car come from?<br>我車子的凹痕是哪兒來的？ |
| **lament**<br>[lə`mɛnt]<br>動 悲痛 | lament the death of her son<br>哀悼她兒子的死 | It took her many years to lament the death of her son.<br>她有很多年的時間都處於兒子死去的哀傷中。 |
| **cement**<br>[sɪ`mɛnt]<br>名 水泥 | cover with cement<br>用水泥覆蓋 | They covered the hole with cement.<br>他們用水泥蓋住洞口。 |
| * **implement**<br>[`ɪmplə͵mɛnt] [`ɪmpləmənt]<br>動 實行 名 器具 | farming implements<br>農具 | What kind of farming implements do you need to harvest corn?<br>你收割玉米時需要哪種農具？ |
| **torment**<br>[tɔr`mɛnt] [`tɔr͵mɛnt]<br>動 折磨 名 痛苦 | physically torment<br>肉體折磨 | He physically tormented the little boy.<br>他肉體折磨小男孩。 |
| **rent**<br>[rɛnt]<br>名 租金 動 租 | pay my rent<br>付租金<br>rent a cabin<br>租一間小屋 | I'm not sure if I have enough money this month to pay my rent.<br>我不確定這個月是否有錢付房租。<br>Let's rent a cabin in the woods for the weekend!<br>這個週末在森林裡租個小木屋吧！ |
| **dissent**<br>[dɪ`sɛnt]<br>動 名 不同意 | without dissent<br>無異議 | The main political party surprisingly held a convention without dissent.<br>出乎意料地，主政黨舉行了一場無異議的大會。 |

| 單字 | 片語 | 例句 |
|---|---|---|
| **resent**<br>[rɪˋzɛnt]<br>動 怨恨 | resent her<br>怨恨她 | He resents her for taking his job.<br>他因為被她搶走工作而怨恨她。 |
| **represent**<br>[ˏrɛprɪˋzɛnt]<br>動 象徵、代表 | represent something<br>象徵著什麼 | That picture must represent something.<br>那幅畫必定象徵著什麼。 |
| **consent**<br>[kənˋsɛnt]<br>動 名 同意 | consent to<br>同意 | Will he consent to all the terms in the contract?<br>他會同意合約所有的條款嗎？ |
| **tent**<br>[tɛnt]<br>名 帳篷 | put up their tent<br>搭起帳篷 | It took them a long time to put up their tent.<br>他們花了很久才搭好帳篷。 |
| **content**<br>[kənˋtɛnt] [ˋkantɛnt]<br>形 滿意的 名 內容 | content with<br>對…很滿意 | Are you content with your job?<br>你對你的工作滿意嗎？ |
| **discontent**<br>[dɪskənˋtɛnt]<br>形 不滿的 | discontent with<br>對…不滿意 | She seems to be discontent with the way things are going between them.<br>她似乎不滿意他們之間的狀況。 |
| **extent**<br>[ɪkˋstɛnt]<br>名 程度 | to a certain extent<br>在一定程度上 | To a certain extent, I'm glad he is leaving. 就某種程度而言，我很高興他要離開了。 |
| **vent**<br>[vɛnt]<br>名 動 發洩 | give vent to<br>發洩 | I sometimes give vent to my anger by listening to loud music. 我有時會藉著大聲聽音樂來發洩怒氣。 |

| | | |
|---|---|---|
| **event** [ɪ`vɛnt] 名 事件 | a great event 大事 | The music festival was such a great event! 音樂節是很大的活動！ |
| **prevent** [prɪ`vɛnt] 動 預防 | prevent from 阻止 | The sink strainer will prevent food from clogging the sink. 水槽濾網會防止食物阻塞水槽。 |
| **invent** [ɪn`vɛnt] 動 發明、創造 | invent the telephone 發明電話 | Do you know who invented the telephone? 你知道是誰發明電話的嗎？ |

## ental [`ɛntl̩]

| | | |
|---|---|---|
| **dental** [`dɛntl̩] 形 牙齒的 | a dental operation 牙齒手術 | He needs a dental operation for his wisdom teeth. 他得拔掉智齒。 |
| **accidental** [ˏæksə`dɛntl̩] 形 意外的 | accidental insurance 意外險 | How much does your accidental insurance cover? 你的意外險涵蓋多少？ |
| **incidental** [ˏɪnsə`dɛntl̩] 形 偶然的、附帶的 | an incidental remark 附帶的話 | He made an incidental remark that surprisingly made the group change their mind. 他附帶的話意外讓這群人改變想法。 |
| **coincidental** [koˏɪnsə`dɛntl̩] 形 巧合的 | coincidental meeting 巧合的會面 | I don't think that was a coincidental meeting. 我想那次會面不是巧合。 |

| | | |
|---|---|---|
| **mental**<br>[ˋmɛntḷ]<br>形 精神的、心理的 | ▶ mental disease<br>精神疾病 | ▶ Mental disease is becoming more of a problem that the community has to deal with.<br>精神疾病漸漸成為社區必須處理的問題。 |
| **fundamental**<br>[ˏfʌndəˋmɛntḷ]<br>形 基礎的、主要的 | ▶ the fundamental cause<br>主因 | ▶ What was the fundamental cause of death?<br>死亡的主因是什麼？ |
| **temperamental**<br>[ˏtɛmprəˋmɛntḷ]<br>形 氣質的、喜怒無常的 | ▶ a temperamental attitude<br>喜怒無常的態度 | ▶ He has a temperamental attitude when it comes to his family.<br>一提到他的家人，他的態度就喜怒無常。 |
| **elemental**<br>[ˏɛləˋmɛntḷ]<br>形 自然力的、基本的 | ▶ elemental reasoning<br>基本推論 | ▶ What is the elemental reasoning in your argument?<br>你的論點的基本推論是什麼？ |
| **experimental**<br>[ɪkˏspɛrəˋmɛntḷ]<br>形 實驗性的 | ▶ experimental teaching<br>實驗性的教學 | ▶ That school encourages experimental teaching techniques.<br>那所學校鼓勵實驗性的教學技術。 |
| **sentimental**<br>[ˏsɛntəˋmɛntḷ]<br>形 重感情的、感傷的 | ▶ sentimental about<br>對…重感情<br>a sentimental love story<br>感傷的愛情故事 | ▶ She is very sentimental about her high school friends.<br>她對高中時的朋友很重感情。<br>He loves watching a sentimental love story.<br>他愛看感傷的愛情故事。 |
| * **governmental**<br>[ˏgʌvənˋmɛntḷ]<br>形 政府的 | ▶ a governmental secretary<br>政府的祕書 | ▶ That governmental secretary treats everyone badly.<br>那個政府祕書對每個人都很壞。 |

| | | |
|---|---|---|
| * **environmental** [ɪnˏvaɪrən`mɛntl̩] 形 有關環境的 | ▸ environmental concern 對環境的關心 | ▸ There should be more environmental concern about the ozone layer. 大家應該更關心臭氧層的環境問題。 |
| **monumental** [ˏmɑnjə`mɛntl̩] 形 紀念性的 | ▸ a monumental pillar 紀念柱 | ▸ They constructed a monumental pillar to the people who died in the war. 他們為在戰爭中死去的人建了根紀念柱。 |
| **instrumental** [ˏɪnstrə`mɛntl̩] 形 用樂器演奏的 | ▸ instrumental music 器樂 | ▸ I like instrumental music that doesn't have any words. 我喜歡沒有歌詞的器樂。 |

## enter [`ɛntɚ]

23

| | | |
|---|---|---|
| **enter** [`ɛntɚ] 動 進入 | ▸ enter the park 進入公園 | ▸ From which way did you enter the park? 你從哪條路進入公園？ |
| **center** [`sɛntɚ] 名 中心 | ▸ in the center of 在中心 | ▸ I want to open a store in the center of town. 我想要在市中心開店。 |

## entor [`ɛntɚ]

| | | |
|---|---|---|
| **mentor** [`mɛntɚ] 名 良師益友 | ▸ good mentor 很好的良師益友 | ▸ He's a really good mentor. 他真是個很好的良師益友。 |

| | | |
|---|---|---|
| **inventor**<br>[ɪn`vɛntɚ]<br>名 發明家、創作者 | ▶ an inventor of a drug<br>藥的發明者 | ▶ He got famous being an inventor of a drug that cured cancer.<br>他因發明治療癌症的藥而變得出名。 |

## ential [`ɛnʃəl]

| | | |
|---|---|---|
| **credential**<br>[krɪ`dɛnʃəl]<br>名 證書、證照 | ▶ excellent credentials<br>優秀的證照 | ▶ I think you have excellent credentials for the job.<br>我認為你具有這份工作所需的優秀證照。 |
| **confidential**<br>[ˏkɑnfə`dɛnʃəl]<br>形 祕密的、表示信任的 | ▶ confidential information<br>機密資訊 | ▶ That is confidential information that I cannot give you.<br>那是機密資訊，我無法給你。 |
| **residential**<br>[ˏrɛzə`dɛnʃəl]<br>形 居住的 | ▶ residential area<br>住宅區 | ▶ It's hard to decide on which residential area to live in.<br>很難決定要住在哪個住宅區。 |
| **presidential**<br>[ˏprɛzə`dɛnʃəl]<br>形 總統的 | ▶ presidential election<br>總統大選 | ▶ When is the next presidential election?<br>下一屆總統大選是什麼時候？ |
| **preferential**<br>[ˏprɛfə`rɛnʃəl]<br>形 優先的 | ▶ preferential treatment<br>優先禮遇 | ▶ It's unfair that he gives her preferential treatment.<br>他給她優先禮遇是很不公平的。 |
| **essential**<br>[ɪ`sɛnʃəl]<br>形 必要的、本質的 | ▶ essential difference<br>本質的不同 | ▶ The essential difference lies in the quality.<br>本質的差異反映在品質上。 |

| | | |
|---|---|---|
| **potential**<br>[pə`tɛnʃəl]<br>形 潛在的 名 潛能 | potential investors<br>潛在投資者<br>have potential for<br>有…的潛力 | Please treat the potential investors with respect.<br>請尊重潛在投資者。<br>His coach told him that he had potential for becoming a professional football player.<br>他的教練告訴他，他有成為職業橄欖球員的潛力。 |
| **influential**<br>[ˏɪnflʊ`ɛnʃəl]<br>形 有影響的 | an influential newspaper<br>具影響力的報社 | Her dream is to be a reporter for an influential newspaper.<br>她夢想成為具影響力報社的記者。 |

## ention [`ɛnʃən]

| | | |
|---|---|---|
| * **mention**<br>[`mɛnʃən]<br>動 提到、說起 | mention that<br>提及 | Please don't mention that to anyone else.<br>請不要向其他人提起。 |
| **detention**<br>[dɪ`tɛnʃən]<br>名 拘留 | get detention<br>被拘留 | He got detention for picking on the other kid.<br>他因為找別的小孩的麻煩而被拘留。 |
| * **intention**<br>[ɪn`tɛnʃən]<br>名 意圖 | good intentions<br>善意 | Although he was often clumsy, he always had good intentions.<br>雖然他常常很笨拙，但一直很善良。 |
| * **attention**<br>[ə`tɛnʃən]<br>名 注意 | pay attention to<br>注意 | You'd better pay attention to the teacher.<br>你最好專心聽老師講。 |

| | | |
|---|---|---|
| **prevention** [prɪˋvɛnʃən] 名 防止 | the prevention of fire 火災防範 | Do you know what to do for the prevention of fire? 你知道要如何防範火災嗎？ |
| * **invention** [ɪnˋvɛnʃən] 名 發明 | the invention of this machine 機器的發明 | The invention of this machine made things a lot easier. 這個機器的發明讓事情變得很容易。 |
| * **convention** [kənˋvɛnʃən] 名 會議、習俗 | a teachers' convention 教師大會<br>social conventions 社會習俗 | She went to attend a teachers' convention. 她去參加教師大會。<br>When you go to another country, you need to learn their social conventions. 當你去別的國家時，你需要學習他們的社會習俗。 |
| **intervention** [ˏɪntɚˋvɛnʃən] 名 介入 | military intervention 軍隊介入 | The government ordered a military intervention. 政府指示軍隊介入。 |

## ension [ˋɛnʃən]

| | | |
|---|---|---|
| **comprehension** [ˏkɑmprɪˋhɛnʃən] 名 理解力 | listening comprehension 聽力理解 | I do really well on listening comprehension sections of tests. 我的聽力測驗考得很好。 |
| **apprehension** [ˏæprɪˋhɛnʃən] 名 憂慮 | apprehension over the result 憂心結果 | Does she feel a lot of apprehension over the result? 對於結果，她感到非常憂心嗎？ |

| | | |
|---|---|---|
| * **dimension** [dɪˋmɛnʃən] 名 範圍 | ▶ the dimensions of his problems 他的問題範圍 | ▶ I can't believe the overwhelming dimensions of his problems. 我不敢相信他的問題那麼嚴重。 |
| * **pension** [ˋpɛnʃən] 名 退休金 | ▶ a small pension 小額退休金 | ▶ It's unfair that some people who work hard all their life still receive a small pension. 有些人很努力工作卻只拿到小額退休金，這是很不公平的。 |
| * **tension** [ˋtɛnʃən] 名 緊張 | ▶ nervous tension 神經緊張 | ▶ I have a lot of nervous tension in my back. 我的背部常會神經緊張。 |
| * **extension** [ɪkˋstɛnʃən] 名 伸展、延長 | ▶ extension of the deadline 期限延長 | ▶ Do you think the teacher can give us an extension of the deadline for the paper? 你認為老師能延後我們交報告的期限嗎？ |

## enture [ˋɛntʃɚ]

| | | |
|---|---|---|
| **venture** [ˋvɛntʃɚ] 名 冒險、投機活動 | ▶ a joint venture 合資公司 | ▶ The two big companies came together for a joint venture. 兩大公司已共同成立一家合資公司。 |
| **adventure** [ədˋvɛntʃɚ] 名 動 冒險 | ▶ a space adventure 太空探險 | ▶ He dreams of going on a space adventure someday. 他夢想著有一天去太空探險。 |

## ep [ɛp]

| | | |
|---|---|---|
| **step**<br>[stɛp]<br>名 腳步 | take a few steps<br>走幾步 | I love watching a baby take a few steps.<br>我很愛看嬰兒走路。 |
| **overstep**<br>[ˋovəˋstɛp]<br>動 超出限度 | overstep authority<br>超越權限 | Be careful not to overstep authority.<br>小心不要超越權限。 |
| **doorstep**<br>[ˋdorˏstɛp]<br>名 門階 | on the doorstep<br>在門階上 | They found a baby on the doorstep of their house.<br>他們在自家門階上發現一個嬰兒。 |

## ept [ɛpt]

| | | |
|---|---|---|
| * **accept**<br>[əkˋsɛpt]<br>動 接受、答應 | accept our invitation<br>接受我們的邀請 | Please accept our invitation to the party.<br>請接受我們的邀請參加宴會。 |
| **concept**<br>[ˋkɑnsɛpt]<br>名 概念、觀念 | a new concept<br>新概念 | He came up with a new concept.<br>他想出一個新概念。 |
| * **except**<br>[ɪkˋsɛpt]<br>介 連 除了 | except for<br>要不是… | I would go to the party, except for the fact that I have a presentation tomorrow.<br>要不是我明天有個簡報，我會去參加宴會。 |
| **inept**<br>[ɪnˋɛpt]<br>形 不適當的、無能的 | an inept employee<br>不適任的員工 | The boss fired him because he was an inept employee.<br>他是個不適任的員工，所以老板把他解雇。 |

## eption [ˋɛpʃən]

 24

| | | |
|---|---|---|
| **deception** [dɪˋsɛpʃən] 名 欺騙、欺詐 | ▶ use deception 運用欺詐 | ▶ That political party used deception to promote their cause. 政黨用欺詐達到目標。 |
| * **reception** [rɪˋsɛpʃən] 名 接待、接受 | ▶ an enthusiastic reception 熱情的迎接 | ▶ She was welcomed home from the hospital with an enthusiastic reception. 她出院回家受到熱情的迎接。 |
| **conception** [kənˋsɛpʃən] 名 概念、想法 | ▶ naive conception 天真的想法 | ▶ He has a naive conception that he will never have any problems. 他天真認為他不會有任何問題。 |
| **perception** [pɚˋsɛpʃən] 名 感知、看法 | ▶ my perception of the problem 我對問題的看法 | ▶ My boss doesn't respect my perception of the problem. 我的老板不尊重我對問題的看法。 |
| * **exception** [ɪkˋsɛpʃən] 名 例外 | ▶ an exception to the rule 規則之例外 | ▶ It seems like nothing is absolute and there is always an exception to the rule. 似乎沒有任何事是絕對的，規則總有例外。 |

## er [ɝ]

| | | |
|---|---|---|
| **defer** [dɪˋfɝ] 動 拖延、延期 | ▶ defer her departure 延後出發 | ▶ She will have to defer her departure because of the emergency. 因為有緊急事件，她必須延後出發。 |
| **refer** [rɪˋfɝ] 動 論及、參考 | ▶ refer to 參考 | ▶ If you refer to page 3, you'll see what I'm talking about. 如果你參考第三頁，你就會知道我在講什麼。 |

| | | |
|---|---|---|
| **prefer**<br>[prɪ`fɝ]<br>動 寧可、更喜歡 | prefer to<br>較喜歡 | Do you prefer to do this rather than that?<br>跟那相比，你比較喜歡做這個嗎？ |
| **infer**<br>[ɪn`fɝ]<br>動 推論 | infer a conclusion from the facts<br>從事實推出結論 | By now, you should be able to infer a conclusion from the facts. 現在，你應該可以從這些事實推出一個結論。 |
| **her**<br>[hɝ]<br>代 她的、她 | her child<br>她的小孩 | She has lost her child.<br>她已失去她的小孩。 |

## erge [ɝdʒ]

| | | |
|---|---|---|
| * **merge**<br>[mɝdʒ]<br>動 合併 | merge with<br>與…合併 | That river merges with another river up ahead.<br>那條河在前面與另一條河匯流了。 |
| **emerge**<br>[ɪ`mɝdʒ]<br>動 浮現 | emerge from the water<br>從水面浮出 | He looked tired when he emerged from the water.<br>他從水面浮出時，看起來很累。 |
| **verge**<br>[vɝdʒ]<br>名 邊緣 | on the verge of<br>接近於 | I think she is on the verge of crying.<br>我想她快哭了。 |
| **diverge**<br>[daɪ`vɝdʒ]<br>動 分歧、偏離 | diverge from<br>偏離 | That teacher often diverges from the topic she was originally talking about. 那個老師常常偏離她原本在講的話題。 |

| | | |
|---|---|---|
| **converge**<br>[kən`vɝdʒ]<br>動 會合 | converge on<br>會合在 | They will converge on the hill for a rally.<br>他們將在山上會合參加集會。 |

## ergent [`ɝdʒənt]

| | | |
|---|---|---|
| **emergent**<br>[ɪ`mɝdʒənt]<br>形 緊急的 | emergent situation<br>緊急的狀況 | Do you know what to do in an emergent situation?<br>你知道緊急狀況時要怎麼辦嗎？ |
| **detergent**<br>[dɪ`tɝdʒənt]<br>名 清潔劑 | washing detergent<br>洗潔劑 | This washing detergent is only used for clothing.<br>此洗潔劑僅用來洗衣服。 |

## eria [`ɪrɪə]

| | | |
|---|---|---|
| **bacteria**<br>[bæk`tɪrɪə]<br>名 細菌 | a bacterial infection<br>細菌感染 | He's been really sick with a bacterial infection.<br>他因為細菌感染生病了。 |
| **cafeteria**<br>[ˏkæfə`tɪrɪə]<br>名 自助餐廳 | cafeteria food<br>自助餐伙食 | Most schools' cafeteria food is not very good.<br>大部分學校的自助餐伙食都不太好。 |

## erious [`ɪrɪəs]

| | | |
|---|---|---|
| * **serious** [ˋsɪrɪəs] 形 嚴重的、認真的 | ▶ a serious mistake 嚴重的錯誤 a serious man 認真的男人 | ▶ I've made a serious mistake. 我犯了嚴重的錯誤。 I want a serious man for a boyfriend. 我想要認真的男人當男朋友。 |
| **mysterious** [mɪsˋtɪrɪəs] 形 神祕的 | ▶ mysterious universe 神祕的宇宙 | ▶ She often wonders about the mysterious universe. 她常對神祕的宇宙感到好奇。 |

## erk [ɜk]

| | | |
|---|---|---|
| * **clerk** [klɜk] 名 職員 | ▶ a bank clerk 銀行行員 | ▶ He's been a bank clerk for over 35 years. 他已經當銀行行員超過35年了。 |

## erm [ɜm]

| | | |
|---|---|---|
| **germ** [dʒɜm] 名 微生物、細菌 | ▶ kill germs 殺菌 | ▶ This soap is supposed to be good at killing germs. 這肥皂殺菌效果應該很好。 |
| **term** [tɜm] 名 期限、學期 | ▶ at the end of the term 學期末 | ▶ There is a final exam at the end of the term. 期末有個期末考。 |
| **midterm** [ˋmɪdˏtɜm] 形 期中的 名 期中考 | ▶ midterm exam 期中考 | ▶ Have you studied for your midterm exam yet? 你期中考的書讀了沒？ |

## irm [ɜm]

| | | |
|---|---|---|
| ***firm** [fɜm] 形 穩固的 名 公司 | ▶ law firm 律師事務所 | ▶ He has been working at that law firm for many years now. 他已經在律師事務所工作很多年了。 |
| ***confirm** [kən`fɜm] 動 證實、確定 | ▶ confirm the reservation 確認預約 | ▶ Did you confirm the reservation for our flight? 你有確認我們的機位嗎？ |

## ernal [`ɜnl̩]

| | | |
|---|---|---|
| **maternal** [mə`tɜnl̩] 形 母親的 | ▶ maternal love 母愛 | ▶ Nothing can beat maternal love. 沒有任何東西可以勝過母愛。 |
| **paternal** [pə`tɜnl̩] 形 父親的、父系的 | ▶ paternal grandfather 祖父 | ▶ My paternal grandfather looked exactly like my father when he was younger. 我的祖父年輕時跟我父親很像。 |
| **fraternal** [frə`tɜnl̩] 形 兄弟的、友愛的 | ▶ fraternal love 手足之愛 | ▶ There is a fraternal love between brothers that can't be denied. 兄弟間的手足之愛是無法否認的。 |
| **internal** [ɪn`tɜnl̩] 形 內部的、國內的 | ▶ internal injury 內部傷害 | ▶ He suffered an internal injury while he was playing soccer. 他踢足球時受到內傷。 |
| **eternal** [ɪ`tɜnl̩] 形 永久的、永恆的 | ▶ eternal love 永恆的愛 | ▶ Is there such a thing as eternal love? 有永恆的愛這回事嗎？ |

| | | |
|---|---|---|
| **external**<br>[ɪkˋstɝnḷ]<br>形 外部的、外界的 | ▶ external pressures<br>外界壓力 | ▶ I am getting tired of these external pressures.<br>我開始對這些外界的壓力感到厭煩。 |

## ero [ˋɪro]

| | | |
|---|---|---|
| **hero**<br>[ˋhɪro]<br>名 英雄 | ▶ the national heroes<br>全國英雄 | ▶ Firefighters in New York City were some of the national heroes of the 9-11 incident.<br>紐約的消防隊員是911事件的全國英雄。 |
| **zero**<br>[ˋzɪro]<br>名 零 形 零的 | ▶ zero degrees<br>零度 | ▶ Zero degrees Celsius is the freezing point.<br>攝氏零度是冰點。 |

## erse [ɝs]

25

| | | |
|---|---|---|
| **immerse**<br>[ɪˋmɝs]<br>動 使埋首於 | ▶ immerse yourself in<br>將自己埋首在… | ▶ You shouldn't immerse yourself in computer games.<br>你不應該沉溺於電玩。 |
| **disperse**<br>[dɪˋspɝs]<br>動 驅散、解散 | ▶ disperse the crowd<br>驅散群眾 | ▶ The police tried to disperse the crowd after the game.<br>警察在比賽後試圖驅散群眾。 |
| **verse**<br>[vɝs]<br>名 詩節、韻文 | ▶ verse of a poem<br>詩節 | ▶ I've been trying to memorize the verse of a poem.<br>我一直在努力記住詩節。 |

| | | |
|---|---|---|
| **adverse**<br>[æd`vɜs]<br>形 逆向的、有害的 | ▶ adverse effects<br>不良的影響 | ▶ There were adverse effects of taking that medicine.<br>吃那藥有不良的影響。 |
| **reverse**<br>[rɪ`vɜs]<br>形 顛倒的、相反的 | ▶ in reverse order<br>順序相反 | ▶ Can you tell me the list in reverse order? 你能用相反的順序告訴我清單上的資料嗎？ |
| **diverse**<br>[daɪ`vɜs]<br>形 不同的、互異的 | ▶ a diverse group of people<br>不同團體的人 | ▶ I want to associate with a diverse group of people.<br>我想跟不同團體的人來往。 |
| **universe**<br>[`junə͵vɜs]<br>名 宇宙、全世界 | ▶ in the universe<br>宇宙中 | ▶ Who believes that there are other life forms in the universe?<br>有誰相信宇宙中有其他生物？ |
| **inverse**<br>[ɪn`vɜs]<br>形 相反的 名 相反 | ▶ the inverse of<br>相反 | ▶ What is the inverse of five-fourths?<br>四分之五反過來是多少？ |
| **converse**<br>[kən`vɜs]<br>動 交談 | ▶ converse with<br>跟…交談 | ▶ She wants to converse with the king.<br>她想跟國王講話。 |

## erce [ɜs]

| | | |
|---|---|---|
| * **commerce**<br>[`kɑmɜs]<br>名 商業、貿易 | ▶ overseas commerce<br>海外貿易 | ▶ That company is in the business of overseas commerce.<br>那間公司經營海外貿易。 |

| | | |
|---|---|---|
| **coerce**<br>[ko`ɝs]<br>動 強制 | coerce my friend<br>強迫我的朋友 | I will try to coerce my friend into coming with us.<br>我會設法強迫我朋友跟我們來。 |

## ersion [`ɝʒən]

| | | |
|---|---|---|
| **immersion**<br>[ɪ`mɝʒən]<br>名 沈浸、浸沒 | cultural immersion<br>文化沈浸 | The cultural immersion program is very effective for learning a language. 文化體驗課程對於學習語言有很好的效果。 |
| * **version**<br>[`vɝʒən]<br>名 譯本、版本 | the old version<br>舊版 | This is the old version; I want the new one!<br>這是舊版，我想要新版！ |
| **aversion**<br>[ə`vɝʒən]<br>名 厭惡、反感 | an aversion to meat<br>對肉反感 | Some vegetarians have an aversion to meat.<br>有些素食者對肉反胃。 |
| **conversion**<br>[kən`vɝʒən]<br>名 改變、轉變 | religious conversion<br>宗教的改變 | She has had a religious conversion from Buddhism to Christianity.<br>她的信仰從佛教變成基督教。 |
| **diversion**<br>[daɪ`vɝʒən]<br>名 轉向、消遣 | good diversion<br>好的消遣 | Reading a fun book is a good diversion.<br>閱讀有趣的書是不錯的消遣。 |

## ersity [`ɝsətɪ]

| | | |
|---|---|---|
| **adversity** [əd`vɝsətɪ] 名 逆境、厄運 | in time of adversity 在逆境中 | My mother is always there for me in time of adversity. 當我處於逆境時，媽媽一直支持我。 |
| **diversity** [daɪ`vɝsətɪ] 名 差異、多樣性 | ethnic diversity 種族多樣性 | I enjoy the ethnic diversity of New York City. 我很喜歡紐約的種族多樣性。 |
| **university** [͵junə`vɝsətɪ] 名 大學 | university campus 大學校園 | You should visit the university campus before you decide to go there. 你應該先參觀大學校園再決定要不要去那裡讀。 |

## erson [`ɝsn̩]

| | | |
|---|---|---|
| **person** [`pɝsn̩] 名 人 | young person 年輕人 | That young person offended the older people in the room. 那個年輕人冒犯了屋內的前輩。 |
| **spokesperson** [`spoks͵pɝsn̩] 名 發言人 | spokesperson for the company 公司的發言人 | The spokesperson for the company came by today to talk to the manager. 公司發言人今天前來跟經理談話。 |

## ert [ɝt]

| | | |
|---|---|---|
| * **alert** [ə`lɝt] 名 警戒 形 警覺的 | on the alert 警覺著 | Please be on the alert at all times. 請隨時保持警覺。 |

| | | |
| --- | --- | --- |
| **desert** [dɪ`zɜt] [`dɛzət] 動 拋棄 名 沙漠 | the desert areas 沙漠區 | The desert areas of China are vast and sprawling. 中國沙漠是廣闊蔓延的。 |
| **insert** [ɪn`sɜt] 動 插入 | insert the card 插入卡片 | You must insert the card before you enter your password. 你必須先插卡才能輸入密碼。 |
| **assert** [ə`sɜt] 動 斷言、堅持 | assert oneself 堅持自己的權利 | She has learned to assert herself over the years. 這些年來她已學會堅持自己的權利。 |
| **dessert** [dɪ`zɜt] 名 餐後甜點 | eat dessert 吃甜點 | Do you have enough room in your stomach to eat dessert? 你還吃得下甜點嗎？ |
| **avert** [ə`vɜt] 動 避開 | avert his eyes from 眼神閃避 | I saw him avert his eyes from that girl. 我看到他的眼神閃避那女孩。 |
| **divert** [daɪ`vɜt] 動 使轉向 | divert the opponents 使對手轉向 | Try to divert the opponents by making them think that you are going the other way. 試著讓對手認為你會走另一邊而轉向別處。 |
| **convert** [kən`vɜt] 動 轉變 | convert others to Christianity 使別人改信基督教 | He often tries to convert others to Christianity. 他常常試圖說服別人改信基督教。 |
| **introvert** [`ɪntrə͵vɜt] 名 內向的人 | quiet introvert 安靜內向的人 | I thought he was a quiet introvert, but he went crazy at the party. 我以為他是安靜又內向的人，但是他在派對上玩得很瘋。 |

| | | |
|---|---|---|
| **extrovert** [`ɛkstrovɜt] 名 外向的人 | loud extrovert 高調外向的人 | People sometimes think I'm a loud extrovert. 別人有時會認為我是個高調又外向的人。 |

## erve [ɜv]

| | | |
|---|---|---|
| **nerve** [nɜv] 名 神經 | get on my nerves 使我心煩 | He really gets on my nerves! 他讓我很心煩！ |
| * **serve** [sɜv] 動 服務、供應 | serve dinner 供應晚餐 | My mother serves dinner at 6:30. 我媽媽六點半準備好晚餐。 |
| * **observe** [əb`zɜv] 動 注意到、觀察 | observe class 教學觀摩 | I asked the teacher if I could observe his class. 我要求老師讓我觀摩他上課。 |
| * **deserve** [dɪ`zɜv] 動 應受、該得 | deserve an award 該得獎 | I think that she deserves an award for her bravery. 我認為她的勇氣值得獎勵。 |
| * **reserve** [rɪ`zɜv] 動 保存、預約 | reserve seats 預約座位 | Please reserve seats at the restaurant tonight. 請預約今晚的餐廳。 |
| **preserve** [prɪ`zɜv] 動 保存、醃 | preserve meat 醃肉 | Do you know how to preserve meat? 你知道怎麼醃肉嗎？ |

| | | |
|---|---|---|
| **conserve**<br>[kən`sɝv]<br>動 保存、保護 | conserve energy<br>保持動力 | It is important that you know ways to conserve energy.<br>知道如何保持動力是很重要的。 |

## escent [`ɛsn̩t]

| | | |
|---|---|---|
| **adolescent**<br>[͵ædl̩`ɛsn̩t]<br>名 青少年 形 青春期的 | adolescent problems<br>青春期的問題 | What kind of adolescent problems did you have?<br>你有過什麼樣的青春期問題？ |

## essant [`ɛsn̩t]

| | | |
|---|---|---|
| **incessant**<br>[ɪn`sɛsn̩t]<br>形 不停的、連續的 | incessant rain<br>連綿的雨 | I can't stand the incessant rain in May.<br>我無法忍受五月連綿不絕的雨。 |

## esh [ɛʃ]

| | | |
|---|---|---|
| **flesh**<br>[flɛʃ]<br>名 肉、肉體 | flesh and blood<br>血肉之軀、親人 | My children are my own flesh and blood.<br>我的孩子都是自己的骨肉。 |
| **fresh**<br>[frɛʃ]<br>形 新鮮的 | fresh fruit<br>新鮮水果 | Our house is out of fresh fruit.<br>我們家的新鮮水果吃完了。 |

## esident [`ɛzədənt]

26

| | | |
|---|---|---|
| **resident** [`rɛzədənt] 名 居民 | ▶ New York resident 紐約市民 | ▶ Are you a New York resident? 你是紐約市民嗎？ |
| **president** [`prɛzədənt] 名 總統、總裁 | ▶ president of the company 公司總裁 | ▶ The president of the company is very greedy. 這公司的總裁非常貪婪。 |

## esitant [`ɛzətənt]

| | | |
|---|---|---|
| **hesitant** [`hɛzətənt] 形 遲疑的 | ▶ a hesitant look 遲疑的表情 | ▶ I can tell that he isn't sure because I saw him with a hesitant look on his face. 我可以看出他並不確定，因為我看到他臉上有遲疑的表情。 |

## esque [ɛsk]

| | | |
|---|---|---|
| **picturesque** [ˏpɪktʃə`rɛsk] 形 如畫的、美麗的 | ▶ picturesque scenery 如畫的風景 | ▶ This place looks like it can be used for picturesque scenery in a movie. 這地方風景如畫，可以拍電影了。 |
| **grotesque** [gro`tɛsk] 形 奇怪的、畸形的 | ▶ grotesque wound 奇怪的傷 | ▶ I couldn't look at his grotesque wound. 我無法看著他奇怪的傷。 |

## esk [ɛsk]

|  |  |  |
| --- | --- | --- |
| **desk**<br>[dɛsk]<br>名 書桌 | desk lamp<br>桌燈 | My desk lamp fell and broke.<br>我的桌燈摔壞了。 |

## ess [ɛs]

|  |  |  |
| --- | --- | --- |
| * **access**<br>[`æksɛs]<br>名 接近、進入 | have access to<br>能進入 | He has access to all the rooms in the building.<br>他可以進入屋中所有房間。 |
| * **success**<br>[sək`sɛs]<br>名 成功 | financial success<br>財務上的成功 | Everybody dreams of financial success.<br>每個人都夢想賺大錢。 |
| **excess**<br>[ɪk`sɛs]<br>名 超越、過量 | excess of<br>過度 | There is an excess of corruption in this business<br>這家公司貪污過度。 |
| **confess**<br>[kən`fɛs]<br>動 坦白、告解 | confess to the priest<br>向神父告解 | Her mother made her confess all her sins to the priest.<br>她母親要她向神父告解所有的罪過。 |
| **profess**<br>[prə`fɛs]<br>動 承認、表示 | profess a distaste for<br>表示不喜歡… | He has professed a distaste for Chinese food.<br>他表示不喜歡吃中國菜。 |
| * **less**<br>[lɛs]<br>形 較少的 | less information<br>較少的資訊 | You will receive less information from the magazine than from the Internet.<br>你從雜誌獲得的資訊比網路少。 |

| | | |
|---|---|---|
| **bless**<br>[blɛs]<br>動 保佑 | bless you<br>保佑你 | People in the United States say "bless you" after another sneezes. 美國人會在別人打噴嚏後說「上帝保佑你」。 |
| **nonetheless**<br>[ˌnʌnðəˋlɛs]<br>連 副 但是、仍然 | nonetheless<br>但是 | I hate action movies. Nonetheless, I'll go with you to this one. 我討厭動作片，但我會跟你一起去看這部。 |
| * **unless**<br>[ʌnˋlɛs]<br>連 除非 介 除…外 | unless there is a problem<br>除非有問題 | Unless there is a problem, please stop calling me all the time. 除非有問題，否則請不要一直打給我。 |
| **dress**<br>[drɛs]<br>動 使…穿著 | dress up<br>盛裝打扮 | He will dress up tonight for the banquet.<br>他今晚會盛裝出席晚宴。 |
| **undress**<br>[ʌnˋdrɛs]<br>動 脫衣服 | undress himself<br>脫衣服 | He feels uncomfortable undressing himself in fitting rooms.<br>他覺得在試衣間脫衣服不自在。 |
| **address**<br>[əˋdrɛs]<br>名 住址 動 演說 | address the audience<br>對聽眾演講 | She is very nervous about addressing the audience tonight for her speech.<br>她今晚要對聽眾演講，非常緊張。 |
| **regress**<br>[rɪˋgrɛs] [ˋrigrɛs]<br>動 名 退回、回歸 | regress to an earlier state<br>退化 | I find that his level of speech is regressing to an earlier state because of his illness.<br>我發現他說話的水平因為生病退化了。 |
| * **impress**<br>[ɪmˋprɛs]<br>動 使…印象深刻 | impress me<br>讓我印象深刻 | That doesn't impress me much.<br>那並沒有給我太深的印象。 |

| | | |
|---|---|---|
| **oppress**<br>[ə`prɛs]<br>動 壓迫、壓制 | oppress the lower class<br>壓迫低階者 | Sometimes it is obvious when the upper class is trying to oppress the lower class.<br>高階者試圖壓迫低階者有時是很明顯的。 |
| **suppress**<br>[sə`prɛs]<br>動 鎮壓、抑制 | suppress a laugh<br>忍住笑意 | I tried to suppress a laugh in class, but instead I burst out laughing. 上課時我試著忍住笑意，但反而突然大笑出來。 |
| **express**<br>[ɪk`sprɛs]<br>動 表達 名 快車 | express train<br>快車 | Take the express train; it's much faster than the local one. 搭快車會比普通車快多了。 |
| **stress**<br>[strɛs]<br>名 壓力 動 壓迫 | in times of stress<br>有壓力時 | What helps you the most in times of stress?<br>壓力來時什麼最有用？ |
| **distress**<br>[dɪ`strɛs]<br>名 苦惱、困苦 | in distress<br>困苦 | He saw a woman in distress, and felt as though he needed to be a hero.<br>他看到一位困苦的女性，覺得自己應該成為英雄來幫她。 |
| **possess**<br>[pə`zɛs]<br>動 擁有、持有 | possess powers<br>擁有力量 | A lot of cartoon characters possess special powers.<br>很多卡通主角擁有特殊的力量。 |
| **guess**<br>[gɛs]<br>動 猜測、推測 | guess what<br>猜猜看怎麼著 | Guess what?<br>猜猜看怎麼著！ |

**es [ɛs]**

| | | |
|---|---|---|
| **yes**<br>[jɛs]<br>副 是 名 同意 | ▶ "yes or no" answer<br>「是或不是」的答案 | ▶ I want you to give me a "yes or no" answer.<br>我要你回答我「是」或「不是」。 |

## essful [ˋɛsfəl]

| | | |
|---|---|---|
| **successful**<br>[səkˋsɛsfəl]<br>形 成功的 | ▶ a successful woman<br>成功的女性 | ▶ There are a lot of obstacles in becoming a successful woman. 成為一名成功的女性要通過很多障礙。 |
| **stressful**<br>[ˋstrɛsfəl]<br>形 壓力大的 | ▶ stressful job<br>壓力大的工作 | ▶ Not all stressful jobs are rewarding. 並非所有壓力大的工作都能有應得的報酬。 |

## ession [ˋɛʃən]

| | | |
|---|---|---|
| **succession**<br>[səkˋsɛʃən]<br>名 連續、繼承 | ▶ in succession to<br>繼承 | ▶ He was the first in succession to his father.<br>他是繼承父志的第一人選。 |
| **recession**<br>[rɪˋsɛʃən]<br>名 後退、衰退 | ▶ economic recession<br>經濟衰退 | ▶ Asia has been suffering an economic recession.<br>亞洲受到經濟衰退影響。 |
| **confession**<br>[kənˋfɛʃən]<br>名 告解、坦白 | ▶ confession booth<br>告解亭 | ▶ Catholic churches have confession booths for people to confess their sins to a priest.<br>天主教堂有告解亭，在那裡人們可向神父懺悔。 |

| | | |
|---|---|---|
| * **profession** [prə`fɛʃən] 名 職業 | ▸ a lawyer by profession 專業律師 | ▸ She is a lawyer by profession, but a mother as well. 她是專業的律師，但也是位母親。 |
| **aggression** [ə`grɛʃən] 名 侵略 | ▸ physical aggression 身體上的侵犯 | ▸ You can be arrested for physical aggression against another person. 你可能會因侵犯他人身體被捕。 |
| **progression** [prə`grɛʃən] 名 前進、發展 | ▸ steady progression 穩定的發展 | ▸ It is clear that there is a steady progression from light to dark in this painting. 這幅畫中可以很清楚看到顏色由亮到暗穩定地變化。 |
| **depression** [dɪ`prɛʃən] 名 沮喪、憂鬱症 | ▸ symptoms of depression 憂鬱症的徵兆 | ▸ You better watch out for symptoms of depression and take care of her. 你最好注意她憂鬱症的徵兆，並好好照顧她。 |
| * **impression** [ɪm`prɛʃən] 名 印象 | ▸ under the impression that 以為 | ▸ I was under the impression that you were going to help me. 我以為你會幫我。 |
| **oppression** [ə`prɛʃən] 名 壓迫 | ▸ feeling of oppression 感到壓迫 | ▸ I hate this feeling of oppression. 我討厭這種被壓迫的感覺。 |
| **suppression** [sə`prɛʃən] 名 壓制、禁止 | ▸ suppression of the rally 鎮壓集會 | ▸ The police helped the military with the suppression of the rally. 警方幫軍隊鎮壓集會。 |
| * **expression** [ɪk`sprɛʃən] 名 表達、表情 | ▸ facial expression 臉部表情 | ▸ Which facial expression of his is your favorite? 你最喜歡他的哪個臉部表情？ |

| | | |
|---|---|---|
| **session**<br>[ˋsɛʃən]<br>名 開會 | ▶ court session<br>開庭 | ▶ They are in court session right now.<br>他們正在開庭。 |
| **obsession**<br>[əbˋsɛʃən]<br>名 著迷 | ▶ obsession with you<br>對你著迷 | ▶ He has an obsession with you. Be careful.<br>他對你很著迷，小心點。 |
| **possession**<br>[pəˋzɛʃən]<br>名 擁有、所有物 | ▶ get possession of<br>獲得財物 | ▶ The burglars tried to get possession of the jewels.<br>夜賊試圖偷珠寶。 |

## etion [ˋɛʃən]

| | | |
|---|---|---|
| **discretion**<br>[dɪˋskrɛʃən]<br>名 謹慎、處理權 | ▶ at your own discretion<br>隨意 | ▶ Please use them at your own discretion.<br>請隨意使用它們。 |
| **indiscretion**<br>[ˏɪndɪˋskrɛʃən]<br>名 輕率 | ▶ show indiscretion by<br>表現輕率 | ▶ He had the nerve to show indiscretion by talking about the gang leader.<br>他竟敢輕率地談論幫派首領。 |

## essive [ˋɛsɪv]

| | | |
|---|---|---|
| **excessive**<br>[ɪkˋsɛsɪv]<br>形 過度的 | ▶ excessive charges<br>過度的收費 | ▶ There are some excessive charges on my bill that I have to clear up. 我的帳單有些收費超過，我必須釐清。 |

| | | |
|---|---|---|
| **aggressive** [ə`grɛsɪv] 形 好鬥的 | ▶ aggressive personality 好鬥的個性 | ▶ His aggressive personality got him in a lot of trouble. 他好鬥的個性給他帶來很多麻煩。 |
| * **impressive** [ɪm`prɛsɪv] 形 讓人印象深刻的 | ▶ an impressive show 讓人印象深刻的表演 | ▶ We saw an impressive show last night. 昨晚我們看了一場讓人印象深刻的秀。 |
| **oppressive** [ə`prɛsɪv] 形 壓迫的、專制的 | ▶ oppressive laws 專制的律法 | ▶ Some people think that there are too many oppressive laws that restrict our freedoms. 有些人認為有太多專制的律法限制我們的自由。 |
| **expressive** [ɪk`sprɛsɪv] 形 表達…的 | ▶ expressive smile 表達感受的微笑 | ▶ She has the most expressive smile that can tell you how she feels. 她的笑容可以傳情達意，讓你知道她的感受。 |

## essor [`ɛsɚ]

| | | |
|---|---|---|
| **successor** [sək`sɛsɚ] 名 繼任者、繼承人 | ▶ the successor to the throne 王位繼承人 | ▶ He killed the successor to the throne so he could become king. 他殺了王位繼承人因而當上國王。 |
| **predecessor** [`prɛdɪ͵sɛsɚ] 名 前任、前輩 | ▶ the former predecessor 前任 | ▶ Who was the former predecessor in that managerial position? 誰是前任的管理者？ |
| **oppressor** [ə`prɛsɚ] 名 壓迫者、壓制者 | ▶ cruel oppressor 殘忍的迫害者 | ▶ Everyone knew him as a cruel oppressor. 每個人都知道他是殘忍的迫害者。 |

| | | |
|---|---|---|
| **possessor** [pə`zɛsɚ] 名 持有人 | the possessor of the book 書的持有人 | The possessor of the book will supposedly gain magical powers. 擁有這本書的人據說會得到不可思議的力量。 |

## essy [`ɛsɪ]

| | | |
|---|---|---|
| **messy** [`mɛsɪ] 形 髒亂的、麻煩的 | messy room 髒亂的房間 | Clean up your messy room! 把你髒亂的房間清乾淨！ |

## est [ɛst]

27

| | | |
|---|---|---|
| **best** [bɛst] 形 最好的 | my best friend 我最好的朋友 | I miss my best friend. 我想念我最好的朋友。 |
| * **suggest** [sə`dʒɛst] 動 建議、暗示 | what do you suggest 你建議什麼 | What do you suggest we do for dinner? 你建議我們晚餐要吃什麼？ |
| **chest** [tʃɛst] 名 胸膛 | chest pain 胸痛 | He says he has bad chest pain. 他說他的胸部很痛。 |
| **nest** [nɛst] 名 巢、穴 | bird's nest 鳥巢 | I saw that bird's nest fall out of the tree. 我看到鳥巢從樹上掉下來。 |

| 單字 | 片語 | 例句 |
| --- | --- | --- |
| **pest** [pɛst] 名 害蟲 | garden pests 花園的害蟲 | We need to get some pesticides for our garden pests. 我需要一些殺蟲劑來殺花園的害蟲。 |
| * **rest** [rɛst] 名 動 休息 | take a rest 休息一下 | Let's take a rest here under the tree. 我們在這樹下休息一下吧。 |
| **arrest** [ə`rɛst] 動 名 逮捕 | under house arrest 在軟禁下 | He was under house arrest for 15 years. 他被軟禁了十五年。 |
| **test** [tɛst] 動 名 考試、檢驗 | a blood test 血液測試 | He got a blood test at the doctor's office. 他在醫師的診療室作了血液測試。 |
| * **contest** [`kɑntɛst] 名 爭奪、比賽 | eating contest 大胃王比賽 | Did you see that Japanese eating contest on TV? 你有看電視播的日本大胃王比賽嗎？ |
| **protest** [prə`tɛst] 動 抗議、反對 | protest against 抗議 | They were protesting against war. 他們抗議戰爭。 |
| * **guest** [gɛst] 名 客人 | house guest 過夜的客人 | You are our honored house guest. 你是我們的貴賓。 |
| **quest** [kwɛst] 名 動 追求、探索 | in quest of 尋找 | The hobbit Bilbo was in quest of a sacred ring. 哈比人比爾博尋找魔戒。 |

| | | |
| --- | --- | --- |
| * **request**<br>[rɪ`kwɛst]<br>名 動 要求、請求 | make a request for<br>做出要求 | I'd like to make a request for a song, please.<br>我想要點一首歌。 |
| **conquest**<br>[`kɑŋkwɛst]<br>名 征服、佔領 | virtual conquest<br>實際的佔領 | They almost had a virtual conquest of the whole region.<br>他們幾乎佔領了整個區域。 |
| **vest**<br>[vɛst]<br>名 背心 | vest pocket<br>背心口袋 | What did you find in his vest pocket?<br>你在他背心的口袋找到什麼？ |
| * **invest**<br>[ɪn`vɛst]<br>動 投資、入股 | invest $1000 in stock<br>投資1000美元買股票 | I want to invest a thousand dollars in stock.<br>我想投資一千美元買股票。 |
| **west**<br>[wɛst]<br>名 西方 形 西方的 | West Asia<br>西亞 | The 2006 Asian Games was held in West Asia.<br>2006年亞運在西亞舉行。 |
| **zest**<br>[zɛst]<br>名 熱心、熱情 | with zest<br>熱情地 | She goes to class with zest.<br>她很高興地去上課。 |

## ester [`ɛstɚ]

| | | |
| --- | --- | --- |
| **semester**<br>[sə`mɛstɚ]<br>名 一學期 | this semester<br>這學期 | What new classes are you taking this semester?<br>你這學期要選什麼新課程？ |

| | | |
|---|---|---|
| **tester**<br>[`tɛstɚ]<br>名 試驗員、測試器 | fat tester<br>脂肪測試器 | Our gym has a fat tester.<br>我們的健身房有脂肪測試器。 |

## estor [`ɛstɚ]

| | | |
|---|---|---|
| **ancestor**<br>[`ænsɛstɚ]<br>名 祖宗、祖先 | ancestor worship<br>拜祖先的儀式 | There is little ancestor worship in Western culture.<br>西方文化裡很少有拜祖先的儀式。 |
| **protestor**<br>[prə`tɛstɚ]<br>名 抗議者 | angry protestors<br>氣憤的抗議者 | The angry protestors stayed up all night.<br>氣憤的抗議者整晚沒睡。 |
| * **investor**<br>[ɪn`vɛstɚ]<br>名 投資者、出資者 | a careful investor<br>小心的投資者 | You have to be a careful investor to avoid big losses.<br>你必須小心投資以避免大筆損失。 |

## estion [`ɛstʃən]

| | | |
|---|---|---|
| **suggestion**<br>[sə`dʒɛstʃən]<br>名 建議、暗示 | good suggestion<br>好的建議 | Thanks for your good suggestion.<br>感謝你的好建議。 |
| **digestion**<br>[də`dʒɛstʃən]<br>名 消化 | poor digestion<br>消化不良 | Unfortunately, I have poor digestion.<br>倒楣的是我消化不良。 |

| | | |
|---|---|---|
| **indigestion**<br>[ˌɪndəˋdʒɛstʃən]<br>名 消化不良 | ▶ suffer from indigestion<br>受消化不良之苦 | ▶ He is suffering from indigestion, so he couldn't come today.<br>他消化不良，所以今天不能來。 |
| **congestion**<br>[kənˋdʒɛstʃən]<br>名 擁塞 | ▶ the congestion of traffic<br>交通擁塞 | ▶ The congestion of traffic is worse during the holidays.<br>交通擁擠的情況在假日時更為嚴重。 |
| * **question**<br>[ˋkwɛstʃən]<br>名 問題 動 詢問 | ▶ out of the question<br>不可能的 | ▶ That is out of the question! No way!<br>那是不可能的！門兒都沒有！ |

## et [ɛt]

| | | |
|---|---|---|
| **bet**<br>[bɛt]<br>動 名 打賭 | ▶ wanna bet<br>要打賭嗎 | ▶ I bet you I'm right. Wanna bet?<br>我跟你打賭我是對的，要賭嗎？ |
| **alphabet**<br>[ˋælfəˌbɛt]<br>名 字母系統 | ▶ the Greek alphabet<br>希臘字母系統 | ▶ Does anyone know the Greek alphabet?<br>有誰知道希臘字母系統？ |
| * **get**<br>[gɛt]<br>動 獲得、到達 | ▶ get there<br>到那兒 | ▶ Just follow me, because I know how to get there. 只要跟著我即可，因為我知道如何到那兒。 |
| * **forget**<br>[fəˋgɛt]<br>動 忘記 | ▶ forget everything<br>忘了每件事 | ▶ It's easy to forget everything after a night of drinking too much.<br>晚上喝太多，很容易忘東忘西。 |

| | | |
|---|---|---|
| **jet**<br>[dʒɛt]<br>名動 噴射 | ▶ a jet of water<br>一道水柱 | ▶ That boat shoots out a jet of water from the back.<br>那條船的後面噴出一道水柱。 |
| **net**<br>[nɛt]<br>名 網子 | ▶ a mosquito net<br>蚊帳 | ▶ It would be better if you used a mosquito net tonight.<br>你今晚用蚊帳會比較好。 |
| **pet**<br>[pɛt]<br>名 寵物 | ▶ pet name<br>暱稱 | ▶ What is your pet name?<br>你的暱稱是什麼？ |
| **regret**<br>[rɪˋgrɛt]<br>動名 懊悔、遺憾 | ▶ regret lost opportunities<br>後悔失去的機會 | ▶ I don't want to regret lost opportunities.<br>我不想要為失去的機會後悔。 |
| **set**<br>[sɛt]<br>動 放置、安裝 | ▶ set records<br>創紀錄 | ▶ He set records for being the fastest cyclist in town.<br>他創下了鎮上腳踏車騎最快的紀錄。 |
| **reset**<br>[riˋsɛt]<br>動 重放、重調 | ▶ reset the clock<br>重調時鐘 | ▶ Everyone sometimes wishes that they could reset the clock and start over. 人有時會希望時光能倒流然後從頭來過。 |
| **sunset**<br>[ˋsʌn͵sɛt]<br>名 日落 | ▶ watch the sunset<br>看日落 | ▶ This is a great place to watch the sunset.<br>這是個欣賞日落的好地方。 |
| **upset**<br>[ʌpˋsɛt]<br>動 傾覆 形 心煩的 | ▶ feel upset<br>感到心煩 | ▶ He feels upset.<br>他感到心煩。 |

| | | |
|---|---|---|
| **wet**<br>[wɛt]<br>形 潮濕的 | ▶ get wet<br>弄濕 | ▶ You will definitely get wet on that water ride.<br>玩那水上遊樂設施你肯定會弄濕。 |
| **yet**<br>[jɛt]<br>副 還 連 可是 | ▶ not yet<br>尚未 | ▶ The mail isn't here yet.<br>信還沒送來這兒。 |

## ette [ɛt]

| | | |
|---|---|---|
| **cigarette**<br>[ˌsɪgəˋrɛt]<br>名 香菸 | ▶ cigarette advertisement<br>香菸廣告 | ▶ There are fewer cigarette advertisements these days.<br>這陣子香菸廣告比較少。 |

## eat [ɛt]

| | | |
|---|---|---|
| **threat**<br>[θrɛt]<br>名 威脅、恐嚇 | ▶ carry out his threat<br>進行威脅 | ▶ Do you think he'll carry out his threat?<br>你認為他會進行威脅嗎？ |
| **sweat**<br>[swɛt]<br>名 汗水 動 出汗 | ▶ in a cold sweat<br>冒冷汗 | ▶ She's been in a cold sweat because of her fever.<br>因為發燒的關係，她全身冒冷汗。 |

## ebt [ɛt]

| | | |
|---|---|---|
| **debt**<br>[dɛt]<br>名 債、借款 | in debt<br>負債 | He's in debt to a lot of people.<br>他欠很多人錢。 |

## etch [ɛtʃ]

28

| | | |
|---|---|---|
| **etch**<br>[ɛtʃ]<br>動 蝕刻 | etch in a stone<br>刻在石頭上 | That couple etched their names in a stone.<br>那對情侶將他們的名字刻在石頭上。 |
| **fetch**<br>[fɛtʃ]<br>動 拿來 | fetch the ball<br>撿球 | Her dog is good at fetching the ball.<br>她的狗撿球很厲害。 |
| **sketch**<br>[skɛtʃ]<br>名 動 速寫、素描 | sketch book<br>素描本 | He carries his sketch book around with him at all times.<br>他整天帶著他的素描本。 |
| **stretch**<br>[strɛtʃ]<br>動 伸直、伸長 | stretch out<br>伸展身體 | I like to stretch out on the couch.<br>我喜歡舒展身體躺在沙發上。 |

## etic [ˋɛtɪk]

| | | |
|---|---|---|
| **diabetic**<br>[ˏdaɪəˋbɛtɪk]<br>形 糖尿病的 | diabetic food<br>糖尿病專用食物 | He needs to find diabetic food everywhere he goes.<br>不管到哪裡，他身邊都要有糖尿病專用食物。 |

| | | |
|---|---|---|
| **magnetic** [mæg`nɛtɪk] 形 磁鐵的、磁性的 | magnetic field 磁區 | There is a strange magnetic field here that scientists are studying. 這裡有個奇妙的磁區，科學家們正在研究。 |
| * **apologetic** [ə͵pɑlə`dʒɛtɪk] 形 道歉的、認錯的 | an apologetic letter 道歉信 | He wrote an apologetic letter to the teacher. 他寫一封道歉信給老師。 |
| * **energetic** [͵ɛnɚ`dʒɛtɪk] 形 精力旺盛的 | an energetic person 精力旺盛的的人 | She is such an energetic person who never gets tired. 她總是精力旺盛從不覺得累。 |
| **pathetic** [pə`θɛtɪk] 形 可憐的、可悲的 | a pathetic sight 可憐兮兮的情景 | Look at them getting crushed by the other team. What a pathetic sight. 看他們被另一隊打垮，多可悲的情景。 |
| **sympathetic** [͵sɪmpə`θɛtɪk] 形 同情的 | sympathetic looks 同情的目光 | She gave me sympathetic looks while I was stuttering in class. 當我上課結巴時，她用同情的眼神看著我。 |
| **synthetic** [sɪn`θɛtɪk] 形 合成的 | synthetic rubber 合成橡膠 | The synthetic rubber is waterproof and unbreakable. 這合成橡膠防水且不易破。 |
| **anesthetic** [͵ænəs`θɛtɪk] 名 麻醉劑 形 麻醉的 | under the influence of an anesthetic 在麻醉劑的影響下 | He couldn't remember the surgery because he was under the influence of an anesthetic. 因為受到麻醉的影響，他記不得手術情形。 |
| **athletic** [æθ`lɛtɪk] 形 運動的、體育的 | athletic-looking people 運動型的人 | Athletic-looking people look healthy. 運動型的人看起來很健康。 |

| | | |
|---|---|---|
| **cosmetic**<br>[kaz`mɛtɪk]<br>名 化妝品 形 整容的 | cosmetic surgery<br>整容手術 | She didn't tell anybody about her cosmetic surgery.<br>她不告訴任何人她整容的事。 |
| **genetic**<br>[dʒə`nɛtɪk]<br>形 基因的 | genetic modification<br>基因改造 | The scientists did some genetic modification in the lab.<br>科學家在實驗室做了些基因改造的實驗。 |
| **poetic**<br>[po`ɛtɪk]<br>形 詩的、詩人的 | in poetic form<br>用詩的形式 | Can you re-write this essay in poetic form?<br>你可以用詩的形式重寫這篇散文嗎？ |

## etter [`ɛtɚ]

| | | |
|---|---|---|
| * **better**<br>[`bɛtɚ]<br>形 更好的 | a better man<br>更好的男人 | He is a better man than most.<br>他比大多數的男人好。 |
| * **letter**<br>[`lɛtɚ]<br>名 信、文字 | send the letter<br>寄信 | We need to send the letter away today, or we'll miss the deadline. 我們今天必須寄出這封信，不然就超過期限了。 |
| **newsletter**<br>[`njuz`lɛtɚ]<br>名 商務通訊、報刊 | publish our newsletter<br>出版報刊 | They said they would publish our newsletter!<br>他們說他們想出版我們的報刊！ |

## eater [`ɛtɚ]

| | | |
|---|---|---|
| **sweater**<br>[ˋswɛtɚ]<br>名 毛線衣 | ▸ cashmere sweater<br>喀什米爾羊毛衣 | ▸ I love cashmere sweaters because they are so soft.<br>我喜愛喀什米爾羊毛衣，因為它們很柔軟。 |

## etto [ˋɛto]

| | | |
|---|---|---|
| **ghetto**<br>[ˋgɛto]<br>名 貧民區 | ▸ live in the ghetto<br>住在貧民區 | ▸ A lot of rich people are afraid to live in the ghetto.<br>很多有錢人害怕住在貧民區。 |

## eadow [ˋɛdo]

| | | |
|---|---|---|
| **meadow**<br>[ˋmɛdo]<br>名 草地、牧草地 | ▸ graze in the meadow<br>在草地上吃草 | ▸ Cows like to graze in the meadow.<br>牛喜歡在草地上吃草。 |

## even [ˋɛvn̩]

| | | |
|---|---|---|
| **eleven**<br>[ɪˋlɛvn̩]<br>名 十一 形 十一的 | ▸ at eleven o'clock<br>在十一點 | ▸ He will arrive at eleven o'clock.<br>他將會在十一點抵達。 |
| **seven**<br>[ˋsɛvn̩]<br>名 七 形 七的 | ▸ the seven dwarves<br>七個小矮人 | ▸ "Snow White and the Seven Dwarves" was the first Disney movie. 《白雪公主與七個小矮人》是迪士尼的第一部電影。 |

## eaven [ˋɛvən]

| | | |
|---|---|---|
| **heaven** [ˋhɛvən] 名 天國、天空 | ▸ for heaven's sake 看在上帝的份上 | ▸ Oh, for heaven's sake, don't be such a fool. 哦，看在老天的份上，不要這麼傻。 |

## ever [ˋɛvɚ]

| | | |
|---|---|---|
| **ever** [ˋɛvɚ] 副 從來、至今、究竟 | ▸ happily ever after 此後一直很快樂 | ▸ Most fairy tales end with the words, "happily ever after." 大部分童話故事都會用「從此以後過著幸福快樂的日子」結尾。 |
| **whichever** [hwɪtʃˋɛvɚ] 代 形 無論哪個 | ▸ whichever one 無論哪個 | ▸ Whichever one you choose, it will be OK with me. 不論你選哪個，我都可以。 |
| **clever** [ˋklɛvɚ] 形 聰明的、靈巧的 | ▸ clever story 機智的故事 | ▸ She knows how to tell a clever story. 她很會説機智的故事。 |
| **never** [ˋnɛvɚ] 副 從未、永不 | ▸ a neverending story 永不結束的故事 | ▸ Life is a neverending story. 生命是一個永不止息的故事。 |
| **whenever** [hwɛnˋɛvɚ] 連 副 無論何時、每當 | ▸ whenever I think of you 每當我想起你 | ▸ Whenever I think of you, I get angry. 我只要一想到你就生氣。 |
| **whoever** [huˋɛvɚ] 代 無論誰 | ▸ whoever comes 無論誰來 | ▸ Whoever comes to the party should bring some food. 不管誰來參加派對都要帶些食物。 |

| | | |
|---|---|---|
| **wherever**<br>[hwɛr`ɛvɚ]<br>連 副 無論在哪裡 | ▶ wherever you are<br>無論你在哪裡 | ▶ Wherever you are, come out!<br>不管你在哪裡，都給我出來！ |
| **forever**<br>[fɚ`ɛvɚ]<br>副 永遠 | ▶ forever and ever<br>永遠 | ▶ I will love you forever and ever.<br>我將永遠愛你。 |
| **whatever**<br>[hwɑt`ɛvɚ]<br>代 形 不管什麼 | ▶ whatever you do<br>無論你做什麼 | ▶ Whatever you do when you're gone, don't tell me. 你離開後無論做什麼，都不要告訴我。 |
| **however**<br>[haʊ`ɛvɚ]<br>副 然而、無論如何 | ▶ however old you are<br>不管你多老 | ▶ However old you are, you can still feel young. 不管你多老，都可以保有一顆年輕的心。 |

## ew [ju]

| | | |
|---|---|---|
| **dew**<br>[dju]<br>名 露水 | ▶ morning dew<br>晨露 | ▶ I love the feeling of morning dew on my bare feet.<br>我喜歡光腳沾晨露的感覺。 |
| **few**<br>[fju]<br>形 很少的 | ▶ only a few<br>只有幾個 | ▶ There are only a few people in the room.<br>房間裡只有幾個人。 |
| **curfew**<br>[`kɝfju]<br>名 戒嚴、宵禁 | ▶ make the curfew<br>趕上宵禁 | ▶ If we go to the 8 o'clock movie, will we make the curfew?<br>如果我們去看八點的電影，我們趕得及宵禁前回來嗎？ |

| | | |
|---|---|---|
| **new** [nju] 形 新的、新鮮的 | ▶ turn a new leaf 展開新的生活 | ▶ It's time to turn a new leaf today. 今天是展開新生活的時候了。 |
| **renew** [rɪˋnju] 動 使更新、使恢復 | ▶ renew a contract 更新合約 | ▶ You have to renew your contract for the apartment soon. 你必須儘快更新公寓合約。 |
| **stew** [stju] 動 煮、燉 | ▶ beef stew 燉牛肉 | ▶ My mom makes a really good beef stew. 我媽媽很會燉牛肉。 |

## iew [ju]

| | | |
|---|---|---|
| **view** [vju] 名 觀點 動 觀看 | ▶ in my point of of view 從我的觀點來看 | ▶ In my point of view, it's great! 以我的觀點來看，這很棒！ |
| * **review** [rɪˋvju] 動 名 回顧、復習 | ▶ reviews for the magazine 雜誌的評論 | ▶ She writes reviews for the magazine. 她為雜誌寫評論。 |
| * **interview** [ˋɪntɚ͵vju] 動 名 採訪、面談 | ▶ have an interview with 跟…有面試 | ▶ I have an interview with Sony today. 我今天去Sony面試。 |

## ex [ɛks]

| | | |
|---|---|---|
| **index**<br>[`ɪndɛks]<br>名 索引 | the index finger<br>食指 | What is the index finger most used for?<br>食指通常用來做什麼？ |
| **reflex**<br>[`riflɛks]<br>動 名 反射、反映 | fast reflex<br>快速反射 | He is good at sports because he has fast reflexes.<br>他運動細胞很好，因為他反應很快。 |
| **complex**<br>[`kamplɛks]<br>形 複雜的、合成的 | complex relationships<br>複雜的關係 | It's tough to be in complex relationships.<br>身陷在複雜的關係裡是很棘手的。 |
| **sex**<br>[sɛks]<br>名 性別、性 | have sex with<br>與…發生性關係 | I know that he has sex with a lot of people.<br>我知道他跟很多人發生性關係。 |

## ext [ɛkst]

| | | |
|---|---|---|
| **next**<br>[`nɛkst]<br>形 緊鄰的、貼近的 | next door<br>隔壁 | Someone moved in next door.<br>隔壁有人搬進來。 |
| **text**<br>[tɛkst]<br>名 正文、本文 | this textbook<br>這本課本 | This textbook is so expensive!<br>這本課本好貴！ |
| **context**<br>[`kantɛkst]<br>名 上下文、文章脈絡 | from the context<br>從上下文 | Can you guess what this word means from the context?<br>你可以從上下文猜到這字的意思嗎？ |

# 3. 押 | 韻的單字

## iable [ˋaɪəbl̩]

| | | |
|---|---|---|
| **liable** [ˋlaɪəbl̩] 形易於…的 | ▶ liable to make mistakes 易於犯錯 | ▶ I think you should find someone else to help you because he's liable to make mistakes. 我認為你應該找別人幫忙，因為他容易犯錯。 |
| * **reliable** [rɪˋlaɪəbl̩] 形可信賴、可靠的 | ▶ a reliable source 可靠的來源 | ▶ He got information for the article from a reliable source. 他從可靠的來源獲得文章的訊息。 |
| **unreliable** [ˏʌnrɪˋlaɪəbl̩] 形靠不住的 | ▶ unreliable friend 不可靠的朋友 | ▶ You're an unreliable friend, because you're always late. 你是個不可靠的朋友，因為你老是遲到。 |
| **undeniable** [ˏʌndɪˋnaɪəbl̩] 形無可否認的 | ▶ undeniable truth 不可否認的事實 | ▶ That's the undeniable truth, you'd better accept it. 這是個事實，你最好接受。 |

## iance [ˋaɪəns]

| | | |
|---|---|---|
| **defiance** [dɪˋfaɪəns] 名反抗、挑戰 | ▶ in defiance of 違抗 | ▶ He rebels in defiance of his parents. 他反抗他的父母。 |
| **reliance** [rɪˋlaɪəns] 名信賴、依賴 | ▶ reliance on drugs 對藥物的依賴 | ▶ She needs to overcome her reliance on drugs. 她需要克服對藥物的依賴。 |
| **alliance** [əˋlaɪəns] 名結盟、聯盟 | ▶ forge an alliance with 與…結盟 | ▶ They forged an alliance with the other team. 他們跟另一隊結盟。 |

| | | |
|---|---|---|
| **appliance**<br>[ə`plaɪəns]<br>名 器具、使用 | gas appliances<br>瓦斯器 | They sell gas appliances on the second floor.<br>他們在二樓賣瓦斯器。 |

## ience [`aɪəns]

| | | |
|---|---|---|
| **science**<br>[`saɪəns]<br>名 科學 | science fiction<br>科幻小說 | Do you like to read science fiction?<br>你喜歡看科幻小說嗎？ |

## iant [`aɪənt]

| | | |
|---|---|---|
| **defiant**<br>[dɪ`faɪənt]<br>形 違抗的、大膽的 | a defiant look<br>反抗的眼神 | She gave me a defiant look.<br>她給了我一個反抗的眼神。 |
| **giant**<br>[`dʒaɪənt]<br>形 巨人、巨大的 | a giant TV<br>大型電視 | I want to buy that giant TV.<br>我想買那台大型電視。 |
| **reliant**<br>[rɪ`laɪənt]<br>形 依賴的 | reliant on<br>依賴 | He is reliant on his mother.<br>他依賴他母親。 |

## ient [`aɪənt]

| | | |
|---|---|---|
| * **client** [`klaɪənt] 名 客戶、委託人 | lawyer's client 律師的委託人 | That lawyer's client sued her husband for ten million dollars. 那個律師的委託人向她的先生要求一千萬美金。 |

## ibe [aɪb]

| | | |
|---|---|---|
| **bribe** [braɪb] 動 名 賄賂 | bribe the clerk 賄賂辦事人員 | He bribed the clerk so he could get away with something illegal. 他賄賂辦事人員好從事非法行為。 |
| **scribe** [skraɪb] 動 謄寫 名 抄寫員 | an Egyptian scribe 埃及抄寫員 | All of this artwork was done by an Egyptian scribe. 這件藝術作品全是埃及抄寫員抄出來的。 |
| * **subscribe** [səb`skraɪb] 動 訂閱 | subscribe to a magazine 訂閱雜誌 | Would you like to subscribe to a magazine? 你想要訂閱雜誌嗎？ |
| * **describe** [dɪ`skraɪb] 動 描述 | describe your boyfriend 形容你的男友 | Can you describe your boyfriend? 你能形容一下你的男友嗎？ |
| **prescribe** [prɪ`skraɪb] 動 開藥方 | prescribe medicine for patients 給病人開藥方 | Only doctors are allowed to prescribe medicine for patients. 只有醫生可以給病人開藥方。 |
| **inscribe** [ɪn`skraɪb] 動 銘刻 | inscribed on the wall 刻在牆上 | What is that inscribed on the wall? 那個刻在牆上的是什麼？ |

| | | |
|---|---|---|
| **tribe**<br>[traɪb]<br>名 部落 | ▶ a primitive tribe<br>原始部落 | ▶ We studied a primitive tribe in Anthropology today.<br>今天的人類學課我們研究原始部落。 |

## ibit [ˋɪbɪt]

| | | |
|---|---|---|
| **inhibit**<br>[ɪnˋhɪbɪt]<br>動 抑制、禁止 | ▶ malnutrition inhibits growth<br>營養失調抑制成長 | ▶ You need to eat well because malnutrition inhibits growth.<br>你要吃得好一點，因為營養失調會抑制成長。 |
| **prohibit**<br>[prəˋhɪbɪt]<br>動 明文禁止 | ▶ prohibit smoking<br>禁止吸煙 | ▶ In New York, restaurants prohibit smoking.<br>在紐約，餐廳內禁止吸煙。 |
| **exhibit**<br>[ɪgˋzɪbɪt]<br>動 展示 | ▶ exhibit art<br>陳列藝術品 | ▶ Galleries exhibit art.<br>畫廊陳列藝術品。 |

## ice [aɪs]

| | | |
|---|---|---|
| **ice**<br>[aɪs]<br>名 冰 動 結冰 | ▶ ice cube<br>冰塊 | ▶ Can you put some ice cubes in my drink, please?<br>可以請你在我飲料中加些冰塊嗎？ |
| **dice**<br>[daɪs]<br>名 骰子 | ▶ roll the dice<br>擲骰子 | ▶ It's your turn to roll the dice.<br>換你擲骰子了。 |

| | | |
|---|---|---|
| **suffice**<br>[sə`faɪs]<br>動 足夠 | what will suffice<br>什麼足夠 | What will suffice if it seems like everything I do is no use?<br>如果我做的事是沒用的，那什麼才是夠的？ |
| **sacrifice**<br>[`sækrə͵faɪs]<br>名 動 犧牲 | sacrifice her life<br>奉獻她的一生 | She is willing to sacrifice her life for her children.<br>她情願為了她的孩子奉獻一生。 |
| **slice**<br>[slaɪs]<br>名 薄片 動 切片 | watermelon slice<br>西瓜切片 | Can you give me a watermelon slice?<br>你可以給我一片西瓜嗎？ |
| **mice**<br>[maɪs]<br>名 老鼠 | brown mice<br>褐鼠 | That boy has three brown mice as pets.<br>那個男孩養了三隻褐鼠當寵物。 |
| **nice**<br>[naɪs]<br>形 良好的 | nice weather<br>好天氣 | Everyone loves nice weather.<br>每個人都愛好天氣。 |
| **spice**<br>[spaɪs]<br>名 香料、趣味 | add a bit of spice<br>增添趣味 | How can a person add a bit of spice to their life?<br>人要怎麼在生活中增添趣味呢？ |
| **rice**<br>[raɪs]<br>名 米 | fried rice<br>炒飯 | I'll take Chicken fried rice, please.<br>麻煩給我雞肉炒飯。 |
| * **price**<br>[praɪs]<br>名 價格 | high price<br>高價位 | They charge a very high price to see their show.<br>他們的表演價位很高。 |

| | | |
|---|---|---|
| **vice** [vaɪs] 名 邪惡 形 副位的 | vice president 副總 | The vice president said he would give me a promotion. 副總說他會讓我升遷。 |
| * **advice** [əd`vaɪs] 名 建議 | take advice 接受建議 | It's hard to take advice when you think that you are right. 當你認為你是對的就很難接受建議。 |
| * **device** [dɪ`vaɪs] 名 儀器、設備 | electronic device 電子設備 | Turn off your electronic devices when the plane is taking off and landing. 飛機起降時，要關掉你的電子器材。 |
| **twice** [twaɪs] 副 兩次 | think twice 再思考 | You better think twice before you do something stupid. 在你做傻事前最好三思。 |

## ise [aɪs]

| | | |
|---|---|---|
| **precise** [prɪ`saɪs] 形 準確的 | precise timing 準確的時機 | That machinery has precise timing. 那個機器時間抓得很精準。 |
| **paradise** [`pærə͵daɪs] 名 天堂 | as beautiful as paradise 美如天堂 | Some people say that Bali is as beautiful as paradise. 有些人說峇里島美如天堂。 |
| **merchandise** [`mɜtʃən͵daɪs] 名 商品 | examine the merchandise 檢查商品 | He had to examine the merchandise before he approved it for sale. 他必須在核准銷售前檢查商品。 |

## icial [ˋɪʃəl]



| | | |
|---|---|---|
| **judicial** [dʒuˋdɪʃəl] 形 司法的 | judicial system 司法系統 | Do you understand the judicial system at all? 你真的了解司法系統嗎？ |
| **beneficial** [ˏbɛnəˋfɪʃəl] 形 有益的 | to be beneficial 是有益的 | This method will prove to be beneficial for everyone involved. 這個方式將證實是對每個相關的人有益的。 |
| **official** [əˋfɪʃəl] 形 官方的、正式的 | official report 正式的報告 | When is the official report coming out? 正式的報告何時出爐？ |
| **artificial** [ˏɑrtəˋfɪʃəl] 形 人工、人為的 | artificial sweetener 人工代糖 | He uses artificial sweetener instead of sugar because he has diabetes. 他用人工代糖代替糖，因為他有糖尿病。 |

## itial [ˋɪʃəl]

| | | |
|---|---|---|
| **initial** [ɪˋnɪʃəl] 形 最開始的 | initial stage 最初階段 | We are only in the initial stage of the process. 我們僅在程序的最初階段。 |

## icious [ˋɪʃəs]

| | | |
|---|---|---|
| **malicious** [məˋlɪʃəs] 形 惡意的 | malicious intentions 惡意 | He is an evil man with many malicious intentions. 他是個不懷好意的惡人。 |

| | | |
|---|---|---|
| **delicious** [dɪˋlɪʃəs] 形 美味的 ▶ | a delicious meal 美食 ▶ | I could really go for a delicious meal right now. 我現在好想吃美食。 |
| **suspicious** [səˋspɪʃəs] 形 疑心的 ▶ | be suspicious of 疑心 ▶ | She's suspicious of him because he is treating her differently than he usually does. 她懷疑他，因為他跟平常的態度不一樣。 |
| **vicious** [ˋvɪʃəs] 形 壞的 ▶ | a vicious circle 惡性循環 ▶ | It seems like I'm going in a vicious circle where I exercise a lot, but eat more. 我運動量很大，但吃得更多，好像變成惡性循環。 |

## itious [ˋɪʃəs]

| | | |
|---|---|---|
| **ambitious** [æmˋbɪʃəs] 形 有企圖心的 ▶ | an ambitious dream 遠大的夢想 ▶ | He has an ambitious dream of becoming a professional basketball player. 他懷有成為職業籃球員的遠大夢想。 |
| **nutritious** [njuˋtrɪʃəs] 形 營養的 ▶ | nutritious meal 營養餐 ▶ | Thank you so much for that nutritious meal! 非常感謝你的營養餐！ |

## icit [ˋɪsɪt]

| | | |
|---|---|---|
| **implicit** [ɪmˋplɪsɪt] 形 不言明的 ▶ | implicit consent 默許 ▶ | They didn't agree to it clearly, but I think they had implicit consent. 他們並沒有明確同意，但我想他們已經默許了。 |

| | | |
|---|---|---|
| **explicit**<br>[ɪk`splɪsɪt]<br>形 清楚的 | explicit statement<br>清楚的聲明 | She made an explicit statement about how she wanted it; it should be very clear.<br>她已明確聲明她要的方式，應該是非常清楚才對。 |

## ick [ɪk]

| | | |
|---|---|---|
| **thick**<br>[θɪk]<br>形 厚的、濃的 | thick fog<br>濃霧 | There is a thick fog over the woods.<br>森林裡瀰漫著濃霧。 |
| **kick**<br>[kɪk]<br>動 踢 | kick the ball<br>踢球 | Kick the ball over there!<br>把球踢到那裡！ |
| **lick**<br>[lɪk]<br>動 舔 | lick stamps<br>舔郵票 | I get sick of licking stamps.<br>我討厭舔郵票。 |
| **pick**<br>[pɪk]<br>動 拾起 | pick up<br>拾起 | Can you pick up my mail for me?<br>你可以幫我拿郵件嗎？ |
| **brick**<br>[brɪk]<br>名 磚塊 | a brick wall<br>磚牆 | They hit a brick wall in their car and died.<br>他們開車撞到磚牆身亡了。 |
| **trick**<br>[trɪk]<br>名 詭計、惡作劇 | play a trick<br>惡作劇 | I think they are playing a trick on me!<br>我想他們在對我惡作劇！ |

| | | |
|---|---|---|
| **sick**<br>[sɪk]<br>形 生病的 | ▶ get sick<br>生病了 | ▶ He says he's getting sick so he can't come out with us.<br>他說他生病了，所以不能跟我們一起出去。 |
| **seasick**<br>[ˋsi͵sɪk]<br>形 暈船的 | ▶ feel seasick<br>感到暈船 | ▶ I don't like going on boats because when I do I feel sea-sick.<br>我不喜歡搭船，因為我會暈船。 |
| **homesick**<br>[ˋhom͵sɪk]<br>形 想家的 | ▶ be homesick<br>感到想家 | ▶ You must be homesick.<br>你一定是想家吧。 |
| **lovesick**<br>[ˋlʌv͵sɪk]<br>形 害相思病 | ▶ lovesick boy<br>患相思病的小子 | ▶ He is just a lovesick boy who needs to recover from his relationship. 他只是患了相思病，需要從感情中重新振作。 |
| **airsick**<br>[ˋɛr͵sɪk]<br>形 暈機的 | ▶ feel airsick<br>感到暈機 | ▶ Do you feel airsick when you fly?<br>你搭飛機時會暈機嗎？ |
| **stick**<br>[stɪk]<br>名 棍棒 動 附著 | ▶ stick posters on walls<br>貼海報在牆上 | ▶ He likes to stick posters on the walls in his room.<br>他喜歡在房間的牆上貼海報。 |
| **lipstick**<br>[ˋlɪp͵stɪk]<br>名 唇膏、口紅 | ▶ wear lipstick<br>擦口紅 | ▶ She always wears a lot of lip-stick.<br>她總是擦很多口紅。 |
| **chopstick**<br>[ˋtʃap͵stɪk]<br>名 筷子 | ▶ eat with chopsticks<br>用筷子吃東西 | ▶ Does he know how to eat with chopsticks?<br>他知道怎麼用筷子吃東西嗎？ |

| | | |
|---|---|---|
| * **quick** [kwɪk] 形 副 迅速 | a quick pace ▶ 快步 | ▶ He always walks at a quick pace. 他走路的步伐總是很快。 |

## icken [ˋɪkɪn]

| | | |
|---|---|---|
| **chicken** [ˋtʃɪkɪn] 名 雞、雞肉 | chicken soup ▶ 雞湯 | ▶ A lot of Americans think chicken soup is the best food for nursing a cold. 很多美國人認為雞湯是感冒養病時最好的食物。 |

## icket [ˋɪkɪt]

| | | |
|---|---|---|
| **cricket** [ˋkrɪkɪt] 名 蟋蟀 | cricket sounds ▶ 蟋蟀聲音 | ▶ He loves to hear cricket sounds as he's falling asleep. 他喜歡聽著蟋蟀的聲音進入夢鄉。 |
| **ticket** [ˋtɪkɪt] 名 車、入場票 | ticket booth ▶ 售票亭 | ▶ Go to the ticket booth to pick up your ticket. 到售票亭取票。 |

## ickle [ˋɪkl̩]

| | | |
|---|---|---|
| **trickle** [ˋtrɪkl̩] 動 滴下 名 滴 | trickle down ▶ 滴下 | ▶ She likes to watch the rain trickle down the windows. 她喜歡看雨水從窗戶慢慢流下。 |

| | | |
|---|---|---|
| **tickle** [ˋtɪkḷ] 動 呵癢、逗笑 | ▶ tickle me under my chin 在我下巴呵癢 | ▶ He often makes me mad because he tries to tickle me under my chin. 他常讓我抓狂，因為他老愛在我下巴呵癢。 |

## icycle [ˋaɪsɪkḷ]

| | | |
|---|---|---|
| **bicycle** [ˋbaɪsɪkḷ] 名 腳踏車 | ▶ ride a bicycle 騎腳踏車 | ▶ People say that you can never forget how to ride a bicycle. 人家說騎腳踏車的技巧一輩子都不會忘。 |
| **tricycle** [ˋtraɪsɪkḷ] 名 三輪車 | ▶ tricycle rentals 三輪車出租 | ▶ They have tricycle rentals down by the boardwalk. 他們在木板路旁有提供三輪車出租的服務。 |

## icle [ˋɪkḷ]

| | | |
|---|---|---|
| * **vehicle** [ˋviɪkḷ] 名 交通工具 | ▶ motor vehicle 汽車 | ▶ You need to register your motor vehicle or else it's illegal. 你需要登記你的汽車，否則它就是非法的。 |

## ix [ɪks]

| | | |
|---|---|---|
| * **fix** [fɪks] 動 修理 | ▶ fix a car 修理車子 | ▶ Because he's a mechanic, he knows how to fix a car. 他是技工，所以他知道怎麼修車。 |

| | | |
|---|---|---|
| **mix**<br>[mɪks]<br>動 混合 | mix up<br>混合 | Don't mix up the yellow ones with the red ones.<br>不要把黃色的和紅色的混在一起。 |
| **six**<br>[sɪks]<br>名 六 形 六個的 | six cars<br>六輛車 | There are six cars in the parking lot.<br>停車場有六輛車。 |

## ics [ɪks]

| | | |
|---|---|---|
| **politics**<br>[ˋpɑlətɪks]<br>名 政治 | racial politics<br>種族政治學 | The racial politics in this school are controversial.<br>這間學校的種族政治學頗受爭議。 |

## ict [ɪkt]

31

| | | |
|---|---|---|
| **contradict**<br>[ˌkɑntrəˋdɪkt]<br>動 矛盾、反對 | contradict one another<br>互相反駁 | Although they are on the same team, they always contradict one another. 雖然他們在同一隊，但他們總是互相反駁對方。 |
| **predict**<br>[prɪˋdɪkt]<br>動 預言 | predict the future<br>預言未來 | He claims that he can predict the future.<br>他聲稱他可預知未來。 |
| **conflict**<br>[ˋkɑnflɪkt]<br>名 動 衝突 | in conflict<br>衝突 | The two countries are in conflict.<br>這兩個國家發生衝突。 |

| | | |
|---|---|---|
| **strict**<br>[strɪkt]<br>形 嚴格的 | a strict father ▶<br>嚴謹的父親 | ▶ He is a strict father who doesn't allow his children to make their own decisions. 他是一位嚴厲的父親，不允許他的小孩自己作決定。 |
| **restrict**<br>[rɪˋstrɪkt]<br>動 限制 | restrict to ▶<br>限制 | ▶ The chances to meet the baseball star are restricted only to the members of the fan club. 和棒球明星見面的機會僅限球迷俱樂部會員。 |
| **convict**<br>[kənˋvɪkt]<br>動 判決 | convicted of murder ▶<br>判謀殺罪 | ▶ She was convicted of murder.<br>她被判謀殺罪。 |

## iction [ˋɪkʃən]

| | | |
|---|---|---|
| **addiction**<br>[əˋdɪkʃən]<br>名 上癮 | an addiction to chocolate ▶<br>對巧克力上癮 | ▶ She has an addiction to chocolate that she can't get rid of. 她對巧克力上癮，無法抗拒巧克力的魅力。 |
| **fiction**<br>[ˋfɪkʃən]<br>名 小說 形 假的 | fiction or non-fiction ▶<br>小說或非小說 | ▶ Is this book considered fiction or non-fiction?<br>這本書被認定是小說或非小說？ |
| **friction**<br>[ˋfrɪkʃən]<br>名 摩擦、爭執 | cause friction ▶<br>造成爭執 | ▶ That sensitive issue caused friction in the family.<br>那個敏感話題在家裡造成爭執。 |

## id [ɪd]

| | | |
|---|---|---|
| * **bid**<br>[bɪd]<br>名 動 出價 | high bid<br>出價高 | There was a high bid for that piece of furniture at the auction. 在拍賣會上，有人出高價標了那件傢俱。 |
| **forbid**<br>[fɚ`bɪd]<br>動 禁止 | forbid the children<br>禁止小孩 | She will forbid the children to go out on weekends.<br>她將禁止小孩週末外出。 |
| **kid**<br>[kɪd]<br>名 小孩 | little kids<br>小朋友們 | I think those little kids are going to get into trouble again.<br>我想那些小朋友們又要闖禍了。 |
| **eyelid**<br>[`aɪ͵lɪd]<br>名 眼皮 | close your eyelid<br>閉眼 | Please close your eyelid when putting on your eyeliner.<br>畫眼線時，請閉上眼睛。 |
| **amid**<br>[ə`mɪd]<br>介 在…期間 | amid the chaos<br>在混亂中 | Where did you go amid the chaos?<br>混亂中你去了哪裡？ |
| **pyramid**<br>[`pɪrəmɪd]<br>名 金字塔 | build a pyramid<br>建一座金字塔 | The Egyptians built a pyramid thousands of years ago.<br>埃及人在幾千年前建了一座金字塔。 |

## iddle [`ɪdḷ]

| | | |
|---|---|---|
| **fiddle**<br>[`fɪdḷ]<br>動 虛度 名 小提琴 | fiddle around<br>閒蕩 | The teacher doesn't like it when we fiddle around.<br>老師不喜歡我們閒蕩。 |

| | | |
|---|---|---|
| **middle**<br>[ˋmɪdḷ]<br>形 中間的 名 中央 | in the middle<br>在中間 | We're stuck in the middle of traffic.<br>我們被塞在車陣中。 |
| **riddle**<br>[ˋrɪdḷ]<br>名 謎、難題 | solve a riddle<br>解開謎題 | She needs to solve a riddle to win a prize.<br>她要解開謎題才能贏得獎金。 |

## ittle [ˋɪtḷ]

| | | |
|---|---|---|
| * **little**<br>[ˋlɪtḷ]<br>形 小的 副 少 | little by little<br>逐漸地 | He is improving little by little.<br>他正逐漸地進步。 |
| **belittle**<br>[bɪˋlɪtḷ]<br>動 輕視 | belittle yourself<br>輕視自我 | You shouldn't belittle yourself so much.<br>你不應該這樣輕視自我。 |

## ital [ˋɪtḷ]

| | | |
|---|---|---|
| **hospital**<br>[ˋhɑspɪtḷ]<br>名 醫院 | in the hospital<br>在醫院裡 | She will have to stay in the hospital for two more weeks.<br>她必須在醫院裡多留兩個星期。 |

## ide [aɪd]

| | | |
|---|---|---|
| * **decide** [dɪˋsaɪd] 動 決定 | you decide 你決定 | You decide whether or not we should go. 我們是否應該去由你來決定。 |
| **coincide** [͵koɪnˋsaɪd] 動 巧合 | coincide with 與…一致 | My birthday coincides with Valentine's Day. 我的生日與情人節同一天。 |
| **confide** [kənˋfaɪd] 動 透露 | confide in 對…吐露秘密 | Sometimes it seems hard to find someone to confide in. 有時要找個人談心似乎很難。 |
| **hide** [haɪd] 動 躲藏 | hide and seek 捉迷藏 | Did you like to play hide and seek when you were little? 你小時候喜歡玩捉迷藏嗎？ |
| **collide** [kəˋlaɪd] 動 碰撞、衝突 | vehicles collide 撞車<br>opinions collide 意見衝突 | I saw those two vehicles collide. 我看到那兩部車相撞。<br>Their opinions often collide. 他們的意見時常衝突。 |
| **slide** [slaɪd] 動 名 滑動 | water slide 滑水道 | That amusement park has water slides. 那遊樂園有滑水道。 |
| **landslide** [ˋlænd͵slaɪd] 名 山崩 | caught beneath a landslide 被困在山崩下 | She was caught beneath a landslide. 她因為山崩被壓在底下。 |
| **ride** [raɪd] 動 騎乘 | ride a bus 搭公車 | He rides a bus to school every day. 他每天搭公車去學校。 |

| | | |
|---|---|---|
| **bride**<br>[braɪd]<br>名 新娘 | ▶ bride and groom<br>新娘和新郎 | ▶ The bride and groom decided to have their wedding on another day.<br>新娘與新郎決定在另一天舉行婚禮。 |
| **pride**<br>[praɪd]<br>名 驕傲 | ▶ take pride in his success<br>為他的成功驕傲 | ▶ His mother and father take pride in his success.<br>他的父母親對他的成功很驕傲。 |
| **side**<br>[saɪd]<br>名 邊、側邊 | ▶ on the side<br>另外 | ▶ He makes some money on the side.<br>他另賺外快。 |
| **aside**<br>[əˋsaɪd]<br>副 在旁邊 | ▶ aside from<br>除此之外 | ▶ Aside from the fact that he left his wife, he is a very loyal person. 撇開他離開太太的事實，他是位非常忠誠的人。 |
| **subside**<br>[səbˋsaɪd]<br>動 退去 | ▶ the noise subsided<br>喧鬧平息了 | ▶ After hours of construction, the noise subsided.<br>經過幾個小時的施工後，噪音終於平息了。 |
| **roadside**<br>[ˋrodˏsaɪd]<br>名 路邊 | ▶ along the roadside<br>沿著路邊 | ▶ She picked up two teenage boys along the roadside.<br>她沿著路邊搭載兩個青少年。 |
| **beside**<br>[bɪˋsaɪd]<br>介 在…旁邊 | ▶ beside the table<br>在桌邊 | ▶ Look beside the table.<br>看著桌子的旁邊。 |
| **inside**<br>[ˋɪnˋsaɪd]<br>介 在…之內 | ▶ inside a house<br>在屋內 | ▶ He should be inside his house right now.<br>他現在應該在他的家裡。 |

| | | |
|---|---|---|
| **outside**<br>[ˋautˋsaɪd]<br>介 在…之外 | outside the door<br>在門外 | Who could be outside the door at this hour?<br>這個時候會是誰在門外？ |
| **tide**<br>[taɪd]<br>名 潮汐 | low tide<br>退潮 | It's safer to go swimming during low tide.<br>在退潮時游泳較安全。 |
| **guide**<br>[gaɪd]<br>名 動 引導 | a travel guide<br>旅遊指南 | That is a travel guide to Thailand.<br>那是到泰國的旅遊指南。 |
| **misguide**<br>[mɪsˋgaɪd]<br>動 引入歧途 | misguided children<br>誤入歧途的小孩 | They bring misguided children here.<br>他們帶著誤入歧途的小孩到這裡。 |
| **divide**<br>[dəˋvaɪd]<br>動 劃分、分配 | divide into<br>分成 | What will the reward divide into three ways?<br>獎品將分成哪三種方式？ |
| **provide**<br>[prəˋvaɪd]<br>動 提供 | provide the poor with food<br>提供食物給窮人 | It is noble to provide the poor with food.<br>提供食物給窮人是很高尚的行為。 |
| **wide**<br>[waɪd]<br>形 寬廣的 | wide angle<br>廣角 | You can get a better picture if you take it with a wide angle.<br>如果你拍照時用廣角鏡，可以拍到較好的照片。 |
| * **worldwide**<br>[ˋwɜldˏwaɪd]<br>形 全球的 副 在全球 | a worldwide crisis<br>全球危機 | Do you think the new president can handle this worldwide crisis? 你認為新總統可以處理好這次全球危機嗎？ |

## iter [ˋaɪtɚ]



| | | |
|---|---|---|
| **writer**<br>[ˋraɪtɚ]<br>名 作家 | ▶ a fiction writer<br>小說家 | ▶ He's been a fiction writer for years.<br>他當小說家已經很多年了。 |
| **typewriter**<br>[ˋtaɪp͵raɪtɚ]<br>名 打字機 | ▶ old typewriter<br>老舊的打字機 | ▶ She threw her old typewriter away.<br>她丟掉她老舊的打字機。 |

## idge [ɪdʒ]

| | | |
|---|---|---|
| **bridge**<br>[brɪdʒ]<br>名 橋樑 | ▶ under the bridge<br>在橋下 | ▶ They hid under the bridge until the police left.<br>他們躲在橋下一直到警察離開。 |
| **abridge**<br>[əˋbrɪdʒ]<br>動 刪節、節略 | ▶ abridged version<br>節略本 | ▶ I wish I could find an abridged version of this book.<br>我希望我可以找到這本書的節略本。 |
| **fridge**<br>[frɪdʒ]<br>名 冰箱 | ▶ put it in the fridge<br>把它放進冰箱 | ▶ Don't forget to put it in the fridge, or it will go bad. 不要忘了把它放進冰箱，不然會壞掉。 |

## idity [ˋɪdətɪ]

| | | |
|---|---|---|
| **validity**<br>[vəˋlɪdətɪ]<br>名 正確性 | ▶ prove the validity<br>證明正確性 | ▶ How will you prove the validity of your theory?<br>你要如何證明你理論的正確性？ |

## idle [ˋaɪdḷ]

| | | |
|---|---|---|
| **idle** [ˋaɪdḷ] 形 無益的 | ▶ idle thoughts 妄想 | ▶ Don't listen to my idle thoughts. 不要聽我的妄想。 |

## idol [ˋaɪdḷ]

| | | |
|---|---|---|
| **idol** [ˋaɪdḷ] 名 偶像 | ▶ a pop idol 流行偶像 | ▶ He won't be a pop idol for long. 他不會當流行偶像太久。 |

## ital [ˋaɪtḷ]

| | | |
|---|---|---|
| **vital** [ˋvaɪtḷ] 形 必須的、重要的 | ▶ a vital part 重要的部分 | ▶ This has been a vital part in our decision. 這已經成為我們決定的重要部分。 |

## itle [ˋaɪtḷ]

| | | |
|---|---|---|
| **title** [ˋtaɪtḷ] 名 標題、書名 | ▶ the title of the book 書名 | ▶ Do you know the title of the book? 你知道這本書的書名嗎？ |
| **entitle** [ɪnˋtaɪtḷ] 動 給…標題、賦予 | ▶ entitled to freedom 有自由的權利 | ▶ Don't you think that all kids are entitled to freedom? 你不認為年輕人都應該擁有自由嗎？ |

| | | |
|---|---|---|
| **subtitle** [ˋsʌbˏtaɪtl̩] 名 字幕 | ▶ Chinese subtitles 中文字幕 | ▶ I like foreign movies, but if they don't have Chinese subtitles, I won't be able to understand them. 我喜歡外語片，但如果沒有中文字幕，我會看不懂。 |

## idy [ˋaɪdɪ]

| | | |
|---|---|---|
| **tidy** [ˋtaɪdɪ] 形 整齊的 動 整理 | ▶ tidy room 整齊的房間 | ▶ She is good at keeping a tidy room. 她善於保持房間的整齊。 |
| **untidy** [ʌnˋtaɪdɪ] 形 散亂的 | ▶ untidy garage 髒亂的車庫 | ▶ It took the whole weekend to clean their untidy garage. 他們花了整個週末清理髒亂的車庫。 |

## iday [ˋaɪde]

| | | |
|---|---|---|
| **Friday** [ˋfraɪˏde] 名 星期五 | ▶ Friday night 週五晚上 | ▶ What are you doing on Friday night? 你週五晚上要做什麼？ |

## ief [if]

| | | |
|---|---|---|
| * **chief** [tʃif] 名 主管 形 主要的 | ▶ a chief manager 總經理 | ▶ It took him 36 years to become a chief manager. 他花了三十六年才升為總經理。 |

| | | |
|---|---|---|
| **handkerchief**<br>[ˋhæŋkɚ˒tʃɪf]<br>名 手帕 | ▶ blow into a handkerchief<br>用手帕擤鼻涕 | ▶ The lady across the street was blowing into a handkerchief when she got hit. 這位過馬路的女士被撞到時，在用手帕擤鼻涕。 |
| **thief**<br>[θif]<br>名 小偷 | ▶ catch the thief<br>捉到小偷 | ▶ Did they catch the thief yet?<br>他們捉到小偷沒？ |
| **belief**<br>[bɪˋlif]<br>名 信念、信仰 | ▶ old belief<br>老舊信念 | ▶ I don't know if I trust all those old beliefs. 我不知道我是否相信所有的老舊信念。 |
| **relief**<br>[rɪˋlif]<br>名 緩和、慰藉 | ▶ to my relief<br>鬆了一口氣 | ▶ She ran away from their grasp, to my relief. 她從他們的手中逃走，讓我鬆了一口氣。 |
| **brief**<br>[brif]<br>形 簡短的 | ▶ make it brief<br>長話短說 | ▶ You better make it brief or else they'll get bored.<br>你最好長話短話，不然他們會覺得很無聊。 |
| **grief**<br>[grif]<br>名 悲傷 | ▶ grief stricken<br>悲痛 | ▶ He looks so grief stricken.<br>他看起來很悲痛。 |

## eaf [if]

| | | |
|---|---|---|
| **leaf**<br>[lif]<br>名 葉子 | ▶ red leaf<br>紅色葉子 | ▶ She found a red leaf by her bedroom window.<br>她在房間窗戶發現一片紅色的葉子。 |

## eef [if]

| | | |
|---|---|---|
| **beef** [bif] 名 牛肉 | ▶ beef jerky 牛肉乾 | ▶ I think Taiwanese beef jerky tastes really good. 我覺得台灣牛肉乾很好吃。 |

## if [if]

| | | |
|---|---|---|
| **motif** [mo`tif] 名 主題 | ▶ summer motif 夏天主題 | ▶ The store is starting to prepare a summer motif for their display window. 這家店正開始準備櫥窗的夏天主題。 |

## ield [ild]

| | | |
|---|---|---|
| **field** [fild] 名 田野、領域 | ▶ rice field 稻田 | ▶ There is a rice field right outside town. 城外有稻田。 |
| **shield** [`ʃild] 名 保護 動 避開 | ▶ a shield from the sun 防曬 | ▶ People in Taiwan use umbrellas as a shield from the sun. 台灣人用陽傘防曬。 |
| **yield** [jild] 動 屈服、產生 | ▶ yield to sickness 生病<br>yield fruits 生產水果 | ▶ He doesn't want to yield to sickness, but I don't think he has a choice. 他不想生病，但我想他沒得選。<br>When will the orchard yield fruits? 果園何時生產水果？ |

## iet [`aɪət]

| | | |
|---|---|---|
| * **diet** [ˋdaɪət] 名 飲食 動 節食 | ▶ on a diet 節食 | ▶ He has been on a diet for a long time now. 他已經節食很久了。 |
| **quiet** [ˋkwaɪət] 形 安靜的 | ▶ keep quiet 保持安靜 | ▶ Will you just keep quiet? 你可不可以保持安靜？ |

## iety [ˋaɪətɪ]

| | | |
|---|---|---|
| * **society** [səˋsaɪətɪ] 名 社會 | ▶ secret society 神秘的社會 | ▶ This secret society has been in existence for over 3 hundred years. 這個神秘的社會已存在三百多年了。 |
| * **variety** [vəˋraɪətɪ] 名 多樣化 | ▶ a variety of candy 各種糖果 | ▶ She always has a variety of candy on her coffee table. 她總是在咖啡桌上放各種糖果。 |
| **propriety** [prəˋpraɪətɪ] 名 適當 | ▶ behave with propriety 行為適當 | ▶ When you are at a fancy restaurant, you must behave with propriety. 當你在高級餐廳用餐時，你必須舉止得宜。 |
| **anxiety** [æŋˋzaɪətɪ] 名 焦慮 | ▶ emotional anxiety 情緒的焦慮 | ▶ She suffers from emotional anxiety. 她飽受情緒焦慮的困擾。 |

## ife [aɪf]

| | | |
|---|---|---|
| **life** [laɪf] 名 生命、生活 | life expectancy 壽命 | Life expectancy has become longer as time goes on. 平均壽命已經愈來愈長。 |
| **wildlife** [ˋwaɪld͵laɪf] 形 野生的 名 野生生物 | some wildlife 有些野生生物 | It's too bad that some wildlife are becoming extinct. 有些野生生物正逐漸絕種，真是太糟了。 |
| **knife** [naɪf] 名 刀子 | knife and fork 刀叉 | Do you know how to eat with a knife and fork? 你知道如何用刀叉嗎？ |
| **wife** [waɪf] 名 妻子 | a good wife 好妻子 | He was luckily married to a good wife. 他很幸運娶了個好太太。 |
| **housewife** [ˋhaʊs͵waɪf] 名 家庭主婦 | sad housewife 悲傷的家庭主婦 | She has been a sad housewife for many years. 她多年來一直是個悲傷的家庭主婦。 |

## iff [ɪf]

33

| | | |
|---|---|---|
| **sniff** [snɪf] 動 嗅聞 | sniff a flower 聞花香 | I wish I had time to stop and sniff a flower. 我希望我有時間停下來聞花香。 |
| **stiff** [stɪf] 形 僵硬的、生硬的 | a stiff neck 脖子僵硬 | He has a stiff neck from sitting at the computer all day. 他整天坐在電腦前，所以脖子僵硬。 |

## if [ɪf]

| | | |
|---|---|---|
| **if** [ɪf] 連 假如 | ▶ what if 如果，怎麼辦 | ▶ What if she leaves me? 如果她離開我怎麼辦？ |

## ific [ˋɪfɪk]

| | | |
|---|---|---|
| **Pacific** [pəˋsɪfɪk] 名 太平洋 | ▶ the Pacific Ocean 太平洋 | ▶ Is Taiwan on the Pacific Ocean or the Atlantic Ocean? 台灣位於太平洋或大西洋上？ |
| * **specific** [spɪˋsɪfɪk] 形 明確的 | ▶ a specific theme 明確的主題 | ▶ Remember that you need to keep in mind a specific theme when you're writing an essay. 當你在寫論文時，記住你的腦中要有明確的主題。 |
| **prolific** [prəˋlɪfɪk] 形 豐富的、多產的 | ▶ a prolific writer 多產作家 | ▶ He is well known as being a prolific writer. 他以多產作家之姿出名。 |
| **terrific** [təˋrɪfɪk] 形 極佳的 | ▶ a terrific movie 很棒的電影 | ▶ We saw a terrific movie last night. 我們昨晚看了一場很棒的電影。 |
| **horrific** [hɔˋrɪfɪk] 形 可怕的 | ▶ horrific story 恐怖故事 | ▶ He told us a horrific story about a killer. 他告訴我們一個關於殺手的恐怖故事。 |

## ift [ɪft]

| | | |
|---|---|---|
| **gift**<br>[gɪft]<br>名 禮品、才能 | a gift for painting<br>繪畫的天份 | That little boy has a gift for painting.<br>那個小男孩有繪畫的天份。 |
| **shift**<br>[ʃɪft]<br>動 名 轉移 | shift attention<br>轉移注意力 | Please shift your attention over here.<br>請把注意力轉移到這裡。 |
| **lift**<br>[lɪft]<br>動 舉起 名 電梯 | lift up<br>舉起 | Do you think you can lift up this box for me?<br>你覺得你可以幫我提這一盒嗎？ |
| **shoplift**<br>[ˋʃɑpˏlɪft]<br>動 順手牽羊 | caught shoplifting<br>捉到商店行竊 | She was caught shoplifting at the age of 13.<br>她十三歲時被捉到在店內行竊。 |
| **drift**<br>[drɪft]<br>動 名 漂流 | drift away<br>漂流 | All of his worries and sorrows slowly drifted away.<br>他的煩惱和傷心事全都慢慢消失了。 |
| **swift**<br>[swɪft]<br>形 快速的 | swift feet<br>快步 | She is a fast runner with swift feet.<br>她是個飛毛腿。 |

## ifty [ˋɪftɪ]

| | | |
|---|---|---|
| **fifty**<br>[ˋfɪftɪ]<br>名 五十 形 五十的 | fifty states<br>五十個州 | There are fifty states in the United States of America.<br>美國有五十個州。 |

| | | |
|---|---|---|
| **thrifty**<br>[`θrɪftɪ]<br>形 節儉的 | be thrifty<br>節儉的 | My mom is thrifty so she saves a lot of money.<br>我媽很節儉，所以她存了很多錢。 |

## ig [ɪg]

| | | |
|---|---|---|
| * **big**<br>[bɪg]<br>形 大的 | big plan<br>大計畫 | They have big plans for when they move out to California.<br>他們有搬去加州的大計畫。 |
| **dig**<br>[dɪg]<br>動 挖、挖掘 | dig a hole<br>挖個洞 | When my dog dies, I will dig a hole in my backyard and bury him. 我的狗死掉時，我會在我的後院挖個洞埋了牠。 |
| **pig**<br>[pɪg]<br>名 豬 | pig pen<br>豬欄 | Pig pens usually stink.<br>豬欄通常發出惡臭。 |
| **wig**<br>[wɪg]<br>名 假髮 | wear a wig<br>戴假髮 | He wears a wig every day to cover up his bald spot.<br>他每天戴假髮蓋住禿頭。 |
| **twig**<br>[twɪg]<br>名 細枝、嫩枝 | make fire from twigs<br>用細枝生火 | We learned how to make fire from twigs.<br>我們學習如何用樹枝生火。 |

## ight [aɪt]

| | | |
|---|---|---|
| * **fight**<br>[faɪt]<br>動 名 戰鬥、爭吵 | ▶ fight against the enemy<br>跟敵人對抗 | ▶ You need to reserve your energy to fight against the enemy.<br>你要先儲備能量才能跟敵人對抗。 |
| * **light**<br>[laɪt]<br>名 光線、燈 | ▶ turn on the light<br>開燈 | ▶ It's dark, please turn on the light.<br>很暗，請開燈。 |
| **headlight**<br>[ˋhɛdˏlaɪt]<br>名 車前大燈 | ▶ turn off the headlights<br>關掉車前大燈 | ▶ You should turn off the headlights when another car is coming towards you. 當另一輛車朝你開來時，你應該關大燈。 |
| * **delight**<br>[dɪˋlaɪt]<br>名 欣喜、愉快 | ▶ with great delight<br>很大的樂趣 | ▶ He tortured them with great delight.<br>他拷打他們時感到很大的樂趣。 |
| * **flight**<br>[flaɪt]<br>名 飛行、班次 | ▶ a flight to London<br>往倫敦的班機 | ▶ How long is a flight to London from New York?<br>從紐約飛到倫敦要多久？ |
| * **highlight**<br>[ˋhaɪˏlaɪt]<br>動 突顯 | ▶ highlight the problem of<br>強調…的問題 | ▶ We need to highlight the problem of theft in our next meeting. 我們需要在下次會議中強調偷竊的問題。 |
| **flashlight**<br>[ˋflæʃˏlaɪt]<br>名 手電筒 | ▶ bring a flashlight<br>帶著手電筒 | ▶ Don't forget to bring a flashlight to our camping trip.<br>露營時不要忘了帶手電筒。 |
| **twilight**<br>[ˋtwaɪˏlaɪt]<br>名 形 黃昏、黎明 | ▶ twilight zone<br>模糊狀態 | ▶ The twilight zone can be characterized as a gray area that's hard to define. 模糊狀態可形容為難以定義的灰色地帶。 |

| | | |
|---|---|---|
| **moonlight** [ˋmun͵laɪt] 名 月光 | in the moonlight 在月光下 | They traveled by camels in the moonlight. 他們在月色中騎駱駝旅行。 |
| **sunlight** [ˋsʌn͵laɪt] 名 日光 | in the sunlight 在陽光下 | She likes to spend most of her days in the sunlight. 她喜歡在陽光下待很久。 |
| **starlight** [ˋstɑr͵laɪt] 名 星光 | by starlight 藉由星光 | He tried to read by starlight. 他試著藉由星光讀書。 |
| **spotlight** [ˋspɑt͵laɪt] 名 聚光燈 | in the spotlight 在聚光燈下 | She gets really nervous when she is in the spotlight. 她在鎂光燈下時真的很緊張。 |
| **daylight** [ˋde͵laɪt] 名 白晝 | in the daylight 在白天 | We can play soccer in the daylight, and watch it on TV at night. 我們可以白天踢足球，晚上看電視播足球。 |
| **might** [maɪt] 名 力量、威力 | use his might 用他的力量 | He used his might to fight the opponent. 他用他的力量對抗對手。 |
| **night** [naɪt] 名 夜 形 夜晚的 | night time 晚上的時光 | What do you do at night time? 晚上你都在做什麼？ |
| **midnight** [ˋmɪd͵naɪt] 名 午夜 | at midnight 在午夜 | He is really scared that ghosts and monsters will come out at midnight. 他很怕半夜鬼和怪物會跑出來。 |

| | | |
|---|---|---|
| **knight**<br>[naɪt]<br>名 騎士 | knight in shining armor<br>穿著閃耀盔甲的騎士 | It is common that a knight in shining armor would save a girl in distress in novels.<br>在小說中，穿著閃耀盔甲的騎士拯救陷入危難的少女是很平常的。 |
| **tonight**<br>[tə`naɪt]<br>名 今晚 | see you tonight<br>今晚見 | I hope to see you tonight.<br>我希望今晚見到你。 |
| **upright**<br>[`ʌp͵raɪt]<br>形 副 直立 | stand upright<br>站直 | My mom always tells me to stand upright.<br>我媽總是告訴我要站直。 |
| * **copyright**<br>[`kɑpɪ͵raɪt]<br>名 版權 | copyright laws<br>著作權法 | He was convicted of breaking copyright laws.<br>他被判決違反著作權法。 |
| * **sight**<br>[saɪt]<br>名 視力、視覺 | out of sight<br>看不見 | The airplane was soon out of sight.<br>飛機很快就不見了。 |
| **foresight**<br>[`for͵saɪt]<br>名 遠見、先見之明 | have foresight<br>有先見之明 | Since she is a fortune teller, she claims to have foresight.<br>她是算命師，所以她聲稱自己有先見之明。 |
| **eyesight**<br>[`aɪ͵saɪt]<br>名 視力 | poor eyesight<br>視力差 | He needs his glasses because of his poor eyesight.<br>他需要眼鏡，因為他視力不好。 |
| * **insight**<br>[`ɪn͵saɪt]<br>名 洞察力、眼光 | show insight<br>表現觀察力 | This paper of yours really shows insight into the issue at hand.<br>你的論文的確點出了既存的問題。 |

| | | |
|---|---|---|
| **tight**<br>[taɪt]<br>形 副 牢固、緊 | ▶ tight jeans<br>緊身牛仔褲 | ▶ Did you see her wearing those tight jeans?<br>你有看到她穿那條緊身牛仔褲嗎？ |

## ite [aɪt]

34

| | | |
|---|---|---|
| **bite**<br>[baɪt]<br>動 名 咬、啃 | ▶ get a bite to eat<br>吃點東西 | ▶ Do you want to get a bite to eat?<br>你想吃點東西嗎？ |
| **cite**<br>[saɪt]<br>動 引…為證 | ▶ works cited<br>引用作品 | ▶ Don't forget to include your "works cited" in your paper.<br>不要忘了在論文中包含參考文獻。 |
| **recite**<br>[rɪˋsaɪt]<br>動 背誦、朗誦 | ▶ recite a poem<br>朗誦一首詩 | ▶ My little sister recited a poem to us after dinner.<br>我小妹晚餐後朗誦一首詩給我們聽。 |
| **excite**<br>[ɪkˋsaɪt]<br>動 刺激、使興奮 | ▶ excite me<br>讓我很興奮 | ▶ It's hard to find things that excite me nowadays.<br>現在要找到讓我興奮的事很難。 |
| **white**<br>[hwaɪt]<br>名 白色 形 白色的 | ▶ the White House<br>美國白宮 | ▶ You can take a tour of the White House.<br>你可以去白宮參觀一下。 |
| **kite**<br>[kaɪt]<br>名 風箏 | ▶ fly a kite<br>放風箏 | ▶ When was the last time you flew a kite?<br>上次你放風箏是何時？ |

| | | |
| --- | --- | --- |
| **satellite** [ˋsætḷˏaɪt] 名 衛星 | place a satellite in orbit 在軌道上安置衛星 | I think that the U.S. government will place a satellite in orbit again soon. 我想美國政府很快就會在太空軌道上再安置一顆衛星。 |
| **polite** [pəˋlaɪt] 形 有禮貌的 | a polite manner 有禮貌的態度 | He always treats his elders in a polite manner. 他通常都很有禮貌地對待他的長輩。 |
| **impolite** [ˏɪmpəˋlaɪt] 形 無禮的 | impolite child 無禮的小孩 | That impolite child told his mother to shut up. 那個無禮的小孩要他母親閉嘴。 |
| **dynamite** [ˋdaɪnəˏmaɪt] 名 炸藥 | plant dynamite 埋炸藥 | I saw him plant dynamite near the warehouse and called the police right away. 我看到他在倉庫附近埋炸藥，就馬上打電話給警方。 |
| **ignite** [ɪgˋnaɪt] 動 點燃、使燃燒 | ignite a fire 點火 | Do you know how to ignite a fire without using matches? 你知道不用火柴怎樣點火嗎？ |
| **finite** [ˋfaɪnaɪt] 形 有限的 | finite resources 有限的資源 | Our company has finite resources so we can't afford to pay for that. 我們公司的資源有限，所以我們付不起那個。 |
| **unite** [juˋnaɪt] 動 統一、使團結 | unite people 使人們團結 | Is there a way to unite people of different beliefs and races? 有沒有方法可以使不同信仰和種族的人們團結起來？ |
| * **write** [raɪt] 動 書寫 | write a letter 寫一封信 | I would like to write a letter to the president. 我想要寫一封信給總統。 |

| | | |
|---|---|---|
| **site**<br>[saɪt]<br>名 地點、場所 | web site<br>網站 | What is the web site for your company?<br>你公司網站是什麼？ |
| **appetite**<br>[ˋæpəˏtaɪt]<br>名 食慾、胃口 | have no appetite<br>沒胃口 | I don't know why I have no appetite today.<br>我不知道為何我今天沒胃口。 |
| **quite**<br>[kwaɪt]<br>副 相當地 | quite well<br>相當好 | He seems to know him quite well.<br>他似乎相當了解他。 |

## ility [ˋɪlətɪ]

| | | |
|---|---|---|
| * **ability**<br>[əˋbɪlətɪ]<br>名 能力、能耐 | natural ability<br>自然的能力 | He has a natural ability to make people laugh.<br>他有種與生俱來讓人發笑的能力。 |
| * **capability**<br>[ˏkepəˋbɪlətɪ]<br>名 能力、才能 | potential capability<br>潛在的才能 | I think he has the potential capability in shooting a gun.<br>我認為他有成為槍手的潛在才能。 |
| **durability**<br>[ˏdjurəˋbɪlətɪ]<br>名 耐久性 | outlasting durability<br>高耐久性 | This battery boasts its outlasting durability.<br>這個電池具耐久性。 |
| **adaptability**<br>[əˏdæptəˋbɪlətɪ]<br>名 順應性、適應性 | social adaptability<br>社會適應性 | Her social adaptability skills are good since she's moved around a lot. 她的社會適應能力很好，因為她常到處旅行。 |

| 單字 | 片語 | 例句 |
|---|---|---|
| * **stability**<br>[stə`bɪlətɪ]<br>名 穩定、穩定性 | emotional stability<br>情緒穩定 | My cousin has problems with his emotional stability.<br>我的堂兄有情緒不穩的問題。 |
| * **credibility**<br>[ˏkrɛdə`bɪlətɪ]<br>名 可信性 | professional credibility<br>專業的可信度 | They are trusted by many customers because of their professional credibility. 因為他們的專業，所以客戶很信賴他們。 |
| **sensibility**<br>[ˏsɛnsə`bɪlətɪ]<br>名 敏感、感性 | maternal sensibility<br>母性的敏感 | She can tell what her children feel because of her maternal sensibilities. 她能看出她的小孩的感覺，是因為她身為母親的敏感。 |
| * **responsibility**<br>[rɪˏspɑnsə`bɪlətɪ]<br>名 責任 | take responsibility<br>負起責任 | You're old enough to take responsibility now.<br>你現在已經長大到足以負起責任了。 |
| * **possibility**<br>[ˏpɑsə`bɪlətɪ]<br>名 可能性 | possibility of success<br>成功的可能性 | Is there any possibility of success?<br>有任何成功的可能嗎？ |
| **impossibility**<br>[ɪmˏpɑsə`bɪlətɪ]<br>名 不可能性 | impossibility for improvement<br>不可能進步 | There is an impossibility for improvement because of her injury.<br>因為她受傷，所以不可能進步。 |
| * **flexibility**<br>[ˏflɛksə`bɪlətɪ]<br>名 靈活、彈性 | flexibility of the arm<br>手臂的靈活 | He has lost the flexibility of his arm after he broke it.<br>在他摔斷手臂後，手臂就不靈活了。 |
| **nobility**<br>[no`bɪlətɪ]<br>名 高貴特質 | country's nobility<br>全國人民的崇高特質 | All of the country's nobility will be there at the festival.<br>人民的優秀特質將在節慶表現出來。 |

|  |  |  |
|---|---|---|
| * **facility** [fə`sɪlətɪ] 名 設備 | cooking facilities 烹煮設備 | I think that the cooking facilities in this restaurant are run-down and unsanitary. 我覺得這家餐廳的烹煮設備年久失修又不衛生。 |
| **humility** [hju`mɪlətɪ] 名 謙卑、謙遜 | act with humility 謙虛地做事 | No matter how proud he is, he always acts with humility. 不論他如何自豪，他總是很謙虛地做事。 |
| **versatility** [ˏvɜsə`tɪlətɪ] 名 多才多藝、多用途 | exceptional versatility 卓越的多才多藝 | He plays the violin with exceptional versatility. 他多才多藝地演奏小提琴。 |
| **hostility** [hɑs`tɪlətɪ] 名 敵意 | hostility toward each other 彼此具敵意 | I don't know how they are going to dissolve their hostility toward each other. 我不知道他們要如何化解對彼此的敵意。 |
| * **utility** [ju`tɪlətɪ] 形 多用途的 名 水電、瓦斯等公共設施 | utility knife 多用途的刀子<br>public utility 公共設施 | You should bring a utility knife with you when you go camping. 當你去露營時，你應該隨身帶著一把多用途的刀。<br>What are the average costs of public utilities in a month? 水電瓦斯一個月的平均費用多少？ |
| **futility** [fju`tɪlətɪ] 名 徒勞無益 | futility of his attempts 他的企圖徒勞無功 | He was so upset after he found out about the futility of his attempts. 他發現他的企圖徒勞無功時，他很沮喪。 |
| **tranquility** [træŋ`kwɪlətɪ] 名 平靜、安寧 | tranquility of the night 夜晚的寧靜 | I appreciate the tranquility of the night. 我喜愛夜晚的寧靜。 |

35

| | | |
|---|---|---|
| **milk**<br>[mɪlk]<br>名 牛奶 | a cup of milk<br>一杯牛奶 | Having a cup of milk before you go to bed will help you sleep.<br>睡覺前喝一杯牛奶有助於睡眠。 |
| **silk**<br>[sɪlk]<br>名 絲 形 絲的 | silk blouse<br>絲質短衫 | My friend gave me a silk blouse for my birthday.<br>我的朋友送我一件絲質短衫當生日禮物。 |

## ill [ɪl]

| | | |
|---|---|---|
| **ill**<br>[ɪl]<br>形 生病的 | become ill<br>生病 | After she became ill, we looked after her day and night.<br>她生病後，我們整天照顧她。 |
| * **bill**<br>[bɪl]<br>名 帳單 | pay the bills<br>付帳 | Sometimes I forget to pay the bills.<br>有時我會忘了付帳。 |
| **fill**<br>[fɪl]<br>動 裝滿、填滿 | fill out the form<br>填表 | Can you help him fill out the form?<br>你能幫忙他填表嗎？ |
| **refill**<br>[riˋfɪl]<br>動 再裝滿 | refill his cup<br>再來一杯 | He just went to the kitchen to refill his cup of coffee.<br>他剛去廚房再倒一杯咖啡。 |
| **fulfill**<br>[fʊlˋfɪl]<br>動 達成 | fulfill a dream<br>達成夢想 | What does it take to fulfill a dream?<br>達到夢想需要什麼？ |

| | | |
| --- | --- | --- |
| **hill**<br>[hɪl]<br>名 小山丘 | go up a hill<br>爬上小山丘 | I watched the pig go up a hill very slowly.<br>我看到一隻豬緩慢走上小山丘。 |
| **chill**<br>[tʃɪl]<br>名 寒冷 | feel a chill<br>感到寒冷 | Is the window open? I feel a chill.<br>窗戶是打開的嗎？我覺得冷。 |
| **downhill**<br>[ˋdaʊnˋhɪl]<br>名 下坡 副 向下 | go downhill<br>往下坡 | How fast do you go downhill when you're skiing?<br>你滑雪時，往下坡的速度有多快？ |
| **uphill**<br>[ˋʌpˋhɪl]<br>名 上坡 副 往上坡 | walk uphill<br>往上坡走 | We walked uphill with ease.<br>我們輕鬆地走上山去。 |
| **kill**<br>[kɪl]<br>動 殺死 | kill an insect<br>殺死昆蟲 | He doesn't have the heart to kill an insect.<br>他無意殺死一隻昆蟲。 |
| * **skill**<br>[ˋskɪl]<br>名 技術、技能 | have a skill<br>有技能 | It seems like everyone here has a skill to sell.<br>這裡每個人似乎都有銷售技能。 |
| **pill**<br>[pɪl]<br>名 藥丸 | take a pill<br>吃藥丸 | Did you take a pill for your stomachache?<br>你胃痛有吃藥丸嗎？ |
| **spill**<br>[spɪl]<br>動 溢出、濺出 | spill over<br>溢出來 | That milk will spill over if you put it there.<br>那牛奶如果放在那兒會溢出來。 |

| | | |
|---|---|---|
| **drill**<br>[drɪl]<br>名 鑽頭、訓練 | fire drill<br>防火演習 | I hate fire drills because you have to evacuate the building and wait outside. 我討厭防火演習，因為必須要撤空大樓到室外等。 |
| **thrill**<br>[θrɪl]<br>名 刺激 動 使興奮 | seek a thrill<br>尋求刺激 | She is always seeking a thrill.<br>她總是在尋求刺激。 |
| **till**<br>[tɪl]<br>介 連 直到…為止 | till Wednesday<br>直到星期三為止 | I have till Wednesday to finish my report.<br>我必須在星期三之前完成我的報告。 |
| **still**<br>[stɪl]<br>副 還是、仍舊 | I still love you<br>我依然愛你 | "I still love you," he said, when he was breaking up with me. 當他跟我分手時，他說：「我依然愛你。」 |
| **standstill**<br>[ˋstændˏstɪl]<br>名 停止、停頓 | come to a standstill<br>陷於停頓 | I think we've come to a standstill.<br>我認為我們已陷入停頓狀態。 |
| **instill**<br>[ɪnˋstɪl]<br>動 循循教導 | instill values<br>逐漸灌輸價值觀 | All parents try to instill values in their children.<br>所有的父母都試著將他們的價值觀灌輸給小孩。 |
| **will**<br>[wɪl]<br>助 將 名 意志 | strong will<br>強烈意志 | He has a strong will to help others.<br>他有很強烈的意志要幫助他人。 |
| **goodwill**<br>[ˋgudˋwɪl]<br>名 善意 | out of goodwill<br>出於善意 | She is so sincere, especially since she does everything out of goodwill. 她是如此真誠，特別是因為她做每件事都是出於善意。 |

| | | |
|---|---|---|
| **freewill**<br>[ˋfri͵wɪl]<br>名 自由意志 | ▶ out of your own freewill<br>出於你自己的自由意志 | ▶ I can't believe you are going to the dentist out of your own freewill.<br>我無法相信你自願去看牙醫。 |

## iller [ˋɪlɚ]

| | | |
|---|---|---|
| **killer**<br>[ˋkɪlɚ]<br>名 殺手、兇手 | ▶ that serial killer<br>連環殺手 | ▶ Everyone is looking for that serial killer.<br>每個人都在找那個連環殺手。 |

## illar [ˋɪlɚ]

| | | |
|---|---|---|
| **caterpillar**<br>[ˋkætɚ͵pɪlɚ]<br>名 毛毛蟲 | ▶ fuzzy caterpillar<br>毛茸茸的毛毛蟲 | ▶ Do you see that fuzzy caterpillar hanging from a string?<br>你有看到那掛在樹鬚上的毛毛蟲嗎？ |

## illion [ˋɪljən]

| | | |
|---|---|---|
| **billion**<br>[ˋbɪljən]<br>名 十億 | ▶ a billion dollars<br>十億元 | ▶ I wish I had a billion dollars.<br>我希望我有十億元。 |
| **million**<br>[ˋmɪljən]<br>名 百萬 | ▶ a million people<br>百萬人 | ▶ There are over a million people who want to be like Madonna.<br>超過百萬人想要像瑪丹娜。 |

| | | |
|---|---|---|
| **trillion**<br>[ˋtrɪljən]<br>名 一兆、無數 | a trillion things<br>一堆事 | There are a trillion things I have to do today.<br>有一堆事我今天必須去做。 |

## illow [ˋɪlo]

| | | |
|---|---|---|
| **pillow**<br>[ˋpɪlo]<br>名 枕頭 | pillow case<br>枕頭套 | My daughter made a pillow case for me.<br>我女兒幫我做了一個枕頭套。 |
| **willow**<br>[ˋwɪlo]<br>名 柳樹 | weeping willow<br>垂柳 | Many people like reading a book under the weeping willow tree.<br>很多人喜歡在垂柳下讀書。 |

## ilt [ɪlt]

| | | |
|---|---|---|
| **tilt**<br>[tɪlt]<br>動 使傾斜 | tilt your head<br>頭斜一下 | Can you tilt your head to the side for me please?<br>可以請你把頭斜一邊嗎？ |
| **guilt**<br>[gɪlt]<br>名 罪、內疚 | feel guilt<br>感到內疚 | He feels guilt for losing his son.<br>他因失去他的兒子感到內疚。 |

## im [ɪm]

| 單字 | 片語 | 例句 |
| --- | --- | --- |
| **dim** [dɪm] 形 微暗的 動 變暗 | dim the light 使燈光暗下來 | Can you dim the light for the movie please? 可以請你把燈光變暗以便看電影嗎？ |
| **him** [hɪm] 代 他 | tell him 告訴他 | Tell him that I hate him. 告訴他我恨他。 |
| **whim** [hwɪm] 名 奇想 | on a whim 一時興起 | She decided to move to New York on a whim. 她一時興起決定搬到紐約。 |
| **skim** [skɪm] 動 掠過、瀏覽 | skim the book 瀏覽一下書 | If you just skim the book, you'll get an idea of what it's like. 如果你瀏覽一下書，你會大概有個了解。 |
| **slim** [slɪm] 形 苗條的 | keep slim 保持苗條 | It must be difficult to keep slim when you live next to a pastry shop. 當你住在點心店隔壁時，想保持苗條的身材必定很難。 |
| **rim** [rɪm] 名 框邊 | basketball rim 籃框 | He can jump up to the basketball rim and can slam dunk the ball. 他能跳到籃框灌籃。 |
| **trim** [trɪm] 動 修剪 | trim trees 修剪樹木 | He had a summer job trimming trees. 他有一個修剪樹木的暑期工作。 |
| **swim** [swɪm] 動 游泳 | go swimming 游泳 | It's so nice to go swimming in the hot weather. 在大熱天游泳很棒。 |

## imb [ɪm]

| | | |
|---|---|---|
| **limb** [lɪm] 名 肢體 | ▶ stretch our limbs 伸展我們的肢體 | ▶ We wanted to stretch our limbs on the airplane, but we couldn't. 我們想要在飛機上伸展肢體，但沒辦法這麼做。 |

## ym [ɪm]

| | | |
|---|---|---|
| **synonym** [ˋsɪnə͵nɪm] 名 同義字 | ▶ match the synonym 配同義字 | ▶ Can you match the synonyms together? 你能將同義字配對嗎？ |
| **antonym** [ˋæntə͵nɪm] 名 反義字 | ▶ what is the antonym 反義字是什麼 | ▶ What is the antonym of "love"? 「愛」的反義字是什麼？ |

## ime [aɪm]

| | | |
|---|---|---|
| **lime** [laɪm] 名 萊姆 | ▶ lime juice 萊姆汁 | ▶ Lime juice is added to many cocktails. 很多雞尾酒都加了萊姆汁。 |
| **crime** [kraɪm] 名 罪行 | ▶ commit a crime 犯罪 | ▶ He was arrested for committing a crime. 他因犯罪被捕。 |
| **bedtime** [ˋbɛd͵taɪm] 名 就寢時間 | ▶ a bedtime story 睡前故事 | ▶ My mother used to tell me a bedtime story as I went to sleep. 我母親過去常在我上床睡覺時跟我說睡前故事。 |

| | | |
|---|---|---|
| **lifetime** [ˋlaɪf͵taɪm] 名 一生、終生 | in a lifetime 在一生 | This is the best experience I've had in my lifetime. 這是我這一生中最好的經驗。 |
| **sometime** [ˋsʌm͵taɪm] 副 某一時候 | sometime ago 從前 | Sometime ago, a little girl lost her parents here. 從前，一位小女孩在這裡與父母失散。 |
| **meantime** [ˋmin͵taɪm] 名 副 其間 | in the meantime 在此時 | What should we do in the meantime? 此時我們應該做什麼？ |
| **overtime** [ˋovɚ͵taɪm] 名 副 加班 | work overtime 加班 | It's tiring to work overtime. 加班很累。 |

| | | |
|---|---|---|
| **daytime** [ˋde͵taɪm] 名 白天 | daytime shows 日間表演 | Which daytime shows do you like? 你喜歡哪一些日間的表演？ |

## imb [aɪm]

| | | |
|---|---|---|
| **climb** [klaɪm] 動 爬、攀登 | climb mountains 爬山 | He likes to climb mountains. 他喜歡爬山。 |

## immer [ˋɪmɚ]

| | | |
|---|---|---|
| **shimmer**<br>[ˋʃɪmɚ]<br>動 發微光 名 閃光 | shimmer in the light<br>燈光下的閃光 | Where does that shimmer in the light come from?<br>那閃光是從哪來的？ |
| **glimmer**<br>[ˋglɪmɚ]<br>動 閃爍不定 名 微光 | glimmer of light<br>閃爍不定的光 | We saw a glimmer of light in the distance.<br>我們看到在遠處有閃爍不定的光。 |
| **swimmer**<br>[ˋswɪmɚ]<br>名 游泳者 | good swimmer<br>好的游泳者 | He is a very good swimmer.<br>他是位很棒的泳者。 |

## imp [ɪmp]

36

| | | |
|---|---|---|
| **limp**<br>[lɪmp]<br>動 跛行 名 跛腳 | limp slightly<br>微跛<br>have a slight limp<br>有輕微跛腳 | She has been limping slightly ever since the accident.<br>自從發生意外後，她走路就有點跛。<br>They are looking for a guy who has a slight limp.<br>他們正在找一位有輕微跛腳的人。 |
| **shrimp**<br>[ʃrɪmp]<br>名 蝦子 | shrimp dumplings<br>蝦餃 | This restaurant's shrimp dumplings are excellent.<br>這餐廳的蝦餃很棒。 |

## imple [ˋɪmpl̩]

| | | |
|---|---|---|
| **dimple**<br>[ˋdɪmpl̩]<br>名 酒窩 | dimples in her cheeks<br>她臉頰的酒窩 | She has two dimples in her cheeks.<br>她的臉頰有兩個酒窩。 |

| | | |
|---|---|---|
| **pimple** [ˋpɪmpḷ] 名 面皰、痘痘 | have a pimple 長痘痘 | He was embarrassed because he had a big pimple on his forehead. 他前額長了顆大痘痘，所以感到不好意思。 |
| **simple** [ˋsɪmpḷ] 形 簡單的 | a simple life 簡單的生活 | They want to lead a simple life. 他們想過簡單的生活。 |

## in [ɪn]

| | | |
|---|---|---|
| **in** [ɪn] 介 在…裡 | in here 在這裡 | You're not allowed to smoke in here. 你不能在這裡抽菸。 |
| **fin** [fɪn] 介 鰭 | shark fin 鯊魚鰭 | Many Chinese people like to eat shark fin. 許多中國人喜歡吃魚翅。 |
| **begin** [bɪˋgɪn] 動 開始 | begin working 開始工作 | When did you begin working? 你何時開始工作的？ |
| **chin** [ɛʃɪn] 名 下巴 | on the chin 在下巴 | You have something on your chin. 你下巴沾了東西。 |
| **thin** [θɪn] 形 薄的、細的、瘦的 | thin woman 瘦女人 | No matter how much she eats, she is still a thin woman. 不論她吃多少東西，她仍然很瘦。 |

| | | |
|---|---|---|
| **within**<br>[wɪˋðɪn]<br>介 在…範圍內 | ▶ within reach<br>在可到達的範圍 | ▶ I think the goal is within reach.<br>我想這目標是在可達成範圍內。 |
| **skin**<br>[skɪn]<br>名 皮膚 | ▶ skin cancer<br>皮膚癌 | ▶ If you don't use suntan lotion, you might get skin cancer.<br>如果你不用防曬乳液，你可能會得皮膚癌。 |
| **pin**<br>[pɪn]<br>名 大頭針、別針 | ▶ pin drop<br>針掉下 | ▶ It's so quiet in here that you can hear a pin drop.<br>這裡安靜到連一根針掉下都聽得到。 |
| **spin**<br>[spɪn]<br>動 紡紗、旋轉 | ▶ spin the wheel<br>轉動輪軸 | ▶ In the game of roulette, you spin the wheel.<br>在輪盤賭局中，你旋轉輪軸。 |
| **grin**<br>[grɪn]<br>動 名 露齒而笑 | ▶ sly grin<br>狡猾的笑 | ▶ He had a sly grin on his face when he looked at us.<br>他在看我們時，臉上有狡猾的笑容。 |
| **sin**<br>[sɪn]<br>名 罪 | ▶ horrible sin<br>可怕的罪 | ▶ Killing someone is a horrible sin.<br>殺人是一件可怕的罪。 |
| **tin**<br>[tɪn]<br>名 錫、馬口鐵 | ▶ tin can<br>錫罐 | ▶ He used a tin can as an instrument.<br>他用錫罐當樂器。 |
| **win**<br>[wɪn]<br>動 獲勝 | ▶ win a game<br>贏得比賽 | ▶ He knows how to win a game.<br>他知道如何贏得比賽。 |

| | | |
|---|---|---|
| **twin**<br>[twɪn]<br>名 孿生兒 | ▶ fraternal twins<br>異卵雙胞胎 | ▶ They are fraternal twins.<br>他們是異卵雙胞胎。 |

## ine [ɪn]

| | | |
|---|---|---|
| **discipline**<br>[`dɪsəplɪn]<br>名 紀律、風紀 | ▶ maintain discipline<br>維持紀律 | ▶ This school teaches the students to maintain discipline at all times. 這學校教學生要時時刻刻維持紀律。 |

## inn [ɪn]

| | | |
|---|---|---|
| **inn**<br>[ɪn]<br>名 小旅館 | ▶ Holiday Inn<br>假日飯店 | ▶ Holiday Inn is an international chain of affordable hotels.<br>假日飯店是家國際知名的連鎖平價飯店。 |

## ince [ɪns]

| | | |
|---|---|---|
| **prince**<br>[prɪns]<br>名 王子 | ▶ prince charming<br>白馬王子 | ▶ Prince charming is a made-up character that does not exist.<br>白馬王子是個虛構的角色，他並不存在。 |
| * **since**<br>[sɪns]<br>連 介 自…以來 | ▶ since December<br>自從十二月 | ▶ He hasn't eaten any meat since December.<br>他自從十二月以來都沒有吃肉。 |

| | | |
|---|---|---|
| *convince [kən`vɪns] 動 說服 | hard to convince 難以說服 | She is hard to convince on this issue. 在這個問題上她是難以說服的。 |

## inch [ɪntʃ]

| | | |
|---|---|---|
| inch [ɪntʃ] 名 英吋 | inch worm 小蟲 | I found an inch worm in my food. 我發現我的食物中有隻小蟲。 |
| pinch [pɪntʃ] 動 捏、擰 | pinch her arm 捏她的手臂 | He would pinch her arm when she laughed too hard. 她笑得太用力時，他會捏她的手臂。 |

## inct [ɪŋkt]

| | | |
|---|---|---|
| *distinct [dɪ`stɪŋkt] 形 區別的、清楚的 | distinct from each other 彼此不同的<br>far from distinct 完全不清楚 | Although these two things look the same, they are distinct from each other. 雖然這兩個東西看起來一樣，但他們是彼此不同的。<br>The picture that you gave me is far from distinct. 你給我的這照片是完全不清楚的。 |
| instinct [`ɪnstɪŋkt] 名 本能、天性 | out of instinct 出於本能 | He has never played tennis before, but today he played very well, out of instinct. 他之前從來沒有打過網球，但出於天份，他今天打得非常好。 |

| | | |
|---|---|---|
| **extinct** [ɪkˋstɪŋkt] 形 滅亡的 ▶ | become extinct 變成滅亡的 ▶ | It is very sad when animals become extinct. 當動物滅亡時，是很令人難過的。 |

## ind [aɪnd]

| | | |
|---|---|---|
| **blind** [blaɪnd] 形 盲的 ▶ | blind in one eye 一隻眼瞎了 ▶ | She was born blind in one eye. 她出生就一隻眼瞎了。 |
| * **find** [faɪnd] 動 找到、發現 ▶ | find out 找出 ▶ | Can you find out where she went? 你能找出她去哪裡了嗎？ |
| * **behind** [bɪˋhaɪnd] 介 在…的後面 ▶ | fall behind 落在後面 ▶ | I'm falling behind in schoolwork. 我的學業落後了。 |
| * **kind** [kaɪnd] 名 種類 形 善良的 ▶ | what kind 哪種 kind people 善良的人 ▶ | What kind of people are going to this party? 哪種人會去這個宴會？ There were a lot of kind people at the party. 在宴會中有很多善良的人。 |
| * **mind** [maɪnd] 名 心智 ▶ | in his mind 在他的心中 ▶ | It is all in his mind that he is not good enough. 在他心中認為自己不夠好。 |
| * **remind** [rɪˋmaɪnd] 動 提醒 ▶ | remind me of 讓我回想起 ▶ | She reminds me of my mother. 她讓我想起我的母親。 |

| | | |
| --- | --- | --- |
| **grind** [graɪnd] 動 磨 名 苦事 | daily grind 每天的苦差事 | Don't you ever get sick of the daily grind? 每天做這苦差事你從不厭煩嗎？ |
| **wind** [waɪnd] 動 轉動、蜿蜒 | wind through 蜿蜒 | The brook winds through the field. 小溪蜿蜒流過原野。 |

## ine [aɪn]

37

| | | |
| --- | --- | --- |
| * **combine** [kəm`baɪn] 動 使結合 | combine our efforts 結合努力 | We need to combine our efforts in order to succeed. 為了成功，我們得結合我們的努力。 |
| **dine** [daɪn] 動 用餐 | dine out 外出用餐 | Let's dine out tonight! 我們今晚出去用餐吧！ |
| * **fine** [faɪn] 形 美好的 動 名 罰 | a fine day 美好的一天 | She said she had a fine day. 她說她度過了美好的一天。 |
| * **define** [dɪ`faɪn] 動 解釋、給…下定義 | define a word 定義一個字 | Can you define a word for me? 你可以幫我定義一個字嗎？ |
| **refine** [rɪ`faɪn] 動 提煉、精製 | refined sugar 精製糖 | He used refined sugar in the cake. 他在蛋糕中加精製糖。 |

| | | |
|---|---|---|
| **confine**<br>[kən`faɪn] [`kɑnfaɪn]<br>動 限制 名 範圍 | confine to<br>限制 | That rule is not confined to children.<br>那個規則不限於孩子們。 |
| **shine**<br>[ʃaɪn]<br>動 發光、擦亮 | shine shoes<br>擦亮鞋 | He shines shoes for a living.<br>他幫人擦鞋為生。 |
| **sunshine**<br>[`sʌn͵ʃaɪn]<br>名 陽光 | in the sunshine<br>在陽光下 | She likes to bask in the sunshine.<br>她喜歡在陽光下曬太陽。 |
| * **decline**<br>[dɪ`klaɪn]<br>動 減少、婉拒 | the crime rate declines<br>犯罪率減少<br>decline my invitation<br>婉拒我的邀請 | The economy is better when the crime rate declines.<br>當犯罪率下降時，經濟就會比較好。<br>I don't know why he declined my invitation.<br>我不知道為何他婉拒我的邀請。 |
| **incline**<br>[ɪn`klaɪn]<br>動 名 傾斜 | steady incline<br>穩定的斜坡 | There is a steady incline up ahead.<br>在前面有個平穩的斜坡。 |
| * **deadline**<br>[`dɛd͵laɪn]<br>名 截止期限 | meet the deadline<br>趕上截止期限 | I'm not sure I can meet the deadline for the report.<br>我不確定我是否可以準時交報告。 |
| * **headline**<br>[`hɛd͵laɪn]<br>名 大標題 | headline news<br>頭條新聞 | What is the headline news for today?<br>今天的頭條新聞是什麼？ |
| **underline**<br>[͵ʌndɚ`laɪn]<br>動 劃底線、強調 | underline the important words<br>在重要的字下劃線 | Don't forget to underline the important words in the text.<br>不要忘了將課文中重要的字劃線。 |

| | | |
|---|---|---|
| **coastline** [ˋkost͵laɪn] 名 海岸線 | ▶ along the coastline 沿著海岸線 | ▶ We often took long drives along the coastline. 我們時常沿著海岸線開車。 |
| **skyline** [ˋskaɪ͵laɪn] 名 天際線 | ▶ beautiful skyline 美麗的天際線 | ▶ You can see the beautiful skyline from the top of that building. 你可以看到美麗的天際線從那棟大樓頂端延伸出來。 |
| **mine** [maɪn] 代 我的 | ▶ all mine 都是我的 | ▶ That candy is all mine! 那顆糖果都是我的！ |
| **nine** [naɪn] 名 九 形 九的 | ▶ nine years old 九歲 | ▶ He moved to France when he was nine years old. 他九歲搬到法國。 |
| **pine** [paɪn] 名 松樹 | ▶ pine tree 松樹 | ▶ They cut down the old pine tree in our backyard. 他們鋸斷了我們後院的老松樹。 |
| **spine** [spaɪn] 名 脊椎 | ▶ down my spine 脊椎下 | ▶ I get chills down my spine when I think about ghosts. 當我想到鬼時，我的背脊都涼了。 |
| **vine** [vaɪn] 名 藤蔓 | ▶ heard it through the grapevine 道聽塗說來的 | ▶ Where did you hear about that? I heard it through the grapevine. 你在哪兒聽說的？我道聽塗說的。 |
| **divine** [dəˋvaɪn] 形 神聖的 | ▶ divine work 神聖的工作 | ▶ The teacher thought that she made divine work with her hands. 這老師認為她親手做了神聖的工作。 |

| | | |
|---|---|---|
| **wine**<br>[waɪn]<br>名 葡萄酒、酒 | wine cellar<br>酒窖 | Their wine cellar must have been worth thousands of dollars.<br>他們的酒窖必定值數千元。 |

## ign [aɪn]

| | | |
|---|---|---|
| * **sign**<br>[saɪn]<br>名 符號 動 簽名 | traffic signs<br>交通號誌<br>sign your name<br>簽名 | Pay attention to the traffic signs when you're driving.<br>當你在開車時，要注意交通號誌。<br>Please sign your name at the bottom of the form.<br>請在這份表格下方簽名。 |
| * **design**<br>[dɪˋzaɪn]<br>動 名 設計 | design costumes<br>設計戲服 | She designs costumes for musicals and plays.<br>她為音樂劇及戲劇設計戲服。 |
| * **resign**<br>[rɪˋzaɪn]<br>動 辭去 | resign his presidency<br>辭去總統之位 | President Nixon was forced to resign his presidency.<br>尼克森總統被迫辭去總統之位。 |
| **cosign**<br>[ˏkoˋsaɪn]<br>動 連署 | cosign this contract<br>連署這份合約 | I need someone to cosign this contract with me.<br>我需要有人跟我一起連署這份合約。 |
| * **assign**<br>[əˋsaɪn]<br>動 分配、分派 | assign tasks to him<br>指派任務給他 | His mother always assigns tasks to him every day.<br>他母親總是每天指派任務給他。 |

## inor [ˋaɪnɚ]

| | | |
|---|---|---|
| * **minor**<br>[ˋmaɪnɚ]<br>形 較小的、次要的 | minor operation<br>小手術 | Don't worry; it's just a minor operation.<br>別擔心，只是小手術。 |

## ing [ɪŋ]

| | | |
|---|---|---|
| * **thing**<br>[θɪŋ]<br>名 東西 | precious thing<br>珍貴的東西 | He stored a precious thing in a safe in the bank.<br>他把貴重物品存在銀行保險箱裡。 |
| **something**<br>[ˋsʌmθɪŋ]<br>代 某事 | buy something<br>買個東西 | I need to buy something for my mother's birthday.<br>我必須買個東西幫我母親慶生。 |
| **anything**<br>[ˋɛnɪˏθɪŋ]<br>代 任何事 | try anything<br>做任何嘗試 | He will try anything to make you like him.<br>他會努力讓你喜歡他。 |
| **everything**<br>[ˋɛvrɪˏθɪŋ]<br>代 每件事 | everything goes<br>開始 | In a clearance sale, every thing goes!<br>清倉大拍賣，開始囉！ |
| **king**<br>[kɪŋ]<br>名 國王 | king of Thailand<br>泰國國王 | Have you ever seen a picture of the King of Thailand?<br>你曾看過泰國國王的照片嗎？ |
| **cling**<br>[klɪŋ]<br>動 黏著、依靠 | cling on to<br>依戀 | She seems to cling on to the past.<br>她似乎依戀著過去。 |

| | | |
|---|---|---|
| **ring**<br>[rɪŋ]<br>名 圈 動 鈴響 | wedding ring<br>結婚戒指<br>ring the bell<br>按鈴 | She never took off her wedding ring.<br>她從來沒有脫下結婚戒指。<br>You should ring the bell before you open the door.<br>你應該在開門前按鈴。 |
| * **bring**<br>[brɪŋ]<br>動 帶來、拿來 | bring along<br>帶來 | Can I bring along a friend?<br>我能帶個朋友來嗎？ |
| **spring**<br>[sprɪŋ]<br>名 春天、水泉 | in spring<br>在春天<br>hot spring<br>溫泉 | Flowers bloom in spring.<br>春天花朵盛開。<br>Some hot springs smell really bad. 有些溫泉很難聞。 |
| **offspring**<br>[`ɔf͵sprɪŋ]<br>名 子女、後代 | bear offspring<br>生育 | Due to complications, she cannot bear offspring.<br>因為併發症，她無法生育。 |
| **earring**<br>[`ɪr͵rɪŋ]<br>名 耳環 | wear earrings<br>戴耳環 | Some people like it when men wear earrings.<br>有些人喜歡男人戴耳環。 |
| **string**<br>[strɪŋ]<br>名 帶子、一連串 | undo the string<br>解開帶子<br>a string of accidents<br>一連串的意外 | Can you please undo the string on the back of my dress for me? 可以請你幫我解開我衣服後面的帶子嗎？<br>With his bad luck and a string of accidents, he didn't dare leave the house. 因為壞運氣和一連串的意外，導致他不敢出門。 |
| **shoestring**<br>[`ʃu͵strɪŋ]<br>名 鞋帶 | tie your shoestring<br>綁鞋帶 | When did you learn to tie your shoestrings?<br>你何時學會綁鞋帶？ |

| | | |
|---|---|---|
| **sing** [sɪŋ] 動 唱歌 | ▶ sing along 跟著唱 | ▶ Do you sing along to certain songs on the radio? 你會跟著收音機裡的歌一起唱嗎？ |
| **sting** [stɪŋ] 動 名 刺、螫、叮 | ▶ bee sting 蜜蜂螫 | ▶ She is allergic to bee stings. 她被蜜蜂叮到會過敏。 |
| **wing** [wɪŋ] 名 翅膀、機翼 | ▶ spread my wings 展開翅膀 | ▶ I sometimes dream that I could spread my wings and fly. 我有時夢想能展翅翱翔。 |
| **swing** [swɪŋ] 動 搖擺、搖盪 | ▶ swing back and forth 前後搖晃 | ▶ They used to swing back and forth on a tree branch like monkeys.他們過去常像猴子一樣在樹枝上前後搖晃。 |

## injure [`ɪndʒɚ]

| | | |
|---|---|---|
| **injure** [`ɪndʒɚ] 動 傷害 | ▶ get injured 受傷 | ▶ He can't play anymore this year because he got injured. 他今年不能再打了，因為他受傷了。 |

## ingle [`ɪŋgl̩]

| | | |
|---|---|---|
| **jingle** [`dʒɪŋgl̩] 名 叮噹聲 | ▶ radio jingle 廣播的串場曲 | ▶ She sang a radio jingle about cat food. 她唱了首有關貓食的廣播串場曲。 |

| | | |
|---|---|---|
| **mingle**<br>[ˋmɪŋgḷ]<br>動 使混合、來往 | ▶ mingle together<br>往來 | ▶ Those two groups don't mingle together.<br>那兩個團體不往來。 |
| **single**<br>[ˋsɪŋgḷ]<br>形 單一的 名 一人 | ▶ a single bed<br>單人床<br>remain single<br>保持單身 | ▶ There is a single bed in this room. 這房間有張單人床。<br>He wants to remain single for the rest of his life.<br>他想單身一人度過餘年。 |

## ingy [ˋɪndʒɪ]

| | | |
|---|---|---|
| **dingy**<br>[ˋdɪndʒɪ]<br>形 骯髒的 | ▶ dingy basement<br>骯髒的地下室 | ▶ I'm afraid to go down into that dingy basement.<br>我很怕下去那骯髒的地下室。 |
| **stingy**<br>[ˋstɪndʒɪ]<br>形 吝嗇的 | ▶ stingy old man<br>吝嗇的老男人 | ▶ He is a stingy old man who no one likes.<br>他是個沒人喜歡的吝嗇老男人。 |

## inister [ˋɪnɪstɚ]

| | | |
|---|---|---|
| * **minister**<br>[ˋmɪnɪstɚ]<br>名 部長、牧師 | ▶ minister of Education<br>教育部長 | ▶ Who is the minister of Education this year?<br>今年的教育部長是誰？ |
| * **administer**<br>[ədˋmɪnəstɚ]<br>動 管理 | ▶ administer a company<br>管理公司 | ▶ He thinks that he can administer the company better than his superiors.<br>他認為他比他的上司更會管理公司。 |

## inity [ˋɪnətɪ]

 38

| | | |
|---|---|---|
| **vicinity** [vəˋsɪnətɪ] 名 附近地區 | in the vicinity 在附近 | I know she is hiding somewhere in the vicinity. 我知道她躲在附近某處。 |
| **affinity** [əˋfɪnətɪ] 名 喜好、傾向 | affinity for flowers 喜好花 | All the men who courted her knew about her affinity for flowers. 所有追求她的男人都知道她喜歡花。 |
| **infinity** [ɪnˋfɪnətɪ] 名 無限、無窮 | infinity of the universe 宇宙的無限 | Aren't you amazed at the infinity of the universe? 你對宇宙的無限不會感到驚奇嗎？ |
| **masculinity** [ˏmæskjəˋlɪnətɪ] 名 男子氣概 | display masculinity 表現男子氣概 | I don't like it when he tries to display his masculinity. 我不喜歡他努力表現他的男子氣概。 |
| **femininity** [ˏfɛməˋnɪnətɪ] 名 女子氣質 | act with femininity 表現得很娘 | He often acts with femininity. 他常常表現得很娘。 |
| **divinity** [dəˋvɪnətɪ] 名 神性 | divinity of God 神性 | Do you believe in the divinity of God? 你相信神嗎？ |

## ink [ɪŋk]

| | | |
|---|---|---|
| **ink** [ɪŋk] 名 墨水 | black ink 黑色墨水 | I got black ink on my shirt. 我的襯衫沾到黑色墨水。 |

| | | |
| --- | --- | --- |
| * **think** [θɪŋk] 動 思考 | think of 思考 | Can you think of anything to do? 你可以想到任何要做的事嗎？ |
| **link** [lɪŋk] 動 名 連接、結合 | web links 網站連結 | There are some useful web links to other related web sites. 有些實用的網站連結可連到其他相關網站。 |
| **blink** [blɪŋk] 動 眨眼睛 | blink your eyes 眨動你的眼睛 | See how long you can go without blinking your eyes. 看看你能多久不眨眼。 |
| **pink** [pɪŋk] 名 粉紅 形 粉紅的 | pink dress 粉紅色的洋裝 | She wore a pink dress to the concert. 她穿件粉紅洋裝去聽音樂會。 |
| **brink** [brɪŋk] 名 邊緣 | on the brink of losing control 在失控邊緣 | He seems to be on the brink of losing control. 他似乎快失控了。 |
| **drink** [drɪŋk] 動 飲、喝 名 飲料 | drink wine 喝酒 | I like to go to my friends' house and drink wine. 我喜歡去我朋友家喝酒。 |
| **sink** [sɪŋk] 動 下沈 | sink to the bottom of the lake 下沈到湖底 | We watched that boat sink to the bottom of the lake. 我們看著那船沈到湖底。 |
| **shrink** [ʃrɪŋk] 動 收縮、躲避 | shrink in size 尺寸縮水<br>shrink from responsibilities 躲避責任 | Our clothes will shrink in size if you put them in the dryer too long. 如果你把我們的衣服放在烘衣機裡太久，它們會縮水。<br>He often shrinks from responsibilities. 他常常逃避責任。 |

| | | |
|---|---|---|
| **stink**<br>[stɪŋk]<br>動 發出惡臭 | stink up<br>發出惡臭 | If you stink up the bathroom, please use the deodorizer.<br>如果你的浴室發臭，請用防臭劑。 |
| **wink**<br>[wɪŋk]<br>動 眨眼 | wink at me<br>對我眨眼 | That handsome boy winked at me!<br>那個帥哥對我眨眼！ |

## inkle [ˋɪŋkḷ]

| | | |
|---|---|---|
| **sprinkle**<br>[ˋsprɪŋkḷ]<br>動 灑、撒 | sprinkle water<br>灑水 | In the summer, he sprinkles water on his face.<br>夏天時，他會在臉上潑水。 |
| **wrinkle**<br>[ˋrɪŋkḷ]<br>名 皺紋 動 起皺紋 | wrinkles around his eyes<br>皺紋在他眼睛周圍 | He looks older now that he has wrinkles around his eyes.<br>他眼睛周圍有皺紋，所以看起來比較老。 |
| **twinkle**<br>[ˋtwɪŋkḷ]<br>動 閃爍 | stars twinkle<br>星星閃爍 | They like to watch the stars twinkle in the sky at night.<br>他們喜歡看星星在夜空中閃爍。 |

## inner [ˋɪnɚ]

| | | |
|---|---|---|
| **inner**<br>[ˋɪnɚ]<br>名 內部 形 內心的 | inner peace<br>內心的平靜 | She said that she has found inner peace.<br>她說她已找到內心的平靜。 |

| | | |
|---|---|---|
| **dinner**<br>[ˋdɪnɚ]<br>名 晚餐、正餐 | ▶ have dinner<br>吃晚餐 | ▶ They will have dinner together at home tonight.<br>他們今晚要在家一起吃晚餐。 |
| **beginner**<br>[bɪˋgɪnɚ]<br>名 初學者 | ▶ beginners' class<br>初學者的班 | ▶ I think I should be in the beginners' class.<br>我想我應該在初級班。 |
| **winner**<br>[ˋwɪnɚ]<br>名 優勝者 | ▶ winner of the prize<br>得獎者 | ▶ The winner of the prize is an Italian director.<br>得獎者是一位義大利導演。 |

## ino [ˋino]

| | | |
|---|---|---|
| **Filipino**<br>[ˏfɪləˋpino]<br>名 菲律賓人、菲律賓語 | ▶ Filipino language<br>菲律賓語 | ▶ Can you speak the Filipino language?<br>你會說菲律賓話嗎？ |
| **casino**<br>[kəˋsino]<br>名 賭場 | ▶ go to the casino<br>去賭場 | ▶ They went to the casino every year for Christmas.<br>他們每年的聖誕節都會去賭場。 |

## int [ɪnt]

| | | |
|---|---|---|
| **hint**<br>[hɪnt]<br>名 暗示、示意 | ▶ give me a hint<br>給我暗示 | ▶ Can you please give me a hint of where you hid it?<br>可以請你暗示我你把它藏在哪嗎？ |

| | | |
|---|---|---|
| **mint**<br>[mɪnt]<br>名 薄荷 | ▶ mint chocolate chip<br>薄荷巧克力片 | ▶ My favorite ice cream flavor is mint chocolate chip. 我最喜歡的冰淇淋口味是薄荷巧克力片。 |
| **print**<br>[prɪnt]<br>名 動 印刷 | ▶ in print<br>印好 | ▶ You can find that book in print only in certain stores.<br>你只能在某些店買到那本書。 |
| **blueprint**<br>[ˋbluˋprɪnt]<br>名 藍圖 | ▶ blueprint for the house<br>房子的藍圖 | ▶ Do you know where we can find the blueprint for the house? 你知道我們可以在哪找到這房子的藍圖嗎？ |
| **fingerprint**<br>[ˋfɪŋgɚˏprɪnt]<br>名 指紋 | ▶ look for fingerprints<br>尋找指紋 | ▶ That detective spent a lot of time looking for fingerprints.<br>那個偵探花了很長的時間尋找指紋。 |
| **footprint**<br>[ˋfʊtˏprɪnt]<br>名 腳印 | ▶ footprints on the ground<br>地上的腳印 | ▶ We followed the footprints on the ground to the warehouse.<br>我們跟著地上的腳印到倉庫。 |

## inter [ˋɪntɚ]

| | | |
|---|---|---|
| **printer**<br>[ˋprɪntɚ]<br>名 印表機 | ▶ color printer<br>彩色印表機 | ▶ I want to buy a color printer to replace my old one.<br>我想買彩色印表機替換我舊的那台。 |
| **winter**<br>[ˋwɪntɚ]<br>名 冬季 | ▶ winter vacation<br>寒假 | ▶ Where are you going on winter vacation?<br>你要去哪過寒假？ |

## inus [ˋaɪnəs]

| | | |
|---|---|---|
| **minus** [ˋmaɪnəs] 介 減 形 減去的 | 1 minus 1 一減一 | One minus one always equals zero. 一減一永遠等於零。 |

## ion [ˋaɪən]

| | | |
|---|---|---|
| **lion** [ˋlaɪən] 名 獅子 | lion's den 獅子窩 | You better stay out of the lion's den if you want to be safe. 如果你想要安全的話，你最好留在獅子窩外。 |

## ip [ɪp]

39

| | | |
|---|---|---|
| **dip** [dɪp] 動 名 浸泡 | dip in 浸泡在 | I'd like to take a dip in the swimming pool. 我想在泡在泳池裡。 |
| **hip** [hɪp] 名 臀部、髖部 | hip bone 髖骨 | He hurt his hip bone playing soccer. 他踢足球時傷了他的髖骨。 |
| **chip** [tʃɪp] 名 炸洋芋片、碎片 | potato chips 洋芋片 | What's your favorite kind of potato chips? 你最喜歡哪一種洋芋片？ |
| **ship** [ʃɪp] 名 船 | abandon ship 棄船 | We must abandon ship now! 我們現在必須要棄船！ |

| | | |
| --- | --- | --- |
| **friendship** [ˋfrɛndʃɪp] 名 友誼 | create new friendships 建立新友誼 | Sometimes it is hard to create new friendships in a new place. 有時在新的環境裡要建立新友誼是很難的。 |
| **hardship** [ˋhɑrdʃɪp] 名 艱難 | during hardship 艱難時 | She tends to lock herself in her room during hardship. 在痛苦時，她會把自已鎖在房裡。 |
| **spaceship** [ˋspesˏʃɪp] 名 太空船 | aboard the spaceship 在太空船上 | The astronauts had an argument aboard the spaceship. 太空人在太空船上發生爭執。 |
| **sportsmanship** [ˋsportsmənˏʃɪp] 名 運動家精神 | good sportsmanship 好的運動家精神 | I like playing against him because he has good sportsmanship. 我喜歡跟他比賽，因為他有良好的運動家精神。 |
| **companionship** [kəmˋpænjənˏʃɪp] 名 伴侶關係 | seek companionship 尋找伴侶關係 | She's trying to seek companionship because she is lonely. 她正試著尋找伴侶關係，因為她很寂寞。 |
| **championship** [ˋtʃæmpɪənˏʃɪp] 名 冠軍身分 | win the championship 贏得冠軍 | They expect to win the championship this year. 他們期待今年能贏得冠軍。 |
| **membership** [ˋmɛmbɚˏʃɪp] 名 會員身分 | apply for membership 申請會員 | What do I need to do to apply for membership? 我需要做什麼才能申請會員呢？ |
| **scholarship** [ˋskɑlɚˏʃɪp] 名 獎學金 | won a scholarship 贏得獎學金 | He won a scholarship to Cambridge University. 他獲得了去劍橋讀書的獎學金。 |

| | | |
|---|---|---|
| **leadership**<br>[`lidəʃɪp]<br>名 領導者的地位 | leadership skills<br>領導能力 | You need to develop your leadership skills in order to get a promotion. 你需要培養你的領導能力以便升遷。 |
| **ownership**<br>[`onəʃɪp]<br>名 所有權 | buy ownership<br>買下所有權 | She will buy ownership of that store, and open a coffee shop. 她將買下那家店的所有權，並開一間咖啡店。 |
| **whip**<br>[hwɪp]<br>動 鞭笞、抽打 | whiplash<br>頸部扭傷 | Because of the car crash, she is suffering from whiplash.<br>她因為車禍的關係，頸部受到扭傷。 |
| **lip**<br>[lɪp]<br>名 嘴唇 | lip stick<br>口紅 | I want to buy a different colored lip stick.<br>我想買一支不同顏色的口紅。 |
| **clip**<br>[klɪp]<br>動 夾住、剪 | clip-on<br>夾式 | He wears a clip-on tie.<br>他戴著夾式領帶。 |
| **rip**<br>[rɪp]<br>動 撕、剝 | rip apart<br>撕開 | She will rip apart all of his pictures when they break up. 他們分手時，她會把他所有的照片都撕毀。 |
| **drip**<br>[drɪp]<br>動 滴下 | drip down<br>滴下 | He stared at the coffee machine, watching the coffee drip down slowly. 他凝視著咖啡機，看著咖啡緩緩滴下。 |
| **grip**<br>[grɪp]<br>動 名 緊握 | strong grip<br>緊握 | He held his racquet with such a strong grip, that his hands were red. 他非常用力緊握著球拍，所以手都變紅了。 |

| | | |
|---|---|---|
| **trip**<br>[trɪp]<br>名 旅行 | take a trip to<br>去…旅行 | Let's take a trip to the beach!<br>讓我們去海邊旅行吧！ |
| **strip**<br>[strɪp]<br>動 剝去 | strip off<br>剝光 | He dreamt that one day she would strip off her clothes in front of him. 他夢想著有一天她能在他面前一絲不掛。 |
| **sip**<br>[sɪp]<br>名 動 啜飲 | take a sip<br>啜飲一小口 | Just take a sip of this love potion, and she'll be yours.<br>只要啜飲一口這愛的魔藥，她將會成為你的。 |
| **tip**<br>[tɪp]<br>名 頂端 動 給小費 | tip of the mountain<br>山頂<br>tip the waitress<br>給女侍者小費 | He tried to plant his flag at the tip of a mountain, but then he cracked. 他試圖把旗子插到山頂上，但後來他放棄了。<br>Don't forget to tip the waitress, or she won't serve you next time you come in.<br>不要忘了給女侍者小費，否則下次你來時，她不會為你服務的。 |
| **fingertip**<br>[ˋfɪŋgɚˏtɪp]<br>名 指尖 | at your fingertips<br>在你的指尖 | The world is at your fingertips so grab it.<br>世界就在你手指尖，要掌握它。 |
| **equip**<br>[ɪˋkwɪp]<br>動 裝備、配備 | well-equipped<br>配備良好的 | She goes to a well-equipped gym, but doesn't do anything but talk to the boys.<br>她去設備良好的健身房，但她什麼運動都不做，只跟男生聊天。 |
| **zip**<br>[zɪp]<br>名 拉鍊 動 拉拉鍊 | zip up your coat<br>拉上外套的拉鍊 | Please zip up your coat. Your shirt is blinding. 請拉上外套的拉鍊，你的襯衫太眩目了。 |

## ipe [aɪp]

| | | |
|---|---|---|
| **pipe**<br>[paɪp]<br>名 導管、煙斗 | ▶ smoking pipe<br>煙斗 | ▶ What did you do with my smoking pipe?<br>你對我的煙斗做了什麼？ |
| **ripe**<br>[raɪp]<br>形 成熟的 | ▶ become ripe<br>變成熟 | ▶ I can't wait until the mangoes become ripe.<br>我等不及芒果成熟。 |
| **stripe**<br>[straɪp]<br>名 條紋 | ▶ striped shirt<br>條紋衫 | ▶ He is a tall man, with blonde hair, blue eyes, pale skin, and he's wearing a striped shirt that looks like a ref's uniform.<br>他長得很高，金髮、藍眼、白皮膚，穿著一件像裁判制服的條紋衫。 |
| **wipe**<br>[waɪp]<br>動 擦拭 | ▶ wipe my eyes<br>擦我的眼睛 | ▶ When I wake up in the morning, I wipe my eyes and try to figure out where I am.<br>我早上醒來時，會擦擦眼，想想自己在哪裡。 |

## ype [aɪp]

| | | |
|---|---|---|
| **type**<br>[taɪp]<br>名 類型 動 打字 | ▶ type with only one hand<br>用一手打字 | ▶ She has learned to type with only one hand.<br>她已經學會用一手打字。 |
| * **stereotype**<br>[ˋstɛrɪə͵taɪp]<br>名 刻板印象 | ▶ racial stereotype<br>種族刻板印象 | ▶ A lot of people believe in racial stereotypes that are unfair and just plain mean.<br>很多人相信不公平且十分惡劣的種族刻板印象。 |

| | | |
|---|---|---|
| **prototype**<br>[`protə͵taɪp]<br>名 原型、標準 | examine the prototype<br>檢查原型 | I asked the boss to examine the prototype and give me her opinion. 我請我老板檢查原型並給予意見。 |

## iption [`ɪpʃən]

| | | |
|---|---|---|
| **subscription**<br>[səb`skrɪpʃən]<br>名 捐款、訂閱 | magazine subscription<br>訂閱雜誌 | He ordered a magazine subscription to "Time" magazine. 他訂閱了時代雜誌。 |
| **description**<br>[dɪ`skrɪpʃən]<br>名 描寫、形容 | beyond description<br>無法描述 | That alien that I saw is beyond description.<br>我看到的那個外星人難以描述。 |
| **prescription**<br>[prɪ`skrɪpʃən]<br>名 處方、規定 | prescription drug<br>處方藥 | That store sells prescription drugs illegally.<br>那間店非法販賣處方藥。 |
| **inscription**<br>[ɪn`skrɪpʃən]<br>名 銘刻、銘文 | inscription on the wall<br>牆上的刻文 | The inscription on the wall says "Go away."<br>牆上刻著「走開」。 |

## ire [aɪr]

| | | |
|---|---|---|
| **dire**<br>[daɪr]<br>形 可怕的、悲慘的 | in dire straits<br>身陷悲慘的困境 | He's been crying all day because he thinks he's in dire straits. 他覺得自己身陷悲慘的困境，已經哭了一整天。 |

| | | |
|---|---|---|
| **fire**<br>[faɪr]<br>名 火 動 射擊 | light a fire<br>點火 | She couldn't light a fire with a match.<br>她不會用火柴點火。 |
| * **hire**<br>[haɪr]<br>名 動 雇用 | taxi for hire<br>供租用的計程車 | Many taxis for hire wait for you outside the airport.<br>許多出租的計程車在機場外等你。 |
| * **admire**<br>[əd`maɪr]<br>動 欽佩、欣賞 | admire nurses for their patience<br>佩服護士的耐心 | I certainly admire nurses for their patience.<br>我當然很佩服護士的耐心。 |
| **vampire**<br>[`væmpaɪr]<br>名 吸血鬼 | turn into a vampire<br>變成吸血鬼 | Sometimes I'm frightened that my friend will turn into a vampire. 有時我很害怕我的朋友會變成吸血鬼。 |
| **aspire**<br>[ə`spaɪr]<br>動 熱望、嚮往 | aspire to be great<br>嚮往成為偉人 | I used to aspire to be great, and then I faced reality.<br>我曾希望成為偉人，但後來我認清了現實。 |
| * **inspire**<br>[ɪn`spaɪr]<br>動 鼓舞、激勵 | inspire the team<br>激勵士氣 | To be a good captain, you need to know how to inspire the team. 要成為一個好隊長，你必須知道如何激勵士氣。 |
| **conspire**<br>[kən`spaɪr]<br>動 同謀、密謀 | conspire against<br>密謀反抗 | I'm not sure why they decided to conspire against me.<br>我不確定為什麼他們決定要密謀反抗我。 |
| **perspire**<br>[pə`spaɪr]<br>動 流汗、辛勞 | constantly perspire<br>不停地流汗 | Even when it's cold out, he constantly perspires.<br>即使天氣冷了，他仍然不停地流汗。 |

| | | |
| --- | --- | --- |
| **desire** [dɪˋzaɪr] 動 名 渴望 | desire for fame 渴望成名 | Her desire for fame got in the way of her studies. 她對成名的渴望妨礙她的求學之路。 |
| **tire** [taɪr] 動 使疲倦、使厭煩 | tire out 讓…十分疲倦 | I know kids tire out their parents, but I think a lot of parents tire out their kids too. 我知道小孩讓父母疲於奔命，但我想很多父母也讓他們的小孩感到很累。 |
| **satire** [ˋsætaɪr] 名 諷刺 | full of satire 充滿諷刺 | That novel is full of satire. 那本小說充滿了諷刺。 |
| * **retire** [rɪˋtaɪr] 動 退休 | retire at an early age 提早退休 | She was lucky enough to retire at an early age. 她是非常幸運的，可以提早退休。 |
| * **entire** [ɪnˋtaɪr] 形 全部的、整個的 | the entire world 全世界 | He had a fear that the entire world would blow up one day. 他害怕有一天世界會爆炸。 |
| * **acquire** [əˋkwaɪr] 動 獲得 | acquire a taste for 開始喜歡 | I have really acquired a taste for “stinky tofu.” 我開始喜歡上臭豆腐了。 |
| * **require** [rɪˋkwaɪr] 動 需要 | require your services 需要你的服務 | When the boss says he requires your services, you should do what he says. 當老板說他需要你的服務時，你應該照他的話做。 |
| **inquire** [ɪnˋkwaɪr] 動 詢問、查問 | inquire about 詢問關於 | She came here to inquire about a weird growth on her toe. 她來這裡詢問腳趾長了怪東西的問題。 |

## irst [ɜst]



| | | |
|---|---|---|
| * **first** [fɜst] 名 第一 形 第一的 | first class 第一堂課、頭等艙 | Flying first class is a luxury. 搭頭等艙是一種奢侈的享受。 |
| **thirst** [θɜst] 名動 口渴、渴望 | thirst for a cold drink 渴望喝冷飲 | This heat is making me feel a thirst for a cold drink. 這個熱度讓我好想喝冷飲。 |

## urst [ɜst]

| | | |
|---|---|---|
| **burst** [bɜst] 動名 爆炸、破裂 | burst out laughing 突然笑起來 | My brother burst out laughing in the middle of the night and woke me up. 我哥半夜突然大笑，把我吵醒。 |

## irth [ɜθ]

| | | |
|---|---|---|
| **birth** [bɜθ] 名 出生 | birth rate 出生率 | The birth rate in the world is declining. 全球出生率正在下降中。 |
| **mirth** [mɜθ] 名 歡笑、高興 | full of mirth 充滿歡笑 | I want to live in a place that's full of mirth. 我想住在充滿歡笑的地方。 |

## earth [ɜθ]

| | | |
|---|---|---|
| **earth**<br>[ɝθ]<br>名 地球 | on earth<br>在地球上 | He is my favorite fat man on earth.<br>他是我在世上最喜歡的胖男人。 |
| **unearth**<br>[ʌn`ɝθ]<br>動 掘出、發現 | unearth the clues<br>找出線索 | She spent years trying to unearth the clues of her ex-boyfriend's murder. 她多年來努力找出前男友兇殺案的線索。 |

## orth [ɝθ]

| | | |
|---|---|---|
| **worth**<br>[wɝθ]<br>名 價值 形 值得 | worth it<br>值得的 | Do you think it's worth it to spend lots of money on shoes?<br>你覺得花很多錢在鞋子上值得嗎? |

## irty [`ɝtɪ]

| | | |
|---|---|---|
| **dirty**<br>[`dɝtɪ]<br>形 髒的 | dirty dishes<br>髒盤子 | Please wash my dirty dishes for me.<br>請幫我洗我的髒盤子。 |
| **thirty**<br>[`θɝtɪ]<br>名 三十 形 三十的 | thirty something<br>三十幾歲 | It seems like most people who are thirty something have families. 好像大部分三十幾歲的人都成家了。 |

## ish [ɪʃ]

| | | |
|---|---|---|
| **dish**<br>[dɪʃ]<br>名 碟、盤 | ▶ main dish<br>主菜 | ▶ The main dish tonight will be cow's intestines served with mixed vegetables.<br>今晚的主菜是牛腸拌蔬菜。 |
| **fish**<br>[fɪʃ]<br>名 魚 | ▶ drink like a fish<br>狂飲 | ▶ If you drink like a fish, you better have someone take you home.<br>如果你狂喝，最好有人帶你回家。 |
| **goldfish**<br>[`gold͵fɪʃ]<br>名 金魚 | ▶ feed the goldfish<br>餵金魚 | ▶ Can you remember to feed the goldfish while I'm gone?<br>我不在時，你會記得餵金魚嗎？ |
| **wish**<br>[wɪʃ]<br>名 願望 動 希望 | ▶ a birthday wish<br>生日願望 | ▶ What is your birthday wish this year?<br>你今年的生日願望是什麼？ |

## ision [`ɪʒən]

| | | |
|---|---|---|
| * **decision**<br>[dɪ`sɪʒən]<br>名 決定 | ▶ make a decision<br>做個決定 | ▶ I can't wait any longer; make a decision or I'm leaving.<br>我不能再等了，做個決定，否則我要走了。 |
| **indecision**<br>[͵ɪndɪ`sɪʒən]<br>名 優柔寡斷 | ▶ indecision of a group<br>團體的優柔寡斷 | ▶ The indecision of a group can waste a lot of time.<br>一群人優柔寡斷會浪費很多時間。 |
| * **precision**<br>[prɪ`sɪʒən]<br>名 精確 | ▶ mechanical precision<br>機器般的精確 | ▶ They put together this car by hand with mechanical precision.<br>他們很精確地用手組合這部車。 |

| | | |
|---|---|---|
| **collision** [kə\`lɪʒən] 名 碰撞 | ▶ collision with a car 與一輛車相撞 | ▶ Thank goodness he survived his collision with a car. 感謝老天他在車禍後生存下來。 |
| **vision** [\`vɪʒən] 名 視力、洞察力 | ▶ man of vision 有遠見之人 | ▶ He is famed for being a man of vision. 他以有遠見出名。 |
| **television** [\`tɛlə͵vɪʒən] 名 電視 | ▶ television set 電視機 | ▶ The television set in our living room blew up. 我們客廳裡的電視機爆炸了。 |
| * **revision** [rɪ\`vɪʒən] 名 修訂、修正 | ▶ after revision 修正後 | ▶ My professor gave me a failing grade on my paper even after revision. 即使在我修正報告後，我的教授還是把我當掉。 |
| **division** [də\`vɪʒən] 名 分開、分割 | ▶ division of property 財產的分配 | ▶ Their family quarreled about the deceased grandfather's division of property. 他們家為了過世祖父的財產分配爭吵。 |
| * **provision** [prə\`vɪʒən] 名 預備 | ▶ make provisions 做準備 | ▶ Wherever you are, you must make provisions. 不論你在哪，你必須隨時做準備。 |
| * **supervision** [͵supɚ\`vɪʒən] 名 管理、監督 | ▶ under strict supervision 在嚴密監督之下 | ▶ In his house, he's under strict supervision. 在他的房子裡，他受到嚴密的監控。 |

## isk [ɪsk]

| | | |
|---|---|---|
| **disk**<br>[dɪsk]<br>名 圓盤 | floppy disk<br>軟碟 | I lost all my files on the floppy disk.<br>我存在軟碟裡的所有檔案都不見了。 |
| **risk**<br>[rɪsk]<br>名 危險、風險 | run the risk of<br>冒…危險 | If you don't practice dancing, you'll run the risk of looking like a fool the next time you dance. 如果你不練習的話，你下次跳舞可能會看起來像個笨蛋。 |

## isky [ˋɪskɪ]

| | | |
|---|---|---|
| **risky**<br>[ˋrɪskɪ]<br>名 危險的、冒險的 | risky business<br>冒險事業 | Dealing drugs is a risky business.<br>買賣毒品是個危險事業。 |

## ism [ˋɪzəm]

| | | |
|---|---|---|
| **racism**<br>[ˋresɪzəm]<br>名 種族歧視 | victim of racism<br>種族歧視的受害者 | You could argue that everyone on this planet has been a victim of racism. 你可以主張這星球上每個人都是種族歧視的受害者。 |
| * **criticism**<br>[ˋkrɪtəˏsɪzəm]<br>名 批評 | harsh criticism<br>嚴厲的批評 | Can you take harsh criticism of your work?<br>你能對你的工作做嚴厲的批評嗎？ |
| **idealism**<br>[aɪˋdiəˏlɪzəm]<br>名 理想主義 | naive idealism<br>天真的理想主義 | Naive idealism doesn't work.<br>天真的理想主義起不了作用。 |

| | | |
|---|---|---|
| **realism** [ˋrɪəlˏɪzəm] 名 現實主義 | ▸ realism period 寫實主義時期 | ▸ She enjoys art from the realism period in France. 她欣賞法國寫實主義時期的藝術。 |
| **socialism** [ˋsoʃəlˏɪzəm] 名 社會主義 | ▸ Marxist socialism 馬克斯社會主義 | ▸ Marxist socialism is still widely studied around the world. 馬克斯社會主義在世上仍被廣泛地研究。 |
| **journalism** [ˋdʒɜnḷˏɪzṃ] 名 新聞業 | ▸ radio journalism 廣播新聞業 | ▸ He is trying to start his career in radio journalism. 他正努力開始他在廣播界的生涯。 |
| **capitalism** [ˋkæpətḷˏɪzəm] 名 資本主義 | ▸ global capitalism 全球資本主義 | ▸ Some people think that global capitalism is the beginning of the end of the world. 有些人認為全球資本主義是世界末日的開端。 |
| **individualism** [ɪndəˋvɪdʒuəlˏɪzəm] 名 個人主義 | ▸ Western individualism 西方個人主義 | ▸ Western individualism can be in opposition to the Chinese sense of community. 西方個人主義與中國共有思想對立。 |
| * **pessimism** [ˋpɛsəmɪzəm] 名 悲觀 | ▸ full of pessimism 充滿悲觀 | ▸ She is so full of pessimism that I have never seen her smile. 她非常悲觀，我從未看過她的笑容。 |
| * **optimism** [ˋɑptəmɪzəm] 名 樂觀 | ▸ lack of optimism 缺乏樂觀 | ▸ His lack of optimism discouraged the group. 他的不樂觀使全隊沮喪。 |
| **communism** [ˋkɑmjuˏnɪzəm] 名 共產主義 | ▸ Chinese communism 中國共產主義 | ▸ What do you know about Chinese communism? 你對中國共產主義知道多少？ |

| | | |
|---|---|---|
| **terrorism** [ˋtɛrə͵rɪzəm] 名 恐怖主義 | fight against terrorism 對抗恐怖主義 | The president is leading the fight against terrorism. 總統率領對抗恐怖主義。 |

## iss [ɪs]

| | | |
|---|---|---|
| **kiss** [kɪs] 動 名 吻 | first kiss 初吻 | When did you have your first kiss? 你的初吻在何時？ |
| **miss** [mɪs] 動 錯過 | miss a train 錯過火車 | Sometimes I want to yell at the top of my lungs when I miss a train. 有時我錯過火車會想放聲大叫。 |
| **dismiss** [dɪsˋmɪs] 動 解雇、解散 | dismiss the cook 解雇廚師<br>class is dismissed 下課 | The head of the household dismissed the cook for the wrong reasons. 主人以不當的理由解雇了廚師。<br>There is nothing that feels as good as when class is dismissed. 沒有什麼事比下課更棒。 |

## issive [ˋɪsɪv]

| | | |
|---|---|---|
| **submissive** [sʌbˋmɪsɪv] 形 服從的、柔順的 | submissive man 服從的男人 | It's odd to see a submissive man in a Chinese family. 在中國家庭裡看到服從的男人是很怪的。 |

# issue [ˋɪʃu]

41

| | | |
|---|---|---|
| **tissue** [ˋtɪʃu] 名 面紙、衛生紙 | tissue paper 衛生紙 | You can buy cheap tissue paper at that store. 你可以在那家店買到便宜的衛生紙。 |
| * **issue** [ˋɪʃu] 動 發佈 名 議題、發行 | the special issue of the magazine 雜誌的特刊<br>a political issue 政治議題 | The special issue of the magazine is already sold out. 雜誌的特刊已經賣光了。<br>He gets loud and excited when a political issue is raised. 當說到政治議題時，他講話大聲又興奮。 |

# ist [ɪst]

| | | |
|---|---|---|
| **fist** [fɪst] 名 拳頭 | clench your fist 握緊你的拳頭 | I saw you clench your fist when you got angry. 我看到你生氣時握緊拳頭。 |
| * **list** [lɪst] 名 表、目錄 | the waiting list 候補名單 | She was put on the waiting list for admission to college. 她被列在進大學的候補名單中。 |
| **mist** [mɪst] 名 薄霧 | through the mist 通過薄霧 | Can you see through the mist? 你可以看穿薄霧嗎？ |
| * **resist** [rɪˋzɪst] 動 抵抗、反抗 | resist the urge 抵抗衝動 | If you want to lose weight, you have to resist the urge of eating too many desserts. 如果你想減重，你必須抵抗吃太多點心的衝動。 |

| | | |
|---|---|---|
| **wrist**<br>[rɪst]<br>名 手腕 | ▶ wrist watch<br>手錶 | ▶ Where can I find a fancy wrist watch for my boyfriend?<br>我可以在哪裡替我男朋友買到別緻的手錶？ |
| * **insist**<br>[ɪn`sɪst]<br>動 堅持 | ▶ insist on<br>堅持 | ▶ My doctor insists on the need for exercise at least 3 times a week. 我的醫生堅持一星期至少要運動三次。 |
| * **consist**<br>[kən`sɪst]<br>動 組成、構成 | ▶ consist of<br>組成 | ▶ That mixture consists of flour, pork, scallions, peaches, and cream. 那個混合物是由麵粉、豬肉、青蔥、桃子和奶油組成。 |
| **persist**<br>[pɚ`sɪst]<br>動 堅持 | ▶ persist on<br>堅持 | ▶ She persists on taking us to the country fair.<br>她堅持帶我們去鄉村市集。 |
| * **assist**<br>[ə`sɪst]<br>動 協助 | ▶ assist someone<br>協助某人 | ▶ How can I assist someone home without any money or transportation? 我要怎麼在沒有錢或交通工具時協助別人回家？ |
| **twist**<br>[twɪst]<br>動 名 扭轉 | ▶ twist my ankle<br>扭到腳踝 | ▶ I think it hurts tremendously when I twist my ankle.<br>我扭到腳踝時痛得不得了。 |
| **exist**<br>[ɪg`zɪst]<br>動 存在、生存 | ▶ exist only on vegetables<br>只靠蔬菜生存 | ▶ Animals that exist only on vegetables are herbivores.<br>只吃蔬菜維生的動物是草食性動物。 |
| **coexist**<br>[`koɪg`zɪst]<br>動 共存 | ▶ coexist harmoniously<br>和諧共存 | ▶ How can animals and humans coexist harmoniously on this planet forever? 動物和人類怎麼可能在這星球上一直和平共存？ |

## istic [ˋɪstɪk]

| | | |
|---|---|---|
| **idealistic** [aɪˏdɪəlˋɪstɪl] 形 理想主義的 | be so idealistic 非常理想主義的 | She is so idealistic in her views. 她的觀點是很理想主義的。 |
| **realistic** [rɪəˋlɪstɪk] 形 現實的 | realistic estimate 現實的判斷 | It's hard to make a realistic estimate of what we will need. 對於我們所需之物做出現實的判斷是很難的。 |
| **unrealistic** [ˏʌnrɪəˋlɪstɪk] 形 不切實際的 | unrealistic goal 不切實際的目標 | You should be careful in making unrealistic goals. 你應該要當心別訂定不切實際的目標。 |
| **optimistic** [ˏɑptəˋmɪstɪk] 形 樂觀的 | optimistic about the future 對未來樂觀 | She feels pretty optimistic about the future. 對於未來她感到相當樂觀。 |
| * **characteristic** [ˏkærəktəˋrɪstɪk] 形 特有的 名 特性 | characteristic of 特有的 | That style of painting is characteristic of that genre. 那畫風是那類作品的特色。 |
| **statistic** [stəˋtɪstɪk] 形 統計的 名 統計值 | statistics for this year 今年的統計數字 | What are the statistics of this year for the sales of this model? 今年這個模型的銷售統計數字是多少？ |
| **artistic** [ɑrˋtɪstɪk] 形 藝術的、美術的 | artistic talent 藝術的天份 | Her many artistic talents surpassed those of her art teachers. 她的藝術天份優於她的藝術老師。 |
| **linguistic** [lɪŋˋgwɪstɪk] 形 語言的、語言學的 | linguistic abilities 語言能力 | He can speak many languages because of his amazing linguistic abilities. 他能講許多語言，因為他有驚人的語言能力。 |

## istory [ˋɪstərɪ]

| | | |
|---|---|---|
| **history** [ˋhɪstərɪ] 名 歷史 | ▶ make history 創造歷史 | ▶ Do you think you can make history by the time you die? 你覺得你能在你死前創造歷史嗎？ |

## ystery [ˋɪstərɪ]

| | | |
|---|---|---|
| **mystery** [ˋmɪstərɪ] 名 神祕的事物 | ▶ mystery novel 推理小說 | ▶ Her favorite kinds of books are the mystery novel. 她喜歡推理小說這類的書。 |

## it [ɪt]

| | | |
|---|---|---|
| **it** [ɪt] 代 它 | ▶ move it 移動它 | ▶ Can you please move it? 可以請你移動它嗎？ |
| **bit** [bɪt] 名 小片、少量 | ▶ a little bit 一點點 | ▶ I'm only concerned a little bit. 我只有一點點擔心。 |
| **fit** [fɪt] 動 與…相稱 形 健康 | ▶ keep fit 保持健康 | ▶ My grandmother, who is 86 years old, still keeps fit. 我祖母八十六歲，仍保持健康體態。 |
| * **benefit** [ˋbɛnəfɪt] 名 利益、義賣 | ▶ go to a benefit 去義賣會 | ▶ We are going to a benefit tonight for breast cancer. 我們今晚要去參加乳癌的義賣會。 |

| | | |
|---|---|---|
| **hit**<br>[hɪt]<br>動 打、打擊 | ▶ hit the wall<br>撞牆 | ▶ He hit the wall on his bicycle.<br>他騎腳踏車撞牆。 |
| **split**<br>[splɪt]<br>動 劈開、切開 | ▶ split up<br>絕交 | ▶ They split up after they had a fight.<br>他們在吵一架後絕交了。 |
| **moonlit**<br>[ˋmunlɪt]<br>形 月光照耀的 | ▶ moonlit nights<br>月光照耀的晚上 | ▶ She often sits outside on her porch, enjoying the moonlit nights. 她常坐在外面的陽台享受月夜的美好。 |
| **sunlit**<br>[ˋsʌnˏlɪt]<br>形 陽光照射的 | ▶ sunlit room<br>陽光照射的房間 | ▶ I love how the living room is a nicely sunlit room.<br>我喜歡客廳有和煦的陽光照射。 |
| * **submit**<br>[səbˋmɪt]<br>動 使服從、提交 | ▶ submit the forms<br>提交表格 | ▶ Where do we submit the forms for the application?<br>我們要在哪交出申請表格？ |
| * **commit**<br>[kəˋmɪt]<br>動 犯罪 | ▶ commit a crime<br>犯罪 | ▶ Would you commit a crime if your life depended on it?<br>如果你藉此維生，你會因而犯罪嗎？ |
| **omit**<br>[oˋmɪt]<br>動 遺漏、刪去 | ▶ omit details<br>遺漏細節 | ▶ He is not thorough; too often he omits details on important things. 他不是很仔細的人，時常在重要的事情上遺漏細節。 |
| * **permit**<br>[pəˋmɪt]<br>動 允許 | ▶ permit them to pass<br>允許他們通過 | ▶ You need to permit them to pass because they are honored guests. 你得准許他們通過，因為他們是貴賓。 |

| | | |
|---|---|---|
| **transmit**<br>[træns`mɪt]<br>動 傳送、傳達 | transmit the signal<br>傳送信號 | We are waiting for them to transmit the signal.<br>我們正等他們傳送信號。 |
| **knit**<br>[nɪt]<br>動 編織 | knit a sweater<br>織毛衣 | He knows how to knit a sweater out of yarn.<br>他知道如何用紗線編毛衣。 |
| **spit**<br>[spɪt]<br>動 吐口水、吐痰 | spit it out<br>一吐為快 | I know you have something to say; please spit it out.<br>我知道你有話要說，請說吧。 |
| * **quit**<br>[kwɪt]<br>動 退出、放棄 | quit smoking<br>戒菸 | He has tried to quit smoking over twenty times, but he just can't do it. 他已試著戒菸二十次以上了，但就是戒不掉。 |
| **acquit**<br>[ə`kwɪt]<br>動 宣告…無罪 | acquit the defendant<br>宣告被告無罪 | The judge acquitted the defendant after long deliberation. 經過冗長的審議，法官宣告被告無罪。 |
| **outwit**<br>[aʊt`wɪt]<br>動 智勝 | outwit the opponent<br>以機智勝過對手 | My coach taught me how to outwit the opponent during the game. 我的教練教我要怎麼在比賽中以機智勝過對手。 |

## itch [ɪtʃ]

| | | |
|---|---|---|
| **itch**<br>[ɪtʃ]<br>名 癢 動 發癢 | scratch an itch<br>抓癢 | It's hard not to scratch an itch.<br>很難不抓癢。 |

| | | |
|---|---|---|
| **ditch**<br>[dɪtʃ]<br>名 溝 | ▶ in a ditch<br>在溝渠中 | ▶ We found him hiding in a ditch, all scared and muddy.<br>我們發現他躲在溝渠中，又怕又髒。 |
| **pitch**<br>[pɪtʃ]<br>動 投擲 | ▶ pitch a ball<br>投球 | ▶ She can pitch a ball so fast it will surprise you.<br>她投球投得很快，會讓你嚇一跳。 |
| * **switch**<br>[swɪtʃ]<br>名 動 開關、轉換 | ▶ switch on the lights<br>打開電燈 | ▶ I was sleeping alone, and then I woke up because someone switched on the lights.<br>我正在睡，後來因為有人打開電燈我就醒了。 |

## ith [ɪθ]

| | | |
|---|---|---|
| **blacksmith**<br>[ˋblæk͵smɪθ]<br>名 鐵匠 | ▶ go to the blacksmith<br>找鐵匠 | ▶ Not many people nowadays go to the blacksmith.<br>現在會去找鐵匠的人不多了。 |

## yth [ɪθ]

| | | |
|---|---|---|
| **myth**<br>[mɪθ]<br>名 神話 | ▶ ancient myth<br>古代神話 | ▶ Do you believe in all of the ancient myths?<br>你相信所有的古代神話嗎？ |

## ither [ˋɪðɚ]

| | | |
|---|---|---|
| **wither** [ˋwɪðɚ] 動 枯萎、凋謝 | ▶ wither away 枯萎 | ▶ Nobody wants to watch his or her loved ones wither away. 沒有人想看著所愛的人變得衰弱。 |

## itic [ˋɪtɪk]

42

| | | |
|---|---|---|
| * **critic** [ˋkrɪtɪk] 名 批評家、評論家 | ▶ film critic 電影評論家 | ▶ I saw a film critic yesterday on TV talking about the politics of movies. 我昨天看電視上有位電影評論家在談論電影的政治。 |

## ytic [ˋɪtɪk]

| | | |
|---|---|---|
| * **analytic** [ˏænḷˋɪtɪk] 形 解析的、分析的 | ▶ analytic reasoning 解析的推論 | ▶ How does someone accurately test your analytic reasoning? 要如何準確地測試你的解析推論？ |

## itical [ˋɪtɪkḷ]

| | | |
|---|---|---|
| * **political** [pəˋlɪtɪkḷ] 形 政治的 | ▶ political reform 政治革新 | ▶ What kind of political reform does he plan to undertake in this campaign? 他計劃在這活動中進行哪種政治革新？ |
| * **critical** [ˋkrɪtɪkḷ] 形 批評的 | ▶ critical of 愛批評的 | ▶ She is so critical of everyone and everything. 她很愛批評每個人每件事。 |

| | | |
|---|---|---|
| **hypocritical** [ˏhɪpəˋkrɪtɪkḷ] 形 偽善的 | ▶ be so hypocritical 非常偽善的 | ▶ He is so hypocritical because he yells at others for smoking, but he smokes too. 他很偽善，因為他對別人抽菸很有意見，可是他自己也抽菸。 |

## ition [ˋɪʃən]

| | | |
|---|---|---|
| * **exhibition** [ˏɛksəˋbɪʃən] 名 展覽、展示會 | ▶ pottery exhibition 陶器展 | ▶ There is a pottery exhibition today at the university. 今天大學有個陶器展。 |
| * **tradition** [trəˋdɪʃən] 名 傳統 | ▶ follow tradition 遵守傳統 | ▶ My parents expect me to follow tradition even though I belong to a different generation. 我的父母期望我遵守傳統，即使我屬於不同的世代。 |
| **addition** [əˋdɪʃən] 名 附加 | ▶ in addition to 除…之外 | ▶ He answers the telephone in addition to bringing tea or coffee to his superiors. 除了倒茶或咖啡給上司外，他也接電話。 |
| * **edition** [ɪˋdɪʃən] 名 版本 | ▶ second edition 第二版 | ▶ This book has done so well, that there is a second edition coming up. 這本書賣得很好，即將有第二版。 |
| **expedition** [ˏɛkspɪˋdɪʃən] 名 遠征、考察 | ▶ expedition to South America 到南美考察 | ▶ They made an expedition to South America and stayed there for good. 他們到南美考察，並永遠留在那裡。 |
| **condition** [kənˋdɪʃən] 名 情況、條件 | ▶ in good condition 狀況好 | ▶ This piano is old, but still in good condition. 這鋼琴雖老舊，但狀況仍然很好。 |

| | | |
|---|---|---|
| **audition** [ɔˋdɪʃən] 名聽覺、試聽 | audition for plays 戲劇的試鏡 | She has tried out for all of the auditions for plays in town. 她參加過城裡所有的戲劇試鏡會。 |
| **nutrition** [njuˋtrɪʃən] 名營養、滋養 | good nutrition 好的營養 | You need to follow good nutrition in order to stay healthy. 你要有好的營養以維持健康。 |
| **acquisition** [ˌækwəˋzɪʃən] 名獲得、取得 | language acquisition 學會語言 | The best way for language acquisition is to study a language in that country. 學會語言最好的方式是在該國學該語言。 |
| **transition** [trænˋzɪʃən] 名過渡、變遷 | tough transition 棘手的過渡時期 | It has been a tough transition moving to a new place. 搬到一個新地方會經歷很棘手的過渡時期。 |
| * **position** [pəˋzɪʃən] 名位置、地位 | high position 地位高 | He is almost immune to the law because of his high position. 因為他的地位很高，他幾乎免受法律的限制。 |
| **composition** [ˌkɑmpəˋzɪʃən] 名寫作、作曲 | musical composition 音樂作曲 | She dreams of becoming famous for her musical composition. 她夢想成為有名的音樂作曲家。 |
| **disposition** [ˌdɪspəˋzɪʃən] 名性格、性情 | lazy disposition 懶惰性格 | His lazy disposition turned off most girls. 他懶惰的個性讓大多數女孩倒胃口。 |
| * **repetition** [ˌrɛpəˋtɪʃən] 名重複 | without repetition 不重複 | Why can't I make you understand what I am saying without repetition? 為何我不能一次就讓你了解我在說什麼？ |

| | | |
|---|---|---|
| * **competition** [ˌkɑmpəˋtɪʃən] 名 競爭 | ▶ close competition 實力相近的競爭 | ▶ This race has been a close competition. 這比賽是實力相近的競爭。 |
| **superstition** [ˌsupɚˋstɪʃən] 名 迷信 | ▶ believe in superstition 迷信 | ▶ Sometimes I wish I didn't believe in superstitions. 有時我希望我不迷信。 |
| **tuition** [tjuˋɪʃən] 名 教學、學費 | ▶ tuition fees 學費 | ▶ The tuition fees at that school are too high; I'll be in debt forever! 那間學校學費太高，我將欠債一輩子！ |

## ician [ˋɪʃən]

| | | |
|---|---|---|
| **magician** [məˋdʒɪʃən] 名 魔術師 | ▶ amateur magician 業餘魔術師 | ▶ The amateur magician made many mistakes, so he became a comedy act instead. 業餘魔術師犯了很多錯，所以反而成為搞笑演出。 |
| * **technician** [tɛkˋnɪʃən] 名 技術人員 | ▶ computer technician 電腦技師 | ▶ The computer technicians at my company play games all the time. 我公司的電腦技師整天玩電動。 |
| **musician** [mjuˋzɪʃən] 名 音樂家 | ▶ talented musician 天才音樂家 | ▶ She is a talented musician, but she doesn't practice enough. 她是位天才音樂家，但她練習不足。 |
| * **politician** [ˌpɑləˋtɪʃən] 名 政治人物 | ▶ crooked politician 欺詐的政客 | ▶ It's a shame there are so many crooked politicians in the world. 世上有這麼多欺詐的政客真是件憾事。 |

## ission [ˋɪʃən]

| | | |
|---|---|---|
| * **mission** [ˋmɪʃən] 名 任務 | on a mission 出任務 | She is on a mission to conquer the world. 她的任務是征服世界。 |
| * **admission** [ədˋmɪʃən] 名 許可 | admission to a university 大學入學許可 | If you receive admission to a university, you should be proud. 如果你收到大學入學許可，你應該感到自豪。 |
| **submission** [sʌbˋmɪʃən] 名 屈從 | brought to submission 屈服 | He was brought to submission from the torture. 他在酷刑下屈服。 |
| **commission** [kəˋmɪʃən] 名 佣金、委任 | pay commission 付佣金 | You have to pay commission, if a broker finds you an apartment. 如果房屋仲介幫你找到公寓，你就必須付佣金。 |
| **permission** [pɚˋmɪʃən] 名 允許、許可 | get permission 獲得許可 | Why do I have to get permission from my parents even at the age 45? 為何我都45歲了還必須得到我父母的允許？ |
| **intermission** [ˏɪntɚˋmɪʃən] 名 間歇、暫停 | during intermission 在休息期間 | There are snacks in the hallway during intermission. 中場休息時間大廳有點心可用。 |
| **transmission** [trænsˋmɪʃən] 名 傳送、傳達 | radio transmission 廣播傳送 | The radio transmission is fuzzy and unclear. 廣播傳送得很模糊，不清楚。 |

## ival [ˋaɪvl̩]

| | | |
|---|---|---|
| **rival**<br>[ˋraɪvl̩]<br>名 競爭者 | your rival<br>你的競爭者 | I heard that your rival really hates you.<br>我聽說你的競爭者真的很恨你。 |
| * **arrival**<br>[əˋraɪvl̩]<br>名 到達 | arrival in Taipei<br>到達台北 | Ever since his arrival in Taipei, he's been talking about meeting you.<br>他一到台北就一直說要跟你見面。 |
| **revival**<br>[rɪˋvaɪvl̩]<br>名 甦醒、復活 | revival of the seventies<br>七十年代的復古 | This lounge looks like a revival of the seventies.<br>這休息室看起來是七十年代的復古風格。 |
| **survival**<br>[sɚˋvaɪvl̩]<br>名 倖存、殘存 | survival of the fittest<br>適者生存 | Do you believe in Darwin's theory of the survival of the fittest?<br>你相信達爾文的適者生存論嗎？ |

## ive [ɪv]

| | | |
|---|---|---|
| * **live**<br>[lɪv] [laɪv]<br>動 活 形 活的 | live longer<br>活得較久 | People now live longer than people did before.<br>人類現在比以前活得久。 |
| * **forgive**<br>[fɚˋgɪv]<br>動 原諒、寬恕 | forgive someone<br>原諒某人 | What does it take for you to forgive someone?<br>你會因為什麼原諒別人？ |
| * **give**<br>[gɪv]<br>動 給 | give someone something<br>給某人某物 | I gave my brother a basketball jersey for his birthday.<br>我送我哥一件籃球衣當生日禮物。 |

| | | |
|---|---|---|
| **outlive** [aʊtˋlɪv] 動 比…活得長 | ▶ outlive your children 比你的小孩活得久 | ▶ It's a terrible feeling to outlive your children. 比自己的小孩活得久感覺很可怕。 |

## iver [ˋaɪvɚ]

| | | |
|---|---|---|
| **diver** [ˋdaɪvɚ] 名 潛水者 | ▶ scuba diver 潛水者 | ▶ He is a scuba diver in the summer and a snow boarder in the winter. 在夏天他是位潛水者，冬天則是滑雪者。 |
| **driver** [ˋdraɪvɚ] 名 駕駛員 | ▶ bus driver 公車司機 | ▶ My school bus driver used to give us candy when we got off the bus. 我學校校車司機過去常在我們下車時給我們糖果。 |
| **screwdriver** [ˋskru͵draɪvɚ] 名 螺絲起子 | ▶ use a screwdriver 使用螺絲起子 | ▶ You need to use a screwdriver to get those screws in. 你要用螺絲起子才能將螺絲旋入。 |

## ivor [ˋaɪvɚ]

| | | |
|---|---|---|
| **survivor** [sɚˋvaɪvɚ] 名 倖存者、生還者 | ▶ last survivor 最後一位倖存者 | ▶ On the adventure to find the sacred treasure, the last survivor died on the way home. 在找尋聖物的冒險旅程中，最後一位倖存者死在回家的路上。 |

## iver [ˋɪvɚ]

| | | |
|---|---|---|
| **shiver** [ˋʃɪvɚ] 動名 發抖、打顫 | ▶ shiver from the cold 冷到發抖 | ▶ I saw him shiver from the cold, and gave him a blanket. 我看他冷到發抖，就給他一件毛毯。 |
| **liver** [ˋlɪvɚ] 名 肝臟 | ▶ liver damage 肝損傷 | ▶ You can get liver damage from drinking too much alcohol. 你喝太多酒會傷肝。 |
| **deliver** [dɪˋlɪvɚ] 動 投遞、傳送 | ▶ deliver a package 送包裹 | ▶ She has to leave early to deliver a package. 她必須早點離開去送包裹。 |
| **quiver** [ˋkwɪvɚ] 動 顫抖、發抖 | ▶ quiver from fear 怕得發抖 | ▶ I was still quivering from fear after the ghost disappeared. 鬼消失後，我仍然怕得發抖。 |

## ivity [ˋɪvətɪ]

43

| | | |
|---|---|---|
| **creativity** [ˏkrieˋtɪvətɪ] 名 創造力 | ▶ lack of creativity 缺乏創造力 | ▶ He told me my painting showed a lack of creativity. 他告訴我，我的畫缺乏創造力。 |
| * **activity** [ækˋtɪvətɪ] 名 活動 | ▶ activity center 活動中心 | ▶ We will meet at the activity center tonight at 6:00 pm. 今晚六點我們將在活動中心見面。 |
| **objectivity** [ˏɑbdʒɛkˋtɪvətɪ] 名 客觀性 | ▶ use objectivity 用客觀性 | ▶ Please use objectivity in your judgment when you look at your friend's work. 在看你朋友的作品時，請客觀判斷。 |

| | | |
|---|---|---|
| **productivity** [ˏprodʌk`tɪvətɪ] 名 生產力 | ▶ high productivity 高生產力 | ▶ There are high productivity levels in this factory, but the workers are overworked. 這工廠有高生產力的水準，但員工卻超時工作。 |
| **sensitivity** [ˏsɛnsə`tɪvətɪ] 名 敏感性 | ▶ low sensitivity 低敏感性 | ▶ Her eyes have a low sensitivity to light. 她的眼睛對光的敏感度很低。 |

## iz [ɪz]

| | | |
|---|---|---|
| **showbiz** [`ʃobɪz] 名 娛樂性行業 | ▶ in showbiz 娛樂業 | ▶ There are a lot of sacrifices you must make in showbiz. 在娛樂業你要付出很多代價。 |
| **quiz** [kwɪz] 名 考查、測驗 | ▶ pop quiz 流行歌曲測驗 | ▶ The teacher gave us a pop quiz in class today. 今天老師上課時給我們作流行歌曲測驗。 |

## is [ɪz]

| | | |
|---|---|---|
| **is** [ɪz] 動 是 | ▶ she is 她是 | ▶ She is funny, pretty, smart, happy, and kind-hearted. 她搞笑、漂亮、聰明、快樂，並且好心。 |
| **his** [hɪz] 代 他的、他的東西 | ▶ his stuff 他的東西 | ▶ You better not touch his stuff or he'll kill you. 你最好不要碰他的東西，否則他會殺了你。 |

## ize [aɪz]

| | | |
|---|---|---|
| * **criticize** [ˋkrɪtɪˏsaɪz] 動 批評、批判 | criticize a friend 批評朋友 | Sometimes you have to criticize a friend if you want to help them. 有時你必須批評朋友，如果你想幫他們。 |
| * **apologize** [əˋpɑləˏdʒaɪz] 動 道歉、認錯 | apologize for your mistake 為你的錯誤道歉 | It's important that you apologize for your mistakes. 為自己的錯誤道歉是很重要的。 |
| **sympathize** [ˋsɪmpəˏθaɪz] 動 同情、憐憫 | sympathize with a friend 體諒朋友 | It feels good to sympathize with a friend over things you both experience. 跟朋友有相同經驗而能體諒朋友是件感覺很好的事。 |
| * **realize** [ˋrɪəˏlaɪz] 動 了解、實現 | realize the truth 了解事實 | He doesn't realize the truth of the matter. 他不了解事情的真相。 |
| * **specialize** [ˋspɛʃəlˏaɪz] 動 專攻 | specialize in 專攻 | What do you specialize in? 你專攻什麼？ |
| **socialize** [ˋsoʃəˏlaɪz] 動 交際 | socialize with 與…交際 | She doesn't like to socialize with them. 她不喜歡跟他們交際。 |
| **penalize** [ˋpinl̩ˏaɪz] 動 對…處刑 | penalize for 處刑 | You will be penalized for bearing false witness. 你會因作偽證而被處刑。 |
| **capitalize** [ˋkæpətl̩ˏaɪz] 動 用大寫書寫、利用 | capitalize on 利用 | Let's capitalize on the fact that they will be in a weak position. 讓我們利用他們即將處於弱勢的事實。 |

| | | |
|---|---|---|
| **stabilize**<br>[ˋstebl̩ˏaɪz]<br>動 使穩定 | ▶ stabilize the crowd<br>穩定人群 | ▶ The police and security guards tried to stabilize the crowd.<br>警察及保全試圖穩定人群。 |
| **mobilize**<br>[ˋmobl̩ˏaɪz]<br>動 動員、調動 | ▶ mobilize people<br>調動人員 | ▶ It's tough to mobilize people especially if they don't want to move. 調動人員是很棘手的，尤其是如果他們不想移動。 |
| **sterilize**<br>[ˋstɛrəˏlaɪz]<br>動 消毒 | ▶ sterilize the needle<br>消毒針 | ▶ You must sterilize the needle before using it.<br>你必須在使用針前消毒它。 |
| **fertilize**<br>[ˋfɝtl̩ˏaɪz]<br>動 使肥沃 | ▶ fertilize the land<br>使土地肥沃 | ▶ The farmers here fertilize the land with cow manure.<br>這裡的農夫用牛糞施肥。 |
| **utilize**<br>[ˋjutl̩ˏaɪz]<br>動 利用 | ▶ utilize space<br>利用空間 | ▶ In small apartments, it's wise to utilize space well.<br>在小公寓裡，善用空間是明智的。 |
| **idolize**<br>[ˋaɪdl̩ˏaɪz]<br>動 把…當偶像崇拜 | ▶ idolize a rock star<br>把搖滾明星當偶像 | ▶ Most girls idolize a rock star at some point in their lives.<br>大部分的女孩在人生某階段會崇拜搖滾明星。 |
| **organize**<br>[ˋɔrgəˏnaɪz]<br>動 組織、安排 | ▶ organize a conference<br>安排會議 | ▶ It will take a lot of planning to organize a conference.<br>安排會議需要很多規劃。 |
| **recognize**<br>[ˋrɛkəgˏnaɪz]<br>動 認出、認識 | ▶ recognize talent<br>辨識天才 | ▶ His job is to recognize talent, and develop their skills.<br>他的工作是辨識天才，並培養他們的才能。 |

|  |  |  |
|---|---|---|
| **colonize** [ˋkɑlə͵naɪz] 動 殖民 | colonize a country 殖民一個國家 | She thinks it is evil to colonize a country. 她認為殖民一個國家是邪惡的。 |
| * **summarize** [ˋsʌmə͵raɪz] 動 總結、概述 | summarize a paragraph 總結文章 | The teacher made the students summarize a paragraph for homework. 老師要學生總結文章作為功課。 |
| * **characterize** [ˋkærəktə͵raɪz] 動 描繪…的特性 | characterize that situation 描繪那狀況 | How would you characterize that situation? 你會怎麼描繪那個狀況？ |
| * **authorize** [ˋɔθə͵raɪz] 動 授權給、批准 | authorize our entrance 批准我們進入 | We waited for the doorman to authorize our entrance. 我們等著守門人讓我們進入。 |
| * **memorize** [ˋmɛmə͵raɪz] 動 記住、背熟 | memorize a poem 記住詩 | She has memorized a poem to recite for him. 她已經把詩背熟，可唸給他聽了。 |
| * **prize** [praɪz] 名 獎賞、獎金 | win the first prize 獲得第一名 | She wants to win the first prize so badly that she will cheat. 她非常想獲得第一名，所以她要作弊。 |
| **size** [saɪz] 名 尺寸、大小 | small-sized 小尺寸 | May I have a small-sized Coke, please? 可以請你給我一杯小可嗎？ |
| **dramatize** [ˋdræmə͵taɪz] 動 戲劇化 | dramatize a novel 將小說改編成戲劇 | That dancing group will dramatize a novel and perform it at school. 那個舞團將把小說搬上舞台，並在學校表演。 |

# ise [aɪz]

| | | |
|---|---|---|
| * **exercise**<br>[ˋɛksɚˏsaɪz]<br>動 名 運動、練習 | ▶ exercise routine<br>運動排程 | ▶ Is your exercise routine appropriate for your age?<br>你的運動排程適合你的年齡嗎？ |
| * **compromise**<br>[ˋkɑmprəˏmaɪz]<br>動 名 妥協、和解 | ▶ make a compromise<br>做出妥協 | ▶ They will make a compromise over where they will eat for dinner.<br>他們會對於晚餐要在哪吃做出妥協。 |
| **despise**<br>[dɪˋspaɪz]<br>動 鄙視、看不起 | ▶ despise a person<br>看不起一個人 | ▶ It's unhealthy to despise a person.<br>看不起一個人是不健康的。 |
| * **rise**<br>[raɪz]<br>動 升起、上漲 | ▶ rise out of bed<br>起床 | ▶ What time do you rise out of bed?<br>你何時起床？ |
| **arise**<br>[əˋraɪz]<br>動 升起、上升 | ▶ arise from<br>自…升起 | ▶ A phoenix will arise from the ashes.<br>鳳凰將浴火重生。 |
| **sunrise**<br>[ˋsʌnˏraɪz]<br>名 日出 | ▶ watch the sunrise<br>看日出 | ▶ We should wake up early and watch the sunrise.<br>我們應該早點起來看日出。 |
| * **comprise**<br>[kəmˋpraɪz]<br>動 包含 | ▶ comprise of<br>包括 | ▶ This mix is comprised of nuts, chocolate chips, and granola bits. 這個混合物包含核果、巧克力片和格蘭諾拉燕麥捲片。 |
| * **advertise**<br>[ˋædvɚˏtaɪz]<br>動 為…做廣告 | ▶ advertise something<br>為某物做廣告 | ▶ How can you advertise something like cigarettes, without playing the devil? 你要怎麼廣告香菸之類的東西而不觸法？ |

| 單字 | 片語 | 例句 |
|---|---|---|
| **guise** [gaɪz] 名 偽裝、外觀 | guise of someone 某人的裝扮 | I saw the guise of someone I know from school, outside my house. 我看到我家外面有人的裝扮很像我認識的學校朋友。 |
| **disguise** [dɪsˋgaɪz] 動 假扮、偽裝 | disguise as 假扮成 | He was disguised as a mailman. 他偽裝成郵差。 |
| * **advise** [ədˋvaɪz] 動 勸告、忠告 | advise someone to 建議某人 | It's not nice to advise someone to do something dangerous. 建議別人做危險的事是不好的。 |
| * **devise** [dɪˋvaɪz] 動 設計、發明 | devise a plan 設想計劃 | We should devise a plan to get out of here. 我們應該設法離開這裡。 |
| **televise** [ˋtɛlə͵vaɪz] 動 電視播送 | televise the ceremony 電視播送典禮 | They will televise the ceremony on channel five. 他們將在第五頻道轉播典禮。 |
| * **revise** [rɪˋvaɪz] 動 修訂、校訂 | revise your essay 修訂你的文章 | If you revise your essay, it will be a work of genius. 如果你修改你的文章，它將會成為絕妙之作。 |
| * **supervise** [ˋsupɚvaɪz] 動 監督、管理 | supervise the staff 管理員工 | He supervises the staff, and the staff hates him. 他管理員工，所以員工恨他。 |
| * **wise** [waɪz] 形 有智慧的、聰明的 | wise woman 聰明的女人 | You will grow up to be a wise woman someday. 有一天你會長大變成一個聰明的女人。 |

| | | |
|---|---|---|
| **likewise**<br>[ˋlaɪk͵waɪz]<br>副 照樣地、也 | do likewise<br>同樣地做 | If you do likewise, you will succeed.<br>如果你也這麼做，你會成功的。 |
| **unwise**<br>[ʌnˋwaɪz]<br>形 不明智的、愚蠢的 | unwise decision<br>不智的決定 | Everybody makes unwise decisions sometimes.<br>每個人有時會做出不智的決定。 |
| **otherwise**<br>[ˋʌðɚ͵waɪz]<br>副 除此以外、否則 | otherwise known as<br>除此以外也稱為 | This gadget is otherwise known as a knife sharpener.<br>這小器具也稱為磨刀器。 |

## izzle [ˋɪzḷ]

| | | |
|---|---|---|
| **drizzle**<br>[ˋdrɪzḷ]<br>動 下毛毛雨 | only drizzle<br>只下毛毛雨 | It's only drizzling.<br>只有下毛毛雨。 |
| **sizzle**<br>[ˋsɪzḷ]<br>動 發出嘶嘶聲 | sizzle on a hot plate<br>在熱盤上嘶嘶作響 | I love to watch my steak sizzle on a hot plate.<br>我喜歡看牛排在熱盤上嘶嘶作響。 |

# 4. 押 O 韻的單字

| | | |
|---|---|---|
| **video** [ˋvɪdɪˏo] 名 錄影、錄影節目 | a video tape 錄影帶 | I saw a video tape of my husband and another woman holding hands. 我看到我先生和別的女人手牽手的錄影帶。 |
| **stereo** [ˋstɛrɪo] 名 立體音響 | stereo equipment 立體音響裝置 | We can use this stereo equipment to hold a party. 我們可以用這個立體音響設備舉辦派對。 |
| * **info** [ˋɪnfo] 名 通知、消息 | personal info 個人資料 | Please write down your personal info on the form. 請在表格內寫下你的個人資料。 |
| **go** [go] 動 去、離去 | go away 離開 | I want you to go away. 我要你走開。 |
| **ago** [əˋgo] 副 在…以前 | three years ago 三年前 | Three years ago, the man escaped from prison. 三年前，這個男人從監獄逃走了。 |
| **radio** [ˋredɪˏo] 名 收音機 | car radio 車上收音機 | On the car radio, he heard that the police were looking for him. 他從車上收音機中聽到警察正在找他。 |
| **studio** [ˋstjudɪˏo] 名 工作室 | art studio 藝術工作室 | He went to his art studio and decided to express himself through his art. 他到藝術工作室去，決定用他的作品表現自己。 |
| **portfolio** [portˋfolɪˏo] 名 卷宗夾、公事包 | put together a portfolio 集結作品 | He put together a portfolio of his work and went to see an art dealer. 他帶作品集去見藝術業者。 |

| | | |
|---|---|---|
| * **ratio**<br>[ˋreʃo]<br>名 比、比例 | the ratio of 3:1<br>三比一的比例 | The art was split between paintings and sculptures, by the ratio of 3:1. 這藝術作品的繪畫與雕塑比例是三比一。 |
| **buffalo**<br>[ˋbʌfḷˏo]<br>名 水牛 | water buffalo<br>水牛 | The dealer thought his best work was a sculpture of a water buffalo. 業者認為他的最佳作品是水牛雕塑。 |
| **hello**<br>[həˋlo]<br>名 感 哈囉 | hello again<br>哈囉 | When I saw her today, she said "hello, again."<br>當我今天看到她時，她說：「哈囉。」 |
| **no**<br>[no]<br>形 副 不、沒有 | no friends<br>沒有朋友 | She is used to having no friends.<br>她習慣沒有朋友。 |
| **so**<br>[so]<br>副 這麼 連 因此 | so what<br>那又怎樣 | A: He bought a million dollar house and a new car. B: So what?<br>A：他買了一棟一百萬的房子和一輛新車。B：那又怎樣？ |

## ow [o]

| | | |
|---|---|---|
| **bow**<br>[bo]<br>名 弓 | bow and arrow<br>弓和箭 | I went to a summer camp where they taught me how to use a bow and arrow.<br>我參加夏令營，在那裡他們教我怎麼射箭。 |
| **rainbow**<br>[ˋrenˏbo]<br>名 彩虹 | over the rainbow<br>在彩虹那端 | There must be a better place somewhere over the rainbow.<br>彩虹那端一定有個更美好的地方。 |

| | | |
|---|---|---|
| **show**<br>[ʃo]<br>動 展示 名 表演 | show off<br>賣弄 | He often shows off his body to impress girls.<br>他常常賣弄他的身體，加深女孩子對他的印象。 |
| **low**<br>[lo]<br>形 低的 | in a low voice<br>小聲 | During the test, he told me the answers in a low voice.<br>考試時他小聲告訴我答案。 |
| **blow**<br>[blo]<br>動 吹、刮 | blow out the candle<br>吹蠟燭 | The birthday boy has to blow out the candles on the cake.<br>生日的小男孩必須把蛋糕上的蠟燭吹熄。 |
| * **below**<br>[bə`lo]<br>介 在…下面 副 下面 | below the ground<br>地面下 | Sometimes I get scared thinking about all the little creatures below the ground. 有時我想到地底下的小生物就害怕。 |
| **flow**<br>[flo]<br>名 流 動 流動 | a flow chart<br>流程圖 | Do you know how to draw a flow chart, or what it is used for? 你知道怎麼畫流程圖，或者它是用來做什麼的嗎？ |
| **overflow**<br>[ˏovə`flo]<br>動 氾濫 | overflow with people<br>人滿為患 | That dance club is so popular that it is overflowing with people.<br>那個舞蹈社很受歡迎，人爆多。 |
| **glow**<br>[glo]<br>動 發光、洋溢 | glow with happiness<br>幸福洋溢 | I know she loves him so much because she glows with happiness when she's with him.<br>我知道她很愛他，因為跟他在一起時她幸福洋溢。 |
| * **slow**<br>[slo]<br>形 慢的、緩緩的 | a slow walker<br>慢走者 | He gets impatient when he is walking with a slow walker.<br>他跟腳程慢的人一起走路會不耐煩。 |

| | | |
|---|---|---|
| **mow** [mo] 動 除草 | mow the lawn ▸ 剪草 | ▸ It's your turn to mow the lawn. 輪到你剪草了。 |
| **know** [no] 動 知道、認識 | know each other ▸ 彼此認識 | ▸ Do you know each other? 你們互相認識嗎？ |
| **snow** [sno] 名 雪 動 下雪 | in the snow ▸ 在雪中 | ▸ Don't forget to wear your snow suit and boots when you play in the snow. 在雪地裡玩時，不要忘了穿雪衣和雪鞋。 |
| **row** [ro] 名 排、列 | in a row ▸ 一排、一連串 | ▸ She won the skating championship five years in a row. 她連續贏了五年的溜冰冠軍。 |
| **crow** [kro] 名 烏鴉 | black crow ▸ 黑烏鴉 | ▸ Some people think it is bad luck to see a black crow. 有些人認為看到烏鴉是不幸的。 |
| **grow** [gro] 動 成長、種植 | grow up ▸ 成長 | ▸ When are you going to grow up? 你什麼時候才會長大？ |
| **throw** [θro] 動 投、擲 | throw a ball ▸ 投球 | ▸ He can throw a ball so far that it's annoying to go fetch it. 他可以把球丟得很遠，以致於去撿回來讓人覺得很煩。 |
| **tow** [to] 動 拖、拉 | tow away your car ▸ 將車子拖走 | ▸ It takes a lot of effort, time, and money to get your car back after they tow away your car. 他們拖吊你的車後，你要領回是很費力費時費錢的。 |

## ough [o]

| | | |
|---|---|---|
| **dough** [do] 名 生麵糰 | ▶ raw dough 生麵糰 | ▶ Raw dough needs to be baked or fried in order to be eaten. 生麵糰需要烤過或炸過才能吃。 |
| **though** [ðo] 連 副 雖然、儘管 | ▶ though it seems 儘管似乎 | ▶ Though it seems you like me, I know you hate me. 儘管你似乎很喜歡我，但我知道其實你恨我。 |
| * **although** [ɔl`ðo] 連 雖然、儘管 | ▶ although you're nice 雖然你很好 | ▶ Although you're nice, I'm not attracted to you. 雖然你是個好人，但我對你沒有感覺。 |

## o [u]

| | | |
|---|---|---|
| * **do** [du] 動 做 | ▶ do homework 做功課 | ▶ Stop watching TV, and do your homework! 不准再看電視，去做功課！ |
| * **undo** [ʌn`du] 動 解開、打開 | ▶ you can't undo 無法回復 | ▶ You can't fix something you can't undo. 有些事覆水難收。 |
| **overdo** [ˏovɚ`du] 動 做得過分 | ▶ decorations are overdone 裝飾太過 | ▶ The party's decorations are overdone. 宴會的裝飾太過度。 |
| **hairdo** [`hɛrˏdu] 名 髮型 | ▶ a new hairdo 新髮型 | ▶ She came in today with a new hairdo. 今天她換了個新髮型。 |

| | | |
|---|---|---|
| **outdo** [ˏaut`du] 動 勝過、超越 | outdo him 勝過他 | He is competitive in his English class, but I always outdo him. 他在英文課表現很好，但我總是勝過他。 |
| * **who** [hu] 代 誰 | who cares 誰在乎 | Who cares if no one likes me? 誰在乎我是不是沒人愛？ |
| * **to** [tu] 介 向、往、到 | from morning to night 從早到晚 | She is so busy from morning to night. 她從早到晚都很忙。 |
| **into** [`ɪntu] 介 到…裡 | into the house 進入房子 | I saw a bear go into the house! 我看到一隻熊進入房子！ |

## oo [u]

| | | |
|---|---|---|
| **taboo** [tə`bu] 名 禁忌 形 禁忌的 | taboo subject 忌諱的主題 | She always brings up taboo subjects and makes people around her feel uncomfortable. 她總是說到忌諱話題，讓她周遭的人很不舒服。 |
| **bamboo** [bæm`bu] 名 竹子 | bamboo furniture 竹製傢俱 | It's hard to find good and cheap bamboo furniture in the United States. 在美國想找到又好又便宜的竹製傢俱是很難的。 |
| * **shampoo** [ʃæm`pu] 動 洗髮 名 洗髮精 | a bottle of shampoo 一瓶洗髮精 | Please get me a bottle of shampoo when you go to the store. 你去店裡時，請幫我買一瓶洗髮精。 |

| | | |
|---|---|---|
| **too**<br>[tu]<br>副 太、也 | too young ▶<br>太年輕 | She is too young for you! ▶<br>她對你而言太年輕了！ |
| **tattoo**<br>[tæ`tu]<br>名 動 紋身、刺青 | a tattoo of a dragon ▶<br>龍的刺青 | He has a tattoo of a dragon on his back. ▶<br>他的背上刺了一條龍。 |
| **zoo**<br>[zu]<br>名 動物園 | in the zoo ▶<br>在動物園裡 | My friends got lost in the zoo. ▶<br>我的朋友們在動物園裡迷路了。 |

## ou [u]

| | | |
|---|---|---|
| **you**<br>[ju]<br>代 你、你們 | thank you ▶<br>謝謝你 | Thank you very much. ▶<br>非常感謝你。 |

## ough [u]

| | | |
|---|---|---|
| **through**<br>[θru]<br>介 穿過、通過 | run through the woods ▶<br>穿過森林 | We ran through the woods screaming because we thought a wolf was chasing us. ▶<br>我們尖叫著穿過森林，因為我們以為有一隻狼在追我們。 |

## oach [otʃ]

| | | |
|---|---|---|
| **coach**<br>[kotʃ]<br>名 教練 | football coach<br>足球教練 | The football coach at our school is really popular but dumb. 我們學校的足球教練很受歡迎但很腦殘。 |
| **cockroach**<br>[ˋkɑk͵rotʃ]<br>名 蟑螂 | a large cockroach<br>大蟑螂 | I saw a large cockroach under the sink!<br>我看到水槽底下有一隻大蟑螂！ |
| **reproach**<br>[rɪˋprotʃ]<br>動 名 責備、斥責 | look of reproach<br>責備的眼神 | Please don't give me that look of reproach, mom.<br>媽，請不要用責備的眼神看著我。 |
| * **approach**<br>[əˋprotʃ]<br>動 接近、靠近 | approach the house<br>靠近房子 | Someone is approaching the house.<br>有人靠近房子。 |

## oax [oks]

 45

| | | |
|---|---|---|
| **coax**<br>[koks]<br>動 哄誘 | coax a smile from a girl<br>哄女生笑 | He is so charming, that he doesn't have to try to coax a smile from a girl.<br>他很迷人，不需要哄女生笑。 |
| * **hoax**<br>[hoks]<br>名 動 欺騙、愚弄 | turn out to be a hoax<br>結果是騙人的 | That diet on TV turned out to be a hoax.<br>電視上那個減肥食品是騙人的。 |

## ob [ɑb]

| | | |
|---|---|---|
| **job**<br>[dʒab]<br>名 工作、職業 | a good job<br>一份好工作 | It's hard to find a good job now.<br>現在要找到一份好工作很難。 |
| **mob**<br>[mab]<br>名 暴民、烏合之眾 | face a mob<br>面對暴民 | Do you think you can face a mob by yourself?<br>你認為你可以自己面對暴民嗎？ |
| **snob**<br>[snab]<br>名 勢利鬼 | a snob<br>勢利鬼 | She is a snob that looks down on everyone.<br>她是一個看不起每個人的勢利鬼。 |
| **rob**<br>[rab]<br>動 搶劫 | rob him of his money<br>搶他的錢 | She is only going out with him to rob him of his money.<br>她跟他出去只是在削他的錢。 |
| **throb**<br>[θrab]<br>動 名 跳動、抽痛 | his leg is throbbing<br>他的腿在抽痛 | Someone pushed him down and he broke his leg, so his leg is throbbing. 他被推下去跌斷了腿，所以他的腿正在抽痛。 |
| **heartthrob**<br>[`hart͵θrab]<br>名 心跳、迷戀對象 | her heartthrob<br>她迷戀的對象 | Brad Pitt has been her heart-throb for years.<br>布萊德彼特是她多年來迷戀的男人。 |
| **sob**<br>[sab]<br>動 名 嗚咽、啜泣 | sob in the corner<br>在角落啜泣 | Don't sob in the corner; it'll be alright.<br>不要在角落啜泣，沒事的。 |

## obby [`abɪ]

| | | |
|---|---|---|
| **hobby** [ˋhɑbɪ] 名 嗜好 | ▶ hobby of collecting stamps 集郵的嗜好 | ▶ He has a hobby of collecting stamps. 他有集郵的嗜好。 |
| **lobby** [ˋlɑbɪ] 名 大廳、門廊 | ▶ hotel lobby 飯店大廳 | ▶ Meet me in the hotel lobby at six p.m. 晚上六點在飯店大廳見。 |

## obe [ob]

| | | |
|---|---|---|
| * **globe** [glob] 名 球、地球 | ▶ in many parts of the globe 全球許多地方 | ▶ People practice Hinduism in many parts of the globe. 全球很多地方的人信印度教。 |
| **earlobe** [ˋɪr͵lob] 名 耳垂 | ▶ long earlobes 長耳垂 | ▶ Chinese say that long ear-lobes are good luck. 中國人說有長耳垂是福氣。 |
| **robe** [rob] 名 罩袍 | ▶ long robe 長袍 | ▶ She was wearing a long robe when she got shot. 她被射殺時穿著長袍。 |
| **wardrobe** [ˋwɔrd͵rob] 名 衣櫥 | ▶ in the wardrobe 在衣櫥裡 | ▶ You can find my boots in the wardrobe. 你可以在衣櫥裡找到我的靴子。 |
| **bathrobe** [ˋbæθ͵rob] 名 浴袍 | ▶ red bathrobe 紅色浴袍 | ▶ My wife and I have matching red bathrobes. 我太太和我有相同的紅色浴袍。 |

| | | |
|---|---|---|
| **probe**<br>[prob]<br>名 探針 | ▶ pass the doctor a probe<br>遞給醫生探針 | ▶ The nurse passed the doctor a probe.<br>護士遞給醫生探針。 |

## oble [ˋobḷ]

| | | |
|---|---|---|
| **noble**<br>[ˋnobḷ]<br>形 高貴的 | ▶ noble man<br>高尚的人 | ▶ That noble man saved my life.<br>那位高尚的人救了我。 |

## obal [ˋobḷ]

| | | |
|---|---|---|
| * **global**<br>[ˋglobḷ]<br>形 全世界的 | ▶ global economy<br>全球經濟 | ▶ The global economy is taking over local economies.<br>全球經濟正逐漸取代地方經濟。 |

## obile [ˋobɪl]

| | | |
|---|---|---|
| **mobile**<br>[ˋmobil]<br>形 可動的、移動式的 | ▶ mobile phone<br>行動電話 | ▶ Nowadays it's rare not to have a mobile phone.<br>現在沒有行動電話是很稀奇的事。 |
| **immobile**<br>[ɪmˋmobil]<br>形 不能動的、固定的 | ▶ immobile statue<br>固定的雕像 | ▶ You can't move that immobile statue.<br>你無法移動那座固定的雕像。 |

## ocal [ˋokḷ]

| | | |
|---|---|---|
| **focal**<br>[ˋfokḷ]<br>形 焦點的 | ▶ focal point<br>焦點 | ▶ Learning new vocabulary is the focal point of this book.<br>這本書的焦點在於學習新字彙。 |
| * **local**<br>[ˋlokḷ]<br>形 本地的 | ▶ local residents<br>本地居民 | ▶ The local residents here complain about the stench of the sewer.<br>本地居民抱怨下水道的惡臭。 |
| **vocal**<br>[ˋvokḷ]<br>形 聲音的 | ▶ vocal cord<br>聲帶 | ▶ You might strain your vocal cord if you yell for a while.<br>如果你大叫個一會兒，你的聲帶可能會受損。 |

## osity [ˋɑsətɪ]

| | | |
|---|---|---|
| **curiosity**<br>[͵kjʊrɪˋɑsətɪ]<br>名 好奇心 | ▶ out of curiosity<br>出於好奇心 | ▶ Out of curiosity, are you married?<br>出於好奇問一下，你結婚了嗎？ |
| **generosity**<br>[͵dʒɛnəˋrɑsətɪ]<br>名 寬宏大量、慷慨 | ▶ countless generosities<br>不勝枚舉的慷慨行為 | ▶ I can't thank you enough for your countless generosities.<br>你不勝枚舉的慷慨行為令我無以銘謝。 |

## ock [ɑk]

| | | |
|---|---|---|
| **peacock**<br>[ˋpikɑk]<br>名 孔雀、愛炫耀者 | ▶ beautiful peacock<br>美麗的孔雀 | ▶ I saw a beautiful peacock next to the lake.<br>我在湖邊看見一隻美麗的孔雀。 |

| | | |
|---|---|---|
| **dock**<br>[dɑk]<br>名 碼頭、港區 | on the dock<br>在碼頭上 | There are several food stands on the dock.<br>碼頭上有些攤子。 |
| **shock**<br>[ʃɑk]<br>名 動 衝擊、震動 | shocking news<br>令人震撼的消息 | We didn't know how to react to the shockings news. 這個震撼的消息讓我們不知如何反應。 |
| **aftershock**<br>[ˋæftɚˏʃɑk]<br>名 餘震 | probability of aftershocks<br>餘震的可能 | There is a high probability of aftershocks in the next 2 weeks.<br>接下來兩個星期餘震的可能性很高。 |
| * **lock**<br>[lɑk]<br>動 名 鎖 | lock up<br>鎖起來 | Make sure to lock up the doors before you leave.<br>你離開前要確定門有鎖好。 |
| * **block**<br>[blɑk]<br>動 阻礙 名 街區 | block up<br>阻礙 | You're blocking up the entry-ways; move aside.<br>你擋住入口了，閃到旁邊去。 |
| **roadblock**<br>[ˋrodˏblɑk]<br>名 路障、障礙物 | put up roadblocks<br>設置路障 | You have to detour and use another route because they put up roadblocks over there. 你必須繞道走別條路，因為那裡設了路障。 |
| **clock**<br>[klɑk]<br>名 時鐘 | alarm clock<br>鬧鐘 | I slept through my alarm clock this morning.<br>今天早上我睡過頭了。 |
| **gridlock**<br>[ˋgrɪdˏlɑk]<br>名 交通阻塞、僵局 | stuck in gridlock<br>塞在車陣中 | It's very bad to be stuck in gridlock and in a hurry.<br>趕時間時塞在車陣中感覺很糟。 |

| | | |
|---|---|---|
| **flock**<br>[flɑk]<br>名 羊群、群 | ▶ flock of sheep<br>羊群 | ▶ The wolf chased the flock of sheep in the fields.<br>狼在原野上追逐羊群。 |
| **mock**<br>[mɑk]<br>動 嘲弄、模仿 | ▶ mock other people<br>嘲笑他人 | ▶ It's not nice to mock other people.<br>嘲笑他人是不好的。 |
| **knock**<br>[nɑk]<br>動 碰擊、打 | ▶ knock on the head<br>打頭 | ▶ We knocked the thief on the head with a baseball bat.<br>我們用球棒打小偷的頭。 |
| **sock**<br>[sɑk]<br>名 短襪 | ▶ pair of socks<br>一雙襪子 | ▶ The pair of socks I'm wear-ing now have holes in them.<br>我穿的這雙襪子有破洞。 |
| * **stock**<br>[stɑk]<br>動 貯存 名 股票 | ▶ stocks of the company<br>公司的股票 | ▶ As an employee, you will get stocks of the company.<br>身為員工你將會獲得公司的股票。 |

## ocket [ˋɑkɪt]

| | | |
|---|---|---|
| **pocket**<br>[ˋpɑkɪt]<br>名 口袋 | ▶ a pocket dictionary<br>口袋型字典 | ▶ He always carries around a pocket dictionary.<br>他總是隨身帶著小字典。 |
| **pickpocket**<br>[ˋpɪk͵pɑkɪt]<br>名 扒手 | ▶ three pickpockets<br>三名扒手 | ▶ Three pickpockets surrounded me and took my watch, wallet, and necklace. 三名扒手圍住我，拿走我的手錶、錢包和項鍊。 |

| | | |
|---|---|---|
| **rocket**<br>[`rakɪt]<br>名 火箭 | send a rocket to the moon<br>將火箭發送到月球 | We tried to send a rocket to the moon.<br>我們努力將火箭發送到月球。 |

## ocracy [`akrəsɪ]

| | | |
|---|---|---|
| **democracy**<br>[dɪ`makrəsɪ]<br>名 民主 | new democracy<br>新的民主國家 | This government is a new democracy.<br>這個政府是新的民主國家。 |
| **aristocracy**<br>[ˏærəs`takrəsɪ]<br>名 貴族、特權階級 | old aristocracy<br>舊貴族階級 | There are people of the old aristocracy here at this function.<br>這場宴會裡有舊貴族階級的人。 |
| **autocracy**<br>[ɔ`takrəsɪ]<br>名 獨裁、專制制度 | overthrow the autocracy<br>推翻專制制度 | The rebels are trying to overthrow the autocracy.<br>反抗軍正試圖推翻專制制度。 |

## ocrisy [`akrəsɪ]

| | | |
|---|---|---|
| **hypocrisy**<br>[hɪ`pakrəsɪ]<br>名 偽善、虛偽 | hypocrisy of the government<br>政府的虛偽 | I don't think we can ever rectify the hypocrisy of the government.<br>我認為我們無法糾正政府的虛偽。 |

## ottle [`atl̩]

| | | |
|---|---|---|
| **bottle** [ˋbɑtḷ] 名 瓶子 | ▶ a bottle of water 一瓶水 | ▶ Where can I buy a bottle of water around here? 這附近哪裡可以買到瓶裝水？ |

## odel [ˋɑdḷ]

| | | |
|---|---|---|
| * **model** [ˋmɑdḷ] 名 模型、原型 | ▶ airplane model 飛機模型 | ▶ He loved to play with airplane models when he was a young boy. 他還是小男孩時愛玩飛機模型。 |

## ode [od]

| | | |
|---|---|---|
| * **code** [kod] 名 代號、密碼 | ▶ send the message in code 用密碼傳送訊息 | ▶ They sent the message in code so I can't read it. 他們用密碼傳送訊息，所以我無法解讀。 |
| **decode** [ˋdiˋkod] 動 解碼 | ▶ decode the telegram 解讀電報 | ▶ Can you decode the telegram for me? 你可以幫我解讀電報嗎？ |
| **explode** [ɪkˋsplod] 動 使爆炸、爆發 | ▶ watch a bomb explode 看到炸彈爆炸 | ▶ Have you ever watched a bomb explode before? 你之前曾看過炸彈爆炸嗎？ |
| * **mode** [mod] 名 方法 | ▶ mode of travel 旅行的方式 | ▶ What's your mode of travel? 你的旅行方式是哪一種？ |

## oad [od]



| | | |
|---|---|---|
| * **load** [lod] 動 裝載 名 載重 | load up the truck 裝貨到卡車 | They loaded up the truck with illegal firearms. 他們將非法軍火裝到卡車上。 |
| **unload** [ʌn`lod] 動 卸下貨物 | unload the ship 卸船上的貨 | It took hours to unload the ship. 卸船上的貨要花好幾個小時。 |
| **road** [rod] 名 路、公路 | on the road 在旅途中 | We have been on the road for two months. 我們已經旅行兩個月了。 |
| **crossroad** [`krɔs͵rod] 名 十字路口 | reach a crossroads 到達十字路口 | When you reach a crossroads up ahead, take a left. 你到前面的十字路口時向左轉。 |
| **toad** [tod] 名 蟾蜍 | a large toad 大蟾蜍 | A large toad jumped in front of me and I stepped on it. 大蟾蜍跳到我面前，我就把它踩住。 |

## odge [ɑdʒ]

| | | |
|---|---|---|
| **dodge** [dɑdʒ] 動 名 閃開、躲開 | dodge the ball 躲開球 | You better dodge the ball when he throws it at you or you'll be really hurt. 當他朝你丟球你最好躲開，不然你會受傷。 |

## odious [`odɪəs]

| | | |
|---|---|---|
| **melodious** [mə`lodɪəs] 形 旋律優美的 | the melodious notes 旋律優美的曲調 | The melodious notes soothed me. 旋律優美的曲調安撫了我。 |

## ody [`adɪ]

| | | |
|---|---|---|
| **body** [`badɪ] 名 身體 | his whole body 他的全身 | He had hives all over his whole body. 他全身上下長了蕁麻疹。 |
| **somebody** [`sʌm͵badɪ] 代 某人 名 重要人物 | somebody in television 電視界大人物 | She wants to meet somebody in television before she dies. 她想在死前見到電視界的大人物。 |
| **antibody** [`æntɪ͵badɪ] 名 抗體 | virus antibody 病毒抗體 | Scientists are still looking for the virus antibody. 科學家仍在尋找病毒抗體。 |
| **embody** [ɪm`badɪ] 動 體現、使具體化 | embody the spirit of freedom 實踐自由精神 | Some people would argue that the United States of America does not embody the spirit of freedom. 有些人認為美國沒有實踐自由精神。 |
| **nobody** [`nobadɪ] 代 沒有人 名 小人物 | a nobody 默默無聞的人 | I don't want to be a nobody when I grow up. 當我長大後，我不想成為默默無聞的人。 |
| **anybody** [`ɛnɪ͵badɪ] 代 任何人 | didn't meet anybody 沒遇見任何人 | She didn't meet anybody there. 她在那裡沒遇見任何人。 |

| | | |
|---|---|---|
| **everybody** [ˋɛvrɪˏbɑdɪ] 代 每個人 | ▶ everybody agrees 每個人都同意 | ▶ Everybody agrees with him. 每個人都同意他。 |

## aughty [ˋɔtɪ]

| | | |
|---|---|---|
| **haughty** [ˋhɔtɪ] 形 高傲的、傲慢的 | ▶ haughty attitude 高傲的態度 | ▶ He has a haughty attitude that makes everyone hate him. 他高傲的態度讓每個人都討厭他。 |
| **naughty** [ˋnɔtɪ] 形 頑皮的、淘氣的 | ▶ a naughty boy 頑皮的小男孩 | ▶ He didn't get anything for Christmas from Santa Claus because he was a naughty boy. 他沒有拿到聖誕老人送的禮物，因為他是頑皮的小男孩。 |

## off [ɔf]

| | | |
|---|---|---|
| **off** [ɔf] 副 離開、切斷 | ▶ turn off 離開 | ▶ Turn off the freeway at exit 3. 在三號出口下高速公路。 |
| **kickoff** [ˋkɪkˏɔf] 名 開球、開始 | ▶ kickoff of the soccer game 足球賽開球 | ▶ I don't want to miss the kick-off of the soccer game. 我不想錯過足球賽開球。 |
| **liftoff** [ˋlɪftˏɔf] 名 起飛、發射 | ▶ liftoff of a space shuttle 太空梭發射 | ▶ Many people wait for hours to see the liftoff of a space shuttle. 許多人等了好幾小時要看太空梭發射。 |

| | | |
|---|---|---|
| **cutoff** [ˋkʌtˏɔf] 名 切斷 | cutoff point 臨界點 | What is the cutoff point for the incoming government funds? 政府資金收入的臨界點是什麼？ |

## ough [ɔf]

| | | |
|---|---|---|
| **cough** [kɔf] 名 動 咳嗽 | have a cough 咳嗽 | She has had a cough for almost a week. 她已經咳嗽快一個禮拜了。 |

## often [ˋɔfən]

| | | |
|---|---|---|
| **often** [ˋɔfən] 副 常常、時常 | very often 時常 | He goes to see his grandmother in the nursing home very often. 他常去療養院看他的祖母。 |
| **soften** [ˋsɔfən] 動 變柔和 | soften the blow 使打擊變小 | She tried to think of someway to soften the blow of breaking up with him. 她努力想辦法讓跟他分手的打擊不那麼大。 |

## offin [ˋɔfɪn]

| | | |
|---|---|---|
| **coffin** [ˋkɔfɪn] 名 棺材 | wood coffin 木製棺材 | That funeral home over there specializes in wood coffins. 那邊那家殯儀館專製木製棺材。 |

## og [ɔg]

| | | |
|---|---|---|
| **dog**<br>[dɔg]<br>名 狗 | dog food<br>狗食 | He sometimes eats dog food to disgust his friends.<br>有時他吃狗食讓他的朋友作嘔。 |
| **watchdog**<br>[`watʃ͵dɔg]<br>名 看門狗、監視人 | a mean watchdog<br>暴躁的看門狗 | There is a mean watchdog at that house that will eat you alive if you try to break in.<br>在那房子有隻暴躁的看門狗，如果你試圖闖入，牠會把你活生生吃掉。 |
| **fog**<br>[fɔg]<br>名 霧氣 | the heavy fog<br>濃霧 | We were scared because we couldn't see anything through the heavy fog.<br>濃霧之中我們看不到任何東西，所以我們很害怕。 |
| **log**<br>[lɔg]<br>名 原木、日誌 | made with logs<br>用原木製成<br>the details in the log<br>日誌中的細節 | Look for a cabin made with logs at the edge of the river.<br>在河邊尋找用原木做的小屋。<br>They looked through the details in the log of the sunken ship, but still couldn't tell why the ship sunk.<br>他們看過了沈船的日誌細節，但仍然無法確定為何船會沈沒。 |
| **catalog**<br>[`kætəlɔg]<br>名 目錄 | summer catalog<br>夏季型錄 | Did you see that cute pink strapless dress in the summer catalog?<br>你有看到夏季型錄裡那件可愛的粉紅色無肩帶洋裝嗎？ |
| **clog**<br>[klɔg]<br>動 堵塞 | clog with<br>被…堵塞 | I think the shower drain is clogged with hair.<br>我想浴室排水孔被頭髮堵住了。 |

| | | |
|---|---|---|
| **frog**<br>[frɔg]<br>名 青蛙 | ▶ slimy frog<br>黏答答的青蛙 | ▶ He used to keep slimy frogs as pets.<br>他曾經養過黏答答的青蛙當寵物。 |

## ogue [ɔg]

| | | |
|---|---|---|
| * **dialogue**<br>[ˋdaɪə͵lɔg]<br>名 對話 | ▶ written in dialogue<br>以對白寫成 | ▶ Plays are mostly written in dialogue.<br>劇本大部分以對白寫成。 |
| **monologue**<br>[ˋmɑnl̩͵ɔg]<br>名 獨白 | ▶ in her monologue<br>在她的獨白 | ▶ She professed her love for the villain in her monologue.<br>她在獨白中表示她對壞人的愛。 |
| **prologue**<br>[ˋpro͵lɔg]<br>名 序言 | ▶ the prologue to the play<br>戲劇的序言 | ▶ The prologue to the play included some background of the story.<br>戲劇的序言包括故事的一些背景。 |

## oggy [ˋɑgɪ]

| | | |
|---|---|---|
| **foggy**<br>[ˋfɑgɪ]<br>形 多霧的、模糊的 | ▶ a foggy morning<br>多霧的早晨 | ▶ I like waking up in a foggy morning.<br>我喜歡在多霧的早晨醒來。 |
| **smoggy**<br>[ˋsmɑgɪ]<br>形 煙霧彌漫的 | ▶ a smoggy city<br>煙霧彌漫的城市 | ▶ London is a smoggy city.<br>倫敦是座煙霧彌漫的城市。 |

## ogical [ˋɑdʒɪkḷ]

| | | |
|---|---|---|
| **logical** [ˋlɑdʒɪkḷ] 形 合邏輯的 | ▶ a logical result 合邏輯的結果 | ▶ This was a logical result of their former actions. 他們前次行動的結果合乎邏輯。 |
| **illogical** [ɪˋlɑdʒɪkḷ] 形 不合邏輯的 | ▶ an illogical explanation 不合邏輯的解釋 | ▶ Some people don't believe that things can happen with an illogical explanation. 有些人不相信會有不合邏輯的事情發生。 |
| **astrological** [ˏæstrəˋlɑdʒɪkḷ] 形 占星學的 | ▶ astrological sign 星座 | ▶ Since my astrological sign is Pisces, people say I'm romantic. 因為我的星座是雙魚座，所以大家都說我很浪漫。 |

## ography [ˋɑgrəfɪ]

| | | |
|---|---|---|
| **geography** [ˋdʒɪˋɑgrəfɪ] 名 地理學、地形 | ▶ world geography 世界地理學 | ▶ We studied world geography when I was in ninth grade. 我們九年級時上世界地理學。 |
| **biography** [baɪˋɑgrəfɪ] 名 傳記 | ▶ read a biography 閱讀傳記 | ▶ Their new assignment is to read a biography on anyone they choose. 他們新的作業是閱讀自選的人物傳記。 |
| **autobiography** [ˏɔtəbaɪˋɑgrəfɪ] 名 自傳 | ▶ Mark Twain's autobiography 馬克吐溫的自傳 | ▶ Mark Twain's autobiography fascinated a lot of people. 馬克吐溫的自傳讓許多人著迷。 |
| **photography** [fəˋtɑgrəfɪ] 名 攝影 | ▶ wildlife photography 野生生物的攝影 | ▶ She wants to take wildlife photography seriously and make it a career. 她想認真看待野生生物攝影這件事情，並以此為職志。 |

## ogue [og]



| | | |
|---|---|---|
| **rogue** [rog] 名 流氓 | young rogue 年輕流氓 | The police look for young rogues who are up too late at night. 警察尋找深夜還在閒晃的年輕流氓。 |
| **vogue** [vog] 名 流行、時髦 | Vogue magazine Vogue雜誌 | Vogue magazine is one of the oldest fashion magazines in print. Vogue雜誌是出刊最久的時尚雜誌之一。 |

## oice [ɔɪs]

| | | |
|---|---|---|
| * **choice** [tʃɔɪs] 名 選擇 | make a choice 作個抉擇 | You have to make a choice between him and me. 你必須在他和我之間作個抉擇。 |
| **rejoice** [rɪˋdʒɔɪs] 動 欣喜、高興 | rejoice at the good news 為好消息高興 | After he found out about his sister's marriage, he rejoiced at the good news. 知道姊姊結婚的好消息後他很高興。 |
| * **voice** [vɔɪs] 名 聲音 | cheerful voice 愉快的聲音 | It's so nice to hear your cheerful voice over the phone. 聽到你在電話那頭愉快的聲音真好。 |

## oid [ɔɪd]

| | | |
|---|---|---|
| **tabloid** [ˋtæblɔɪd] 名 小報 | read the tabloids 閱讀小報 | She thinks that reading the tabloids is the same thing as reading the news. 她認為看小報跟看新聞是一樣的事。 |

| | | |
|---|---|---|
| **Polaroid**<br>[`polə͵rɔɪd]<br>名 拍立得 | Polaroid film<br>拍立得底片 | I ran out of Polaroid film and had to get more. 我用完了拍立得底片，必須再買一些。 |
| **void**<br>[vɔɪd]<br>形 空的、缺乏的 | void of interest<br>缺乏興趣 | My children are void of interest when it comes to studying Science.<br>我的小孩對學習科學缺乏興趣。 |
| * **avoid**<br>[ə`vɔɪd]<br>動 避開、避免 | avoid an accident<br>避免車禍 | Please avoid an accident when driving your car by being extra careful, OK? 開車請格外小心，以免發生車禍，好嗎？ |

## oil [ɔɪl]

| | | |
|---|---|---|
| **oil**<br>[ɔɪl]<br>名 油、石油 | out of oil<br>沒油 | Please run to the store because we're out of oil.<br>請快跑去店裡，因為我們沒油了。 |
| **boil**<br>[bɔɪl]<br>動 沸騰、烹煮 | boil an egg<br>煮顆蛋 | She boils an egg for breakfast every day.<br>她每天煮顆蛋當早餐。 |
| **spoil**<br>[spɔɪl]<br>動 損壞、寵壞 | spoil their child<br>寵壞他們的小孩 | They spoil their child by getting him everything he wants.<br>他們寵壞小孩，讓他予取予求。 |
| **turmoil**<br>[`tɝmɔɪl]<br>名 騷動、混亂 | in turmoil<br>在混亂中 | The political situation in that country is in turmoil.<br>這個國家的政治情勢處於一片混亂。 |

| | | |
|---|---|---|
| **broil**<br>[brɔɪl]<br>動 烤、炙 | broiled potatoes<br>烤馬鈴薯 | My mom makes really good broiled potatoes.<br>我媽會做很好吃的烤馬鈴薯。 |
| **soil**<br>[sɔɪl]<br>名 土壤 | fertile soil<br>肥沃的土壤 | There is no fertile soil in the desert.<br>沙漠中沒有肥沃的土壤。 |

## oyal [ˋɔɪəl]

| | | |
|---|---|---|
| **loyal**<br>[ˋlɔɪəl]<br>形 忠誠的、忠心的 | loyal to her husband<br>對丈夫忠誠 | She has been loyal to her husband all of her life.<br>她終其一生對丈夫忠誠。 |
| **disloyal**<br>[dɪsˋlɔɪəl]<br>形 不忠誠的 | disloyal behavior<br>不忠誠的行為 | He punished her for disloyal behavior.<br>他處罰她不忠誠的行為。 |
| **royal**<br>[ˋrɔɪəl]<br>形 王室的 | the royal family<br>皇家 | The royal family in England gets a lot of attention from the media.<br>英國皇家獲得媒體很多的關注。 |

| | | |
|---|---|---|
| **coin**<br>[kɔɪn]<br>名 硬幣 | foreign coins<br>外幣 | He collects foreign coins as a hobby.<br>蒐集外幣是他的嗜好。 |

| | | |
|---|---|---|
| * **join**<br>[dʒɔɪn]<br>動 連結 | join together<br>連結在一起 | If you join together the two sides, it will form a circle.<br>如果將兩邊接在一起，會變成一個圓圈。 |

## oint [ɔɪnt]

| | | |
|---|---|---|
| **joint**<br>[dʒɔɪnt]<br>名 關節 動 連接 | knee joint<br>膝關節 | She went to the hospital to fix her knee joint.<br>她去醫院復健她的膝關節。 |
| * **point**<br>[pɔɪnt]<br>名 尖端、得分、要點 | get to the point<br>直截了當 | Would you just get to the point and stop wasting everyone's time?<br>你可以直截了當，不要再浪費大家的時間了嗎？ |
| **checkpoint**<br>[ˋtʃɛkˏpɔɪnt]<br>名 檢查站 | checkpoints on the border<br>邊境檢查哨 | If you are carrying anything illegal, you should be careful at the checkpoints on the border of a country.<br>如果你帶著違法物品，在邊境檢查哨時要小心點。 |
| * **appoint**<br>[əˋpɔɪnt]<br>動 任命、指派 | appoint him as manager<br>任命他為經理 | She is hoping that they will appoint him as manager so she can get a promotion too. 她正希望他們任命他為經理，這樣她也得以升遷。 |
| * **viewpoint**<br>[ˋvjuˏpɔɪnt]<br>名 觀點、見解 | from my viewpoint<br>從我的觀點 | From my viewpoint, you can do anything you want that won't hurt others.<br>從我的觀點來看，你能做任何你想做的事，只要不傷害別人。 |

| | | |
|---|---|---|
| **ballpoint**<br>[ˋbɔlˏpɔɪnt]<br>名 圓珠尖 | ballpoint pen<br>原子筆 | They say you need a ballpoint pen to fill out this application.<br>他們說你填申請表需要原子筆。 |
| **pinpoint**<br>[ˋpɪnˏpɔɪnt]<br>名 針尖 動 找出 | pinpoint the problem<br>找出問題 | You can't solve anything without first pinpointing the problem. 你不先找出問題是解決不了任何事的。 |
| **disappoint**<br>[ˏdɪsəˋpɔɪnt]<br>動 失望、使破滅 | disappoint his father<br>使他的父親失望 | He is afraid to disappoint his father.<br>他害怕讓他父親失望。 |

## oke [ok]

| | | |
|---|---|---|
| **choke**<br>[tʃok]<br>動 使窒息、阻塞 | choke to death<br>窒息致死 | He threatened to choke her to death.<br>他威脅要讓她窒息而死。 |
| **joke**<br>[dʒok]<br>名 玩笑、戲謔 | tell a joke<br>講個笑話 | Sometimes it's good to tell a joke to break the ice.<br>有時講個笑話打破沈默是好的。 |
| * **smoke**<br>[smok]<br>名 煙 動 抽菸 | smoke a pipe<br>抽煙斗 | He likes to smoke a pipe after dinner.<br>他喜歡在晚餐後抽煙斗。 |
| **poke**<br>[pok]<br>動 戳、撥弄 | poke at the ashes<br>撥弄灰燼 | After we lit a fire, he spent the rest of the night poking at the ashes. 在我們點火後，他整個晚上都在撥灰燼。 |

| | | |
|---|---|---|
| **stroke**<br>[strok]<br>名動 打、擊 | heat stroke<br>激烈心跳 | I had a heat stroke walking around for hours on a hot summer day. 我在炎熱的夏日走了好幾個小時，心跳劇烈。 |
| **sunstroke**<br>[ˋsʌnˏstrok]<br>名 中暑 | get sunstroke<br>中暑 | She got sunstroke sunbathing in Jamaica.<br>她在牙買做作日光浴時中暑。 |
| **provoke**<br>[prəˋvok]<br>動 挑釁、導致 | provoke discussion<br>引起討論 | A controversial topic will provoke discussion.<br>一個爭議的主題將引起討論。 |

## olk [ok]

| | | |
|---|---|---|
| **folk**<br>[fok]<br>形 民間的、民眾的 | folk song<br>民謠 | We learned folk songs in school.<br>我們在學校學民謠。 |
| **yolk**<br>[jok]<br>名 蛋黃 | the yolk of an egg<br>蛋黃 | The yolk of an egg has more protein than the egg whites.<br>蛋黃比蛋白有更多的蛋白質。 |

## oken [ˋokən]

| | | |
|---|---|---|
| **unbroken**<br>[ʌnˋbrokən]<br>形 未打破的 | unbroken record<br>未打破的紀錄 | He set an unbroken record for most wins by a rookie pitcher.<br>他創下新人投手最多勝的紀錄。 |

| | | |
|---|---|---|
| **outspoken** [aut`spokən] 形 坦率的、直言的 | ▶ outspoken person 坦率的人 | ▶ She likes to be an outspoken person on certain issues. 她喜歡在某些問題上坦率直言。 |
| **broken** [`brokən] 形 損壞的、破碎的 | ▶ broken window 破損的窗 | ▶ He had to pay for the broken window he broke at the store. 他在店裡打破窗子，必須負擔費用。 |
| **heartbroken** [`hartˏbrokən] 形 悲傷的 | ▶ a heartbroken girl 悲傷的女孩 | ▶ She is just a heartbroken girl who is looking for a rebound date. 她只是個悲傷的女孩，正在尋找重新振作的日子。 |

## oker [`okɚ]

| | | |
|---|---|---|
| **smoker** [`smokɚ] 名 吸菸者 | ▶ a heavy smoker 老菸槍 | ▶ He has been a heavy smoker for over forty years now. 他是個菸齡超過四十年的老菸槍。 |
| **poker** [`pokɚ] 名 撲克牌遊戲 | ▶ play poker 玩撲克牌 | ▶ My grandparents like to invite their friends over and play poker. 我的祖父母喜歡邀請他們的朋友來家裡玩撲克牌。 |
| * **broker** [`brokɚ] 名 經紀人、代理人 | ▶ real estate broker 不動產代理人 | ▶ The real estate broker said she could sell this house by June. 不動產代理人說她可以在六月前賣出這房子。 |
| **stockbroker** [`stakˏbrokɚ] 名 股票經紀人 | ▶ a young stockbroker 年輕的股票經紀人 | ▶ A young stockbroker in New York got arrested for drugs the other day. 紐約一名年輕股票經紀人不久前因吸毒被捕。 |

## olar [ˋolɚ]

| | | |
|---|---|---|
| **polar** [ˋpolɚ] 形 北極的、極地的 | a polar bear ▶ 北極熊 | ▶ Have you ever seen a polar bear hunt for food? 你曾看過北極熊獵食嗎？ |
| **solar** [ˋsolɚ] 形 太陽的 | solar energy ▶ 太陽能 | ▶ Soon cars will be powered by solar energy. 不久後車子將會用太陽能發動。 |

## old [old]

| | | |
|---|---|---|
| * **old** [old] 形 老的、舊的 | an old man ▶ 老人 | ▶ She hit an old man on the street in her car. 她在街上開車撞到一個老人。 |
| **bold** [bold] 形 大膽的 | a bold speech ▶ 大膽的演說 | ▶ The class president made a bold speech about the bureaucracy of the school. 班長針對校方官僚體制發表大膽演說。 |
| * **cold** [kold] 形 冷的 | a cold drink ▶ 冷飲 | ▶ I would die for a cold drink right now. 我現在想喝冷飲想死了。 |
| **scold** [skold] 動 責罵 | scold her children ▶ 責備她的小孩 | ▶ She had to scold her children for stealing. 她必須責備她小孩的偷竊行為。 |
| **fold** [fold] 動 摺疊、交疊 | fold the laundry ▶ 摺洗好的衣服 | ▶ I hate folding the laundry. 我討厭摺洗好的衣服。 |

| | | |
|---|---|---|
| **gold**<br>[gold]<br>名 金、金色 | gold bracelet<br>金手鐲 | He bought a gold bracelet for his girlfriend as an anniversary present. 他買金手鐲送女友作為週年紀念禮物。 |
| * **hold**<br>[hold]<br>動 握著、保持 | hold a knife<br>握著刀子 | I saw him hold a knife to his wife.<br>我看到他握著刀對著他太太。 |
| **household**<br>[ˋhaus͵hold]<br>名 家庭 形 家用的 | household soap<br>家用香皂 | You can use any household soap to wash your hands.<br>你可以用任何一塊家用香皂洗手。 |
| **threshold**<br>[ˋθrɛʃhold]<br>名 門檻、開端 | on the threshold of<br>在…的開端 | I think he is on the threshold of losing his mind.<br>我認為他正開始喪失他的心智。 |
| **withhold**<br>[wɪðˋhold]<br>動 抑制、隱瞞 | withhold information<br>隱瞞消息 | I know the government is withholding information from us.<br>我知道政府對我們隱瞞消息。 |
| **mold**<br>[mold]<br>名 模子、模型 | candle mold<br>蠟燭模型 | We learned how to make candle molds in art class today.<br>我們今天在美術課學會怎麼做蠟燭模型。 |
| **untold**<br>[ʌnˋtold]<br>形 未透露的 | an untold secret<br>未透露的秘密 | It's difficult to keep an untold secret.<br>守口如瓶很難。 |

## oulder [ˋoldɚ]

| | | |
|---|---|---|
| **shoulder** [ˋʃoldɚ] 名 肩膀 | ▶ put his head on her shoulder 把他的頭放在她肩上 | ▶ He was so surprised when she told him to put his head on her shoulder. 當她要他把頭放在她的肩上時，他很驚訝。 |

## ole [ol]

48

| | | |
|---|---|---|
| **hole** [hol] 名 洞 | ▶ hole in the wall 牆上的洞 | ▶ Please call the repairman to fix the hole in the wall. 請叫修理人員來修補牆上的洞。 |
| **peephole** [ˋpipˏhol] 名 窺視孔 | ▶ peephole in the door 門上的窺視孔 | ▶ She looked through the peephole in the door to see who knocked on her door. 她透過門上的窺視孔看誰在敲門。 |
| **keyhole** [ˋkiˏhol] 名 鑰匙孔 | ▶ peep through the keyhole 透過鑰匙孔窺探 | ▶ He peeped through the keyhole to see her naked in the bathroom. 他透過鑰匙孔偷看她在浴室內一絲不掛。 |
| **mole** [mol] 名 痣 | ▶ benign mole 良性痣 | ▶ Don't worry; the doctor said it is a benign mole. 別擔心，醫生說它是良性的痣。 |
| **pole** [pol] 名 柱、竿 | ▶ fishing pole 釣魚竿 | ▶ You need a different fishing pole to fish for freshwater fish than for saltwater fish. 與鹹水魚相較下，你要用不同的釣魚竿釣淡水魚。 |
| **role** [rol] 名 角色 | ▶ the leading role 主角 | ▶ The youngest girl took the leading role of the play. 最年輕的女孩擔任戲劇的主角。 |

| | | |
|---|---|---|
| **flagpole** [ˋflægˏpol] 名 旗竿 | tall flagpole 高旗竿 | She climbed that tall flagpole all the way to the top and yelled at the top of her lungs. 她一路爬到旗竿頂端，放聲大叫。 |
| **sole** [sol] 形 唯一的 | the sole heir 唯一的繼承人 | She is the sole heir to his property and assets. She's going to be rich! 她是他財產唯一的繼承人，她將成為有錢人！ |
| **console** [kənˋsol] 動 安慰、撫慰 | console him with soft words 輕聲細語安慰他 | I tried to console him with soft words but he still cried like a baby. 我試著輕聲細語安慰他，但他仍哭得像小嬰兒。 |

## oll [ol]

| | | |
|---|---|---|
| **roll** [rol] 動 名 滾動、轉動 | roll out the red carpet 鋪紅地毯 | Why do they only roll out the red carpet for celebrities? 為何他們只有在名人來時才鋪紅毯？ |
| **scroll** [skrol] 名 卷軸、名冊 | ancient Chinese scroll 古代的中國卷軸 | She studies ancient Chinese scrolls. 她研究古中國卷軸。 |
| * **enroll** [ɪnˋrol] 動 記入名冊、登記 | enroll in school 登記入學 | Today is the last day to enroll in school. 今天是登記入學最後一天。 |
| **unroll** [ʌnˋrol] 動 展開 | unroll the map 展開地圖 | The explorer unrolled the map on the table. 探險家在桌上展開地圖。 |

| | | |
|---|---|---|
| **stroll**<br>[strol]<br>名 散步 | take a stroll<br>散步 | Let's take a stroll in the park and hold hands.<br>讓我們在公園牽手散步吧。 |
| **toll**<br>[tol]<br>名 通行費、使用費 | pay a toll<br>付通行費 | You have to pay a toll at the end of the bridge.<br>你必須在橋端付通行費。 |

## olic [ˋalɪk]

| | | |
|---|---|---|
| **symbolic**<br>[sɪmˋbalɪk]<br>形 象徵的、符號的 | symbolic image<br>象徵的意像 | Can you find some symbolic images in this picture?<br>你能在這幅圖中找到象徵的意像嗎？ |
| **workaholic**<br>[ˏwɝkəˋhalɪk]<br>名 工作狂 | obsessive workaholic<br>過度工作狂 | She has been an obsessive workaholic lately.<br>她最近已經成了過度工作狂。 |
| **alcoholic**<br>[ˏælkəˋhalɪk]<br>形 含酒精的、酗酒的 | alcoholic beverage<br>含酒精的飲料 | Her face gets really red after drinking one alcoholic beverage.<br>她喝了含酒精飲料後臉變得很紅。 |
| **chocoholic**<br>[ˋtʃɔkəhalɪk]<br>名 嗜食巧克力者 | a skinny chocoholic<br>很瘦的嗜食巧克力者 | I don't know how he can be a skinny chocoholic. 我不知道他怎麼可以愛吃巧克力又那麼瘦。 |

## olish [ˋalɪʃ]

| | | |
|---|---|---|
| **abolish**<br>[ə`balɪʃ]<br>動 廢除 | ▶ abolish slavery<br>廢除奴隸制 | ▶ Even though they abolished slavery, racism is still prevalent today. 即使他們廢除了奴隸制度，今天種族歧視仍普遍存在。 |
| **demolish**<br>[dɪ`malɪʃ]<br>動 毀壞 | ▶ demolish the city<br>毀壞城市 | ▶ That big corporation will demolish the city and take it over. 那間大公司將毀壞城市並接管它。 |
| **polish**<br>[`palɪʃ]<br>動 磨光 | ▶ polish silver<br>磨亮銀器 | ▶ It'll take a long time to polish silver that has been sitting in the attic for 50 years.<br>把已經放在閣樓五十年的銀器磨亮是需要花很長的時間的。 |

## olly [`alɪ]

| | | |
|---|---|---|
| **folly**<br>[`falɪ]<br>名 愚蠢、愚行 | ▶ the follies of his youth<br>他年輕時的蠢事 | ▶ I don't know if the follies of his youth will be forgiven or forgotten. 我不知道他年輕的蠢事是否會被原諒或遺忘。 |
| **holly**<br>[`halɪ]<br>名 冬青 | ▶ wreath made out of holly<br>冬青做的花環 | ▶ She bought a wreath made out of holly to hang on the door.<br>她買了冬青做的花環掛在門上。 |
| **jolly**<br>[`dʒalɪ]<br>形 快活的、高興的 | ▶ jolly laugh<br>開懷大笑 | ▶ Everyone loved his jolly laugh.<br>每個人都愛他的開懷大笑。 |

## olo [`olo]

| | | |
|---|---|---|
| **solo**<br>[ˋsolo]<br>名 獨奏曲 | ▶ play three solos<br>演奏三首獨奏曲 | ▶ During the recital, she played three solos.<br>獨奏會時她演奏三首獨奏曲。 |

## ology [ˋɑlədʒɪ]

| | | |
|---|---|---|
| **ecology**<br>[ɪˋkɑlədʒɪ]<br>名 生態學、生態 | ▶ major in Ecology<br>主修生態學 | ▶ She majors in Ecology and is an activist. 她主修生態學並且是個行動主義者。 |
| **anthropology**<br>[ˏænθrəˋpɑlədʒɪ]<br>名 人類學 | ▶ Anthropology exam<br>人類學考試 | ▶ I haven't studied at all for my Anthropology exam!<br>我完全沒準備人類學考試！ |
| **archaeology**<br>[ˏɑrkɪˋɑlədʒɪ]<br>名 考古學 | ▶ study archaeology<br>研究考古學 | ▶ He continues to study archaeology even in his retirement.<br>即使退休後他還是繼續研究考古學。 |
| **geology**<br>[dʒɪˋɑlədʒɪ]<br>名 地質情況 | ▶ the geology of this area<br>這個區域的地質 | ▶ There has been fascinating research regarding the geology of this area. 關於這個區域的地質已經有些有趣的研究。 |
| **psychology**<br>[saɪˋkɑlədʒɪ]<br>名 心理學 | ▶ a degree in Psychology<br>心理學的學位 | ▶ A degree in Psychology is not enough to become a psychiatrist. 取得心理學的學位不足以成為精神病專家。 |
| **biology**<br>[baɪˋɑlədʒɪ]<br>名 生物學 | ▶ biology professor<br>生物學教授 | ▶ My biology professor discovered a certain kind of molecule in blood cells. 我的生物學教授在血球裡發現某一種分子。 |

| | | |
|---|---|---|
| **sociology** [ˌsoʃɪˋɑlədʒɪ] 名 社會學 | ▶ a Sociology major 社會學主修生 | ▶ He was a Sociology major in college. 他在大學主修社會學。 |
| * **technology** [tɛkˋnɑlədʒɪ] 名 技術 | ▶ state-of-the-art technology 現代化技術 | ▶ State-of-the-art technology costs a lot of money. 現代化技術成本很高。 |
| **criminology** [ˌkrɪməˋnɑlədʒɪ] 名 犯罪學 | ▶ Criminology class 犯罪學課 | ▶ What did you learn in your Criminology class about thieves? 關於小偷，你在犯罪學課學到了什麼？ |
| **chronology** [krəˋnɑlədʒɪ] 名 年表 | ▶ chronology of events 活動日程表 | ▶ Do you remember the chronology of events that day? 你記得那天的活動日程表嗎？ |
| **zoology** [zoˋɑlədʒɪ] 名 動物學 | ▶ Zoology course 動物學課程 | ▶ They teach a Zoology course here over the summer. 夏季期間他們在這裡教動物學課程。 |
| * **apology** [əˋpɑlədʒɪ] 名 道歉 | ▶ apology for my rudeness 為我的無禮道歉 | ▶ Please accept my apology for my rudeness. 我為我的無禮道歉，請你接受。 |
| **astrology** [əˋstrɑlədʒɪ] 名 占星術 | ▶ follow astrology 信星座占卜 | ▶ Do you follow astrology? 你信星座占卜嗎？ |

## olve [ɑlv]

| | | |
| --- | --- | --- |
| * **solve** [sɑlv] 動 解決、溶解 | solve the problem 解決問題 | We can solve the problem by ourselves. 我們可以自行解決問題。 |
| **resolve** [rɪ`zɑlv] 動 名 決心、決意 | with resolve 決心 | He always pursues his goals with resolve. 他總是決心追求他的目標。 |
| **dissolve** [dɪ`zɑlv] 動 分解、使溶解、解散 | dissolve the marriage 離婚 | She is trying to dissolve the marriage by having an affair. 她以搞婚外情為由設法離婚。 |
| **evolve** [ɪ`vɑlv] 動 發展、演變成 | evolve to a new system 發展成新體制 | Do you think that our government can evolve to a new system soon? 你認為我們的政府能很快地發展成新體制嗎？ |
| **revolve** [rɪ`vɑlv] 動 旋轉、使旋轉 | revolve the wheels 驅動輪子 | You need to revolve the wheels of your car every few years. 你每幾年就需要驅動你的車子。 |
| **involve** [ɪn`vɑlv] 動 涉入、牽涉 | involve me in your quarrel 把我捲入你們的爭吵 | Please don't involve me in your quarrel. 請不要把我牽扯進你們的爭吵中。 |

## oly [`olɪ]

| | | |
| --- | --- | --- |
| **holy** [`holɪ] 形 神聖的 | holy matrimony 神聖的婚姻生活 | You have promised to love me forever in holy matrimony! 你答應過要在神聖的婚姻生活中永遠愛我！ |

## alm [ɑm]

| | | |
|---|---|---|
| **balm**<br>[bɑm]<br>名 鎮痛軟膏 | lip balm<br>護唇膏 | My lips are so chapped, cracked, and dry that I need to apply some lip balm. 我的雙唇粗糙裂開又乾燥，所以我得擦些護唇膏。 |
| **calm**<br>[kɑm]<br>形 鎮靜的 動 使鎮定 | calm down<br>冷靜點 | Will you please calm down and take a deep breath?<br>可以請你冷靜點，做個深呼吸嗎？ |
| **palm**<br>[pɑm]<br>名 手掌、手心 | in his palm<br>在他的手掌中 | He was holding a bunch of little beetles in his palm.<br>他把一群甲蟲握在他的手掌中。 |

## omb [ɑm]

| | | |
|---|---|---|
| **bomb**<br>[bɑm]<br>名 炸彈 動 轟炸 | drop a bomb<br>投炸彈 | I hope that they won't drop a bomb on us when we go to war. 我希望當我們上戰場時，他們不會向我們投炸彈。 |

## oma [`omə]

| | | |
|---|---|---|
| **coma**<br>[`komə]<br>名 昏睡、昏迷 | in a coma<br>在昏迷狀態 | After the accident, he went in a coma.<br>車禍後，他呈現昏迷狀態。 |
| **diploma**<br>[dɪ`plomə]<br>名 文憑、學位證書 | a high school diploma<br>高中文憑 | It's hard to get a good job without a high school diploma.<br>沒有高中文憑是很難獲得一份好工作的。 |

| | | |
|---|---|---|
| **aroma** [ə`romə] 名 香氣 | the sweet aroma 香味 | Do you smell the sweet aroma of my mom's cooking? 你有聞到我媽媽煮菜的香味嗎？ |

## ome [om]

49

| | | |
|---|---|---|
| **dome** [dom] 名 圓頂、圓蓋 | the dome of that church 教堂的圓頂 | The dome of that church is famous. 那間教堂的圓頂很有名。 |
| * **home** [hom] 名 家、故鄉 | work at home 在家工作 | She wants to work at home so she can look after her baby. 她想在家工作，這樣才能照顧她的嬰兒。 |
| **metronome** [`mɛtrə͵nom] 名 節拍器 | use a metronome 使用節拍器 | We were taught to use a metronome when playing the piano. 我們學到彈鋼琴時要用節拍器。 |
| **Rome** [rom] 名 羅馬 | in Rome 在羅馬 | There are so many things and places to see in Rome. 羅馬有很多東西和地方可以欣賞。 |
| **syndrome** [`sɪn͵drom] 名 併發症狀 | Down's syndrome 唐氏症 | My friend from school had Down's syndrome. 我學校的朋友有唐氏症。 |

## oam [om]

| | | |
|---|---|---|
| **foam** [fom] 名 泡沫 | ▶ foam on the beer 啤酒泡沫 | ▶ You know you didn't pour the beer right if there is a big layer of foam on the beer. 如果啤酒上有一大層泡沫，你就知道你倒的方式錯了。 |
| **roam** [rom] 動 漫步、流浪 | ▶ roam around 漫步 | ▶ When we were in high school, we liked to roam around town. 我們高中時喜歡在城裡漫步。 |

## omb [om]

| | | |
|---|---|---|
| **comb** [kom] 名 梳子 動 梳理 | ▶ comb my hair 梳頭髮 | ▶ My dad always made fun of me for not combing my hair. 爸總是取笑我不梳頭髮。 |

## oem [`oɪm]

| | | |
|---|---|---|
| **poem** [`poɪm] 名 詩 | ▶ write a poem 寫詩 | ▶ Don't you ever write a poem when you feel sad? 你傷心時不會寫詩嗎？ |

## ometer [`ɑmətɚ]

| | | |
|---|---|---|
| **speedometer** [spi`dɑmətɚ] 名 速度計 | ▶ car speedometer 車子計速器 | ▶ Take a look at your car speedometer! You're going 50 miles over the speed limit! 看一下你的車子計速器！你快超過速限五十哩了！ |

| | | |
|---|---|---|
| **odometer** [o`damətɚ] 名 里程計 | ▶ set back the odometer 調回里程數 | ▶ He tried to set back the odometer so his father couldn't tell that he took his car out for a drive. 他試著調回里程數，這樣他父親就不知道他開他的車到外面兜風。 |
| * **thermometer** [θɚ`mamətɚ] 名 温度計 | ▶ disposable thermometer 拋棄式溫度計 | ▶ We use disposable thermometers in our house. 我們家用拋棄式溫度計。 |
| **barometer** [bə`ramətɚ] 名 氣壓計 | ▶ look at the barometer 看氣壓計 | ▶ If you look at the barometer, you can tell if it's going to rain or not. 如果你看氣壓計，就可以知道是否將要下雨。 |

## omic [`amɪk]

| | | |
|---|---|---|
| **comic** [`kamɪk] 名 漫畫 形 喜劇的 | ▶ comic book 漫畫書 | ▶ My parents won't let me read comic books until I finish my homework. 在我完成功課前，我的父母不會讓我看漫畫書。 |
| **atomic** [ə`tamɪk] 形 原子的、核武器的 | ▶ atomic bomb 原子彈 | ▶ There is a museum in Hiroshima to document the effects the atomic bomb had, and to promote world peace. 在廣島有個紀念館，記載著原子彈的影響，並推動世界和平。 |
| * **economic** [ˏikə`namɪk] 形 經濟上的 | ▶ economic crisis 經濟危機 | ▶ This worldwide economic crisis has major repercussions for everyone. 這場全球性的經濟危機對每個人都有重大的影響。 |

## ommy [ˋamɪ]

| | | |
|---|---|---|
| **mommy**<br>[ˋmamɪ]<br>名 媽咪 | ▶ my mommy<br>我的媽咪 | ▶ My mommy is a busy woman.<br>我的媽咪是一位忙碌的女性。 |

## ami [ˋamɪ]

| | | |
|---|---|---|
| **tsunami**<br>[tsuˋnamɪ]<br>名 海嘯 | ▶ deadly tsunami<br>致命的海嘯 | ▶ That deadly tsunami hit the fishing village two years ago.<br>兩年前，那次致命的海嘯席捲漁村。 |

## once [wʌns]

| | | |
|---|---|---|
| **once**<br>[wʌns]<br>副 一次、曾經 | ▶ all at once<br>突然 | ▶ There were people clapping and throwing stuff at the performers all at once. 突然有人鼓掌，並且丟東西給表演者。 |

## ond [and]

| | | |
|---|---|---|
| **bond**<br>[band]<br>名 動 結合、聯結 | ▶ bond together<br>結合在一起 | ▶ The glue bonds together both sides of the paper.<br>膠水將紙的兩面黏在一起。 |
| **fond**<br>[fand]<br>形 喜歡的、愛好的 | ▶ fond of music<br>喜愛音樂 | ▶ She is fond of music.<br>她喜愛音樂。 |

| | | |
|---|---|---|
| **blond** [bland] 形 白膚金髮的 | ▶ the blond man 白膚金髮的男人 | ▶ The blond man flirted with all the women he met. 這個白膚金髮的男人跟所有遇過的女人調情。 |
| **pond** [pand] 名 池塘 | ▶ in the pond 在池塘裡 | ▶ There are plenty of carp and tadpoles in the pond. 池塘裡有很多鯉魚和蝌蚪。 |
| * **respond** [rɪ`spand] 動 回答、反應 | ▶ respond to this letter 回覆此封信 | ▶ Please respond to this letter as soon as possible. 請儘速回覆此封信。 |
| * **correspond** [ˌkɔrɪ`spand] 動 符合、一致 | ▶ correspond with 與…一致 | ▶ His beliefs correspond with his actions. 他的信仰與他的行為一致。 |
| * **beyond** [bɪ`jand] 介 在…之外 | ▶ beyond recognition 無法認出 | ▶ This town has developed at such a rapid pace that it's now beyond recognition. 這城市發展得如此快速，現在已經讓人認不出來了。 |

## onder [`andɚ]

| | | |
|---|---|---|
| **ponder** [`pandɚ] 動 仔細考慮、衡量 | ▶ ponder the problem 思考問題 | ▶ He took a walk in the park to ponder the problem. 他在公園散步以思考問題。 |

## ander [`andɚ]

| | | |
|---|---|---|
| **squander**<br>[ˋskwɑndɚ]<br>動 浪費、揮霍 | ▶ squander an opportunity<br>浪費一個機會 | ▶ She tends to squander an opportunity when it comes along.<br>當機會來時，她容易浪費掉。 |
| **wander**<br>[ˋwɑndɚ]<br>動 漫遊、閒逛 | ▶ wander the streets<br>在街上閒逛 | ▶ When I was kicked out of the house, I wandered the streets.<br>當我被趕出屋外時，我在街上閒逛。 |

## one [on]

| | | |
|---|---|---|
| **bone**<br>[bon]<br>名 骨頭 | ▶ broken bone<br>骨折 | ▶ No one knows why her broken bone never healed.<br>沒人知道為什麼她骨折從沒復原。 |
| **phone**<br>[fon]<br>名 電話 動 打電話 | ▶ phone call<br>電話 | ▶ You have a phone call from Greece.<br>你有一通希臘打來的電話。 |
| **headphone**<br>[ˋhɛd͵fon]<br>名 頭戴式耳機 | ▶ pair of headphones<br>一副耳機 | ▶ I need a new pair of headphones because I lost my old ones on the beach.<br>我需要一副新的耳機，因為我在海邊弄丟了原來那副。 |
| **telephone**<br>[ˋtɛlə͵fon]<br>名 電話 動 打電話 | ▶ on the telephone<br>電話中 | ▶ He has been talking on the telephone for hours with his new girlfriend. 他已經跟他新女友講電話講好幾小時了。 |
| **microphone**<br>[ˋmaɪkrə͵fon]<br>名 擴音器、麥克風 | ▶ talk into a microphone<br>對著麥克風講 | ▶ When you present your speech, be sure to talk into a microphone.<br>當你演講時，切記對著麥克風。 |

| | | |
|---|---|---|
| **saxophone**<br>[ˋsæksə͵fon]<br>名 薩克斯風 | ▶ a new saxophone<br>新的薩克斯風 | ▶ His parents bought him a new saxophone because they broke his other one.<br>他的父母幫他買了新的薩克斯風，因為他們把他的另一把弄壞了。 |
| **lone**<br>[lon]<br>形 孤單的 | ▶ a lone ranger<br>孤單的漫遊者 | ▶ He has been a lone ranger all his life.<br>終其一生他都是個孤單的漫遊者。 |
| **alone**<br>[əˋlon]<br>形 副 單獨、獨自 | ▶ live alone<br>獨自生活 | ▶ She likes to live alone in the countryside.<br>她喜歡自己一人住在鄉下。 |
| **clone**<br>[klon]<br>名 動 複製 | ▶ clone humans<br>複製人類 | ▶ Soon they will be able to clone humans and everything else.<br>很快地，他們將能複製人類以及每個事物。 |
| **hormone**<br>[ˋhɔrmon]<br>名 荷爾蒙 | ▶ male hormone<br>男性荷爾蒙 | ▶ There are some male hormones in females.<br>女性身上會有一些男性荷爾蒙。 |
| * **postpone**<br>[postˋpon]<br>動 使延期 | ▶ be postponed to Saturday<br>延期至週六 | ▶ The football game will be postponed to Saturday because of the rain.<br>因為下雨，橄欖球賽將延至週六。 |
| **prone**<br>[pron]<br>形 有…傾向的 | ▶ prone to headaches<br>經常頭痛 | ▶ She is prone to headaches, so she always comes prepared with medicine. 她經常頭痛，所以總是隨身準備好藥。 |
| **tone**<br>[ton]<br>名 音調 | ▶ in a high tone<br>高聲 | ▶ She sings in a high tone.<br>她高聲唱歌。 |

| | | |
|---|---|---|
| **stone** [ston] 名 石頭 | made of stone 石頭做的 | The furniture in the back yard is made of stone. 後院的傢俱是石頭做的。 |
| **tombstone** [ˋtum͵ston] 名 墓碑、墓石 | written on the tombstone 寫在墓碑上 | There is something strange written on the tombstone. 墓碑上寫著很奇怪的事。 |
| **milestone** [ˋmaɪl͵ston] 名 里程碑 | a milestone in human history 人類歷史的里程碑 | The atomic bomb can be seen as a milestone in human history. 原子彈可被視為人類歷史上的里程碑。 |
| **zone** [zon] 名 地帶、地區 | economic zone 經濟區 | That area is a special economic zone where free trade occurs between China and Taiwan. 那個地區是一個特別的經濟區，在那裡中國與台灣自由貿易。 |
| **ozone** [ˋozon] 名 臭氧 | ozone layer 臭氧層 | Don't you ever worry about the ozone layer and humans' destroying it? 你不擔心人類破壞臭氧層嗎？ |

## oney [ˋʌnɪ]

| | | |
|---|---|---|
| **honey** [ˋhʌnɪ] 名 蜂蜜 | honey jar 蜂蜜罐子 | Winnie the Pooh likes to eat his honey out of a honey jar. 小熊維尼喜歡吃他罐子裡的蜂蜜。 |
| **money** [ˋmʌnɪ] 名 錢 | make money 賺錢 | How do you make money? 你怎麼賺錢的？ |

## onth [ʌnθ]

| | | |
|---|---|---|
| **month** [mʌnθ] 名 月、一個月 | last month ▶ 上個月 | ▶ Last month he made more money than he made last year. 上個月他賺的錢比去年還多。 |

## own [on]

| | | |
|---|---|---|
| **own** [on] 形 自己的 動 有 | my own car ▶ 我自己的車 | ▶ When I can save enough money, I want to buy my own car. 當我存夠錢時，我想買自己的車。 |
| **unknown** [ʌn`non] 形 未知的 | an unknown artist ▶ 不知名的藝術家 | ▶ This famous painting was done by an unknown artist. 這幅名畫出自不知名的藝術家。 |

## oan [on]

| | | |
|---|---|---|
| * **loan** [lon] 名 動 借出 | student loan ▶ 學生貸款 | ▶ Many students in the United States must get student loans to pay for their higher education. 很多美國學生必須申請學生貸款以付高等教育的學費。 |
| **moan** [mon] 名 動 呻吟、抱怨 | moan and groan ▶ 抱怨 | ▶ Stop moaning and groaning about school. 不要再抱怨學校的事了。 |
| **groan** [gron] 名 動 呻吟、抱怨 | groan in pain ▶ 痛苦地呻吟 | ▶ After he fell from the tree, he groaned in pain. 他從樹上掉下來後，痛苦地呻吟。 |

| | | |
|---|---|---|
| * **long** [lɔŋ] 形長的、遠的 | for a long time 長久以來 | For a long time she didn't talk to anybody because of her shyness. 長久以來她因為害羞而不跟任何人說話。 |
| * **along** [ə`lɔŋ] 介沿著 副向前 | walk along 沿著…走 | If you walk along this road, you will end up at the train station. 如果你沿著這條路走，最後會走到火車站。 |
| * **belong** [bə`lɔŋ] 動屬於 | belong to different generations 屬於不同的世代 | My parents, my brother, and I all belong to different generations. 我的父母、哥哥和我屬於不同的世代。 |
| **lifelong** [`laɪf͵lɔŋ] 形一輩子的 | lifelong friendship 一輩子的友誼 | We've created lifelong friendships. 我們已經建立了一輩子的友誼。 |
| **prolong** [prə`lɔŋ] 動延長 | prolong life 延長壽命 | There are many theories and superstitions in ways to prolong life. 有很多延長壽命的理論和迷信。 |
| * **strong** [strɔŋ] 形強壯的、堅強的 | a strong woman 堅強的女人 | He wants to marry a strong woman. 他想要跟堅強的女人結婚。 |
| **headstrong** [`hɛd͵strɔŋ] 形固執的、任性的 | headstrong actions 任性的行為 | Her headstrong actions offended many people. 她任性的行為得罪了很多人。 |
| * **wrong** [rɔŋ] 形錯誤的 | take this the wrong way 見怪 | Please don't take this the wrong way, but I don't like you. 請別見怪，但我不喜歡你。 |

| | | |
|---|---|---|
| **song** [sɔŋ] 名 歌曲 | sing songs 唱歌 | Children learn to sing songs in pre-school. 小朋友在幼稚園學習唱歌。 |

## onish [`ɑnɪʃ]

| | | |
|---|---|---|
| **admonish** [əd`mɑnɪʃ] 動 告誡、警告 | admonish the kid 警告小孩 | I saw the father admonish the kid who broke the plates in the restaurant. 我看到爸爸警告在餐廳打破盤子的小孩。 |
| **astonish** [ə`stɑnɪʃ] 動 使吃驚、使驚訝 | astonished at the news 對新聞很吃驚 | We were so astonished at the news that we screamed until the neighbors came. 我們對新聞感到很吃驚，所以一直到鄰居來才停止尖叫。 |

## onk [ɔŋk]

| | | |
|---|---|---|
| **honk** [hɔŋk] 動 鳴喇叭 名 喇叭聲 | honk his horn 按喇叭 | He always honks his horn when he's driving. 他開車時總是按喇叭。 |

## only [`onlɪ]

| | | |
|---|---|---|
| **only** [`onlɪ] 形 唯一的 副 只 | only son 獨生子 | He is a spoiled only son. 他是被寵壞的獨生子。 |

## onomy [ˋanəmɪ]

| | | |
|---|---|---|
| * **economy** [ɪˋkanəmɪ] 名 節約、經濟 | economy class 經濟艙 | Flying in the economy class seats is so much cheaper than flying first class. 經濟艙的座位比頭等艙便宜很多。 |
| **astronomy** [əsˋtranəmɪ] 名 天文學 | astronomy club 天文社 | She joined the astronomy club in her high school. 她高中時參加天文社。 |
| **autonomy** [ɔˋtanəmɪ] 名 自治、自治權 | ruled by autonomy 自治 | Some countries that are ruled by autonomy succeed. 有些自治國家很成功。 |

## onor [ˋanɚ]

| | | |
|---|---|---|
| **honor** [ˋanɚ] 名 榮譽 動 尊敬 | be an honor to 是光榮的 | It would be an honor to go to the president's house. 能去總統官邸是很光榮的。 |
| **dishonor** [dɪsˋanɚ] 名 動 侮辱、丟臉 | dishonor your ancestors 丟祖先的臉 | In Chinese culture, there is a lot of concern about dishonoring your ancestors. 中國文化中，人們會非常擔心讓祖先蒙羞。 |

## ood [ʊd]

| | | |
|---|---|---|
| * **good** [gʊd] 形 好的、有益的 | my good friends 我的好朋友 | My good friends will support me for the rest of my life. 我的好友會在我往後的人生支持我。 |

| | | |
|---|---|---|
| **hood**<br>[hud]<br>名 頭巾、車蓋 | the hood of their car<br>他們的車蓋 | Those teenagers often hang out on the hood of their car.<br>那些青少年經常在他們車子的車蓋上逗留。 |
| * **childhood**<br>[ˋtʃaɪld͵hud]<br>名 童年 | her early childhood<br>她幼年時期 | She accomplished an impressive amount in her early childhood. 她在幼年時期就很有出息。 |
| **likelihood**<br>[ˋlaɪklɪ͵hud]<br>名 可能性 | the likelihood of<br>可能性 | What is the likelihood of you becoming my wife?<br>你成為我太太的可能性是多少？ |
| **livelihood**<br>[ˋlaɪvlɪ͵hud]<br>名 生計 | earn a livelihood<br>謀生 | He earned a livelihood by selling purses on the street.<br>他在街上賣錢包謀生。 |
| **wood**<br>[wud]<br>名 木材 形 木製的 | a wood chair<br>木椅 | She carved a wood chair in her garage.<br>她在車庫裡刻了張木椅。 |
| **Hollywood**<br>[ˋhɑlɪ͵wud]<br>名 好萊塢 | Hollywood stars<br>好萊塢明星 | Everybody compares their own beauty to that of Hollywood stars.<br>每個人都跟好萊塢明星比美。 |

## oodle [ˋudl̩]

| | | |
|---|---|---|
| **noodle**<br>[ˋnudl̩]<br>名 麵條 | instant noodles<br>速食麵 | Although instant noodles are yummy and inexpensive, they are also unhealthy.<br>雖然泡麵好吃又不貴，但是不健康。 |

## oof [uf]

| | | |
|---|---|---|
| **aloof** [ə`luf] 副 形 遠離 | stand aloof 疏離 | People think he's weird because he always stands aloof in big buildings. 人們認為他很怪，因為他在大樓裡總是保持疏離。 |
| **roof** [ruf] 名 屋頂、車頂 | fix the roof 修屋頂 | Please fix the roof. There is a big leak in my living room. 請修好屋頂，我的客廳有一個很大的裂縫。 |
| * **proof** [pruf] 名 證據 | give me some proof 提供我一些證據 | Can you give me some proof that she murdered her husband? 你可以提供我一些她謀殺她先生的證據嗎？ |
| **soundproof** [`saʊnd͵pruf] 形 隔音的 | soundproof studio 隔音工作室 | They spent so much money on building a soundproof studio in their basement. 他們花了許多錢在地下室蓋一間隔音工作室。 |
| **fireproof** [`faɪr`pruf] 形 防火的、耐火的 | fireproof building 防火大樓 | This is supposed to be a fireproof building. 這應該是棟防火大樓。 |

## ook [ʊk]

| | | |
|---|---|---|
| * **book** [bʊk] 名 書 動 預訂 | read a book 讀書<br>book a flight 訂機票 | One of her hobbies is to read a book in the bathtub. 她的嗜好之一是在浴缸中讀書。<br>If you want cheaper airfares, you should book a flight as soon as possible. 如果你想要便宜的票價，你應該儘早訂機票。 |

| | | |
|---|---|---|
| **notebook**<br>[ˋnotˏbʊk]<br>名 筆記本、筆電 | in a notebook<br>在筆記本裡 | He tends to get lost drawing in his notebook.<br>他容易忘我地在筆記本上畫圖。 |
| **checkbook**<br>[ˋtʃɛkˏbʊk]<br>名 支票簿 | lose my checkbook<br>遺失支票本 | I lost my checkbook and had to report it to the bank.<br>我遺失了支票簿，一定要通知銀行。 |
| **textbook**<br>[ˋtɛkstˏbʊk]<br>名 教科書、課本 | buy textbooks<br>買教科書 | You have to buy textbooks in college.<br>在大學你必須買教科書。 |
| * **cook**<br>[kʊk]<br>動 烹調 名 廚師 | cook fish<br>煮魚<br>a good cook<br>好廚師 | Do you know how to cook fish? 你知道怎麼煮魚嗎？<br>I want to marry a good cook.<br>我想要嫁給好廚師。 |
| **hook**<br>[hʊk]<br>動 扣住 名 掛鉤 | hook the back of my dress<br>扣住衣服後面 | Can you please hook the back of my dress? I can't reach it.<br>可以請你幫我扣一下衣服後面嗎？我碰不到。 |
| * **look**<br>[lʊk]<br>動 看、注意 | look over<br>仔細檢查 | Will you look over this report for me?<br>你會幫我仔細檢查這份報告嗎？ |
| **overlook**<br>[ˏovɚˋlʊk]<br>動 眺望、寬容 | overlook his mistakes<br>寬容他的錯誤 | She naturally overlooks his mistakes because she's infatuated with him. 她很自然地寬容他的錯，因為她迷戀著他。 |
| **outlook**<br>[ˋautˏlʊk]<br>名 展望、看法 | outlook on life<br>對生活的態度 | I admire the ancient Greek outlook on life.<br>我欣賞古希臘人對於生活的態度。 |

| | | |
|---|---|---|
| **nook** [nʊk] 名 角落 | ▶ every nook and cranny 每個角落 | ▶ The police searched every nook and cranny for illegal weapons. 警方搜尋每個角落查緝非法槍械。 |

## ool [ul]

| | | |
|---|---|---|
| * **cool** [kul] 形 涼快的 動 變涼 | ▶ cool down 變涼 | ▶ Let's find an air-conditioned store to cool down in. 讓我們找間有冷氣的店涼快一下。 |
| **fool** [ful] 名 傻瓜 動 愚弄 | ▶ fool a lot of people 愚弄很多人 | ▶ She fools a lot of people by appearing nice, but she is actually mean. 她用表面的友善欺騙很多人，但事實上她是很惡劣的人。 |
| * **school** [skul] 名 學校 | ▶ go to school 去上學 | ▶ He has been going to school for over 20 years. 他已經上學超過二十年了。 |
| **pool** [pul] 名 水塘 | ▶ swimming pool 游泳池 | ▶ They are so lucky because they have a swimming pool in their house. 他們很幸運，因為他們家裡有游泳池。 |
| * **tool** [tul] 名 工具 | ▶ carpentry tools 木匠工具 | ▶ My dad bought a new set of carpentry tools to build an extra room off the garage. 我爸買了一組新的木匠工具要在車庫旁多蓋一間房間。 |
| **stool** [stul] 名 凳子 | ▶ sit on a stool 坐在凳子上 | ▶ I get tired sitting on a stool for too long. 我坐在凳子上太久覺得很累。 |

| | | |
|---|---|---|
| **boom** [bum] 名動 繁榮 | boom in sales 業績迅速增長 | There has been a boom in sales this year. 今年的業績迅速成長。 |
| **doom** [dum] 名 厄運 動 注定 | doomed to fail 注定失敗 | He has the worst luck; I think he's doomed to fail. 他運氣非常不好，我想他注定失敗。 |
| **bloom** [blum] 名動 開花 | in full bloom 盛開 | Let's go to the park this weekend, the flowers are in full bloom. 我們這個週末去公園吧，花朵都盛開了。 |
| **room** [rum] 名 房間 | in my room 在我的房間 | I locked myself in my room when my parents yelled at me. 每當我父母吼我時，我都把自己鎖在房裡。 |
| **broom** [brum] 名 掃帚 | a new broom 新掃帚 | I need a new broom to sweep the floors with. 我需要新掃帚好打掃地板。 |
| **groom** [grum] 名 新郎 動 打扮 | bride and groom 新娘與新郎<br>groom himself for the party 為了宴會打扮 | The bride and groom's families seem to clash. 新娘與新郎的家族似乎不搭。<br>Since he was trying to impress a girl, he took hours grooming himself for the party. 他想在宴會裡讓女孩印象深刻，所以他花了好幾小時打扮自己。 |
| **mushroom** [ˋmʌʃrum] 名 蘑菇 | shitake mushrooms 香菇 | She likes shitake mushrooms, but she doesn't like other kinds of mushrooms. 她喜歡香菇，但她不愛其他種蘑菇。 |

| | | |
|---|---|---|
| **classroom**<br>[ˋklæsˏrum]<br>名 教室 | ▶ in the classroom<br>在教室裡 | ▶ Everybody saw them kissing in the classroom.<br>每個人都看到他們在教室裡接吻。 |

## omb [um]

| | | |
|---|---|---|
| **tomb**<br>[tum]<br>名 墓碑、墓 | ▶ tombstone<br>墓碑 | ▶ They had a family tombstone made before they died.<br>他們在死前建造了家族墓碑。 |
| **womb**<br>[wum]<br>名 子宮、發源地 | ▶ in her womb<br>在她的子宮裡 | ▶ She could feel the baby kicking in her womb. 她可以感覺到小嬰兒在她子宮裡踢來踢去。 |

## oon [un]

| | | |
|---|---|---|
| **typhoon**<br>[taɪˋfun]<br>名 颱風 | ▶ big typhoon<br>強烈颱風 | ▶ A big typhoon hits Taiwan about once a year.<br>強烈颱風一年大約侵襲台灣一次。 |
| **saloon**<br>[səˋlun]<br>名 交誼廳、酒吧 | ▶ in the saloon<br>在酒吧裡 | ▶ In the old west of the United States, people used to drink and gamble in the saloon.<br>過去在美國西部，人們在酒吧裡喝酒賭博。 |
| **balloon**<br>[bəˋlun]<br>名 氣球 | ▶ blow up the balloon<br>吹破氣球 | ▶ She has a fear of blowing up the balloon, because she's afraid it'll pop. 她害怕氣球會被吹破，因為她很怕它發出砰的一聲。 |

| | | |
|---|---|---|
| **moon**<br>[mun]<br>名 月球、月亮 | full moon<br>滿月 | People do strange things when there is a full moon.<br>人們在滿月時會做奇怪的事。 |
| **honeymoon**<br>[ˋhʌnɪˏmun]<br>名 蜜月、蜜月旅行 | go for your honeymoon<br>去度蜜月 | Where do you want to go for your honeymoon?<br>你想去哪裡度蜜月？ |
| **noon**<br>[nun]<br>名 中午 | at noon<br>在中午 | We have lunch break at noon.<br>我們在中午有吃飯休息時間。 |
| **afternoon**<br>[ˋæftɚˋnun]<br>名 下午、午後 | afternoon tea<br>下午茶 | The British have a custom of taking afternoon tea.<br>英國人有喝下午茶的習慣。 |
| **spoon**<br>[spun]<br>名 湯匙 動 舀取 | silver spoon<br>銀湯匙 | He has expensive silver spoons in his silverware collection.<br>在他的銀器收集品中有很昂貴的銀湯匙。 |
| **soon**<br>[sun]<br>副 不久、很快地 | as soon as possible<br>儘快 | Please reply as soon as possible.<br>請儘快回覆。 |
| **monsoon**<br>[mɑnˋsun]<br>名 印度的雨季 | monsoon season<br>雨季 | Don't go there in May because you should try to avoid monsoon season. 不要在五月時去那裡，因為你應該避開雨季。 |
| **cartoon**<br>[kɑrˋtun]<br>名 卡通、連環漫畫 | watch cartoons<br>看卡通 | She spent most of her time away from school watching cartoons. 她下課後大部分的時間都在看卡通。 |

## oup [up]

| | | |
|---|---|---|
| * **group** [grup] 名 團體 | a group of people 一群人 | They gathered a group of people together for the ceremony. 他們聚集一群人參加典禮。 |
| **regroup** [rɪˋgrup] 動 重新組合 | time to regroup 重新組合的時候 | After finding each other, we knew it was time to regroup. 在找到彼此後，我們知道該重新結合了。 |

## oot [ʊt]

| | | |
|---|---|---|
| * **foot** [fʊt] 名 腳、足 | on foot 走路 | He is going to go to the supermarket on foot. 他要走路去超市。 |
| **barefoot** [ˋbɛr͵fʊt] 形 赤腳的 | a barefoot kid 赤腳的小孩 | We saw a barefoot kid running alongside the road. 我們看到赤腳的小孩沿著路邊奔跑。 |

## ut [ʊt]

| | | |
|---|---|---|
| * **put** [pʊt] 動 放 | put on 穿上 | Put on your clothes now! 現在穿上你的衣服！ |
| **input** [ˋɪn͵pʊt] 名 動 輸入 | give input 告知 | I want you to give me input on how I'm doing. 我想要你告訴我我做得怎樣。 |

## ooth [uθ]

| | | |
|---|---|---|
| * **booth** [buθ] 名 公用電話亭 | phone booth ▶ 公用電話亭 | ▶ He slept in a phone booth all night. 他整晚都睡在公用電話亭。 |
| * **tooth** [tuθ] 名 牙齒 | tooth paste ▶ 牙膏 | ▶ He used to brush his teeth without using tooth paste. 他以前不用牙膏刷牙。 |

## outh [uθ]

| | | |
|---|---|---|
| **youth** [juθ] 名 青少年時期 | in my youth ▶ 在我青少年時期 | ▶ In my youth, I did a lot of crazy things. 青少年時期，我做了很多瘋狂的事。 |

## op [ɑp]

| | | |
|---|---|---|
| **cop** [kɑp] 名 警察 | kill a cop ▶ 殺警察 | ▶ It is a major felony to kill a cop. 殺死警察是重罪。 |
| **hop** [hɑp] 動 跳過 | hop over ▶ 跳過 | ▶ When you walk on a sidewalk, there are occasionally things you must hop over. 當你走在人行道時，偶爾你得跳過擋路的東西。 |
| **chop** [tʃɑp] 動 砍、劈 | chop wood ▶ 砍柴 | ▶ She used to chop wood for fire. 她以前常砍柴生火。 |

| | | |
|---|---|---|
| * **shop** [ʃɑp] 名 商店 動 購物 | coffee shop 咖啡館 | Meet me at our favorite coffee shop at 3. 三點在我們喜愛的咖啡館碰面。 |
| * **workshop** [ˋwɝk͵ʃɑp] 名 工場、研討會 | a two-day workshop 兩天研討會 | We had to attend a two-day workshop on diabetes. 我們必須參加關於糖尿病的兩天研討會。 |
| **pawnshop** [ˋpɔn͵ʃɑp] 名 當鋪 | go to a pawnshop 去當鋪 | You can go to a pawnshop to buy and sell old things. 你可以去當鋪買賣舊東西。 |
| **barbershop** [ˋbɑrbɚ͵ʃɑp] 名 理髮店 | at the barbershop 在理髮店 | Every morning he got his face shaved at the barbershop. 每天早上他會去理髮店讓人刮鬍子。 |
| **mop** [mɑp] 名 拖把 動 用拖把拖洗 | mops for cleaning the floor 清潔地板的拖把<br>mop the floor 拖地板 | Please buy some mops for cleaning the floor when you go to the store. 你去商店時請買一些清地板的拖把。<br>She mopped the floor because the child spilt his milk. 小朋友打翻了牛奶，所以她把地拖一拖。 |
| **crop** [krɑp] 名 作物 動 收成 | harvest the crop 收割作物 | It's time to harvest the crop! 收割的時候到了！ |
| **drop** [drɑp] 名 滴 動 落下 | drop off 睡著 | I dropped off during the math class. 上數學課時我睡著了。 |

| | | |
|---|---|---|
| **raindrop** [ˋren͵drɑp] 名 雨滴 | falling raindrops 落下的雨滴 | She loves the feeling of falling raindrops on her face. 她愛雨滴落到臉上的感覺。 |
| * **top** [tɑp] 名 頂部 | on the top of the hill 在山頂 | I will be really tired if I ever get to the place on the top of the hill. 如果我到山頂上我會很累。 |
| **rooftop** [ˋruf͵tɑp] 名 屋頂 | on the rooftop 屋頂上 | There are chimneys on the rooftops of some Western homes. 西邊房子的屋頂有煙囪。 |
| **hilltop** [ˋhɪl͵tɑp] 名 山頂 | a hilltop village 在山頂的村莊 | He dreams to find a hilltop village, and spend the rest of his life there. 他夢想找到一座山頂村莊，在那度過餘年。 |
| * **stop** [stɑp] 動 停止 | stop sign 停止標示 | Look out for the stop sign! 注意停車號誌！ |

## ope [op]

52

| | | |
|---|---|---|
| * **cope** [kop] 動 對付、處理 | cope with 處理 | I'm sorry you have to cope with the difficult situation of losing a loved one. 我很遺憾你必須面對失去摯愛的困境。 |
| **scope** [skop] 名 範圍、領域 | the scope of the novel 小說的範圍 | The scope of the novel is limited, since it is written by a little boy. 小說範圍是受限的，因為它是個小男孩寫的。 |

| | | |
|---|---|---|
| **telescope**<br>[ˋtɛlə͵skop]<br>名 望遠鏡 | ▶ look through a telescope<br>透過望遠鏡看 | ▶ You can only see some planets when you look through a telescope. 當你用望遠鏡觀看時，只能看到一些星球。 |
| **microscope**<br>[ˋmaɪkrə͵skop]<br>名 顯微鏡 | ▶ look through a microscope<br>透過顯微鏡看 | ▶ The scientist must look through a microscope to see bacteria or other small cells and molecules. 科學家必須用顯微鏡看細菌或其他細胞分子。 |
| **horoscope**<br>[ˋhɔrə͵skop]<br>名 占星術 | ▶ read the horoscope<br>看星座運勢 | ▶ She makes a point to read the horoscope in the newspaper every morning.<br>她每天早上都要看報紙的星座運勢。 |
| **dope**<br>[dop]<br>名 麻藥、毒品 | ▶ sell dope<br>賣毒品 | ▶ It's depressing to see people sell dope to children. 看到有人賣毒品給小孩是很令人沮喪的。 |
| * **hope**<br>[hop]<br>名 動 希望、期望 | ▶ a hope of success<br>成功的希望 | ▶ There is still a hope of success for our business.<br>我們的生意仍有成功的希望。 |
| **envelope**<br>[ˋɛnvə͵lop]<br>名 信封 | ▶ address the envelope<br>寫上收件人地址 | ▶ Don't forget to address the envelope before mailing it.<br>寄信前別忘了信封上要寫收件地址。 |
| **slope**<br>[slop]<br>名 傾斜、坡度 | ▶ a steep slope<br>陡坡 | ▶ We climbed a steep slope to get to the hotel.<br>我們爬上陡坡到了飯店。 |
| **rope**<br>[rop]<br>名 繩索 | ▶ tie the rope<br>把繩索綁住 | ▶ She tied the rope tightly to make sure it wouldn't come undone.<br>她把繩索牢牢綁住以確保不會鬆開。 |

| | | |
|---|---|---|
| **tightrope**<br>[ˋtaɪtˏrop]<br>名 繃索 | ▶ walk a tightrope<br>走繃索 | ▶ The gangsters made the girl walk a tightrope over a pit full of alligators. 歹徒讓女孩走繃索，底下坑洞全是短吻鱷。 |

## oap [op]

| | | |
|---|---|---|
| **soap**<br>[sop]<br>名 肥皂 | ▶ bar of soap<br>一塊香皂 | ▶ This bar of soap has given me an allergic reaction.<br>這塊香皂讓我過敏。 |

## opic [ˋapɪk]

| | | |
|---|---|---|
| **tropic**<br>[ˋtrapɪk]<br>形 熱帶的 | ▶ the Tropic of Cancer<br>北回歸線 | ▶ Where is the Tropic of Cancer?<br>北回歸線在哪裡？ |
| * **topic**<br>[ˋtapɪk]<br>名 題目、話題 | ▶ topic sentence<br>主題句 | ▶ You must have a topic sentence for each paragraph of your essay. 你論文的每一段都必須有個主題句。 |

## opper [ˋapɚ]

| | | |
|---|---|---|
| **copper**<br>[ˋkapɚ]<br>名 銅、銅幣 | ▶ copper coins<br>銅幣 | ▶ There are copper coins made in this mint here.<br>這裡這家造幣廠有製造銅幣。 |

| | | |
|---|---|---|
| * **shopper**<br>[ˋʃapɚ]<br>名 顧客 | bargain shopper<br>想買便宜貨的顧客 | If you are a bargain shopper, you know factory outlet stores really well. 如果你是想買便宜貨的人，你就會很清楚工廠直營店。 |
| **grasshopper**<br>[ˋgræsˏhapɚ]<br>名 蚱蜢 | a lot of grasshoppers<br>很多蚱蜢 | There are a lot of grasshoppers that are keeping me awake because they are so loud. 有很多蚱蜢讓我睡不著，因為他們很吵。 |

## option [ˋapʃən]

| | | |
|---|---|---|
| **option**<br>[ˋapʃən]<br>名 選擇、選擇權 | have an option<br>有選擇權 | You have an option: you can stay or you can go.<br>你有選擇權，看是要留下或離開。 |
| **adoption**<br>[əˋdapʃən]<br>名 採納、領養 | put a child up for adoption<br>把小孩給人收養 | They did not want to put a child up for adoption, but they couldn't take care of the child themselves. 他們不想把小孩給人收養，但他們無法自己照顧小孩。 |

## opy [ˋapɪ]

| | | |
|---|---|---|
| **copy**<br>[ˋkapɪ]<br>名 複製品 動 複製 | make a copy<br>複製一份 | Please make a copy of that report for me. I lost mine.<br>請幫我印一份報告，我的不見了。 |

## oral [ˋorəl]

| | | |
|---|---|---|
| **oral**<br>[ˋorəl]<br>形 口頭的 | an oral exam<br>口頭測驗 | At the end of the year, we have an oral exam that is worth 30 percent. 年底我們有個佔百分之三十的口頭測驗。 |
| **floral**<br>[ˋflorəl]<br>形 花的、似花的 | a floral pattern<br>花紋 | He hates my blue dress with a floral pattern on it.<br>他討厭我的藍色衣服上有花紋。 |

## oral [ˋɔrəl]

| | | |
|---|---|---|
| **moral**<br>[ˋmɔrəl]<br>形 道德的 名 道德 | a moral issue<br>道德議題 | Abortion is a moral issue.<br>墮胎是個道德議題。 |
| **amoral**<br>[eˋmɔrəl]<br>形 與道德無關的 | an amoral person<br>沒道德觀的人 | He is an amoral person who follows few rules. 他是個沒道德觀的人，不太遵守規則。 |
| **immoral**<br>[ɪˋmɔrəl]<br>形 不道德的 | an immoral man<br>不道德的男人 | The church has called him an immoral man for cheating on his wife. 教會因他對妻子不忠，認為他是不道德的男人。 |

## orch [ortʃ]

| | | |
|---|---|---|
| **porch**<br>[portʃ]<br>名 門廊、入口處 | porch light<br>門廊燈 | We bought a new porch light that costs us only 10 dollars.<br>我們買了一個新的門廊燈，只花了十元。 |

| | | |
|---|---|---|
| **torch**<br>[tortʃ]<br>名 火把、手電筒 | ▶ carry a torch<br>拿火把 | ▶ During the Olympics, there is always someone who carries a torch.<br>奧運時會有人拿聖火。 |

## ord [ɔrd]

| | | |
|---|---|---|
| **cord**<br>[kɔrd]<br>名 細繩、電線 | ▶ pull out an electrical cord<br>拔出電線 | ▶ You must pull out an electrical cord if it is close to your bathtub. 如果電線離浴缸很近，必須把它拔出來。 |
| * **record**<br>[rɪ`kɔrd]<br>動 記錄 | ▶ record everything<br>記錄每件事 | ▶ She recorded everything happening on her trip.<br>她把旅行發生的一切都記錄下來。 |
| **discord**<br>[`dɪskɔrd] [dɪs`kɔrd]<br>名 動 不和諧 | ▶ the discord of his music<br>音樂的不和諧 | ▶ The discord of his music angered his neighbors.<br>他的音樂很吵，惹惱了他的鄰居。 |
| * **afford**<br>[ə`fɔrd]<br>動 買得起 | ▶ afford to pay the price<br>付得起這個價錢 | ▶ I'm not sure if I can afford to pay the price of that coat.<br>我不確定我是否付得起那件外套的價錢。 |
| **chord**<br>[kɔrd]<br>名 弦、感情 | ▶ strike a chord<br>打動 | ▶ My boyfriend tried to strike a chord with my parents by buying them flowers. 我男朋友送花給我父母，試圖打動他們。 |
| * **landlord**<br>[`lænd͵lɔrd]<br>名 地主、房東 | ▶ pay the landlord<br>付錢給房東 | ▶ It's almost time to pay the landlord the rent.<br>快到付房租給房東的時候了。 |

## oard [ord]

| | | |
|---|---|---|
| * **board** [bord] 名 木板、船舷 | on board 在船上 | They danced, ate, played games, and slept on board the cruise ship. 他們在遊艇上跳舞、吃飯、玩遊戲跟睡覺。 |
| **aboard** [ə`bord] 副 介 在船上、上船 | go aboard the ship 上船 | If I go aboard the ship, I'll get seasick. 如果我搭船，我會暈船。 |
| **cardboard** [`kɑrd͵bord] 名 硬紙板 | a cardboard box 硬紙箱 | Some homeless people live in the streets in a cardboard box. 有些無家可歸的人露宿街頭睡在硬紙箱裡。 |
| **scoreboard** [`skor͵bord] 名 記分板 | look at the scoreboard 看記分板 | Look at the scoreboard! Our team is winning by 20! 你看記分板！我們隊贏了二十分！ |
| **dashboard** [`dæʃ͵bord] 名 汽車儀器板 | on the dashboard 在汽車儀錶板上 | All the stuff she kept on the dashboard of her car was stolen. 她留在車裡儀錶板上的東西都被偷了。 |
| **billboard** [`bɪl͵bord] 名 廣告牌 | advertise on a billboard 在看板登廣告 | I think it would be a good idea if we advertise on a billboard along the highway. 我認為在公路旁的看板登廣告是個好主意。 |
| * **keyboard** [`ki͵bord] 名 鍵盤 | play keyboards 演奏鍵盤 | She plays keyboards for the band. 她在團裡是鍵盤手。 |

## ard [ɔrd]

| | | |
|---|---|---|
| **ward**<br>[wɔrd]<br>名 監禁、病房 | ▶ the isolation ward<br>隔離監禁 | ▶ The isolation ward in prison seems like the worst punishment. 監獄裡的隔離監禁似乎是最嚴厲的懲罰。 |
| **reward**<br>[rɪˋwɔrd]<br>動 報答 名 酬金 | ▶ collect a reward<br>領取酬金 | ▶ You can collect a reward sometimes for bringing in someone's lost pet. 把別人走失的寵物帶回來，有時可以收到酬金。 |
| * **toward**<br>[təˋwɔrd]<br>介 朝、向 | ▶ move toward the center<br>移向中心 | ▶ We were told to move toward the center of the room and shake hands. 我們被告知要往房間中心移動然後握手。 |

## order [ˋɔrdɚ]

| | | |
|---|---|---|
| * **order**<br>[ˋɔrdɚ]<br>名 順序 動 命令 | ▶ in alphabetical order<br>按字母順序 | ▶ Put the names in alphabetical order.<br>把名字按字母順序排列。 |
| **border**<br>[ˋbɔrdɚ]<br>名 邊緣、接界 | ▶ on the border of<br>瀕於… | ▶ I'm on the border of going insane.<br>我快發瘋了。 |
| **recorder**<br>[rɪˋkɔrdɚ]<br>名 錄音機 | ▶ tape recorder<br>錄音機 | ▶ We recorded our recital with a tape recorder.<br>我們用錄音機錄下我們的獨奏。 |

## orter [ˋɔrtɚ]

| | | |
|---|---|---|
| **shorter** [`ʃɔrtɚ] 形 更矮的 | ▶ a shorter vacation 更短的假期 | ▶ Spring break is a shorter vacation than summer break. 春假比暑假還短。 |
| **porter** [`pɔrtɚ] 名 搬運人員 | ▶ pay the porter 付費給搬運人員 | ▶ You have to pay the porter a tip. 你必須付小費給搬運人員。 |
| * **reporter** [rɪ`pɔrtɚ] 名 記者 | ▶ become a reporter 成為記者 | ▶ Her lifelong dream is to become a reporter. 她一生的夢想是成為記者。 |
| * **supporter** [sə`pɔrtɚ] 名 支持者、援助者 | ▶ strong supporter of animal rights 動物權利的強力支持者 | ▶ He is not only a vegetarian, but also a strong supporter of animal rights. 他不僅是素食者，也是動物權利的強力支持者。 |

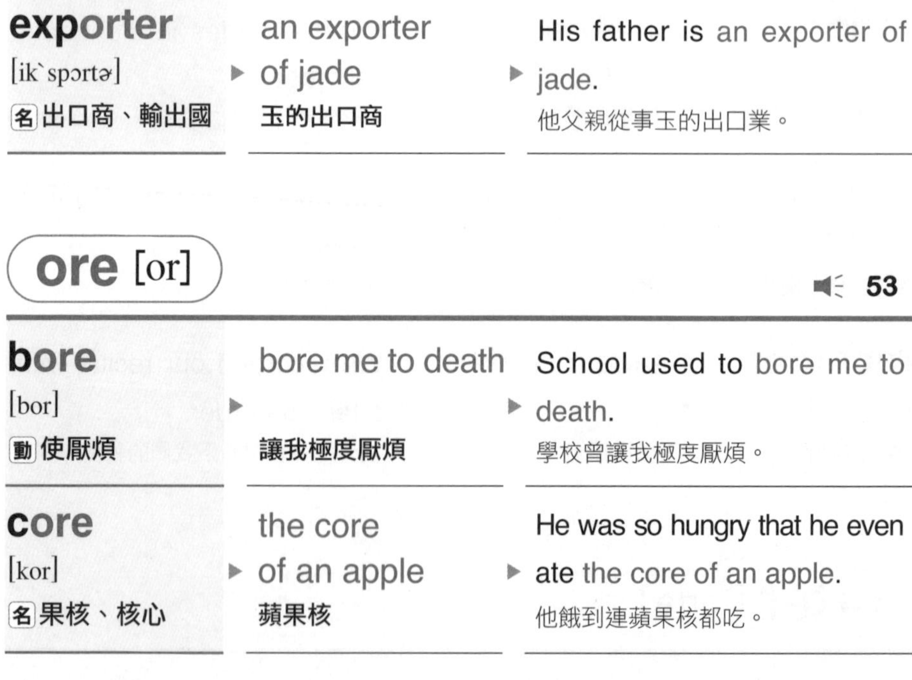

| | | |
|---|---|---|
| **exporter** [ik`spɔrtɚ] 名 出口商、輸出國 | ▶ an exporter of jade 玉的出口商 | ▶ His father is an exporter of jade. 他父親從事玉的出口業。 |

## ore [or]

53

| | | |
|---|---|---|
| **bore** [bor] 動 使厭煩 | ▶ bore me to death 讓我極度厭煩 | ▶ School used to bore me to death. 學校曾讓我極度厭煩。 |
| **core** [kor] 名 果核、核心 | ▶ the core of an apple 蘋果核 | ▶ He was so hungry that he even ate the core of an apple. 他餓到連蘋果核都吃。 |

| | | |
|---|---|---|
| * **score** [skor] 名 成績、分數 | ▶ get a low score 得到低分 | ▶ I can't afford to get a low score on my final exam. 我期末考不能考低分。 |
| **adore** [ə`dor] 動 敬重、愛慕 | ▶ adore someone 愛慕某人 | ▶ Once he really adores someone, he becomes obsessed with her. 一旦他真的愛上一個人，他會著迷於她。 |
| * **before** [bɪ`for] 介 在…以前 | ▶ before the examination 考試前 | ▶ Eat something light before the examination. 考前要吃輕淡的東西。 |
| * **therefore** [`ðɛr͵for] 副 因此、所以 | ▶ therefore 因此 | ▶ I hate working; therefore, I don't have much money. 我討厭工作，所以我沒有很多錢。 |
| **chore** [tʃor] 名 家庭雜務 | ▶ do chores 做家事 | ▶ My mom makes me do chores like washing the dishes and cleaning the toilet. 我媽讓我做家事，像是洗碗和打掃廁所。 |
| **seashore** [`sɪ͵ʃor] 名 海岸 | ▶ walk along the seashore 沿著海岸散步 | ▶ He used to walk along the seashore to find seashells. 他曾沿著海岸散步找貝殼。 |
| **ashore** [ə`ʃor] 副 在岸上 | ▶ come ashore 來到岸上 | ▶ They wait for their fishermen to come ashore, but unfortunately, the fishermen were lost at sea. 他們等待他們的漁夫上岸，但不幸的是，漁夫在海中遇難了。 |
| **explore** [ɪk`splor] 動 探索、探險 | ▶ explore a foreign land 探索國外 | ▶ She loves the excitement of exploring a foreign land. 她喜歡探索國外的刺激感。 |

| | | |
| --- | --- | --- |
| * **more** [mor] 形更多的 副更 | more than enough 過多 | I think you used more than enough sugar in your coffee. 我想你的咖啡加了太多糖。 |
| **furthermore** [`fɝðɚ`mor] 副此外、再者 | furthermore 此外 | You are mean and nasty. Furthermore, your breath stinks. 你卑鄙，下流，而且你的呼吸很臭。 |
| **forevermore** [fɚˏɛvɚ`mor] 副永遠地 | love me forevermore 永遠愛我 | She said she would love me forevermore. 她說她會永遠愛我。 |
| * **ignore** [ɪg`nor] 動不顧、忽視 | ignore their advice 不顧他們的勸告 | If you ignore their advice, you are responsible for your actions. 如果你不顧他們的勸告，你就要對自己的行為負責。 |
| **snore** [snor] 動名 打鼾 | loud snores 鼾聲很大 | I can't sleep in the same room as him because of his loud snores. 我無法和他睡在同一間房間，因為他的鼾聲很大。 |
| **Singapore** [`sɪŋgəˏpor] 名新加坡 | travel to Singapore 到新加坡旅遊 | He often travels to Singapore for business. 他常常去新加坡出差。 |
| **sophomore** [`sɑfm̩or] 名二年級學生 | sophomore in college 大二生 | She already has a book published, and she's only a sophomore in college. 她的書已經出版，而她只是大二生。 |
| **sore** [sor] 形痛的 | a sore throat 喉嚨痛 | A sore throat is usually the first sign of a cold. 喉嚨痛通常是感冒的第一個徵兆。 |

| | | |
|---|---|---|
| **eyesore** [ˋaɪ͵sor] 名 難看的東西 | an eyesore 難看的東西 | Those bright colored outfits are an eyesore. 那些鮮豔的服裝很難看。 |
| **restore** [rɪˋstor] 動 恢復、修復 | restore your strength 恢復體力 | You should rest here to restore your strength. 你應該在這兒休息一下恢復體力。 |

## or [ɔr]

| | | |
|---|---|---|
| **decor** [deˋkɔr] 名 裝飾 | modern decor 現代裝潢 | She likes the modern decor of this restaurant. 她喜歡這家餐廳的現代裝潢。 |
| **abhor** [əbˋhɔr] 動 厭惡、憎惡 | abhor dishonesty 厭惡不誠實 | You better not lie to him, because he is a man who abhors dishonesty. 你最好不要對他說謊，因為他很痛恨不誠實。 |

## oar [or]

| | | |
|---|---|---|
| **uproar** [ˋʌp͵ror] 名 騷動、吵鬧 | in an uproar 一片嘩然 | They were all in an uproar because everyone was offended by the show. 他們一片嘩然，因為那場秀讓每個人都很不舒服。 |
| **soar** [sor] 動 升騰、高飛 | soar into the sky 上升到天空 | I saw the hawk soar into the sky when the hunters shot at it. 當獵人獵鷹時，我看到老鷹飛升到空中。 |

## our [or]

| | | |
|---|---|---|
| **downpour** [ˋdaʊnˏpor] 名 傾盆大雨、豪雨 | ▶ the sudden downpour 驟然大雨 | ▶ There was a sudden downpour of rain when we were walking home. 當我們走路回家時，突然下起大雨。 |

## oor [or]

| | | |
|---|---|---|
| **indoor** [ˋɪnˏdor] 形 室內的 | ▶ an indoor swimming pool 室內游泳池 | ▶ They are so rich; they even have an indoor swimming pool! 他們很有錢，連室內游泳池都有！ |
| **outdoor** [ˋaʊtˏdor] 形 戶外的、野外的 | ▶ go outdoors 去戶外 | ▶ I want to go outdoors for some fresh air. 我想去戶外呼吸新鮮空氣。 |

## orge [ɔrdʒ]

| | | |
|---|---|---|
| **forge** [fɔrdʒ] 動 鍛造、偽造 | ▶ forge a signature 偽造簽名 | ▶ She forged her father's signature on the credit card bills. 她在信用卡帳單上偽造她爸的簽名。 |
| **gorge** [gɔrdʒ] 動 狼吞虎嚥 | ▶ gorge yourself on food 狂吃 | ▶ Sometimes it feels good to gorge yourself on food. 有時狂吃的感覺很好。 |

## orial [ˋorɪəl]

| | | |
|---|---|---|
| **memorial** [mə`morɪəl] 名 紀念物 形 追悼的 | ▶ a memorial hall 紀念大廳 | ▶ They built a memorial hall for the late owner of the house. 他們為這房子已故的所有人建造紀念大廳。 |

## oric [`ɔrɪk]

| | | |
|---|---|---|
| **caloric** [kə`lɔrɪk] 形 熱量的 | ▶ caloric intake 熱量的攝取 | ▶ If you don't want to gain weight, you should keep your caloric intake below about 2000. 如果你不想增重，你的熱量攝取應在2000卡以下。 |
| **historic** [hɪs`tɔrɪk] 形 歷史上著名的 | ▶ historic event 歷史上著名的事件 | ▶ This will be a historic event if we can make it happen. 如果我們能讓它發生，這將是歷史上著名的事件。 |
| **prehistoric** [ˏprihɪs`tɔrɪk] 形 史前的 | ▶ prehistoric evidence 史前證據 | ▶ There is prehistoric evidence that dinosaurs once roamed the earth. 有史前證據可證明恐龍曾在地球漫步。 |

## orify [`orəˏfaɪ]

| | | |
|---|---|---|
| **glorify** [`glorəˏfaɪ] 動 讚美、美化 | ▶ glorify the past 美化過去 | ▶ It's easy to glorify the past even though there is much pain and regret. 美化過去是很容易的，儘管過去有很多痛苦和悔恨。 |

## orrify [`ɔrəˏfaɪ]

| | | |
|---|---|---|
| **horrify**<br>[ˋhɔrə͵faɪ]<br>動 使恐懼 | ▶ horrify the children<br>使小孩恐懼 | ▶ The haunted house horrified the children.<br>鬼屋讓小孩恐懼。 |

## orious [ˋorɪəs]

| | | |
|---|---|---|
| **glorious**<br>[ˋglorɪəs]<br>形 光榮的、榮耀的 | ▶ win a glorious victory<br>贏得光榮的勝利 | ▶ I watched my favorite basketball team win a glorious victory. 我看到我最喜歡的籃球隊贏得光榮的勝利。 |
| **victorious**<br>[vɪkˋtorɪəs]<br>形 勝利的 | ▶ still victorious<br>依然勝利 | ▶ The team was still victorious even though its star player was injured. 即使明星球員受傷，這支隊伍還是獲勝了。 |
| **notorious**<br>[noˋtorɪəs]<br>形 惡名昭彰的 | ▶ notorious for<br>以…惡名昭彰 | ▶ That woman over there is notorious for treating her children badly. 那邊那個女人因對她的小孩很壞而惡名昭彰。 |

## ority [ˋɔrətɪ]

54

| | | |
|---|---|---|
| * **authority**<br>[əˋθɔrətɪ]<br>名 權力、當局 | ▶ the school authorities<br>學校當局 | ▶ The school authorities punished him for defacing school property.<br>學校當局懲罰他破壞學校公物。 |
| **inferiority**<br>[ɪnfɪrɪˋɔrətɪ]<br>名 劣勢、次級 | ▶ inferiority complex<br>自卑感 | ▶ He has an inferiority complex where he's trying to hide his insecurity. 他有自卑感，所以他試圖隱藏他的不安全感。 |

| | | |
|---|---|---|
| **superiority**<br>[sə,pɪrɪ`ɔrətɪ]<br>名 優勢、上等 | ▶ feeling of superiority<br>優越感 | ▶ Her feeling of superiority is unfounded.<br>她的優越感是毫無理由的。 |
| **seniority**<br>[sin`jɔrətɪ]<br>名 老資格、年資 | ▶ in order of seniority<br>按年資順序 | ▶ They lined us up in order of seniority.<br>他們按年資把我們排成一列。 |
| * **priority**<br>[praɪ`ɔrətɪ]<br>名 居前、優先 | ▶ top priority<br>最優先的事 | ▶ The safety of the people is the police's top priority.<br>人們的安全是警方的首要責任。 |
| * **majority**<br>[mə`dʒɔrətɪ]<br>名 大多數 | ▶ majority of the group<br>團體中大多數 | ▶ The majority of the group voted for a new leader.<br>團體中大多數的人投給新的領導者。 |
| * **minority**<br>[maɪ`nɔrətɪ]<br>名 少數 | ▶ ethnic minority<br>少數種族 | ▶ The aborigines in Taiwan are an ethnic minority.<br>台灣原住民是少數種族。 |

## orium [`orɪəm]

| | | |
|---|---|---|
| **auditorium**<br>[,ɔdə`torɪəm]<br>名 觀眾席、禮堂 | ▶ school auditorium<br>學校的禮堂 | ▶ They hold the annual benefit in the school auditorium.<br>他們在學校禮堂舉辦年度義賣會。 |

## ork [ɔrk]

| | | |
|---|---|---|
| **cork**<br>[kɔrk]<br>名 軟木塞 | cork of a bottle<br>瓶塞 | You must pull out the cork of a bottle to pour the wine out!<br>你必須拔掉瓶塞才能倒出酒來！ |
| **fork**<br>[fɔrk]<br>名 叉子 | use knives and forks<br>用刀叉 | Most people use knives and forks to eat steak.<br>大多數的人用刀叉吃牛排。 |
| **pork**<br>[pɔrk]<br>名 豬肉 | pork chop<br>豬排 | His mom makes the best pork chops I have ever eaten.<br>他媽媽做的豬排是我吃過最棒的。 |

## orm [ɔrm]

| | | |
|---|---|---|
| **dorm**<br>[dɔrm]<br>名 宿舍 | live in the dorm<br>住在宿舍 | She lived in the dorm during her college years.<br>大學期間，她都住在宿舍。 |
| * **form**<br>[fɔrm]<br>名 形狀、形式 | art form<br>藝術形式 | What kind of art form do you create?<br>你創作的藝術是哪種形式？ |
| * **reform**<br>[ˌrɪˋfɔrm]<br>名 動 改革 | economic reform<br>經濟改革 | A country needs to go through economic reform often.<br>一個國家需要常經歷經濟改革。 |
| * **uniform**<br>[ˋjunəˌfɔrm]<br>形 一致的 名 制服 | uniform size<br>統一的尺寸<br>wear a uniform<br>穿制服 | This shirt comes in one uniform size. 這襯衫只有一種尺寸。<br>She has to wear a uniform to work. 她必須穿制服工作。 |

| | | |
|---|---|---|
| * **inform**<br>[ɪn`fɔrm]<br>動 通知 | ▶ inform her<br>通知她 | ▶ Will you please inform her about the change of schedule?<br>可以請你通知她行程改了嗎？ |
| **conform**<br>[kən`fɔrm]<br>動 符合、遵守 | ▶ conform to the latest trends<br>順應最新趨勢 | ▶ She is a fashion victim who conforms to the latest trends.<br>她是流行的奴隸，老是跟著流行跑。 |
| * **perform**<br>[pɚ`fɔrm]<br>動 執行、演出 | ▶ perform the operation<br>執行手術<br>perform on stage<br>在舞台上演出 | ▶ The doctor did not seem to be concentrating when he was performing the operation.<br>醫生在開刀時，似乎不專心。<br>He gets stage fright when he performs on stage.<br>他在舞台上表演時感到怯場。 |
| **transform**<br>[træns`fɔrm]<br>動 使改變、使轉化 | ▶ transform it into something else<br>使它變成其他東西 | ▶ He doesn't like his clay model; he wants to transform it into something else.<br>他不喜歡他的黏土模型，想把它變成其他東西。 |
| **platform**<br>[`plæt͵fɔrm]<br>名 平台、月台 | ▶ wait on the platform<br>在月台上等候 | ▶ Someone tried to talk to me while we were waiting on the platform for a train.<br>我們在月台等火車時，有人試圖跟我攀談。 |
| **norm**<br>[nɔrm]<br>名 基準、規範 | ▶ not the norm<br>不是常態 | ▶ This weather is not the norm.<br>這天氣不是常態。 |
| **storm**<br>[stɔrm]<br>名 暴風雨 動 猛衝 | ▶ storm out of the room<br>衝出房間 | ▶ She stormed out of the room because she was so angry.<br>她因為很生氣所以衝出房間。 |

| | | |
|---|---|---|
| * **brainstorm** [`bren,storm] 動名 集思廣益 | ▶ brainstorm ideas 集思廣益 | ▶ We had to brainstorm ideas for our research project. 我們必須針對研究專題集思廣益。 |
| **thunderstorm** [`θʌndɚ,storm] 名 大雷雨 | ▶ big thunderstorm 大雷雨 | ▶ A big thunderstorm hit the city and 7 people were hit by lightning. 大雷雨襲擊城市，有七人被閃電打到。 |
| **snowstorm** [`sno,storm] 名 暴風雪 | ▶ weather a snowstorm 平安度過暴風雪 | ▶ The biggest concerns are to stay warm and safe when weathering a snowstorm. 要平安度過暴風雪，最需要保持溫暖和安全。 |

## arm [ɔrm]

| | | |
|---|---|---|
| * **warm** [wɔrm] 形 溫暖的、熱情的 | ▶ a warm person 熱情的人 | ▶ She is a warm person who makes everyone feel comfortable. 她是個熱情的人，讓每個人都感到舒服。 |
| **swarm** [swɔrm] 名動 成群、群集 | ▶ a swarm of bees 成群的蜜蜂 | ▶ Since he was allergic to bees, when a swarm of bees surrounded him and stung him, he quickly died. 因為他對蜜蜂過敏，所以當成群蜜蜂圍叮他時，他很快就死亡。 |
| **lukewarm** [`luk`wɔrm] 形 微溫的、冷淡的 | ▶ lukewarm water 微溫的水 | ▶ I asked for a cup of hot coffee! This is lukewarm water! 我要一杯熱的咖啡！這是溫的！ |

## ormal [`ɔrml̩]

| | | |
|---|---|---|
| **informal** [ɪn`fɔrml̩] 形 非正式的 | an informal agreement 非正式的協議 | They had an informal agreement, and one of them broke it. 他們達成非正式的協議，其中有人違反了此協議。 |
| * **formal** [`fɔrml̩] 形 正式的 | dress formally 穿著正式 | This restaurant requires you to dress formally. 這餐廳要求你穿正式的衣著。 |
| * **normal** [`nɔrml̩] 形 正常的、標準的 | normal pace 正常的速度 | I walk at a normal pace. 我用正常的速度走路。 |
| **abnormal** [æb`nɔrml̩] 形 不正常的 | abnormal behavior 不正常的行為 | My dog has been showing signs of abnormal behavior; I'm worried. 我的狗狗出現不正常行為的跡象，我很擔心。 |

## ormer [`ɔrmɚ]

| | | |
|---|---|---|
| **former** [`fɔrmɚ] 形 從前的、前任的 | the former president 前任董事長 | The former president of the company got fired because he stole money from the company. 公司前任董事長因為盜用公款被開除。 |
| **reformer** [rɪ`fɔrmɚ] 名 改革者 | a social reformer 社會改革者 | Being a social reformer is hard work and gives little pay. 當社會改革者是件辛苦的工作，得到的報酬也很少。 |
| **performer** [pɚ`fɔrmɚ] 名 演出者、演奏者 | circus performer 馬戲團表演者 | He dreamt of becoming a circus performer when he was young. 年輕時，他夢想成為馬戲團表演者。 |

## orn [ɔrn]

| | | |
|---|---|---|
| **born**<br>[bɔrn]<br>形 出生的、天生的 | born in the USA<br>生於美國 | I was born in the USA.<br>我生於美國。 |
| **newborn**<br>[ˋnju͵bɔrn]<br>形 新生的 | a newborn baby<br>新生兒 | Be gentle with a newborn baby.<br>對新生兒要溫柔。 |
| **corn**<br>[kɔrn]<br>名 玉米 | an ear of corn<br>一穗玉米 | She had an ear of corn and a sandwich for lunch.<br>她午餐吃玉米和三明治。 |
| **popcorn**<br>[ˋpɑp͵kɔrn]<br>名 爆米花 | a bag of popcorn<br>一包爆米花 | Please get me a bag of popcorn and a Coke. I'll go get our seats in the theater.<br>請幫我買爆米花和可樂，我要進電影院找我們的位子。 |
| **scorn**<br>[skɔrn]<br>名 動 輕蔑、藐視 | with scorn<br>以藐視的眼光 | He looked at her with scorn. They must have had a fight.<br>他用藐視的眼光看她，他們一定吵過架。 |
| **adorn**<br>[əˋdɔrn]<br>動 裝飾 | adorned with flowers<br>用花裝飾 | The tables and walls in the dining room were adorned with flowers.<br>飯廳的桌子和牆面用花裝飾。 |
| **horn**<br>[hɔrn]<br>名 角、喇叭 | honk your horn<br>鳴喇叭 | Honk your horn if someone gets in your way.<br>如果有人搶你的車道，你就按喇叭。 |
| **worn**<br>[wɔrn]<br>形 破舊的、磨壞的 | worn out<br>破舊的 | Those shoes are so worn out; throw them out!<br>那些鞋子很破舊了，丟了吧！ |

## arn [ɔrn]

| | | |
|---|---|---|
| * **warn** [wɔrn] 動 警告 | warn me of 警告我 | She warned me of sticking my hands in the dog cage. 她警告我不要把手放在狗籠裡。 |
| **forewarn** [forˋwɔrn] 動 預先警告 | give a forewarning 發出預警 | The weather station gave a forewarning that a tornado was coming through the area. 氣象站發出預警，龍捲風即將通過本地區。 |

## orse [ɔrs]

| | | |
|---|---|---|
| **endorse** [ɪnˋdɔrs] 動 背書、簽署 | endorse the check 簽支票 | You have to endorse the check on the back in order to get the cash for it. 你必須在支票背面簽名才能兌現。 |
| **horse** [hɔrs] 名 馬 | ride a horse 騎馬 | Can you ride a horse on your own? 你可以自己騎馬嗎？ |

## orce [ɔrs]

| | | |
|---|---|---|
| **force** [fɔrs] 名 力量 動 強迫 | air force 空軍 | She wanted to be in the air force after watching the movie "Top Gun." 她在看完《捍衛戰士》這部電影後想成為空軍。 |
| **reinforce** [ˏriɪnˋfɔrs] 動 增援、加強 | reinforce the walls 使牆更堅固 | My father reinforced the walls with buttresses. 我父親用扶壁使牆更加堅固。 |

| | | |
|---|---|---|
| **divorce** [də`vɔrs] 動 名 離婚 | divorce his wife 與他太太離婚 | He will divorce his wife once he finds out she's having an affair. 一旦他發現他太太有外遇，他會跟她離婚。 |

## ource [ors]

| | | |
|---|---|---|
| **source** [sors] 名 源頭、來源 | water source 水源 | The nearest water source is at the Free Reservoir. 最近的水源是在自由水庫。 |
| **resource** [rɪ`sors] 名 資源 | natural resources 自然資源 | Environmentalists are worried about depleting our natural resources. 環保人士擔心我們的自然資源耗竭。 |

## ort [ɔrt]

55

| | | |
|---|---|---|
| **escort** [`ɛskɔrt] 動 護衛 名 護航隊 | escort home 護送回家 | When I stay out late, I like to be escorted home. 當我在外頭待很晚時，我喜歡有人送我回家。 |
| * **short** [ʃɔrt] 形 矮的、短的 | shortcoming 缺點 | It's easy to overlook the shortcomings of someone you love. 忽略所愛的人的缺點是很容易的。 |
| **port** [pɔrt] 名 港、港口 | an important port 重要港口 | Keelung is an important port for Taiwan. 基隆是台灣重要的港口。 |

| | | |
| --- | --- | --- |
| **deport** [dɪ`pɔrt] 動 驅逐 | get deported 被驅逐 | Some foreigners get deported for illegal activities. 有些外國人因非法活動被驅逐。 |
| * **report** [rɪ`pɔrt] 動 名 報告 | book report 閱讀心得報告 | In elementary school, I had to do one book report a month. 小學時，我一個月必須寫一次閱讀心得報告。 |
| **import** [ɪm`pɔrt] 動 進口 | imported apples 進口的蘋果 | I like imported apples from Japan. 我喜歡日本進口的蘋果。 |
| * **airport** [`ɛr͵port] 名 機場 | airport terminal 機場航站 | Which airport terminal do you have to go to? 你必須去哪個機場航站？ |
| * **sport** [spɔrt] 名 運動 | team sport 團隊運動 | Some people prefer team sports to individual sports. 有人較喜歡團隊運動勝於個人運動。 |
| * **transport** [træns`pɔrt] 動 運輸 | transport goods 運送貨物 | That company transports goods by trucks. 那家公司用卡車運貨物。 |
| * **passport** [`pæs͵pɔrt] 名 護照 | carry a passport 帶護照 | When you are traveling, remember to carry a passport. 當你旅行時，記得帶護照。 |
| * **export** [ɪks`pɔrt] 動 出口 | export rice 出口米 | Does this country export rice? 這國家出口米嗎？ |

## orth [ɔrθ]

| | | |
|---|---|---|
| **north**<br>[nɔrθ]<br>名 北方 形 北方的 | ▶ North Star<br>北極星 | ▶ If you recognize the North Star, you should be able to get your bearings. 如果你能辨識北極星，你應該就可以找到方位。 |

## ourth [orθ]

| | | |
|---|---|---|
| **fourth**<br>[forθ]<br>形 第四的 名 第四 | ▶ the fourth quarter<br>第四節 | ▶ The two teams are tied in the fourth quarter, with one minute remaining. 兩隊在第四節只剩一分鐘時打成平手。 |

## ortion [`ɔrʃən]

| | | |
|---|---|---|
| **portion**<br>[`pɔrʃən]<br>名 分配、等份 | ▶ one portion<br>一份 | ▶ I'd like one portion of the Chef's special, please.<br>我想要一份主廚特餐，謝謝。 |
| **contortion**<br>[kən`tɔrʃən]<br>名 扭曲 | ▶ contortion of the body<br>身體扭曲 | ▶ We saw some dancers do weird contortions of the body.<br>我們看到有些舞者的身體做出奇怪的扭曲。 |
| **distortion**<br>[dɪs`tɔrʃən]<br>名 變形 | ▶ the distortion of the face<br>臉變形 | ▶ Some diseases will contribute to the distortion of the face.<br>有些疾病會讓人臉變形。 |

## orty [`ɔrtɪ]

| | | |
|---|---|---|
| **forty**<br>[ˋfɔrtɪ]<br>形 四十的 名 四十 | forty students<br>四十個學生 | There will be forty students going on the field trip to Hualien. 將有四十個學生去花蓮作實地考察之旅。 |
| **sporty**<br>[ˋspɔrtɪ]<br>形 喜歡運動的 | a sporty girl<br>愛運動的女孩 | She is a sporty girl who is competitive and strong.<br>她是個愛運動的女孩，好勝心強又強壯。 |

## ory [ˋorɪ]

| | | |
|---|---|---|
| * **category**<br>[ˋkætə͵gorɪ]<br>名 種類 | category of music<br>音樂的種類 | What category of music does this song fall under?<br>這首歌是什麼類型？ |
| **glory**<br>[ˋglorɪ]<br>名 光榮 | honor and glory<br>榮耀與光榮 | Do you believe that there is honor and glory in war?<br>你認為戰爭中有榮耀與光榮嗎？ |
| **obligatory**<br>[əˋblɪgə͵torɪ]<br>形 義務的、必須的 | attendance is obligatory<br>出席是必須的 | You have to go to the meeting; attendance is obligatory.<br>你必須去開會，出席是必須的。 |
| **explanatory**<br>[ɪksˋplænə͵torɪ]<br>形 解釋的 | self-explanatory<br>明顯的 | The directions should be self-explanatory.<br>指示應該要明顯。 |
| **laboratory**<br>[ˋlæbrə͵torɪ]<br>名 實驗室 | research laboratory<br>研究室 | He's worked at the same research laboratory for the past 50 years. 他過去五十年一直都在相同的研究室工作。 |

| | | |
|---|---|---|
| **conservatory**<br>[kən`sɝvəˏtorɪ]<br>名 温室、音樂學校 | ▶ music conservatory<br>音樂學校 | ▶ She went to study at the music conservatory.<br>她去音樂學校讀書。 |

## osal [`ozḷ]

| | | |
|---|---|---|
| * **proposal**<br>[prə`pozḷ]<br>名 提議、求婚 | ▶ marriage proposal<br>求婚 | ▶ He wanted to have the perfect marriage proposal, but she ended up rejecting him.<br>他想有最完美的求婚過程，但結果是她拒絕了他。 |
| **disposal**<br>[dɪ`spozḷ]<br>名 處理、處置 | ▶ garbage disposal<br>廢物處理裝置 | ▶ Don't put really big things in the garbage disposal or else it will break. 不要把很大的東西放在廢物處理裝置裡，不然它會壞掉。 |

## ose [os]

| | | |
|---|---|---|
| **dose**<br>[dos]<br>名 一劑 | ▶ a dose of medicine<br>一劑藥 | ▶ She took a dose of medicine before dinner, and fell asleep.<br>她晚餐前吃了藥，然後就睡著了。 |
| * **close**<br>[klos]<br>形 近的、親密的 | ▶ close friends<br>親密的朋友 | ▶ We have been close friends since the first grade. 自從一年級開始，我們就是很親密的朋友。 |
| * **diagnose**<br>[`daɪəgnos]<br>動 診斷 | ▶ diagnose the illness<br>診斷病情 | ▶ The doctor couldn't diagnose the illness because of its contradictory symptoms.<br>因為症狀矛盾，醫生診斷不出病情。 |

# ose [oz]

| | | |
|---|---|---|
| **hose** [hoz] 名 水龍帶 | fire hose ▶ 消防軟管 | Only use a fire hose when necessary. ▶ 只有必要時才用消防軟管。 |
| * **those** [ðoz] 代 那些 形 那些的 | those shoes ▶ 那些鞋子 | I love those shoes you're wearing! ▶ 我愛你穿的那雙鞋子！ |
| * **close** [kloz] 動 關閉 | close the door ▶ 關門 | It's cold outside; close the door behind you. ▶ 外面很冷，請關上身後的門。 |
| **enclose** [ɪn`kloz] 動 圍住、圈起 | bill enclosed ▶ 內含帳單 | There is a bill enclosed in that letter. ▶ 那封信內含帳單。 |
| **nose** [noz] 名 鼻子 | runny nose ▶ 流鼻涕 | She didn't have any tissues for her runny nose, so she wiped her nose on her sleeve. ▶ 她沒有衛生紙可以擦鼻涕，所以她用袖子擦。 |
| **pose** [poz] 名 姿勢 動 擺姿勢 | strike a pose ▶ 擺個姿勢 | I bet you can strike a pose even though you're not a model. ▶ 我敢打賭你會擺姿勢，即使你不是模特兒。 |
| **impose** [ɪm`poz] 動 打擾、徵稅 | impose on you ▶ 打擾你 | I don't want to impose on you and your family; I'm leaving soon. ▶ 我不想打擾你和你的家人，我很快就會離開了。 |
| **decompose** [ˌdikəm`poz] 動 分解 | decomposed body ▶ 腐爛的屍體 | There was a decomposed body under the bed. ▶ 床下有具腐爛的屍體。 |

| | | |
|---|---|---|
| * **propose**<br>[prə`poz]<br>動 提議 | propose to a girl<br>向女孩求婚 | He has proposed to a girl more than once.<br>他已經向女孩求婚不下一次。 |
| * **oppose**<br>[ə`poz]<br>動 反對 | opposing side<br>反對的一方 | Even though he's on the opposing side, we are good friends.<br>雖然他是反對的一方，但我們仍是好朋友。 |
| * **suppose**<br>[sə`poz]<br>動 以為、認為應該 | suppose that<br>以為 | I suppose that you have been good.<br>我以為你過得很好。 |
| **dispose**<br>[dɪ`spoz]<br>動 配置、處理 | dispose of the trash<br>丟掉垃圾 | My brother never disposes of the trash in our apartment.<br>我哥從未在我們公寓裡丟垃圾。 |
| **expose**<br>[ɪk`spoz]<br>動 使暴露於、揭露 | expose the truth<br>揭露事實 | The detective will expose the truth of the scandal.<br>偵探將揭露醜聞的真相。 |
| **rose**<br>[roz]<br>名 玫瑰花 | a dozen roses<br>一打玫瑰 | He bought her a dozen roses for no special occasion. 沒有特別的理由，他送了她一打玫瑰。 |
| **prose**<br>[proz]<br>名 散文 | written in prose<br>以散文寫成 | Most of her work was written in prose.<br>她大部分作品是散文形式。 |

## oss [ɔs]

| | | |
|---|---|---|
| * **boss**<br>[bɔs]<br>名 老板、上司 | nice boss<br>好老板 | Working in a company with a nice boss makes a difference.<br>在有好老板的公司工作差別很大。 |
| * **loss**<br>[lɔs]<br>名 喪失 | loss of memory<br>喪失記憶 | She suffered from a loss of memory after the accident.<br>自從車禍後她就喪失了記憶。 |
| **floss**<br>[flɔs]<br>動 用牙線潔牙 | floss your teeth<br>用牙線清潔牙齒 | You should floss your teeth every day.<br>你應該每天用牙線清潔牙齒。 |
| **gloss**<br>[glɔs]<br>名 光澤 | lip gloss<br>潤澤唇膏 | Her lip gloss made her lips look shiny.<br>她的潤澤唇膏讓嘴唇晶亮有光澤。 |
| **cross**<br>[krɔs]<br>名 十字形 動 越過 | cross the street<br>過馬路 | Look both ways before you cross the street.<br>過馬路前要看兩邊來車。 |
| **across**<br>[ə`krɔs]<br>介 穿過 副 在對面 | across the street<br>穿過馬路 | There is a Japanese restaurant across the street.<br>馬路對面有家日本料理店。 |
| **crisscross**<br>[`krɪs͵krɔs]<br>名 十字形 | crisscross design<br>十字形設計 | The crisscross design is popular this year.<br>十字形設計今年很流行。 |
| **toss**<br>[tɔs]<br>動 拋、拌 | tossed salad<br>涼拌沙拉 | I hear the tossed salad here is delicious.<br>我聽說這裡的涼拌沙拉很好吃。 |

## auce [ɔs]

| | | |
|---|---|---|
| **sauce** [sɔs] 名 調味醬、樂趣 | ▶ soy sauce 醬油 | ▶ There is too much soy sauce in this dish. 這道菜放很多醬油。 |

## ossom [ˋɑsəm]

| | | |
|---|---|---|
| **blossom** [ˋblɑsəm] 名 花 | ▶ blossoms of a tree 樹上的花 | ▶ The blossoms of a tree in spring bring a certain kind of peace and happiness. 春天樹上的花帶來一種和平快樂的感覺。 |

## ost [ost]

56

| | | |
|---|---|---|
| **host** [host] 名 主人、主辦人 | ▶ the host country 主辦國 | ▶ There is so much competition to be the host country for the Olympic Games. 要成為奧運的主辦國競爭很激烈。 |
| **ghost** [gost] 名 幽靈、鬼 | ▶ believe in ghosts 相信有鬼 | ▶ I hear some stories that make me believe in ghosts. 我聽到一些故事，讓我相信有鬼。 |
| * **most** [most] 形 最多的 副 最 | ▶ most of all 尤其 | ▶ I love playing sports, reading, and making friends. Most of all, I love traveling. 我愛運動、讀書，和交朋友。我尤其喜愛旅行。 |
| * **almost** [ˋɔlˏmost] 副 幾乎 | ▶ almost done 幾乎完成了 | ▶ The cake is almost done! 蛋糕幾乎做好了！ |

| | | |
|---|---|---|
| **utmost**<br>[ˋʌt͵most]<br>形 極度的 名 極度 | utmost importance<br>極為重要 | It is of utmost importance that you do not tell anybody about our secret. 事關重大，你不要告訴任何人我們的秘密。 |
| **innermost**<br>[ˋɪnɚ͵most]<br>形 最深處的 | her innermost feelings<br>她最深處的感覺 | She told her psychiatrist her innermost feelings. 她把最深處的感覺告訴她的心理醫師。 |
| **post**<br>[post]<br>名 郵政 動 投寄 | post office<br>郵局 | I need to go to the post office and buy some stamps.<br>我需要去郵局買些郵票。 |

## oast [ost]

| | | |
|---|---|---|
| **boast**<br>[bost]<br>動 誇耀 | boast about<br>誇耀 | Most people don't like him because he boasts about his wealth non-stop. 大部分人都不喜歡他，因為他老是誇耀他的財富。 |
| **coast**<br>[kost]<br>名 沿海地區 | along the coast<br>沿著海岸 | We drove along the coast at night.<br>晚上我們沿著海岸開車。 |
| **roast**<br>[rost]<br>動 烤、烘 | roast a chicken<br>烤雞 | Her grandmother roasted a chicken for dinner.<br>她的祖母晚餐烤了一隻雞。 |
| **toast**<br>[tost]<br>名 吐司 | a piece of toast<br>一片吐司 | She only eats a piece of toast for breakfast.<br>她早餐只吃一片吐司。 |

## ost [ɔst]

| | | |
|---|---|---|
| * **cost** [kɔst] 名 費用 動 花費 | ▶ cost of a meal 一餐的花費 | ▶ The cost of a meal in Taiwan normally is cheaper than the cost of a meal in the United States. 台灣一餐的花費通常比美國一餐還要便宜。 |
| * **lost** [lɔst] 形 遺失的、迷途的 | ▶ lost child 迷路的小孩 | ▶ There was a poor lost child crying in the supermarket. 超市裡有個可憐的迷路小孩在哭。 |
| **frost** [frɔst] 名 霜 動 結霜 | ▶ frost over 結霜 | ▶ It was so cold last night; this morning the windows were frosted over. 昨晚很冷，今早窗戶結霜了。 |

## aust [ɔst]

| | | |
|---|---|---|
| **exhaust** [ɪg`zɔst] 動 耗盡、排氣 | ▶ exhaust system of my car 車子的排氣系統 | ▶ There is something wrong with the exhaust system of my car, because black smoke is coming out of it. 我的車排氣系統有點問題，因為它一直冒黑煙。 |

## osure [`oʒɚ]

| | | |
|---|---|---|
| **exposure** [ɪk`spoʒɚ] 名 暴露 | ▶ exposure to the sun 曝曬在陽光下 | ▶ Exposure to the sun for long periods of time is damaging to your skin, especially if you don't wear sun block. 長期曝曬在陽光下會對你的皮膚造成傷害，特別是如果你沒擦防曬油。 |

| | | |
|---|---|---|
| **closure**<br>[ˋkloʒɚ]<br>名 關閉、結束 | ▸ the closure of the deal<br>交易的結束 | ▸ We came to the closure of the deal by giving the other party an extra sum of money.<br>我們給予對方額外一筆錢而結束了這場交易。 |
| **composure**<br>[kəmˋpoʒɚ]<br>名 平靜、鎮靜 | ▸ lose his composure<br>失控 | ▸ He has a bad temper and will lose his composure pretty often.<br>他的脾氣很壞，常會情緒失控。 |

## ot [ɑt]

| | | |
|---|---|---|
| **robot**<br>[ˋrobɑt]<br>名 機器人 | ▸ robots in the future<br>未來的機器人 | ▸ Hopefully there will be robots in the future which will do our household chores. 希望未來會有機器人幫我們做家事。 |
| **mascot**<br>[ˋmæskɑt]<br>名 吉祥物 | ▸ the football team's mascot<br>足球隊的吉祥物 | ▸ The football team's mascot is a bear.<br>足球隊的吉祥物是熊。 |
| **dot**<br>[dɑt]<br>名 點 動 用點構成 | ▸ dotted line<br>虛線 | ▸ Usually on perforated paper, there is a dotted line to help you tear the portion off. 通常打孔紙上會有虛線方便你撕下來。 |
| * **hot**<br>[hɑt]<br>形 熱的 | ▸ hot weather<br>天氣熱 | ▸ Do you prefer to be in hot weather, or in cold weather?<br>你較喜歡天氣熱還是天氣冷？ |
| **shot**<br>[ʃɑt]<br>名 射擊、開槍 | ▸ fatal gun shot<br>致命的一槍 | ▸ That day, one fatal gun shot ended the woman's life.<br>那一天，致命的一槍結束了那女人的生命。 |

| | | |
| --- | --- | --- |
| **bloodshot**<br>[ˋblʌdˏʃɑt]<br>形 充血的、血紅的 | bloodshot eyes<br>充血的眼睛 | Her bloodshot eyes make her look tired or drunk.<br>她充血的眼睛讓她看起來很累，或像是喝醉了。 |
| **snapshot**<br>[ˋsnæpˏʃɑt]<br>名 動 快照 | old snapshot<br>舊照片 | I found an old snapshot of my mother when she was young in the garage. 我在車庫發現我母親年輕時的舊照片。 |
| * **lot**<br>[lɑt]<br>名 很多 | a lot of money<br>很多錢 | That designer dress costs a lot of money.<br>那件設計師品牌服裝很貴。 |
| **plot**<br>[plɑt]<br>動 策劃 名 情節 | plot of a story<br>故事的情節 | If you don't understand the plot of a story, you're missing the point. 如果你不懂故事情節，你就錯過了重點。 |
| **knot**<br>[nɑt]<br>名 打結 | tie a knot<br>打個結 | She learned how to tie a knot at age 3.<br>她三歲就學會如何打結。 |
| **snot**<br>[snɑt]<br>名 鼻涕 | snot coming out of your nose<br>鼻涕流出來 | You better blow your nose; I can see snot coming out of your nose! 你最好擤擤鼻涕，我看到你的鼻涕流出來了！ |
| **pot**<br>[pɑt]<br>名 鍋、一壺之量 | a pot of tea<br>一壺茶 | My mother always has a pot of tea ready for guests.<br>我母親總是準備好一壺茶招待客人。 |
| **teapot**<br>[ˋtiˏpɑt]<br>名 茶壺 | Chinese teapot<br>中式茶壺 | She only drinks Oolong tea so she uses Chinese teapots, instead of Western ones.<br>她只喝烏龍茶，所以她用中式茶壺不用西式的。 |

| | | |
|---|---|---|
| **jackpot**<br>[ˋdʒækˏpɑt]<br>名 累積賭金 | hit the jackpot<br>贏得賭金 | Everyone dreams of hitting the jackpot someday.<br>每個人都夢想有一天能贏得賭金。 |
| **rot**<br>[rɑt]<br>動 名 腐爛 | rot away<br>爛掉 | Your teeth will rot away if you don't take care of them.<br>如果你不好好照顧你的牙齒，它們會爛掉。 |

## ought [ɔt]

| | | |
|---|---|---|
| **ought**<br>[ɔt]<br>助 應當、應該 | ought to study<br>應該用功 | He knows he ought to study for the exams, but he is addicted to his computer game.<br>他知道他應該用功準備考試，但他沈迷於電玩。 |

## ota [ˋotə]

| | | |
|---|---|---|
| **quota**<br>[ˋkwotə]<br>名 配額、定額 | the production quota<br>生產配額 | We have to make 400 more shirts in one hour to make the production quota!<br>我們必須在一小時內製作四百多件襯衫才能達到生產配額！ |

## ote [ot]

| | | |
|---|---|---|
| **dote**<br>[dot]<br>動 溺愛 | dote on his son<br>溺愛他的兒子 | He dotes on his son so much that he often forgets he has a daughter. 他很溺愛他的兒子，常忘了他還有女兒。 |

| 單字 | 片語 | 例句 |
| --- | --- | --- |
| **anecdote**<br>[ˋænɪk͵dot]<br>名 軼事 | a few anecdotes<br>一些軼事 | My friend told me a few anecdotes about her trip to jail.<br>我的朋友告訴我一些她入獄的軼事。 |
| **antidote**<br>[ˋæntɪ͵dot]<br>名 解毒劑 | an antidote to snakebites<br>解蛇毒劑 | If you are ever bitten by a poisonous snake, you better buy an antidote to snakebites as soon as possible. 如果你被毒蛇咬了，你最好儘快買解蛇毒劑。 |
| **remote**<br>[rɪˋmot]<br>形 遙遠的、偏僻的 | remote control<br>遙控器<br>a remote village<br>偏僻的村莊 | We fight over the remote control when we watch TV together. 我們一起看電視會搶搖控器。<br>Ever since he left the city, he has been living in a remote village all alone. 自從他離開城市後，他一直獨自住在偏僻的村莊。 |
| * **promote**<br>[prəˋmot]<br>動 晉升、促進 | be promoted<br>升遷 | My supervisor told me that I would be promoted by the end of this year if I worked hard enough. 我的主管告訴我，如果我努力工作，今年底會被升遷。 |
| * **note**<br>[not]<br>名 筆記、便條 | take notes<br>記筆記 | He fell asleep while he took notes in class.<br>他上課記筆記時睡著了。 |
| **footnote**<br>[ˋfʊt͵not]<br>名 註腳 | the footnote<br>註腳 | She described a literal definition and a personal definition in one of the footnotes in her paper. 她在論文中的註腳註明了原義及個人的定義。 |
| **quote**<br>[kwot]<br>動 引用、引述 | quote his speech<br>引用他的言論 | I know she quoted his speech in her presentation.<br>我知道她在簡報中引用他的言論。 |

| | | |
|---|---|---|
| * **vote**<br>[vot]<br>動 投票 | vote for<br>投給 | Who you vote for can be personal and private.<br>你要投給誰是很個人的。 |
| **devote**<br>[dɪ`vot]<br>動 奉獻給 | devote myself to<br>專心於 | This month I'm going to try to devote myself to eating healthily.<br>這個月我要致力吃得健康點。 |

## oat [ot]

57

| | | |
|---|---|---|
| **oat**<br>[ot]<br>名 燕麥 | oat bran<br>燕麥片 | Oat bran is high in fiber.<br>燕麥片有高纖成份。 |
| **boat**<br>[bot]<br>名 小船 | row a boat<br>划船 | How much longer will it take to row the boat to the shore?<br>划船到岸上還要多久？ |
| **lifeboat**<br>[`l ɪf͵bot]<br>名 救生艇 | 12 lifeboats<br>十二艘救生艇 | On this cruise ship, there are only 12 lifeboats.<br>遊艇上只有十二艘救生艇。 |
| **steamboat**<br>[`stim͵bot]<br>名 汽船 | take a steamboat<br>搭汽船 | We took a steamboat along the river when we went to New Orleans.<br>我們搭汽船沿著河到紐奧良。 |
| **raincoat**<br>[`ren͵kot]<br>名 雨衣 | wear a raincoat<br>穿雨衣 | She prefers to wear a raincoat instead of carrying an umbrella.<br>她喜歡穿雨衣勝於帶雨傘。 |

| | | |
|---|---|---|
| **goat**<br>[got]<br>名 山羊 | ▶ goat cheese<br>羊酪 | ▶ Goat cheese is crumbly, and stinky with a strong taste.<br>羊酪易碎，並有很強的臭味。 |
| **scapegoat**<br>[ˋskep͵got]<br>名 替人頂罪者 | ▶ blame on a scapegoat<br>責怪替人頂罪的人 | ▶ It's not fair how they blame their troubles on a scapegoat and never take responsibility for themselves. 他們把問題怪到別人頭上卻從不負責是很不公平的。 |
| **float**<br>[flot]<br>動 漂浮 | ▶ float away<br>漂走 | ▶ My hat fell into the water and I watched it float away.<br>我的帽子掉進水裡，我看著它漂走。 |
| **afloat**<br>[əˋflot]<br>形 漂浮著的 | ▶ get the boat afloat<br>讓船漂浮著 | ▶ They had to clog up the hole, in order to get the boat afloat.<br>他們必須把洞塞住才能讓船浮著。 |
| **throat**<br>[θrot]<br>名 喉嚨 | ▶ clear his throat<br>清他的喉嚨 | ▶ He cleared his throat in the middle of his performance.<br>他在表演中途清喉嚨。 |

## oth [oθ]

| | | |
|---|---|---|
| **both**<br>[boθ]<br>形 副 兩者皆 | ▶ both Mary and John<br>瑪麗和約翰都 | ▶ Both Mary and John like to play Scrabble.<br>瑪麗和約翰都喜歡玩拼字遊戲。 |

## oath [oθ]

| | | |
|---|---|---|
| **oath**<br>[oθ]<br>名 誓言 | take an oath<br>發誓 | I had to take an oath to tell the truth before I testified.<br>作證前，我必須發誓說實話。 |

## owth [oθ]

| | | |
|---|---|---|
| **growth**<br>[groθ]<br>名 生長、發育 | retard growth<br>減緩成長 | That method will only retard growth of our sales.<br>那種方式只會減緩我們的銷售成長。 |

## oth [ɔθ]

| | | |
|---|---|---|
| **cloth**<br>[klɔθ]<br>名 布 | a damp cloth<br>濕布 | Use a damp cloth to wipe the dining room table.<br>用濕布擦餐桌。 |

## other [ˋʌðɚ]

| | | |
|---|---|---|
| **other**<br>[ˋʌðɚ]<br>形 其他的 代 其他 | other ways<br>其他方式 | I think we can find other ways to please him.<br>我想我們可以找到其他方式討好他。 |
| **mother**<br>[ˋmʌðɚ]<br>名 母親 | mother tongue<br>母語 | English is my mother tongue.<br>英語是我的母語。 |

| | | |
|---|---|---|
| **grandmother**<br>[ˋgrænd͵mʌðɚ]<br>名 祖母 | grandmother's cooking<br>祖母的烹飪 | There's nothing like grandmother's cooking. 沒有任何東西跟我祖母做的菜一樣好。 |
| **godmother**<br>[ˋgɑd͵mʌðɚ]<br>名 教母 | taken care of by my godmother<br>由我教母照顧 | I was taken care of by my godmother until I was in college.<br>我的教母照顧我直到大學。 |
| **stepmother**<br>[stɛp͵mʌðɚ]<br>名 繼母 | evil stepmother<br>邪惡的繼母 | Cinderella was taken advantage of by her evil stepmother.<br>灰姑娘被她邪惡的繼母欺負。 |
| **smother**<br>[ˋsmʌðɚ]<br>動 使窒息 | smother with kisses<br>用吻讓人窒息 | I love it when my girlfriend smothers me with kisses.<br>我好愛我女朋友吻得我無法呼吸。 |
| **another**<br>[əˋnʌðɚ]<br>形 另一 代 另一個 | another chance<br>另一個機會 | Please give me another chance to make it up to you.<br>請給我另一個機會補償你。 |
| **brother**<br>[ˋbrʌðɚ]<br>名 兄弟 | younger brother<br>弟弟 | Her younger brother made fun of her outfits.<br>她弟弟取笑她的衣服。 |

## otic [ˋɑtɪk]

| | | |
|---|---|---|
| **chaotic**<br>[keˋɑtɪk]<br>形 混亂的 | chaotic party<br>混亂的派對 | Last night we went to a chaotic party in a warehouse. 昨晚我們去倉庫參加一個混亂的派對。 |

| | | |
|---|---|---|
| **narcotic**<br>[nar`katɪk]<br>形 麻醉性的 | a narcotic drug<br>麻醉藥 | Cocaine is a narcotic drug.<br>古柯鹼是麻醉性藥品。 |
| **antibiotic**<br>[ˌæntɪbaɪ`atɪk]<br>形 抗生的 | a course of antibiotics<br>抗生素的療程 | Depending on your illness, a doctor could prescribe a course of antibiotics.<br>醫生可視你的病情開抗生素療程。 |
| **idiotic**<br>[ˌɪdɪ`atɪk]<br>形 白癡的 | an idiotic idea<br>愚蠢的主意 | He suggested an idiotic idea of breaking into the zoo at night. 他建議在晚上闖入動物園，真是愚蠢的主意。 |
| **patriotic**<br>[ˌpetrɪ`atɪk]<br>形 愛國的 | patriotic songs<br>愛國歌曲 | There are many patriotic songs that I don't know.<br>有很多我不知道的愛國歌曲。 |
| **hypnotic**<br>[hɪp`natɪk]<br>形 催眠的 | hypnotic method<br>催眠方式 | Some psychiatrists use the hypnotic method in their sessions. 有些心理醫師會在療程中使用催眠方式。 |
| **neurotic**<br>[njʊ`ratɪk]<br>形 神經過敏的 | neurotic fears<br>神經質的恐懼 | Lately she has some neurotic fears about being watched.<br>最近她只要被看就會很神經質地感到害怕。 |
| **exotic**<br>[ɛg`zatɪk]<br>形 異國的、奇特的 | exotic dress<br>奇特的服裝 | Fashion shows often have different exotic dresses for each season. 流行秀每季通常會有不同的奇特服裝。 |

## otion [`oʃən]

| | | |
|---|---|---|
| **lotion** [ˋloʃən] 名 護膚液 ▶ | suntan lotion 防曬乳 ▶ | Don't forget to put on your suntan lotion when you're out on the beach! 到海邊時，不要忘了擦防曬乳！ |
| **motion** [ˋmoʃən] 名 移動 ▶ | slow motion 慢動作 ▶ | There is one scene from the movie that he would watch over and over in slow motion. 電影裡有一幕他會一再用慢動作觀賞。 |
| * **emotion** [ɪˋmoʃən] 名 情感 ▶ | strong emotions 強烈情感 ▶ | He has strong emotions that he can't control. 他無法控制自己強烈的情感。 |
| **commotion** [kəˋmoʃən] 名 動亂 ▶ | cause a commotion 造成動亂 ▶ | Their fight in the restaurant caused a commotion, and the manager kicked them out. 他們在餐廳裡打架造成一陣混亂，經理就把他們開除了。 |
| **notion** [ˋnoʃən] 名 概念、想法 ▶ | the old-fashioned notion 過時的想法 ▶ | The old-fashioned notion that children don't have rights is starting to change. 小孩沒有權利的古板想法已經開始改變。 |

## ocean [ˋoʃən]

| | | |
|---|---|---|
| **ocean** [ˋoʃən] 名 海洋 ▶ | the Pacific Ocean 太平洋 ▶ | I flew across the Pacific Ocean to see you. 我飛過太平洋來看你。 |

## otton [ˋɑtn̩]

| **cotton**<br>[ˋkatn̩]<br>名 棉、棉花 | ▶ cotton T-shirt<br>棉質T恤 | ▶ He wore a cotton T-shirt under his other shirts.<br>他在別件襯衫裡穿了棉質T恤。 |
|---|---|---|

## ottery [ˋatərɪ]

| **lottery**<br>[ˋlatərɪ]<br>名 獎券 | ▶ play the lottery<br>玩樂透 | ▶ Many people in Taiwan are playing the lottery.<br>台灣很多人在玩樂透。 |
|---|---|---|
| **pottery**<br>[ˋpatərɪ]<br>名 陶器 | ▶ a piece of pottery<br>一件陶器 | ▶ She gave me a piece of pottery from Japan.<br>她給我一件日本的陶器。 |

## otto [ˋato]

| **motto**<br>[ˋmato]<br>名 座右銘 | ▶ company motto<br>公司座右銘 | ▶ "The customer is always right." is a common company motto.<br>「顧客至上」是常見的公司座右銘。 |
|---|---|---|

## ouble [ˋʌbl̩]

| * **double**<br>[ˋdʌbl̩]<br>形 雙的 | ▶ a double room<br>雙人房 | ▶ We got a double room for the night.<br>我們晚上住雙人房。 |
|---|---|---|

| | | |
|---|---|---|
| * **trouble** [ˋtrʌbḷ] 名 動 麻煩 | get into trouble 惹麻煩 | Don't get into trouble while you're at school! 在學校時別惹麻煩！ |

## ubble [ˋʌbḷ]

| | | |
|---|---|---|
| **bubble** [ˋbʌbḷ] 名 氣泡 | blow bubbles 吹泡泡 | It's still fun to blow bubbles every once in a while. 偶爾吹泡泡仍然很有趣。 |
| **rubble** [ˋrʌbḷ] 名 粗石、碎石 | a heap of rubble 一堆碎石 | There is a large heap of rubble across the street. 馬路對面有一大堆碎石。 |

## ouch [aʊtʃ]

| | | |
|---|---|---|
| **ouch** [aʊtʃ] 感 哎喲 | Ouch! That hurts! 哎喲！很痛！ | Ouch! That hurts! Stop hitting me! 哎喲！很痛！別打我了！ |
| **couch** [kaʊtʃ] 名 長沙發 | sit on the couch 坐在長沙發上 | It's relaxing to sit on the couch and watch TV. 坐在長沙發上看電視很輕鬆。 |
| **pouch** [paʊtʃ] 名 錢包 | small pouch 小錢包 | She had a small pouch full of money hidden away in her room. 她把裝滿錢的小錢包藏在她房間裡。 |

| | | |
|---|---|---|
| **crouch** [ˋkrautʃ] 動 蹲伏 | ▶ crouch next to the wall 蜷伏在牆邊 | ▶ We saw the tiger crouch next to the wall of its cage and growl. 我們看到老虎蜷伏在籠子的牆邊咆哮。 |
| **vouch** [vautʃ] 動 擔保、保證 | ▶ vouch for 保證 | ▶ I can vouch for my good friends. 我可以為我的好朋友作擔保。 |

## oud [aʊd]

58

| | | |
|---|---|---|
| * **loud** [laʊd] 形 大聲的 | ▶ a loud voice 很大的聲音 | ▶ I heard a loud voice outside the hall. 我聽到大廳外有很大的聲音。 |
| **aloud** [əˋlaʊd] 副 大聲地 | ▶ cry aloud 哭得很大聲 | ▶ It feels good to cry aloud sometimes. 有時放聲大哭感覺很好。 |
| **cloud** [klaʊd] 名 雲 | ▶ dark storm clouds 黑色暴風雲 | ▶ I see some dark storm clouds up ahead. We better get inside. 我看到頭頂上有些黑雲，我們最好快進去。 |
| * **proud** [praʊd] 形 驕傲的 | ▶ proud of 以…為傲 | ▶ Her parents are very proud of her. 她的父母很以她為傲。 |

## owd [aʊd]

| | | |
|---|---|---|
| **crowd**<br>[kraʊd]<br>名 人群 動 擁擠 | a crowd of<br>很多<br>▶ crowd the platform<br>擠滿月台 | There was a crowd of people surrounding the robbery.<br>有很多人圍繞著搶劫現場。<br>▶ It's really annoying when people crowd the platform waiting for a train. 等火車時有很多人擠在月台上真的很討厭。 |
| **overcrowd**<br>[ˏovɚˋkraʊd]<br>動 過度擁擠 | overcrowded<br>▶ city<br>過度擁擠的城市 | Tokyo is an overcrowded<br>▶ city.<br>東京是個過度擁擠的城市。 |

## ounce [aʊns]

| | | |
|---|---|---|
| **ounce**<br>[aʊns]<br>名 盎司、少量 | ounce of<br>▶ chicken<br>一點雞肉 | Eating an ounce of chicken<br>▶ every day is good for you.<br>每天吃一點雞肉對你有好處。 |
| **bounce**<br>[baʊns]<br>動 彈回 | bounce off<br>▶<br>彈出去 | The sound in this hall bounces off the walls and makes an<br>▶ echo.<br>這大廳裡的聲音碰到牆反彈出去產生回音。 |
| **renounce**<br>[rɪˋnaʊns]<br>動 聲明放棄 | renounce<br>▶ his religion<br>聲明放棄宗教信仰 | He renounced his religion after seeing the death of his<br>▶ parents.<br>在他父母去世後，他聲明放棄他的宗教信仰。 |
| **announce**<br>[əˋnaʊns]<br>動 宣佈 | announce<br>▶ the winner<br>宣佈冠軍 | Quickly! They are going to announce the winner of the<br>▶ contest soon!<br>快點！他們就快要宣佈比賽冠軍！ |

| | | |
|---|---|---|
| **pronounce**<br>[prə`naʊns]<br>動 發音 | ▶ pronounce this word<br>發這個字的音 | ▶ Do you know how to pronounce this word?<br>你知道這個字如何發音嗎？ |

## ound [aʊnd]

| | | |
|---|---|---|
| **round**<br>[raʊnd]<br>形 圓的 | ▶ round shaped<br>圓形的 | ▶ I'm looking for a round shaped table.<br>我正在找圓形的桌子。 |
| **found**<br>[faʊnd]<br>形 找到的 動 建立 | ▶ already found<br>已被找到了 | ▶ Stop looking for it; it's already found.<br>別找了，已經找到了。 |

## owned [aʊnd]

| | | |
|---|---|---|
| **renowned**<br>[rɪ`naʊnd]<br>形 有名的 | ▶ renowned for<br>以…出名 | ▶ This restaurant is renowned for its atmosphere, not its food. 這餐廳有名的是它的氣氛，不是它的食物。 |

## our [aʊr]

| | | |
|---|---|---|
| * **our**<br>[aʊr]<br>代 我們的 | ▶ our lives<br>我們的生命 | ▶ We need to cherish our lives.<br>我們必須愛惜我們的生命。 |

| | | |
|---|---|---|
| * **hour** [aʊr] 名 小時、時間 ▶ | after hours 營業時間後 ▶ | There is an after hours party at another club. 在另一家俱樂部裡有場營業時間後的派對。 |
| **flour** [flaʊr] 名 麵粉 ▶ | plain flour 中筋麵粉 ▶ | Add some plain flour to the mixture and mix it well. 加一些中筋麵粉好好攪拌。 |
| **sour** [saʊr] 形 酸的 ▶ | a sour taste 酸味 ▶ | I don't know why there is a sour taste in my mouth. 我不知道為何我的嘴巴會有酸酸的味道。 |
| **devour** [dɪˋvaʊr] 動 狼吞虎嚥 ▶ | devour his food 狼吞虎嚥吃東西 ▶ | He looks like an animal when he is hungry and he devours his food. 他餓起來狼吞虎嚥的樣子看起來就像動物。 |

## owér [ˋaʊɚ]

| | | |
|---|---|---|
| **Mayflower** [ˋmeˏflaʊɚ] 名 五月花號 ▶ | aboard the Mayflower 登上五月花號 ▶ | Protestants from England went aboard the Mayflower to come to America. 來自英國的新教徒登上五月花號來到美國。 |
| * **power** [ˋpaʊɚ] 名 權力 ▶ | in power 當權 ▶ | There are presently two people in power now in my social organization. 目前在我的社會組織裡有兩位當權者。 |
| **horsepower** [ˋhɔrsˏpaʊɚ] 名 馬力 ▶ | a 120 horsepower engine 120匹馬力的引擎 ▶ | He wants to buy a 120 horsepower engine for his car. 他想幫他的車子買個一百二十匹馬力的引擎。 |

| | | |
|---|---|---|
| **willpower**<br>[ˋwɪlˏpaʊɚ]<br>名 意志力 | sheer willpower<br>全心的意志力 | She lost forty pounds by using her sheer willpower not to overeat. 她用全心的意志力節制飲食，減了四十磅。 |
| **empower**<br>[ɪmˋpaʊɚ]<br>動 授權、使能夠 | empower people with<br>使人們能夠… | Education empowers people with knowledge.<br>教育讓人們有知識。 |
| **superpower**<br>[ˏsupɚˋpaʊɚ]<br>名 超強力量 | possess superpower<br>擁有超強力量 | Spiderman and Superman possess superpowers.<br>蜘蛛人和超人擁有超強的力量。 |
| **overpower**<br>[ˏovɚˋpaʊɚ]<br>動 擊敗、制伏 | overpowering smell<br>無法忍受的味道 | There is an overpowering smell of stinky feet in this room. 在這房間裡有令人無法忍受的腳臭味。 |
| **tower**<br>[ˋtaʊɚ]<br>名 塔 | bell tower<br>鐘塔 | They used to meet at the bell tower at night for a secret date.<br>他們曾在夜晚約在鐘塔祕密約會。 |

## ouse [aʊs]

| | | |
|---|---|---|
| **house**<br>[haʊs]<br>名 房子、家庭 | house keeper<br>管家 | Some people hire house keepers to clean the house.<br>有些人雇用管家打掃房子。 |
| **madhouse**<br>[ˋmædˏhaʊs]<br>名 吵鬧的場所 | absolute madhouse<br>吵雜的場所 | This protest turned out to be an absolute madhouse!<br>這場抗議結果成了鬧哄哄的活動！ |

| | | |
|---|---|---|
| **warehouse**<br>[ˋwɛr͵haus]<br>名 倉庫 | empty warehouse<br>空倉庫 | The children found an empty warehouse and went inside.<br>小孩發現有個空的倉庫就進去了。 |
| **lighthouse**<br>[ˋlaɪt͵haus]<br>名 燈塔 | a lighthouse keeper<br>燈塔看守員 | A lighthouse keeper must be alert at all times.<br>燈塔的看守員必須全天候警戒。 |

## out [aʊt]

| | | |
|---|---|---|
| **out**<br>[aut]<br>副 形 出外、在外 | go out<br>出去 | Will you go out with me on a date?<br>你要跟我出去約會嗎？ |
| **about**<br>[əˋbaut]<br>介 關於 副 四周 | about me<br>關於我<br>walk about<br>四處走走 | I want you to know everything about me.<br>我想要讓你知道關於我的每一件事。<br>We walked about for hours.<br>我們四處走走了好幾個小時。 |
| **scout**<br>[skaut]<br>名 動 尋找、偵察 | scout for<br>尋找 | The dog is scouting for a missing child.<br>這隻狗正在尋找失蹤的小孩。 |
| **handout**<br>[ˋhændaut]<br>名 傳單、講義 | read the handout<br>讀講義 | We had to read the handout for homework, but I lost it somewhere. 我們必須讀講義才能做功課，但我不知它掉到哪了。 |
| **throughout**<br>[θruˋaut]<br>介 遍及 | throughout history<br>整個歷史 | Throughout history, there has always been evil.<br>歷史上總是有邪惡存在。 |

| | | |
|---|---|---|
| **shout**<br>[ʃaut]<br>動名 喊叫 | shout loudly<br>大叫 | If you keep on shouting loudly, the neighbors will call the police!<br>如果你一直大叫，鄰居會叫警察！ |
| **without**<br>[wɪ`ðaut]<br>介 無、沒有 | without a word<br>一聲不響 | She left town without a word to anyone.<br>她沒跟任何人說一聲就離開鎮上了。 |
| **knockout**<br>[`nɑk͵aut]<br>名 擊倒對手 | by knockout<br>擊倒對手 | The boxer won the match by knockout.<br>拳擊手擊倒對手贏了比賽。 |
| **lookout**<br>[`luk`aut]<br>名 監視、注意 | on the lookout for<br>密切注意著 | Watch out! That gang is on the lookout for you!<br>小心！那群歹徒正在密切注意你！ |
| **pout**<br>[paut]<br>動名 噘嘴 | pout on her face<br>噘嘴 | Look at that pout on her face! She's upset now.<br>你看她噘起嘴來了！她現在很沮喪。 |
| **dropout**<br>[`drɑp͵aut]<br>名 退學者 | high school dropout<br>高中退學生 | It's hard to find a good job as a high school dropout.<br>高中中輟生很難找到一份好工作。 |
| **spout**<br>[spaut]<br>動 噴出 | spout out<br>噴出、滔滔不絕 | She should keep her mouth shut because she tends to spout out things she shouldn't say. 她應該閉嘴，因為她容易說出不該說的事。 |

## oute [ut]

| | | |
|---|---|---|
| **route** [rut] 名 路線 | take this route 走這條路 | Take this route to the shopping center. 走這條路去購物中心。 |

## outh [aʊθ]

| | | |
|---|---|---|
| **mouth** [maʊθ] 名 嘴 | a big mouth 大嘴巴 | He has a big mouth; don't tell him any secrets. 他是個大嘴巴，不要告訴他任何秘密。 |
| **south** [saʊθ] 名 南方 | face south 面向南方 | Her apartment faces south. 她的公寓面向南方。 |

## ove [ov]

59

| | | |
|---|---|---|
| **stove** [stov] 名 火爐、暖爐 | hot stove 熱火爐 | Be careful. The hot stove will burn you. 小心點，這熱火爐會燙到你。 |

## ove [ʌv]

| | | |
|---|---|---|
| * **above** [ə`bʌv] 介 在…之上 | above all 最重要的 | I love my friends and my job and my life. Above all, I love my husband. 我愛我的朋友，我的工作和我的生活。最重要的是，我愛我先生。 |

| | | |
|---|---|---|
| **dove**<br>[dʌv]<br>名 鴿、温和派人士 | white dove<br>白鴿 | White doves are a symbol for peace.<br>白鴿是和平的象徵。 |
| * **love**<br>[lʌv]<br>名 愛情 動 愛 | fall in love with<br>愛上… | He fell in love with another woman.<br>他愛上另一個女人。 |
| **glove**<br>[glʌv]<br>名 手套 | baseball glove<br>棒球手套 | My dad got me a new baseball glove.<br>我爸買給我一副新的棒球手套。 |

## ove [uv]

| | | |
|---|---|---|
| * **move**<br>[muv]<br>動 移動、搬動 | move out<br>搬出去 | I told him to move out of the house.<br>我要他搬出這房子。 |
| **remove**<br>[rɪ`muv]<br>動 搬開、移除 | remove from<br>移除 | Please remove the tag from the dress.<br>請將這衣服的標籤拿掉。 |
| * **prove**<br>[pruv]<br>動 證明 | prove true<br>證明是真的 | If your theory proves true then you are a genius!<br>如果你的理論可證明是真的，你就是個天才！ |
| * **approve**<br>[ə`pruv]<br>動 贊成 | approve of<br>贊成 | My parents don't approve of my choice in clothes.<br>我父母不贊成我選的衣服。 |

| | | |
|---|---|---|
| **disapprove**<br>[ˏdɪsəˋpruv]<br>動 不贊成 | ▶ disapprove of<br>不贊成 | ▶ Her friends disapprove of her new boyfriend.<br>她的朋友不喜歡她新交的男朋友。 |

## over [ˋovɚ]

| | | |
|---|---|---|
| * **over**<br>[ˋovɚ]<br>介 越過 形 結束的 | ▶ run over<br>輾過<br>game over<br>遊戲結束 | ▶ Unfortunately, her precious dog got run over by a car.<br>不幸的是她心愛的狗狗被車輾過。<br>Game over, you lose.<br>遊戲結束了，你輸了。 |
| **turnover**<br>[ˋtɝnˏovɚ]<br>名 翻轉、流動率 | ▶ high turnover rate<br>高搬遷率 | ▶ This neighborhood has a high turnover rate.<br>這社區搬遷率高。 |
| **leftover**<br>[ˋleftˏovɚ]<br>名 殘餘物 | ▶ eat leftovers<br>吃剩菜 | ▶ I hate eating leftovers for dinner three nights in a row.<br>我討厭連續三天晚餐都吃剩菜。 |

## ow [aʊ]

| | | |
|---|---|---|
| **bow**<br>[baʊ]<br>名 動 鞠躬 | ▶ take a bow<br>鞠躬 | ▶ The ballerina took a bow after her wonderful performance.<br>芭蕾舞女演員在精采演出後鞠躬。 |
| **cow**<br>[kaʊ]<br>名 母牛 | ▶ milk from a cow<br>牛奶 | ▶ He likes goat's milk rather than milk from a cow.<br>他喜歡羊奶而非牛奶。 |

| | | |
|---|---|---|
| **meow**<br>[mɪˋaʊ]<br>名 貓叫聲 | the cat's meow<br>貓的叫聲 | Last night the cat's meows kept me up all night.<br>昨晚貓叫聲讓我整晚沒睡。 |
| **how**<br>[haʊ]<br>副 連 怎樣、怎麼 | how come<br>怎麼會 | How come you never come and visit me anymore?<br>為何你不再來看我了？ |
| **somehow**<br>[ˋsʌm͵haʊ]<br>副 不知怎麼地 | somehow<br>不知怎麼地 | Somehow she felt uneasy.<br>不知怎麼地她感到不自在。 |
| **anyhow**<br>[ˋɛnɪ͵haʊ]<br>副 不管怎樣 | anyhow<br>不管怎樣 | Anyhow, let's change the subject.<br>不管怎樣，我們換個主題吧。 |
| **allow**<br>[əˋlaʊ]<br>動 允許、准許 | allow me to explain<br>允許我解釋 | Please allow me to explain why I have been late every day the past week. 請允許我解釋為何我過去這個星期每天遲到。 |
| **now**<br>[naʊ]<br>名 現在 副 馬上 | right now<br>馬上 | I could eat a whole box of chocolate right now.<br>我現在就可以吃下整盒巧克力。 |
| **eyebrow**<br>[ˋaɪ͵braʊ]<br>名 眉毛 | raise his eyebrows<br>挑眉 | He raised his eyebrows to express his interest in the subject. 他的眉表示他對這個話題很有興趣。 |
| **kowtow**<br>[ˋkaʊˋtaʊ]<br>名 動 叩頭 | kowtow to<br>叩頭 | It is not customary to kowtow to others in American society. 在美國社會裡沒有對別人叩頭的習俗。 |

| | | |
|---|---|---|
| **vow**<br>[vaʊ]<br>名 誓言 動 發誓 | take a vow<br>發誓 | They made me take a vow never to tell anyone about the murder. 他們要我發誓絕不告訴任何人關於謀殺案的事。 |

## owder [ˋaʊdɚ]

| | | |
|---|---|---|
| **powder**<br>[ˋpaʊdɚ]<br>名 粉末 | baby powder<br>嬰兒痱子粉 | She likes to use baby powder over her body after she showers. 她喜歡在洗澡後用嬰兒痱子粉灑遍全身。 |

## oward [ˋaʊɚd]

| | | |
|---|---|---|
| **coward**<br>[ˋkaʊɚd]<br>名 懦夫 | be a coward<br>是個懦夫 | Don't be a coward! Fight like a man!<br>不要像個懦夫！像個男人一樣戰鬥！ |

## owing [ˋoɪŋ]

| | | |
|---|---|---|
| **showing**<br>[ˋʃoɪŋ]<br>名 陳列、放映 | showing of a film<br>放映電影 | There will be a showing of a film in the school's auditorium tonight.<br>今晚學校大禮堂將放映電影。 |
| **flowing**<br>[ˋfloɪŋ]<br>形 流暢的 | flowing handwriting<br>流暢的筆跡 | You can tell by the flowing handwriting that Beth wrote this note. 你可從流暢的筆跡看出是貝絲寫的便條。 |

| | | |
|---|---|---|
| **glowing**<br>[ˋgloɪŋ]<br>形 熱烈的 | ▶ face is glowing<br>臉上展露熱情 | ▶ Every time she's with him, her face is glowing. 每當她跟他在一起時，臉上就會展露熱情。 |
| **knowing**<br>[ˋnoɪŋ]<br>形 會意的 | ▶ give a knowing look<br>給個會意的眼神 | ▶ He gave her a knowing look that he understood the gesture. 他給了她會意的眼神，表示他了解手勢的意思。 |

## oing [ˋoɪŋ]

| | | |
|---|---|---|
| **ongoing**<br>[ˋɑnˏgoɪŋ]<br>形 前進的 | ▶ an ongoing process<br>前進過程 | ▶ Recovering from trauma is an ongoing process that isn't easy.<br>從創傷中走出並不是容易的過程。 |
| **outgoing**<br>[ˋaʊtˏgoɪŋ]<br>形 外向的、外出的 | ▶ an outgoing person<br>外向的人 | ▶ She is an outgoing person who always meets new people.<br>她是個外向的人，總是認識新朋友。 |
| **easygoing**<br>[ˋizɪˏgoɪŋ]<br>形 隨和的 | ▶ an easygoing person<br>隨和的人 | ▶ He is an easygoing person who takes things as they come.<br>他隨遇而安，是個隨和的人。 |

## owel [ˋaʊəl]

60

| | | |
|---|---|---|
| **bowel**<br>[ˋbaʊəl]<br>名 腸 | ▶ Irritable Bowel Syndrome<br>腸易激綜合症 | ▶ Irritable Bowel Syndrome is a physical and mental disease that does not have a cure yet. 腸易激綜合症是生理及心理的疾病，目前還沒有治療方法。 |

| | | |
|---|---|---|
| **towel**<br>[ˋtauəl]<br>名 毛巾 | ▶ bath towel<br>浴巾 | ▶ Can you get me a clean bath towel from the closet? 你可以從衣櫃裡幫我拿條乾淨的浴巾嗎？ |
| **vowel**<br>[ˋvauəl]<br>名 母音 | ▶ sound a vowel<br>發母音 | ▶ It's hard to sound a vowel that is not in your mother tongue.<br>要發一個你母語中沒有的母音很難。 |

## oul [aul]

| | | |
|---|---|---|
| **foul**<br>[faul]<br>形 骯髒的 | ▶ foul language<br>髒話 | ▶ I will not tolerate foul language in my classroom.<br>我無法忍受在我班上有人講髒話。 |

## own [aun]

| | | |
|---|---|---|
| **down**<br>[daun]<br>副 向下 | ▶ write down<br>寫下 | ▶ Please write down your name and number.<br>請寫下你的名字和號碼。 |
| **touchdown**<br>[ˋtʌtʃˏdaun]<br>名 著陸、達陣 | ▶ get a touchdown<br>達陣得分 | ▶ The other team got a touchdown with only one minute left in the game.<br>另一隊在終場前一分鐘達陣得分。 |
| **breakdown**<br>[ˋbrekˏdaun]<br>名 故障、崩潰 | ▶ mental breakdown<br>精神崩潰 | ▶ After the death of her parents, she had a mental breakdown.<br>她的父母去世後，她精神崩潰。 |

| | | |
|---|---|---|
| **crackdown**<br>[ˋkræk͵daʊn]<br>名 動 取締、痛擊 | ▶ crackdown on crime<br>**取締犯罪** | ▶ The mayor of this city wants to crackdown on crime.<br>這市長想要取締犯罪。 |
| **sundown**<br>[ˋsʌn͵daʊn]<br>名 日落 | ▶ at sundown<br>**在日落** | ▶ Vampires and other nocturnal creatures start to come out at sundown. 吸血鬼和其他夜行性怪物在日落後開始出來活動。 |
| **letdown**<br>[ˋlɛt͵daʊn]<br>名 失望 | ▶ what a letdown<br>**真失望** | ▶ What a letdown! I was expecting to get a lot more money for New Year's. 真失望！我原本以為過年能拿到更多錢的。 |
| **meltdown**<br>[ˋmɛlt͵daʊn]<br>名 核反應爐熔毀 | ▶ danger of meltdown<br>**熔毀的危險** | ▶ The engine is too hot and there is a danger of meltdown.<br>引擎太熱了，有熔毀的危險。 |
| **countdown**<br>[ˋkaʊnt͵daʊn]<br>名 倒數計時 | ▶ countdown to the New Year<br>**新年倒數計時** | ▶ We went to Times Square in NYC to watch the famous countdown to the New Year.<br>我們去紐約時代廣場參加有名的新年倒數計時。 |
| **gown**<br>[gaʊn]<br>名 禮服 | ▶ wedding gown<br>**結婚禮服** | ▶ Her wedding gown cost her almost two million dollars.<br>她的結婚禮服花了她近兩百萬元。 |
| **clown**<br>[klaʊn]<br>名 小丑、丑角 | ▶ sad clown<br>**悲傷的小丑** | ▶ I saw a sad clown walking down the street.<br>我看到悲傷的小丑沿著街道行走。 |
| **crown**<br>[kraʊn]<br>名 王冠 動 為…加冕 | ▶ crown a beauty queen<br>**為選美皇后加冕** | ▶ The judges said it was hard to crown a beauty queen because they were all beautiful. 評審說很難選出選美皇后，因為大家都很美。 |

| | | |
|---|---|---|
| **drown**<br>[draʊn]<br>動 解愁、淹沒 | drown his sorrows<br>解愁 | By drinking lots of alcohol, he's trying to drown his sorrows. 他試圖借酒澆愁。 |
| **frown**<br>[fraʊn]<br>動 皺眉 | frown upon<br>不被贊成 | Drugs are frowned upon in the majority of the world.<br>毒品在多數人眼中是不被贊成的。 |
| * **town**<br>[taʊn]<br>名 市鎮 | go to town<br>去鎮上 | We will go to town to find the book we are looking for.<br>我們要去鎮上找我們正在找的書。 |
| **Chinatown**<br>[`tʃaɪnə͵taʊn]<br>名 中國城 | eat in Chinatown<br>在中國城吃東西 | Let's eat in Chinatown for dinner.<br>我們在中國城吃晚餐吧。 |
| * **downtown**<br>[͵daʊn`taʊn]<br>名 城市商業區 | go downtown<br>去市中心 | I want to go downtown and go shopping.<br>我想去市中心購物。 |

## ox [ɑks]

| | | |
|---|---|---|
| **ox**<br>[ɑks]<br>名 牛 | ox tail soup<br>牛尾湯 | He likes his mother's ox tail soup.<br>他喜歡他媽媽煮的牛尾湯。 |
| * **box**<br>[bɑks]<br>名 箱、盒 | a box of<br>一盒 | I'd like to buy a box of cigarettes please.<br>我想買一盒香菸，謝謝。 |

| | | |
|---|---|---|
| **lunchbox**<br>[ˋlʌntʃbɑks]<br>名 午餐飯盒 | ▶ bring a lunchbox<br>帶午餐便當 | ▶ She brings a lunchbox to school every day.<br>她每天帶午餐便當到學校。 |
| **mailbox**<br>[ˋmelˏbɑks]<br>名 信箱 | ▶ open his mailbox<br>打開他的信箱 | ▶ He opens his mailbox every day, but gets no mail.<br>他每天打開他的信箱，但都沒有信。 |
| **fox**<br>[fɑks]<br>名 狐、狡猾的人 | ▶ sly fox<br>狡猾的人 | ▶ She is one sly fox who's beautiful, smart, and tricky. 她是個狡猾的人，漂亮、聰明又難以捉摸。 |
| **chickenpox**<br>[ˋtʃɪkɪnˏpɑks]<br>名 水痘 | ▶ get the chickenpox<br>得到水痘 | ▶ Everyone gets the chickenpox once in their lifetime.<br>每個人一生中都會得一次水痘。 |
| **sox**<br>[sɑks]<br>名 短襪 | ▶ Boston Red Sox<br>波士頓紅襪隊 | ▶ My favorite baseball team in America is the Boston Red Sox. 我最喜歡的美國棒球隊是波士頓紅襪隊。 |

## oy [ɔɪ]

| | | |
|---|---|---|
| **boy**<br>[bɔɪ]<br>名 男孩 | ▶ boyfriend<br>男朋友 | ▶ My boyfriend loves me, but he likes to look at other pretty girls too. 我男朋友愛我，但他也喜歡看其他漂亮的女孩。 |
| **joy**<br>[dʒɔɪ]<br>名 歡樂、高興 | ▶ jump for joy<br>高興得跳起來 | ▶ When he found out that he won the lottery, he jumped for joy. 當他知道贏了樂透，他高興得跳起來。 |

| | | |
|---|---|---|
| **enjoy** [ɪn`dʒɔɪ] 動 欣賞、享受 | enjoy yourself 過得快活 | You need to learn how to enjoy yourself. 你必須學會過得快活。 |
| * **employ** [ɪm`plɔɪ] 動 雇用 | employ some new workers 雇用一些新人 | That company wants to employ some new workers. 那間公司想雇用一些新人。 |
| * **annoy** [ə`nɔɪ] 動 惹惱、使生氣 | annoy me 讓我生氣 | For some reason, that boy really annoys me. 因為某種理由，那個男孩真的讓我很生氣。 |
| **toy** [tɔɪ] 名 玩具 | a toy gun 玩具槍 | My little cousin wants to play with a toy gun. 我的小表弟想玩玩具槍。 |
| **buoy** [bɔɪ] 名 浮標、救生圈 | life buoy 救生圈 | Thank god there was a life buoy on the boat. 感謝上天船上有救生圈。 |

## oise [ɔɪz]

| | | |
|---|---|---|
| * **noise** [nɔɪz] 名 聲響、噪音 | make a noise 製造噪音 | Don't make a noise. The baby is sleeping. 不要製造噪音，小嬰兒正在睡覺。 |
| **poise** [pɔɪz] 動 使平衡 名 姿態 | poise the vase 使花瓶平衡<br>graceful poise 優雅的姿態 | We tried to poise the vase on the unstable table. 我們試著讓花瓶在不穩的桌上平衡。<br>She is good at ballet because she has graceful poise. 她姿態優雅，是個很好的芭蕾舞者。 |

# 5. 押 U 韻的單字

## ub [ʌb]



| | | |
|---|---|---|
| * **club** [klʌb] 名 俱樂部 | ▶ a tennis club 網球俱樂部 | ▶ Since we lived in the city, we had to join a tennis club to play tennis. 因為我們住在都市，必須參加網球俱樂部才能打網球。 |
| **pub** [pʌb] 名 酒吧 | ▶ go to the pub 去酒吧 | ▶ Let's go to the pub and have a beer. 讓我們去酒吧喝杯啤酒吧。 |
| **rub** [rʌb] 動 磨擦 | ▶ rub off 擦掉 | ▶ You can rub off a temporary tattoo. 你可以擦掉暫時性的刺青。 |
| **scrub** [skrʌb] 動 名 用力擦洗 | ▶ scrub the toilet 洗廁所 | ▶ Your punishment is to scrub the toilet. 你的懲罰是去洗廁所。 |
| **bathtub** [ˋbæθˏtʌb] 名 浴缸 | ▶ clean the bathtub 清洗浴缸 | ▶ I'm going to clean the bathtub and take a nice, hot bath. 我要把浴缸洗乾淨，然後洗個舒服的熱水澡。 |

## ubber [ˋʌbɚ]

| | | |
|---|---|---|
| **rubber** [ˋrʌbɚ] 名 橡膠 | ▶ made of rubber 橡膠做成的 | ▶ These tires are made of rubber. 這些輪胎是橡膠做成的。 |

## ubby [ˋʌbɪ]

| | | |
|---|---|---|
| **chubby** [ˋtʃʌbɪ] 形 圓胖的 ▶ | chubby cheeks 圓胖的臉頰 ▶ | People think she is fat, but she just has chubby cheeks. 大家都覺得她胖，其實她只是臉頰圓。 |

## ube [jub]

| | | |
|---|---|---|
| **cube** [kjub] 名 立方體 ▶ | ice cube 冰塊 ▶ | Can you get some ice cubes from the freezer? 你可以從冷凍庫拿些冰塊來嗎？ |
| **tube** [tjub] 名 管狀物 ▶ | a tube of toothpaste 一條牙膏 ▶ | I accidentally squeezed a tube of toothpaste on my shirt. 我不小心將牙膏擠到我的襯衫上。 |

## uck [ʌk]

| | | |
|---|---|---|
| **duck** [dʌk] 名 鴨子、鴨肉 ▶ | roast duck 烤鴨 ▶ | He won't eat roast duck because he used to feed ducks at a pond. 他不吃烤鴨，因為他過去常在池塘餵鴨子。 |
| **suck** [sʌk] 動 吸吮 ▶ | suck up 吸收<br>suck his thumb 吸拇指 ▶ | That vacuum cleaner can suck up anything, even a quarter. 那個吸塵器能吸任何東西，甚至是一枚硬幣。<br>At age 9, he was still sucking his thumb and holding a blanket. 他九歲的時候還在抱毯子吸大拇指。 |

| | | |
|---|---|---|
| **truck** [trʌk] 名 卡車 | ▶ truck stop 卡車餐廳 | ▶ I need to stop at a truck stop off the highway to use the bathroom. 我得下高速公路到卡車餐廳上個廁所。 |

## ucky [`ʌkɪ]

| | | |
|---|---|---|
| **lucky** [`lʌkɪ] 形 幸運的 | ▶ wear a lucky charm 戴著幸運飾物 | ▶ She always wears her lucky charm when she takes a test. 考試時她總是戴著幸運飾物。 |

## uct [ʌkt]

| | | |
|---|---|---|
| **abduct** [æb`dʌkt] 動 綁架 | ▶ abduct a boy 綁架男孩 | ▶ He abducted a rich boy for ransom money. 他綁架家裡有錢的男孩來勒索贖金。 |
| * **deduct** [dɪ`dʌkt] 動 扣除 | ▶ tax-deductible 免稅的 | ▶ If you give to charity, your donation will be tax-deductible. 如果你捐錢給慈善機構，你的捐款將可免稅。 |
| * **conduct** [kən`dʌkt] [`kɑndʌkt] 動 引導 名 品行 | ▶ good conduct 良好品行 | ▶ Good conduct comes from discipline and respect. 良好的品行來自教養及尊重。 |
| **obstruct** [əb`strʌkt] 動 阻塞 | ▶ obstruct the road 阻塞道路 | ▶ That car accident obstructed the road. 那場車禍造成道路阻塞。 |

| | | |
|---|---|---|
| * **instruct** [ɪn`strʌkt] 動 指示、教導 | ▶ instruct people in 指導人們 | ▶ As a martial arts instructor, he instructs people in defending themselves through karate. 身為武術指導，他教大家用空手道保護自己。 |
| * **construct** [kən`strʌkt] [`kɑnstrʌkt] 動 建造 名 構想 | ▶ construct a house 建造一間房子 | ▶ She constructed a house with sticks. 她用柴枝蓋了一間房子。 |

## uction [`ʌkʃən]

| | | |
|---|---|---|
| * **production** [prə`dʌkʃən] 名 生產 | ▶ auto production 自動化生產 | ▶ The auto production industry worldwide keeps on changing. 全世界自動化生產產業一直在改變。 |
| * **introduction** [ˏɪntrə`dʌkʃən] 名 介紹 | ▶ make an introduction 作個介紹 | ▶ I'd like to make an introduction of my sister. This is Emily. 我來介紹我姊姊，這位是Emily。 |
| **destruction** [dɪ`strʌkʃən] 名 破壞 | ▶ cause serious destruction 造成嚴重的破壞 | ▶ The earthquake caused serious destruction in my town. 地震對鎮上造成嚴重的破壞。 |
| * **instruction** [ɪn`strʌkʃən] 名 教學、講授 | ▶ 2 hours of instruction 兩小時的教學 | ▶ Her piano teacher gives her two hours of instruction every other day. 她的鋼琴老師每隔一天教她兩個小時。 |
| * **construction** [kən`strʌkʃən] 名 建造 | ▶ under construction 在建造中 | ▶ Stay away from this building because it's under construction. 遠離這棟建築物，因為它正在建造中。 |

## uctive [ˋʌktɪv]

| | | |
|---|---|---|
| **productive** [prəˋdʌktɪv] 形 有成效的 | ▶ to be productive 是有成效的 | ▶ It's hard to be productive when it's just nice outside. 當它只是外表很好時，是很難有實際的成效的。 |
| **destructive** [dɪˋstrʌktɪv] 形 毀滅性的 | ▶ destructive behavior 毀滅性的行為 | ▶ They are worried about their son's destructive behavior. 他們擔心兒子的毀滅性行為。 |

## uctor [ˋʌktɚ]

| | | |
|---|---|---|
| **conductor** [kənˋdʌktɚ] 名 售票員 | ▶ conductor on the train 火車上的售票員 | ▶ I don't have enough time to buy a ticket at the booth. I'll just buy it from the conductor on the train. 我沒時間在售票亭買車票，會直接跟火車上的售票員買。 |
| * **instructor** [ɪnˋstrʌktɚ] 名 教員、教練 | ▶ scuba diving instructor 潛水教練 | ▶ My scuba diving instructor in Bali couldn't speak English, so I was scared. 我在峇里島的潛水教練不會說英語，所以我很害怕。 |

## ud [ʌd]

| | | |
|---|---|---|
| **bud** [bʌd] 名 芽、花苞 | ▶ bud of flower 花苞 | ▶ She would make birthday cards out of buds of flowers. 她會用花苞作生日卡片。 |
| **mud** [mʌd] 名 泥 | ▶ wash off the mud 洗掉泥巴 | ▶ Wash off the mud on your shoes before you come in. 你進來之前先洗掉鞋子上的泥巴。 |

## ood [ʌd]

| | | |
|---|---|---|
| **blood** [blʌd] 名 血液 | new blood 新成員 | Our boss hired a new woman to be our receptionist. It's nice to have new blood in the office. 我們老板雇了一位新女性當接待員，辦公室裡有新成員很棒。 |
| **flood** [flʌd] 名 洪水 | lost in the flood 消失在洪水裡 | The little girl got lost in the flood. 小女孩消失在洪水裡。 |

## uddha [`ʊdə]

| | | |
|---|---|---|
| **Buddha** [`bʊdə] 名 佛陀、佛 | pray to Buddha 拜佛 | Sometimes he goes to the temple at night to pray to Buddha. 有時他晚上會去廟裡拜佛。 |

## uddle [`ʌdl̩]

| | | |
|---|---|---|
| **huddle** [`hʌdl̩] 動 名 擠作一團 | huddle together 擠在一起 | During time outs, the team huddled together to discuss what to do next. 比賽暫停時，隊員們擠在一起討論接下來該怎麼做。 |
| **puddle** [`pʌdl̩] 名 水坑 | puddle of water 水坑 | She likes to step in puddles of water to splash others walking on the street. 她喜歡踏進水坑把水濺到街上的路人。 |

## ubtle [`ʌtl̩]

| | | |
|---|---|---|
| **subtle**<br>[ˋsʌtḷ]<br>形 微妙的 | a subtle change<br>些微的改變 | I like your haircut. It's a subtle change, but it makes you look different.<br>我喜歡你新剪的髮型，雖然只是些微的改變，但讓你看起來不一樣。 |

## uttle [ˋʌtḷ]

| | | |
|---|---|---|
| **shuttle**<br>[ˋʃʌtḷ]<br>名 太空梭、穿梭運輸 | space shuttle<br>太空梭<br>a shuttle service<br>接駁服務 | Apollo 13 was a space shuttle that went through some technical difficulties. 阿波羅十三號是一架高難度技術的太空梭。<br>You can take a shuttle service from the train station to the airport.<br>你可以從火車站搭接駁巴士至機場。 |

## uddy [ˋʌdɪ]

62

| | | |
|---|---|---|
| **buddy**<br>[ˋbʌdɪ]<br>名 夥伴、好朋友 | my buddy<br>我的好朋友 | You'll always be my buddy.<br>你會一直是我的好朋友。 |
| **muddy**<br>[ˋmʌdɪ]<br>形 泥濘的 | muddy water<br>泥濘的水 | This river is not clear; instead it's filled with muddy water.<br>這條河不乾淨，充滿泥濘的水。 |

## udy [ˋʌdɪ]

| | | |
|---|---|---|
| * **study**<br>[`stʌdɪ]<br>動 學習 | study English<br>學英文 | How long have you studied English?<br>你學英文多久了？ |

## ude [ud]

| | | |
|---|---|---|
| * **include**<br>[ɪn`klud]<br>動 包括、包含 | service charge is included<br>內含服務費 | You don't need to give a tip; the service charge is included already.<br>你不用給小費，服務費已內含。 |
| * **conclude**<br>[kən`klud]<br>動 推斷、結束 | conclude from<br>從…推斷<br>conclude our meeting<br>結束我們的會議 | What can you conclude from this argument?<br>你能從這論點中做出什麼結論？<br>We will conclude our meeting when the discussion is over.<br>當討論結束時，我們將結束會議。 |
| * **exclude**<br>[ɪk`sklud]<br>動 把…排除在外 | exclude from<br>從…排除在外 | Please don't exclude me from the activities.<br>請不要把我從活動中排除。 |
| **delude**<br>[dɪ`lud]<br>動 欺騙 | delude everyone<br>欺騙每個人 | He deluded everyone about his identity.<br>他欺騙每個人他的身份。 |
| **allude**<br>[ə`lud]<br>動 暗示、提及 | allude to<br>提到 | In this book, the author alludes to a mythical figure in ancient Greece. 在這本書中作者提到一位古希臘神話人物。 |
| **nude**<br>[n(j)ud]<br>形 裸的 | a nude beach<br>天體海灘 | He has always dreamt of going to a nude beach.<br>他一直夢想能去天體海灘。 |

| | | |
|---|---|---|
| **rude**<br>[rud]<br>形 粗野的 | ▶ rude remark<br>無禮的評論 | ▶ She got really angry after he made that rude remark about her appearance.<br>在他對她的外表做了無禮的評論後，她真的火大了。 |
| **crude**<br>[krud]<br>形 未經加工的 | ▶ crude oil<br>原油 | ▶ You're not supposed to use crude oil on your skin.<br>你不能用原油擦你的皮膚。 |
| **intrude**<br>[ɪn`trud]<br>動 侵入、打擾 | ▶ intrude on<br>打擾 | ▶ This is a private meeting; you are intruding on us.<br>這是私人會議，你打擾到我們了。 |
| **longitude**<br>[`lɑndʒə`t(j)ud]<br>名 經度 | ▶ latitude and longitude<br>經緯度 | ▶ Give me the latitude and longitude coordinates of your whereabouts.<br>給我你所在位置的經緯度。 |
| **solitude**<br>[`sɑlə͵t(j)ud]<br>名 孤獨 | ▶ live in solitude<br>獨居 | ▶ He preferred to live in solitude, rather than with someone else.<br>他喜歡獨居勝於跟別人一起生活。 |
| **latitude**<br>[`lætə͵t(j)ud]<br>名 緯度 | ▶ at the same latitude<br>在相同的緯度 | ▶ I don't know which city is at the same latitude as Taipei.<br>我不知哪個城市跟台北位於相同的緯度。 |
| **altitude**<br>[`æltə͵t(j)ud]<br>名 高度、海拔 | ▶ an altitude of<br>海拔 | ▶ When we fly in an airplane, we reach an altitude of around 30,000 feet. 當飛機飛行時，我們到達海拔約三萬呎的高度。 |
| **gratitude**<br>[`grætə͵t(j)ud]<br>名 感激 | ▶ express gratitude<br>表達感激 | ▶ He expressed his gratitude by inviting us out to dinner.<br>他邀請我們到外面吃晚餐以表達他的感激。 |

| | | |
|---|---|---|
| * **aptitude** [ˋæptə͵t(j)ud] 名 傾向、資質 ▶ | aptitude test 性向測驗 ▶ | You have to take an aptitude test in order to get into some schools. 你必須做性向測驗才能就讀某些學校。 |
| * **attitude** [ˋætət(j)ud] 名 態度 ▶ | bad attitude 不好的態度 ▶ | I think that you have a bad attitude. 我覺得你的態度不好。 |

## ood [ud]

| | | |
|---|---|---|
| * **food** [fud] 名 食物 ▶ | eat food 吃東西 ▶ | He eats food almost constantly. 他幾乎不斷地吃東西。 |
| **seafood** [ˋsi͵fud] 名 海鮮 ▶ | allergic to seafood 對海鮮過敏 ▶ | She is allergic to seafood; if she accidentally eats seafood, she passes out. 她對海鮮過敏；如果她不小心吃了海鮮，她就會昏倒。 |
| * **mood** [mud] 名 心情 ▶ | in a good mood 好心情 ▶ | It's hard to tell whether he is in a good mood or bad mood. 很難看出他心情好還是心情壞。 |
| **brood** [brud] 名 動 沈思 ▶ | brood over your problems 沈思你的問題 ▶ | How do you brood over your problems? 你怎麼沈思你的問題？ |

## u [u]

| | | |
|---|---|---|
| **flu**<br>[flu]<br>名 流行性感冒 | in bed with the flu<br>因流行性感冒躺在床上 | He had to spend a week in bed with the flu. 因為流行性感冒，他必須在床上躺一星期。 |
| **Peru**<br>[pə`ru]<br>名 秘魯 | live in Peru<br>住在秘魯 | She had a dream that she lived in Peru.<br>她曾夢想自己住在秘魯。 |

## udge [ʌdʒ]

| | | |
|---|---|---|
| **judge**<br>[dʒʌdʒ]<br>動 審判、判決 | judge the case<br>審判案子 | If you are biased, it wouldn't be fair for you to judge the case. 如果你存有偏見，你審判案子就不會公平。 |

## ue [ju]

| | | |
|---|---|---|
| **cue**<br>[kju]<br>名 動 提示 | miss your cue<br>沒看到提示 | You'd better not miss your cue tonight during the play; this is an important performance for us. 你今晚演出時最好注意提示，這場表演對我們很重要。 |
| * **due**<br>[dju]<br>形 到期的、由於 | due date<br>到期日<br>due to<br>由於 | When is the due date for this library book?<br>這本圖書館的書借到何時？<br>He often got sick and feeble due to his lowered immunity.<br>由於他的免疫力很低，所以他時常生病身體虛弱。 |

| | | |
|---|---|---|
| **barbecue**<br>[ˋbɑrbɪkju]<br>名 動 烤肉 | ▶ have a barbecue<br>烤肉(BBQ) | ▶ She is going to have a barbecue on the roof of her apartment.<br>她要在她的公寓屋頂烤肉。 |
| **overdue**<br>[ˋovɚˋdju]<br>形 過期的 | ▶ overdue telephone bill<br>過期的電話帳單 | ▶ You better pay that overdue telephone bill, or your phone service will be cut off.<br>你最好去付過期的電話帳單，不然你的電話會被切斷。 |
| **hue**<br>[hju]<br>名 顏色、色澤 | ▶ red hue<br>紅色 | ▶ The hair color put a red hue in your hair.<br>這個染髮劑會讓你的頭髮變紅。 |
| **avenue**<br>[ˋævə͵nju]<br>名 通道 | ▶ 5th Avenue<br>紐約第五大道 | ▶ 5th Avenue in New York City is famous for its shopping.<br>紐約第五大道是有名的購物區。 |
| **sue**<br>[s(j)u]<br>動 控告、提出訴訟 | ▶ sue him for<br>對他提出控告 | ▶ I am going to sue him for stealing my idea.<br>我要對他剽竊我的點子提出控告。 |
| **pursue**<br>[pɚˋs(j)u]<br>動 追求、從事 | ▶ pursue a career<br>致力於事業 | ▶ She wants to pursue a career in modeling.<br>她想致力於模特兒事業。 |

## uel [ˋjuəl]

| | | |
|---|---|---|
| **duel**<br>[ˋdjuəl]<br>名 動 決鬥 | ▶ a duel with<br>與…的決鬥 | ▶ He is going to have a duel with his enemy today.<br>今天他將跟敵手有場決鬥。 |

| | | |
|---|---|---|
| **fuel**<br>[ˋfjuəl]<br>名 燃料 | ▶ fuel for the airplane<br>飛機燃料 | ▶ In the movie, the fuel for the airplane was running on empty and the pilot was dead. 電影裡，飛機燃料耗盡，飛行員也死了。 |

## ual [ˋjuəl]

| | | |
|---|---|---|
| **dual**<br>[ˋdjuəl]<br>形 雙重的 | ▶ dual citizenship<br>雙重公民身份 | ▶ Some Taiwanese have dual citizenship.<br>有些台灣人有雙重公民身份。 |

## uff [ʌf]

| | | |
|---|---|---|
| **cuff**<br>[kʌf]<br>名 袖口 | ▶ off the cuff<br>不加準備 | ▶ He made some off the cuff remarks about her boyfriend.<br>他對她男友做了一些即興的評論。 |
| **handcuff**<br>[ˋhænd͵kʌf]<br>動 給…戴上手銬 名 手銬 | ▶ handcuff him<br>給他戴上手銬 | ▶ You better handcuff him or he'll run away.<br>你最好給他戴上手銬不然他會逃走。 |
| **stuff**<br>[stʌf]<br>名 材料 動 裝填 | ▶ get a lot of stuff<br>買很多東西 | ▶ We should take the car because I need to get a lot of stuff at the grocery store. 我們應該要開車，因為我得在雜貨店買很多東西。 |

## ough [ʌf]

| | | |
|---|---|---|
| **rough**<br>[rʌf]<br>形 粗糙的 | rough hands<br>粗糙的雙手 | He has rough hands from working as a construction worker. 因為他是位建築工人，所以他有雙粗糙的手。 |
| * **enough**<br>[ə`nʌf]<br>形 副 名 足夠 | quite enough<br>相當夠 | I think there's quite enough of salt in this food.<br>我想這食物的鹽相當夠了。 |
| **tough**<br>[tʌf]<br>形 棘手的 | a tough job<br>棘手的工作 | It's a tough job calming him down.<br>讓他平靜下來是棘手的工作。 |

## uffle [`ʌfl̩]

| | | |
|---|---|---|
| **shuffle**<br>[`ʃʌfl̩]<br>動 拖著腳步走 | shuffle across the room<br>拖著腳步走過房間 | The children shuffled across the room.<br>小朋友拖著腳步走過房間。 |
| **muffle**<br>[`mʌfl̩]<br>動 使聲音模糊 | muffled voices<br>模糊的聲音 | I hear muffled voices in the room next door.<br>我聽到隔壁房間隱約有什麼聲音。 |

## ug [ʌg]

| | | |
|---|---|---|
| **bug**<br>[bʌg]<br>名 蟲子、故障 | tiny bug<br>小蟲子<br>computer bug<br>電腦(程式)錯誤 | There is a tiny bug on my desk. 我的桌上有隻小蟲子。<br>Computer bugs are going around the school.<br>電腦錯誤在學校裡肆虐。 |

| | | |
|---|---|---|
| **hug** [hʌg] 動名 擁抱 | hug each other 擁抱彼此 | I saw them hug each other on the street last night. 我昨晚看到他們在街上擁抱彼此。 |
| **mug** [mʌg] 名 馬克杯 | coffee mug 咖啡馬克杯 | She has been using the same coffee mug for forty years now. 她用同一個咖啡馬克杯四十年了。 |
| **rug** [rʌg] 名 地毯 | woolen rug 羊毛地毯 | The woolen rug by the door is all dirty and torn. 門口的羊毛地毯又髒又破。 |
| **shrug** [ʃrʌg] 動名 聳肩 | shrug off 不理會 | Just shrug off the creeps and ignore them. 別理爛人，當作沒看見。 |
| **tug** [tʌg] 動 用力拉拖 | tug the drawer 用力拉抽屜 | She kept on tugging the drawer, but it was stuck. 她一直用力拉抽屜，可是抽屜卡住了。 |

## uge [judʒ]

| | | |
|---|---|---|
| **refuge** [ˋrɛfjudʒ] 名動 避難 | take refuge 避難 | It's important to have places where people can take refuge. 有地方能讓人們避難是很重要的。 |
| **huge** [hjudʒ] 形 龐大的 | a huge amount of money 大筆錢 | There is a huge amount of money missing from my bank account. 我的銀行帳戶遺失了一大筆錢。 |

## uggle [ˋʌgḷ]

 63

| | | |
|---|---|---|
| **smuggle** [ˋsmʌgḷ] 動走私 | ▶ smuggle drugs 走私毒品 | ▶ The police caught him smuggling drugs across the border. 警察抓到他在邊境走私毒品。 |
| **struggle** [ˋstrʌgḷ] 動奮鬥、鬥爭 | ▶ struggle for 為…奮鬥 | ▶ She is struggling for the rights of orphan children. 她正為孤兒的權利奮鬥。 |

## ull [ʊl]

| | | |
|---|---|---|
| **bull** [bʊl] 名公牛 | ▶ take the bull by its horns 不畏艱難 | ▶ You have to take the bull by its horns and just do it. 你必須不畏艱難地去做。 |
| * **full** [fʊl] 形充滿的 | ▶ full of 充滿 | ▶ She is full of lies. 她滿口謊言。 |
| * **pull** [pʊl] 動拉 | ▶ pull the door open 把門拉開 | ▶ Pull the door open, don't push it. 把門拉開，不要用推的。 |

## ool [ʊl]

| | | |
|---|---|---|
| **wool** [wʊl] 名羊毛 | ▶ made of wool 羊毛做的 | ▶ This sweater that my mom knit for me is made of wool. 我媽織給我的這件毛衣是羊毛的。 |

## ulsive [ˋʌlsɪv]

| | | |
|---|---|---|
| **repulsive** [rɪˋpʌlsɪv] 形 使人反感的 | ▶ a repulsive man 使人反感的男人 | ▶ He is a repulsive man who is unsanitary, mean, and perverted. 他是個令人反感的男人，不衛生、卑鄙又性變態。 |
| **impulsive** [ɪmˋpʌlsɪv] 形 衝動的 | ▶ act impulsively 衝動地行動 | ▶ Don't act impulsively; think before you act. 不要衝動行事，在你做之前先想想。 |
| **compulsive** [kəmˋpʌlsɪv] 形 難以抑制的 | ▶ a compulsive overeater 暴食症者 | ▶ She can't help being a compulsive overeater, so she went to the doctor. 她沒辦法克制暴食症，所以她去看了醫生。 |

## ult [ʌlt]

| | | |
|---|---|---|
| **cult** [kʌlt] 名 教派、崇拜 | ▶ dangerous cult 危險的教派 | ▶ My parents told me to stay away from the dangerous cult, but I couldn't. 我的父母告訴我要遠離危險的教派，但我沒辦法。 |
| **occult** [əˋkʌlt] 形 神祕的 | ▶ occult powers 神秘的力量 | ▶ He possesses occult powers and he can't control them. 他擁有神秘的力量而無法加以控制。 |
| * **difficult** [ˋdɪfəˌkʌlt] 形 困難的 | ▶ rather difficult 相當困難 | ▶ It seems rather difficult to discuss anything with him. 和他討論任何事似乎都相當困難。 |
| **adult** [əˋdʌlt] 名 成年人 | ▶ behave like an adult 行為像成人 | ▶ Please behave like an adult and you will be treated with respect. 請你表現得像個成人，你才會被尊重。 |

| | | |
|---|---|---|
| * **result** [rɪ`zʌlt] 名結果 動 導致 | result from 起因於… | We don't know what the problem resulted from. 我們不知道問題的起因是什麼。 |
| **insult** [`ɪnsʌlt] [ɪn`sʌlt] 名 動 侮辱 | an insult to 侮辱 insult you 侮辱你 | He said an insult to my brother. 他說了侮辱我兄弟的話。 I don't mean to insult you. 我無意侮辱你。 |
| * **consult** [kən`sʌlt] 動 請教 | consult a doctor 請教醫生 | You should consult a doctor about your symptoms. 你應該請教醫生你的症狀。 |

## ulture [`ʌltʃɚ]

| | | |
|---|---|---|
| * **culture** [`kʌltʃɚ] 名文化 | culture shock 文化衝擊 | He is suffering from culture shock; he's still not used to being in a foreign place. 他正受文化衝擊之苦，他還不習慣在外國的感覺。 |
| **agriculture** [`ægrɪˌkʌltʃɚ] 名農業 | study agriculture 研究農業 | She studied agriculture in college. 她大學時讀農業。 |

## um [ʌm]

| | | |
|---|---|---|
| **scum** [skʌm] 名渣 | the scum of the earth 地球的人渣 | She told him that he was the scum of the earth. 她跟他說他是地球的人渣。 |

| | | |
|---|---|---|
| **gum**<br>[gʌm]<br>名 樹膠、口香糖 | chew gum<br>嚼口香糖 | You're not supposed to chew gum on the MRT in Taiwan.<br>你不能在台灣的捷運上嚼口香糖。 |
| **hum**<br>[hʌm]<br>動 哼曲子 | hum a song<br>哼歌 | He must be happy today because I caught him humming a song. 他今天一定很高興，因為我聽到他在哼歌。 |
| **slum**<br>[slʌm]<br>名 貧民窟 | live in the slums<br>住在貧民窟 | Although he's rich now, he grew up living in the slums.<br>雖然他現在很富有，但他是在貧民窟長大的。 |
| **rum**<br>[rʌm]<br>名 蘭姆酒 | drink rum<br>喝蘭姆酒 | She loved to drink rum on the porch.<br>她喜歡在陽台上喝蘭姆酒。 |
| **drum**<br>[drʌm]<br>名 鼓 動 打鼓 | beat the drums<br>打鼓 | She went to the pub to hear the drummer beating the drums.<br>她去酒吧聽鼓手打鼓。 |
| * **sum**<br>[sʌm]<br>名 金額 動 總結 | a large sum of money<br>一大筆錢<br>sum up<br>總結 | I won a large sum of money in the contest.<br>我在比賽中贏得一大筆錢。<br>Can you sum up the plot of the story?<br>你可以總結這故事的情節嗎？ |

## umb [ʌm]

| | | |
|---|---|---|
| **succumb**<br>[səˋkʌm]<br>動 屈服 | succumb to<br>屈服 | He always succumbs to her pleas, even if they are unreasonable. 他總是屈服於她的懇求，即使是不合理的。 |

| | | |
|---|---|---|
| **dumb**<br>[dʌm]<br>形 啞的、愚笨的 | play dumb<br>裝傻 | Don't play dumb; you know what's going on.<br>不要裝傻，你知道發生什麼事。 |
| **thumb**<br>[θʌm]<br>名 拇指 | all thumbs<br>笨手笨腳 | When it comes to sports, she's all thumbs.<br>她是個運動白痴。 |
| **numb**<br>[nʌm]<br>形 麻木的 | feel numb<br>感到麻木 | She felt numb after the doctor gave her a shot.<br>醫生幫她打了一針後她感到麻木。 |
| **crumb**<br>[krʌm]<br>名 麵包屑 | bread crumbs<br>麵包屑 | I told you not to eat in bed! Look at all the bread crumbs on the sheets!<br>我跟你說過不要在床上吃東西！看看掉在床單上的麵包屑！ |

## ome [ʌm]

| | | |
|---|---|---|
| * **come**<br>[kʌm]<br>動 來 | come across<br>偶然碰到 | I came across a nice shirt yesterday.<br>我昨天無意間看到一件好看的襯衫。 |
| * **become**<br>[bɪˋkʌm]<br>動 變成、成為 | become cold<br>變冷 | The weather became cold gradually.<br>天氣逐漸變冷。 |
| * **overcome**<br>[ˏovəˋkʌm]<br>動 戰勝、克服 | overcome the obstacles<br>克服障礙 | We must overcome the obstacles in life.<br>我們必須克服生活中的障礙。 |

| | | |
|---|---|---|
| * **outcome** [ˋaʊt͵kʌm] 名 結果 | ▶ final outcome 最後的結果 | ▶ The final outcome of the game was 2-0. 比賽最後結果是二比零。 |

## umble [ˋʌmbḷ]

| | | |
|---|---|---|
| **fumble** [ˋfʌmbḷ] 動 亂摸、摸索 | ▶ fumble about 摸索 | ▶ I saw him fumble about in the dark looking for something. 我看到他在黑暗中摸索找東西。 |
| **humble** [ˋhʌmbḷ] 形 謙遜的、卑微的 | ▶ humble background 卑微的背景 | ▶ Although he came from a humble background, he's one of the most powerful men in the world today. 雖然他出身卑微，但他可是當今最有影響力的人之一。 |
| **jumble** [ˋdʒʌmbḷ] 動 使混亂 | ▶ jumble up 混在一起 | ▶ Her words get jumbled up when she tries to say something. 當她試著說話時，她的字句含糊不清。 |
| **mumble** [ˋmʌmbḷ] 動 含糊地說 | ▶ mumble his words 口齒不清 | ▶ I can't understand him because he mumbles his words. 我聽不懂他說啥，因為他口齒不清。 |
| **crumble** [ˋkrʌmbḷ] 動 粉碎 | ▶ crumble into pieces 粉碎成片狀 | ▶ That piece of pie crumbled into pieces when I stuck my fork in it. 我用叉子叉那塊派時，它碎成片狀。 |
| **grumble** [ˋgrʌmbḷ] 動 抱怨 | ▶ grumble about 抱怨 | ▶ When we scolded him for being irresponsible, he grumbled about our audacity. 當我們罵他不負責任時，他抱怨我們膽大妄為。 |

| | | |
|---|---|---|
| **tumble**<br>[ˋtʌmbḷ]<br>動 跌倒 | tumble down the stairs<br>跌下樓 | He accidentally missed a step and tumbled down the stairs.<br>他不小心沒踩到台階跌下樓了。 |
| **stumble**<br>[ˋstʌmbḷ]<br>動 絆倒 | stumble on the sidewalk<br>在人行道絆倒 | We saw an old man stumble on the sidewalk, holding a bottle of whisky.<br>我們看到一位老人在人行道絆了一跤，手裡握著瓶威士忌。 |

## ummer [ˋʌmɚ]

| | | |
|---|---|---|
| **summer**<br>[ˋsʌmɚ]<br>名 夏天 | summer vacation<br>暑假 | What are you doing for your summer vacation?<br>你的暑假要怎麼過？ |

## omer [ˋʌmɚ]

| | | |
|---|---|---|
| **newcomer**<br>[ˋnjuˋkʌmɚ]<br>名 新來的人 | a newcomer to<br>新人 | Forgive his ignorance because he is a newcomer to this organization. 原諒他的無知，因為他是這組織的新人。 |

## ummy [ˋʌmɪ]

64

| | | |
|---|---|---|
| **dummy**<br>[ˋdʌmɪ]<br>名 模型人 | use a dummy<br>用模型人 | They use a dummy driver when they are testing how a car crashes. 他們用模型人充當駕駛，測試車子衝撞時的狀況。 |

| | | |
|---|---|---|
| **mummy**<br>[ˋmʌmɪ]<br>名 木乃伊 | ▶ find a mummy<br>發現木乃伊 | ▶ Some archeologists found a mummy in a desert when they were looking for dinosaur bones.<br>一些考古學家在找恐龍骨時，在沙漠中發現木乃伊。 |
| **yummy**<br>[ˋjʌmɪ]<br>形 好吃的 | ▶ tastes yummy<br>嚐起來很好吃 | ▶ This food tastes yummy! Can I have some more?<br>這食物嚐起來很好吃！我可以再多吃點嗎？ |
| **tummy**<br>[ˋtʌmɪ]<br>名 肚子、胃 | ▶ tummy ache<br>肚子痛 | ▶ I have a tummy ache from eating that too fast.<br>我吃東西吃太快肚子痛。 |

## umor [ˋjumɚ]

| | | |
|---|---|---|
| **humor**<br>[ˋhjumɚ]<br>名 幽默 | ▶ sense of humor<br>幽默感 | ▶ She has a really good sense of humor.<br>她很有幽默感。 |
| **tumor**<br>[ˋtjumɚ]<br>名 腫瘤 | ▶ a benign tumor<br>良性腫瘤 | ▶ Everyone was worried, but the doctor said that it's just a benign tumor. 大家都很擔心，但醫生説只是良性腫瘤。 |

## ump [ʌmp]

| | | |
|---|---|---|
| **bump**<br>[bʌmp]<br>動 碰、撞 | ▶ bump into<br>無意中遇到 | ▶ We bumped into Dan the other day.<br>我們不久前無意間遇到丹。 |

| | | |
|---|---|---|
| **dump**<br>[dʌmp]<br>動 傾倒 | dump the trash<br>倒垃圾 | Please dump the trash on your way out.<br>請在你外出時倒垃圾。 |
| **jump**<br>[dʒʌmp]<br>動 跳躍 | jump over<br>跳過 | The dog jumped over the fence.<br>這狗跳過籬笆。 |
| **lump**<br>[lʌmp]<br>名 塊狀 | lump in my throat<br>喉嚨有硬塊 | I got a lump in my throat when it was my turn to give a presentation. 輪到我做簡報時，我的喉嚨像卡了硬塊說不出口。 |
| **slump**<br>[slʌmp]<br>動 名 下跌 | slump in sales<br>銷售衰退 | There has been a slump in sales this year.<br>今年的銷售衰退。 |

## un [ʌn]

| | | |
|---|---|---|
| **bun**<br>[bʌn]<br>名 小圓麵包 | steamed bun<br>饅頭 | There are many types of steamed buns in Chinese food. 中式食物中有很多種饅頭。 |
| * **fun**<br>[fʌn]<br>名 娛樂、樂趣 | have fun<br>玩得愉快 | Have fun at the amusement park!<br>希望你在遊樂園玩得愉快！ |
| **gun**<br>[gʌn]<br>名 槍 | aim a gun at<br>用槍瞄準 | I would never aim a gun at a person.<br>我絕不會用槍瞄準人。 |

| | | |
|---|---|---|
| **shotgun** [ˋʃɑt͵gʌn] 名 獵槍 | shoot a shotgun ▶ 用獵槍射擊 | ▶ He shot a shotgun through the roof when burglars came into his house. 當夜賊闖進他家時，他用獵槍射穿屋頂。 |
| **shun** [ʃʌn] 動 躲開、避開 | shun others ▶ 避開別人 | ▶ We don't know why he shuns others all the time and keeps to himself. 我們不知道為何他一直避開別人，獨來獨往。 |
| * **run** [rʌn] 名 動 跑 | on the run ▶ 在逃 | ▶ She's been on the run for a while because she stole some gangsters' money. 她因為偷了歹徒的錢，跑路一陣子了。 |
| * **sun** [sʌn] 名 太陽 | lie in the sun ▶ 躺在陽光下 | ▶ I love to lie in the sun and relax on the beach. 我喜歡躺在海灘上曬太陽放鬆心情。 |

## on [ʌn]

| | | |
|---|---|---|
| **son** [sʌn] 名 兒子 | raise a son ▶ 撫養兒子 | ▶ It's hard to raise a son alone. 獨自撫養兒子是很辛苦的。 |
| **grandson** [ˋgrænd͵sʌn] 名 孫子 | live with his grandson ▶ 跟孫子一起生活 | ▶ He lives with his grandson since his wife passed away. 自從他太太去世後，他就跟他的孫子一起生活。 |
| **ton** [tʌn] 名 噸、很重的分量 | weigh a ton ▶ 重得很 | ▶ This bag weighs a ton! 這個袋子重得很！ |

## unch [ʌntʃ]

| | | |
|---|---|---|
| **bunch**<br>[bʌntʃ]<br>名 串、束 | a bunch of<br>一捆 | There were a bunch of punks outside the store.<br>店外有一捆木頭。 |
| **hunch**<br>[hʌntʃ]<br>名 預感、直覺 | just a hunch<br>只是直覺 | I don't know how I knew where to find him. It's just a hunch. 我不清楚我是怎麼知道去哪找他的，只是種直覺。 |
| **lunch**<br>[lʌntʃ]<br>名 午餐 | have lunch<br>吃午餐 | Let's have lunch together sometime.<br>我們找個時間一起吃午餐吧。 |
| **punch**<br>[pʌntʃ]<br>動 名 用拳猛擊 | punch him in the face<br>毆打他的臉 | We saw her punch him in the face.<br>我們看到她毆打他的臉。 |
| **brunch**<br>[brʌntʃ]<br>名 早午餐 | have brunch<br>吃早午餐 | She has brunch every Sunday with her father.<br>她每週日都跟她父親一起吃早午餐。 |

## unction [`ʌŋkʃən]

| | | |
|---|---|---|
| * **function**<br>[`fʌŋkʃən]<br>動 名 作用 | function as<br>作為 | This bottle can also function as a flower vase.<br>這個瓶子也能當花瓶用。 |
| **malfunction**<br>[mæl`fʌŋkʃən]<br>名 故障 | system malfunction<br>系統故障 | We don't know why there is a system malfunction.<br>我們不知道為何系統會故障。 |

| | | |
|---|---|---|
| **junction** [ˋdʒʌŋkʃən] 名 連接、接合點 | ▶ at the junction of 在交接處 | ▶ Meet me at the junction of Pine and 2nd Street. 跟我在杉樹街與第二街口碰面。 |
| **conjunction** [kənˋdʒʌŋkʃən] 名 結合 | ▶ in conjunction with 結合 | ▶ We use this workbook in conjunction with this textbook. 我們將這本練習簿和這本教科書結合使用。 |

## und [ʌnd]

| | | |
|---|---|---|
| **fund** [fʌnd] 名 基金 | ▶ raise funds 募款 | ▶ We are raising funds for our friend's surgery. 我們正在為我們朋友的手術費募款。 |

## under [ˋʌndɚ]

| | | |
|---|---|---|
| * **under** [ˋʌndɚ] 介 在…下方 | ▶ under control 在掌控中 | ▶ Everything is under control. Don't worry. 每件事都在掌控中，別擔心。 |
| **thunder** [ˋθʌndɚ] 名 雷聲 | ▶ thunderstorm 大雷雨 | ▶ There is a thunderstorm coming up. 有場大雷雨即將到來。 |
| **blunder** [ˋblʌndɚ] 名 大錯 | ▶ commit a blunder 做錯事 | ▶ He committed a blunder when he met his girlfriend's parents for the first time. 當他第一次跟女朋友的父母見面時，他犯了大錯。 |

## onder [ˋʌndɚ]

**wonder**
[ˋwʌndɚ]
動 想知道 名 驚奇
▶ do wonders
有神奇的效果
▶ This moisturizing lotion does wonders for your skin.
保濕化妝水對皮膚有神奇的效果。

## ung [ʌŋ]

**lung**
[lʌŋ]
名 肺臟
▶ black lung
黑肺病
▶ He has black lung from smoking.
他因抽菸得了黑肺病。

## oung [ʌŋ]

* **young**
[jʌŋ]
形 年輕的
▶ young adult
年輕人
▶ A young adult could be a teenager to a person in their early twenties. 年輕人指的是青少年到二十幾歲的人。

## ong [ʌŋ]

* **among**
[əˋmʌŋ]
介 在⋯之中
▶ among his classmates
在他的同學之間
▶ He was the smartest kid among his classmates.
他在同學之間是最聰明的小孩。

## ongue [ʌŋ]

| | | |
|---|---|---|
| **tongue** [tʌŋ] 名 舌頭、語言 | foreign tongue 外語 | I can't understand him; he's speaking a foreign tongue. 我聽不懂他的話，他在說外語。 |

## unge [ʌndʒ]

| | | |
|---|---|---|
| **plunge** [plʌndʒ] 動 投入、衝進 | plunge into 跳入 | Some people just plunge into a swimming pool. 有些人直接跳進游泳池。 |

## onge [ʌndʒ]

| | | |
|---|---|---|
| **sponge** [spʌndʒ] 名 海綿 | with a sponge 用海綿 | You should wash the bathtub with a sponge. 你應該用海綿清洗浴缸。 |

## unger [ˋʌŋgɚ]

| | | |
|---|---|---|
| * **hunger** [ˋhʌŋgɚ] 名 飢餓 動 渴望 | hunger strike 絕食抗議<br>hunger for 渴望 | They are on a hunger strike for education reform. 他們絕食抗議要求教育改革。<br>He hungers for success. 他渴望成功。 |
| * **younger** [ˋjʌŋgɚ] 形 較年輕的 | a younger sister 妹妹 | That 4 year old girl tells her mother that she wants a younger sister. 那個四歲的女孩跟媽媽說她想要個妹妹。 |

## ungle [ˋʌŋgḷ]



| | | |
|---|---|---|
| **jungle** [ˋdʒʌŋgḷ] 名 叢林 | in a jungle ▸ 在叢林 | ▸ I had a nightmare that I was lost in a jungle. 我作了個迷失在叢林裡的惡夢。 |

## union [ˋjunjən]

| | | |
|---|---|---|
| * **union** [ˋjunjən] 名 結合、工會 | join a union ▸ 加入工會 | ▸ You should join a union if you want to be protected at the workplace. 如果你想在工作場合受到保障，你應該加入工會。 |
| **reunion** [riˋjunjən] 名 重聚 | high school ▸ reunion 高中同學會 | ▸ She told lies at her high school reunion. 她在高中同學會上說謊。 |

## unity [ˋjunətɪ]

| | | |
|---|---|---|
| * **unity** [ˋjunətɪ] 名 單一性、團結 | promote unity ▸ 促進團結 | ▸ This gathering will promote unity between the two groups. 這次聚會將可促進兩個團體的團結。 |
| **immunity** [ɪˋmjunətɪ] 名 免疫力 | acquire ▸ immunity 獲得免疫力 | ▸ If you take antibiotics too often, you will acquire immunity to them. 如果你太常攝取抗生素，你會對其產生免疫力。 |
| * **community** [kəˋmjunətɪ] 名 社區、共同體 | academic ▸ community 學術界 | ▸ He never found his place in the academic community, although he was a professor. 雖然他是一位教授，他卻不曾在學術界找到自己的定位。 |

| | | |
|---|---|---|
| * **opportunity** [ˏɑpɚ`tjunətɪ] 名 機會 | pass up an opportunity 放棄機會 | Don't pass up an opportunity to learn about different things. 別放棄可以學習不同事物的機會。 |

## unk [ʌŋk]

| | | |
|---|---|---|
| **hunk** [hʌŋk] 名 大片 | hunk of bread 一大片麵包 | He ripped off a big hunk of bread and gave it to me. 他偷了一大片麵包給我。 |
| **chunk** [tʃʌŋk] 名 厚塊 | a chunk of chocolate 一塊巧克力 | I ate a big chunk of chocolate for breakfast. 我吃了一大塊巧克力當早餐。 |
| * **junk** [dʒʌŋk] 名 廢棄物 | junk mail 垃圾郵件 | I think junk mail is a major waste of paper. 我認為垃圾郵件非常浪費紙張。 |
| **trunk** [trʌŋk] 名 樹幹 | the trunk of a tree 樹幹 | She liked to sit at the trunk of a tree and read. 她喜歡坐在樹幹旁讀書。 |

## onk [ʌŋk]

| | | |
|---|---|---|
| **monk** [mʌŋk] 名 僧侶 | Buddhist monks 和尚 | We saw some Buddhist monks on a roller coaster at the amusement park. 我們在遊樂園看到一些和尚坐雲霄飛車。 |

## unnel [ˋʌnḷ]

| | | |
|---|---|---|
| **funnel** [ˋfʌnḷ] 名 漏斗 | through a funnel 通過漏斗 | He drank his beer through a funnel. 他透過漏斗喝啤酒。 |
| **tunnel** [ˋtʌnḷ] 名 隧道、地道 | go through a tunnel 穿過隧道 | She gets scared when she goes through a tunnel. 穿過隧道時她很害怕。 |

## unny [ˋʌnɪ]

| | | |
|---|---|---|
| **bunny** [ˋbʌnɪ] 名 兔子 | little bunny 小兔子 | She has a little bunny as a pet. 她養隻小兔子當寵物。 |
| **funny** [ˋfʌnɪ] 形 有趣的、好笑的 | a funny joke 好笑的笑話 | He tells many jokes, but seldom does he tell a funny joke. 他常常說笑話，但很少有好笑的。 |
| **sunny** [ˋsʌnɪ] 形 陽光充足的 | sunny day 晴天 | It's a beautiful sunny day today. 今天是美好的晴天。 |

## unt [ʌnt]

| | | |
|---|---|---|
| **hunt** [hʌnt] 動 獵取 | go hunting 打獵 | He goes hunting for fun. 他去打獵是為了好玩。 |

| | | |
|---|---|---|
| **manhunt** [ˋmænˏhʌnt] 名 搜索 | conduct a manhunt for 進行搜索 | The police conducted a manhunt for an escaped convict. 警方搜索逃跑的犯人。 |
| **blunt** [blʌnt] 形 鈍的 | blunt knife 鈍的刀子 | We need a knife sharpener for our blunt knives. 我們需要用磨刀器磨我們的鈍刀。 |

## unter [ˋʌntɚ]

| | | |
|---|---|---|
| **hunter** [ˋhʌntɚ] 名 獵人 | deer hunter 獵鹿人 | He is a deer hunter who hunts deer to eat and sell. 他是個獵鹿人，以此為食和賣錢。 |

## up [ʌp]

| | | |
|---|---|---|
| * **up** [ʌp] 副 向上 | up and down 上下 | The children rode the elevator up and down for hours. 小朋友搭電梯上下好幾個小時了。 |
| * **cup** [kʌp] 名 杯子 | a cup of 一杯 | Can you get me a cup of water please? 可以請你給我一杯水嗎？ |
| **teacup** [ˋtiˏkʌp] 名 茶杯 | fill her teacup 倒滿她的茶杯 | The maid filled her teacup with hot jasmine tea. 少女在她的茶杯裡倒滿熱茉莉花茶。 |

| | | |
| --- | --- | --- |
| **hiccup** [ˋhɪkʌp] 名動 打嗝 | stop hiccupping 停止打嗝 | Some say that you should drink 12 sips of water to stop hiccupping. 有些人說喝十二口的水就可以止住打嗝。 |
| * **makeup** [ˋmekˏʌp] 名 構成、化妝 | chemical makeup 化學構造<br>stage makeup 舞台妝 | What is the chemical makeup of this kind of plastic? 這種塑膠的化學構造是什麼？<br>It takes her at least an hour to put on her stage makeup. 她至少要花一個小時化舞台妝。 |
| **lineup** [ˋlaɪnˏʌp] 名 列隊 | in a lineup 在一排人之中 | She had to pick out the assailant in a lineup. 她必須在一排人之中找出攻擊者。 |
| **breakup** [ˋbrekˋʌp] 名 瓦解 | the breakup of their marriage 婚姻瓦解 | He felt responsible for the breakup of their marriage. 他覺得他們的婚姻瓦解他有責任。 |
| * **backup** [ˋbækˏʌp] 名動 備份 | backup the file 備份檔案 | You better backup the file in case anything happens to it. 你最好備份檔案以防發生任何意外。 |
| * **checkup** [ˋtʃɛkˏʌp] 名 檢查 | get a checkup 作個檢查 | I need to get a checkup because I haven't gone to the doctor in years. 我需要作個健康檢查，因為好幾年沒有看醫生了。 |
| **pickup** [ˋpɪkˏʌp] 名 收集、小卡車 | pickup truck 小貨車 | He bought a pickup truck so he could carry his construction materials. 他買了一輛小貨車好載他的建築材料。 |
| * **setup** [ˋsɛtˏʌp] 名動 設定、安裝 | setup the computer 安裝電腦 | I'm so excited I got a new computer. All I have to do is setup the computer first. 我很興奮買到新電腦。首先我得先安裝電腦。 |

| | | |
|---|---|---|
| **blowup**<br>[`blo`ʌp]<br>名 爆炸、放大照片 | ▶ blowup of the building<br>大樓爆炸 | ▶ We saw the blowup of the building.<br>我們看到大樓爆炸。 |

## upid [`jupɪd]

🔈 66

| | | |
|---|---|---|
| **cupid**<br>[`kjupɪd]<br>名 邱比特 | ▶ play cupid<br>扮演邱比特 | ▶ He tried to play cupid by setting me up with a girl.<br>他試著扮演邱比特，幫我跟一位女孩牽線。 |
| **stupid**<br>[`stjupɪd]<br>形 笨的 | ▶ a stupid person<br>愚笨的人 | ▶ She has no tolerance for a stupid person.<br>她無法忍受愚笨的人。 |

## upiter [`upətɚ]

| | | |
|---|---|---|
| **Jupiter**<br>[`dʒupətɚ]<br>名 木星、宙斯神 | ▶ Planet Jupiter<br>木星 | ▶ We saw Planet Jupiter through the telescope.<br>我們透過望遠鏡看到木星。 |

## upil [`jupḷ]

| | | |
|---|---|---|
| **pupil**<br>[`pjupḷ]<br>名 學生、瞳孔 | ▶ one of my best pupils<br>我最優秀的學生之一 | ▶ That girl from Brazil was one of my best pupils. 那個從巴西來的女孩是我最優秀的學生之一。 |

## upper [ˋʌpɚ]

| | | |
|---|---|---|
| **supper** [ˋsʌpɚ] 名 晚餐 | have supper 吃晚餐 | Where are you going to have supper tonight? 今晚你要去哪裡吃晚餐？ |

## uppy [ˋʌpɪ]

| | | |
|---|---|---|
| **puppy** [ˋpʌpɪ] 名 小狗 | lost puppy 走失的小狗 | We put up flyers all over our neighborhood with a picture of our lost puppy. 我們在附近張貼附有走失小狗照片的傳單。 |
| **yuppy** [ˋjʌpɪ] 名 雅痞 | stuck-up yuppy 高傲的雅痞 | She is a stuck-up yuppy who only socializes with other yuppies. 她是一個高傲的雅痞，只跟其他雅痞交際。 |

## upt [ʌpt]

| | | |
|---|---|---|
| **abrupt** [əˋbrʌpt] 形 突然的 | an abrupt change 突然的改變 | There has been an abrupt change in our schedule. 我們的行程突然有了改變。 |
| **erupt** [ɪˋrʌpt] 動 噴出、爆發 | watch the volcano erupt 看火山爆發 | People come here to watch the volcano erupt. 人們來這看火山爆發。 |
| * **bankrupt** [ˋbæŋkrʌpt] 形 動 破產 | go bankrupt 破產 | I will go bankrupt if I don't start making money soon. 如果我不快開始賺錢我就要破產了。 |

| | | |
|---|---|---|
| **interrupt**<br>[ˏɪntəˋrʌpt]<br>動 打斷、阻礙 | ▶ interrupt you<br>打斷你 | ▶ I don't mean to interrupt you, but do you have a minute?<br>我無意打斷你，你有空嗎？ |
| **corrupt**<br>[kəˋrʌpt]<br>形 貪污的 | ▶ corrupt politician<br>貪污的政客 | ▶ It's almost inevitable to have some corrupt politicians in the government. 政府機構幾乎不可避免地會有一些貪污的政客。 |
| **disrupt**<br>[dɪsˋrʌpt]<br>動 使分裂、使中斷 | ▶ disrupt the gathering<br>中斷集會 | ▶ Please don't disrupt the gathering; this is a very important meeting. 請不要打斷集會，這是個很重要的會議。 |

## urable [ˋjʊrəbl̩]

| | | |
|---|---|---|
| **curable**<br>[ˋkjʊrəbl̩]<br>形 可醫治的 | ▶ a curable disease<br>可醫治的疾病 | ▶ We hope that one day AIDS will become a curable disease. 我們希望有一天愛滋病會變成可醫治的疾病。 |
| **incurable**<br>[ɪnˋkjʊrəbl̩]<br>形 不可救藥的 | ▶ an incurable disease<br>不治之症 | ▶ It's tough knowing someone with an incurable disease.<br>知道有人得了不治之症很令人遺憾。 |
| **durable**<br>[ˋdjʊrəbl̩]<br>形 耐用的 | ▶ durable material<br>耐用材 | ▶ This is made out of durable material that should last a long time. 這是耐久材製成的，應該可以用很久。 |

## ural [ˋʊrəl]

| | | |
|---|---|---|
| **plural**<br>[ˋplurəl]<br>形 複數的 | plural noun<br>複數名詞 | The plural noun for "man" is "men."<br>man的複數名詞是men。 |
| **rural**<br>[ˋrurəl]<br>形 農村的 | rural area<br>農村地區 | She prefers to live in a rural area where it is quiet and peaceful. 她較喜愛住在靜謐安寧的農村地區。 |

## urance [ˋjurəns]

| | | |
|---|---|---|
| **endurance**<br>[ɪnˋdjurəns]<br>名 忍耐 | a test of endurance<br>耐力測試 | Swimming laps can be a test of endurance.<br>來回游幾圈可以當耐力測試。 |
| * **insurance**<br>[ɪnˋʃurəns]<br>名 保險 | life insurance<br>壽險 | It is important that you buy life insurance for your child.<br>為你的小孩買壽險是很重要的。 |
| **assurance**<br>[əˋʃurəns]<br>名 保證 | self assurance<br>自信 | His self assurance makes others feel comfortable around him. 他的自信讓其他人在他身旁感到自在。 |

## urb [ɝb]

| | | |
|---|---|---|
| **suburb**<br>[ˋsʌbɝb]<br>名 郊區 | live in the suburbs<br>住在郊區 | She wants to live in the suburbs when she has kids.<br>她有小孩時想住在郊區。 |

| | | |
|---|---|---|
| **curb**<br>[kɝb]<br>名 人行道的邊欄 | run over the curb<br>輾過人行道的邊欄 | He ran over the curb when he turned the corner in his car. 當他開車轉過街角時，輾過了人行道的邊欄。 |
| * **disturb**<br>[dɪs`tɝb]<br>動 妨礙、打擾 | disturb the peace<br>妨礙安寧 | Those kids disturb the peace in our neighborhood at night.<br>那些小孩妨礙我們這一帶晚上的安寧。 |

## erb [ɝb]

| | | |
|---|---|---|
| **herb**<br>[hɝb]<br>名 藥草 | Chinese herbs<br>中藥 | He bought some Chinese herbs for his cold.<br>他買了一些中藥治感冒。 |
| **superb**<br>[sʊ`pɝb]<br>形 極好的 | a superb performance<br>很棒的表演 | That was a superb performance of the play. Congratulations! 很棒的表演，恭喜你！ |
| **verb**<br>[vɝb]<br>名 動詞 | verb phrases<br>動詞片語 | It's hard to learn all of the verb phrases in English.<br>學會英文所有的動詞片語是很難的。 |
| **adverb**<br>[`ædvɝb]<br>名 副詞 | pick out an adverb<br>找出副詞 | Can you pick out an adverb in the sentence?<br>你可以在這句裡找出副詞嗎？ |

## urch [ɝtʃ]

| | | |
|---|---|---|
| **church** [tʃɜtʃ] 名 教堂 | go to church 上教堂 | That family goes to church every Sunday. 那家人每週日上教堂。 |

## earch [ɜtʃ]

| | | |
|---|---|---|
| **search** [sɜtʃ] 動 搜查 | search for 搜尋 | The police have been searching for the missing girl for over 20 years. 警方已經搜尋失蹤的女孩超過二十年了。 |
| **research** [rɪ`sɜtʃ] 動 名 研究 | do research 做研究 | I'm going to the library to do research. 我要去圖書館做研究。 |

## urtle [`ɜtl̩]

| | | |
|---|---|---|
| **turtle** [`tɜtl̩] 名 海龜、龜 | slow as a turtle 慢得像隻龜 | Hurry up! You are as slow as a turtle. 快點！你慢得像隻龜。 |

## ertile [`ɜtl̩]

| | | |
|---|---|---|
| **fertile** [`fɜtl̩] 形 多產的、肥沃的 | fertile land 肥沃的土地 | They have been trying to find fertile land where they can grow crops. 他們一直在找可以栽培作物的肥沃土地。 |

## urdy [ˋɝdɪ]



| | | |
|---|---|---|
| **sturdy** [ˋstɝdɪ] 形 堅固的 | a sturdy table 堅固的桌子 | We need a sturdy table to set up the computer on. 我們需要堅固的桌子好在上面安裝電腦。 |

## ure [jʊr]

| | | |
|---|---|---|
| * **cure** [kjʊr] 動 名 治療 | a cure for 治療法 | Is there a cure for this illness? 這個疾病有治療方法嗎？ |
| * **secure** [sɪˋkjʊr] 形 安全的 | feel secure 感到安全 | She doesn't feel secure walking alone at night in the city by herself. 她覺得晚上獨自一人走在城裡不安全。 |
| **obscure** [əbˋskjʊr] 形 晦澀的 | obscure meaning 晦澀的含義 | His keen and intelligent mind can find obscure meanings in most art. 他機敏聰明的心靈能看出大部分藝術中晦澀的含義。 |
| **insecure** [ˏɪnsɪˋkjʊr] 形 不安全的 | insecure person 不安的人 | She is an insecure person who cannot take criticism without being offended. 她是個不安的人，一經批評就覺得不舒服。 |
| **manicure** [ˋmænɪˏkjʊr] 名 動 修指甲 | get a manicure 修指甲 | I'm going to the nail salon to get a manicure. 我要去美容院修指甲。 |
| * **endure** [ɪnˋdjʊr] 動 忍耐 | endure pain 忍痛 | He can endure a lot of pain. 他能忍受很多痛苦。 |

| | | |
|---|---|---|
| **brochure** [bro`ʃjʊr] 名 小冊子 | ▶ seasonal brochure 週期性的冊子 | ▶ They put out a seasonal brochure for their line of clothing. 他們為自家服裝出版週期性刊物。 |
| **pure** [pjʊr] 形 純粹的 | ▶ pure sugar 純糖 | ▶ This kind of candy is made up of pure sugar, artificial flavoring, and coloring. 這種糖果是由純糖、人工香料和色素組成的。 |
| **impure** [ɪm`pjʊr] 形 不純的 | ▶ impure drugs 不純的藥品 | ▶ You should be careful of the impure drugs that they sell here. 你應該小心他們這兒銷售的不純藥品。 |
| * **mature** [mə`tjʊr] 形 成熟的 | ▶ a mature attitude 成熟的態度 | ▶ You need to have a mature attitude in the office for others to respect you. 在辦公室你必須有成熟的態度，別人才會尊重你。 |
| **immature** [ˏɪmə`tjʊr] 形 未成熟的 | ▶ immature for her age 以她的年紀而言不成熟 | ▶ She is 45 years old, but she is immature for her age. 她45歲，但以她的年紀而言她不夠成熟。 |

## ure [ʊr]

| | | |
|---|---|---|
| * **sure** [ʃʊr] 形 確信的 | ▶ sure of 確信 | ▶ Are you sure of this? 對此你確信嗎？ |
| * **ensure** [ɪn`ʃʊr] 動 保證 | ▶ ensure fair treatment 保證公平的對待 | ▶ Can this new policy ensure fair treatment to everybody? 這個新政策可以保證公平對待每個人嗎？ |

| | | |
|---|---|---|
| **unsure**<br>[ˏʌnˋʃʊr]<br>形 無把握的 | feel unsure<br>感到沒把握 | I feel unsure about this new teacher we have.<br>我對我們這位新老師沒有把握。 |
| * **assure**<br>[əˋʃʊr]<br>動 向…保證 | assure you of<br>向你保證 | I assure you of our quality and our good customer service. 我向你保證我們的品質及良好的客戶服務。 |
| **reassure**<br>[ˏriəˋʃʊr]<br>動 使放心、再保證 | reassure me<br>向我再次保證 | My friends reassured me that everything would be OK.<br>我朋友向我再次保證一切都會沒事。 |

## our [ʊr]

| | | |
|---|---|---|
| **tour**<br>[tʊr]<br>名 旅遊 | take a tour<br>遊覽 | Let's take a tour of the building.<br>讓我們參觀這棟大樓吧。 |
| **detour**<br>[ˋditʊr]<br>名 動 繞道 | make a detour<br>繞道 | We have to make a detour because there is construction up ahead.<br>我們必須繞道，因為前面在施工。 |
| **your**<br>[jʊr]<br>代 你的、你們的 | your life<br>你的生活 | Only you can make decisions about your life.<br>只有你能決定你的生活。 |

## urf [ɝf]

| | | |
|---|---|---|
| **surf**<br>[sɜf]<br>動 衝浪、上網 | ▶ go surfing<br>衝浪 | ▶ Did you go surfing last week-end?<br>你上週末有去衝浪嗎？ |

## urious [ˋjʊrɪəs]

| | | |
|---|---|---|
| * **curious**<br>[ˋkjʊrɪəs]<br>形 好奇的 | ▶ curious about<br>對…好奇 | ▶ He is curious about the way things work around here.<br>他對這附近的風俗習慣很好奇。 |
| **furious**<br>[ˋfjʊrɪəs]<br>形 狂怒的 | ▶ furious at<br>狂怒 | ▶ She will become furious at me if I don't help her out.<br>如果我不幫她，她會對我大發雷霆。 |

## url [ɜl]

| | | |
|---|---|---|
| **curl**<br>[kɜl]<br>動 使捲曲 | ▶ curl her hair<br>捲頭髮 | ▶ She wakes up early in the morning to curl her hair.<br>她早上很早起床捲頭髮。 |
| **hurl**<br>[hɜl]<br>動 猛力投擲 | ▶ hurl at<br>猛投 | ▶ He took that ball and hurled it at my face.<br>他拿那顆球朝我的臉猛丟過來。 |

## earl [ɜl]

| earl [ɜl] 名伯爵 | ▸ Earl Grey Tea 伯爵茶 | ▸ Earl Grey Tea is a British tea taken with milk. 伯爵茶是加鮮奶的英式茶。 |
|---|---|---|
| pearl [pɜl] 名珍珠 | ▸ pearl necklace 珍珠項鍊 | ▸ She got disappointed when she found out her pearl necklace was a fake. 當她發現她的珍珠項鍊是假的時，她很失望。 |

## irl [ɜl]

| girl [gɜl] 名女孩 | ▸ a cute girl 可愛的女孩 | ▸ When she was little, she was a cute girl. 她小時候是個可愛的女孩。 |
|---|---|---|
| whirl [hwɜl] 動名 旋轉 | ▸ the dancer whirled 舞者旋轉 | ▸ The dancer whirled around and around until she fell down. 舞者不斷旋轉直到她跌倒。 |
| twirl [twɜl] 動使快速轉動 | ▸ twirl batons 轉動指揮棒 | ▸ In the parade, some girls twirled batons. 遊行裡，有些女孩轉動指揮棒。 |

## urn [ɜn]

| urn [ɜn] 名甕、缸 | ▸ ceramic urn 陶瓷甕 | ▸ His ceramic urn is placed in a temple. 他的陶瓷骨灰甕被放在廟裡。 |
|---|---|---|

| | | |
|---|---|---|
| * **burn** [bɝn] 動 燃燒 | burn wood 燃燒木柴 | In the winter, they burn wood in the fireplace to heat their house. 冬天時，他們在壁爐裡燃燒木柴讓房子暖和。 |
| **sunburn** [ˋsʌn͵bɝn] 動 名 曬傷 | sunburned skin 曬傷的皮膚 | It feels good to put Aloe Vera on sunburned skin. 在曬傷的皮膚上擦蘆薈感覺很好。 |
| * **turn** [tɝn] 動 轉動、改變 | turn into 變成 | I don't want to turn into a bad person when I get older. 當我年紀大一點時，我不想變成壞人。 |
| * **return** [rɪˋtɝn] 動 返回 | return to 返回 | Let's return to our original plan. 讓我們回到原來的計劃。 |
| **overturn** [͵ovɚˋtɝn] [ˋovɚ͵tɝn] 動 名 傾覆 | overturn the boat 使船翻覆 | He purposely overturned the boat when I wasn't looking. 我沒顧著時，他就故意讓船翻覆。 |

## ern [ɝn]

| | | |
|---|---|---|
| * **concern** [kənˋsɝn] 動 關於、涉及 | concern you 涉及你 | That matter doesn't concern you. 那件事跟你無關。 |
| **intern** [ɪnˋtɝn] 名 實習生 | only an intern 只是實習生 | He cannot make important decisions about patients because he's only an intern. 關於病人的事，他不能做重要的決定，因為他只是實習醫生。 |

| | | |
|---|---|---|
| **stern**<br>[stɜn]<br>形 嚴格的 | stern look<br>嚴厲的表情 | Her stern look gives me an insecure feeling.<br>她嚴厲的表情讓我感到不安。 |

## earn [ɜn]

| | | |
|---|---|---|
| * **earn**<br>[ɜn]<br>動 賺得、贏得 | earn a living<br>謀生 | How will you earn a living when you grow up?<br>當你長大你要怎麼謀生？ |
| * **learn**<br>[lɜn]<br>動 學習 | learn from<br>從…學習 | You must try to learn from your mistakes.<br>你必須試著從錯誤中學習。 |
| **yearn**<br>[jɜn]<br>動 渴望、嚮往 | yearn for<br>渴望 | I yearn for a long vacation.<br>我渴望放長假。 |

## urry [`ɜɪ]

| | | |
|---|---|---|
| **scurry**<br>[`skɜɪ]<br>動 急匆匆地跑 | scurry away<br>急忙跑走 | The cockroach scurried away when I tried to step on it.<br>當我試圖踩蟑螂時，它急忙跑掉了。 |
| **furry**<br>[`fɜɪ]<br>形 毛皮的 | furry animal<br>有毛動物 | She likes to pet furry animals.<br>她喜歡撫弄有毛的動物。 |

| | | |
|---|---|---|
| **blurry**<br>[ˋblɝɪ]<br>形 模糊的 | ▶ a blurry memory<br>模糊的記憶 | ▶ I only have a blurry memory of my childhood.<br>我只有模糊的童年記憶。 |

## orry [ˋɝɪ]

| | | |
|---|---|---|
| **worry**<br>[ˋwɝɪ]<br>動 擔心 | ▶ worry about<br>擔心 | ▶ Don't worry about it.<br>別擔心。 |

## ury [ˋjʊrɪ]

| | | |
|---|---|---|
| **fury**<br>[ˋfjʊrɪ]<br>名 狂怒 | ▶ in his fury<br>在狂怒中 | ▶ In his fury he hit his own children.<br>在狂怒中他打自己的小孩。 |

## us [ʌs]

68

| | | |
|---|---|---|
| **us**<br>[ʌs]<br>代 我們 | ▶ meet us<br>跟我們見面 | ▶ Where will you meet us tonight for dinner?<br>今天晚餐你要在哪兒跟我們見面？ |
| **bus**<br>[bʌs]<br>名 巴士 | ▶ on the bus<br>在公車上 | ▶ Someone threw up on the bus, and it smelled bad. 有人在公車上嘔吐，味道很難聞。 |

| | | |
|---|---|---|
| **plus** [plʌs] 介 加上 | ▶ 1 plus 1 一加一 | ▶ Everyone should know what 1 plus 1 is. 每個人都應該知道一加一等於多少。 |

## uss [ʌs]

| | | |
|---|---|---|
| * **discuss** [dɪ`skʌs] 動 討論 | ▶ discuss with 與…討論 | ▶ We will discuss the plans with everyone before we make a decision. 我們會在做決定前跟每個人討論計劃。 |
| **fuss** [fʌs] 名 動 忙亂、大驚小怪 | ▶ make a fuss 大驚小怪 | ▶ Please don't make a fuss about it. 請不要對此大驚小怪。 |

## use [jus]

| | | |
|---|---|---|
| * **use** [jus] 名 使用 | ▶ use of violence 使用暴力 | ▶ The use of violence is a sign of weakness. 使用暴力是軟弱的象徵。 |
| **abuse** [ə`bjus] 名 濫用、虐待 | ▶ physical abuse 肉體的虐待 | ▶ No one should accept physical abuse in a marriage. 沒有人應該在婚姻中受到肉體虐待。 |

## uce [jus]

| | | |
|---|---|---|
| **deduce** [dɪˋdjus] 動 推論 ▶ | deduce from 從…推論 ▶ | What can you deduce from this text? 你可以從這段文字推論出什麼？ |
| * **reduce** [rɪˋdjus] 動 減少 ▶ | reduce waste 減少浪費 ▶ | We need to reduce waste on our planet. 我們需要減少地球上的浪費。 |
| * **produce** [prəˋdjus] [ˋprɑdjus] 動 生產 名 產品 ▶ | produce cars 生產車子 ▶ | That country has produced cars for more than a century. 那個國家生產車子已超過一世紀了。 |
| * **introduce** [ˏɪntrəˋdjus] 動 介紹 ▶ | introduce me to 介紹我給… ▶ | Please introduce me to your new friend. 請介紹我給你的新朋友認識。 |

## use [juz]

| | | |
|---|---|---|
| **accuse** [əˋkjuz] 動 指控 ▶ | accuse me of 指控我 ▶ | They accused me of stealing the money. 他們指控我偷錢。 |
| * **excuse** [ɪkˋskjuz] 動 原諒 名 藉口 ▶ | excuse me 原諒我 ▶ | Will you excuse me please? 請你原諒我好嗎？ |
| * **refuse** [rɪˋfjuz] 動 拒絕 ▶ | refuse the offer 拒絕 ▶ | She offered to help out with money, but he refused the offer. 她想出錢幫忙，但他拒絕了。 |

| | | |
|---|---|---|
| * **confuse** [kən`fjuz] 動 使困惑 | confuse me ▶ 讓我搞混 | ▶ All of the information confuses me. 這些資訊把我給搞混了。 |
| **muse** [mjuz] 動 沈思 名 靈感 | musical muse ▶ 音樂的靈感 | ▶ She thinks of him as her musical muse. 她認為他是她的音樂靈感。 |
| **amuse** [ə`mjuz] 動 使歡樂 | amuse the audience ▶ 取悅觀眾 | ▶ He is a natural in amusing the audience. 他天生就會取悅觀眾。 |
| **misuse** [mɪs`juz] 動 誤用、濫用 | misuse his time ▶ 濫用他的時間 | ▶ Since he spends all of his extra time in the video arcade, his parents think that he misuses his time. 他把空閒時間都花在電玩店，他父母因而認為他濫用時間。 |

## uise [uz]

| | | |
|---|---|---|
| **bruise** [bruz] 名 動 瘀傷 | a few bruises ▶ 一些瘀傷 | ▶ She got a few bruises on her arms from the game. 因為比賽她的手臂有些瘀傷。 |
| **cruise** [kruz] 動 巡航、漫遊 | cruise along the coast ▶ 沿海漫遊 | ▶ It's nice to cruise along the coast in a fancy car. 在拉風的車裡沿海漫遊很棒。 |

## ush [ʌʃ]

| 單字 | 片語 | 例句 |
| --- | --- | --- |
| **hush** [hʌʃ] 動 使安靜 | hush the crying child 使在哭的小孩安靜 | They hushed the crying child by playing with him. 他們跟哭泣的小孩玩讓他安靜下來。 |
| **blush** [blʌʃ] 動 臉紅 | cheeks blush 臉頰很紅 | Her cheeks blush when she gets embarrassed. 當她不好意思時，她的臉頰變很紅。 |
| **flush** [flʌʃ] 動 臉紅、用水沖洗 | flush the toilet 沖馬桶 | Don't forget to flush the toilet after you use it. 你上完廁所時，別忘了沖一下馬桶。 |
| * **rush** [rʌʃ] 名 繁忙 動 匆忙 | rush hour 尖峰時刻 | It's annoying to be stuck in traffic during rush hour. 尖峰時刻塞在路上感覺很討厭。 |
| **brush** [brʌʃ] 動 刷洗 名 刷子 | brush my teeth 刷牙 | I try to brush my teeth at least twice a day. 我試著每天至少刷兩次牙。 |
| **toothbrush** [ˋtuθ͵brʌʃ] 名 牙刷 | disposable toothbrush 可棄式牙刷 | Some hotels give you a disposable toothbrush. 有些飯店會提供拋棄式牙刷。 |
| **crush** [krʌʃ] 動 名 壓壞 | crush the box 壓壞盒子 | My dog crushed the box and tore it apart with its teeth. 我的狗壓壞盒子，並用牙齒撕裂它。 |

## ush [uʃ]

| | | |
|---|---|---|
| **bush**<br>[buʃ]<br>名 灌木 | beat around the bush<br>拐彎抹角 | Just tell me. We don't have time to beat around the bush. 就直接告訴我，我們沒有時間拐彎抹角。 |
| **ambush**<br>[`æmbuʃ]<br>名 動 埋伏、伏擊 | set an ambush<br>設埋伏 | The group set an ambush on that little town.<br>這群人在那小鎮上設了埋伏。 |
| * **push**<br>[puʃ]<br>動 推動、推進 | push ahead<br>往前進 | It's important to push ahead in times of discouragement.<br>在氣餒時能往前邁進是很重要的。 |

## usion [`juʒən]

| | | |
|---|---|---|
| **fusion**<br>[`fjuʒən]<br>名 熔化、融合 | a fusion of<br>融合 | This restaurant serves a fusion of Asian and Indian food.<br>這家餐廳的菜融合亞洲及印度風味。 |
| **illusion**<br>[ɪ`ljuʒən]<br>名 錯覺、幻覺 | create an illusion<br>產生錯覺 | The show created an illusion of being in another world.<br>這場表演讓人產生身處在另一個世界的錯覺。 |

## usk [ʌsk]

| | | |
|---|---|---|
| **dusk**<br>[dʌsk]<br>名 薄暮、黃昏 | at dusk<br>在黃昏 | She likes to take a long walk at dusk.<br>她喜歡在黃昏時散步。 |

| | | |
|---|---|---|
| **robust** [rə`bʌst] 形 強健的 | robust man 強健的男人 | She wanted to date a robust man who could protect her physically. 她想跟可以保護她的強健男人約會。 |
| **dust** [dʌst] 名 灰塵 | a layer of dust 一層灰塵 | The piano collected a layer of dust since no one played it for years. 有好幾年都沒人彈鋼琴，它因而積了一層灰。 |
| **gust** [gʌst] 名 一陣強風 | a gust of wind 一陣狂風 | A gust of wind blew our tree down. 一陣狂風吹倒我們的樹。 |
| **disgust** [dɪs`gʌst] 名 動 厭惡 | disgust me 讓我感到噁心 | Eating innards and other weird animal parts disgusts me. 吃內臟和其他奇怪的動物部位讓我感到很噁心。 |
| * **just** [dʒʌst] 副 正好、只是 | just because 只是因為 | She left town just because she wanted to. 她離開鎮上只是因為她想。 |
| * **adjust** [ə`dʒʌst] 動 調整 | adjust to 調整 | She became good at adjusting to different surroundings. 她調適不同環境的能力變得很好。 |
| **unjust** [ʌn`dʒʌst] 形 不公平的 | unjust sentence 不公平的判決 | People protested the unjust sentence of the innocent man. 人們抗議對無罪男人的不公平判決。 |
| * **must** [mʌst] 助 必須 | must-see 非看不可 | That movie is a must-see. 那部電影非看不可。 |

| | | |
|---|---|---|
| **rust**<br>[rʌst]<br>名 鏽 動 生鏽 | ▶ gather rust<br>生鏽 | ▶ That metal will gather rust if you leave it in the rain.<br>如果你任憑那金屬淋雨，它會生鏽。 |
| **crust**<br>[krʌst]<br>名 麵包皮、地殼 | ▶ crust of bread<br>麵包皮 | ▶ We fed a crust of bread to birds in the park.<br>我們在公園用麵包皮餵鳥。 |
| **thrust**<br>[θrʌst]<br>動 用力推 | ▶ thrust him<br>用力推他 | ▶ We watched the police thrust him against the wall.<br>我們看到警察用力推他到牆邊。 |
| * **trust**<br>[trʌst]<br>動 信任 | ▶ trust me<br>相信我 | ▶ You will have to trust me if you want me to help you.<br>如果你要我幫你，你就必須相信我。 |
| * **entrust**<br>[ɪn`trʌst]<br>動 委託 | ▶ entrust you with<br>委託你 | ▶ Do you think I can entrust you with my valuables?<br>你想我可以委託你我的貴重物品嗎？ |
| **distrust**<br>[dɪs`trʌst]<br>動 不信任 | ▶ distrust people<br>不信任人 | ▶ He tends to distrust people who look innocent.<br>他不信任看起來頭腦簡單的人。 |

## uster [`ʌstɚ]

| | | |
|---|---|---|
| **blockbuster**<br>[`blɑk͵bʌstɚ]<br>名 轟動一時的事物 | ▶ a real blockbuster<br>風靡一時的鉅片 | ▶ The movie “Titanic” was a real blockbuster.<br>電影《鐵達尼號》是一部風靡一時的鉅片。 |

| | | |
|---|---|---|
| **muster** [ˋmʌstɚ] 動 召集、鼓起 | ▶ muster up 鼓起 | ▶ She had to muster up her courage to report the crime. 她必須鼓起勇氣揭發罪行。 |

## ustle [ˋʌsl̩]

| | | |
|---|---|---|
| **hustle** [ˋhʌsl̩] 動 名 趕緊、奔忙 | ▶ hustle and bustle 繁忙喧鬧 | ▶ He likes the hustle and bustle of the city. 他喜歡都市的繁忙喧鬧。 |
| **rustle** [ˋrʌsl̩] 動 沙沙作響 | ▶ the leaves rustled 葉子沙沙作響 | ▶ The leaves rustled as they fell to the ground. 葉子落到地面時沙沙作響。 |

## uscle [ˋʌsl̩]

| | | |
|---|---|---|
| **muscle** [ˋmʌsl̩] 名 肌肉 | ▶ develop your muscles 使你的肌肉成長 | ▶ After you break a limb, you must develop your muscles slowly. 你摔傷手腳後，必須慢慢地讓肌肉成長。 |

## ut [ʌt]

| | | |
|---|---|---|
| * **but** [bʌt] 連 但是 介 除…以外 | ▶ nothing but 只不過 | ▶ He is nothing but a loser. 他只不過是個失敗者。 |

| | | |
|---|---|---|
| **rebut** [rɪˋbʌt] 動 反駁 | ▶ rebut his argument 反駁他的論點 | ▶ I couldn't think of what to say to rebut his argument. 我想不到要說什麼來反駁他的論點。 |
| * **cut** [kʌt] 動 切、砍 | ▶ cut his hand 切到他的手 | ▶ He cut his hand on a pair of scissors. 他的手被剪刀剪到。 |
| **haircut** [ˋhɛr͵kʌt] 名 理髮 | ▶ get a haircut 理髮 | ▶ It's time to get a haircut. 該理髮了。 |
| * **shortcut** [ˋʃɔrt͵kʌt] 名 捷徑 | ▶ take a shortcut 走捷徑 | ▶ We can take a shortcut this way. 我們可以往這邊抄近路。 |
| **gut** [gʌt] 名 腸子 | ▶ puke his guts out 吐得很嚴重 | ▶ The food went bad so he puked his guts out. 這食物壞了，所以他吐得很嚴重。 |
| * **shut** [ʃʌt] 動 關上 | ▶ shut the window 關上窗戶 | ▶ Shut the window; it's cold outside. 把窗戶關上，外頭很冷。 |
| **nut** [nʌt] 名 核果、難題 | ▶ a hard nut to crack 難以對付的人 | ▶ I can't figure him out; he's a hard nut to crack. 我搞不懂他，他是個難以對付的人。 |
| **strut** [strʌt] 動 高視闊步 | ▶ strut your stuff 大顯身手 | ▶ If you are a model or look like one, you probably strut your stuff. 如果你是模特兒或看起來像塊料，你就可能大顯身手。 |

## utch [ʌtʃ]

| | | |
|---|---|---|
| **Dutch** [dʌtʃ] 名 荷蘭語 形 荷蘭的 | ▶ Dutch people 荷蘭人 | ▶ Dutch people colonized Taiwan centuries ago. 幾個世紀以前荷蘭人殖民台灣。 |
| **clutch** [klʌtʃ] 動 抓住 | ▶ clutch at 抓住 | ▶ He is still clutching at an unrealistic dream. 他還在做不切實際的夢。 |
| **crutch** [krʌtʃ] 名 拐杖 | ▶ walk on crutches 靠拐杖走路 | ▶ Since he broke his leg, he has to walk on crutches for a while. 自從他摔斷腿後，他有一陣子必須靠拐杖走路。 |

## uch [ʌtʃ]

| | | |
|---|---|---|
| * **much** [mʌtʃ] 形 許多 副 非常 | ▶ very much 非常 | ▶ I like this very much. 我非常喜歡這個。 |
| * **such** [sʌtʃ] 形 這樣的、如此的 | ▶ such a beautiful girl 如此美的女孩 | ▶ You are such a beautiful girl. 你真是個美麗的女孩。 |

## ouch [ʌtʃ]

| | | |
|---|---|---|
| * **touch** [tʌtʃ] 動 名 接觸 | ▶ keep in touch with 與…保持聯絡 | ▶ You should keep in touch with your old friends. 你應該與你的老朋友保持聯絡。 |

| | | |
|---|---|---|
| **tribute** [ˋtrɪbjut] 名 進貢、敬意 | pay tribute to 向…致敬 | We'd like to pay tribute to our parents by raising our glasses. Cheers! 我們要舉杯向父母致敬，乾杯！ |
| * **attribute** [əˋtrɪbjut] 動 歸因於 | attribute to 歸因於 | This water damage is attributed to the leak in the roof. 這片水漬是因為屋頂裂縫造成。 |
| **cute** [kjut] 形 可愛的 | a cute baby 可愛的嬰兒 | He was a cute baby. 他曾是可愛的嬰兒。 |
| **acute** [əˋkjut] 形 尖銳的、劇烈的 | acute pain 劇痛 | The acute pain will go away after you take some of these pills. 你吃這些藥後劇痛就會消失了。 |
| * **execute** [ˋɛksɪˏkjut] 動 實行 | execute the policy 實行政策 | The police didn't execute the policy until it came into effect. 警察直到政策生效後才執行。 |
| **prosecute** [ˋprɑsɪˏkjut] 動 起訴 | prosecute for 起訴 | The District Attorney will prosecute for the victim of the crime. 地方檢察官將為受害者起訴。 |
| **persecute** [ˋpɝsɪˏkjut] 動 迫害 | persecute people 迫害人民 | Governments often persecute people. 政府常迫害人民。 |
| **refute** [rɪˋfjut] 動 駁斥 | refute the argument 反駁論點 | I have to think of how I'm going to refute the argument. 我必須思考要怎樣反駁論點。 |

| | | |
|---|---|---|
| **mute**<br>[mjut]<br>形 沈默的 動 減輕 | mute the sound<br>降低音量 | Please mute the sound on the TV. I'm trying to sleep.<br>請降低電視的音量，我正想睡覺。 |
| * **commute**<br>[kə`mjut]<br>動 通勤 | commute between<br>在…之間通勤 | It takes me 2 hours to commute between my house and my workplace. 從我家到工作的地方兩地通勤要花兩小時。 |
| **compute**<br>[kəm`pjut]<br>動 計算 | compute the bill<br>算帳 | I think I need a calculator to compute the bill.<br>我想我需要用計算機來算帳。 |
| * **dispute**<br>[dɪ`spjut]<br>動 名 爭論 | dispute over<br>爭論 | They had a dispute over the game.<br>他們對比賽有所爭論。 |
| * **substitute**<br>[`sʌbstə,tjut]<br>動 代替 名 代替物 | substitute for<br>代替 | She will substitute for the sick English teacher.<br>她將幫生病的英文教師代課。 |
| **institute**<br>[`ɪnstətjut]<br>名 協會、研究院 | research institute<br>研究所 | That research institute has the best equipment.<br>那所研究所有最好的設備。 |

## ute [ut]

| | | |
|---|---|---|
| **parachute**<br>[`pærə,ʃut]<br>名 降落傘 | open the parachute<br>打開降落傘 | Teach me how to open the parachute before I jump!<br>在我跳之前教我怎麼打開降落傘！ |

| | | |
|---|---|---|
| **salute** [sə`lut] 動致敬 | salute an officer 向軍官致敬 | You should salute an officer of high ranking. 你應該向高階軍官致敬。 |
| **flute** [flut] 名長笛 | play the flute 演奏長笛 | She plays the flute in her school band. 她在學校樂隊演奏長笛。 |
| * **pollute** [pə`lut] 動污染、弄髒 | pollute people's minds 污染人心 | Some political groups will pollute people's minds with propaganda. 有些政治團體用宣傳手法污染人心。 |
| * **absolute** [`æbsə͵lut] 形絕對的 | absolute ruler 專制統治者 | Fewer countries nowadays have absolute rulers than before. 比起以前，現在的國家較少有專制統治者。 |
| **resolute** [`rɛzə͵lut] 形堅決的 | a resolute person 堅決的人 | I need a resolute person to do the job. 我需要堅決的人做這工作。 |

## oot [ut]

| | | |
|---|---|---|
| **boot** [but] 名靴子 | high-heeled boots 高跟靴子 | Her high-heeled boots attracted a lot of people's attention. 她的高跟靴子吸引了很多人的注意。 |
| **shoot** [ʃut] 動發射 | shoot an arrow 射箭 | You can practice how to shoot an arrow here in this field. 你可以在這場上練習如何射箭。 |

| | | |
|---|---|---|
| **loot**<br>[lut]<br>動 掠奪、搶劫 | loot the store<br>搶劫商店 | Some people looted the store when the riot broke out.<br>當暴動發生時，有些人搶劫商店。 |
| **root**<br>[rut]<br>名 根 動 根除 | root of<br>…的根源<br>root out<br>徹底根除 | The root of the problem is in the unstable foundation.<br>問題的根源是基礎不穩定。<br>We should root out the bad ones in the group.<br>我們應該根除團體中的不良份子。 |
| **uproot**<br>[ʌp\`rut]<br>動 根除 | trees have been uprooted<br>樹被連根拔除 | These trees have been uprooted and taken away because of construction. 因為要大興土木，所以這些樹被連根拔起運走。 |

## uit [ut]

| | | |
|---|---|---|
| **recruit**<br>[rɪ\`krut]<br>動 徵募 | recruit new members<br>召募新會員 | They are recruiting new members for the club.<br>他們正為俱樂部召募新會員。 |
| * **suit**<br>[sut]<br>名 套裝 動 適合 | suit us<br>適合我們 | I think that this will suit us.<br>我認為這個會適合我們。 |
| * **pursuit**<br>[pɚ\`sut]<br>名 追求 | in the pursuit of<br>為了追求 | She lied and cheated her colleagues in the pursuit of her promotion at work. 為了要在工作上升遷，她說謊並欺騙她的同事。 |
| **lawsuit**<br>[\`lɔˏsut]<br>名 訴訟 | file a lawsuit<br>提起訴訟 | You can file a lawsuit against him, but it will cost you time and money. 你可以對他提起訴訟，但那將花費你的時間及金錢。 |

## uter [`jutɚ]

| | | |
|---|---|---|
| **commuter** [kə`mjutɚ] 名 通勤者 | commuter train 通勤火車 | He takes the commuter train every day to work. 他每天搭通勤火車去上班。 |
| * **computer** [kəm`pjutɚ] 名 電腦 | a laptop computer 筆記型電腦 | She brings a laptop computer to class to take notes. 她上課帶筆記型電腦做筆記。 |

## utor [`jutɚ]

| | | |
|---|---|---|
| **tutor** [`tjutɚ] 名 家庭教師 | English tutor 英文家教 | Many foreigners who come to Taiwan become an English tutor to make extra money. 很多來到台灣的外國人當英文家教賺外快。 |

## ution [`juʃən]

| | | |
|---|---|---|
| **retribution** [ˏrɛtrɪ`bjuʃən] 名 報應 | seek retribution 進行報復 | After he gets out of the hospital, he will seek retribution by suing the assailant. 他出院後將控告攻擊他的人作為報復。 |
| * **contribution** [ˏkantrə`bjuʃən] 名 貢獻 | make a contribution to 對…有貢獻 | Try to make a contribution to your household chores. 試著幫忙做家事。 |
| * **distribution** [ˏdɪstrə`bjuʃən] 名 分配 | even distribution 平均分配 | There is an even distribution of girls and boys in the room. 房間裡的男女人數均等。 |

| **institution** [ˌɪnstəˋtjuʃən] 名 制度、機構 | ▸ | mental institution 精神療養院 | ▸ | After attempting suicide, his parents sent him to a mental institution. 在他企圖自殺後，他的父母把他送到精神療養院去。 |
|---|---|---|---|---|

## ution [ˋuʃən]

| | | | | |
|---|---|---|---|---|
| * **pollution** [pəˋluʃən] 名 污染 | ▸ | air pollution 空氣污染 | ▸ | The air pollution in Taiwan is pretty bad. 台灣的空氣污染很嚴重。 |
| * **solution** [səˋluʃən] 名 解答 | ▸ | a solution to 解決…的辦法 | ▸ | We need to find a solution to the problem. 我們需要找到解決問題的辦法。 |
| **evolution** [ˌɛvəˋluʃən] 名 演化 | ▸ | evolution of man 人類的進化 | ▸ | The evolution of man has been studied through artifacts. 透過手工藝品可研究人類的進化。 |
| * **revolution** [ˌrɛvəˋluʃən] 名 革命 | ▸ | carry out a revolution 實行革命 | ▸ | Governments prepare for the chance that someone might carry out a revolution. 政府作好準備以防有人革命起義。 |

## utter [ˋʌtɚ]

| | | | | |
|---|---|---|---|---|
| **utter** [ˋʌtɚ] 動 表達、說 | ▸ | utter a word 說話 | ▸ | Be quiet. Don't utter a word. 安靜，不要說話。 |

| | | |
|---|---|---|
| **butter**<br>[ˋbʌtɚ]<br>名 奶油 | ▶ spread butter<br>塗奶油 | ▶ I need a knife to spread butter on my bread.<br>我需要用把刀把奶油塗在麵包上。 |
| **clutter**<br>[ˋklʌtɚ]<br>名 雜亂、散亂 | ▶ clean up the clutter<br>打掃雜亂 | ▶ My mother told me to clean up the clutter in my room.<br>我的母親叫我要打掃我的房間。 |
| **flutter**<br>[ˋflʌtɚ]<br>動 拍翅 | ▶ flutter their wings<br>拍動翅膀 | ▶ Birds flutter their wings to fly.<br>鳥兒振翅飛翔。 |
| **mutter**<br>[ˋmʌtɚ]<br>動 低聲嘀咕 | ▶ mutter a word<br>低聲說話 | ▶ He muttered a word that I couldn't understand.<br>他低聲喃喃，我無法理解。 |
| **stutter**<br>[ˋstʌtɚ]<br>動 名 結巴 | ▶ have a stutter<br>有口吃 | ▶ She went to a speech therapist because she has a stutter.<br>她因為口吃去看語言治療師。 |

## uzzle [ˋʌzl̩]

| | | |
|---|---|---|
| **puzzle**<br>[ˋpʌzl̩]<br>動 使迷惑 名 拼圖 | ▶ jigsaw puzzle<br>拼圖玩具 | ▶ It took me three years to finish that jigsaw puzzle.<br>我花了三年才完成那幅拼圖。 |

# 單字尾韻索引

# 單字索引

## A

## D

## F

## G

## M

## N



## O

## P

## S

## U



## V

## W



## Y



## Z

# MEMO

MEMO

NEW TOEIC必考單字快速記憶/Carolyn G. Choong
著. -- 二版. -- 臺北市：笛藤出版, 2021.07
面； 公分
ISBN 978-957-710-826-5(平裝)
1.多益測驗 2.詞彙
805.1895 110011518

2022年9月5日二版 第2刷 定價460元

NEW TOEIC
附MP3音檔連結
必考單字 快速記憶

| | |
|---|---|
| 著者 | Carolyn G. Choong |
| 譯者 | Melody |
| 編輯 | 羅金純・伍曉玥・葉艾青 |
| 封面設計 | 王舒玗 |
| 總編輯 | 賴巧凌 |
| 編輯企劃 | 笛藤出版 |
| 發行人 | 林建仲 |
| 發行所 | 八方出版股份有限公司 |
| 地址 | 台北市中山區長安東路二段171號3樓3室 |
| 電話 | (02) 2777-3682 |
| 傳真 | (02) 2777-3672 |
| 總經銷 | 聯合發行股份有限公司 |
| 地址 | 新北市新店區寶橋路235巷6弄6號2樓 |
| 電話 | (02)2917-8022・(02)2917-8042 |
| 製版廠 | 造極彩色印刷製版股份有限公司 |
| 地址 | 新北市中和區中山路二段380巷7號1樓 |
| 電話 | (02)2240-0333・(02)2248-3904 |
| 印刷廠 | 皇甫彩藝印刷股份有限公司 |
| 地址 | 新北市中和區中正路988巷10號 |
| 郵撥帳戶 | 八方出版股份有限公司 |
| 郵撥帳號 | 19809050 |

# 末等魂師

## 第2部

## 2 就是讓你想不到

銀千羽—著
希月—繪

## 人物介紹

### 端木玖

身分：端木家族嫡系九小姐
等級：一星魂師（兼：三星聖武師）
個性：從低調變高調
寵物：焱、磊、寶寶
配件：硫金、流影、小狐狸頭飾、黑色連帽披風

### 紅色小狐狸

身分：魔獸
年紀：不明
特長：被玖玖抱在懷裡睡覺
出場印象：疑似魔獸火狐狸的紅毛小狐狸
新技能：燒光想傷害玖玖的人

## 仲奎一

身分：煉器師
等級：天魂師（傳說中）
個性：樂觀、詼諧、誠信

## 樓烈

身分：疑似聲名赫赫的煉器師
年紀：不明
特長：吃魚、喝酒、教徒弟
出場印象：黑黑灰灰的浮屍一具
口頭禪：我不是壞人
（內心附註：是帥哥）

## 北御前

身分：玖父託付之人，來歷神秘
魂階：五星天魂師
武器：黑色長槍
出場印象：外表約三十歲的紫衣帥美男
口頭禪：不能把小玖養歪了

## 端木風

身分：端木世家嫡系六少爺，
也是本代子弟中第一天才
好友：夏侯駒
特長：護玖狂魔

## 端木傲

身分：端木家族嫡系四少爺
年紀：三十二歲
魂階：天魂師
新技能：妹控兄長實習中
出場印象：冷漠正直的男人
外型：黑髮黑眼的酷型帥青年，氣質沉穩

## 夏侯駒

身分：夏侯皇朝四皇子，
　　　天魂大陸十大天才之一
外型：沉默寡言的俊青年
個性：熱心開朗，有點悶騷
好友：端木風、端木傲
新技能：認識某少女後發現自己往吃貨發展

## 星流

原名：陰星流
身分：原為陰家子弟，現已離族
等級：二星聖魂師
個性：低調、忠誠
契約獸：不明
配件：黑色連帽披風、黑刀

## 寶寶

品種：不明
外型：發育不良的盲眼小狗
專長：汪汪嗚嗚叫、吃

## 雪長歌

身分：東州五少之一，東雪城少城主，東州最俊美的優雅貴公子
特徵：玉冠烏髮，一身白衣，出塵脫俗
個性：優雅、腹黑
武器：長弓
好友：海宇越

# 目錄

## ◆地理簡介◆

東州，天魂大陸三州之一。

西以一道橫亙大陸的天塹——東星山脈，與中州相鄰；以東則為一片無邊無際的海洋。

東州境內，魔獸無數，分散在陸地與水域。

人族聚居，由北到南，則以東雪城、東海城、東明城、東林城、東岩城等五城，為主要居地。

五城的存在，除了保護人族的生存空間，也維持東州的穩定，使海上魔獸，無法任意欺上岸……

# 第十二章 囂張大小姐也有怕的人?!

狂風捲起風雪漫天，比暴風雪來臨時更蔽人耳目。

即使在場的人都是魂師與武師，實力不凡，但面對這陣狂躁風雪，依然不由自主地後退半步，偏掩視線。

刺骨風雪吹過，像將現場已經觸發的火藥味瞬間冷凍！

短短眨眼時間過後，眾人再度睜開眼。

所有人同時一瞬間呆愣，神情有點兒恍惚。

彷彿在懷疑自己是不是眼花、看錯了？

幾息之前，東明玉凌恃強而來，還帶著兩名聖階護衛。

所以他們預想中，接下來的畫面，是東明玉凌欺負一名弱小的少女，而那名少女被打落倒地，受傷又流血，只能憤怒和委屈，還得求饒。

根據過去的經驗，結果都是這樣的。

東明城之主唯一的女兒，行事作風太出名了！

出名到只要她一出現，所有認得她的人——紛紛避讓。

沒有家底、沒有點兒勢力背景的人，真的是不要隨便出現在她面前，免得被誤傷。

然而此刻，他們所看見的，是那名應該害怕、受傷和求饒的少女，不但沒有受傷流血、沒有憤怒委屈和求饒，反而站得直挺挺。

她好整以暇、悠然以待地舉著劍，看似一點攻擊性也沒有，但平舉的劍尖，已幾乎抵觸到東明玉凌的咽喉。

殺機暗藏！

銳氣橫生！

原該氣燄張狂、恃強得意的東明玉凌，此刻一動也不動，面無表情。

張揚高傲的氣燄同時停頓。

兩名聖階護衛，也暫時不敢動手。

囂張的和被欺負的對象，好像——顛倒過來了。

這和他們想像的完全不一樣！

這個世界變化得會不會也太快了，讓人完全想像不到！

這情況，怎麼想都不可能發生啊！

偏偏，就這麼發生了。

還就在他們的面前。

白雪皚皚的大街。

冷冽的風，送著不斷飄落的細雪，一陣、一陣地吹。

上萬人聚湧的廣場，此時寂靜無聲。

喝出制止的聲音、同時急忙由遠處急奔而來的幾人一來到近處，就不由得在測試台前十丈內的安全範圍落地、收聲，沒急著往前靠近。

測試台上的武者、魂師們，一旁的岩華與林燁，和街道上圍觀的眾人沒有注意到這些，只覺得——他們需要冷靜地、冷靜地回想一下。

那把劍，什麼時候冒出來的？

又是怎麼被她擺到東明玉凌的咽喉前的？

她到底怎麼反制的？

他們明明一直看著，怎麼就漏掉這個最精采的畫面?!

啊！那陣風！

風吹雪什麼時候都有，為什麼就偏偏那個時候來！

所有人咬牙又扼腕，非常惋惜。

但是也有人，非常憤怒。

「這是妳第二次拿劍指著我了。」奇怪的是，身為當事人的東明玉凌竟然沒有第一時間就怒上眉峰，反而神情冷然地看著她。

負責保護東明玉凌的兩名護衛不發一語，卻悄悄接近兩人的位置，謹慎而戒備地想伺機救人。

沐沐的眼神掃過他們，讓兩人悄然的動作頓時停下，她這才悠悠然將注意力轉向東明玉凌。

「然後呢？」

搞清楚，是她先挑釁的，不然誰想拿劍跟她玩？

有這種空閒時間，她還不如陪焱和磊呢！

「妳敢傷我，我會讓妳生不如死！」東明玉凌冷笑。

生不如死？

沐沐的表情頓了一下，有點兒難以形容地看著她。

「妳這是什麼表情？」

「一言難盡的表情。」

旁觀眾人：「……」他們的心情才一言難盡。

不是要打起來嗎？

結果就這?!

聽起來像聊天。

但是，感覺又好像有濃濃火藥味。

最重要的是：那隻持劍的手臂，一點抖都沒有，依然穩穩地指著東明玉凌的咽喉。

只要前進一分，東明玉凌一定見血。

這就是即使兩名聖階護衛近在咫尺，卻不敢輕易出手救人，只能按兵不動的原因。

「什麼意思？」

「就是，我懷疑妳的腦袋可能有問題。」沐沐一臉嚴肅正經。

「妳……」東明玉凌一動，劍鋒的冷意，頓時襲得她又定在原地。

「我？」沐沐笑了。「我很好，但我勸妳不要隨便生氣。劍鋒無眼，我不動，如果妳偏偏受傷了，那是妳的問題，可不要賴我。」

不等東明玉凌開口，她又接著道：

「不過就算妳賴我，也不奇怪。像妳這種個性，大概就是不管發生什麼事，『全大陸的人都錯了，妳也不會錯；就算是妳錯，那也是別人的錯造成的，不關妳的事』。

「所以，跟妳講道理、論對錯，那是浪費時間，不如直接來說說，妳要怎麼讓我放過妳吧！」

現在，是東明玉凌的命在她手上，該著急的人不是她。

「妳想怎麼樣？」示意自家小姐先別開口，陽右問道。

「你們又想怎麼樣？」找麻煩的，可是他們。

沐沐覺得自己是無辜的路人甲，招人恨實在太沒道理。

不過有些人攻擊別人，本來就不講道理。尤其在這個講究實力、推崇強者、沒有太多人權法律約束的大陸，每天找別人麻煩、和被別人找麻煩的事多得不得了，她也不用太意外。

反正，她有本事打回去就行了。

「妳先放開小姐。」陽右說道。

沐沐瞄了他一眼。

「放開她，然後讓她再攻擊我？」她看起來很像笨蛋嗎？

「能讓我記住，是妳的榮幸。」東明玉凌高高在上的表情。

沐沐：「……」她覺得，她可能是笨蛋。

跟個嬌氣滿身、行事囂張、目中無人的城主家大小姐講什麼道理？是根本沒道理可講啊。

人家覺得自己出身高貴，身分一報出來，全人類都要跪服謙讓恭敬她，尊她的話為聖旨、神諭，只能照辦、不能違抗拖延。

簡稱：重度公主病患者。

想跟這種人講道理、論是非，是比緣木求魚還緣木求魚吧！

要她講良心、意識到自己有點錯，那大概……就像白天想見鬼一樣。

不，可，能。

作夢比較快！

那要怎麼辦呢？

「嗚嗚。」一直安靜待在她肩上的寶寶輕輕地嗯兩聲。

砍了她。

沐沐表情一頓。

這意思她懂了。

但——她有教寶寶暴力嗎？

應該沒有。

但是她在牠面前一直有和人打架——罪過罪過。

「放開小姐，一切到此為止。」陽左說道。

「不可能！」

沐沐還沒開口，東明玉凌先反對。

「小姐。」陽左皺眉。

「我就不信她敢殺我。」東明玉凌挑釁地看著她。「我不管妳是誰，敢讓雪長歌護著妳，妳就得死！」

果然沒道理可講。

沐沐挑眉，笑了。

「那妳還是先死吧。」

脖子都在她劍尖下了還威脅她，這是腦袋不清楚了吧！

「別傷小姐！」兩名聖階護衛異口同聲。

東明玉凌冷哼一聲。

「想殺我，作夢！」

她身上魂師印一閃，右手同時一揮。

「鏘」一聲。

長劍被揮開，東明玉凌立刻欺身向前反攻。

這是開外掛啊！利用魂器欺負人！

被攻擊的沐沐足尖一蹬、飛身避退的同時，劍勢連揮，劍尖擊在東明玉凌的雙手上，發出「鏘鏘鏘鏘」的聲響。

因為兩人的對招帶動陣陣氣流，銳利地旋向四周，讓觀戰的人群不得不隨著兩人的移動而移動。

眾人這才發現，東明玉凌的手臂上——

「是護具！」魂器！

「天魂師。」東明城的大小姐有這樣的修階，實在不用太意外——但是，有點嫉妒。

「三星魂器？」

「不對，至少四星。」根據雙方攻擊力道判斷的。

有人倒抽口氣。

「四星?!」四星魂器只作成護具?!不對，是她身上的護具就是四星魂器了?!

好貴！

買不到！

再想一下，她身上一定不只這一組護具……

財大氣粗！

「不愧是東明城的大小姐……」每天為修練資源忙忙碌碌的魂師們真是連嫉妒都嫉妒不起來。

東明城主的愛女，真是缺什麼都不缺錢、缺東缺西就是不缺魂器。

他們恨有錢人。

他們恨不缺魂器的人。

因為，他們兩者都很缺！

「難道你們不覺得，這個陌生的少女也很不一樣嗎？」

對喔！

面對東明玉凌一點都不害怕還敢直接拿劍戳的人，跟他們這些普普大眾怎麼會一樣？

而且，她手上的劍對上四星魂器，一點都不落下風。

這器階，至少也是四星吧！

隨便拿出武器就能對抗四星魂器的人，怎麼可能跟弱小、受欺負這種詞扯上關係？

他們先嫉妒一下那把劍——不是，是先嫉妒一下這個少女，怎麼隨便就有能對抗四星魂器的武器啊！

而且現在，她她她，她還能跟天魂師的東明大小姐打得不相上下?!

所以，這名少女的實力——至少天階。

眾人默了一下。

看到這裡，他們突然覺得，最應該被擔心的，是自己吧！

辛辛苦苦認真修練好幾年，有的人終於跨入天階、有的還在地階徘徊，而她們兩個，已經不知道天階幾級了。

個人實力，比他們強。

勤勤懇懇做任務好幾年，想買個三星魂器都得看運氣，人家早就已經把四星魂器拿上手了，而且身上不知道還有幾個？

反觀他們，有一個魂器就珍惜得不得了哇！

簡直同情自己。

「別同情自己了，快追呀！」就他們這聊天兼自我可憐的這一會兒，那兩個已經打到快不見人影啦。

為了看後續，一群人立刻向前追。

可惜沒多久，就又被前面的人潮堵住了，有人追、有人退，原本井然有序的街道，因為這場架，整個混亂起來。

「別擠！」

「你擋到我了！」

「是你擋到我！」

「那麼大聲幹嘛？想打架？」

「打就打，誰怕誰?!」

「哼！」呼呼、哈哈！推來推去。

「喂，別擠……」碰！

被打到了。

簡直無妄之災！

那，被打了就自認倒楣？

想得美！

當然是打回去！

於是，擠來擠去的人變成打來打去，一小群一小群混戰成一團，很快變成全體混戰。

只是這種混戰，始終保持在測試台前十丈外，沒有人敢越過線。

此時，測試台上的測試已經暫時停止，即使東雪城的人沒有介入，卻都在觀看這場戰鬥。

對戰中的兩人，已經晉升到空中。

即使雪下得愈來愈大，也止不住愈來愈混亂的街道，還有更多的人，因為在空中對戰的兩人而湧過來。

一來，就看見飄在半空中的兩人身影倏來倏去，「鏗鏗鏘鏘」的聲音不斷傳來。

一聲接一聲，一聲比一聲猛烈。

魂器交接迸出的火花與飄落的雪花混成一團，在空中形成一層白茫茫的霧色，讓人看不清楚。

唯一能確定的，是目前兩人打得不相上下，誰也沒占上風。

「果然都是天階！」看著她們打上天的遠處圍觀者，忍不住感嘆。只有天階，才能不靠任何外物騰空。

「你這是廢話。」一都拿四星魂器來用了，地階以下的魂力根本撐不住。而且，以今天的場合來說，天階高手還會少嗎？

看看測試台旁的公告吧！

「又兩個天階，那秘境還有我們的分嗎？」她們打成怎麼樣不重要，重要的是，他們這些小武師們還有機會進秘境撿運氣嗎？

天階那麼多，地階都只能回家藏了啊。他們這些勉強搆上地階的人……

「個人沒資格、組隊也不成，那我們就跟團。」

實力不足，人數來湊。

傭兵團，也是有名額的。

而匆匆趕來，卻停在測試台十丈內的幾人，沒有在一開始跟上去，此時隨著戰鬥的升級，也被重重人潮擋住。

若不是他們關心的人在半空中，讓他們能看得見她的情況，恐怕他們就真的要打過去了。

但是，現在這種情況，他們也不能放心。

雖然東明玉凌傷不了她，但是，那兩個聖階護衛，還在底下虎視眈眈，準備出手。

「都亂了，不如……我們飛過去。」一躍躍欲試的神情。

「這個……」你冷靜一點，不要看到有架打就想往前衝。

先以眼神制止好友，然後看向測試台。

測試台十丈範圍內禁空、禁戰。

敢在這裡亂飛，等同公然挑釁東雪城的權威，是想被趕出去，還是想被射下來？

「……」一時忘記這件事。

都怪空中戰打得太有感染力了，讓他拳頭很想動——那兩個護衛是很好的對手啊……可惜，要給地主面子，只能先忍著。

太難了。

見好友忍住，某人稍稍放心。

很好，總算勸住了。

其實看見這種情景，最該激動到想衝向前的人應該不是他們，而是剛才放狂風的那兩個才對呀。

但是不知道為什麼，那兩個現在看起來冷靜得不得了，半點衝向前的意思也沒有，莫非……他們平常表現出來的關心、一路趕來著急到差點連半夜都不休息的焦慮都是假的？

咳，這純粹是亂想。

恐怕他們現在已經在心裡把東明家的人大卸八塊千萬遍了。

同一時間，測試台上，負責今天報名事宜的幾名長老和相關人員們，也在環視全場。

有人皺眉，表示很不高興；也有人心寬一點，當成看熱鬧。

比較盡責的，就是防衛在四周的護衛兵們了，個個蓄勢待發，只等長老下令，他們就出手肅清全場。

「這種日子，在這裡搗亂，簡直沒把東雪城放在眼裡。」

「有東明玉淩，會出亂子，一點都不奇怪。」東明城大小姐的名聲，整個東州誰沒聽過？

偏偏以她的身分，目前東雪城還真不好對她做出什麼嚴厲處置。

少城主可以不給她面子，直接在城門外趕人。

他們嘛……最好還是留點兒餘地，免得在此時就讓兩城的關係直接惡化成敵人。

倒不是怕跟東明城翻臉，而是，時機不適宜。

想到這裡，他們也不禁有點兒哀怨。

他們家的少城主，他們引以為傲。少城主的為人處事品貌實力，完全沒有可挑剔的地方。

簡直就是少城主中的少城主，輾壓其他四城——對，他們就是這麼自信。

這絕對不是他們自誇，而是事實。

但就是少城主這脾氣有點太……「耿直」了點兒。

唉，為了想這個形容詞，簡直是要難死他們了。

他們一群修練至上的魂師武師們，哪裡會去研究怎麼說話才好聽？

但是，那是自家的少城主呀，不能有損少城主英明神武氣質高上偉岸光耀實力強大的形象，更不能把自家自豪的少城主給形容得掉價，最後，也不能太浮誇、太不切實際。

所以，這兩個字，已經是他們能想到的極致了。

少城主的脾氣，就是面對不想應付的人，沒什麼耐心；面對會胡攪蠻纏的人，沒當場打昏對方，算他心情好。

身為一城少主，這種作風沒什麼問題。

再囂張傲氣一點也是可以的。

高高在上、少有敗績、體體面面，也是身為少城主的標準配備呢。

也多虧了一直以來，少城主的實力都很強，向來只有他揍別人沒有被別人揍的分兒，不然……

他們日常操心的事，就得多一件了。汗。

想得太遠了，趕緊把注意力拉回現在的狀況。

起因雖然——好像是他家少城主，但是他家少城主現在人不在場，這兩個人，倒是很明顯有點違反東雪城的城規了。

「不管嗎？」

「當然管。」不管的話，東雪城的面子往哪兒擺？「不過，待會兒再管。」

「這樣好嗎？」

看那兩個在半空中對戰的人，已經從近身戰到稍微拉開距離的大招，對周遭事物的破壞力大大增加。

再多等一下，只怕這條街道上的屋宅要遭殃了。

「沒關係。有人就有爭鬥，亂個幾次，習慣就好。」只要是在可控範圍內，就當是他們守在這裡每天為人做測試的休息時間了。

「跟東明玉凌對戰的人，是誰？」其中一名觀戰的長老問道。

小姑娘的實力，很可以呀！

「不認識。」

「少城主應該認識。」

「對了，跟少城主一起回城的，除了林燁、岩華兩位少城主之外，還有一男一女，小姑娘是那個女的。」

「在城外，這兩個人已經發生過一次衝突了吧？」

「哦～～」說到這裡，眾人頓時異口同聲，發出一種「你懂我懂大家都懂，但是不能說出來」的聲音。

但還是有人不懂。

「怎麼了嗎？」發生什麼事了？

為什麼大家的表情都怪怪的？

「這個嘛，你會知道的。」才成為護衛隊長沒幾年，不知道是正常的；等這次秘境的事結束，他就什麼都知道了。

「上面的可以先不管，但下面要控制一下。」另一位長老說道，以眼神示意還一臉疑惑的隊長。

隊長秒懂。

「是。」他立刻飛下測試台，伸手一揮，一隊護衛隨即跟著他行動。

眼看測試台上的長老沒有插手的意思，剛才好不容易被勸住的人，看著愈打愈遠、而且愈打愈激烈的兩人，又蠢蠢欲動了。

就在他要行動之前，他的肩膀被按住了。

就在被按住的同時，他一轉身，立刻脫離對方的掌握，一臉戒肅的表情在看清來人時，一愣。

然後，立刻眼神一瞪。

「你……」

「別衝動。」來人低聲說道。

在爭執一開始的時候，他被示意別出手，然後就發現這四個人了。趁著人群混亂潛過來，果然是有必要的。

「嗯？」為什麼要聽你的？

話說看到這個人，他戰意都升起來了。

來人有點無奈。

「她不想剛來東雪城就鬧得人盡皆知。」但是有現在這一齣，她想低調大概是不太可能了。

而且，這四個人一來，她的偽裝也搖搖欲墜……

但願等會兒她不要太鬱悶。

「東明玉凌為什麼找她麻煩？」一直沒開口、神情很冷的兩兄弟，其中一個開口問了。

「大概是……亂吃醋吧。」

亂、吃、醋?!

兩兄弟眉眼一冷。

在他們不知道的時候，到底誰敢想誘拐他們年幼單純、涉世未深的妹妹?!

等等，東明玉凌，吃醋？

東州的「名人名事」，他們剛好記得……

好、呀！

罪魁禍首，他們知、道、了！

就在兩兄弟一邊關心空中的戰況、一邊暗暗盤算該怎麼算這筆帳的時候，北方突然瞬移來一道身影，橫身介入空中的對戰。

立身雙方中央，雙手分兩邊，一撥、一擋。

「鏘！」

「砰！」

空中兩聲響，擋下雙方的攻擊，來人魂力一震，將兩人各自逼退。

然後，他朝下方喝了一句：

「住手。」

威嚴的一聲喝，不需要提高聲量，聲波便足以震懾眾人。

下方同樣混戰的群眾，漸漸拉開彼此的距離，順勢被不久前介入爭戰的護衛們以極快的速度分開、停戰。

暫時從戰鬥狀態中脫離，他們抬頭一看——

只見來人頎長的身形，身著藏青色並繡以神秘圖紋的衣袍，他昂身而立，明明有著一張俊雅斯文、極有親和力的容顏，卻常年是不苟言笑、令人不由生畏的神情……

頓時，看熱鬧的澎湃心情像被正在下的雪花急凍、激動到發昏的腦袋像被雷打到，瞬間回神！

在東州混、來過東雪城的人，幾乎沒有不認識他的。

東雪城中，主管護衛隊的長老——衡無非。

個性公正嚴謹，有實力並且有權力在不經城主同意的情況下，驅逐任何在東雪城內鬧事的人。

這位長老不常出現，但一出現，必然代表東雪城的絕對秩序！

眾人的表情瞬間木然了。

表面上散發出我很正直我很守規沒有無故生事的鎮定，內裡哀哀叫地對自己發出靈魂的拷問：

他們在哪？

他們在幹什麼？

他們怎麼能在東、雪、城、裡、打、群、架?!

腦袋是被白花花的雪花給下昏了嗎?!

來人一到，不只把在場眾人嚇回神，同時也讓護衛們的行動個個有效率起來，很快控制住局勢。

緊接著，待在測試台上的人們，也有點心虛，但是很盡力保持抬頭挺胸，表達出自己不心虛的模樣。

一連串的變故，也讓站在禁戰區看戲的「觀眾們」差點傻眼。

從混亂到安靜，只需要眨眨眼、再眨眨眼的時間。

這麼混亂起來的狀況就這樣停了？

哦～來人如果是這位，那，就一點都不奇怪了。

現場突然安靜下來，只有雪花依然不停地往下飄落。

沐沐不急著再打，只是隱約朝北方空中看了一眼，然後就把注意力，轉向眼前的這個人。

大家，好像都很怕他啊！

他很可怕嗎？

剛才卸招的力道，控制得實在太剛好。

不但完全卸掉她們兩人的攻擊，同時也分開她和東明玉凌。

震開她們的力道，完全是一樣的。

能把實力控制到這種程度的人，沐沐是第一次遇到。

看著另一頭，同樣沒有意圖再出手的東明玉凌，沐沐更好奇了。

這是連東明玉凌都會「尊重」的人喔……

這件事不但是沐沐發現了，底下一堆人也發現了，紛紛驚奇。

原來天不怕地不怕，只有她找人麻煩、沒人敢找她麻煩的東明城大小姐，也有怕的人啊……眾人不禁對空中的人投去崇敬的眼神。

不愧是傳說中除了城主之外，東雪城中最強的男人，鎮場效果一流。

無非長老威武！

被崇敬眼神包圍的無非長老，面不改色地站在空中，先掃了下方的人一眼。

「再鬧，驅逐出城。」

不必刻意威嚴或者提高語調，剛才趁亂打成一團又一團的眾人，立刻自覺肅顏肅行。

空中的人——管她們打成怎樣，比起看熱鬧，進秘境的資格當然是更重要的。熱鬧不看了。

立即的，測試過的人自覺站到街道邊，讓出道路不越界。

還沒測試的人，則趕緊再回去排隊——而且是排得整整齊齊，連間隔距離都很一致，以行動充分表達出三個重點：

我們沒有鬧。

我們沒有違反規定。

剛才那樣純粹是不得已的被拖累的絕對不是我們自願的我們絕對沒有在東雪城

搞事的膽子我們很守規矩噠。

底下的人老實了，無非長老再往測試台看了一眼。測試台看戲的、沒看戲的，趁機休息的、趁機做什麼奇怪事的長老及東雪城護衛們，紛紛各回各位，繼續手頭上的事。

「下一個。」剛才看得最起勁、甚至都拖延護衛隊，延緩他們阻止混亂的長老，正好是負責叫號的，回到原座後，他立刻以嚴肅的表情、沒有情緒的語氣叫來下一位做登記。

旁邊的人紛紛低頭，掩飾一言難盡的表情。

剛才看戲看得最歡快的是你，現在最嚴肅、嚴正工作的也是你，這變臉也變得太快了吧！

負責點名叫號的長老回給他們一個很有深意的眼神。

你們難道就「變臉」變得不快？

看看你們自己正襟危坐的表情、雙手放在桌上一副一直在工作並沒有站起來偷懶的態度。

大家半斤八兩就不必互相漏氣了。

他們：「……」

只能說，無非長老的眼神，不只對外人很有威懾力，對自家人的威懾力也一樣足足的。

這證明，即使同樣都叫「長老」，差別也是很大的。

無非長老再往測試台前的「禁戰區」看一眼，確定沒人敢再趁亂鬧事了，最後，才把注意力放到空中的兩個人身上。

負手在後，他先看向沐沐。

沐沐眨了下眼，也睜著眼睛回看他，一點都沒有被他充滿威懾力的眼神給嚇到，也完全沒有氣弱或避開視線。

倒是不經意望向測試台方向時，她稍稍心虛了下，迅速將注意力轉回到眼前的場面。

無非長老看著她的眼神幾不可辨地閃了下，然後再偏轉過頭，看向東明玉凌。

東明玉凌沒有與他對視，在他看過來的時候，眼簾微低了低。

「東明玉凌，見過無非長老。」

這位，是連她父親也不願意輕易招惹的對象，加上小時候曾經「不愉快」的相處經驗，讓東明玉凌的囂張作風，明顯收斂。

沐沐看得有點驚奇。

沒想到那麼張揚的東明城大小姐，也有表現出這麼謙遜有禮的時候耶。

「妳對東雪城可有不滿？」

「……沒有。」

「那為何在這裡擾亂測試？」

「……」見到討厭的人一時沒忍住，忘了這位的存在。不過，東明玉凌是絕對不會認錯的。

在無非長老再次詢問的時候，兩道身影同時一飛身，來到自家小姐身邊。

「小姐見到仇人一時氣憤，並沒有擾亂測試的意思，請無非長老見諒。」陽右態度很客氣。

「東雪城的規矩，你們知道。」沒有什麼見不見諒，對無非長老來說就是：一切照規矩辦事。

「這次是我們忽略了，並沒有挑釁東雪城城規的意思，這一次，小姐是特地為東雪城慶典而來，在這期間，我方會尊重東雪城城規，不會再輕犯，請無非長老網開一面。」陽右軟下語氣說道。

東州五城，明面上分地而立，五城平等。

但實際上，城與城之間的實力也是有差距的。

東雪城，恰恰就是東明城人唯一不敢任意放肆的地方。

無非長老看著他們好一會兒，才道：

「秘境開啟時，東明城人最後才能進入。」

兩名聖階長老一震，連東明玉凌都驚訝地抬起頭，開口就想反駁……

「或者，你們想現在就離開？」無非長老淡淡再加一句。

三人頓時閉上嘴。

但是東明玉凌依然憤憤不平。

「那她呢？」打架，一個人可打不成。

這個沐沐拿劍想殺她，難道還能沒有任何處罰嗎？

「她排在妳前面。」

也就是說，目前入境順序，東明城倒數第一，而沐沐，就是倒數第二。

算起來，兩人受的懲罰是一樣的。

但是東明玉淩不滿意：

「為什麼她能比我先入秘境？」

「因為主動挑事的人，是妳。」這是無非長老解釋的最後一句了，再囉嗦他就要直接趕人了。「現在，你們各自回去。在秘境開始之前，若再有任何擾亂城中秩序者，輕則驅逐出城，重則依規究辦！」

最後一句，不只是對她們，也是對所有人。

敢犯東雪城城規者，絕不輕饒！

在測試台前排隊以及周遭所有聽見的人：「……」

秘境裡的時間和外面不一樣，外面慢了一點，秘境得過去多少時間?!

損失時間，等於損失尋寶找機緣以及修練的時間——肉痛！

秘境開啟前，還、還是乖一點吧！

沐沐：「……」

呃，要不要表明一下，她連入境資格，都還沒拿到呢！

◈

東雪城城主府後山，看著水晶映象裡對戰的兩人，身著一件雪白絨毛披風，有著一頭白色長髮、容顏卻有些模糊的男子神態淡然，眼神注視其中一名被帽兜擋住容貌的少女。

當看到測試場恢復秩序，雙方也各自離開後，男子手一收。

浮在空中的巨大映象也隨之消失，化為一顆小珠子，落回男子的手裡。

「她就是你帶回來的人？」男子問道。

除去面貌，兩人氣質相似、身形相似，身上的穿著也很相似。

差別只在於：前者似乎比後者稍高一些。

而穿著上，前者是一身白，後者則是有著一頭黑髮，一身白裘毛絨中，綴以銀灰色的邊帶。

「是我請回來的貴客。」他糾正道。

「她讓魔獸，和武師定下契約了？」男子想到，那個披著暗色披風的小女娃，在帽兜掉落後，露出的紅色髮飾。

紅色……狐狸……啊……

不，應該不是因為這個。

但是，她竟然這個……呵，該不會真是「他」吧……

「是。」

這絕對是天魂大陸上聞所未聞的大事件，他有請海宇越暫時保密，但這件事，遲早會被傳出去的。

男子點了點頭。

表面平靜，但眼裡卻有一道光彩閃過。

她，如果真是……

不急。

再等等。

「父親，最近幾年，東明城的人似乎愈來愈囂張了。」他的語氣裡沒有氣憤，反倒像在思考。

「敢囂張，有兩種可能。」

「一種是沒腦子，一種是——有底氣。」他說著小時候，父親對他說過的話。

雖然他看東明玉淩的行為，很想說她沒腦子。

但是東明城主卻不是一個簡單的人。

他敢放任自己的女兒這樣行事，絕對不是單純縱容女兒，而且，東明玉淩真的沒腦子嗎？

她的囂張，一直在她自身安全無虞的前提下——只看那兩個聖階護衛，總是寸步不離地跟著她，就可以判斷了。

男子沒回答，他就自己又接著說：

「難道，就因為東海城？」

「那就很夠了。」男子淡聲說道。

東海城若有危，也將是東州之危，甚至是整個天魂大陸之危。

要維護人族的安全，需要武力、需要大量的魂器。

在中州和西州，有著諸多煉器師；大多數的煉器師，都依附煉器師公會，使得公會的公信力，足以凌駕各個家族。

但在東州，煉器師公會的公信力，不如一個東明城。

東明城，就是東州人眼中的煉器師聖地。

這其中雖然有煉器師公會在東州的分會不多的原因，但是東明城本身煉製售出的魂器品質與數量都高於公會，也是重要因素。

另外，東明城城主本身就是一名極高明、極受擁護的煉器師，也是一個重要原因。

「父親，我們不管嗎？」

「暫時不必理會。」男子說道。「慶典期間，要保證一切如常，讓秘境順利開啟。」

至於關閉……男子突然有種預感，或許這一次之後，東雪城，將不再有寒玉秘境了。

「是，父親。」他知道秘境的重要性。

「另外，」想到兒子常常被糾纏，男子罕見地發揮父愛的關心，多說了一句：「東明城的人如果找你麻煩，你想怎麼做都可以，留點裡子給東明縉瀾就行了。」

其他人也許將東明縉瀾看得很重，但在男子眼裡，東明城城主跟其他人也沒什麼不同。

不在意東明城的那些作風，只是懶得理會，以及時機未到而已。

但是，敢在東雪城囂張，顯然也是不把他看在眼裡。

那麼，東明城的面子就不必留了。

這句話的意思，當兒子的一聽就懂。

裡子，也就是留條命就行。

父親這是……對東明城也很看不順眼了吧！

# 第十三章　終於見面

無非長老的出現，讓因為測試而人群混亂的北城區，再度恢復秩序，沒有人敢再胡鬧，連亂跑都不敢，走路都規規矩矩。

能用走的，絕對不會跑，看起來守秩序得不得了。就算無非長老已經離開了，也沒有人再敢製造混亂。

由此可見無非長老的震懾力，真的是威武。

就在大家排隊裝乖的時候，東明玉凌一行人、沐沐，也悄然離開測試台範圍。之後隨著離開的，還有好幾個人。

沒有熱鬧可看，離開了多少人也沒人太注意，這裡，本來就有許多人會來來去去，根本不必太在意。

但還是有人注意到了。

「好像有人不見了。」剛剛在測試台前，不准動武的範圍裡，明明有好幾個看起來很厲害的人。

「對呀！剛才有人喊『住手、誰敢傷她』的！」他還特別看了那個人一眼。一看，實力很強。

再看，跟他站在一起的人，也很有高手的氣息。

結果，從頭到尾到現在散場了，也沒看見他們出手呀！

而且，這幾個人都是生面孔，雖然好像有點眼熟，但是確實不認識。

應該是從其他州來的人。

「難道是怕了？」

「會嗎？」怕事的人，會喊那麼大聲？

「不管他們，那些人不在更好。」熱鬧是閒閒沒事的時候才看的，現在他們的重點，是在測試、在結果啊！

能不能進秘境，才是他們的頭號大事。

但是，有沒有資格進秘境，顯然不是剛才還在場中某些人的大事。

如：東明城大小姐，東岩城、東林城的少主……

東雪城給了其他四城一定數量的名額，他們就算不來測試，一樣可以進秘境……

羨慕啊。

有後台的人，就是幸福。

不過進了秘境後，還是拚實力。

但說到實力……就讓他們又悲傷了！

為什麼這一次會出現這麼多奇奇怪怪的天階，甚至聖階高手，把入境的名額都快霸光了啊！

難道今年，他們這些普普天階、地階的人，只能看著秘境流口水了嗎？

◈

趁機溜走。

沐沐回到自己居住的客棧小院房間，關閉小院，門窗關緊緊，一個人抱著寶寶在房間裡來來回回，走來走去。

哥哥們竟然來了！

而且看樣子好像比她還早到。

她被逮到了！

想起自己「不告而別」……

當時她是覺得，自己做的決定是很有道理的。

堂堂正正。

理直氣壯。

現在嘛……

兩個字：心虛。

三個字：很心虛。

四個字：非常心虛。

心、心虛什麼她也不知道……

明明她也沒做錯什麼事……幹嘛跑呀？

雖然、雖然剛才那種時候，的確是速速離開為上策。

但是這一跑，好像她真的做錯什麼不得了的大事了呀！

跑了就是輸了呀……

「嗚嗚嗚嗚～」她呻吟一聲，就著椅子坐了下來、趴在桌上，順手把寶寶也放在桌上。

「嗚？」寶寶不啃靈晶了，闔閉的眼睛代表不了任何情緒，但是牠端著好奇又不解的表情，對著她。

媽媽發出的聲音跟牠一樣耶。

媽媽也會說牠的話嗎？

但是牠怎麼聽不懂？

沐沐也看著牠。

「寶寶，我好像做錯事了要怎麼辦？」

「嗚！」玖，不會錯！

寶寶對她可真有信心。

感覺到她好像很……怕？沮喪？沒精神？呃……好多情緒好像很複雜，寶寶不是很懂。

不過玖不開心，這個牠懂。

「嗚。」玖不要怕。

想了想，又叫一聲：

「嗚！」寶寶保護妳。

「嗚嗚嗚。」把讓媽媽不開心的人踢飛，這樣就會開心了。玖不要怕，寶寶踢。

沐沐看著牠，伸出短短的小後腿，做了個踢的動作。

「……」噗。

很想笑怎麼辦？

不行，要忍住，寶寶會難過。

沐沐抱回寶寶，揉揉牠的毛。

「寶寶，放心，沒事的。」真有人想欺負她的話……她的字典裡怎麼會有「被欺負」這三個字？

「嗚？」牠歪著頭。

牠有感覺玖的心情變好了。

為什麼呀？

「你繼續吃吧。」她安撫寶寶。

寶寶感覺到她的心情變很好，比剛才打架時還好，寶寶放心了，低頭繼續啃靈石。

沐沐低笑了一聲。

要是哪天她得靠寶寶保護她，那得是多慘的時候啊？現在牠還是好好啃靈石、好好長大吧……

「嗯?!」有人來了！不止一個！

屋外，有好幾道身影從空中落了下來。

「呃……」沐沐又趴了回去，很乾脆的決定：放棄治療。

出來混的，都是要還的。

再讓她賴一下，一分鐘後她就面對現實。

「嗚嗚？」玖的心情又不好了耶。

為什麼呀？

寶寶「嗑嗑嗑」地啃著靈石，這情緒變化得實在太快了，牠，不懂。

客棧所屬，小院客房區的上空，通行令一閃，五道人影從空中落了下來，小院再度關上。

至於其他好奇的目光、想看熱鬧的、想探查消息的人……在客棧所屬範圍外，就被警戒的守衛全數擋下。

這裡是直屬城主府的特殊客棧，無關人等不得擅闖。

執意擅闖者……後果自負。

至於那五人也不全是客棧的住宿客人，為什麼能暢通無阻？

啊，因為他們有「內人」帶路啊。

身帶直接開啟小院的信物，可以直通客院，守衛們確認是住客無誤，自然根本就不攔人。

「就在裡面嗎？」很雀躍的語氣。

「應該是。」

「那我……」往裡面衝。

「石昊，等等。」拉住興奮的某人。

「為什麼呀？」他都等到現在了，還被拉住。

石昊很不滿地瞪姬雲飛。

就算是竹馬好朋友，一直擋他，他也是要瞪的。

「人家在休息，我們也先休息。」不由分說，拉走某人。

「啊？為什麼呀……」他等很久了，還要等啊？他並不想休息……

等很久算什麼？

請看一看左邊那兩位的表情。

那是悶著氣很久了啊！

為了避免成為無辜躺災的路人甲，他們兩個還是再等等吧，先到外面。

給久別重聚的兄妹讓出一點痛哭流涕的時間啊！

嗯，今天又是日行一善的一天，姬雲飛覺得自己真是個好人。

現場剩三個人。

「她就在裡面。」看著端木風與端木傲，流星主動開口道。

兩個神情有些相似的兄弟，齊齊轉頭看向他。

這傢伙，一路跟著妹妹。

這傢伙……妹妹沒見他們卻帶著這傢伙……離家出走?!

「……」感覺危機在逼近。

「我先回房，不打擾你們和沐沐，你們……慢聊。」速速離開現場，奔出小院，轉往隔壁小院的客房。

開門、進門、關門、上鎖。小院也關閉。

動作迅速確實、一氣呵成。

流星也是很有危機意識……不是，是日行一善的好人。

在奔向自己居住的小院時，先退出來的兩人眼明腳快，不由分說地也跟著蹭進了他的小院。

他們沒有住這裡，一時之間也不好再去訂房，更不想回去原來住的地方，所以，請發揮「老朋友的同鄉情」，收留一下。

好歹他們三人現在是「同病相憐」，流星也只好收留這兩個人了。

石昊雖然還有點不想放棄，但是基於人家是「兄妹重聚」……他還是憮憮地被姬雲飛拉進去了，看起來好委屈。

忍、等，太難了。

但是，做人要有同理心。

不打擾人家兄妹重聚。

另一個重點是：不識相一點可能會先面臨兄弟檔混合雙打。

這三人先後跑了，兄弟倆瞪人的視線一頓，默默轉向關閉的房門。

兩人同時跨步，來到門前。

從門外，聽不見門內傳出任何聲響。

妹妹……就在裡面。

神情冷肅的端木傲，抬手就要敲門時，卻被身旁的端木風拉住。

端木傲望向他，眼帶詢問。

端木風只搖了下頭，就轉向關閉的門，開口：

「小玖，妳不打算見我們嗎？」

房間內，還趴在桌上的沐沐一驚，幾乎整個人跳起來。

寶寶啃靈晶的動作一頓。

感覺到玖跳了一下。

牠也……跳一下。

呆呆的模仿動作，瞬間惹笑了沐沐。

深吸口氣，沒再多想，她抬手一揮。

闔閉的房門頓時自動打開。

兩名身高相仿、形貌有些相似，氣質卻完全不同的男子，頓時出現在她眼前。

緊張、擔憂、忐忑、又特別心虛的心情頓時統統退到後面，只剩下欣喜的神情，露了出來。

「四哥、六哥。」笑靨如花。

小玖，就在幾步遠的眼前。

不是方才的遠遠望著、看著她和別人戰鬥、她沒有發現他們的單方面注視。

不是她戴著小小的偽裝，用斗篷遮掩自己的模樣。

是她一身輕裝無偽，俏然嫣然。

而他們，都平安的、真切的，就在彼此眼前，看著對方。

兩人一路以來累積在心裡的擔心與掛念，到此刻才終於真的放下。

從她眼裡透出來的，真真切切的欣喜，讓兩人心中一暖。

「小玖。」

「小玖。」

兩人同時出聲、張開手，同時向前一步，然後發現彼此同樣的動作，向前的步伐一頓。

誰先？

在兩人以眼神決鬥、用來決定誰先的舉動之前，沐沐先向前，一手拉一個，一起坐到桌旁。

端木風、端木傲：「……」

一起進門，他們完全不用決鬥了。

兩人又看向她。

她立刻把寶寶抱下來放到腿上。

然後從儲物戒裡掏出平時從三色綠木上收集後製成的飲品，以及各種點心，放在哥哥們面前。

「哥哥，先吃吃喝喝。」呃……這樣說對嗎？

不管，吃東西最大。

兄弟倆無語地看著她。

這一桌吃吃喝喝當真讓人看起來就很有食欲，他們差點就真的動手了……等等！

吃吃喝喝可以等一下，沒抱到妹妹，他們之前腦子裡在想的東西回來了，首先——要訓她一頓。

怎麼可以什麼都不說丟下哥哥就跑……

就在兩人打算開口的時候，寶寶啃靈晶的動作一頓。

嗯？

嗅嗅。

沒有聞過的味道耶。

寶寶一個念頭間就把靈晶收了起來，前腳趴近媽媽面前的桌子，頭一湊近，就是再嗅嗅。

這舉動太搶眼了，兩人的眼神，又轉向這隻……閉著眼的小狗？

盲眼？

是天生缺陷，還是發育不良？

「這是……」

魔獸？

但好像沒有感覺到牠身上有任何力量的波動。呃……不對，有，一點點力量波動，若有似無的。

有這麼弱的魔獸？

要真是魔獸……

等等，妹妹身邊不是有隻紅色狐狸嗎？牠呢？

「牠叫寶寶，是我不久前契約的魔獸。」

還真是。

兩人的表情頓時有點糾結了。

這隻魔獸，會不會太弱了？

她在對敵時，這隻魔獸完全是拖後腿的吧？

「寶寶，這個是我四哥、這是六哥，打招呼。」雖然牠看不見，沐沐完全不介意，一樣介紹。

寶寶一聽，立刻往兩人所在的位置嗅了一下，然後：

「嗚嗚。」

「……」聽不懂。

但兩人無奈的神情同時一頓。

「咦？」

兩人神識裡，同時冒出一句驚疑。

這讓兩人的神情一頓，後又露出一喜。

沐沐好奇地看著兩個哥哥。

「小玖……」

又一次同時開口。

這次沒有費事再想什麼對決，兩人身上同時光芒一閃。

一條金色的龍，以著三分之一人身的長度，像圍巾一樣，掛在端木風的肩膀上。

另一邊，一隻大約有三個巴掌大的青色玄龜，出現在端木傲的手上，然後一跳……就跳到他右邊的肩膀上。

嗯，這個高度很可以。

兩隻動物、四顆大大的眼睛，就注視著對面的兩腳動物——人族。

對面那個，表情一點也沒有害怕的樣子，同樣睜著大大的眼睛——雖然數量上輸了，不過眼睛的大小和好奇度一點也不輸。

雙方就這樣互相對看。

金龍龍鱗金燦燦。

玄龜龜殼青亮亮。

寶寶好像感覺到什麼，就算眼睛沒睜開，同樣坐得直挺挺，頭左轉一下、右轉一下，輪流「看」著這兩隻盯著牠媽媽看的獸獸。

雖然個子比人家小很多……

一隻，是身體長到可以捲牠兩三圈。

一隻，是身體寬得可以把牠壓扁扁。

但是牠，沒在慫的。

沒有眼睛，也依然跟牠們看來看去。

被金龍盤掛著的端木風，表情雖然不變，但內心簡直要被這三隻笑死。

「小玖。」他喚道。

「有！」她肅然直挺挺。

「這是我的魔獸伙伴，金嘯。妳叫牠『金』就可以。」他對小玖說道。

「這是我的魔獸伙伴，青玄。妳叫牠『青』就可以。」端木傲也說道。

「之前因為牠們在修練，一直在睡覺，所以遲遲沒介紹給妳。這是我們的妹妹，小玖。」端木風為雙方介紹完畢。

他也沒想到會這麼巧，金和青，會在同一個時間「睡醒」，剛好可以讓小玖見見牠們。

金嘯這才收回眼神，轉而看向自己的契約者。

「端木風，妳妹妹……還不錯。」金嘯自認為牠的眼光是很高的，這個人族……實力是還不錯。

以同齡兩腳人族來說，差不多笑傲同年齡層了。

不過稍微稱讚了一下妹妹之後，要特別嫌棄一下：

「就是這隻，太弱了。」指寶寶。

這話一出，旁邊的青色玄龜也點點頭。

「她，很好。牠，弱！」青玄簡短地對自家契約者，端木傲說道。

但是牠的評價和旁邊的那條一樣，牠有點嫌棄。

牠一點都不想跟某龍「神同步」。

嫌棄？

牠金龍大人都還沒嫌棄這隻渾身只剩下「殼」的龜，這隻只剩殼的龜竟然敢先嫌棄牠?!

金色的銳利大眼和青色的幽幽雙眼，互相瞪視起來。

一邊瞪視，還一邊互相嫌棄。

敢嫌棄我?!

不能接受被嫌棄的對方嫌棄的兩獸，開始用傳音互相叫囂。

你那什麼眼神，本龍眼神比你好、比你能幹！

你才什麼眼神，本龜眼睛比你精明、比你厲害！

呿，本龍能上天！

呿，本龜能下海！

本龍攪風攪雨不在話下！

本龜翻雲覆雨輕輕鬆鬆！

本龍一鞭足以把你甩成天邊一顆星！

本龜一鎮你再會飛也休想逃！

本龍的字典裡沒有「逃」這個字！

本龜的詞典裡沒有「被甩」這兩個字！

本龍＆％＄＃＠︿……

本龜＄％︿＃＠︿……

最後。

本龍懶得跟你這隻萬年睡龜計較。哼！

是本龜不與你這條萬年笨龍計較。哼！

兩個契約主：「……」

滿腦子的槽點不知道該從哪裡吐起。

這兩隻互相叫囂得太起勁了，沒發現沐沐開始用有趣的眼神看著牠們，就連寶寶，也用像「打開新大門」的表情認真聽。

最後，寶寶用一句話總結：

「牠們，吵。」

嗯?!

一個「吵」字，把轉頭哼向一邊的兩獸給吸引過來了。

這麼個弱獸竟然說牠們吵?!

不對！

「你能聽到我的傳音?!」金龍和玄龜同時說道，然後神情一頓，又互相不滿地瞪了對方一眼。

我為什麼要跟這條龍（這隻龜）說同樣的話？

哼！

「吵。」寶寶點點頭，再說一次牠的評價。

金龍和玄龜的神情頓時扭曲了。

被隻比自己弱……不對，是被一隻跟自己根本沒得比的魔獸嫌吵，真是孰可忍孰不可……

「不是吵，牠們是在交流感情。」沐沐一本正經地糾正自家寶寶。

交流……感情？

交流什麼感情？

本龍（本龜）跟這隻才沒有感情！

一龍一龜同時大聲傳音。

「嗚？」是這樣嗎？

「是！」這語氣，鏗鏘有力！

寶寶一臉思考。

「要把自己的意思表達完整，對方才會懂呀。牠們平時一定很少說話，所以一見面，就要多說一點。」多溝通有助於增進感情。

「嗚，嗚。」原來是這樣，寶寶懂了。

不好奇了，拿出靈晶，繼續啃。

一龍、一龜，雙雙瞪著牠。

心情和幾分鐘之前的契約者同步了──滿心的槽點不知道該從哪裡吐起。

本龍（本龜）才不吵，也不想多講話，更不是和這長條（這殼）在交流感情，我們是在互相嫌棄！

但是，兩兄弟卻關注到一點。

「小玖，妳聽見牠們在說話？」端木風問。

「聽得見呀。」她抱回趴在桌邊的寶寶，摸摸牠的頭。

寶寶就賴在她懷裡了，表情很舒服、很溫順。

「寶寶也聽得見？」

「對。」寶寶自己回答，發音不是很標準。

聽到契約主問到這個問題，立刻暫停互相嫌棄、把注意力轉回來的一龍一龜，同樣注意聽。

光顧著互相嫌棄差點忘了問這件事。

「牠能聽見你們傳音？」端木傲看著這隻……犬？

如果能聽見別人的傳音，那……就算牠很弱，也不算一無可取啊。

等等，牠剛才是說話了，不是嗚嗚啊。

「嗚嗚？」寶寶一臉懵，完全不知道現在重點在哪裡。

金龍伸長頭，靠近寶寶細看。

「嗚嗚嗚嗚！」驚慌失措。

陌生又強大的氣息接近，寶寶愜意的神情立刻變成慌張，一翻身，猛往沐沐懷裡鑽。

兩個男人加兩隻自認強大的魔獸，四顆腦門上瞬間各自滑下三條線，面無表情。

才剛覺得這隻魔獸可能沒那麼廢，還是有點特長的，但是下一秒牠就用事實告訴你，牠就是那麼廢，有特長也補不過來。

金龍忍了忍，還是沒忍住。

「妹妹，妳要不要考慮換一隻魔獸？」

突然多了一個「哥哥」，小玖無語了下。

就連哥哥們也看著她。

寶寶，就更是緊緊趴在她腿上，小小的腳掌還抓著她的衣服。

她拍拍牠，然後看向金龍：

「不用了。」雖然理解他們的想法，不過她是不會做出「半途棄養」這種事的。

「為什麼？」

魔獸崇尚強者。

人族也以強者為尊。

太弱的人或獸在別人眼裡，沒有價值。

牠雖然不會做欺負弱小這種事——除非那個弱小自己找揍，但是也絕對不會給自己找個弱小的東西帶在身邊。

像妹妹這樣不但契約了一隻弱小、發育不良、有殘缺的魔獸，還對牠那麼照顧的理由，金龍覺得自己想破頭都想不出來。

「我遇到寶寶的時候，牠還是一顆蛋，被人追著跑，我答應牠，如果牠能靠自己破蛋出來，我就會一直養著牠，不讓別人欺負牠。」她一邊安撫寶寶，看著牠把剛才沒啃完的靈晶再拿出來啃，一邊對他們說道。

主要是解釋給哥哥們聽的。

她看得出來，弱弱的寶寶讓哥哥們有點擔心。

魔獸，關乎一名魂師的戰力。

他們就擔心有危險時，寶寶幫不上忙，還會變成小玖的拖累。

但是對她而言，並沒有所謂拖不拖累。

她對寶寶有承諾，而寶寶也很爭氣。

雖然當時很狼狽，還弱得人人皆知，但牠還是靠自己破蛋出世了。

牠做到了，那她就會把寶寶當同伴，不會因為任何理由放棄或嫌棄牠。

金龍一聽完，就沒話說了。

相反的，牠還覺得有點高興。

雖然不同類別，但是寶寶也是魔獸。

魔獸和人族之間，可以是仇人、敵人，也可以是最親密的伙伴。

能看到有人這麼重視承諾，不嫌棄弱小的魔獸，也不嫌牠累贅地照顧牠，金龍還是有點高興的。

所以金龍大人毫不吝嗇地給了小玖一句讚美：

「妹妹，妳不錯。」

「妹妹，妳不錯。」青色玄龜也說道。

「你學我?!」金龍大人瞪。

「是你搶了我的話。」青色玄龜悠悠然回道。

「哼，跟屁蟲。」金龍大人懶得理什麼都慢吞吞的一坨殼。

「又不是趕投胎搶那麼快做什麼？」青色玄龜又悠悠然地回道。

「你詛咒我?!」金龍大人想拍桌。

什麼投胎？本龍活得好好的，投什麼胎?!這塊殼會不會說話?!

「……我只是比喻。再說，我也沒說是你呀。」金龍這就是……人族常說的：自動對號入座呀。

「你少給本龍轉移話題，敢說不敢承認嗎？」是魔獸就坦白一點，別說那種一肚子彎彎曲曲的兩腳人族拐彎抹角。

是獸，就要乾脆一點！

玄龜大人一時被噎住。

牠認為自己是很有智慧的回答。

但是在這個不懂得欣賞「智慧」的金龍面前，就變成陰謀詭計了。

玄龜大人微妙地覺得自己懂了「對牛彈琴」這四個字的涵義。

「哼！」成功讓龜沒話說，金龍大人很滿意，注意力又轉回到妹妹和這隻弱幼獸身上。

雖說欣賞妹妹「不棄養」的品性，但是這幼獸，真的太弱了呀！

金龍大人看著啃靈晶的寶寶，嘆一口氣。

不過，有靈晶啃、有人抱、還順毛，這幼獸的「犬生」是不是太幸福了點兒？

熟知自家契約獸性情的端木風與端木傲兄弟，卻很高興。

這兩隻，在魔獸中血統純正。

愈高等的魔獸，愈難有人可以入牠們的眼、讓牠們稱讚，就算與人族契約、或是被契約，也有可能發生無視契約主的狀況。

根據過去經驗，這兩隻對於看不入眼的人與獸，不但無視，甚至連看都不會看一眼，更加不會開口說話。

但是對小玖，這兩隻讚美之外，而且在她面前不但開口說話，還吵起來。

這代表牠們認可小玖了，否則是不會在她面前這麼放鬆的。

忽然，金龍飄了起來，繞著小玖飛了一圈。

嗅嗅。

「金，你在做什麼？」端木風有種把金龍扯回來的衝動。

就算欣賞，也不可以隨便靠妹妹這麼近！

妹妹是女的，金龍是雄性生物！

金龍瞄了自家契約主一眼，不太想理會這個「護妹狂」哥哥，反而轉向青色玄龜。

「你有感覺到嗎？」

青玄本來是很想直接回一句：「你是龍不是狗，嗅什麼嗅?!」但是……

青玄突然也飄了起來，繞著小玖飛一圈，做出和金龍一樣的動作。

嗅嗅。

端木傲眼角頓時抽了一下，努力放輕語氣：

「青，你在、幹什麼?」幸虧端木傲很有自制力，這句話才不至於變成咬牙切齒。

金和青沒理，一同飛高了點，看見微微飄動的紅色髮飾……

兩獸一僵，「咻」一下，瞬間飛回自家契約主身上趴好。

「你、你你，你妹妹身上怎麼會有這種東西?!」兩隻獸異口同聲，連結巴程度和想尖叫的語氣都一樣。

但是這回金龍沒嫌棄了，和隻龜說同樣的話?那不重要。

「什麼東西？」端木颩和端木傲往小玖頭上看了一眼。

不就是……小狐狸頭像的髮飾嗎?

下面還綴了九條紅色毛流蘇，像垂了九條尾巴。

「挺好看的。」端木颩說道。

「很可愛。」端木傲說道。

很搭小玖白瓷色的五官。

配上黑色的、軟軟的髮色，讓小玖看起來更加可愛，還有一點俏皮的活潑感，真的很搭。

不過，就算沒有髮飾，小玖本來就是最可愛的妹妹，沒有之一。

金龍和玄龜第一次同時產生一種疑惑：我家契約主莫非是傻的？

咳！

不能這樣說。

如果契約主是傻的，那和他們契約的牠們，豈不是也是傻的？

本龍（本龜）英明睿智，怎麼可能是傻的？一定是契約主見識少。

「那不是普通的髮飾。」金龍看向小玖，「那是……魔獸送妳的吧？」

「嗯。」小玖點點頭。

紅色狐狸頭？

「那隻紅色小狐狸?!」端木風立刻想到了。

「嗯。」小玖再點點頭。

「那隻小狐狸……很厲害？」端木傲回想。

「它，」青指著那個髮飾，「讓我覺得很有壓力。」

金龍在一邊，難得沒有和玄龜唱反調，跟著點點頭。

端木風和端木傲有點驚訝。

身為契約主，當然知道自家魔獸的等級，能讓金和青感到壓力，表示小狐狸的血脈……在金和青之上?!

「小玖，小狐狸究竟是什麼魔獸？」端木傲和小玖同行過一段時間，完全沒有感覺到小狐狸……有很厲害呀？

牠很懶……一直要小玖抱著，才是端木傲對牠最深的印象。

「就狐狸呀。」小玖直覺回答。

兩獸心聲：這回答，真是太強大了。

是狐狸沒錯，但那是普通的狐狸嗎?!

「魔獸等級呢？」端木風細問。

小玖一臉無辜：「……不知道。」

兩獸看向她，不知道還敢收魔獸的禮物，很大膽啊……不是，是不知道還契約……等等！

「那隻狐狸，也是妳的契約獸？」金龍覺得，自己發現一個大問題。

「大概……是吧。」小玖不是很確定。

兩兄弟及兩獸：「……」有這麼迷糊的嗎？

「到底是不是？」這次是端木傲細問。

小玖想了想。

「應該是。」不是她主動契約的就是了。

金龍瞪大眼……雖然牠的眼睛本來就很大了。

「端木風，妳家妹妹契約兩隻獸！」

「很奇怪嗎？」小玖不解地問。

「沒有很奇怪，是很稀奇。」金龍又飄了起來，繞著小玖飛一圈——特別注意，飛的高度沒有超過那個狐狸髮飾。

青色玄龜解釋：

「一般來說，一個人，只會契約一隻魔獸，要契約第二隻，必須先和第一隻解除契約。」

一來，要契約魔獸並不容易，能有一隻已經很好，還想要第二隻？作什麼美夢呢！

另外，一般魂師想契約兩隻魔獸的結果，通常不是成功契約魔獸成為眾魂師羨慕嫉妒恨的對象，而是魂師自我魂力崩潰。

後果，輕則變成不能自理的傻子、重則喪生或被魔獸給吞了，成為眾魂師口耳相傳的笨蛋。

二來，魔獸之間，基本上是一山不容二虎，尤其當後者比前者血脈強悍時，魔獸的驕傲，是寧死也不肯服從人族的。

「所以如果妹妹可以契約兩隻魔獸……」金龍飄回端木風身上，「至少表示兩點：一是妹妹天生魂力強大，二是那隻狐狸的血脈等級，應該很高——至少在我和這隻龜之上。」

第二點，金龍大人是很不願意承認的。

本龍是那麼輕易自動承認不如別隻獸的嗎？

但是事實是這樣的時候，金龍大人也不是那種不能接受事實、只會找理由自我欺騙、死不承認的蠢獸。

「真的？」端木傲問青。

青點了下頭。

「金龍說的是真的。」

玄龜同樣高傲，但是金龍都能面對事實了，牠當然也有這種勇氣。

「這隻，」指寶寶，「雖然弱，但也不是輕易和人契約的魔獸。牠會選擇妹妹，也就表示，牠是臣服於狐狸的。」當然也不排除，因為寶寶是在妹妹身邊孵化的，第一個接觸的人、熟悉的氣味就是妹妹，所以視妹妹為母親。

不過這樣一來，牠會跟隨妹妹，卻不會成為妹妹的契約魔獸。

想了想，又補充一句：

「還有，牠雖然弱，但是血脈等級，和我們是差不多的。」以種族數量來說，這隻還更稀有。

這隻小魔獸有這麼強?!

端木風與端木傲齊齊看向寶寶。

「嗚？」被注視了，寶寶啃靈晶的動作一頓，牠後腿動了動，小心地把自己移動得更貼近小玖一點。

「……」這麼膽小的幼獸真的和金（青）同等級?!

莫非，他們平常都太高估金（青）了?

被契約主用懷疑的目光掃了一眼，金龍和玄龜突然福至心靈，莫名就懂了這一眼的涵義。

竟、然、被、小、看、了。

「血脈和發育不良是兩回事，不要把本龍（本龜）和這隻弱幼獸放在一起比！」吼！

端木風、端木傲兩兄弟對看一眼，很順地就點點頭了。

「我知道，你很強。」

一個摸金龍、一個摸玄龜。

順便拿起桌上的點心，餵幾口。

自家的契約魔獸，還是要哄的。

金龍和玄龜：「……」雖然不滿意，但是勉強可以接受。

畢竟是自家契約主，不會哄人……哄獸，所以動作、語氣都那麼生硬，身為魔獸還是要包容一下的。

是說，這點心挺好吃的呀。咔滋咔滋。

一龍一龜瞬間變小，飛到點心盤裡，一獸霸一盤，開吃。

小玖撐著下巴，偷笑。

「嗚嗚。」摸摸。

寶寶也要安慰。

小玖摸摸牠的頭。

寶寶立刻滿足了，繼續啃靈晶。

「小玖，那隻狐狸呢？」真是的，話題都被帶偏了。

趁著愛吵架的魔獸都去「忙了」，端木風立刻問道。

「他……和北叔叔一樣，都離開了。」小狐狸離開，她只是有點不捨得，也有種莫名的預感，他們一定會再見的。

但北叔叔的離開，她是真的有些不習慣。

儘管恢復神智不算太久，但是自她出生以來，一直是北叔叔在照顧她，不是父女，卻勝似父女。

在她還傻乎乎的時候，只有北叔叔一直在帶著她，無論她有沒有回應，他教她熟悉這個世界、教她修練，一遍、兩遍、三遍……不厭其煩。

即使過去習慣一個人，但這十五年的陪伴，不只是記憶，也是她的真實經歷，在她心裡，留下很深的痕跡。

「北叔叔不在，哥哥陪妳。」端木風用力揉揉她的頭。

頭髮有點亂了，小玖有點哀怨地看著他。

端木風這回沒被妹妹的哀怨騙走，立刻接著問：

「那，為什麼不跟哥哥說一聲就走？」

這一問，兩個哥哥都用眼神瞪著她。

如果沒有什麼好理由的話……

哼哼。

在這種瞪視下，小玖眼神飄了飄。

……心虛。

# 第十四章　妹妹的心思，哥哥要懂得

不告而別。

就算再多正當的理由，再美化、再多為對方好的原因，還是不告而別。

本質上，就是一種辜負。

小玖遲疑了半晌，還是實話實說：

「我……就是……不想連累你們。」

「連累？」

感覺，哥哥們瞪視她的眼神，有點兇。

就為這點微不足道的理由？

「陰月華死在我手上。越階殺神，那些家族……不會放過這件事，一旦我出現、再和你們見面，他們也不會放過你們。」

人心，無論是在哪個世界，都是一樣的。

貪、利。

無人能避免。

能自制的人，終究是少數。

自認為高高在上的家族，雖然表面上做不出強逼的事，但是不代表不會暗地裡行使一些手段。

即使她對端木家族沒有什麼留戀，但不可否認，她是「端木」玖。

在重視家族出身的天魂大陸，只要沒有被除名，她出自端木家，仍然是端木家的一分子。

若她沒有出現，其他人或許不會做什麼。

但若她一出現，那些人會做出什麼事，就很難說了。

事實證明，她的判斷也是對的。

因為那一戰後，她直接消失，連星流也不見蹤影。

其他家族就算想追問，只要端木家族與師兄不回應，那他們做不出太多有失分寸的事。

這樣一來，四哥、六哥和師兄的安全，就會有一定的保障。

「讓他們來。」端木傲面無表情。

「這種事，不需要擔心。」端木風根本不把這種事放在心上。

以仲奎一身為煉器師的地位，就更不擔心這種事了。

仲奎一的師父雖然久未出現，但「天魂大陸第一煉器師」的號召力，對其他家族的震懾力還是很足的。

這種小事，小玖根本不必要擔心。

「可是，我怕。」小玖定定地看著他們，「如果你們因為我而受到傷害，我不會原諒自己。」當然，更不會原諒那個敢下手的人。

「保護妹妹，本來就是身為哥哥該做的事，沒有什麼拖不拖累。如果今天是我和四哥有了麻煩，妳會撇清關係、轉身就走，只求自己安全嗎？」端木風簡直哭笑不得。

小玖的心思，在來東州的路上，他就想明白了。被「拋棄」的怒火，經過趕路，其實剩下的也沒多少。

相信四哥也是一樣。

但是見了面，該質問的還是要質問，該問的要問、該罵的還是要罵，最重要的，是要改變小玖這種想法。

是親人，還怕拖累嗎？

這種麻煩，又不是因為小玖犯了錯或做得不好。相反的，是做得太好，才惹了別人的眼。

但在那種情況下，她有能力，難道不救四哥嗎？

如果不是小玖横插一手，當時在場的各家族成員的死傷會更加慘重。

偏偏有些人不懂感恩，只懂利益。

他們，為何要因為別人的貪念就放棄自己在意的親人？

追根究底，現在的他和四哥，即使已經是別人眼中的「高手」，但對比整個中州，還是太弱了。

「能平安，當然要平平安安的。」小玖反駁。

「修行路上，想要變強、想要繼續修練，哪裡不危險？」端木風才不信小玖會不明白這個道理。

「妳一聲不吭地跑走，我們很擔心。」端木傲直白地說道。

看他們一路追來，把休息的時間壓縮到最短，就知道他們有多著急。

「而且，妳把端木家想得太弱了。」端木風笑著點點她的額頭。

端木家族能一直維持在中州的地位，數千年來不曾動搖，靠的絕對不是以和為貴。

而是——實力。

「妳是不是擔心，家族會因為多方壓力，選擇把妳交出去？」端木傲想到之前三叔搞出的事。

然而聽到這句話，端木風立刻望著她，「妳認為，家族會捨棄妳？」

小玖默了默。

顯然是了。

端木風和端木傲一時無語。

「爺爺不會那樣做的。」端木傲說道。

是嗎？

小玖懷疑。

「妳不信任家族，也是正常的。」端木風卻很理解。

他大概能猜出小玖的想法和心思。

與其被捨棄，不如一開始……就不給誰捨棄自己的機會。

也可以說，端木家族，從來不是小玖的選擇。

「六弟！」不幫爺爺說話，也不要火上澆油啊。

「四哥，小玖離開帝都至少十年，也幾乎不曾見過祖父。無論是小時候的她，或是現在的她，都沒有受到太多家族的栽培與保護，她對家族沒有信任感，也是正常的。」而且，小玖還受到很多欺負。

幼時的小玖，是被家族放棄的，被族長——也就是祖父，親口逐出帝都，到偏遠的西州生活。

一直陪著她、照顧她的，並不是端木家族的族人。

更不用說，後來當小玖一恢復神智之後，面對族人的第一件事，就是成為親人手中利益交換的籌碼。

天知道當時他一收到消息的時候有多生氣，多擔心自己趕回帝都的時候已經來不及阻止。

幸好，小玖好了，也有了實力保護自己。

她只是對家族無感，卻沒有記恨家族，端木風都覺得，北叔叔真的把小玖教得太好了。

至少端木風非常喜愛現在開朗、有點俏皮的妹妹。

他一點都不希望小玖的心裡，是存在仇恨的，那樣太辛苦，她也不會開心的。

想到三叔的作為，端木傲也無語了。

「妳對家族不信任我能理解，妳怕拖累我們的心情，我也能明白。但是身為哥哥，並不希望被妹妹拋棄，妳懂得的吧？」端木風看著妹妹，眼神微瞇地盯著她。

小玖年紀還小，會一時想不開、會「鑽牛角尖」、會想獨立、會有點小脾氣，都是正常的。

踏上修練一途，他不反對妹妹自立自強，但是「不能拋棄哥哥」這一點，是必須要讓小玖深刻記住的。

「……懂。」在這種注視下，小玖有點艱難地點點頭。

換位思考，大概她——也不會高興。

「所以，妳要答應我，以後無論發生什麼事，絕對不可以因為怕連累哥哥，就不告而別、離家出走。」

「這個……」

「答應我。」這是要求，不是選擇。

「如果……不答應呢？」她小小聲地問。

「我派金跟著妳，寸步不離，好嗎？」端木風微笑。

……莫名有點冷。

「我答應。」小玖只能同意。

隨身被金龍跟著……這畫面，她不想看。

端木風滿意。

「那，哥哥不生氣了吧？」小玖立刻又問。

「當然還生氣。」端木風立刻收起笑臉。

「……」六哥變臉太快了。六哥過河拆橋。

「的確不能那麼容易原諒妳這次拋棄哥哥的行為。」端木傲也說道。

「喔。」小玖反省。

人果然不能做虧心事呀。

一虧心，就心虛，理不直、氣不壯，想幫自己爭取一下都沒立場。

就算、就算只是不想連累哥哥，她也還是有點……太沒心肝了。

她不喜歡道別的場面。

可同樣，也不喜歡她關心的人，不告而別。

如果北叔叔、小狐狸不告而別……

嗯，想揍人。

想到這裡，小玖不只心虛，還愧疚。

己所不欲，勿施於人。

這樣的處世之道，是她一貫奉行的。

即使已經離開那個教她為人處世之道的世界，她也沒有忘記。

所以，她很慎重地對著哥哥們說：

「對不起。讓你們擔心了。」而且好像，也丟給哥哥們不小的麻煩。

那些世家的人如果「魯」起來，用武力還好解決，打一架就是；但如果軟磨硬泡，應付起來就很煩人。

她不喜歡煩人的事。

把煩人的事丟給一直護她的哥哥，雖然是因為知道這些難不倒哥哥，可是，卻也有仗著哥哥們不會不管、不會真的生氣，所以有恃……無恐。

她以前從來不會把自己的麻煩丟給別人的。

現在……居然養成壞習慣了！

嗚，她明明成熟穩重，連報仇都可以算計得絲毫無差，現在怎麼好像變幼稚了？

換了個世界，年紀縮水個子縮水實力縮水知識縮水常識縮水，所以腦袋也縮水了？

明明她一向都是自己的事自己處理的，現在，好像會依賴北叔叔和哥哥們?!

依賴？

這很不符合以前父親對她的教育。

身為獨生女，又沒有其他同族的人互相扶持，在那個需要處處防備的時代，這兩個字是絕對不會出現在她的生命裡的。

可是在這裡，她卻不自覺有了這種心態。

好像，因為北叔叔的照顧、因為有會護著她的哥哥，她不用事事周全，也可以……任性一點？

任性？

這兩個字竟然會出現在她身上？小玖有點不太能接受這個事實……

任性＝恣意＝妄為＝招麻煩。

她才不招麻煩，都是麻煩找上她……

小玖這麼乾脆地認錯，然後表情變來變去，一點都沒有之前沉穩、八風吹不動、好像發生什麼都不足以讓她動容的樣子，讓兩個哥哥看著覺得新奇之餘，又覺得欣慰。

這樣，才像一個十幾歲的妹妹。

會有情緒、會不安、又反省，即使把歪理變成理直氣壯，卻不會去做什麼仗勢欺負別人的事。

不像某城的某大小姐。

不對不對，身為哥哥，是寧可妹妹去欺負別人，也不要她被別人欺負的。

小玖有本事不被別人欺負，很好。

如果小玖會欺負別人，那一定是別人的錯。

身為愛護妹妹的哥哥，看妹妹的濾鏡就是這麼厚。

端木風起身，抱了一下妹妹，又揉揉她的頭。

「哥哥不要妳道歉，只要妳記住，妳是我的妹妹，任何時候，都不要忘記哥哥。」

身為哥哥，會為妹妹擔心是應該的。

但是，不要這種不知道妹妹在哪裡的擔心，更不要妹妹為了怕連累自己就不告而別。

「無論是招了麻煩，還是惹了仇家，妳是我的妹妹，就沒有『連累』這兩個字，只有一起承擔。」端木傲也說道。

端木風抱完、揉完，換他。

……難怪六弟一直摸摸他妹的頭。

柔柔軟軟，妹妹又乖巧。

多揉幾下頭，才放手。

小玖趕緊撥撥頭髮，抓綁一下，就恢復髮型。

幸好她沒有整什麼複雜華麗的髮型，不然這下，肯定一頭亂髮。

哥哥們……是什麼習慣啊？

她很高興有哥哥們的關心，但是這習慣，能不能改改？

接收到妹妹有點哀怨的眼神，哥哥們的眼神飄忽了下。

揉揉乖巧妹妹的頭，是疼愛妹妹的表現，是一種身為哥哥的滿足感。

他們是絕對不會放棄這項權利的。

為免妹妹繼續糾結這件事，端木風轉移她的注意力。

「小玖，這個給妳。」拉過她的手，一只儲物手環，放在她的掌心裡。

「這是？」

「祖父要我們交給妳的。」端木傲說道。

小玖偏著頭，露出問號表情。

「這是從北叔叔帶妳回來開始，祖父為妳留存的修練資源。」

「我不缺這個。」小玖把手環推回去。

她對端木家族並沒有太多留戀，也不覺得端木家有欠自己什麼。既沒有付出，當然不應該索取。

「小玖，妳是端木家九小姐，妳的父親，是現今端木家主四子——端木定煌，僅就這一點，妳就有資格收下。」端木風說道。

「可是……」

「小玖，祖父知道我和六弟會來找妳，所以特地交給我們，轉交給妳。」端木傲也說道。

祖父當時說：

「無論她怎麼想，她都是我的孫女，你們有的修練資源，她同樣也有。就算是……我這個祖父，對她的一點心意。至於她回不回來，由她吧！你們都不要勉強她。」

小玖愣了下。

這個……便宜祖父，好奇怪。

把那麼小的她驅離中州、不聞不問，感覺不像對她有祖孫之情。

但是他卻特地去見師兄，又特地要哥哥們轉交東西，感覺，又好像是關心她的。

好……矛盾又糾結的老人家喔！

但是，也不能怪他不親自交給她，小玖沒忘記是自己先搞「失蹤」的。

她敲敲自己的頭，這習慣好像不太好。

「先收下吧！要是妳真的不想要，以後見到祖父的時候，再還給他。」端木風直接包住她的手掌，握住那只儲物手環。

端木傲在一旁，很贊同地一點頭。

這種小事，就不要猶豫那麼久了。

「好吧。」她收下儲物手環。

妹妹沒有糾結太久，端木風很滿意，然後話題一轉……

「接下來，我們來說說，妳和東明玉淩之間的事。」

「我沒有惹她。」小玖立刻自白。

「這個我知道。」更沒忘記，要尋機會找到那個「禍害」算帳。「妳到東雪城來，是想進寒玉秘境吧？」

「嗯。」小玖點頭。

「東明玉凌不是一個大方的人，等妳們都進了秘境，一旦遇上，她一定不會放過妳。」

「我不怕她。」進寒玉秘境有年歲限制，東明玉凌的聖階護衛，是進不去的。

「如果單只有她，妳可能不必擔心，但是，她是東明城的大小姐，東明城城主的寶貝愛女。」端木風特別強調。

小玖一想就懂了。

「所以，有人會因為東明城，幫著她對付我？」就算是這樣，小玖也沒有什麼害怕的感覺。

不就是群毆嗎？

打不了，她還跑不了嗎？

她不會傻傻地執著。

「不要小看一個煉器師的號召力。」端木傲提醒，「天魂大陸上，武師的修練者相當多，在中州有煉器師公會，煉器師也相對比較多，妳可能不覺得煉器師有什麼了不起。

「但是妳想想，前陰家家主能讓那麼多人聽從於她、能號令陰家、能在煉器師公會有那麼高的地位，除了其他因素，主要的根本原因，和她本身是一名高明的煉器師是分不開的。」

一個陰家，就攪得整個中州大混亂，她本人更是只差一步就要掌控整個中州……如果不是突然出現小玖這個變數，現在的中州會變成怎麼樣，實在不好說。

直到現在，各家族和各公會，還在處理那場大戰後遺留的後續問題。一般人的生活就算恢復正常，在這過程中損失的，以及那些喪失的武師、魂師，進而引起的各城勢力更迭，都還不算完全平靜。

這也是那些家族的家主、長老們，暫時不敢離開家族的原因。

就連他和六弟，如果不是祖父支持，他們也無法在這種時候就離開中州，來到這裡。

「而在東州，東明城是煉器大城，東明城城主本身更是唯一出自東州、以東州為鄉的聖階煉器師，在東州的地位與重要性，可以說是五城最高；他的號召力，甚至可以動搖東州。」

東州，是三州中最看重實力的地方。

有實力，走到哪裡都人人敬重。

實力不夠，就難以在東州立足。

東明玉淩雖然天賦好，卻也不是最好，但是卻能在東州橫著走，囂張惹事，沒多少人敢管，為什麼？

就因為，她的父親，是東明城城主。

為什麼岩華那麼看不慣東明玉淩，也忍著沒有與她發生正面衝突？

不就是因為擔心東明城城主一怒之下，會斷了對東岩城的武器供應。

端木傲接著道：

「還有，東州鄰近海域，海上的魔獸比陸地上的更加兇殘，也更仇視人族。以東海城為首的沿海諸城，一直都以守衛天魂大陸之陸地，不讓海上魔獸上岸肆虐為己任。因此，在獸潮來時，東明城有提供一定數量的魂器支援東海城的義務，讓東海城依市價購買。」

這就刷了東明城的好名聲。

「東明城提供魂器，東海城出資購買，所以東明城在東州的名聲很好？」小玖聽完，確認似地問道。

「是。」兩個哥哥點頭。

小玖一臉深思。

「那東海城呢？」

「東海城怎麼了？」端木風一時沒抓到妹妹問話的重點。

「東明城有好名聲，東海城沒有嗎？」

「當然有。」原來是問這個。「東州五大城中，名聲最大的就屬東海城，其次是東明城。只不過數千年來，歷任東海城都帶領東州眾武師、魂師們對抗海獸，大家都習慣了。」自然不會再突出東海城的名聲。

獸潮來時，以東海城為首。

但無論何時，東明城都絕對是修練者心中很重要、很有價值、不可或缺的存在。

「東明城城主，很有心機啊。」小玖感慨。

心機？

「他煉器，提供給東海城，錢有了、名聲也有了、連大家的感激都撈到了，一舉三得，還不夠有心機嗎？」

反觀東海城，出錢出力出人，結果是錢花了，名聲與感激被東明城反襯得黯淡無光。

真，有點慘。

端木風、端木傲：「……」很有道理。

但是不是哪裡不對？

「小玖，人生在世，盡一己之力，不一定要求有名聲和別人的感謝的。」端木傲個性清正，很快從小玖的話裡回過神來。

差點被帶偏了。

小玖的想法不能說是錯。

東海城難道從來沒有想到這些嗎？

當然有。

只是不以為意罷了。

每個人看中的不同。

東明城要的，可能是財富、名聲與地位。

而東海城要的，一直以來只有一個——就是天魂大陸的安寧。

這其中，東雪城、東林城、東岩城，明裡暗裡，也是出錢出人出力，與東海城共同守衛天魂大陸。

不然，五年一次獸潮、百年一次大獸潮，光靠東海城的人力、物力，早就撐不下去了。

「人各有志，懂。」小玖嚴肅點點頭。

有人求名、求利。

有人求和平。

大家都得償所願，很好。

端木風、端木傲：「……」總覺得妹妹的想法好像有哪裡不對。

「人各有志」這四個字是這麼用的嗎？

等等，又偏了話題。

「總之，在東州，有很多人願意和東明家牽上關係，憑這一點，就有很多人會幫東明玉凌，明白吧？」端木風終於把自己要說的重點表達完畢，表情很慎重，內心抹了抹不存在的虛汗。

心累。

第一次發現，要跟妹妹溝通，不容易。

以前妹妹不會說話、不會回應，乖乖巧巧的，讓他覺得，只要妹妹能回應他一句，就算變成頑劣妹妹也沒關係。

但現在……沒關係。

只要妹妹好好的，哥哥挺得住！

努力……不被妹妹帶偏話題。

「嗯，明白。」哥哥說得很認真，小玖也很認真地應了。「但是，忍讓很傷身的。」嘆氣。

端木風、端木傲：「……」這句話，有點耳熟。

好像是他們找麻煩或被找麻煩時，比較常聽見的話。

為什麼我家乖巧的妹妹會那麼熟練地說這句話?!

那個星流帶著我家乖巧的妹妹一路到東州到底都教了妹妹什麼?!

突然想到，他們雖然疼愛妹妹，但實際上和妹妹相處的時間並不多。

尤其是妹妹「正常」了之後。

端木傲好歹與小玖同行過一陣子，對妹妹缺乏「常識」的狀態有所了解，對她直來直往的言行，也有點心理準備。

「小玖，強龍不壓地頭蛇。」端木傲輕聲提醒。

並不是要教妹妹一直忍讓，只是在東雪城，他們不占天時地利。不久後東海城即將面臨獸潮，這個時候誰都不希望發生什麼事讓東明城拖延交付武器的時間，影響到東海城，甚至整體人族的戰力。

「聽起來，東明城的人，好像很囂張……不對，是真的很囂張。」想到東明玉凌兩次一言不和，當場動手。

這麼囂張，真的不會讓人想打他們一頓嗎?

「東州有東州的生存方式，我們畢竟不在這裡久留，不要貿然介入比較好。當然，如果她真的太不客氣，小玖也不用一直讓著，能打贏就打，不是我們主動找別人麻煩，就不用怕。」雖然是想勸妹妹避著點兒，但是看著妹妹乖巧可愛又漂亮的小臉，端木風還是捨不得妹妹委屈。

「六弟。」這和他們之前商量的不一樣。

「四哥，我捨不得。」一句話，端木傲就懂了。

「好吧，但是要以自己的安全為先。」後面一句，是對小玖叮嚀的。

算了，都惹了，就不畏首畏尾。

若沒有一往直前的勇氣，怎麼繼續修練之路？

「真的可以嗎？」

「可以。」

「可能會連累你們喔。」

「沒關係。」哥哥，本來就要護著妹妹，尤其是他們這麼疼的妹妹。

「喔。」小玖覺得，自己可以放心了。

下一次，爭取把敢找她麻煩的人，一次打趴。

哥哥們莫名覺得冷了一下。

嗯，錯覺吧。

不過，一說不用忍讓，小玖眼神都亮了，他和四哥，好像真的考慮太多了。

但誰教他們是為妹妹操心的哥哥，多想一點，總是沒錯的——這怎麼很像老父親才有的感言？

被人讚為少年天才、風華正茂的端木風，拒絕把自己想像成糟老頭。「小玖，妳對寒玉秘境了解多少？」

「有寒玉、有魔獸。」

嗯嗯，還有？

沒有了。

望著妹妹臉上「已經答完」的表情，端木風無語了下。

趁著兄妹三人在說話，悄悄把桌上的吃吃喝喝全部一掃而空的金嘯和青玄，趴在盤子裡看著自家契約主那難以言喻的表情。

兩獸默默交流：

妹妹有說錯嗎？

沒有。就是簡短了一點。

有重點不就行了嗎？

呃，不是重點的也很重要。

那些太囉嗦的東西不知道也沒關係。

牠有實力，不怕！

青玄無語了。

看這傢伙的表情就知道牠在想什麼，這傢伙到底知不知道什麼是「謀定而後動」？

只會一招「勇往直前」，早晚會趴地的。

牠覺得再跟這傢伙混在一起，牠的智慧都要被拉低了。

金嘯才覺得，跟這什麼都慢吞吞的傢伙再混下去，牠的英勇威武都要被「慢」沒了。

這實在太有損牠英明神武、霸氣轟轟的魔獸形象。

對妹妹的這種表現，端木傲有點懷念。

沒有常識的妹妹很鬧心，但是，很可愛。

端木傲覺得這個可以，他不介意。

所以他很習慣地就開始說道：

「寒玉，是寒玉秘境特有的礦晶，對魂師而言，有滌清神魂、厚實魂力之效，就要注意有人會開始偷襲、攔路搶劫。

是遇到了就絕對不放過的修練物資。所以如果妳在秘境裡找到寒玉，卻被人知道了，

「另外，寒玉秘境的入口只有一個，但是進入之後，卻通常不會在同一個地方，也有可能妳一入境，就遇上找麻煩的人，或是比妳先入境卻埋伏起來等著偷襲妳的人。所以即使入境後，四下無人，也不要放鬆警惕。」

端木風接著道：

「寒玉秘境很大，裡面有各種地形、各種環境，即使沒有人埋伏，妳也要注意自己被傳送到的地方有沒有危險。」

寒玉秘境十年一開，他上回來東州正好遇到，也湊了回熱鬧，結果一入境，就掉到沼澤區。

幸好及時飛出來，不然……

沼澤裡一大堆張開嘴的兇猛沼鱷歡迎你一生留下喔！

至於端木傲進的那次，是一入境就出現在沙漠——正好是沙蟲的窩，於是立刻被一大群沙蟲追著跑。

那一次，絕對創下青玄有生以來，速度最快、一點都不慢吞吞的龜生快速紀錄，至今難以打破。

小玖以同情的眼神看著兩個哥哥。

這隨機傳送的運氣，實在不能說是好啊。

「我們這還算不錯，我聽過有人直接掉進火山口，然後和岩漿底的火蟾相親相

愛合而為一的。」端木風說道。

以資證明，他的運氣，真的不算糟。

「我也有聽說，有兩個互不認識的人剛巧被傳送到同一個地方，結果兩個人因為想互相暗算對方而打起來，然後……就沒有然後了。」鷸蚌相爭，漁翁得利。

這件事會爆出來，就是那個撿到便宜的「漁翁」得意說出來的。

然後，這個漁翁也沒有活著從那一次的秘境開啟裡走出來。

只能說，當漁翁者，人恆漁翁之。

這三個人沒有被傳送到危險地，但還是就把一生送給秘境了，相形之下，他只是和青玄多「用力」地跑了一點路。

端木傲覺得，他的運氣應該也不能算糟。

小玖：「……」所以進入秘境就是一種——我雖然運氣不好，但有人運氣比我更糟的大比拚？

這個秘境有點坑。

不過哥哥們的意思她懂了。

簡單總結，入境頭一關三要點：

第一，落點不定。

第二，來自秘境天然環境與生物攻擊的危險。

第三，跟人落在同一個地方有被偷襲的危險。

「小玖好聰明。」聽完妹妹的總結，兩個哥哥很滿意。

「……」雖然被稱讚了但是並沒有高興的感覺。

哥哥們都說得那麼清楚了，如果她還聽不懂，這智商就真的太讓人著急了。

看出她無語的表情，端木風笑著揉揉她的頭。

他們就是覺得妹妹好聰明呀！

這是來自哥哥們的偏愛、哥哥們私心的滿足，誰來抗議都沒用，包括妹妹本人。

揉完頭，他繼續道：

「有關秘境，還有兩點要注意：第一，秘境開啟時間是三天，時間一到，所有還活著的入境者——無論當時是在什麼狀況下、在哪裡、在做什麼事，都會中斷，立刻被傳送出來。」

所以，如果剛好在那個時候遇到危險，只要撐到被傳送出境的時間，就安全了。

一出秘境，是不允許爭鬥的，違者——無非長老將會特別問候你，誰來說情都沒用，一切按東雪城城規處理。

當然，如果人離開東雪城，那想怎麼殺、怎麼死、怎麼搶，無非長老就懶得理你了。

比較悲劇的是那種正要挖到寶，結果就差那麼一瞬——被送出來了！

那就……撓心撓牆、痛哭流涕都沒用。

周遭的人只會安慰你：下次再來吧，它一定還會在那裡等著你。順便東扯西拉、明的暗的套一下話，是在哪裡可以挖寶？

「不過，雖然說是三天，但是秘境裡的時間和外界流速不同，秘境外三天，等於秘境內三十天，這個時間差，妳要記得。」端木傲繼續補充。

「另外，秘境裡有各種環境，有炎熱如沙漠、也有寒凍遍地的極地、濕黏陰暗布滿毒物的沼澤，以及綠草如茵的山谷……等等。

「再者，寒玉秘境裡雖然有寒玉礦，但隨著一次次的開啟，寒玉礦也愈來愈難遇到，但是寒玉，卻關係到能不能進入寒玉秘境的『內境』。」

「內境？」秘境中，還有秘境啊？

「『內境』是我們為了區分才有的說法，其實是指秘境中的一處秘地。」端木風接著說道：「秘境一開，我們所有人入境，在秘境裡可以待足三十天。秘境裡靈氣濃郁，就算不去找任何天材地寶，就在秘境裡找一個安全的地方閉關三十天修練，也是很值得的。」

據說，在秘境修練三十天，至少可以抵在外面閉關修練一年。

只是很少人真的這樣做。

入秘境了不去尋寶，只為閉關修練……安全是很安全，但是也太浪費了！

「但是，在秘境中得到寒玉的，可以在最後六天進入秘境中的一個秘地，通關裡面的關卡或度過危機，可以得到一項寶物。

「這個寶物可能是魔獸蛋，可能是魂器或武器，也有可能是可以用來煉器的罕見煉材，或是能提高修為的靈晶、能提升實力的修練方法，更甚至是……在天魂大陸上失傳已久的丹藥……等等。

「麻煩的是，寒玉必須放在身上，不能放在任何儲物器裡。也就是說，在第二十四天，得到寒玉的人必須把寒玉戴在身上，否則就無法被傳送到秘地……」

「所以第二十四天，大概也是進入秘境最危險的一天，因為得到寒玉的人，很有可能被人搶。」小玖已經想到了。

「對。」端木風點頭。

我的妹妹果然很聰明。

「……」坑！

如果這個秘境有主，那設計這種環節的人，簡直是信手一拈就挑起人性的醜陋，絕對的惡趣味啊。

不過六哥說的話裡有一個重點。

「丹藥？」還是早已失傳的？「不會過期吃壞肚子嗎？」

還有，丹藥是天魂大陸「失傳已久」的東西？

小玖有一種，她要開啟惡補天魂大陸歷史的預感。

端木風、端木傲：「……?!」

小玖這發言真是……他們還沒吃壞肚子，已經先感覺到被噎住、吞不下去了。

不過端木傲很認真地想了一想。

「丹藥出現的次數不多，也有人把丹藥放到拍賣會上去換靈晶，沒聽說過有人吃壞肚子。」或者被毒死的。

「保鮮效果這麼好啊！」小玖一臉讚嘆。

寒玉秘境，保守估計已經存在數千年。

一顆藥放了數千年都沒壞……這是多麼不可思議的保鮮度啊！防腐之效堪稱冠絕古今。

不過……真的有保存這麼久的方法嗎？

小玖非常好奇呀！

不過「保鮮效果」四個字，讓兩個哥哥再度被噎著了。

我的妹妹看事情的角度真是……清奇。

好像，妹妹也不是那麼乖巧的感覺……有種身為哥哥未來即將不時頭很痛的預感。

但是沒關係，哥哥撐得住。

兩個哥哥同時伸出手，一前一後揉了下小玖的頭髮，然後把在盤子裡睡著的契約獸收回體內的契約空間裡。

再一看，窩在小玖腿上啃靈晶的弱幼獸，不知道什麼時候也睡著了，關鍵是，睡著了還保持靈晶放在嘴裡啃的動作。

這到底是有多愛吃靈晶啊?!

端木風伸出手，想把靈晶拿開……

「嗚……」寶寶抖了一下，翻轉過身，並且縮了縮身體，窩在小玖懷裡，繼續睡。

小玖忍著笑，摸摸寶寶的頭，然後拿掉牠嘴裡的靈晶。

結果，寶寶什麼反應也沒有，就任由靈晶被拿走，然後身體更縮成一團，窩著睡更熟。

「睡著了竟然也能分辨危險的嗎？」端木風有點驚訝。

這小獸，警惕性很強啊！

但這種警惕性，絕對不像一隻弱獸該有的。

金嘯說：寶寶是和牠們同等級的魔獸。

看起來真的是啊！

「牠能成長嗎？」端木傲也有點好奇地伸出手。

不出意外，在他碰到寶寶之前，寶寶即使沒醒，還是縮著身體，更往小玖懷裡鑽鑽鑽。

「應該可以吧。」小玖不太確定。

不過寶寶拿著靈晶啃著啃著，從腳都站不穩，啃到現在四腳放開、爬上爬下沒問題，那表示，寶寶比剛出生時健壯很多，那應該是可以長大的吧！

「要不，我讓青玄訓練一下牠？」端木傲覺得，現階段這隻弱寶寶是幫不上妹妹的忙。

那他幫著養一下。愛啃靈晶？沒問題，他可以提供。

讓同為魔獸的青玄訓練一下，說不定可以讓寶寶早點有自保能力。

這樣在小玖與人打鬥時，牠就不會是小玖的負擔。

「不用了，讓牠自然成長吧。」小玖笑著道，她知道四哥的好意。

「本來，我們想和妳一起進入秘境……」

「不用了，哥哥。」小玖趕緊打斷他。「我是倒數第二個才能進秘境的，你們不要陪我等。」太浪費時間了呀，而且……

「而且，妳還不想曝光身分，對吧？」端木風已經看穿她的想法了。

小玖呵呵陪笑。

在來的時候，他們兩人已經從星流那裡聽說「沐沐」兩個字。再加上小玖之前一打完架就跑、星流又阻止他們幫忙——不用說，他們兩個也猜到原因了。

星流比他們早知道小玖在想什麼——有點不爽。

這必須打兩架才夠！

避在自己房裡的星流突然覺得冷了一下。

「對了哥哥，我還沒上測試台，為什麼無非長老會做出這種處分？」小玖好奇兼轉移話題地問道。

至於東明玉凌……

不必上測試台，光是她的身分，入秘境的名額絕對有她。

「妳到東雪城，是雪長歌邀請妳來的吧？」端木風不答反問。

「嗯。」當然，岩華和林燁也有分。

「那他有送妳什麼信物嗎？」端木風再問。

「有。」小玖一翻手，一個刻著古字體的白色令牌，就出現在她的手掌上。

「這個，是雪長歌的私人信物，有這個，妳就是東雪城的貴客，可以自由進出城主府，可以參加東雪城內舉辦的各種活動——包括各種宴會、拍賣會，也包括進入寒玉秘境。」所以，無非長老的處分，真不是隨便說說的。

只是，就算雪長歌身為少城主，這樣的信物也只有三個。

沒想到他會這麼快就把其中一個送給小玖。

難道……端木風和端木傲對看一眼，同時看到彼此眼中的懷疑。

他對小玖有什麼企圖？

看來，這個人也必須打兩架才夠！

小玖：「……」東西果然不能亂收。

她低頭望了望手裡的令牌，總覺得這東西，還有什麼別的功用或者代表意義，有點麻煩……

「別擔心，他敢送，妳就收，是他邀請妳來的，送妳個像通行證一樣的東西也是應該的。再說，他是東雪城少主，妳也是端木家九小姐，身分不比他差，他的信物也沒什麼了不起的。」端木風安慰妹妹。

「對。」端木傲跟著補聲。

不是太重要的人，小玖不用太在意，知道吧？

什麼「東州貴公子」的……東州的少城主至少有五個，雪長歌也不過是其中之一，沒什麼了不起的，知道吧？

兩個哥哥努力輕描淡寫，務求妹妹不要把人記得太牢，免得惦記上什麼人。

妹妹還小，這種惦記完全不必要。嗯，就是這樣。

「哦，我知道了。」小玖似懂非懂。

總覺得，哥哥們好像在緊張什麼啊……

「這幾天，城裡一定還會亂，妳先別出門，好好休息，我們……嗯？」端木風還想說什麼，卻聽見屋外天空，傳來幾聲猶如沉物破空的轟隆聲。

「隆隆，轟，隆隆……」

端木風與端木傲對看一眼，三兄妹立刻打開門到屋外。

這陣轟隆聲，驚到的不只是他們。在他們的房門打開後，隱約聽見四周一道接著一道的開門聲、疑惑聲、驚呼聲，此起彼落，向外延伸。

像是原本沉睡中的東雪城，一瞬間全被叫醒了，所有人都在觀望。

轟隆聲後，只見夜色中，遠方天際出現明顯的閃電。

烏沉沉的天空，看不見雲層。

清晰的電痕，一道接著一道，劃開天色，不規則地來回閃動。

「嘶哩！嘶哩！」

透過閃電，他們紛紛感覺到，有什麼出現在雲層裡了。

「這是？」端木傲突然想到什麼，轉頭望向端木風。

「莫非是……」端木風一臉驚訝的神色，同樣回望。

秘境?!

但是距離秘境開啟，應該還有五天，怎麼會現在就出現了?!

# 第十五章　寒玉秘境

同一時間，城主府。

雪長歌匆匆來到府前演武場，就見一道白色的修長身影，立在夜色下，微微仰望天際。

「父親。」

隨之，一道身影飄忽而來，隨後定身在廣場上，緩緩落下。

「城主、少城主。」

「長歌見過無非長老。」雪長歌微彎一禮。

衡無非回了一禮，然後看向城主。

「秘境提前出現了。」

這是從來沒有過的情況。

「無妨。」城主淡淡一點頭，像是一點都不驚訝。「去通知所有人，天亮後繼續測試，依修為取前一百人，發給入境玉牌，明日巳時初，在城北廣場集合，憑玉牌進入秘境。城內的秩序，你多費心。」

「分內之事。那我先去安排了。」城主一令，衡無非沒有二話，一如來時，飛身離開。

「父親，玉牌一發完，城裡會亂吧？」雪長歌幾乎可以想見無非長老與護衛隊會忙碌成什麼樣子。

「不會。」城主語氣依然平淡，不覺得這是什麼大事。

「不會？」雪長歌不太信。

秘境名額，除了五大城內定，對外只有一百名，原本依測試標準選出後，沒有排上的人可以在城內長老的見證下以實力挑戰，搶得玉牌，取得進入秘境的機會。

現在實力挑戰的機會沒了，入境又只認玉牌，那些沒拿到玉牌的……還不想盡辦法偷矇拐騙搶。

這麼一來，秩序肯定亂。

城主緩緩道：

「在給玉牌的時候，無非一定會記得交代，城內不得滋事、不得違反城規，否則……取消入境資格。」

這句話太有威懾力了。

雪長歌相信，一定沒有人敢明目張膽鬧事了。

但是，明的不能，暗的呢？

「修行路上，總是充滿各種危險與機遇的，年輕人，要有披荊斬棘的決心哪。」城主低聲一笑，轉身回房。

雪長歌無語。

為何他會覺得，他那看似不食人間煙火、萬事不縈於心的父親，才是最想看戲的人？

◈

秘境提早開啟！

這個消息一出，簡直炸翻了一干還沒有去測試台的魂師、武師們，立刻在天一亮就奔赴測試台。

一如雪長歌的預測，當一百位名額確定後，當天晚上城裡非常不平靜。

不小心走過哪個角落，說不定還會聞到血腥味，或者聽到什麼奇奇怪怪的交易與搶牌計畫。

但是沒有人敢冒著惹怒無非長老的危險，公然鬧事或是把傷心的動靜弄大，驚動城衛。

於是，一夜就這麼「平靜」地過去了。

當天微微亮的時刻，空無一人的城北廣場，悄悄出現了人影。

一個接一個。

不管天地間一片雪白，也不管現在的溫度是不是冷得讓人發抖，安靜的廣場，漸漸變得吵嚷起來。

才到辰時，廣場已經來了超過萬人，三三兩兩地散在廣場周圍。

有獨自一人的、有傭兵團的，也有來自其他四城的人。

一下子就把廣場擠得讓人有種「到處都是人」的錯覺。

雖然不是人人都有入境玉牌，但這其中，一定有拿到玉牌的人。

不知道這些人是今天一早趕來、還是一拿到玉牌就偷偷躲在這附近，等待開啟時間，免得被搶。

這種情形，每十年就要上演一次。

「又來了。」

「嗯？」

「這些人有九成以上根本沒有入境資格，這麼早跑來這裡湊熱鬧，真是有夠閒。」她雙手環胸、肩靠城壁，語氣嫌棄。

雖然沒人拿出玉牌，但這些人之中，一定還有人想打玉牌的主意，想趁秘境開啟前，把入境資格搶到手。

「寒玉秘境開啟，是東州的大事，也是東雪城的大事，有很多人湊熱鬧，也很正常。」觀看秘境開啟，也是一種長見識啊。

「你怎麼不說，是有人想趁亂搞事？」

「啊，這種可能當然也有。」他語氣感嘆，「不過，有無非長老鎮場，我不認為想搞事的人能搞出什麼事。」

「他們可以在無非長老到來之前先搞事。」她抬槓道。

「那來不及了。」他一副遺憾的語氣。

「來不及什麼？」他那副遺憾的語氣，像去參加誰的葬禮……呸呸，她還想去秘境裡有好運氣，別想這種不好的事。

「無非長老早就來了。」

「在哪裡？」她立刻站正，東瞧西望、上看下看。

沒看見。

「別找了，就算無非長老來了，他沒現身，我們是找不到的。」他扳正她轉來轉去的臉，免得脖子轉太多次，會累。

「別亂摸。」她鼓著表情，拍開他的手，抬摃道：「找不到人，你就不能肯定人已經來了。」

她連城衛都沒看見。

「無非長老是個負責任的人，就算還沒到，他也一定在注意這裡的狀況，不允許任何人搗亂的。」他家的老爹是多麼地羨慕東雪城城主，能找到這麼一個勞動楷模……不是，是這麼一個負責任又能力卓絕的大長老啊！

有了無非長老，不知道省了東雪城多少事。

他家老爹甚至一度想挖角……可惜沒成功。

「你說的，也對。」她想了想，還是贊同他的話。「可惜無非長老不是我們城的人……」

聽說她家老父親也打過主意的啊！

可惜被一口拒絕，害她家老父親受打擊到差點蹲牆角。

好歹考慮一下啊……一口拒絕顯得他們城有多差一樣，連考慮一下的價值都沒有……傷心。

呃，好吧，比起東雪城的美，他們城……是粗獷了點兒。

東雪城雖然好像沒有東明城那麼豪，但對他們倆的城來說，已經是豪了。

然後，東雪城城主……實力像是比他倆的爹要厲害一點。

實力，就是一切。

綜上三點，無非長老不考慮，好像也是正常的。

「唉。」她低頭，沮喪。

「乖，別難過。」他很盡責地立刻抱過自家未婚妻，拍拍安撫。「雖然沒有無非長老，但是我們城裡現在的長老也很好，大家互相信任，相處才能長久。」

實力固然重要，能不能處得來也很重要。

像是，東明城城主很厲害，很有實力，煉器能力在東州更是無人能出其右。

但是如果他要來他們倆的城？他們會很高興嗎？

恐怕會連自家城都不想回去了。

「嗯，你說的有道理。」她想了想，也對，沮喪的心情立刻飛走，這才發現……「你幹嘛？」

「安慰妳。」

「我還需要你安慰?!」我推……沒推開，再推。

他順勢放開了，露出哀怨的表情。

「妳用完就丟，太沒良心了。」

「我、我、什麼用完、就丟?!」簡直不敢相信，他這是誣蔑！「明明是你趁機占我便宜！」

「嗯，那當然。」他一副理所當然樣。

她瞪眼，看他。

他笑得一臉溫柔，看她。

「……笑這麼好看，想誘拐誰呀？」她別開眼，咕噥。

「誘拐妳呀。」他聽到了。

「本少城主是那麼容易被誘拐的嗎?!」立刻把奇怪的感覺丟一邊，傲嬌地嗆了一句。

「是不好拐啊。」他點點頭，又嘆氣。

所以他到現在還沒拐成功。

他家未婚妻一點都不溫柔。

但是，他稀罕啊。

這能怎麼辦呢？

只好繼續……有機會就占便宜、有機會就誘拐，爭取早一天，能真正把人拐回家啊！

「別以為你嘆氣、露出失落的表情，我就會同情你、呆呆被你拐。」她瞄他一眼。

「我這是真情流露。」就算是想拐人，也是真情實意的。

她竟然認為他裝可憐？

他捧著胸口，覺得自己的心被傷到了。

跟在兩人身邊的人：「……」他們家的少城主，戲真多。

周遭的人都在偷看他們啦！

少城主想打情罵俏、膩乎乎的，他們能怎麼辦？

好想假裝不認識……

「是嗎？要不要我安慰一下你？」忽視其他人奇怪的眼神，她瞇起眼，亮出武器。

別人在想什麼和她沒關係，她很能忽略的。

「呃……也可以。」被捶一下，他應該、撐得住吧。

「你無聊啊！」她把武器收了回去，沒好氣地又瞪他一眼。

「不無聊。」他笑了，再補一句：「有妳就不無聊。」

「我看你是真的欠揍了。」她沒好氣地回了一句，然後轉頭看了看四周，掩飾一下不自在，努力不臉紅。「沐沐怎麼沒有來？」

「可能，她覺得早來，也是要等。」這兩天他們沒去找沐沐，但是沐沐卻有訪客。

他有點猜到，沐沐的身分……但，先不要告訴她好了。

「她早點來，我們還可以聊一下啊。」她還可以提醒沐沐進了秘境後，要小心什麼呢！

「妳忘了，無非長老罰她的事了嗎？」如果她仔細找一下，會發現，東明玉凌也還沒來。

依照入境順序，這倒數第一和倒數第二，就算準時來都得等，更何況現在，還沒到入境的時間呢！

「也對。」她不找人了，背靠著牆。「沐沐沒來，我好無聊。」

「……」未婚妻滿心滿眼都是別的……女人，這叫身為未婚夫的他情何以堪？

他這會兒很認真思考，有機會要不要和沐沐打一架，她的存在，把他襯托得更沒存在感了呀。

突然，他看到幾個熟悉的人。

「他們果然也來了。」

「誰？」她抬頭看他。

很好，把未婚妻的注意力轉回自己身上，成功。

「他們。」他指了一個方向。

她順著望過去。

「端木風、石昊、姬雲飛、夏侯駒……」數一數七、八個，她嘖嘖出聲。「中州那些傢伙，都來了呀。」

都是熟面孔。

「面熟」之交有，但深交沒有的同輩人。

「中州的情況現在比較穩定了，他們也就有空來了。」說起來，也是中州各家族解決得快，否則陰家的事，未必不會蔓延到東州來。

那就有點可怕了。

雖然不欣賞，但是不得不說，陰月華真的是一個有實力、有手段，也不介意使手段的一族之長。

重點是，她還是個不介意用魅力交友的人，和她有交情的一些人，大家知道的、和不知道的高手，很難說有多少。

這樣的人很難纏，作為敵人，會讓對方不得不提高警惕，免得一不小心就被暗算了。

不過她現在死了，也不知道有多少人會想替她報仇……

想了想，他又笑了，跟自家未婚妻分享一下小道消息：

「據說，他們之中有幾個，是偷溜、離家出走的。」當然，這真的是沒有證實的消息。

就算是真的，那些家族也不會真的往外說呀！

自家優秀子弟離家出走，他們不要面子的嗎？

「為什麼？」她好奇地問。

「可能……跟端木家有關係。」

「端木家?!」她的眼神，立刻鎖定兩個人。

端木風、端木傲。

端木家這一代天賦最好的兩個人。

跟他們有關？

不會吧，這兩個人有那麼大的魅力？

呃……她承認這兩個人的天賦和實力的確很好，但石昊那些人也不差呀，應該不至於因為這兩個人就離家出走……

「是他們的妹妹。」她在想什麼，都寫在臉上了，看得他哭笑不得。

「喔。」她立刻理解地點點頭。

這才對嘛！

這位打死陰月華的猛人，其實不只是他們，她也很有興趣呀！

「你們兩個怎麼在這裡？」匆匆趕回東海城、又匆匆趕來的海宇越，昨天晚上才終於在城門宵禁前入城。

也才得知，秘境竟然提早開啟了?!長歌那個沒義氣的，都沒有給他一點內幕消息……

「唷！」她打了個招呼，「你的動作還算快嘛。」

「差點來不及。」海宇越老實地說，然後想到……這兩個人也是沒義氣的，都沒有通知他秘境的事。

他昨天進城、得了消息、匆匆休息後，就又趕著來集合。到了這裡，還找了一下，才看見這兩個人。

是說，這兩個人，一個是東岩城少城主、一個是東林城少城主，在這種場合躲在角落像什麼話？

「趕上就好，不然你就吃虧了，我們也很吃虧。」他拍了下海宇越的肩，順便指了個方向。

海宇越順著看過去，就看到中州那幾個人。

「他們也來了。」而且來的人數，竟然還挺齊全的。

「所以呀，如果你沒趕上，我們就吃虧了。」東明玉淩不算，就他、華兒，跟長歌。

才三個人，就算東雪城是長歌的地盤也沒用，人數差太多了。

端木風那幾個人的實力，可不輸他們呢！

海宇越算一下人數比，黑線。

「就算加上我，也不夠吧。」

「多一個你，就多一分力量。」他正色道，覺得他們四個人，互相是有那麼點信任度的。

海宇越差點想不優雅地翻白眼。

進了秘境，會不會遇上很難說，就算多一分力量，這一分力量也不一定用得上吧，不過……

「如果入秘境後，找到寒玉，盡量搶到手。」海宇越以魂力形成屏障，阻絕其他人的聽力後，才低聲對兩人說。

「怎麼了？」海宇越嚴肅的語氣，讓林燁和岩華也跟著嚴肅起來。

「海域的狀況……有點不尋常，我父親擔心……『那一位』，可能會出現。」

「真的?!」林燁和岩華表情一肅。

「那一位，已經超過百年沒出現，這次，很有可能。」雖然他沒真正遇過，但身為東海城的少城主，對海域的狀況，那是從小就必須熟記的常識，尤其是那種需要特別警惕的，沒遇過也得記熟，並且十二萬分警戒。

林燁與岩華對看一眼，心情有點沉重。

東海城城主不會說沒把握的話。

這件事，在東州不算是秘密，但隨著時間流逝，可能大部分人不會放在心上，但是五大城的重要人員，都不敢忘記。

「這件事，你告訴長歌了嗎？」林燁問道。

海宇越點點頭。

「嗯，他昨天晚上就知道了。」

比起這兩個人，雪長歌還是比較像「好朋友」一點的。

昨天他一入城，雪長歌就到城門口迎接他，並且幫他安排好住處。

而這兩個人，是根本不管他什麼時候到吧！

真的是誤交損友……

「那這回進秘境，真的得拚運氣、靠實力了呀。」岩華感嘆地道。

「正合妳意吧！」不要以為我沒看到妳躍躍欲試的表情啊。

「遇上寒玉，難道你不搶？」想搶到寶的心情，大家都一樣，你也只是比較會掩飾而已呀。

「華兒說得對。」林燁負責附和。

海宇越看了他一眼。

能不能有點自己的想法，不要老是只會附和自己的未婚妻？

林燁微笑。

就是因為你有這種想法，所以才到現在都沒有未婚妻呀。

海宇越：「……」跟個「未婚妻至上」的人討論這種問題，他絕對是昨天晚上沒睡飽腦袋糊塗了。

但是必須澄清一點，他沒有未婚妻，才不是因為這、種、原、因。

算了，這種事沒必要多爭論，反正他自己明白就行了。

「入秘境後，照舊嗎？」這才是海宇越特地來找他們的重點大事。

「可以。」岩華想了想，點頭。

「我也可以。」華兒都同意了，林燁當然沒有其他意見。

所以照舊，就是入秘境後，落處不定、也不一定會碰到自己人，他們先口頭約定，若是遇上就彼此幫忙一下，也可以作伴同行，絕對不能互相捅刀。

他們三城，除了自己外，各有五個內定名額，既然約好，那當然是互相認識一下，免得認錯人。

「另外，遇上東明城的人，能避則避。」海宇越提醒。

「為什麼？」岩華不平衡。

海宇越丟個眼神給林燁。

你的未婚妻，你自己搞定。

林燁牽著岩華的手，走到一邊邊，低聲說道：

「我們在秘境的時間有限，收穫當然是愈多愈好，在秘境裡跟東明城的人糾纏，太浪費時間了。」

這點距離，阻擋不了海宇越的耳力。

就算林燁小小聲地說，他還是聽到了，並且暗暗佩服。

真不愧是最了解自家未婚妻的男人，連勸人的話都說得很有藝術啊。

如果林燁分析一堆利害關係什麼的，岩華可能還是會聽，但肯定不高興。

但如果這樣說……

「好吧。」果然，岩華就聽進去了，並且沒有不高興。

但是岩華這時候也發現自己的手，被林燁牽握在手裡了。

「喂，你幹嘛？」趁她不注意的時候，占她便宜喔！

「沒有，我只是覺得，我們的悄悄話別讓人聽見比較好，所以才牽妳走遠一點。」林燁面不改色地說道。

「那現在可以放手了吧？」岩華瞇起眼。

膽敢不放，她就揍人。

「當然。」林燁立刻放開手。

逗人要適可而止，他很懂得。

岩華滿意，但發現兩人站太近了。

她立刻跨開一步、眼神一轉，一片雪花就飄落在她臉上，然後，終於看見她等了一早上的人出現了。

「是沐沐！」她才要走過去，眼角同時瞥見一道身影飛掠而來，落在廣場前的城牆上。

「無非長老來了。」林燁向前拉住她，免得她衝出去。

沐沐的位置，在廣場的另一邊，離他們有點遠呢！這時候不適合再穿越中央的空曠區跑過去了。

另外，東明玉凌也來了。

同樣在兩名聖魂師侍衛的陪伴下，額外帶著五名東明城的魂師，出現在與沐沐相隔一片城牆的地方。

在看見沐沐時，她冷冷地瞥了一眼，然後不再理會她。

沐沐也看見哥哥們、岩華等三人，還有……東明玉凌。

總覺得她那一瞥，像在用眼神放狠話——等到了秘境裡，看還有誰能救妳！

根據哥哥們的說法，入秘境後很考驗運氣呀。

她要不要先用祈福法替自己加持一點好運？

無非長老一現身，隱藏在周圍的城衛同時一個個也從暗處現身，各自站在不同的方位，頓時吸引了所有人的注意。

以這些方位的位置來看，完全可以將整個廣場納入察控範圍。

另外，還有四名長老分站在無非長老側後方，神情嚴肅，不發一語。

「巳時到。」無非長老完全沒有多餘的廢話，直接說道：「秘境開啟。」

他一說完，在他身後的四名長老，立刻縱身浮上半空，分立在空中，四人雙手同時結印，身上同時亮起魂師印。

聖魂師！

而且是九階聖魂師！

相當於四名天魂大陸頂階高手同時發力，四道魂力由四個方位，同時射向天際雲層。

淡色的灰白天空之下，厚厚雲層，層層疊疊。

在四道魂力的衝擊之下，雲層開始一層一層散開，首先顯露出的，是一道道細微的閃光——是閃電?!

從稀稀疏疏，變成漸漸匯聚。

在雲層之上，那一道道閃電，濃密聚成虹光般的色彩，拉長成一道圓形的開口。

四名聖魂師手訣再變，以魂力將開口穩定住，然後才收勢稍微退開，保持在有意外發生時，他們隨時可以出手穩住開口的位置。

秘境開口顯現，但整個秘境卻不知道是不是真的藏在厚厚的雲層裡。

無非長老見狀，才開口說道：

「現在開始入境。」

話聲一落，立刻有人直接縱身上天，就飛入開口……

「啊啊……」

一聲慘嚎，第一個衝進去的人，竟然就在開口被閃電繞身，電成黑炭、電成灰。

在廣場上第一次看到這種景象的人，瞬間目瞪口呆。

這個開口有毒……不是，有危險！

這麼危險還能進去嗎？

要撐得過不會電成黑炭，才能入境?!

「這個閃電……」沐沐抬頭研究中。

似乎不是真的，但又真的把人給電成黑炭。

剛才那個人變成黑炭前，全身電流亂竄，是真的。

「那道門，大概可以說是秘境身分辨識的關卡。」跟在她身側的星流低聲說道。

「你怎麼知道？」

「我來過一次。」

對喔！

星流和哥哥們的年紀相差不大，哥哥們來過，星流的確也有可能來過。

不過這麼說來……

「所以你們都來過？」就是他們這一群，在中州很有名的「世家公子們」。

「一半以上都來過。」星流點點頭，「中州和東州看起來似乎很少往來，但其實不是這樣的。家族勢力之間，交情也許不一定有想像中那麼好，但是各家的子弟，是很常出門歷練的，尤其是晉升天階後，多半都會跨州闖蕩一下。」

中州如此，東州這些少城主們，也到中州闖蕩過，只不過大多數都不那麼高調而已。

這也是給各家子弟的一個考驗。

在異州，只靠實力，不靠家族與背景。

在異州，有沒有闖出名號是其次，多見識不同類型的修練者、多見識不同的環境與人事，增加自己的閱歷與應變能力，就是一種成長。

「這個門的事，應該不是秘密吧？」

「不算。」

「那剛才那個人……」

「雖然不是秘密，但也不是每個人都知道，尤其是第一次來東雪城或者第一次入秘境的人，就可能不知道。」畢竟東雪城，也沒有把這個「常識」到處宣揚，就導致這個狀況，大概只有進過秘境的人才知道。

「不過，也有可能他知道，但是想賭一下運氣，或者覺得自己可以靠實力通過那道門。」於是，就衝了。

沐沐無語了下。

而在廣場上，有一半的人對這副景象，一點都不感到驚訝。

在廣場另一頭的岩華更是小小打了個呵欠。

「每次都有這種勇士。」這語氣，真的很敬佩。

東雪城是東州五城裡最不允許有人搗亂的地方，有無非長老在場，可能讓人在他面前偷溜入境嗎？

作夢吧！

喔，不對，已經當鬼去了。

不過這種勇士，好像每次都有，這樣的精神，也是很讓人佩服的了。

這個時候，無非長老才繼續道：

「擁有入境玉牌的人，依序向前。」神色不變、語氣不變，就好像他這句話，是很正常地接著上一句說的。

至於剛才有人偷衝這件事……完全無視。

沐沐：「……」

無非長老，說話大喘氣是會死人的您知道嗎？

啊不過，大概是知道的，因為人已經死了。

因為無非這句話，廣場上開始冒出一陣竊竊討論聲，想混水摸魚偷溜入境的人，這一瞬間的感覺只有——想罵人！

以及後悔。

他們應該早點下手搶一塊玉牌啊！

下一次、下一次一定要記得……但好像記得也沒有用，下一次他們就超過能夠入境的年紀了，根本連爭入境的資格都沒有。

「入境時，請各位把玉牌握在手中。」無非長老竟然很善良地提醒一句。

心塞。

潛台詞就是：如果擁有玉牌，但是卻放在儲物器裡……下場，請參照剛才那個勇敢向前衝的人。

這回大家都聽懂了。

沒聽懂的也看到前面入境中的人的動作，連忙跟隨。

要是好不容易搶到入境資格，結果卻因為沒拿好玉牌被電成灰，那簡直是太冤了。

擁有玉牌者，一個個平安穿過那道被電流覆蓋的開口，直到第五十名也入境後，來自中州的一群人，以及東海城、東岩城、東林城的人，同時縱身飛向天際。

這種隨意騰空的本領，還是很讓地級以下的修練者羨慕的。

而另一方天際，也有另一組人趕來，為首的正是——雪長歌。

看著他們，沐沐將手從斗篷裡伸了出來，揮了揮。

空中竟然好幾個人同時回她一個揮手。

在空中揮手的人，頓時一懵，互相看一看，但沒有說什麼，統一又轉頭飛向秘境開口。

這一群四、五十個人，完全不帶猶豫的，全都衝向開口。

不過幾息時間，四、五十個人已經全數入境；緊接著，則是後五十位玉牌持有者。

廣場上的人依舊非常多，無非長老則看向沐沐與星流兩個人。直接以眼神示意，表示他們兩人可以進去了。

「……」無非長老真是惜言如金啊！

但沐沐和星流也沒耽擱，兩人一同縱身，直接飛向開口，黑色的身影，頓時消失在虹光閃爍的開口裡。

一通過虹光開口，沐沐只覺一陣失重，她正在……往下掉！

# 第十六章　一株跑路的……

被絢爛虹光亮得不得不閉上的眼一睜開，就看見一片白。

其他的，什麼也看不見。

但隨著她往下掉，那片白漸漸變得稀疏，讓她可以稍微看見一點……藍。

天空嗎？

沐沐心念一動，一把飛劍頓時出現在她腳下，緩住了向下掉落的速度，她也終於能看清楚眼前的景物。

晴天，白雲，遠山飄渺。

近處，一棟棟灰色的高樓群，嵌掛著各色招牌與字樣，光鮮亮麗。

一條條筆直的水泥道路，擠滿一輛輛四輪大小房車。

一棵棵默默存在的行道綠樹，點綴著生生不息與清新……

風聲、人聲、煞車聲、鐵道鳴聲。

熙熙攘攘。

車水馬龍。

這種平和與安詳的熟悉氣氛，讓她的神情，有一陣的恍惚。

不知道什麼時候，就落了地，踩在人行道上。

她無意識地舉步，往前走。

身邊經過的人、車，店家的歡迎聲、吆喝聲，與錯落的交談聲。

許多人低著頭，不時在手機上按著什麼，偶爾抬起頭來看一看，腳步不停，來去匆匆。

突然，她手裡握著的東西響了起來。

她一看，手……機？

她下意識按開。

「喂，院長，開會的時間到了，您什麼時候會到實驗室？」

實驗室？

她忽然清醒了下。

實驗室，她記得……已經被她親手炸掉了，怎麼還有？

四周景象突然變化。

天色，霧濛濛。

空氣中，瀰漫著塵土與荒蕪的氣息。

一棟棟高樓大廈，到處是損毀、裂痕，充斥著破敗。

那些筆直的公路、蜿蜒的鐵道，隨處可以看見裂縫、崩塌與斷軌。

整座城市，被厚厚的塵沙覆蓋，即使偶有不完整的車胎印、腳印，看起來也像是破敗已久。

不見人影，不聞車聲。

靜靜默默。

沉寂荒蕪。

曾經的繁華，只留在曾經見識過的人的記憶裡。

現如今，連海市蜃樓的幻影都沒留下。

她緩緩走著。

時而躍過斷裂的地面，穿過一棟又一棟樓廈。

咚，咚，咚，咚。

單調而細微的腳步聲，是這座城市還存在的唯一聲音。

忽然，一陣吉普車的引擎聲，挾帶著因為路面不平的跳動與衝撞聲，霸氣強橫而來。

又猛然停在她身邊，車內的人跳了起來。

「院長，您怎麼在這裡?!」

她不答。

立刻有人下車來，快步伸手要拉她。

「這裡危險，我們立刻送您回去，您的父母親……」

她卻退了一步，眨了下眼。

畫面再度一變。

她看不見。

似乎是因為閉著眼。

但是，卻聽見兩個不同的聲音……

「她，是我的孫女？」

「是的。」

「我兒子……」

「他很好。」頓了頓。「但處境比較不穩定，所以，要我帶她回來，讓她在這裡成長。」

「是嗎……她叫什麼名字？」

「有，單一字：『玖』。端木玖。」

「玖，小玖。」

一聲呼息似的輕淡笑意，她感覺，有人在摸她的臉頰。

她皺了下眉。

觸感粗粗的，不舒服。

「竟然嫌棄爺爺，看來，不是個很乖的小孩。」玩笑似地抱怨。

「……」她只是個小嬰兒，皮膚柔柔嫩嫩的，你手那麼粗，她不躲不嫌棄才怪。

「你要留下嗎？」

「嗯。」

「那麼，小玖就交給你照顧吧。」

「嗯？」

「端木家族……太多人了，她留在我身邊，太過顯眼。我相信……你可以照顧好她。」

因為，他是他的兒子託付的人。

也因為，看似平和的天魂大陸，漸漸變得暗潮洶湧，連他的兒子，似乎都不安分。

「如果有一天，帝都不安全了……我會讓你帶小玖離開，你能保證她的安全吧……」

兩個大人的聲音，像催眠曲，把她給……聽睡了。

當她再度醒過來的時候，就又聽見另一個聲音，年輕、充滿溫暖。

「這就是小玖嗎？」

感覺，她被人換著抱了。

抱她的人有點小心翼翼，但是……不舒服。

她動了動，就察覺有人調整了一下她的姿勢。

嗯，懷抱雖然一樣，但勉強還可以。

「好可愛！」好軟、好小。

乖乖巧巧的，餓了渴了只會「哼哼」幾聲，不會大哭個不停，也不會怎麼哄都哄不聽。

跟其他弟弟妹妹都不一樣。

「妹妹一定很聰明。」

那些小時候特別鬧、特別會吵、又不聽話的弟弟妹妹，長大後也沒有多聰明。

妹妹這麼小，就不吵不鬧，但是餓了渴了還是懂得出聲，特別體貼人，一定也特別聰明。

「萬一她不聰明，還笨笨的呢？」

「那我保護她。」

這樣看來，他還得再加倍認真修練，提升實力，這樣以後才能好好照顧妹妹，當妹妹的靠山……

沐沐——也就是端木玖，忍不住笑了，緩緩睜開眼。

所有剛才看見的繁華都市、破敗遺跡，與交談的人聲，統統消失。

入目的，是布滿白色花朵的翠綠山谷。

舉目望去，像是無邊無際。

花草地的遠處，有地勢略高的山丘，林木扶疏；再遠的盡頭，似有山幢隱隱，又似什麼都沒有。

四周寂靜無人。

應該說，連小腿高都沒有的花草地，也藏不了人。

所以……應該是沒有被埋伏這樣的擔憂了。

只有偶爾襲來的風，吹過矮低花草間，發出的「沙沙」聲響。

她抬頭看著上方。

剛才，她就是不知道從上方的哪個破洞掉下來的吧？

但現在，它是一片蔚藍的天空，什麼破洞的，並沒有，大概是一種往下掉所產生的錯覺。

似假，又似真。

若說剛才的景象是假，但她卻真切觸摸得到手機，聞得見破敗的氣息，感覺得到被抱著的溫暖。

若說是真，所有的景象都不留痕跡，就連現在所見的一切、一開始那種下墜的感覺，都不一定就是真的。

雪長歌送她的令牌，還在她的手上。

她手一握，將令牌收回儲物空間裡。

嗯，總算令牌是真的。

再以魂力感覺了一下。

巫石裡，焱、磊和寶寶，三隻擠在一起玩疊疊樂，而在疊來疊去的同時，寶寶還不忘啃靈石。

然而，焱卻突然抬起頭。

「啾？」玖玖？

她以魂力安撫了一下敏感的焱，才退出巫石。

小玖神思一穩，正要跨出步伐，打算探索一下的時候才發現……

她就站在被花草包圍的近中央位置。

沒有來時踩踏的痕跡、沒有花草間的小徑，簡稱：無路可走。

現在一跨步，就是踩到小花小草，比辣手摧花還殘忍。

因為辣手摧花只是折了花、折了莖，養護一下，大概還是能救回來的。

但這一踩下去，長在地面上的花與莖肯定都沒了，還能不能救回來，就很難說了。

她突然笑了，將魂力散向四周。

掠過草葉、拂過花瓣。

突然一陣風吹來。

「沙……沙……沙……」

咦？

好像，有魂力的波動。

沒有人，也沒有魔獸，難道……

她眼神轉向右邊，感覺，吹起的風好像停頓了一下。

找到了！

她沒有移動，也沒有做什麼，只是將魂力鎖定在右側方大約一丈半的地方，然後，悄悄放出了焱和磊。

焱與她心神相通，帶著磊立刻撲過去。

紅光一閃，焱倏飛過去，焰一般的光影，迅速距離她一丈半的位置，圍成一道火牆。

「哇哇！」

一陣爆炸式的哭聲傳來，嚇了沐沐好大一跳。

一朵不起眼的小白花，好像咻一下，竄進土裡?!

接著，是第二聲爆哭——

「哇哇哇！」

小白花又冒了出來，花瓣折彎了好幾瓣，像撞到什麼東西折到的。

不過花瓣卻沒有掉。

只是整枝花朵搖搖晃晃，像撞到……頭後，在頭暈？花的頭？

花瓣？花心？整朵花？

「哇～哇～哇～」哭聲持續。

所以這宏亮的哭聲，真的是花朵發出的啊。

連花都會發出聲音喔，真的很奇妙。

不過想到焱的「啾」、磊的「喔」、寶寶的「嗚」……嗯，淡定。

緊接著，她就看到這朵花跳了一下，整株連根跳出地面，然後花根像風火輪一樣，捲起來往沒有火的地方飛竄！

「啾啾！」焱立刻繞著花朵飛一圈。

四面八方，都是火。

小花底下的風火輪滾這邊、又滾那邊，一碰到火就又滾回來，四面八方每一處都跑。

小玖就看見一朵花形狀的魔獸在焱圍成的圓圈裡奔過來又跑過去。

簡直像滾來滾去。

最後，牠突然又一跳，就竄入地下了！

小玖挑了挑眉。

牠還滿聰明的嘛。

地面行不通，就往下。

但是牠大概忘記了，這一招牠剛才……

「哇～哇～哇～」

果然，牠立刻又竄出來。

花瓣看起來……又蔫彎了一點兒，可憐兮兮。

眼見四面八方跑不掉，地面下又不知道為什麼硬到牠跑不過去，上面……還有一隻鳥虎視眈眈。

真的跑、跑不掉。

「花生」以來第一次遇到這種情況，小花……只能繼續哭了。

「哇……哇……哇……」

牠一邊大哭，哭聲宏亮，但花瓣，卻微微又捲了捲。

像在偷瞄她的反應。

而花下的根，小小範圍地動來動去，像隨時都要滾成風火輪跑人……不，跑花。

小玖覺得很有趣。

這朵花，有點賊啊！

不過，也有點幼稚。像寶寶……的智商。

不對，寶寶比牠機靈多了。

但牠也比寶寶……有活力。

有活力，等於活動力佳，等於破壞力強。

小玖終於動了，朝小花走了過去。

小花抖了一下，往後退了幾步，又不敢退太多，因為……後面有火啊！

「啾啾！」玖玖，可以燒了牠了嗎？

小花瞬間僵直。

「等一下好了。」她回了一句，就看見小花好像鬆了口氣，連哭聲都小了很多。

難道小花聽得懂焱的話？

不過小花還是很戒備地看著她，看著她……穿過火焰朝自己而來，小花頓時又抖了兩下。

「嗚嗚……哇哇……」小花又哭了。

不同於之前是被嚇到的哭，還有想讓別人放鬆戒備的大哭，這回的哭聲，是真的傷心害怕了。

就在小花哭的時候，牠所站的地方，土面變成石頭了。

小花都驚呆了。

……硬，邦，邦。

牠用根，戳一下、再戳一下。

立刻抖抖地縮了回去。

小玖判斷，這種模樣，大概就像人的腳踢到石頭，痛得縮回去差不多。

當地面石化後，磊冒了出來，坐在小花對面。

小花被嚇到往後一跳……

「哇啊……」又往回跳了一點。

嗚嗚，葉子被火燒到，雖然沒燒壞，但是好痛痛！

「哇哇哇……」小花……流眼淚?!

沐沐瞪大眼，然後面無表情。

因為小花，真的從花心裡，冒了一滴滴白色透明的水滴，落到地面上……變成霧白色的？

水珠會變色？

小玖覺得，自從看見小花後，她的植物世界觀面臨重塑中。

還有，剛才哇哇大哭，卻只有聲音沒有水滴；現在大哭，卻掉了水滴……

所以，剛才的大哭，是假的吧？

磊好奇地伸出手，撿了好幾顆水滴，放在手掌上看了半天沒看出什麼，就拿給沐沐。

「喔喔。」給玖。

「謝謝磊。」小玖接了過來，雖然沒看出什麼，不過這看起來，很像某種東西，只是……外型完全不像。

「小花，你聽得懂我說的話嗎？」小玖問道。

小花看著她，感覺懵懵懂懂。

牠彎著根坐在地上，沒有哭了，但看起來有點沒精神，整朵花都蔫蔫的。

小玖朝牠走近一步，小花縮了一下，但也沒敢逃……實在是逃不了呀！

再一步……牠突然又哭起來。

「哇哇……不、不要燒……」嚶嚶嚶。

「……」本來不覺得怎麼樣，但是小花一哭，又爆出幼兒聲，她感覺自己像在欺負小朋友……不是，是小幼苗。

「那你好好回答我的問題，我就考慮不燒你。」小玖笑著說。

儘管看起來、聽起來，牠就是株無害的小幼苗。

但是她如果真的以為能在秘境裡跑來跑去、還長出靈識變成生靈的花是無害的，那真的太辜負北叔叔和哥哥們那麼認真幫她補「常識」了。

小花抖了抖。

雖然她在笑，但是牠覺得，這個人……很危險！

但是，牠也有點……想親近她。

她、她有火，好可怕；有、有硬硬的，撞到痛痛；有、有香香……

小花主動靠近她一步，迷迷暈暈的，很舒服……

「啾！」一聲。

小花突然嚇醒！

就見剛才紅色的飛飛，停在這個人的肩上，親膩地蹭蹭這個人，但是，兇兇地，看著牠。

小花立刻被嚇退一步。

小玖伸手摸了摸焱，然後感覺到一股崇拜的……「目光」？來自小花。

「……」大概是因為，她敢摸火？

焱的威懾力，果然很足。

「要乖乖回答我的問題嗎？」她再問一次。

「回、回答。」牠怕怕地說道。

想靠近她，又因為焱在而怕怕。

牠那三條根，一隻向前，一隻就向後，一隻在中間搖擺，看得人都替牠糾結。

「你過來一點。」

小花猶猶豫豫。

「啾！」快點！

小花立刻向前，就在她面前，整隻花直挺挺的，正襟危坐。

「……」焱比她有威懾力。

「啾啾。」放心，牠不乖乖回答，我就燒牠。

焱還特別乖巧地蹭了蹭她，一點都不兇神惡煞。

看來，有時候兇一點果然是有必要的。

雖然小花看起來像被惡霸欺負威脅的小可憐，但是她有種直覺，那是在焱面前才這樣。

小花，絕對不弱小。

靠得這麼近，她也才發現，原來小花有三層花瓣。

最外圍、也最明顯的一圈，是白色的，有九瓣；第二層是半透明的粉色，有六瓣；第三層，也是最上面一層，是透明帶著黑，有三瓣。

最中央，則是花芯，呈現半透明狀。

花朵以下，是筆直的花莖，直連至……牠的三條花根，莖上有著三枚葉瓣，全是青翠的綠色。

花朵正對著她，像正看著她，一動也不敢動。

「你是誰？」她問道。

「我，是我呀。」

小玖思考：這是「我，就是我」的意思？

這語言程度，好像比寶寶還難懂。

「這裡是哪裡？」她換一個問題。

「我家。」這個答案特別響亮、特別清楚。

牠真的很認真在回答。

但是，真的很文不對題。

萬萬沒想到，她有一天也會發生問不下去的情況。

這還能怎麼問呢？

小玖覺得自己需要冷靜一下。

拿出茶水和甜點，吃了一口，然後喝茶。

小花很好奇，偷偷伸長根，目標，那杯茶水……沾到了。

嗯，熱熱的，不喜歡。

牠一下子就把根收回去了。

小玖看得有趣，心念一動，換一杯冷的出來。

牠又把根伸過去……冰冰涼涼的，牠喜歡！

牠花影一晃，整朵花都進去了。

冰冰涼涼的感覺，讓蔫了的小花，恢復三成精神。

「……」沐沐一臉深思。

這是杯子裡插著一朵花？

以及，小花很喜歡冰涼的東西，這應該是牠的習性吧。

「喔喔。」磊突然從土裡冒了出來，手裡拿著一塊霧白色的石頭。

方才現身之後，確定小花跑不掉了，磊就鑽入地下，朝牠覺得怪異的方向而去，然後……把手上的東西交給她。

「這是？」

「我的！」小花突然從杯子裡撲出來，結果……

焱擋住了。

「啾啾！」休想搶玖玖的東西！

「哇哇哇！」那是我的！

「啾啾！」磊帶回來，是玖玖的。

「哇哇哇！」我的！「哇……」小花急哭了，又開始掉水滴。

小玖果斷地把石頭往小花的葉子上一塞。

「哇……」哭聲頓停。

小花的三瓣綠葉顫顫巍巍地頂著石頭。

重……

但是很堅持地頂著不放棄。

過了一會兒實在受不了，牠把石頭放在地下，盤著根坐了上去。

小花因為大哭掉水滴而蔫了的精神，開始以眼睛可以辨識的程度快速恢復。

尋根
國際名廚 Nobu 的
真味信念
李昂・韓良憶・初聲怡
著
用信念探尋人間真味，
用料理體現百味人生。

奇特的是，那塊石頭，從被小花坐的位置開始慢慢變得透明。等小花完全恢復時，石頭已經有三分之一從霧白色變成透明了。

「這是……寒玉?!」

# 第十七章　再加一隻

這種特性太明顯了，而且入境之前，哥哥們還特別介紹過這東西，讓小玖沒見過也立刻想到了。

「磊，你在哪裡找到的？」

「喔喔喔。」地下，有很多。

「我、我、我的！」小花結結巴巴地說道，生怕被搶走。

「你的？」

「嗯……嗯！」小花用力點頭，然後又說：「花，我的，這裡，我的。」意思是：這裡的花都是牠的，這片山谷是牠的地盤。

「這裡只有你？」

「嗯。」這個答案，也是沒結巴、沒猶豫。

小玖想了想——

「以前有人進來過嗎？」

「有。」

「那些人呢？」

「吃、吃、吃掉……了。」小花小小聲。

這個答案有點驚悚。

「怎麼吃？」

「他們……作夢，睡、睡著。沒、沒了。」

「你讓他們作夢，然後在夢裡，就醒不過來，你吃的……」想到寒玉的功效，「是人的靈魂？」還是魂力？

「不好吃。」小花的抱怨，也是沒結巴、沒猶豫的。

「……」都吃光光了還嫌棄難吃，小花很能啊！不過……「所以，你剛才也想吃我？」

她看見的景象，說是作夢，也可以說是幻境；魂入幻境不回，身體自然慢慢消亡。

「呃……」小花整朵都往下垂。

「如果我沒醒過來，就會被你吃掉了吧？」小玖笑笑地看著牠。

小花抖了抖。

「妳……妳……很香，想、想近一點，捨、捨不得……」小花有點迷惑，不太會表達。

但是焱只聽出一個意思，怒了。

「啾啾！」竟然想吃玖玖，壞！燒牠！

小玖連忙抱住要飛出去的焱，免得牠放火。

「焱，不氣哦。」

「啾啾！」氣！

一副要脫出小玖的手掌衝出去的樣子。

「哇哇哇！」沒有要吃沒有要吃沒有要吃。

小花咻地躲到寒玉的後面，巴不得整朵花縮成一團剛好被寒玉擋住，驚嚇得花瓣都要抖下來了。

「燚，不氣，牠是想，但是沒有真的要吃我。」

「啾啾！」連想也不可以！要燒！

玖玖是牠罩的，他們好不容易一起活過來，誰敢傷害玖玖，牠一定放火！

因為被小玖拉住，燚捨不得太過掙扎，乾脆朝著小花，一噴火……

「哇哇……」小花躲躲躲，真的蜷成一團，躲在寒玉後。

燚的火……把寒玉都給燒掉一角。

小花驚呆了。

一時不知道到底是少了寒玉比較傷心，還是差點被燒到比較驚嚇。

「沒、沒沒、沒有、吃……不不、不要、燒偶……」嗚嗚嗚。

「啾！」哼！

「燚，好了，別生氣喔，乖～」小玖哄道：「我知道剛才看到的一切，都是假的。」

雖然一開始真的有點恍惚，不過她在落地之前，就知道是假的了。

「啾？」真的？

「嗯。」小玖很肯定地點頭。「因為那裡，沒有燚呀。有我，怎麼可能沒有燚呢？所以一定是假的。」

所以，都是焱的功勞。

而且，幻境中的人還提到她的父母……即使再想念，她也不願意讓幻境繼續下去。

假的，便是假的。

見到了，一時會開心，但更多的，是傷心，和再一次的失去。

所以，她主動地跳開了那個幻境。

不讓幻境主宰自己的情緒。

不沉溺，不貪戀，便不會給別人坑自己、與讓自己掉入陷阱的機會。

「啾啾，啾啾。」小玖的話，讓焱很滿意。

沒錯，有玖玖就有牠；沒有牠，一定是假的。玖玖好聰明！

焱終於不氣了。

牠開始覺得這朵花很笨。

這朵小花要慶幸沒真的動口吃玖玖，否則，牠早就在玖玖有危險的時候飛出來把這朵花燒成花灰了。

想到這裡，焱又哼哼了兩聲，然後轉頭埋進玖玖懷裡。

要抱抱才能消氣。

一看到焱被抱抱了，磊立刻跑過來。

「喔喔！」要抱抱！

不只磊，連被留在巫石空間裡的寶寶都不啃靈晶了，「嗚嗚」個不停。

牠也要抱抱！

「……」甜、甜蜜的負荷。

好吧，都抱抱。

一手撈起磊、一邊讓寶寶出來，三隻一起團抱在懷裡。

被團住的三隻，自己疊成一排。

最靠近玖玖、占據最好位置的是焱，然後磊趴在焱的背上，寶寶又趴在磊的背上，讓玖玖用手臂環起來。

都被抱到了。

三隻小的都不鬧了，很滿足。

看到這一大三小很快樂的樣子，小花悄悄把自己從寒玉後面移了出來，有一種……很想也撲過去的渴望。

「一、一起。想、想一起……」牠小小聲，不太懂怎麼能明白形容出自己的心情。

只知道，牠們三個，疊在一起，好有趣。

牠、牠也想要……一、一起疊……

寶寶突然轉身，跳了下去，前腳一隻抓靈晶、一隻抓著小花，然後又跳回原來的位置，趴在磊的背上。

小花再一次驚呆了。

「啾？」焱眼神不善地盯著小花。

「不、不吃……花、花乖……」牠、牠沒有要吃了，不要、不要燒牠……

小花怕到抖，三條根蜷緊寶寶的一隻前腳。

「喔喔喔。」牠不好，焱不喜歡牠，不要抓著牠。

磊很有同伴情地勸著寶寶。

寶寶望向小玖。

「嗚？」要放掉牠嗎？

「放掉吧。」小玖回道。

「嗚。」寶寶要放開……

「不要、放，不要、放。」根莖都纏著寶寶的前腳。

「……」小玖想撫額。

這句「不要放」，硬是變成「不要」、「放」。

雖然可以猜到小花的意思，但還是覺得……好好笑。

小花都急得又要抖、又要哭，就不要糾正牠的語病了。

「小花，你生長在這裡，很安全，但我們是要離開的，不能一直待在這裡。」小玖耐心地說道。

雖然她到東雪城的時間不長，但也聽說了不少關於入秘境會有的狀況，卻從沒有聽過，寒玉秘境裡有這樣一座山谷。

再加上小花說的，基本上她猜測，過去也有人來過這裡，但都變成……小花的「養分」了。

沒有人活著離開，也就沒有人知道這裡。

以小花目前的智慧來說，這裡對小花來說是個很好的成長之地，也是很安全的地方。

但是她不同。

入秘境有時間限制，她還要和哥哥們、星流會合，不能一直留在這裡。

「想、想一起……和、和你們……」小花聽懂了，有點害羞地說道。

「啾！」焱不高興。

「喔！」磊跟著不高興。

寶寶看著前面兩個，動了動被蜷住的前腳，要和焱、磊行動一致，所以想丟開小花，但是小花蜷緊緊。

「嗚！」丟不掉。

「啾！」燒！

「不要不要不要……」小花怕焱怕得要死，但還是蜷緊緊，對小玖說：「石……都給妳，一、一起走。」

「……」雖然智力像幼兒，但小花也懂得賄賂啊！

小花跳到小玖手上，用根，刺了她的手指一下。

小玖身上的魂師印頓時浮現。

小玖一凜，本來想把魂師印收回，中斷契約，但是她才一停頓，就感覺到小花強烈的意識。

想要……想要……一起……

那是一種像是遇到可以作伴的同伴，不想放棄，不想再自己一朵花孤孤單單的強烈祈願。

於是，小玖放開魂力，就讓契約繼續。

小花也被魂師印包裹住，小花的意念與記憶，自動傳給了小玖。

不一會兒，魂師印消失，主僕契約成立。

小花一掃剛才蔫蔫的模樣，整株花變得精神奕奕，花色鮮潤，傳達很開心的情緒。

其中變化最大的，是牠的第二層花瓣，從透明微微帶粉，變成淺粉色的半透明花瓣了。

接收完小花的記憶，小玖終於知道牠是什麼了。

「幻魂花。」竟然真的有，而且在這裡遇上?!

「啾？」焱不解地看著她。

「母親……」這一世，未曾謀面的，「託北叔叔轉交給我的東西裡，有關於小花的記載。」

藏魂一族的密書寫著：

幻魂花。花瓣三層，天生靈物。

寒礦為育，魂氣為食，萬載千難，蘊靈而生。

寒礦，殷實、清淨魂力之物。冥界獨有。

幻魂花之魂，初生之株，卻能蔓生無數，自成一方，為植獸王者。

無味無息，入人魂識，擅織幻境，幻中為食。

風雷不驚、水火不浸，魂氣所在，魂花所依。

唯，親近一人，懼一人、一物。

但是在密書中，完全沒有記載誰見過幻魂花；親近的人是誰，懼何人、何物，也都沒有細說。

除此之外，小玖也注意到「冥界」兩個字。

這個冥界，不是以前所普知的那個——亡者才能去的世界，普稱地府、地獄之類。

而是另一個種族所居之地。

但是到目前為止，天魂大陸並沒有人提起過。

是她還不到知道的層次，還是這片大陸，並沒有人知道？

「啾啾！」見小玖一臉沉思，焱突然飛過去，踩了小花一下。

「哇哇！」痛痛痛痛！

「焱！」小玖回神，連忙抓住牠，安撫道：「只是一滴血而已，我沒事，你看，連傷口都沒有。」

「啾啾啾！」焱還是很激動。

在焱眼裡，小花就是一隻弱雞。

牠竟然讓一隻弱雞在牠面前傷了玖玖……雖然只有一滴血。

但也是受傷了！

「焱，只是契約，不算受傷。」

依密書裡形容的那段話，幻魂花絕對不是一株和善的花。

她沒有忽略那句「魂氣所在，魂花所依」。

這絕對不是指幻魂花需要依託魂氣為生，而是指有魂氣的地方，幻魂花就無所不在。

要知道，這世界有魂力的，不是只有人啊！

從小花主動傳給她的記憶裡，來到這裡的，不是只有人，還有魔獸。

但無一能活著從這裡離開。

小花對這些入侵者，可是一點都不留情的。

也曾經有實力比較高強的人，與心性比較單純的魔獸從幻境中脫離，但他們都沒有機會見到幻魂花本體，就直接被這滿地的花與草攻擊，默默變成這些花草的養料了。

只能說，「植獸王者」四個字，絕對不只是一句花樣般的漂亮形容，而是實力壓倒性的形容。

她現在也完全了解，為什麼小花會主動契約了。

因為，牠太寂寞了。

從出生開始，牠就是自己一朵花。

就算有人來、有獸來，都很惹牠討厭，還有想搶牠的礦的，簡直是壞蛋中的壞蛋！

不用說，這些人與獸都在幻境裡失去魂力，然後變成山谷的養分了。

小花大部分的時間都在睡覺，只有牠的地盤被什麼闖進來的時候，牠才會醒來教訓人。

有時候不想睡了，牠就在這裡跑來跑去，要這裡的花花們開花給牠看，也很能讓牠開心。

如果一直只有牠一朵花，牠不知道有什麼不好。

但是看到焱、磊和寶寶三隻一起玩、互相支援，牠就……也很想跟著一起玩。

雖然焱很可怕。

但是想一起玩，不想自己單獨一朵花的這種心情，努力壓過害怕。

至少、至少寶寶很和善，主人、主人也很和善。

而且，大家都變成主人的獸了，焱應該就不會燒牠了吧！

小花的想法，就是這麼有點小奸詐的天真。

「啾啾！」不喜歡，玖玖不要跟牠玩！

焱巴住小玖不放。

「但是，牠現在是我們的一分子了，怎麼辦呢？」小玖有點苦惱。

焱幽幽地轉過頭，看著小花。

小花一跳，咚咚咚就滾到寶寶身後，躲。

寶寶啃靈晶的動作一頓，眼睛沒睜開，卻也望著牠。

小花伸長根，把剛才的寒玉拉過，用葉子遞給寶寶。

「送、送給你。」

寶寶嗅嗅。

比較香耶。

抱著靈晶，牠有點猶豫。

焱不喜歡牠。

因為焱不喜歡，所以磊也不喜歡。

但是玖和牠契約了。

嗯……那牠要討厭牠？還是跟牠一起玩？

寶寶覺得，這是牠「獸生」中，第一次遇到的重大困難選擇題。

於是，牠轉向小玖。

「嗚？」可以收嗎？

小玖：「……」

自己覺得選擇有重大困難，於是交給別人選。

很好，很強大。

「嗚嗚？」可以嗎？

看樣子，是很想收了。

小玖只好點點頭。

「可以。」

「嗚嗚！」寶寶開心地撲抱住寒玉，開啃。

但即使啃著寒玉，牠也沒把靈晶丟到一邊，而是好好收著。

不浪費，愛惜食物。

「啾！」焱不開心了。

小玖把焱抱了過來。

「牠沒有真正傷害我們，就原諒牠一次。以後小花不乖的時候，你可以教牠呀。」

「啾啾。」妳不可以太疼牠。

「好。」

「啾啾啾。」要最愛我最疼我，牠們都要排在我後面。

「好。」

「啾–啾。」那，好吧。

「謝謝焱。」親一下。

「啾啾。」嘿嘿。

焱一下子就開心了，飛到小花面前，開始教育——

「啾啾啾啾。」我最大，磊第二，寶寶第三，你第四。

「嗯嗯。」小花——整朵花都在點頭。

「啾啾啾啾。」在玖玖身邊，要聽她的話，以保護玖玖為第一要務。

「好的。」小花，繼續點頭。

「啾啾。」對小玖不好的人，可以吃。

「好。」這一句，小花認真點頭。

「啾啾啾啾。」玖玖永遠是對的，就算決定得不好，也一定是別人不好，都是別人的錯。

「一定是別人的錯。」小花認真附和。

小玖汗。

焱這樣教，不會把小花教歪了嗎？

但是小花這麼認真又毫不遲疑的態度，讓焱覺得，還可以。

「啾！」好了，其他的以後再說。

「好的呀。」小花乖巧地回道，然後一回頭一回頭看著小玖，「我可以把我的家搬走嗎？」

家？

小玖聯想到，當初磊要跟著焱走的時候，搬進巫石空間裡的「家當」。

「如果搬得走，可以。」要一視同仁哪。

小花很高興，立刻透過契約的神魂相連，讓小玖看到自己家的樣子。

「整片山谷都搬？」小玖看完後，默了默，才問道。

小花的家，除了她目前所看見的整片花草地，也包括遠處隱在山嵐後的山峰，以及……

地面下十丈以下的整片寒玉礦。

數量之多、礦埋之深，以小玖的魂力，竟然還無法一次看透。

而且有的寒玉顏色，不只是霧白，而是白得……看不透。

以魂力去看，就是一顆小石子投入深淵，入得了深淵，卻看不清整個深淵有多大、多深。

小玖將魂力收了回來。

寒礦為育。

她看了小花一眼。

小花的本體，也許不是花，而是寒玉？

花，和石頭。

真的是同一個東西嗎？

可惜的是，小花現在才初生期，靈智生成不久——這個「不久」，以人類時間來算可能是很長的時間，但是對小花來說，可能只是一點點時間，讓牠對自己的情況，了解不深。

算了，這個奇幻的、已經打破她不少三觀的世界，有很多秘密，等該知道的時候，就自然會知道了，現在不用急。

現在的問題是，這麼大的家當，她搬得了嗎？

「主人，可以開始搬了嗎？」小花期待地看著她。

「這個……」巫石空間裝得下嗎？

「主人，妳開空間，我自己搬。」

「好。」就試試，搬不進去再說。

小花向前，把葉子搭在小玖手上，一人一花，神魂一念……

「咚！」

地面一陣震動，突然就空了一個大洞！

「啾！」

「喔！」

「嗚！」

「哇……」

一時沒有防備，四隻全部踩空，爆出四聲尖叫！

小玖雙手撈撈抱抱，把四隻統統撈抱到懷裡，然後身影一閃。

一大四小，瞬間消失在原地。

山谷之外。

突然進來兩百個人，寒玉秘境各處都是一陣雞飛狗跳。

有掉火山口的、掉泥坑的，沒掉坑但出現在山林被獸追的、被送到沙漠迷路走不出來的、掉水裡剛好撈到一顆蛋還來不及高興就被追殺的、還有被埋伏被反殺的……

也有幸運地被傳到安全地點，收穫第一項戰利品的。

各種狀況頻繁發生，在入境的第一個地點，就死傷了近五分之一的入境者。

所有脫離危險的人，都立刻離開第一個地點。

療傷的療傷、尋找寶物的尋找寶物，不管前往哪個方向，相遇的狀況都大大減少。

但在秘境十天之後，他們都不約而同聽見一聲大響——

「砰！」

還伴隨著一陣震動。

這陣震動不只是正在趕路的人被震撼到，就連正在不同打鬥中的很多人，都被震得先暫時休戰。

「那個方向是？」

「有這個地方嗎？」

「那裡是哪裡？」

「去看看！」

分散在秘境各處的人，只要不是沒辦法移動、或者正在打鬥的人，不約而同都往震動的方向奔去。

這時，分別由三個不同方向往消失的山谷飛奔的男人們，心裡只有一個念頭——

「會是小玖嗎？」

巫石空間變大了！

原本巫石空間就很大，無論是空間大小與成長性，遠不是天魂大陸所有的儲物器可比。

小玖覺得，即使身為巫石的主人，她都還沒有完全了解巫石空間的由來與用途。

不過現在，她又看到了一部分。

原本巫石裡就闢出的巫族族祠，她自己的居住地，與闢出土地種植她之前收集的樹木、糧種等等，並沒有改變。

改變的，是四周被白霧覆蓋住、無法前往的地方，清晰了一部分。

小花的山谷，就原原本本、完完整整地占據一塊地方了。

即使還有很大部分依然被白霧覆蓋住，但現在所看見的範圍，已經可以媲美一座城池！

一看見山谷，小花歡呼一聲，三條花根瞬間變身風火輪，直接朝山谷滾動著奔去了。

速度之快，差點連焱都沒追上。

由此可見，小花真的是很會「跑路」。

落在後面的小玖，沒有急著去山谷，反而轉身就朝族祠而去，簡單祭拜行禮，又觀察了一下黑大的情況之後，才回到原處。

山谷那邊傳來奔跑和……挖地的聲音，只有寶寶還留在原地。

「你怎麼沒去？」小玖彎身，把正在啃寒玉的寶寶抱了起來，一起朝山谷走去。

寶寶啃寒玉的速度，比啃靈晶慢很多。

該不會消化不良吧？

她摸摸牠的肚子。

嗯，不算鼓，但也沒有扁扁。

因為每天一直啃靈晶，寶寶身上的皮毛，真的是愈來愈光滑柔軟，就連呆呆的臉上，也有了生動的表情。

「等，玖。」寶寶停啃，回道。

小玖側耳傾聽焱的聲音，只聽見哼哼幾聲，沒有小花的哇哇叫聲。

「聽起來，焱應該已經沒有不高興了。」

「嗯嗯。」寶寶點頭。

「寶寶喜歡小花嗎？」小玖沒忘記，最初，就是寶寶去抓住小花的。

「不。」寶寶竟然搖頭。「牠，一個；寶寶，以前，一個。」說得簡短，不過小玖聽懂了。

寶寶雖然沒有開眼，看不見，但是牠對四周生物的情緒，卻有一種特別敏銳的洞察力。

寶寶並沒有特別喜歡小花，牠最喜歡的只有一個——玖玖。

但是小花那時候的強烈情緒，牠感覺到了。因為曾經雷同的心情，才讓牠去抓花。

自己待在蛋裡，覺得自己可能出不了蛋、活不了了的感覺，有多複雜牠不懂，牠只知道，想活著。

玖玖是牠有意識以來，遇到的人和獸之中，唯一沒有對牠喊契約、喊吃的人，而且保護了牠。

雖然和小花那種怕只剩自己一朵花的心情有點不太一樣。

可是牠想活著的強烈度，和小花想要同伴的期待強烈度，是差不多的。

一開始只是想讓小花不孤單一下，才去抓花，後來小花想加入牠們，牠直覺，小花對玖玖是有用的，所以就沒有反對了。

「寶寶開心嗎？」好像養了寶寶後，她最常做的事，就是提供靈晶讓牠啃。

現在看來，靈晶不是寶寶唯一的口糧啊！

寒玉顯然更好。

寒玉不是她的，她即將養不起寶寶了嗎？

「開心。」寶寶不肯寒玉了，直接撲進她懷裡，蹭蹭。

吃東西只是順便，吃什麼寶寶都可以的，跟玖玖在一起才是最重要的。

「啾啾！」本來在追著小花跑的焱，發現玖玖來了，而且還……抱寶寶，牠也要抱！

飛著撲過去！

「啾啾！啾啾！」抱抱！抱抱！

小玖下意識站穩。下一刻……

「喔喔！喔喔！」抱抱！抱抱！

她的小腿被抱住了。

玖玖心想：果然。

有焱飛撲，磊的撲抱還會遠嗎？

一上一下，完全不打架。

幸好她已經很有經驗地提前站穩，不然就要跌倒了。

不過她少算了一個，現在還多了一朵小花。

「抱！」呃……裝飾也可以。

本來小花是想自己跳進主人手上，被主人手握著或抱著都可以，但是……主人抱焱啊！

不能跟焱搶。

所以牠移動移動位置，改跳到主人上臂，把自己偽裝成一枚別針——小花牌點綴黑斗篷的飾品。

耶，大家都一起了。嘿嘿。

小花自己偷著樂。

小玖覺得，如果他們這一大四小的造型換一換，她即將成為一棵聖誕樹。

囧。

但，她還是把這四小給帶在身上了。

焱和磊放肩上，寶寶依舊抱著，小花是自己掛在她斗篷上大約右上臂的位置，徹底把自己當成一朵別針花了。

焱在她肩上開心叫道——

「啾啾啾！」玖玖，有巫石的氣息！

「巫石？」

「啾啾啾啾！」嗯，當時為了護住我們，巫石壞掉了，還沒有完全找回來，但是這裡有巫石的氣息。

小玖記得這件事。

而且來到天魂大陸後，巫石裡的一切也與過去不同。

看得見的，她瞭若指掌。

被白霧覆蓋的，她看不見、也無法走近，無論她朝白霧的方向走了多久，白霧永遠都距離她很遠。

在與黑大契約、收回失落的部分巫石後，巫石空間就改變過一次。

現在，是第二次。

這意思，她很懂。

第一，得把失落的巫石碎片尋回。

第二，要找北叔叔，連帶找的是——親生父母。

第三，小狐狸。

第四……以後如果還有，就是第四了。

把小狐狸排第三，完全是因為……排序純按熟識先後，無其他意義，請勿多作聯想。

總之，未來很長一段時間，大概就是個「找找找」的歲月，有萬里尋叔、萬里尋父母、萬里尋石，還有萬里尋狐。

想到這裡，小玖心中只有無數烏鴉飛過。

啊，啊，啊，啊。

在一個不熟的世界開啟尋人之旅，這是要把世界走透透的意思啊！

無語。

「啾啾？」玖玖不開心嗎？

找回巫石碎片，不好嗎？

「開心。」小玖偏過頭，臉頰摩挲了下焱身上的羽毛。

「啾？」可是玖玖看起來不像開心。

「沒有不開心，只是有點鬱悶。」小玖嘆氣。

「啾？」焱不太懂。

「要找的東西太……不對，是要找的東西和人，太多了呀。」重點是，還都是那種……不知道在哪裡的找。

「啾啾。」玩，找是順便。

焱可看得太開啦！玩，而且是和玖玖在一起玩，那才是重點，找東西找人是順便。

磊立刻附和。

「喔喔。」玩，找是順便。

「……」磊的立場就是——焱的立場就是磊的立場。

這如果是投票表決，得一等於二，真是太占便宜了！

「嗚嗚。」玖在哪裡，就在那裡。

好的，這句話是，小玖在哪裡，寶寶就跟到那裡。

「我我，還有我！」本來想安靜當根別針的小花，連忙也補充說道，生怕說慢一點，牠的新主人和新小伙伴就沒了。

「啾！」哼！

焱還沒忘記之前小花放幻境想傷害玖玖的事。

牠特別記仇。

「一起。」小花瑟縮了一下，小小聲地說。

小玖：「……」

有一種惡霸欺負小可憐的既視感。

「放心，焱，我就是感嘆一下。」無論要不要找什麼東西或人，既然來到這裡，不好好歷練一番，就太可惜了。

「啾。」感覺到玖玖的心情恢復，焱就開心了。

「焱，你在哪裡感覺到巫石的氣息？」小玖問。

「啾啾。」地底。

「地底……寒玉礦？」不要告訴她，她家祖傳巫石，竟然還可以出產這麼高級的礦料。

「啾。」嗯哪。

「那以前怎麼沒有？」

「啾啾。」不知道。

「……」心裡有口槽不知道從哪裡吐起，「所以巫石碎片，成了寒玉礦嗎？」

「啾。」應該不是。

焱想了想。

「啾啾啾。」其實剛才出來的時候，我就覺得，有巫石的氣息。

剛才出來……出巫石空間的時候?!

所以，難道寒玉秘境，融合了巫石碎片嗎?!

不是巫石碎片成了寒玉礦，而是融合了巫石碎片的秘境，衍生出寒玉礦，所以寒玉礦上才有巫石的氣息。

這要怎麼收回啊？

# 第十八章　秘境爭鬥

寒玉秘境的開啟，並沒有讓東雪城變得沉寂。

相反的，在秘境開啟之後，東雪城又湧入了另一波人潮。

這些人，都是為了等待三天後的秘境關閉，期待到時候，能買到或得到寒玉，或者其他從秘境裡帶出來的東西。

根據過去經驗，從秘境裡被帶出來的東西，無論是煉材或是魔獸內丹、毛皮、肉質等等，其對修練的有益度、煉成器後的等級，都比在天魂大陸上獵得的同等煉材或魔獸要高。

因為大批外人的湧入，城衛們一點都不敢放鬆。

這種時候，要是城裡鬧出什麼事，不只鬧事的人要倒楣，他們同樣會因為防衛不當而被懲處倒大楣。

所以，除了被安排守在秘境周圍的人以外，負責守衛城內安全的城衛們，一點都不敢放鬆，對於巡守的日常職務更是加倍認真。

東雪城，城主府。

靜觀寒玉秘境方向的東雪城城主，接到了東海城城主的來訊。

一接通專門用來聯絡的魂器，兩人面對面。

「你看起來很悠閒哪。」

還有空煮水，泡那個……不知道什麼，但是喝起來很好喝的東西，坐姿還是放鬆不防備的，這明顯就是太平安穩、一點緊急事都沒有的模樣，看得東海城城主真是……

羨慕、嫉妒、恨。

「普通。」

「最近秘境開啟，你應該很忙才對呀？」

要說各大城主最不喜歡的事，就是有人來搗亂。

東州各城大部分的時間都是很忙的，要修練、要找資源、要處理城中內務、要應付外來事故……

這種不得已、為了提升實力與大陸安全的事，麻煩一點他們都認了。

但要是無緣無故、逞一時之氣，或者為什麼私人目的，就破壞各城秩序者，各大城主都不會輕易放過的。

「不用。」

有夠簡短的回答。

但是這意思，在通訊器對面的人懂。

有一個足以震懾各方的執法長老，身為城主的人，自然就很輕鬆了。

……東海城城主覺得自己的拳頭有點癢。

「目的。」一眼見主動發訊的某人有點火氣上飆的模樣，東雪城城主提醒道。

拳頭很癢的某人立刻回神。

……不能揍。

除了因為兩人距離很遠，現在根本揍不到人之外，重點是，他也沒有把握能揍到這個閒到讓人氣得牙癢癢的某城主。

這一點他覺得很謎。

每次找東雪城城主，沒有一次他是在修練狀態的，對於城務，更是「城主有事，長老服其勞」這句話貫徹到底。（當然，長老有事誰會服其勞、誰會忙到翻？本城主哪有空注意那麼多！）

總之，東雪城城主在他的印象中，就是一個字：閒。

閒到整年都窩在他那城主府裡，哪兒都不去，能不動彈就不動彈……這真的有一方強者的樣子嗎？

偏偏，論實力，誰也不會小看東雪城城主。

最主要的是，他現在有求於人，不能太囂張。

於是，東海城城主收起一頓腹誹和發癢的拳頭，正色道：

「你那裡，還有寒玉嗎？」

「有。」

「有多少可以賣？」

「兩萬份。」

「這麼少？」他皺眉。

兩萬份，聽似很多，但其實也就夠兩萬個人用，還是一次性的。

這對動輒數萬、數十萬混戰的東海城來說，可以說是杯水車薪，完全不夠用。

「針對性使用，未必不夠用。」東雪城城主自然知道東海城城主為什麼要寒玉，所以也沒有小氣。

兩萬份，是東雪城儲藏中能拿出來的最大分量。

寒玉秘境雖然十年一開，不算久，但每次能入境的人並不算多，能回收的寒玉也不算多，再加上礦是需要有時間累積醞釀的，就算上百年，都不一定能成長出一份寒玉礦。

這也是寒玉秘境中，寒玉被找到的量愈來愈少的主要原因。

「如果『他』真的出來，準備再多，都不一定夠用。」只能盡量準備。

「除了寒玉，應該也有能抗靈魂攻擊的魂器。」東雪城城主友善地提供另一個方向。

「……」東海城城主的表情，一言難盡？

「怎麼？」難道東明城城主不賣嗎？

不應該呀。

這種能刷好名聲的機會，東明城城主再不願意也不會明著拒絕吧，那是明顯給別人黑自己名聲的把柄。

精明的東明城城主，不可能做這種事。

東海城城主的表情更加……一言難盡了。

「……買不起。」

東明城城主是這麼說的：

「實在不是本城不願意支援，而是因為這類魂器的成本太高，就算是東明城，也承擔不起四、五星級以上魂器大量消耗……」

說到這裡，東明城城主語氣一轉：

「但是，東海城的安全，關乎整個天魂大陸的安全，如今需要支援，東明城也義不容辭。這樣吧，只要貴城能提供煉材，或是足夠的報酬，本城一定召集煉器師，全力為東海城煉器，支援東海城所需。」

轉述完，東海城城主還在通訊器前，拿出東明城開出的「煉材需求及報酬」，攤開給東雪城城主看。

聽完，東雪城城主也：「……」然後輕聲笑了。

「你還笑得出來？」東海城城主皺眉。

「這的確像是東明城城主會說的話。」占著大義、說著委屈、拿著實際的好處，名聲有了、利也有了、別人的感激也有了，一舉好幾得。

是沒錯。

那又怎樣？

代表說這話的人是東明城城主無誤，不是被人假冒的嗎？

老子並不在乎東明城城主有沒有被假冒。

只要他能提供足夠的魂器並且不要獅子大開口，就算他是假的老子也認他是真的。

然而，這是作夢。

事實是，人是真的，要的報酬也是真的，這種報價，簡直是要本城主傾家蕩產！

不對，是「傾城」蕩產！

「也許，人家就是這種打算呢。」東雪城城主的話，別有深意。

「什麼意思？」東海城城主眉眼一橫。

東雪城城主不答，自己想像。

東海城城主臉黑了。

「他這是……不想藏了吧？」

「大概吧。」東雪城城主漫不經心地回道：「你知道，人在悲傷中，總會做出一些失去理智或瘋狂的事，想讓人也體會一下悲傷或者瘋狂的感覺。」

東海城城主先是想了一下，然後直眼瞪著他。

「你、你……」

「嗯？」東雪城城主特優雅地回了一個疑問音。

你這句話，翻成現況，白話就是：

你知道，一個男人在死了老婆之後，總是會做出讓別人也死老婆的事，讓別人跟他一樣也沒有老婆。

東海城城主覺得胃疼。

「這麼形容他，不怕他找你算帳嗎？」

「他可以來。再者，你要告訴他嗎？」

「……」這天沒法聊了。

但還是得聊下去。

「東明城那邊先不論，兩萬份，你幫我準備好吧。」

「可以。」

「謝了。」目的達成，東海城城主這才掐斷通訊。

東雪城城主看向窗外，秘境所在的方向。

秘境藏在厚厚的雲層裡，除了依然虹光閃動的入口，再看不見其他。別人的視線，會被雲層擋住，他卻不會。

心念一動，他的眼睛驀然變了顏色。

厚厚的雲層在他眼裡，宛若不存在，只留下懸浮於空中、宛如空島般的寒玉秘境。

秘境開啟到現在，已經過了一天半，除了半天前秘境有過一陣晃動，差點把守著秘境的城衛嚇個半死，以為秘境要掉下來，一個個準備逃命和叫救命之後，就再沒動靜。

這應該是秘境有哪個地方被搬空，結果引起空間動盪，才引發的震動吧？是誰這麼有能耐呢……

◈

巫石收回什麼的，暫時沒什麼好想法，就先放著吧！

小玖的心態很平穩，不急。

她沒忘記，她還在秘境裡呢！

把燚、磊和寶寶留在巫石空間裡，小玖一出來，整個人又往下掉！

這次小玖可沒有享受什麼失重感了，放出「流影」，直接馭劍停在半空。

不過這個「半空」的高度，實際上是之前的地面，也是她進入巫石空間前停留的地方。

小花的家一搬，不但直接搬空整座山谷，連地面下都不放過，直接挖空逾千丈。

地面這麼突然被搬空，從花草滿地的山谷，變成宛如地坑般的地形，一點都不奇怪，不過……

位置相同，景況卻大不相同。

小玖看著地面，表情陷入思考。

地坑，應該是很完整的吧？

為什麼現在她看見的，是一片的坑坑巴巴，還有各種風吹火焚、被什麼硬物刺過砍過刨過的痕跡？

空氣中，還有未散盡的血腥味，不濃，像是留存有一段時間了，但現場沒有任何人傷亡的蹤跡。

她感覺，如果不是因為整個山谷都搬空，讓這裡留下幾百里的空曠地，現在絕對不會只有地面坑坑巴巴而已。

小玖駕著劍，緩緩往下，觀察四周的同時，漸漸降到最底的地方。

打鬥痕跡很亂，像是什麼招都有，遍布四周。

四周還留下的腳步痕跡也很亂，有點辨不清方向；也有可能，是散亂的腳步痕跡四面八方都有。

小玖想起小花收起山谷時，發出的聲響……大概是，那一聲吸引了很多人來，結果不知怎麼著就打得亂七八糟。

寸草不留，塵土凌亂，難以判斷方向。

「小花，你可以判斷，往哪裡去的人最多嗎？」小玖問道。

繞在小玖右上臂，偽裝別針的小花從斗篷裡探出頭，像是吸了一口氣，然後指了一個方向。

「那裡。」

「為什麼？」小玖好奇地問。

「味道最雜、最不好聞。」小花嫌棄地回道。

這種判斷方式，也是很強大。

「好啦，謝謝小花。」小玖一笑，摸摸牠的花瓣。

小花嘻嘻一笑，然後縮回去了。

小玖將帽兜蓋好，駕著流影，就往小花所指的方向飛去。

◈

十天前，秘境突來的地震，幾乎吸引了半數以上入境的人聚集，然後以東明城和東岩城、東林城，三城少城主為首，分成兩方陣營，爆發一場混戰，還波及到中立的第三方。

那些沒有選擇立場，身後又沒有強大勢力庇護的人，一律被當成是東明城的敵人，不是被打得投降，就是在逃中。

山林裡，兩道人影互相攙扶著往深山裡跑。

其中一名女子明顯受傷較重，另一名身穿黃色戰鎧的男子在逃的同時，也邊想辦法模糊形跡，但絲毫不敢放緩速度。

「東明城……是瘋了嗎？」

其實她更想說的是：是東明玉凌瘋了嗎?!

「大概不是瘋，是不想忍了。」他保持理智地回道。

「在這裡發瘋，對……她，有什麼、好處?!」傷口的疼痛，讓她連話都沒辦法一口氣說完。

好處很多。

最大的好處，大概就是可以一次解決他們這些不跟她站在同一邊的人。

至於壞處……那是離開秘境之後的事。人家秘境外的靠山很硬，不怕被找麻煩……

但是不能這樣回，不然她還不得原地爆炸。

而且，他也有些想不通。

如果說要解決掉他們這些妨礙的人，像他這樣以傭兵為職的人或許還沒什麼，但是東明城主要的目標，分明是放在其他四城上……雖然現身的只有東林城和東岩城兩城的人。

四城少主並不是那麼好對付的，東明玉淩為什麼還拉攏那麼多人，對他們緊追不放？

「把東西搶到手，就是她的好處。」有可能是這樣。

儘管心裡很疑惑、不安感很濃，但是表面上，黃鎧男子還是以很鎮定的語氣對她說道。

「呵！」女子的笑聲非常有諷刺意味。

即使表達不滿、傷況嚴重，也沒有耽誤她的速度。

逃命啊。

就是只要還有「命」，就得拚命「逃」。

只要想活命，就得豁出命。

可惜兩人再怎麼逃、再怎麼快，還是快不過天生就是山林裡速度王者的……

魔獸?!

「喵吼。」

兩人一驚。

是魔豹獸！

獸階不高，卻擅長追蹤。

隨即，一道修長的獸影從後方輕跳，就躍到兩人面前，擋住去路。

「喵吼！」

叫聲很萌。

身形也不是很有威懾力。

但是，牠仍然是不折不扣的魔獸，對敵時不能掉以輕心！

兩人隨即往轉回頭。

後方來人已經追到他們身後。

魔豹獸不可怕。

可怕的是牠偵察與追蹤的速度，讓他們在山林裡無論做多少隱藏，都很容易被找到。

追來的兩人面容與穿著都有些相似，個子相差一點點，分站兩邊，與魔豹獸形成三方合圍。

「兩位，束手就擒吧！」個子較高的那人說道。

這樣一直跑，他們得一直追，實在相當浪費時間，完全沒有意義。又逃不掉，何必浪費力氣？

「作夢！」廢話不多說，她身上魂師印一閃，暗灰色鎧甲鎧化上身，她出拳就攻向說話的人。

「柔柔冷靜……」黃鎧男子阻止不及，卻沒遲疑地立刻攻擊另一個人。

被忘記在後方的魔豹獸觀察兩方戰鬥後，突然撲向左邊！

「柔柔！」黃鎧男子立刻轉身，朝魔豹獸轟出一拳。

魔豹獸敏捷地跳開。

同一時間，一記閃光擊向黃鎧男子，黃鎧男子閃避不及，瞬間被打傷。

「呃！」

「猴子……啊！」一分心，女子也受了傷。

兩人都再度負傷，退了好幾步後靠在一起，擦去唇角的血跡後，喘息著背靠背。

黃鎧男子心裡著急，但臉色一點變化也沒有。

這兩個人的魂階比他和柔柔高，他們本就幾乎沒有勝算，再加上魔豹獸的追蹤天賦，想逃走，又是難上加難。

「喵吼！」魔豹獸一樣守在他們後方，斷絕他們想直接逃跑的去路。

而那兩個人，緩緩靠近他們。

「猴子……」她低聲喚道。

他握了一下她的手。

他了解她的個性。

她不會投降。他也不會。

她眼神一定！

「真是浪費我們的……」個子較矮的那追兵才以嫌棄的語氣開口，猴子與柔柔兩人立刻出手。

「風拳！」

「大地……震！」

兩招合擊，直接朝那兩人攻擊。

放完招，也不管有沒有擊中，兩人毫不遲疑轉身：

「走！」

「喵吼！」魔豹獸立刻跳過來。

猴子立刻再轟出一拳。

「喵吼！」魔豹獸靈巧地避開，並且立刻朝猴子撲去！

猴子立刻推開在他身側的柔柔，雙手交叉在身前形成一道氣牆，擋下魔豹獸；魔豹獸再撲！

「猴子！」

「快走！」

「不行！」她不會拋下他。

「你們兩個，都別想走！」

擋下合擊之招，兩人立刻再追過來，一個攔住一個。

「你們兩個誰都跑不了。」

被反擊的兩人惱羞成怒，下手再沒留情，拿出弩型魂器，一人對準一個……

「轟天一擊！」

「雷霆之怒！」

魔豹獸瞅準時機跳開，兩道光束自魂器口爆射而出，擊向兩人。

猴子與柔柔見狀，果斷應變。

「鎧化！」不管反擊、也不留餘裕，全部魂力，都加乘化為最強防禦……但是魂器發出的攻擊威力更大。

「唔！」

「呃！」

光束擊破兩人的防禦，直中兩人；兩人再度被擊飛後落地，重傷到一時間站不起來。

「柔柔……」顧不得自己的傷勢，男子摔落地後，只看向身邊的人。

「猴……子……」她咬著唇，忍著痛，一時之間卻動不了。

「真是自找苦吃。」一擊得中，追來的兩人手中的魂器依然對準他們，一步步接近。

「真可惜，你們的命得留在這裡。下輩子投胎的時候，千萬記得，不要得罪小姐。」個子較高的那個人笑著說道。

「不要廢話，動手。」另一人卻覺得，囉嗦容易出狀況，快快解決這邊，取了東西，他們才能回去覆命。

「嗯。」

想到任務獎勵，兩人舉起魂器，輸入魂力，再度發出一擊……

猴子立刻擋在柔柔面前，以僅剩的魂力反擊。

只見魂器發出的光束輕而易舉擊散猴子發出的反擊，直擊而來，猴子轉身抱住柔柔……

明知道擋不住，他還是以身護住她。

「猴子……」無法動彈的柔柔，一瞬間只想到，如果以前她就不和他吵，該有多好……

就在兩人閉眼等待最後一刻時，一道劍光從左側疾閃而來，擋下光束。

「轟！」

一聲轟炸，餘波爆向四周。

「唔……」猴子抱著柔柔，被轟炸的餘波衝著滾了好幾圈。

雖然被餘波砸到很痛，滾地也滾出擦挫傷，但這點痛，跟真被魂器發出的光束打中的傷比起來，根本不算是傷。

他們，被救了?!

一穩住自己，猴子立刻張開眼，轉身坐起的同時，仍然將柔柔護在身後，但是一看到來人，他呆了。

「猴子大哥、溫副團長，好……巧啊！」

# 第十九章 救人是一項體力活兒

只見來人依然一身黑色斗篷，只露出一張白皙漂亮，又特別年輕的臉龐。很熟的臉。

猴子何止是呆，他是瞪著眼，結巴：

「妳、妳……」沐沐！

溫柔柔也看向來人，同時，一眼就認出來。

「是妳……」沐沐！

但下一秒，猴子和溫柔柔都變了臉色。

「妳快走！」

「呃？」一來就被趕？

「快走！」猴子對她使眼色。

他和柔柔就算逃不過，也不能連累她。

「沐沐」轉頭看著還舉著魂器的兩人，以及……那隻魔豹獸。

在她的眼神轉向魔豹獸的時候，魔豹獸疑似抖了幾抖。

「妳是誰？」個子較矮的男人謹慎地問道。

「他們是東明城派來的人，要追殺所有不聽從東明城的人。」眼看她不肯走，猴子也以最簡短的話告訴她現在的情況。

「沐沐」疑惑地看著他們。

「在秘境裡還可以這樣做？」組團追殺？

而且，東明城有進來很多人嗎？

她記得每個城進來的人，都是有限定人數的。

「廢話少問，妳是誰？妳想與東明城為敵嗎？」個子較高的男人顯然沒耐性好好說，直接詰問道。

「才沒有、才不是、你別亂說。」「沐沐」瞪大眼，立刻否認三連發，語氣就是「我是無辜的你不要誣賴我」的那種。

猴子、柔柔：「……」這否認聽起來並不是很有誠意，但是他們不說。

這語氣，有充分表現出不與東明城為敵的態度，那兩個男人聽得還算滿意。

「那就讓開，還有，要宣誓效忠東明玉凌小姐。」個子較高的男人說道。

「……」她覺得，東明城的人腦子似乎不太好。

她看了猴子大哥和溫副團長一眼，發現兩人臉上的表情，是有一半呆滯、一半的一言難盡。大概內心的想法和她一樣。

她可能得把話講得明白點兒。

「宣誓效忠東明玉凌……」她看向那兩人，臉上忽然微笑，「那是不可能的。」

然後就看到，那兩個男人臉上微笑的表情一變。

「妳要我們！」

「沒有啊。」她超無辜。

「不肯效忠東明玉凌小姐，就是與東明城為敵！」

「……」這作風，有種熟悉感。

順我者昌，逆我者亡。

跟某個女人真的有點像……啊，現在做這種事的主使者，也是一個女人。

「沐沐，妳快走！」幾句話的時間，足夠讓猴子恢復一點氣力，與柔柔相互扶著站起來，重新站到沐沐身邊，想把她擋在身後。

身為傭兵，沒有讓同伴替自己面對危險，甚至喪命的怕事，只有危險自己承擔的覺悟。

「他們想要寒玉、想要我們效忠東明玉凌，否則只能死。」柔柔恨恨地說。

「這麼囂張？」「沐沐」驚訝，「其他城……都沒有意見嗎？」

雖然秘境探寶，各安天命。

要是在秘境裡沒了命，出了秘境其他人也不能隨意追究——這算是大家公認的通則。

不過這種通則在某些人眼裡，是屬於「別人要遵守，我例外」的那種。

像五大城少城主這樣身分的人進了秘境，基本上會被傷、被設陷阱，但應該沒人敢殺。

東明玉凌這麼做，難道是看準其他人……都不如東明城實力雄厚，所以殺了不會被找麻煩？

不對，是就算被找麻煩、秋後算帳之類的，她也不怕?!

原來在這裡，也是沒背景，沒人權啊……

被「沐沐」以同情的眼光掃了一眼，猴子福至心靈，像是懂了她在想什麼，頓時有點憋屈。

「我們是傭兵公會的代表。」雖然有點走後門，但他和柔柔也是通過公會篩選後能入秘境的人。

只不過公會選人的標準不單純看實力，還看應變力與其他綜合能力。

雖然此時此刻，應變力再好也沒能派上用場。

剛才能逃過一劫，要歸功於……他們運氣不錯。

等等，現在不是解釋這個的時候！

「總之，他們兩人手上的魂器很厲害，妳快走！」猴子回過神來，再度催促道。

「是嗎？」「沐沐」回過頭，眼神看著那兩把魂器。

根據剛才的那攻擊判斷，這是兩把像弓弩般外型的武器，配上宛如小型炸彈般的攻擊強度。

「那是東明城煉製出來的魂器？」她問猴子。

「對。」而且是四星魂器中，最有名的「閃雷弓」。

「那好。」「沐沐」轉向那兩人，「我沒有想與東明城為敵，不過東明城也不要找我的麻煩，現在，你們立刻離開，你們好、我好、大家都好。」給他們一次選擇的機會。

那兩人簡直氣笑了。

這絕對是他們倆加入東明城後，第一次遇到有敢在他們兄弟面前這麼放話的人。

個子較矮的那個瞬間魂力入閃雷弓：

「不服從者，死……！」

話聲一落，一道閃雷般的光束，風馳電閃地轟向「沐沐」。

猴子和柔柔的心一繃！

「沐沐」卻半步也沒有移動，心念微轉間，隱在身側的流影劍旋轉到她身前，完全擋下光束。

「轟……」

只爆了一聲。很響，但很短。

然後，就無聲了。

光束完全被消弭，連轟炸的威力都消失。

猴子和柔柔簡直不敢相信，剛才把他們兩人轟到只剩一口氣的閃雷攻擊，這樣就不見了?!

有點恍恍惚惚。

難道是他們真的太弱了?!

恍惚到懷疑人生的不只是猴子和柔柔，連那兩兄弟都是！

他們眼花了吧！

不然就是閃雷弓故障了！

再不然就是他們魂力配合得不好，沒讓閃雷弓發揮出原來的威力！

「沐沐」伸手握住劍柄，手腕微轉，長劍一揮。

剛才為了救人太匆促了，並沒有完全擋下光束。

還有餘波，就表示力量比她想像中大；這次就剛好。

完全消弭閃雷弓的攻擊，不留一點餘波。

「這就是閃雷弓的威力？」這是東明城所製，四星魂器的威力。

她的劍，好好的，完全沒受影響。

「不可能！」個子較高的那個，同樣閃雷弓一擊。

「轟……」

「沐沐」信手一揮，劍勢直接揮散了閃雷弓發出的光束。

個子較矮的那個男人見狀，悄悄看了魔豹獸一眼。

魔豹獸站起來，四隻腳動了動，後半身微微下壓有要撲過去的態勢，但「沐沐」在握劍間，頭上紅色髮飾微閃，魔豹獸立刻趴下來，一動也不動。

如果仔細看，還會發現，魔豹獸不時顫抖一下、顫抖一下。

沒想到魔豹獸竟然沒有服從命令，個子較矮的男人皺起眉，再度看向魔豹獸，身上魂師印湧現。

魔豹獸又站了起來，但是沒有服從攻擊的命令，反而頭朝天空，叫了一聲：

「喵吼……！」

既委屈，又害怕。

「沐沐」轉頭看了牠一眼。

魔豹獸立刻趴下，任憑主人怎麼命令，牠就是不動。

這情形看得個子較矮的男人簡直氣炸。

「迅豹！」

魔豹獸看了主人一眼，轉頭就想跑，但隨即……

「喵吼……」

這次不是裝威武的可愛吼音，而是含著痛苦的吼叫，並且在吼叫聲中，魔豹獸前腳像掩住耳朵似地蓋在頭上，整隻豹蜷縮在地。

「這是？」

「被契約的魔獸不聽主人的命令，因為與契約相違背，所以牠很痛苦。」猴子一看就知道原因，同時也覺得疑惑。

被簽下主僕契約的魔獸，是不能違背主人命令的。以前，也從來沒有聽過契約魔獸會不聽主人的命令。

除非是遇到血脈等級比牠高的魔獸……但那也只是讓魔獸害怕而影響實力，卻不會讓魔獸不聽命令才對。

現在這又是什麼狀況？

現場沒有其他魔獸，沒有獸壓制獸呀！

總不會是契約過程中出現什麼問題，導致魔獸不聽話吧？

還是這個契約主平常做主人太失敗，虐待魔獸，導致魔獸不想聽他的？

猴子懷疑的眼神，就朝那個人掃過去了。

「迅豹！」男人又叫了一聲，語氣充滿不悅。

「喵吼……」魔豹獸的叫聲依然充滿痛苦與抗拒。

不一會兒，魔豹獸的耳朵，竟然開始流血了。

猴子和柔柔頓時驚愕住。

魔豹獸的主人則是臉色都變了，撤回魂力不敢再強下命令。

要契約魔獸不難，但要活捉魔獸契約卻並不容易，等級愈高的魔獸，愈不會輕易臣服，所以即使是天階以下的魔獸，仍然有大批魂師爭搶著要契約。

魔豹獸雖然等級不高，卻是一隻有著特殊天賦的魔獸，他一點都不想就這麼失去。

他一撤回命令，魔豹獸雖然還在流血，但表情明顯不痛苦了，就趴在原地不動。

男人臉色不善地轉向「沐沐」。

他從來沒有遇過這種情況，就連他的哥哥，也被這種情況嚇了一跳。他同時意識到，他們兄弟兩人，可能攔不住這個……少女。

「妳是誰？妳對我的魔獸做了什麼？」

「我做了什麼？」她才覺得莫名其妙。

「不是妳，我的迅豹怎麼會變那樣？」他心痛地看著還縮趴在地上的魔豹獸。

沒看過魔獸會抖怕成這樣的。

他的迅豹雖然不是攻擊特別厲害的魔獸，好歹也是威風凜凜、氣勢昂昂的，哪裡有過這樣像隻小奶貓的弱小樣？

在場的人，只有她最不熟根底，也是她出現後，迅豹才出現這種奇怪的模樣。

不是她，還能是誰？

「我連碰都沒碰到牠，能對牠做什麼？」她反問。

「就是妳！」不聽任何辯解。

「沐沐」看著他，覺得這人大概歇斯底里了。

這種情況下，是沒什麼道理可說的，於是她直接轉向那個個子高一點的男人。

「這是你弟弟吧，你不管他一下的嗎？」純粹用相似的五官和個子來判斷誰兄誰弟。

「我弟弟說錯了嗎？」恰巧他們兄弟倆，真的是兄長高一點，所以哥哥就反問了。

不管弟弟有沒有說錯，做哥哥的都要站弟弟這邊。

「他說錯了，他誣賴我。」她一臉嚴肅。

「我弟弟沒有說錯，就算有誣賴妳……我們是敵人，誣賴妳不是很正常的嗎？」敵人都是錯的。

「沐沐」吃驚地轉向猴子和溫副團長。

「這樣胡說八道……是可以的嗎？」她感覺自己的是非觀和做人的底線受到衝擊了。

因為是敵人，所以用什麼手段、怎麼誣賴都可以？

被「沐沐」這麼年輕純真的眼神一看，猴子本來見怪不怪的老傭兵心態立刻一整，某種使命感上身……

不能教壞年輕的小幼苗。

傭兵有傭兵的，簡單直接的生存之道。

「這個，沐沐啊，人有很多種，有特別好的人，也有特別小人的人。特別好的人容易養虎為患，特別小人的人時時都想捅我們一刀，這兩種我們都不要學，只要記住一點，對我們不好的，打回去就好了。」不管對方想誣賴還是想幹嘛，是敵人，揍扁他就對了。

沐沐：「……」

容她為以後猴子大哥的小孩的教育……憂慮一下。

在他身邊的溫柔柔聽到他的話，忍不住捏住他的腰肉，一扭。

痛痛痛痛痛……

猴子差點叫出來，幸好及時忍住。

不然就太丟臉了！

但溫柔柔一記眼刀子橫過去。

你想把人家乖乖巧巧的小女生，教育成一個暴力女嗎?!

我、我哪有？

他這、這不是實話實說嗎？他們一向都這樣的啊！總不能教小沐沐要寬宏大量吧？

那小沐沐還不得被這兩兄弟給吞了。

再說，本來這兩兄弟就欠揍！

別忘了這兩兄弟一路追他們、把他們打成重傷，只差一點點，柔柔就要死了。

這他怎麼能忍?!

柔柔的神情有一瞬間不自在。

看懂猴子的意思，她扭他腰肉的手，就不自覺放鬆了。

「那、那也不能教壞小女生……」

她……看起來嬌滴滴的，像是世家貴族教養出來的千金，跟她這樣風裡來、水裡去的女傭兵，截然不同。

溫柔柔並不以自己的生活方式為苦，也不會嫉妒別人的出身好。

雖然她平常行事霸道又直接，她卻不是個嫉妒心強，又沒事就找別人麻煩的那種人。

相反的，對於像沐沐這樣一看起來就生活得很好、無憂無慮、出門又有隨從保護的小女生，她會欣賞，會希望她維持這樣的面貌久一點。

美好，是不應該被破壞的。

「柔柔，妳……不要把沐沐想得太純良。」猴子有點艱難地說。

他對柔柔的了解不是一天、兩天，也知道她現在會怎麼想，但是，一個身邊只有一個隨從、敢跑來東州闖蕩、又敢在傭兵營地面不改色看他們打架、還敢跟東明城少城主單挑的小女生，真的沒那麼膽小。

雖然看沐沐的外表，很容易把她當成是單純不解世事、需要人保護的小女生——他也差一點點想偏。

但是回想一下遇到沐沐後，短短兩天她所做出來的事……人真的不能貌相。

要時時保持警惕和清醒，才不會誤判，把小老虎當成小貓咪。

瞬間，猴子不內疚了。

可惜溫柔柔不能體會他內心的糾結。

「她比我們純良。」溫柔柔也想到那天搶營地的事了，不過沒像猴子一樣想很多。

猴子：「……」

好、好吧，柔柔高興就好。

這樣的柔柔，也是很單純的，要好好保護。

「你們，真敢無視我們兄弟啊！」魔豹獸出問題，他們兩兄弟也沒有急著動手，就讓他們聊。

「我這是體諒你們需要時間呢！」「沐沐」笑咪咪的，然後問猴子：「你們恢復得怎麼樣？」

猴子一聽就懂。

但是溫柔柔先搶答了：

「再和他們打一場沒問題。」

身為天魂師，即使受重傷，恢復起來也是很快的。

即使還沒辦法發揮十成的戰力，但六、七成可以了，絕對不會成為拖累。

「那就準備一下吧。」

「準備什……」猴子才開口要問，就見遠方天空，好幾道人影飛閃而來。

那兩兄弟笑了。

好的，這下不必問，猴子也懂了。

「猴子。」溫柔柔的神情瞬間緊繃。

從不同方向而來的六、七道人影，眨眼間來到眼前。

「明二甲、明二乙，你們兩個在拖什麼？」其中一人看了現場狀況後，皺著眉開口問道。

不過就是多了一個小女娃，值得他們倆發訊請求支援？

「你們兩個這種速度，不行啊……」另一人也笑著說道。

這兩個人的實力還不如他們呢！這麼久竟然還沒搞定，還得發求援傳訊，以後可別再說他們兄弟聯手有多強多不敗的話了。

明二甲聽了臉有點黑，瞬間就想出口反駁，但卻被明二乙拉住，還聽見他面不改色地說：

「二對二，我們兄弟倆沒問題，多出來的一個交給你們。」

「真的沒問題嗎？」懷疑。

「沒問題。」肯定。

他們是請求支援，也沒想到一次會來你們這麼多人呀。

收到求援傳訊而來支援的七個人臉有點黑。

叫他們七個大男人去對付一個看起來就沒成年的小女娃，這是看不起他們，還是太看得起這小女娃？

偏偏，明二乙還一本正經地補了一句：

「一切以完成任務為優先。」手段不論。

別忘了大小姐說的話。

「哼！」來支援的人暫時不說話了，轉身手臂一震，一柄長刀出現在他手裡，飛身就朝「沐沐」攻擊。

沒能好好把那兩兄弟取笑一頓，那就搶點功勞，這股火氣，就發洩在敵人身上了。

「沐沐」橫劍一擋的同時，身形飄開數十丈的同時，明二甲兄弟倆立刻攻向猴子與溫柔柔。

其他六人對看一眼，就往「沐沐」的方向追去。

「沐沐！」猴子是想去幫忙，但和溫柔柔再度被兩兄弟攔下，再加上魔豹獸突然能動了，立刻也撲了過來。

這種情況，讓他和溫柔柔根本分不了心。

「卑鄙！」

明二甲冷笑。

「呵，在戰場上，只有勝負，只要得到結果，其他不重要。」「欺負弱小」這四個字，在任務面前完全不存在。

「猴子，先解決他們。」不然，他們根本別想去幫「沐沐」。

「嗯！」猴子被明二甲纏住。

而且一下子被七人圍住，雖然只有其中四人先出手，但「沐沐」眼觀四面、聽聲辨位，雙劍在手，劍勢完全沒有停過。

以一敵四，瞬間過了好幾息，但她卻完全沒落下風，面對魂技遠攻、武技近攻，一點都不慌亂。

旁觀的三人有點驚訝。

這小女娃沒有他們想的那麼弱小啊！

「天武師？」看著她以雙劍應對四人，劍勢俐落、劍招變化快速，旁觀的三人中，唯一一名武師挑了挑眉道，顯然對她很感興趣。

天魂師大陸眾所皆知，武師與魂師，同階而論，對武師的實力評價，通常不如魂師。

但現在，她卻是以武師之力，力抗四名魂師，這當然叫同為武師的他感到非常有趣。

撇去同伴一事，他絕對是挺武師的。

不知道能不能拉攏這個小女娃，讓她一起投效東明城……

「別想了。」身旁人一看就知道他在想什麼，立刻打破他的幻想，「你們比較慢來不知道，這位……跟大小姐有仇的。」

他比其他人都早到東雪城，剛好就親眼見識大小姐找人家麻煩，在測試台前打得混亂的那一幕。

就算這個小女娃願意和解、效忠東明城，大小姐也絕對不會同意的。

「跟大小姐有仇?!」武師的表情怪怪的。

雖然他效忠東明城、聽命於大小姐，但對於大小姐的行事作風，他不說了解十分，也有七、八分。

通常「和大小姐有仇」——這幾個字翻譯過來的意思就是，大小姐看她不順眼、大小姐找她麻煩、大小姐想殺了她。

武師覺得自己內心有一句髒話不好現在罵出口。

為了手上這支媲美四星魂器的長槍，他把自己賣到別人家的屋簷下。人在屋簷下，不能與屋主作對。只能忍痛放棄招攬小女娃的心思。

「這樣不行，時間浪費太多了。」另一名旁觀魂師說道。

是他太高估這群隊友的實力，還是他沒了解過這幾個隊友的實力？

四打一，竟然過了上百招還不相上下——這太丟天魂師的臉了。

「我拒絕。」武師先表示。

同是天魂師，而且還是只差一點點就晉階聖階的天魂師，四打一已經很失身分，更何況……等等！

四打一。

只差一點點就晉聖階。

旁觀三人同時想到這一點，同時表情僵了一下，同時沉默。

「我有想錯嗎？」武師很嚴肅地問。

「應該沒有。」他身旁的天魂師回道。

「沒有。」最後開口的那位天魂師也終於說道。

三人的眼神，同時咻地看向戰況。

依然是四打一。

四人分立四個方向，不是輪流出招，就是兩、三人合招，總之，就是沒有給敵人一絲喘息的空間，各種天魂技連環攻。

反觀那名小女娃，只靠一雙劍，卻毫無間隙地擋下從不同方向來的攻擊，偶爾還有空可以反擊一下，打亂四名天魂師攻擊的節奏。

如果說這是打成平手，他們會驚訝，但也不至於太驚訝。

但事實是，她一對四，不但攻守分明，而且無論面對快攻連攻近攻遠攻，都沒有露出一絲絲慌亂。

握劍的雙手，看似慢，實則小到每一個旋轉的動作，都不白費力氣，一定剛好讓劍揮在攻或守的位置。

而且，她身上的衣袍的飄動弧度，很小。

這代表她連移動，也是最短的距離，連移動的力氣都沒有浪費。

氣息絲毫不亂。

她的臉上，雖然沒有露出輕鬆的表情，卻也沒有任何緊張與戒慎，甚至，她還能有空隙瞄瞄另一邊的戰況。

難怪明二甲、明二乙要發出求援訊息。

就這樣二對二，明明魂階勝過對方、魂器等級也高，偏偏打這麼久都沒能把對方打趴下。

也是兩個沒用的。

不過那邊的戰況很明顯看得出來，明二甲、明二乙兩人是占上風的，贏是遲早的事；麻煩的是這邊……

「這個小女娃，到底哪裡冒出來的？」就身為武師的實力評斷，他實在很欣賞她。

偏偏她和他們不同立場。

還有，這麼厲害的少女，怎麼之前都沒聽說？

「不知道。」武師身邊的魂師說道：「我只知道她會來到東雪城，是被雪少城主邀請來的……」

好的，他們明白了。

原來她是這樣跟大小姐有仇的。

跟雪少城主走得太近，就是和大小姐作對啊！

「太可惜了。」武師嘆息。

雖然他得承認小女娃的實力很強，但是單憑她要對上大小姐，那絕對是沒有活路的。

「別感嘆了，動手吧！」另一名魂師說道。

三人默契一定，同時飛身向前，加入戰局。

如果說剛才四攻一是採十字交叉攻擊，那麼現在，是混了三角聯合，不但攻勢加強，攻擊力道也更大。

如果說剛才四人合攻的戰術，是一招接一招，那麼現在就是一招一招接一招、一招接一招一招……完全打亂了攻擊的節奏，卻將攻勢變得更加密集，同時各種魂器的攻擊也不斷輪流。

「沐沐」挑了下眉，執劍的雙手變招更快。

「主人，要不要讓我來？」小花在她腦海裡問道。

這麼幾個人，這麼弱小，牠噴一點花霧，保證他們全部昏昏死死，別想再起來欺負主人。

「不用。」你暫時藏著比較好。

她有一種直覺，小花能藏到現在沒被發現，是牠藏得好；但如果小花被發現，可能會引起一些想不到的危險和事件。

目前的她，感覺還不到可以無視麻煩的時候。

「好吧。」小花有點失望。

幫不上主人的忙，心酸。

「你幫我看著猴子大哥他們，別讓他們被殺了。」偷偷地，懂吧！

「沒問題！」小花開心了。

短短幾句話的時間，七人已經各自攻擊了一輪。

「鏘、碰、轟、鏗、隆、咚、喝！」

「沐沐」一一擋下，然後在與小花說完話後，雙劍突地合併，劍勢一轉，劍光橫掃前方四人。

守在她後方位置的武師臉色一變。

「快避開！」

但，來不及了。

不用武師喊他們也知道要閃，但是劍光之疾、範圍之廣，讓他們根本避不開，只能擋。

「呃！」「啊！」「噗！」「啊……」

四人即使鎧化、用魂器反擊，依然被劍光刺傷，在空中噴出四道血痕。

在後方的三人臉色都變了。

「這不是四星武器?!」

「她……不是天武師?!」

最後一人在震驚後一回神，就是直接放出訊號。

「你……」武師震驚地看著他。

「留下她！」說完，他立刻轉換位置，直接出手。「風掃無邊！」一串風刃，射向沐沐。

另兩人一聽，同樣變動方位，一前一後緊接著發出攻擊。

那四個已經傷了，而且……短時間內竟然站不起來。

原先七人合圍，現在變成三方守位，把她困在中央。

以剛才的劍光判斷，他們三個要打敗她的機率很低。務實一點，只要能困住她，撐到其他人來，就不算他們失敗。

想困住她？

來不及了。

已經知道他們的實力，以及攻擊方式的「沐沐」，合而為一的雙劍再度分離，身影快速轉移，直接反擊！

「呃、呃！」兩聲悶哼，兩名魂師身上的鎧甲被削開，鎧化頓時失敗。

兩隻魔獸化光顯現了出來，獸身上流著血，又化光遁入主人的魔獸空間裡養傷。

唯一擋住劍沒受傷的，只剩那名天武師。

「鏘」一聲，長槍擦過劍身，爆出點點銀芒。

武師手一轉，長槍橫掃。

「沐沐」向後退的同時，手中長劍卻飛射而出，直接劃傷武師持槍的手臂，再飛回她手上。

「唔……」武師想擋，卻沒擋住。

一擊得中，「沐沐」沒再追擊，偏轉過頭，劍身一掃，明二甲突然感覺一陣心悸。

「快退開！」明二乙一喊，手中魂器同時射出，打偏了劍光。

明二甲險險躲過致命一擊。

就這麼一息時間，猴子趁機出掌：

「大地印！」

巨大的掌印，轟向明二乙。

明二乙要避開，卻不知道為了什麼，身形突然停頓，就被轟中。

「呃！」

「弟弟！」明二甲要衝過去，卻被溫柔柔擋住。

魔豹獸瞬間跳到自家主人面前。

「喵吼！」對著猴子兇猛地吼叫。

猴子沒有遲疑，巨大的掌印直接再轟。

「碰……」

「迅豹！」明二乙眼睜睜看著自己的魔獸被轟飛，又掉落地面，血跡從牠的嘴角流了出來。

「喵……嗚……」牠想爬起來，但是爬不起來。「喵嗚嗚……」

明二乙看得眼睛都紅了，拿出魂器，憤怒地一擊。

炫目的光束又粗又急，直射猴子。

猴子立刻後退、防禦。

正纏住明二甲一通拳掌亂砸，不讓他去救明二乙的溫柔柔見狀，下一拳立刻轟向光束。

「碰、轟……」

猴子還是被光束擊中，同時又被轟退，胸口的劇痛差點讓他連站都站不穩。

「猴子！」

「我沒事……」差點連話都說不出來。

傷很重，但是沒有生命危險。沒事。

要感謝柔柔打散了一點魂器攻擊的力道。

就這一息分神的時間，明二甲的魂器，已經對準溫柔柔，轟！

「柔柔！」猴子臉色一變！

溫柔柔心神一凜，回身同時也迅速退開，拉長距離以便應變。

就在魂器的光束要擊到溫柔柔前，一道身影伴隨一支長劍，劍身直接劈散了光束，又迅疾向前，凌空一劃……

「啊……」

四星魂器當場被長劍削斷，明二甲表情痛苦地抱著頭大叫。

「大哥！」明二乙飛撲過來，想伸手扶著大哥，卻根本抓不住痛得抱頭不斷掙扎的明二甲。

溫柔柔只愣了一下，就飛向猴子，扶住他。

兩人這才有空打量那兩兄弟。

「啊、啊、啊……」明二甲還在大叫。

而剛才一劍砍斷魂器的人，正俏生生地站在那裡……等等！

兩人視線再轉，看向那邊那七個——有躺著、有跪著，還有抱傷流血虛弱的……看起來就戰得七葷八素很混亂。

眼神再咻……地，直接看回一身乾淨俐落，這麼一通打鬥後還衣袍整齊、沒多少混亂，看起來一點都不像打過架的某人。

這畫面落差有點大。

「……」他們是不是太小看沐沐的實力了?

「沒事吧？」

「沒……」猴子和溫柔柔正要回答，卻發現周圍突然冒出許多人來，一看就知道和他們不是同一掛的。

不，我們有事了！

「沐沐」沒有看，只是輕輕嘆了一口氣。

「救人真是一項體力活兒。」一波打完又一波。

好辛苦！

# 第二十章 她，那個傳說中的猛人?!

打了四個，加三個，再加兩個。

嗯，以一對多又連續打，跑來跑去，真的挺辛苦的……喂！

這個是重點嗎?!

除了四周又被包圍起來之外，遠處天邊出現一道人影，邁著步伐，看似緩步，移動距離卻極大地朝這裡走來。

幾息之間，已經從千里遠之外來到近前。

於此同時，在他之後，又圍來不少天階高手，初步估算至少數十個人。

看到在場九人的慘狀，有一半的天魂師暗自嘖嘖。

以多欺少還被打成這樣，真是丟天魂師的臉啊！

雖然他們也是天魂師。

不過天魂師和天魂師之間，是有差別的。咱跟這群「倒地」的實力，不同掛！

另一半的天魂師覺得奇怪，對手就這三個，兩個低階天魂師加一個小女娃，也不像多厲害的樣子啊，是怎樣打可以打出這樣一個全軍覆沒的結果？

「沐沐」右手的劍舉在身前，劍身的光芒映在她清麗的臉龐上。

她的眼神，直接看向最後落地的那個人。

他雙手背負在後，俊雅的五官、含帶傲然的氣質，沒有眼高於頂的態勢，卻也沒有將在場的人看在眼裡。

眼神狀似隨意地掃過四周，最後，卻停在身著黑色斗篷、一手舉劍的少女身上。

「東明一鉑。」猴子低語。

「東明一鉑?!」溫柔柔驚訝地低呼一聲。「是他?!」你確定?

「嗯，我曾經見過他一次，不會認錯。」雖然這個人已經五年沒在東州出現，但他是東明城的人無誤。

據說，他原本是東明氏族的旁支，居住地極為偏遠，因為天賦極佳，自幼被接入東明城特別培養。

當初他成名的時候，聲勢、實力之大，不比現在的五大少城主差。

不過他在名揚東州兩年後，又突然宣布閉關，消聲匿跡。

那之後……就是五大少城主先後名聲鵲起，直到現在。

猴子原本沒太在意，但現在細想，這一前一後、一隱一現，是……在避開少城主們嗎?

「猴子。」醒醒！

管他什麼成名什麼避開什麼玩消失的，現在的重點，是這人出現了，他們危險了！快想辦法！

猴子苦笑。

如果說之前還有一點點機會可以邊戰邊走，現在則是完全沒有機會跑了。

除了硬拚，只有投降一途。

妳想投降嗎？

不！

要投降又何必撐到現在？要她憋屈地活著，她寧願堂堂正正地打一場，或敗或亡，她都不後悔。

「鉑少爺。」原先受傷的七人看見來人，在稍微恢復一點氣力之後，都起身走到他面前，低頭行禮。

「退下吧。」東明一鉑說道。

七人在眾人的眼神注視中，默默退到後面。

身為魂師（武師），哪會沒輸過？

沒事。小事。

沒什麼大不了的。

今天他笑我，明日我笑他。

總有機會笑回來，別把他們當回事。

自覺丟臉的七人，內心自我安慰。不管別人怎麼想，反正他們是繃著臉，就算尷尬也不露出來。

七人一退後，其他人正式圍了上來。

幾十個人，根本不必分方位，就可以把他們三人團團圍住。

「怕嗎？」猴子問。

這種情況，能逃出來的機率相當低了。沒想到掙扎到最後，還是這樣的結果。

「怕什麼？要這麼多人才能抓住我們，我們夠有面子了。」沒什麼，溫柔柔把擔心豁出去，不怕！

而且，能讓東明城出動這麼多人抓他們兩個——呃，加上「沐沐」——也算是創紀錄了。

「妳是何人？」東明一鉑問道。

從到這裡開始，即使有和其他人說話，但他的注意力，始終在她身上。

他的確看不出她修練的等級。

但能打敗「明二」這一階段的天魂師，也足夠證明她的實力了，會是聖階嗎？

「唔，路人小傭兵？」她還真想了一下，發現要介紹自己，挺難的。雖然這答案聽起來怪怪的，但這答案真的是實話。

她是路人沒錯！純粹因為救人才捲進這個奇怪的追殺事件。

到東州後，她的確是個小傭兵沒錯——最初級的那一種。

猴子、溫柔柔：「……」表情扭曲了一下。

雖然她說的是實話，但怎麼聽起來就是那麼彆扭？

猴子覺得，東明一鉑搞不好會認為沐沐在耍他。

「名字？」果然，東明一鉑皺眉了，覺得她這回答很沒有誠意。

「沐沐。」

沐沐？表妹提到的女人。

一個讓雪長歌另眼相待的女人。

表妹的不高興以後再說，現在任務為重。

「他們兩人是我們的任務目標，妳要干擾我們嗎？」東明一鉑再問一次。

「什麼任務？」打到現在，她只顧著救人，連為什麼打起來都還沒完全弄清楚……

對了，剛才那七個有說：「宣誓效忠東明玉淩。」任務，就這?!

才回想完，就聽見東明一鉑以清冷的語氣說道：

「交出所得的寒玉，宣誓效忠東明城；拒絕者，死。」或者，只要能在秘境內逃過東明城的追殺，就算他贏。

不過，到目前為止，除去其他四城的人、或與四城少主一起同行的人，也就這兩個人撐最久了。

現在，再加上一個她。

「……」她握劍的手不穩了下。

滿滿的中二風。

她差點以為自己夢迴某掌中戲。

只差沒「順……啥生，逆……啥亡」了。

妥妥的反派言行。

嗯，不對，拿這個反派人物來比喻不太好，因為他太難死了，這種追殺戲碼，她絕對不想看它變成連續劇。

「妳的回答？」東明一鉑給她一次選擇的機會。

「都不要。」

「都不要？」

「就是：都不選。」她再說一次，然後還特別問猴子：「東明城給了選擇就要選，東州有這條規則嗎？」

「沒有。」猴子秒答。

「都不選，那就默認是第二種。」東明一鉑身上光芒一閃，全身瞬間化出火紅色鎧甲，飛身向前的同時，一拳揮出。

一道熊熊火焰竄向沐沐。

沐沐挪步移轉，輕易避開火焰，還分神想著，看起來斯文的人，打起架來一點都不斯文，很粗暴啊！

才分心了一下，東明一鉑的第二道火拳已經來到面前。

沐沐舉劍擋拳。

「碰！」

強悍的拳風，颯動了沐沐的斗篷，露出斗篷下的水藍勁裝。

東明一鉑的拳頭冒出火焰，熾熱的高溫，映紅兩人的面容。

沐沐劍身迴轉，甩開火焰、也拉開距離。

東明一鉑再追上，沐沐再後退後，卻反步向前，劍拳再度對擊！

「碰……碰碰……碰碰碰……」

連續好幾擊，引發一聲比一聲浩大的炸裂聲。

同一時間，圍住猴子與溫柔柔的其他人，同時對兩人發出天魂技，含帶各種元素的攻擊全都轟向兩人。

沐沐立刻後退，放出手上的雙劍，一左一右繞著猴子和溫柔柔迅即迴旋半圈，擋下大部分的攻擊。

「乒乒乒乒……」

震耳的交擊聲中，東明一鉑的火拳又到。

沐沐同樣出拳回擊。

「碰！」轟轟……

熾烈的焰火隨著兩拳相接而爆射四散，撼聲不絕。

不只震撼了在場的人，同時吸引了近百里外聽見這陣聲響的人。

同一時間，擋下大部分攻擊的雙劍，在空中交錯後隨即反擊向兩邊，兩道劍氣橫掃過那群包圍成圈的天魂師們，瞬間打敗了包圍的合勢，還傷了幾乎四分之一的天魂師。

東明一鉑眼底一驚，手上快速出拳。

沐沐卻連連後退閃避，不再硬碰硬，同時雙劍隨著她的心緒回到她手上。一握劍，劍氣隨出，迎向火拳。

「咻……轟！」

猴子與溫柔柔則在包圍的合勢被打亂時，趁隙找個方向狂奔逃離。

部分天魂師立刻追上。

不是他們不講義氣，而是發現在目前的情況下，他們連自己都無法保全，反而變成沐沐的累贅，讓她分心。

逃離，不只為了活命、不使沐沐分心，同時也為了能吸引一些追兵，減輕一點沐沐的負擔。

在拳劍再度交擊時，東明一鉑卻說：「妳的朋友，拋下妳了。」

「喔。」她漫不經心地應了一聲。

「不覺得被背叛嗎？」火拳上，火勢加大。

「不會呀。」

「為什麼？」

「他們活著，才不枉我出手救人。如果我想救人，可他們還是死了，那才是浪費力氣。」

「即使妳會因此死在這裡？」

「我不會死的呀。」她回得輕巧。

「這麼自信？」東明一鉑身上的魂師印湧動，聖階的威壓，讓退到一邊的天魂師們都感覺到壓迫感。

她卻絲毫不受影響。

「妳果然是聖階武師。」東明一鉑不算太意外地道。

明二那七人，敗得不冤。

「這很重要嗎？」她雙劍一揮，逼得東明一鉑不得不後退。

他特別看一眼她手上的劍。

「五星……神器?!」

東明一鉑含著驚訝的話聲才落，就聽見不遠處「碰……轟」一聲。

緊接著，是去追猴子和溫柔柔的天魂師，快速地奔回來。

「鉑大人……啊！」才開口，身後一股旋風追到，頓時掃飛了他。

東明一鉑身形一動，將要飛遠的天魂師拉回來。

同時，那股旋風一停，一道身影顯現了出來。

緊隨在後的，是猴子與溫柔柔，以及……

一群東明一鉑在這時候並不想遇見的人。

隨風到來的男人，在看見不遠處的熟悉身影時，悄悄地鬆了口氣。

然而，由對面隨即傳來一陣迅捷的腳步聲，就在東明一鉑身後，同樣出現了一群魂師們。

隔著一大群人，聽到各種乒乓聲而趕到的兩方隊伍一看見對方，眼裡同時浮現四個大字：

冤家路窄！

也可以說是：得來全不費功夫。

「岩華！」

「東明玉淩！」

終於找到妳了！

「怎麼，不跑了嗎？」

「妳跑我都不會跑！」

「是嗎？那上回是誰被打得落荒而逃？」

「那是因為我覺得多看妳一眼就傷眼。」

「那上回被我燒掉鎧甲的人又是誰？」

「要不是妳偷襲，妳想燒到本少城主……作夢！」

這兩方人，中間隔著一大群天魂師跟兩個正在對戰的人，完全沒有對她們造成任何阻礙，只一看到對方，立刻就互相叫囂吵起來。

真的，挺忙的。

火氣也挺大。

沐沐覺得，錯過一場大混戰，感覺好像錯過了很多有趣的事……

「碰！」

沐沐及時舉劍擋住。

東明一鉑的聲音就在耳邊：

「這是妳第二次分心了。」

沐沐旋劍揮開東明一鉑。

陌生男人，不要靠她太近！

她先瞪了他一眼，然後似乎想到什麼，表情立刻變成一臉委屈樣，轉身嗚嗚地，收起劍時也飛撲進某人的懷抱裡。

圍觀眾人：「……」啊這？

接著就聽見：

「哥哥，他們欺負我！嚶嚶嚶！」

圍觀眾人：「……」懵！

神轉折！

不只圍觀眾人懵，認出她的人也懵。

與她打得不相上下的東明一鉑，更懵。

這被欺負了、委屈了找哥哥的弱小樣，跟剛才和他打得一來一往、鎮定自若的自信樣，未免差太多了！

而她這一撲，所有認得「哥哥」的人，表情再加一個懵。

這傢伙有妹妹?!

呃，也不能這麼說，以他出身的家族，沒有兄弟姐妹才奇怪了。

只是，他會帶妹妹出門……不對不對，這個妹妹根本沒有跟在他身邊，這會兒算是偶遇吧。

他們應該疑惑的是，他有跟哪個妹妹這麼接近？

以前，他有提過哪個妹妹嗎？

但是下一刻，讓他們更懵的事發生了。

只距離「哥哥」三步遠、臉上沒有表情的男人，突然舉步走向前，伸手摸摸她的頭，問道：

「東明一鉑嗎？」

「哥哥……」本來埋著臉的「沐沐」抬起頭，看著另一個哥哥，有點心虛、有點無辜的表情。

「乖，不怕。」他輕聲安撫一句，隨即轉身一跨——轉眼到東明一鉑面前，單鐧一擊！

「鏘！」東明一鉑以手臂擋住，火焰隨即燃上玄鐧。

「嗤……」

玄鐧卻沁出水流，澆息火焰，水火一觸，發出嗤嗤聲響。

「端木傲！」東明一鉑認出來人。

端木傲卻一語不發，沒有執鐧的另一手伸出一揮，一股令人窒息的威壓宛如千萬斤壓在東明一鉑身上。

東明一鉑差點站立不穩，突然全身爆出火焰！

端木傲以鐧一擋，旋身退回原來位置。

這幾下乾淨俐落，看得其他人都差點呆住了。

「四哥？」她擔心地喚道。

「放心，小試一下而已，沒事。」端木傲雲淡風輕地說道。

她沒想到四哥動作這麼快，有點內疚。

「沒事。」端木風拍拍她，「妹妹被欺負了，哥哥打上門去，不是應該的嗎？」

端木傲理所當然地點點頭。

目標：務必讓小玖明白，她是有靠山的，哥哥是可靠的。

順便：再次刷清一下之前被小玖救的印象，四哥還是很有實力的。

原本撲在哥哥懷裡的沐沐，現在改站在兩個哥哥中央，特別抱住端木傲的手臂偎靠了一下。

「謝謝四哥。」她小小聲地說。

端木傲微揚了下唇角。

旁觀眾人：「……」

看到總是萬年臉上沒表情的人，笑了。

而且，兄妹？兄、妹?!

他們是兄妹，這兩隻是端木家最出名的兩隻，所以她是……

另一邊，端木傲停戰暫退，東明一鉑身上火焰頓消，同時嚥下喉間的血腥味，並沒有繼續追擊。

短短幾招來回，看似平手，但當事人都知道，東明一鉑算是吃了虧。

若不是之前和沐沐交戰耗費太多體力與魂力，他不會這麼輕易被端木傲所傷。

但不可否認，端木傲的實力，比他預估得高。

這讓他對大小姐的計畫，又有了更多不贊同感。

但是事已至此，不贊同也無用，必須做保守的打算。

心思轉念間，東明一鉑連同與他同行的天魂師們也退到另一邊，與後方來人會合。

「大小姐。」他站到她面前。

「表哥，沒事吧？」

面的人。

「那就好。」她點了點頭，東明一鉑就站到她側後方。她則抬起頭，環視了對面的人。

「端木傲、端木風，你們要管東州的事嗎？」

天魂大陸三州，各行其事。雖然自由往來，但各州事務，外州人一向不予參與。

像端木傲和端木風這種中州家族的嫡系子弟，更是要避免，免得引起兩州之間的衝突。

這是各州幾大家族與幾大城之間的默認原則。

然而她這句話一問，平常總是溫和有禮的端木風，臉上的笑意突然更深了一些。

深得有點讓人覺得……反常。

端木風還沒回答，在「哥哥」兩個字後，岩華突然抬起頭：

「沐沐，妳是端木家的人?!」

這個問題，沐沐一臉嚴肅地思考。

岩華：「……」這個思考的表情是個什麼事？

她只是問一個問題而已，簡單的「是」或「不是」，就一個答案，要想這麼久嗎？

最後，想很久的沐沐，竟然還給她來個：

「是，也不是。」

岩華想打人。

但是對著那張臉，打不下去。

「什麼意思？」暴躁。

「我姓端木，可是從小是個小廢材，所以這個……不太好意思說自己的姓氏，會丟家族的臉啊。」嘆氣。

這是很真實，但是最微不足道的原因之一。

端木風、端木傲：「……」雖然這大概是實話，但是總感覺妹妹在忽悠人。

但身為哥哥，是不拆自己妹妹台的。

所以他們不說。

所有人：「……」她這樣的，是小廢材？

到底是端木家的標準太嚴格，還是他們其實都是大廢材？不對，可能他們連「廢材」這兩個字都搆不上。

端木家的標準，已經高到這種程度了嗎？

但是岩華認真聽、認真信了。

「原來如此，這個心情，我懂。」她嘆了一口氣，覺得自己跟沐沐，果然很有緣。

林燁、旁觀者：「……」

不是，妳懂了什麼？

身為東州有名的、一言不合就開打的暴力少城主之一……不對，沒有之一，她就是唯一的。

這種自報名號會覺得小丟臉而不敢報名號的事，和妳有什麼關係？妳不是都一向直接報名號、或者「本姑奶奶」、「本少城主」的嗎？

附帶一提，雖然還有一個加強版——屬於那種看不順眼、心情不美、想打人就打人還可以隨時組一團人幫她打的，那不是少城主，那是有權有勢有靈晶、高高在上的大小姐。

遇到這種的，別說他們普通魂師，就是家裡有礦的都不一定惹得起……

「那妳的名字是什麼？」岩華問道。

旁邊的人，也打開耳朵仔細聽。

「玖。」她看著岩華，笑得萌萌噠：

「端木玖。」

哦，端木玖啊。

嗯，果然姓「端木」。

端木家族嫡系，好像……是有這個名字。

天魂大陸上有名的大家族好幾個，記不清楚別人家嫡系的名字，只是彷彿有那麼一點印象，這也是正常的。

畢竟也沒有人閒到沒事就去背別人家的族譜嘛！

當然對於別人家族特別厲害、天賦特好的子弟，像端木風、端木傲，別家的夏侯駒、石昊、姬雲飛……等等這種特別有名，他們就記住了。

但端木玖……

總覺得很陌生、但又覺得好像有聽過，是在哪裡聽過呢……啊！

同一時間，好幾個人都瞬間抬起頭，互相看了一眼。

「我想起來，我在哪裡聽過了。」

「我也想起來了。」聽說的當下，他還很不信呢！

現在，更不信了……不，是根本不想信呀。

「端木玖？」

岩華狐疑的眼神，加上旁邊那些懷疑、震驚、不信的眼神，同時唰唰地落在端木玖身上。

三個多月前，一則消息，從中州火速席捲整個天魂大陸。

中州大戰。

陰氏家族密謀一統中州，號令所有勢力。

煉器師公會被架空，陰家獨大。

神階高手一人獨挑眾大家族。

各大老牌家族差一點點就被掀翻，中州差一點點改朝換代。

危急之際，一名神秘女子忽至，改寫戰局。

本來面對神階高手大家都有點絕望了，結果卻半途殺出個人，把這個神階給幹掉了。

那之後直到現在，這則消息都還是各個大小飯館酒館討論度最高的話題。

雖然陰家主的陰謀他們很不欣賞，但不得不說，成為神魂師與神武師，是所有修練者的夢想；單就這點而言，陰家主的這份實力和天賦，也是很讓他們佩服和羨慕的。

但更奇葩的，是剛準備震撼整個大陸的神魂師，一顯露出實力，竟然就折戟沉沙了。

而讓陰家家主含恨的，不但是一名女子，還非常年輕，簡直讓人懷疑這則消息是不是在開玩笑！

但事實是，消息是真的，不是開玩笑。

這位猛人，真的存在！

這個猛人，還是端木家被放逐出去的有名廢材啊！

然而有一天，這個廢材，以打敗大陸頂級高手的姿態，逆襲了。

打敗神階，簡直比成為神階還要更讓人視為神！

「妳……妳……」至少數十隻手指，指著端木玖，抖抖抖，不是因為害怕驚嚇，而是不敢相信。

主角。

神秘女子。

就這麼冒出來了。

突然地出現在他們眼前。

激動的情緒，難以置信的眼神，包括猴子、溫柔柔、岩華、林燁等人，都被這個領悟炸得暈暈乎乎。

「端木玖！」

# 第二十章
# 她，那個傳說中的猛人?!

「中州的傳說！」

「打敗神階的猛人！」

小玖：「……」

除了名字，後面兩句跟她沒有關係！

# 第二十一章 敵方、我方，大會合

不能怪他們突然太激動。

實在是這件事從發生、到後來，短短幾個月，引起中州太多的變動。

從以陰家家主為首的家族、公會勢力，公開叫戰皇室、端木家族等家族的勢力，幾乎把中州勢力分成兩方。

在陰家家主死亡後，陰氏家族重整，連帶的各大家族、各大公會，上上下下幾乎全被掀翻了一遍。

中州各家族勢力排名雖然沒有多少變動，但清查出與陰家家主有關的人數，卻出乎各大勢力的預料，讓所有人全捏把冷汗……

這絕對是數百年，甚至可以說是近千年以來，最轟動三州的大事件。

首先，是眾人怎麼也沒想到，豔名與實力齊名在外的陰家家主，竟然越過許多成名的聖階九級高手，率先突破了卡住許許多多聖階修練者的桎梏，成為神魂師。

更萬萬沒想到，陰家家主有那麼大的野心。

他們不在中州，對中州也不熟，但是試想一下如果這件事情發生在東州……呸呸，這麼喪的事情千萬不要發生。

這位被放逐到西州偏遠小城的端木家嫡系，以這種幾乎輾壓所有人的實力，揚出名聲，讓所有這一代的大陸天才，相形見絀。

但是，真的是她嗎？

傳言，有沒有誇張、有沒有避重就輕呢？

實在是，她太年輕了！

而且看起來也實在沒有高手的那種威壓特質——雖然她的實力，好像真的很不錯……

「妳是那個端木玖？」岩華終於冷靜一點，雙手環胸問道。

「端木玖，還有分這個和那個嗎？」小玖一臉疑惑。

被抓語病的岩華：「……」

「不要想轉移我的問題，妳是端木家九小姐、殺了陰月華的那個端木玖？」好好回答，不然連朋友都沒得做喔！

「嗯。」小玖點頭。

這麼乾脆就承認，讓岩華肚子裡預備的火氣突然卡住。

好一會兒，岩華找回氣勢，繼續質問：

「為什麼一開始不說？」

「怕麻煩啊。」小玖特誠實。

「那後來我們到東雪城，那麼要好了，為什麼還不說？」

「我是不是那個端木玖，很重要嗎？」小玖反問。

岩華表情頓了下。「當然。」

「那我不是端木玖，妳就不和我做朋友了嗎？」

「當然不是。」一開始她交朋友的，是「沐沐」。

「那如果我是端木玖，妳會改變對我的態度嗎？」

「當然不會！」頂多多看她兩眼。

「一開始瞞著妳，我很抱歉，後來沒澄清，是不想多惹麻煩，只想做個傭兵多歷練。」小玖轉向其他人，「林少城主、猴子大哥、溫副團長，瞞著你們，我在這裡，也說聲抱歉。」

「沒、沒關係。」猴子和溫柔柔不覺得這有什麼，但是對於「沐沐」的真實身分，還有點震驚待消化。

等他回去告訴鬍子，鬍子一定也會驚訝得跳起來的。

「妳隱瞞身分，我能了解。」林燁狀似無意地掃了對面一眼，然後對岩華說：「她和流星兩個人，來到東州闖蕩，勢單力薄的，又有中州那裡的事，如果她不化名，危險會增加很多倍。」

「要你多解釋。」難道她想不到嗎？只是有點不開心而已。

但是她這麼老實地道歉，岩華也就不多計較，但是……

「沐沐是化名，你該不會也是吧？」岩華的目標，轉向不知道什麼時候來到三兄妹身後的「流星」。

「星流。」他言簡意賅地回道。

岩華：「……」這個化名真是太不走心了。

「星流？」林燁則一臉思考。「陰家……」

星流點點頭。

林燁就不說了。

「陰家？」岩華看向林燁。

「沒什麼。」林燁轉移自家未婚妻的注意力，「我們的麻煩，還沒解決完呢！」

他們這邊震驚到差點想尖叫，東方一鉑那邊的人，反應也差不多。

有人震驚、有人懷疑、有人不信。

端木玖能和鉑大人打得不相上下，他們承認，她的確有實力，但這實力能打敗神階嗎？

在這裡的人，當然不全是以東明城的名額進秘境的人，更多的，是參加資格測試而得到入境資格的人。

也是在進秘境，東明玉凌挑起對立之後，他們才猛然發現，原來入秘境的自由名額中，有一半以上，都和東明城有關係。

不是效忠東明城、就是被東明城收買。

沒遇到長歌和海宇越，就連東雪城和東海城的人，也只遇到一、兩個，不知道他們被傳到秘境的哪個角落，希望不是中了什麼埋伏或跌到什麼坑裡出不來，不然就太沒面子了。

如果不算端木風這些非東州的人，光是東岩城、東林城，以及傭兵和其他獨立的修練者聯合起來，也沒有東明城的人數多。

現在東明玉凌也來了，林燁不認為她會放棄這個對付他和岩華的好機會。

否則，她也不必在一開口，就先質問端木風和端木傲的立場了。

端木風當然聽見東明玉凌的質問，但是，直到看著妹妹回答完大家的問題，他才轉回頭。

端木傲沒有把注意力一直放在小玖身上，而是把主要的關注焦點放在東明玉凌一行人，留意他們有沒有偷襲。

東明玉凌，直直看著他，內心，是很不習慣的隱忍。

「大小姐，冷靜。現在不適合處理……也不適合暴露身分，先以任務為要。」東明一鉑不得不傳音提醒。

從「端木玖」三個字被說出來，東明玉凌幾乎就要直接開打，但現在，真的不是好時機。

人不夠，實力也不明，時間、地點都不對，這口氣，必須忍。

東明玉凌深吸口氣，才能讓自己不看她，只盯著端木風。

「在秘境裡肆意擊殺魂師，就是妳說的『東州的事』？」

「我並沒有讓人傷害中州的人，不是嗎？」她避開中州的人，已經給了中州面子。

禮尚往來，該懂吧！

「我們兄妹對東州的事不感興趣，但是在秘境裡遇到認識的人被追殺，總是不能見死不救？」

「所以，你要插手？」

「妳在秘境裡的這種作為，東雪城主、衛長老，會同意嗎？」

「少拿他們來說事，本大小姐不是被嚇大的。」

「那，妳何必問？」本少，也不是怕事的。

東明玉凌瞪視端木風，身上火焰隱隱。

端木風眼神平靜，周身無風自起。

就在兩人蓄勢待發、準備開戰的時候，一道聲音，由遠方突然冒了出來：

「喲～這是……在幹嘛？」

◇

突來的聲音，讓在場的人頓時一陣緊繃。

他們沒有發現有人來！

但一看見來人，端木風、林燁這邊稍微放鬆一些；東明玉凌那邊的魂師們，卻更戒備了。

而剛才開口的人，追著自己的同伴往端木風……不，是端木玖的方向跑去。

小玖就這麼眼睜睜看著人，跑到她面前。

端木風和端木傲直接就想擋人，但看到是某人，才忍住沒擋住妹妹。

而跑到小玖面前的人，也不說話，就一直看著她。

後面追來的男子，看著自家竹馬兄弟的行為，簡直無語凝噎。

「九小姐，我是姬雲飛，他是石昊，妳還記得嗎？」石昊不開口，姬雲飛只能趕緊自我介紹，免得把人嚇跑了。

「記得。」小玖點點頭。

因為這句話，石昊明顯開心了，然後看看現場的氣氛。

「打架嗎？」石昊式的說話法，只有重點，沒有主詞名詞形容詞客氣語，只有動詞。

只要她點頭，他立刻亮武器！

姬雲飛頭痛，不得不幫忙解釋：

「他的意思是，如果要和……他們打，」指東明城的人，「阿昊和我都會幫忙的。」

「先等一下。」小玖說道。

石昊一聽，就看了看她周圍，找到她側後方的空隙，就站了過去，一副「他們是一伙人」的模樣。

姬雲飛想捂臉，但還是跟著一起站過去。

他的竹馬兄弟，真是太不含蓄了。

岩華看到現在才出現的這群人，差點翻白眼。

「你們兩個，也太慢了。」

「來得早，不如來得巧。」

跟石昊與姬雲飛一起來的，是東雪城與東海城的人，尤其是一直沒出現的雪長歌與海宇越，總算也出現了。

「怎麼回事？」海宇越問道。

「她搞出來的。」岩華示意他，看看某人。

林燁則低聲簡短地將雙方對立的事情說了一遍。

雪長歌一聽完，就看向東明玉凌：

「東明城要打，東雪城奉陪。」一下子就把問題擺到明面上，要變成城與城之間的對立。

說到底，那些追殺行動，也算是個人自願參與，秘境內本就生死自負，要因為這一點而追究東明城，理由有點不夠明確。

但要阻止這種行動，還是可以的。

東明一鉑立刻看向東明玉凌，擔心她一時意氣用事。

但是，東明玉凌只是冷笑了聲。

「要保這些人，你這個少城主也真是夠忙的。雪長歌，這次，本小姐給你面子，但沒有下次。我們走。」說完，東明玉凌帶著人就離開了。

乾脆俐落得讓人有點錯愕。

看見雪長歌，也沒有特別再要雪長歌做什麼。

東明玉凌，莫非是被什麼刺激過度，反常了?!

因為有東明城的人虎視眈眈，他們這一行數十個人沒再分開，而是在秘境裡找

了個地方作為營地。

想離開去找尋寒玉或魔獸的人，任憑自願。

需要養傷的人，在這裡也不必擔心再被追擊。

而他們幾個人，卻是聚在一起。

在找營地的路上，雪長歌與海宇越，也知道小玖的身分了，忍不住驚奇地多看她好幾眼。

但是兩人倒是沒有多詢問什麼——人家的哥哥就在旁邊，而且看起來是那種非常護短的哥哥。

碰到這種人時，妹妹的情況不能亂問。

萬一哪句話說得不好，讓哥哥們想揍人，那就不好了。

不想介入東州內鬥的端木風，把妹妹牽在身邊，和端木傲兩人一左一右，把妹妹護在中間。

而在他們周圍，是星流、石昊、姬雲飛三人。

「東明玉凌這次跑得倒快。」沒能把上回不得不先撤退的帳要回來，岩華有點不開心。

「形勢比人強。再說，我們在她眼裡，大概只能算是『前菜』，她的重點，應該是接下來的事。」林燁說道。

內境。

能不能進內境，看之前個人的收穫；能在內境裡得到什麼，看個人幸不幸運。

這就不用多說。

林燁比較想知道的是，海宇越和長歌，對東明城的行動，有什麼看法？

「大概，是想一統東州，或者站在東州的頂點，讓我們四城，都尊東明城為首吧。」雪長歌說道，語氣一點都不意外。

「他們這是在大白天睡大覺吧。」岩華哼。

簡稱：作夢！

「有這種可能。」仔細思考過後，林燁跟雪長歌有相同的推測。

「他們憑什麼？」岩華不服氣地問。

「魂器，武器。」而且是大量的。

這兩個詞，讓岩華頓時憋屈。

為什麼唯恐天下不亂的人，偏偏握有讓人最心動的籌碼？

「東明城這麼囂張，是真的一點都不擔心我們出去後找他們麻煩嗎？」岩華真的暴躁。

就算東明城煉器天下第一，他們也有天下第二、第三可以找，才不要看他們囂張的臉色過日子。

決定了，她出去要揍人揍東明玉凌一頓！

林燁眉心一跳。

光看她的表情，就知道她在想什麼，深深覺得那不是個好主意的林燁只好拍拍自家未婚妻以示安慰，但話一句都沒多說，免得火上澆油。

岩華不是不懂，只是需要發洩一下心裡的憋屈感而已，就讓她想想，自己高興一下。

他們是可以不稀罕東明城，但是東州諸多魂師們、武師們，卻稀罕得很，否則他們也不會在秘境裡被堵了。

「海宇、長歌，你們有什麼想法嗎？」

「目前，能避開與東明玉凌的衝突，就先避開吧。」海宇越說道。

暫時的。

不管東明城想做什麼，他們都需要時間多做一點準備，也需要時間讓東明城的目的明朗化。

就算是真的野心爆發想一統東州……那再來打。

岩華一聽，就瞪著他。

她討厭忍耐！

海宇越覺得自己被瞪很無辜，必須要解釋點什麼：

「東明玉凌敢在秘境裡做這種事，表示他們已經準備很久了。而且嚴格說起來，她並沒有直接針對我們。」

岩華的表情頓了頓。

「是這樣沒錯。但難道沒有針對我們，就可以針對其他人嗎？而且，我們還是打起來了。」

林燁默默提醒：

「沒有針對我們、沒有主動出手，我們就沒有理由找她麻煩，最後會打起來……」是因為妳看不過去東明玉凌刁難人，才出手，結果演變成東明城獨挑東林城與東岩城的對抗戰兼追擊逃跑戰。

岩華一窒。

好像是這樣沒錯。

「東明玉凌太狡猾了！」認真評斷起來，岩華也不是都沒錯的，畢竟一開始也不關她的事，結果她救急變事主了。

不針對東岩城，卻引得東岩城主動出手；東岩城出手了，東林城難道能袖手旁觀嗎？

結果就是，讓東明城有光明正大的理由針對東岩城和東林城。

如果這種情況是預謀的……那東明城的預謀，只是和他們兩城翻臉嗎？

「東明玉凌，是這麼奸詐的嗎？」旁聽到現在，大概聽懂過程的小玖，好奇地問哥哥。

哥哥們……有點為難。

問兩個不關心別人家妹妹或女兒是什麼樣的人、只關心對方實力的直男這種問題，哥哥們實在回答不出來。

同理可推，星流、石昊，同樣回答不出來。

不過他們不是因為不關心別人家妹妹或女兒的個性，他們是對這個女人不感興趣，自然就不會關心這個人做出什麼樣的事。

也就姬雲飛因為家族需要的關係，對各地方的重要人物，與其行事風格，有一定程度的了解。

他很中肯地說：「依照過去東明玉凌的行事風格來判斷，她不是一個擅於謀劃的人。」

如果今天在秘境的人，換成是她的哥哥，那就不用多懷疑，兇手絕對就是他。

「不過秘境裡的事，應該是東明城早就計畫好的。」所以謀劃者是不是東明玉凌不重要，總之這件事，就是東明城搞的鬼。

「這樣做，對東明城有什麼好處？」岩華不明白。

經過這次追殺，進秘境的散修和傭兵死了至少四分之一，雖然他們四城的人損傷不多，但也多少介入這場對抗裡，把他們都得罪光光，難道東明城是想先成為東州公敵嗎？

「好處……」姬雲飛想了想，轉向雪長歌，「雪少城主，內境裡，是不是有什麼我們不知道的秘密？」

過去曾經入內境的人，收穫的確都不小，而且大都比在外境的收穫更大。

並不是能入內境就一定可以得到更多，事實上，入內境的人所能得到的收穫，往往都只有一件，目前還沒有例外過。

如果只是為了得到一樣東西，而搞出這麼一場大陣仗，林燁個人覺得：這不划算吧？

並不是每個人都能進入內境。

為了減少入內境的人來個大掃蕩……這生意會虧本。

除非，還有別的內情。

「可能有，可能沒有，我不確定。」

雪長歌說的是實話，但是大家都看著他。

你家的秘境你說你什麼都不知道，你覺得我們要相信你嗎？

面對大家都不相信的表情，雪長歌默默懷疑，這算不算是他家父親給他挖的坑？

再順便腹誹一句：他家父親，有時候真的挺坑的——坑別人的。

如果真是這樣，當父親要挖坑給兒子踩，當兒子的還能怎麼辦呢？就踩吧。

心懷孝順，雪長歌輕輕嘆口氣。

伸手一張開，一顆圓球出現在他掌心。

長歌輕輕一按……

眾人沒有什麼實質感覺。

小玖卻敏銳地抬起頭。

雖然什麼也看不見，但她知道，有個什麼東西，把他們十個人罩住了。

雪長歌因而看了她一眼。

端木風挑眉。

「小玖，怎麼了？」

「那個，是魂器吧。」指著圓球。

「是。」雪長歌輕笑地點頭。「小玖，妳對魂力的感知很敏銳。」

小玖還沒說什麼，四哥語氣沉沉地開口了：

「小玖？」

才剛知道小玖的真名，就喊得這麼順。

這個名字是他可以這樣喊的嗎？

# 第二十二章　驚喜？

「我聽到你們是這麼喚她的。」但是雪長歌，就這麼清淺地一笑，溫文如水地回答了。

神情語氣，完全無害，彷彿本來就該這麼稱呼，他只是跟從他們的叫法，完全沒有任何不妥。

林燁：「……」這還是那個出塵脫俗、如立雪峰雲端、凡人難近的東雪城少城主嗎？

岩華：「……」第一次發現雪長歌竟然還有這麼無賴的時候，她過去都看錯他了吧！

人家是兄妹，這種叫法沒問題。你呢？

就算你是東雪城少城主，但是對比人家有血緣的兄妹關係，你就是個比路人甲熟一點的，認識的人而已。

叫得這麼親切……

莫非有什麼奇奇怪怪的心思？

不只林燁和岩華這麼想，稍微了解雪長歌行事風格的星流、石昊、姬雲飛也一樣這麼想，更不要說對和妹妹有關的事，警戒雷達會開到最敏銳的端木風和端木傲了。

唯一一個基於是好友而忍住沒吐槽的，只有海宇越了。

這些「好」朋友，雪長歌也是記住了。

還是小玖出聲，打破這陣奇怪的互相注視。

「你這個，是魂器吧？」指那顆圓球。

「對。」

「五星？」

雪長歌驚訝。

「妳看得出來？」

「猜的。」端木玖一笑。

「這顆球有五星?!」岩華瞪眼。

圓乎乎、灰白白，就是一顆普通樣的球，連個特別造型都沒有，這是魂器？還是五星?!

「這球沒有攻擊力，純粹是隱匿和防禦用。」

之所以會有五星這麼高等級，完全是因為煉材本身就有這麼高的等級，而那位煉器師也不浪費材料，就把這兩種功能煉到最高。

「小玖猜得真準。」石昊單純讚美。

小玖笑得有點心虛。

她能說，她這麼猜，是因為這顆圓球的煉製手法她覺得很熟，所以才猜出來的嗎？

雖然還是很懷疑這不起眼的球有那麼厲害，不過雪長歌這麼說，他們也就信了。

同時也猜到，只是說個話還得特別拿這個東西出來，那他接下來的話應該是不適合被別人聽見了。

有秘密聽，特別期待。

「剛才說，內境可能有秘密、也可能沒有，是真的。雖然秘境的開啟一直受東雪城控制，但其實東雪城從來不是秘境的主人，對於秘境的了解，並沒有你們想像中多。」

如果有注意秘境開啟時間的人，大概就會注意到，秘境雖然號稱十年一開，但日期並不是固定的。

就像這一次。

當秘境突然出現，他們也只能提早開啟。

而秘境關閉後，又會自動消失。

東雪城掌握的，也不過就是找到入口，與開啟入口的方法而已。

秘境每次開放的時間，境外三天、境內三十天。

秘境的範圍究竟有多大、秘境裡究竟有些什麼，只怕就算是他的父親，都不一定完全清楚。

「我唯一知道的一點，就是這個秘境曾經有過主人，而這位主人，擁有我們無法想像的威能。

至於秘境的主人是誰、為什麼秘境會只在這裡出現、秘境的主人還在不在，我就不知道了。」

這樣聽起來，好像也沒有什麼不能讓別人聽見的呀，畢竟長歌什麼都不知道，何必刻意用魂器來防止別人偷聽？

「要入內境，需要寒玉，你們都知道吧？」雪長歌問道。

「知道。」大家都點頭。

「那麼，你們有得到寒玉嗎？」

「有。」八個有。

「沒有。」就是岩華和林燁。

岩華不平衡了。

是誰搶了她的運氣？還是她被誰……帶衰了?!

懷疑的眼神，直接看向未婚夫。

「……」未婚夫除了平常用來否認的以外，就是當揹鍋的？

當然不行。

「是東明玉凌害的。」林燁義正詞嚴地說：「如果不是她一直找我們麻煩，我們怎麼會連找寒玉的時間都沒有？」

理所當然地把鍋推過去。

「有道理，都是她的錯。」岩華覺得，她和東明玉凌要算的帳，又多了一條。

其他八人：「……」未婚夫的嘴，哄人的鬼。

雪長歌嘆了口氣，拿出兩塊寒玉，送給林燁和岩華。

「長歌？」兩人訝異。

「沒什麼，你們用得上。」不用謝。

「你找到很多？」岩華想問的是這個。

「……大概不少。」幾十塊有吧。

「怎麼那麼好運?!」

好運嗎？雪長歌嘆了口氣。

「妳以為，我為什麼那麼晚才找到你們？」秘境再大，他找人也沒有這麼遜的好嗎！

「呃……難道……」林燁想到一種可能。

寒玉愈多。

附近的魔獸就會愈難纏。

現在突然發現，雪長歌和海宇越身上的鎧甲，是新換的。

所以這是……

「沼澤魔獸，太難纏了。」想到之前的戰況，海宇越一陣心累。

他和長歌一前一後，正好掉到同一個地方：沼澤。還沒落地，差點就被虎視眈眈的魔獸給咬了，他們兩人當場開打。

打魔獸就算了，打完還得下沼澤挖寒玉。

進秘境來當挖礦工，他和長歌這種運氣，也真的是沒誰有了。

下完沼澤能不換衣服嗎？

身為少城主，形象還是要顧一下的。他懂！

林燁頓時不羨慕他們了。

「辛苦了。」作為被贈送寒玉的人，要感恩這兩人的辛苦。

「辛苦了。」岩華也說道。

雖然她認為，東明玉凌那個女人更麻煩。

可以換的話，岩華還寧願去當挖礦工呢！

「哥哥，你們被傳送到哪裡？」小玖好奇地問道。

應該不會也去挖礦吧？

「爬座山而已，沒什麼。」端木風微笑，好像就這麼簡單。

至於過程中沿路和猴子跳樹比速度、搶寒玉、衣服差點被抓破什麼的，小事，不用說。

「我也沒什麼，就是被凍了一下。」端木傲輕描淡寫地說道。

黑暗暗的冰洞，能不凍人嗎？

幸好青玄不怕凍，拿到寒玉他們就走出來了。

「我搶了個人。」星流被傳送到的地點，正好有寒玉礦，但是有人比他早到，並且還埋伏想殺他。

星流當然就……順手反殺了，拿寒玉走人。

「我搶了一隻魔獸。」石昊覺得跟星流很有緣。

他們都是「搶」的喔！

「原來我最倒楣。」姬雲飛嘆氣。

被傳送進黑翼鵰的鵰巢裡，他一個大成人，就跟剛出生的小幼鵰一樣大，不只被小幼鵰逗著玩耍，還被成鵰追著跑——要跑得過才有命，整整五個時辰啊！

如果不是他在跑出鵰巢的時候，順便掰了巢邊的幾塊寒玉帶著走，可就虧大了。

「小玖，妳被傳送去哪裡？」岩華問道。

「呃，一座山谷，然後看到很多很多花。等我走出來的時候，就遇到猴子大哥和溫副團長被追殺。」端木玖非常簡化地回道。

「就看到花，沒別的？」沒有打架、沒有逃命？

「嗯，主要就是花。」斗篷下，偽裝花別針的小花，悄悄動了動，在主人心裡刷一下存在感。

打架……不用她。逃命的……不是她。

跟其他人比較起來，她的秘境探險……好無趣！

但是岩華立刻轉移位置，坐到她……旁邊的旁邊的旁邊。

因為小玖旁邊和旁邊的旁邊的位置，已經被她哥哥和星流等人占據了。然後宣布：

「我決定了，從現在開始都要跟著妳，這樣我就不用再被追著跑了。」岩華決定黏著小玖了，蹭她的好運氣。

「咳，華兒，這恐怕不行。」林燁輕咳一聲，在雪長歌與海宇越的注視下，立刻也移了位置——到自家未婚妻旁邊。

被丟下的雪長歌和海宇越：「……」重色輕友靠不住。

「為什麼不行？」

「現在能黏，等到進內境的時候，也會分開的。」他提醒道。

內境傳送，是一人一個地點。

入秘境還有可能被前後傳送到同一個位置，但是到內境，完全是個人行動，然後直到秘境關閉，才會被傳送離開。

岩華一聽，有點咬牙。

這個秘境，真是太麻煩了！

「不管，傳送的時候會分開，那就到時候再說。」現在先沾一下好運氣最實際。

「你們都要進內境嗎？」海宇越問道。

「進。」岩華回道。

有寒玉了，當然進。

「寒玉是進內境的憑證，一旦被傳送，寒玉也會消失。如果有多的寒玉……各位還是多留在身邊比較好。」本來海宇越是想勸他們不要進，但他沒有立場這麼說，只能提醒。

岩華一愣，然後就想到她入秘境收到的，她家父親的臨時傳訊。

「能確定嗎？」她正色問。

「不能，只能說，可能性很高。」

那就不能隨便浪費寒玉了……等等，所以雪長歌那麼大方地送他們寒玉，其實不是讓她去內境玩，是……要讓她留著保命的喔！

雪長歌很優雅地對她點了一下頭。

「……」雪長歌這行為是很有朋友情，但她為什麼就是覺得想揍他呢？

從那天東明玉凌主動帶人離開後，雙方的人都沒再碰上。

四天時間，倏忽而過。

藉著都是女生之便，岩華真的很黏小玖，黏得讓端木風和端木傲，都很想敲昏她。

「小玖，妳真的要進去呀？」岩華依依不捨。

小玖，是她長這麼大以來，遇到的第一個讓她覺得可以好好交朋友的女生，就算是打架也不會傷和氣。

沒錯，是打架喔！

黏四天，就打了三次架，只有第一天沒有。

因為岩華實在太好奇小玖的實力了呀。

結果是，打三天，她輸三次。

她真的第一次遇到，可以把劍修練得這麼厲害的人。

岩華佩服之餘，也有點怨念。

小玖一個魂師把武技練得這麼好，這教她這個武師以後怎麼有面子見人呀！

「要進去。」要是不進去，小花會傷心的。

「我捨不得……」岩華哀怨的表情。

「如果妳要進去，我可以送妳寒玉。」

小花有很多，送幾塊……小花不會介意吧？

小花……因為是主人要用，幾塊而已，小花覺得，就當自己什麼都沒看見吧！

「不用。」岩華立刻搖頭。「我對內境沒有那麼多好奇，不過如果妳要送我寒玉，我會很高興收下的。」

她有，她家老爹也有需要呀，多多益善。

她才想著，等小玖進了內境，她就再去找找看，是不是還能找到寒玉。

「那這送妳。」小玖也爽快，直接送她三塊……再多三塊，「妳幫我轉交給林燁。」

「幹嘛對他那麼好？」岩華哼哼。

「他是妳的未婚夫呀，順便的。」

這還差不多。岩華滿意。

「小玖。」端木風喚道。

「六哥。」哥哥一來，小玖很高興地跑過去。

岩華：「……」怎麼有種被拋棄的感覺？

隨即，林燁就從後面，握住她的手。

岩華也就……沒掙開了。

「準備好了嗎？」端木風問。

「好了。」小玖拿出一塊寒玉，握在手上。

端木風撫了撫她微亂的髮絲。

「保護好自己，如果出了秘境，要小心東明城的人。」端木傲慢了一步，沒牽到小玖，就提醒了。

同時，星流、石昊、姬雲飛、雪長歌先後走過來，手上都握著寒玉。

秘境裡，無聲無息。

突然，遠方出現一處沖天光芒，引起寒玉的回應，發出低低的「嗡嗡」鳴聲。

緊接著，每道寒玉都化為一道光，帶著握玉的人直飛向天，瞬間消失了蹤影。

當寒玉的光芒包裹住全身時，小玖只覺得靈魂被什麼震了一下，瞬間失去意識。

不知道過了多久，她的眼瞼動了動。

「啾啾！啾啾！」

著急的叫聲，讓她瞬間睜開眼，只覺得一陣冷。

「啾啾。」

焱落在她身上，發出金紅色光芒，驅散了端木玖周身的低溫。小玖動了動被凍僵的身體，坐了起來。

牠偏著頭，看看四周，神情似乎有些不解。

這是哪裡？為什麼他們到這裡來了呀？

小玖看著四周，也有些不解，感覺好像忘記了什麼，又好像沒有。

四周沒有人，天色昏暗。

奇怪的是，即使在一片黑暗中，仍然看得清楚空中的白色雪花，一片接一片，緩緩往下落。

周圍沒有人、沒有可辨別的事物，能看見的，只有一片雪白，與被積雪覆蓋的樹木，一棵又一棵間隔而立，互不相交。

小玖站了起來，拉緊斗篷。

辨不清方向，便挑了一個方向，抱著焱往前走。

雪層積得太厚，要行走，真的有點困難，但這沒有難倒小玖。

儘管踩進雪層、又拔出來、再往前走的過程有點辛苦。一路往前，偶爾會看見被積雪覆蓋、幾乎要完全看不出原樣的低矮茅草屋，小玖也沒有停下來，繼續往前走。

一路，沒有人聲，連風吹開斗篷，也沒有發出任何聲音，她聽得見的，只有自已踩進雪地，艱難的腳步聲。

「空氣，好冰！」吐一口氣，都吐出白煙，白煙還差點凝固了。

「啾啾。」冷，不喜歡。

雖然也是一片白白的，但是焱本能就知道，這個白白的世界，不是之前那個白白的世界。

那個白白的世界，到處是生之氣息。這裡，卻完全沒有。

不一樣。

「那你先回去。」巫石空間。

「啾啾。」陪玖玖，不回。

玖玖笑了，伸出手。

焱立刻跳到她的手掌心上，一人一鳥緩緩向前走。

白色的雪地，似是一望無際，天色始終昏昏暗暗，讓人看不清楚遠處的情景，四周雙眼所見之處，沒有任何一絲生息。

端木玖不斷前行，在雪地上，留下一人前行的腳印；那一行腳印，隨著她愈走愈遠，又緩緩被落下的雪花覆蓋。

這一片雪色天地，除了她之外，無聲、無息，也無跡。

這種不知前行的去向、不知需要再走多久，愈來愈冷的低溫、愈來愈暗的天色，會引動人心深處，漸漸不安、漸漸害怕起來。

但是玖玖卻沒有害怕，只是保持一定的速度向前走，然後在第三次經過看起來完全一模一樣的白色的茅草屋時，停了下來。

「我們一直在走同樣的地方？」

「啾啾。」焱回給她一副無辜的表情。

焱雖然很聰明，但在玖玖身邊，牠才不管是不是一樣的地方，那不重要。重要的是玖玖在身邊。

牠覺得，好像已經很久很久都沒有像這樣和玖玖在一起了呀，好懷念。沒有搶玖玖的小狐狸、小寶寶，和那朵欠燒的花，好開心，嘻嘻。

玖玖則懷疑地看著這片雪地，不自覺地將魂力集中在眼睛裡，在一片白色雪景裡，似乎有什麼飄閃而過。

緊接著，在昏暗天色的遠方，漸漸出現一道身影，邁步行走而來。

積雪深厚的雪地，完全構不起任何阻礙。

小玖有點羨慕。

當能看見那道身影時，一抹紅色，讓小玖心一跳！

待到微亮可見處，一道修長的紅色身影，霎時出現。

隱在昏暗天色下的臉龐，有著她很熟悉的輪廓。

她頭上的小狐狸髮飾，彷彿因此搖晃了一下。

玖玖眨了下眼，心跳，怦怦的，有些不敢相信地低語：

「蒼冥？」

真的是他！

（待續）

迷你番外

# 鏡頭外的小劇場

「我要挑戰岩華。」石昊突然冒出來這一句，嚇姬雲飛一跳。

「為什麼？」姬雲飛鎮定地問。

「她占了我的位置。」石昊理直氣壯。

占位置？

姬雲飛默默看過去。

岩華，正黏在端木玖身邊。

姬雲飛默默再看回來。

「就算你打贏岩華、把她趕走，你也沒辦法去那個位置的。」

「為什麼？」

「那邊還有兩個人盯著呢！」不要無視人家的哥哥們呀。

「那就再打兩架！」石昊眼神都亮了！

姬雲飛：「……」忘了自家竹馬兄弟最愛的就是打架了，失策！

就在這時候，兩人突然聽見一陣低語……

「她再黏著小玖，打昏她！」

另一人，很慎重點點頭。

姬雲飛、石昊：「……」

他們、他們還是保持遠觀就好，他們不想被打昏啊！

# 作者的話

好久不見，大家。

距離上一集……超過一年（思）……

銀姑娘懺悔。

如果要問這些沒有見面的日子，銀姑娘都在做什麼呢？

那真的大部分的時間，都是：在宅中，度疫情中，寫稿＋看小說＋打混中（踹！）。

真的是非常想念可以出入自由不用擔心的日子呀！

不知道是不是混得太久，連小電都有意見了。

就在銀姑娘決定發奮圖強、一口氣努力的時候，小電它——罷、工、了。

這次真的有嚇銀姑娘一跳。

用了這麼久的小電，銀姑娘第一次遇到——正在使用小電的時候，小電「砰」一聲。

小電熄燈，螢幕黑屏。

銀姑娘當時真是：「……」懵！

現在是怎樣發生了什麼事了為什麼小電砰了電源沒反應了？？？

第一反應：這應該不是硬碟出問題吧！

下一秒立刻安慰自己：只要不是硬碟，無關資料檔，銀姑娘可以！就算有打擊也撐得住。

送修後的結果就是：power燒掉了，小事。

好的，這意思我懂，換新的對吧！卡刷下去就對了。

power嘛，換新，ＯＫ的。

於是很快地換了新power回家了。

然後再開機的時候，嗯，很順，熟悉的windows字樣……

砰！

銀姑娘：「？？？」

默默拔插頭。

回家不到一個小時的小電，再度送修了……

莫非這是在告訴我，玖玖她……不急？

但是銀姑娘很急啊！（編編也很急？）

不過再急，還是得等小電測試好。

再急，還是要從開頭慢慢寫，一字一行慢慢爬～～

這一集寫到後半部分的時候，天氣變熱。

待在電腦前的時間也愈來愈晚。

這段時間陪著玖玖的，是各地camera live的鏡頭。

銀姑娘突然找到樂趣。

比如說，在窗外還暗暗的凌晨三點左右的時分，有的地方，已經四點了，並且天色開始亮了。

在窗外天色還暗暗的四點左右，有的地方，曬著熱度依然很高的陽光，把shopping center各色建築物的影子拉得長長的。

好多人在陽傘的陰影下乘涼，吃漢堡、喝飲料。

在窗外天色開始亮出微曦的凌晨五點時間，有的店家，已經準備好賣品，即將開門營業了。

在窗外天亮的時候，有些城市進入黑夜，有些街道旁的店家很熱鬧、有些交通要道的車流量開始變得很少……

透過鏡頭，發現很多不同的地方，過著和我們不相同的時間、做著不相同的事，讓悶在家很久很久沒出門的銀姑娘發現很多樂趣。

上班日的街道，休假日的街道。

出太陽的時候，下雨的時候，潺潺的流水聲、積著雪的城市……

生活，可能一日復一日，我們覺得沒什麼特別。

然而在不同的人眼裡，就是這樣平凡的日常，也很有意趣。

我想，這樣也是很幸福的吧！

捧著小說，看著不同的風景。

希望你會喜歡玖玖喔！

也歡迎大家到銀姑娘的粉絲團來踩踩。

期待下一集，很快再見ˋ_ˋ

PS：《末等魂師》系列有電子書版喔！歡迎大家到各個電子書平台查詢～（找不到，可以到銀姑娘的粉絲團詢問，銀姑娘會把網址放在那裡喔！）

二〇二二年七月

銀千羽

國家圖書館出版品預行編目資料

末等魂師第 2 部②：就是讓你想不到 / 銀千羽
著 .-- 初版 .-- 臺北市：平裝本． 2022.8 面；公
分（平裝本叢書；第 524 種）（銀千羽作品 9）

ISBN 978-626-96042-5-8（平裝）

863.57 111011422

平裝本叢書第 524 種
銀千羽作品

# 末等魂師 第2部

## ② 就是讓你想不到

作　　者—銀千羽
發 行 人—平雲
出版發行—平裝本出版有限公司
台北市敦化北路 120 巷 50 號
電話◎ 02 27168888
郵撥帳號◎ 18999606 號
皇冠出版社（香港）有限公司
香港銅鑼灣道 180 號百樂商業中心
19 字樓 1903 室
電話◎ 2529-1778　傳真◎ 2527-0904
總 編 輯—許婷婷
執行主編—平靜
責任編輯—張懿祥
美術設計—單宇
著作完成日期— 2022 年 7 月
初版一刷日期— 2022 年 8 月

法律顧問—王惠光律師

讀者服務傳真專線◎ 02-27150507
電腦編號◎ 560009
ISBN ◎ 978-626-96042-5-8
Printed in Taiwan
本書特價◎新台幣 249 元 / 港幣 83 元